The Theatre in History

Sara Siddons.

The Theatre in History

George R. Kernodle

The University of Arkansas Press
Fayetteville · London
1 9 8 9

Designer: Chiquita Babb
Typeface: Linotron 202 Weiss
Typesetter: G & S Typesetters, Inc.
Printer: Edwards Brothers, Inc.
Binder: Edwards Brothers, Inc.

The paper used in this publication meets the minimum
requirements of the American National Standard for
Permanence of Paper for Printed Library Materials
Z39.48-1984. ∞

Library of Congress Cataloging-in-Publication Data

Kernodle, George Riley, 1907–1988
  The theatre in history.

  Bibliography: p.
  Includes index.
  1. Theater—History. 2. Drama. I. Title.
PN2037.K38 1989   792'.09   87-26685
ISBN 1-55728-011-8
ISBN 1-55728-012-6 (pbk.)

Once [men] were fools, I gave them power to think. Through me they won their minds. . . . Seeing they did not see, nor hearing hear. Like dreams they led a random life. They had no houses built to face the sun, of bricks of well-wrought wood, but like the tiny ant who has her home in sunless crannies deep down in the earth, they lived in caverns. The signs that speak of winter's coming, of flower-faced spring, of summer's heat with mellowing fruits, were all unknown to them. From me they learned the stars that tell the seasons, their risings and their settings hard to mark and number, that most excellent device, I taught to them, and letters joined in words. I gave to them the mother of all arts, hard working memory. . . . Best of all gifts I gave them was the gift of healing. For if one fell into a malady there was no drug to cure, no draught, or soothing ointment. . . . Men wasted to a shadow until I showed them how to use the kindly herbs that keep from us disease. . . . Deep within the earth are hidden precious things for men, brass and iron, gold and silver.

—Aeschylus, *Prometheus Bound*

Contents

Contents

Preface

A history is a personal statement. Conscientious and "objective" as one may be, and should be, in the accumulation of facts, a time comes for selection, arrangement, and interpretation, and here the experiences, interests, and preferences of the historian are revealed. In this work I have not tried to conceal these personal factors but rather have been glad of a chance to indulge them.

I have been impressed by the efforts to bring into the modern theatre the spirit of primitive ritual as some directors, especially of the 1960s, have supposed it to be. I have been impressed by the remarkable findings of Egyptologists in this century. My interest has been greatly stimulated by the increasing knowledge of theatre in Asian countries and by its effect on playwrights and directors in the West.

As the title of the book suggests, I have a special interest in placing the theatres of the past in the cultural milieu, for theatre, more than any other art, reflects and illuminates its time.

After centuries of scholarly research, the ancient Greek world and its theatre still pose interesting questions for speculation. Theatre in the Middle Ages seems to me best understood as a demonstration by different classes—villagers, churchmen, merchants, nobles, scholars—of their roles in society. There is always something new in the Renaissance, and the old never ceases to be important.

The Mannerist period in the early seventeenth century is of special interest to twentieth-century man, who finds himself in another age of political and personal turmoil and uncertainty. Though Mannerism has been explored in painting, it has not been used extensively to explain facets of seventeenth-century drama.

The commedia dell' arte is a theatre form that yields interesting results from careful study. In the general pattern of tradition and change, the Baroque period in the late seventeenth and early eighteenth century and the time of the French Revolution with its far-reaching effects in space and time—each has its fascination.

I end my work with the Romantic period of the very late eighteenth century and the first half of the nineteenth century. If I have accomplished what I set out to do, I have given many indications along the way of directions the theatre was to take in the realism, naturalism, and experimentation of the late nineteenth century and the twentieth century.

The amount of material in theatre history is overwhelming, and I have necessarily omitted many aspects, among them the history of particular theatre buildings and a complete account of the career and works of even the most important playwrights and actors. The theatre scholar will be aware of other omissions.

This book is liberally illustrated. I have not only relied on illustrations from many sources but have commissioned drawings by good artists. Among the best of these are the composite pictures of stages and performances. Each combines theatrical features chosen from several sources, and shows more completely than most theatre illustrations the style of a particular period.

Reading the book does not, I think, require a technical knowledge of the theatre. I have wanted to make it available to readers with an interest in theatre but without professional background. Theatre is a universal art and should be accessible to everyone.

Acknowledgments

Most of the material in this book has occupied my leisure hours over a long period of time. Naturally, as I have traveled in Europe, South America, and Asia, principally for research and for viewing plays in their home settings, I have had invaluable benefit from talking with native scholars and drama producers and directors, and from having the interest and professional help of many librarians. To all of these I am deeply grateful. To the following individuals I feel special gratitude:

To Orville Larson for bringing the manuscript to the attention of The University of Arkansas Press. Before this, over a long period of time, his interest in my findings and opinions, his many hours of discussion of them with me, his giving me a chance as a visiting lecturer to try some of them out in his classes, have all been fine contributions. He provided an excellent sketch for my first scholarly book, and he has given careful consideration to my illustrations for this book, contributing also several illustrations I had not found.

To Eleanor King for interpretation of Japanese dance-drama and insights into Asian culture that she had acquired in long periods in Japan and Korea, where she had exchanged her command of Western modern dance for experiences in Eastern dance.

To Martha Sutherland for an artist's understanding of my material and for her skill in making drawings of some important subjects. She has provided a number of illustrations for the book.

To C. Walter Hodges, a British artist and specialist in theatre history, for an illustration showing the probable space and arrangement of the Elizabethan stage.

To Don Wilmeth for compiling a bibliography.

To Portia Kernodle for help in cutting and compacting the manuscript.

To Anne Marie Candido for careful editing of the manuscript and patient assistance in late additions and revisions.

To Cliff Ashby for sharing with me his considerable knowledge of ancient theatre sites in the Middle East.

To Preston Magruder for his tireless attention to many tedious tasks connected with publication.

The Theatre in History

I

Primitive Theatre

Performing space for a sacred Mayan performance, 771 A.D. *Illustration by Norman Johnson.*

Introduction

Where and when did the theatre begin? The answer depends on how theatre is defined. To accept the classic view, that a play is an imitation of a living action performed by rehearsed actors for an expected audience, is to begin theatre history in Athens in 534 B.C., when the stage gave official sanction to an annual contest in tragedies, won the first year by an itinerant actor named Thespis. But there are other views of the beginning of theatre that have received more support from serious students in the twentieth century. One is the ritual theory, which is based on a definition of drama as an organization of movements and sounds designed to stir terrors and ecstasies half-hidden in man's subconscious. A still newer view, based on a definition of drama as one of man's major ways of knowing, is at once more complex and more convincing than either of the other two.

THE THEORY OF RITUAL ORIGINS

The theory of drama as derived from primitive ritual has offered a new view of history as well as a vision of a new theatre in the twentieth century. In this view, the theatre deals with primeval archetypes, myths, and rituals by presenting images of sex, violence, guilt, and wild revelry that elicit a deeper response than the younger images of civilized urban life. Perhaps civilized drama has vitality only as it echoes old motives that haunt the dark recesses of the soul. For two centuries casual tourists and careful anthropologists have ransacked the earth from the South Sea Islands to the jungles of Africa and the mountains of Tibet to bring news of our "contemporary ancestors," convinced by the analogy of biological evolution that all civilized societies have passed through the same primitive condition. For long ages, it has been supposed, tribes of Stone-Age hunters danced around the campfire, casting spells to ward off the terror of thunder, dreams, and ghosts, and prepared for weeks for the rites of spring, when they would kill a human victim in a ritual sacrifice, then dance in frenzied orgies to release the sexual powers and, by magic compulsion, guarantee the fertility of the earth for the coming year. Out of that basic cruel reality, it was supposed, were evolved the arts, especially dance, music, and drama, through several stages. One stage saw the substitution of animal sacrifice for the human victim (witness the myths of Abraham and Isaac and of Iphigenia) and another, the selection of a mock king to preside over the festival and suffer a mock death or be driven out, in a ritual game that led to the invention of drama.

The theory of bloody human sacrifice and orgiastic rites of spring was created in *The Golden Bough* (1890), Sir James Frazer's epic account of his search through the mythology, folklore, and customs of all ages and countries for an explanation of why the priest of Diana at the Roman shrine at Aricia expected to be challenged and killed by the young man who would replace him. When all the pieces fell into place, Frazer had convinced himself that the most important activity of our primitive ancestors was to perform fertility rites every spring and that those rites were partly orgiastic and partly serious and terrifying as they focused on the bloody sacrifice of a human victim. Fully a nineteenth-century man, he was sure that the purpose of religion was to gain practical results: the fertility of crops, cattle, and wives. Frazer's followers were convinced that there was one basic pattern beneath civilized society, and that although European man might try to be rational and polite, his primitive nature lurked just below the surface. The Christian worshiping before an altar was really partaking of the bloody sacrifice on a chopping block; children playing "London Bridge is Falling Down" were really choosing a sacrificial victim; the crowd yelling at a football game was really participating in a contest for the oval head of the victim; the actor putting on his makeup was really putting on a primitive mask to be possessed by a demon.

It is not surprising that Sigmund Freud read Frazer with avidity and offered a psychological explanation of Frazer's theory that each new king replaced the last by killing the old king. Following a guess of Charles Darwin, Freud pictured a primal horde where the sons, suppressed and kept from the women by the fathers, joined together and killed their fathers. It was only a delicate refinement for Theodor Reik to add that Oedipal jealousy of the mother and hatred of the father led to eating the fathers and hence that the basic condition of man was not only murder but cannibalism. *Totem and Taboo* (1913) is not one of Freud's better contributions to anthropology.

Gilbert Murray's adaptation of Frazer to fit his idea of Greek tragedy has become a commonplace of theatre theory. Murray supposed that ritual is much older than drama and that as drama emerges from ritual it not only brings the chorus, dance, and music but preserves, somewhat transformed, the basic patterns of the ritual sacrifice. Murray gave a picture of the progression of the seasons as the year-demon waxed fat and arrogant in his hubris, or pride, then had to be killed and replaced by his son. In the patterns of tragedy, Murray believed he could trace the outlines of an early Greek ritual of spring with such features as the *agon*, or deadly conflict, the sacrifice, the *sparagmos*, or tearing and eating of the victim, the report of the messenger, and the discovery of the hidden heir. The idea of such a ritual seemed very convincing, but classical scholars can find no trace of its existence.

Frazer's great mistake was to confuse symbolic killing with actual killing. There have been wars, massacres, and murders in all ages, but ritual killing is very rare. When the king of Egypt died—a natural death—he was identified with the god Osiris, who had been killed by his brother Seth, the demon of chaos and the desert. The killing was symbolic, however, about as bloody as Christian baptism, which is also a symbol of ritual death and rebirth.

The Frazer picture of a ritual of human sacrifice as belonging to the original condition of man has permeated modern thinking. Mary Renault treated it as historical gospel in her novel *The King Must Die*. In "The Congo," Vachel Lindsay has Christianity exorcise the lingering demons of the African jungle, but Eugene O'Neill has his Emperor Jones lose his confidence as a civilized man and sink in terror before the jungle darkness, primitive drumbeats, and the supposed racial memory of bloodthirsty crocodile gods.

Bertolt Brecht, Antonin Artaud, Peter Brook, Julian Beck, Richard Schechner, Joseph Chaikin, and Jerzy Grotowski—most of the theorists of "new theatre" in the 1960s and 1970s—said that we must return to the spontaneity of primitive play, and, although it seems contradictory, to the orgiastic rhythms and cruel intensities of primitive ritual. When Brook directed Seneca's *Oedipus* for the National Theatre Company in London in 1968, he wanted a ritual ending. After Jocasta had impaled herself with a sword through the womb, a group of revelers danced around a gilded six-foot phallus singing, "Yes, We Have No Bananas." In 1971 the same director produced on the hills of Persepolis, before the tombs of the ancient Persian kings, a spectacular performance in an invented language, exploiting Greek, Persian, and Japanese images of ritual murders, rebellions, and guilts. Not only a new vitality for the theatre but some new spiritual values for mankind were supposed to gush up from the unconscious if the magic rites of primitive theatre could be reconstructed. By bringing the audience into a new participation, the ritual was supposed to strip them of inhibitions and sometimes of clothes.

The myth of ritual drama has opened the eyes of theatre people to the religions and the masks, dances, and dramas of different cultures all over the world. What they borrow is neither cruelty nor frenzy but discipline in performance and rich use of dance and song, especially from the great Oriental traditions. Even though drama did not evolve from ritual but was a parallel form of symbolic expression as old as ritual itself, it is clear that drama and ritual have much in common. A tragedy rouses some of the mixed satisfactions of a spring sacrifice. Francis Fergusson describes *Oedipus the King* as a ritual of locating and driving from the land a pollution, the killer of Laius. The very title of Shakespeare's *Twelfth Night* creates the expectation of revelry and disguises and tricks of the festival at the end of the Christmas season. Besides a celebration of pranks and pastimes and an invocation

7

to Music, "the food of love," it also presents a ritual exorcism of too much care—Olivia's mourning and Malvolio's attempt to stop the revelry. As a ritual to exorcise care and invoke love and revelry, the play had particular pertinence for the audience of 1600, who were facing the rising spirit of Puritanism. Part of the appeal of *The Death of a Salesman* (1949) depends on the basic myth of a son searching for a lost father and finding the secret of his own identity.

A NEWER VIEW OF THE THEATRE

Another view of the nature and origin of theatre, based on a definition of theatre as one of man's major ways of knowing, is for many students of theatre broader, more stimulating, and more convincing than the ritual theory. It directs the mind even farther back, into the Stone Age, and it replaces Frazer's picture of mindless primates attempting by cruel rites to force favor from a mechanical universe with a picture of men of imagination dramatizing their partnership with the gods in a venture toward civilization.

The concept that scientific man is radically different from primitive man is denied by Claude Levi-Strauss. In *The Savage Mind* (1966) he insists that "savage" tribes who use name systems for complex social relationships and the neolithic "savages" who hybridized wheat in the old world and corn in the new world were as scientific as modern man. Levi-Strauss and Joseph Campbell show that myths

Cave drawing of Australian Bushman from Orange Spring. Natives watch stick dancers using long poles to simulate forelegs of animals while spectators clap in accompaniment. *Courtesy the British Library.*

8

Abbé Henri Breuil's drawing of a primitive man (Shaman) disguised as an anthropomorphic god, from a prehistoric cave in the southwestern region of France.

are logical ways of understanding man's historic condition in relation to nature. Primitive religion no longer seems superstitious nonsense but something to be taken seriously by modern man. And the dramatic aspects of worship, too, command respect.

The idea that ritual worship is an act performed in earnest, in full belief, while drama is a later imitation performed in make-believe, assumes that primitive man confused sacred imagery with the divine. Yet what we know of primitive man shows that he understood perfectly well the difference. The man who is initiated knows that his second birth, as he comes from between the legs of an actor dressed as a woman or is shown a small carved figure of a divine nativity mother, is different from his first birth.

THE MASK, THE JOURNEY, AND THE DOORWAY

The simplest images of religious art, and probably the earliest, by which men knew their historic relation with the universe were the mask, the journey, and the doorway. The mask brought the gods to life, the journey brought them into man's world or man into theirs, and the doorway dramatized a transition, especially the death and rebirth at initiation and the birth of the spirit at death.

Sioux dance before a bear hunt, lead by Shaman covered with bear skins.

10

The central image is the mask. Sculptured images could be shown in initiation and carried in processions, just as Kachina dolls representing the gods have been useful in teaching children in the Pueblo lands of the American southwest. The dramatic image of the god seems as basic as any ritual act of supplication, and hence it can be said that ritual was not an earlier form out of which the arts developed but a parallel form.

It has been difficult for people in the Western world to understand the religious mask. Besides the grotesque animal and death-head masks of Hallowe'en, the only mask known in the West has been the black velvet eye-mask of the Venetian carnival and the masked ball. It was a symbol of anonymity, a breach of ordinary communication, hence an invitation to teasing and flirtation without responsibility—the essence of deception and sham. Actors and mimes use masks or white painted faces to secure an alienation from their own daily character, and many actors attest to the trancelike power of the mask.

Demons, of course, must be ugly, but many of the masks of gods and ancestors are awe-inspiring, even shocking images, as though it were more important to show how distant the sacred beings are from daily life than to show them as idealized human faces. Since the sacred was often considered dangerous, even scorching if approached too near, the mask was a protective mediary between man and his gods. A mask could create prestige for a political leader and enable a new chieftain to pick up the continuity with a minimum of interruption as he donned the mask of the dead chieftain and played his roles in public functions.

It is a mark of how far the modern theatre has moved away from nineteenth-century realism that masks have been used in a number of new plays. They can be taken more seriously when one realizes that there is scarcely a primitive society that does not make or use masks and that all the great dramas of early history, from Egypt and Greece to India and Japan, were masked dramas, or, like the Chinese, used painted faces as elaborate as masks.

Many of the masks of the supernatural are animal faces. The reasons for this are not fully known. When early students of anthropology in Australia found clans named for animals, worshiping their ancestor as the spirit of the totem animal, they built up a theory of guilt before the food animal and magic rites for its fertility. But Claude Levi-Strauss has questioned the totem theory by showing that many totem animals were not good to eat but were chosen because they were "good to think," that is, offered sets of interrelated images by which the clans could understand their complex society. Suzanne Langer has shown that by making an image of the totem animal with qualities the clan admires the artist makes an advance in clear thinking.

Did the superior abilities of the animals impress helpless Stone Age man, or did man see animals as an earlier form of life, well adapted to nature and therefore having an older relationship to the gods? Some masks of the Northwest Indians are double: the outer mask of a demon bird opens by hidden strings to show an idealized human face. We can only surmise, and notice that practically all the gods of Egypt take animal form, usually with a human body and an animal mask, and remember that to this day children see themselves and their world in the more distant and symbolic form of animal characters.

It is reasonable to assume that a masked mythological drama, performed in dance and song by actors and choruses of attendants, existed across the Old World from Scandinavia and Spain to the coasts of China and Indonesia. Its subject matter would have been how God entered into the world and transformed it, how man enters the realm of the spirit and is reborn, and how the spirit finally triumphs over death—the points of the Incarnation, Baptism, and Resurrection. The climactic moments in the early drama would occur in the action of crossing

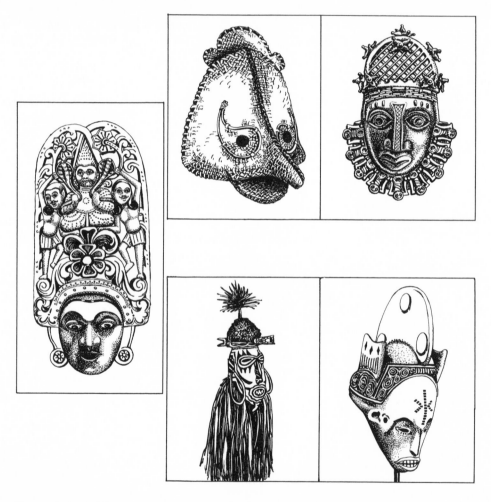

Ten masks from different parts of the world. *Illustration by Ethelyn Pauley.*

the boundary between the profane and the sacred; hence the key images of drama were the procession and the doorway. On every holy day man would enter into the sacred precinct to bring the gods to life, to relive the creation of the world and of man's spiritual realm by bearing the gods in procession out through the sacred doorway into the realm of everyday time and space to bless the fields, flocks, and homes. At the end of the holy day the gods and their tokens would be returned to the sacred precinct. An even more important crossing from time to eternity was man's entrance to the initiation chamber. The doorway became first the mouth of the devouring monster who was to destroy the initiate's childhood self and then the womb from which he was reborn into the world as a son of the divine spirit. For the third crossing, the funeral drama, the doorway was the doorway from the

tomb through which the spirit, reborn in winged form, could ascend to the sky. Today, in the opening of the stage curtain, the opening of a door on stage, and the appearance in stage lights of the actor, we recognize still the mystery of bringing to life an image of the spirit. The Lion Gate at Mycenae still stands from prehistoric times, an entrance to a sacred precinct guarded by two lion spirits, with the sacred triangular symbol of earth (hill) and womb. The Stone-Age burial chambers in Malta and elsewhere provided enclosed space outside the doorway of the tomb, probably for a drama and an audience.

In historic times, any sacred procession partakes of the original entrance of the divine into human life. At Athens, for the festival of Dionysus, a joyous procession brought the cult statue of Dionysus from a suburban shrine where the worship of Dionysus, originally an Oriental god, was first established in Greece. At Bruges every year a Procession of the Holy Blood reenacts the journey of an early Count of Flanders bringing a phial of Christ's blood from the Holy Land. In some early processions a return from the land of the dead developed into a wild dance, with many people in masks of animals and demons. The Middle Ages saw a "Dance of Death" in the cemeteries and into the streets, and the impulse to represent the release of the dead is still seen in the animals and spooks of Hallowe'en.

As we visualize a dramatic procession of primitive times, many people are in mask and costume as sacred attendants; others follow and see as best they can. The episodes within the sacred initiation chamber and the rebirth scenes at the tomb would be seen only by the priest-actors, though, as in medieval church drama, many people would see the ascension of the spirit or the empty tomb. The prominence of viewing platforms at the sides of a sacred path in temples and royal palaces around the world is significant. In the prehistoric palaces which have been restored in Crete, a long sacred way leads to the center of an open place, seemingly intended for performances, where there are steps and platforms on two sides, apparently for seating the royal party. At Angkor Tom in Cambodia, just north of Angkor Wat, several temples overlook a long procession way, as do the pyramid platforms in Mexico and Central America. In the mountains of Peru, there are large circular spaces that were probably theatres, and elsewhere there are large parade ground areas between a pyramid on one side and sectional stone platforms on the other. It may be possible some day to surmise what kind of demonstrations or dance dramas were performed.

THREE DRAMAS OF MAN AND THE GODS

Besides the loose processional forms, with their static gods and marching attendants, we have evidence of three kinds of dramas that presented the great myths of the cosmos—the creation drama, the initiation drama, and the resurrection drama.

The cosmic myth is a map of time leading man back and forth from his daily time to the divine time of eternity, leading him to the beginning of his time in the creation of the world and the establishment of man's estate, leading him to the future for the fulfillment of his time, when time is absorbed in eternity.

The drama of initiation was the central drama of man's partnership with the gods. The neophyte must be symbolically killed in his childhood personality—that is, suddenly and violently separated from his individual past—in order to be

Apache tribal initiation ceremony for young girls reaching puberty. Tribesmen face a ceremonial fire as seven Indian maidens, paired off under blankets with older women (who act as protectors), dance off on the sides. In the center are four masked warriors wearing bizarre headdresses that identify them as mountain spirits. Two small boys act as messengers between the performers and the spectators. *From the collection of the State Museum of History, Oklahoma Historical Society.*

15

reborn as a child of the immortal spirit. He entered the sacred area to be taught the sacred dances and chants of his ancestors, the techniques of hunting and farming, and the social patterns of his tribe, often by the very gods and ancestors who first created them. He must relive the important experiences of the race, indeed the experiences of the cosmos. He must return to the original chaos and watch the drama of the creation of the physical world and his social order in defiance of chaos and death. The doorway was the mouth of the monster of death. Often there were beatings, ordeals, and mutilation as part of the mock killings, and the bodies were thrown over the wall as dead or carried with mourning into the cave-tomb. Among surviving primitive peoples in the modern world, the scars of circumcision and other mutilations are explained as the marks of the monster's teeth. In Ceram, after the novices have entered the door called the crocodile's mouth and are supposed eaten, the women outside are shown bloody garments and told that the youths are dead and will not return. In some Fiji initiations the initiators also undergo the state of death, smearing themselves with the blood and entrails of pigs, and lie down as dead ancestors. The initiates crawl under the row of bodies, until suddenly they come to life and all rush to the river to wash.

In historic time, men and women who came from far and near to be initiated into the mysteries of Eleusis in Greece felt their lives transformed by joy and happiness in this world and the promise of eternal life. They had taken part in Demeter's journey to Hades to bring back Proserpine, the herald of spring, the life of the world. And in Hades, they apparently had seen Dionysus reborn, triumphant over death. In the ruins at Eleusis there are two levels of seats, for scenes on earth and for the underground scenes in Hades.

From what we know of very early history, we surmise that the dramas of prehistoric man showed the triumph of spirit over death. Central was the rebirth of the neophyte after his symbolic death. But that rebirth was part of the recurring drama of the triumph of order over chaos, beginning with the creation of the world and the coming of the savior-leader, the representative of the spirit who entered the world and established an enlightened order for man. In a sophisticated mythological drama, Aeschylus has his Prometheus describe what that transformation from animal to human being had meant to men:

Once [men] were fools, I gave them power to think. Through me they won their minds.
. . . Seeing they did not see, nor hearing hear. Like dreams they led a random life. They had no houses built to face the sun, of bricks or well-wrought wood, but like the tiny ant who has her home in sunless crannies deep down in the earth, they lived in caverns. The signs that speak of winter's coming, of flower-faced spring, of summer's heat with mellowing fruits, were all unknown to them. From me they learned the stars that tell the seasons, their risings and their settings hard to mark and number, that most excellent device, I taught to them, and letters joined in words. I gave to them the mother of all arts, hard working memory. . . . Best of all gifts I gave them was the gift of healing. For if one fell into a malady there was no drug to cure, no draught, or soothing ointment. . . . Men

wasted to a shadow until I showed them how to use the kindly herbs that keep from us disease. . . . Deep within the earth are hidden precious things for men, brass and iron, gold and silver.

And so on through tamed horses, chariots, and sailboats to the summary:

All arts, all goods, have come to men from me.

Prometheus had won that knowledge in defiance of the old natural order, and knowledge could be easily lost, for chaos is waiting, like a shapeless ocean, ready to destroy. The daily triumph of the sun over darkness, the yearly triumph of spring over winter, the triumphant rebirth of each individual, was part of the same pattern as the original triumph of divine order over chaos. Each day that order is broken with sundown; each year has its winter; each individual, each king-chieftain, dies.

While the main plays of creation seem to have been serious celebrations of the triumph of order over chaos, there were provisions for comedy, as part of a controlled element of chaos, in the very creation of the world. Since every festival was a celebration of the coming of order, it must begin in chaos. Holy day became holiday, releasing the wild pranks that had been controlled the rest of the year. Since the time of chaos was before the creation of man, men put on animal masks, as well as fools' caps or other symbols of disorder. Since it was before the differentiation of the sexes, men and women exchanged clothes. It was early discovered that the sun calendar and the moon calendar were not commensurate. The 360-degree circle of the created world-island fitted the 365-day year only if a gap of five days was left between the old year and the new—days outside the established order. In many cultures the new year became a time when a healthy disorder must be danced and dramatized as part of knowing the return of order—the waters of chaos, of unformed vitality, would flow through the gap into the created world and bring it renewed vigor. By another myth, when men found their strict order too burdensome they could return to the irresponsible freedom of an earlier regime. With the American Indians of the southwest, the clown in mudhead mask or makeup is supposed to be left over from the early time when men lived underground. The chief midwinter festival of the Romans was the Saturnalia, a celebration reestablishing the regime of Saturn, who ruled before he was overthrown by Jupiter. All regular rules and restraints were cast off, men dressed as women and women as men, masters obeyed their servants, and everyone celebrated his comic release in revelry. At the end of the festival the symbols of temporary chaos were destroyed or put away and everyone was ready to take up the burdens of society again. Often this controlled chaos was dramatized in the character of a clown-fool, a mock ruler of the revelry. In the dramatization of the creation of the world and the coming of the great savior-teacher, the terrifying monster of ocean and desert was often left offstage. But the clown-fool, symbol of controlled disorder, was a necessary reminder that the local order of each society was a little different

17

from the order of the kingdom next door. Professor William Willsford has shown that as the king is an indispensable symbol of the center of society, so the fool is a symbol of the periphery, where the central order is weakened and exposed to the fringes of the next kingdom. But the fool not only must be kept close to the king but must have a special affinity for the queen or princess, for the queen is regularly from another country and the princess is destined to move to another order when she marries. Order must always find room for incongruity. Primitive men knew quite well the principle of indeterminacy long before anyone had measured the electron.

The crowning drama of prehistoric man was the drama of the future, the birth of the spirit at the funeral, the final triumph over death. It recognized that the body dies but showed the birth of the spirit in a new form, with wings, to fly up and take its place in the sky. This drama, balancing the drama of creation, gave a wide perspective of past and future. It recognized the radical difference between body and spirit; the body must be returned to the earth and the spirit to the sky. The rising spirit, taking a new form, is another rebirth, repeating and completing the birth at the creation of the world and the rebirth in initiation.

The drama of eternal life is the strongest reassurance of the importance of the human order, and it is the oldest drama that has left any trace. Neanderthal man, before the last ice age, perhaps fifty thousand years ago, buried his dead in the drawn-up position. The archeologists guessed that the purpose was to prevent the ghost from walking. A better guess is that the body was put in the embryo position for the drama of the birth of the spirit, so that it might rise facing the morning sun. Small sculptured female figures, with prominent breasts and hips and marked sexual triangle, were discovered in the 1920s and hailed as "Venuses" for some cult of fertility. It seems far more likely that they too were part of the divine nativity drama. Such female figures in Egypt are identified as divine mothers for a rebirth of the spirit.

Winged angels and the stars, so important in Christian imagery and conspicuous in the Easter and Christmas scenes that were the first dramas in the medieval church, are to be found in many religions. The resurrection of an incarnated god and his acceptance in the sky is the final proof that the spirit that had entered the world was of cosmic, eternal importance.

The neophyte can never be the same after seeing the drama of initiation. Henceforth, he must deal with two worlds—the visible world and the unseen world of divine presence—and with two times—the mundane present and *ille tempo*, the mythical time of past and future, of creation and fulfillment. It is not just his superior arrowheads and axes, or even his superior hybrid wheat and corn or his sheepfold walls or his plows and tamed oxen or his control of life, matter, and power that make him truly a man and partner of the gods. In these he is merely a clever animal reveling in his ability to get food, shelter, and protection. He becomes a man and not an animal when he has a vision of his position in time and place. He becomes part of sacred history, related to the center, the navel of the world, where the divine first entered this world and where man has his closest contact with the unseen realm. He knows that the sacred world is around him: north, south, east, and west, above him in the sky, below him under the ground, behind him in history, and ahead of him in eternity. That vision is the subject of his drama.

We now turn to Egypt to see how that vision was reflected in the earliest drama of which there is clear evidence.

Tribal dance drama among Kwakiutl Indians of the Canadian Northwest.
Illustration by David Cuill.

19

The Egyptian Theatre

Egypt achieved the greatest triumph of order and continuity in all history. The founding of the nation came when the king of Upper Egypt conquered Lower Egypt and founded the First Dynasty some time before 3100 B.C. Thereafter, the king was always referred to as the one who unites the two lands. He was installed separately on two thrones, often placed back to back, but he wore a crown that was a combination of the red crown of Lower Egypt and the white crown of Upper Egypt.

After nearly 900 years the Old Kingdom saw a century or so of disintegration, but the patterns were not lost, and the Middle Kingdom, by rallying the old loyalties and symbols, kept order for about a half millennium. Even the invasion of the Hyksos about 1780 B.C. was only an interruption, and beginning in 1580 B.C., the New Kingdom and its successors had nearly a thousand years of triumphant rule as a great empire including much of the Near East. Then the Ethiopians came in from the south, and the Assyrians and Persians from the east, then Alexander in 332 B.C., and at last Caesar and the Romans. Yet each invader ruled by adopting the old religious and political patterns. The old Egypt only disintegrated when the intolerance of early Christianity was backed by the power of Imperial Rome. But the Roman Empire was already in a period of decline; the Arab invasion of 640 A.D. gave the *coup de grâce* to the old civilization of Egypt, and sand and vandals claimed the tombs and temples that had seen man's first major efforts at drama.

The mythology of the Egyptian religion presented a philosophic picture of the cosmic order, a history of the nation of Egypt, and a great drama in which the divine king heals the breach of time caused by the death of his father, reassembles the torn pieces of the past, defeats the ever-threatening demon of chaos, and unites himself with the daily resurrection of the sun and the annual flooding of the Nile. He is reborn as a son and equal of the Supreme Spirit and rules triumphantly over his earthly realm.

In the Egyptian concept of the universe, the Supreme Spirit is eternal and recurrent, like the polar stars that revolve but never set, the sun that triumphs over darkness every morning, or the vegetation that is revived every summer by the flooding of the Nile. As Atum, he was the creator at the beginning of things. Before sexual differentiation came into the world he created Air and Moisture out of

20

himself by spit and masturbation, and they married to bear Geb, the earth, and Nut, the sky. Geb impregnated Nut, who bore the next four gods of the Ennead (the council): Osiris and his wife Isis, and Seth and his wife Nephthys. Osiris and his son Horus are active in the great drama of restoring order to the world. The living king is identified with Horus the son, who presents himself as the center of the drama by conquering the evil Seth and resurrecting his father Osiris, who has been killed by his brother Seth. In the battle Horus loses an eye, which must be recovered, and in the coronation drama his crown or any other offering is called the eye of Horus. Although the damage is recognized in the coronation drama, the battle is in the past. Horus is already triumphant and is collecting his lost eye. In a nativity play he secures the birth of the spirit of his dead father Osiris, which flies up on new-born wings, like the phoenix, to join the imperishable stars. In Egyptian thought there is no break between the seasons, no gap between the generations. When the father dies, the son immediately gathers together the broken segments of the past and dramatizes his own rebirth and his father's ascent to the stars.

The Pyramid Texts, first recorded about 2625 B.C., emphasize repeatedly the unity of father, son, and Supreme Spirit. As in the Christian trinity, the Supreme Spirit begat the son on an earthly mother, the queen. Since all three are one and each derives from the other, the son is spoken of as begetter of himself, begetter of his father, and bull (husband) to his mother. In his eternal form the spirit is beyond change or damage, but as the daily sun he is devoured each night by the underground world and each morning the demon of chaos tries to prevent the opening of the gates of dawn. As living king, he is subject to death, and while his spirit, with new-born wings, may fly up to the stars and his imperishable body be placed in the earth, indicating the union of heaven and earth, yet, since he is living symbol of social order, his death is a break, a triumph of chaos. The son himself is maimed in the battle, and must find and restore the fragmented pieces of the past in order to play his role. He must heal the breach of time.

Egyptian mythology in its dramatic form was a way of knowing the importance of continually restoring the broken fragments of the past and seeing them come to new life as glorious as the sun in its daily triumph over darkness and as richly fertile as the land from the annual flooding of the Nile. Order and continuity were constantly threatened by the demons of chaos, especially the fiery red devil of the western desert, Seth. But the pyramids defied the disintegration of time, and in the Old Kingdom the dramas took place at sunrise on the two-story platform built against the east side of a pyramid.

Like many other peoples, the Egyptians revered one particular stone as a navel of the world, the center of civilization, a sacred spot where the gods first had contact with the world and man. The sacred Benben stone stood at the ancient sacred city, on the hill that first emerged from the surrounding waters of chaos. It was mathematical in form, an equilateral pyramid. To catch and give out the rays

21

of the sun, it was covered with metal foil, and the top of every pyramid and obelisk was a metal-covered Benben stone. The Benben stone was also the nest of the phoenix, a flame from which the spirit could be born and fly up to the stars. Like the pagoda of the Far East and the ziggurat of the Near East, the pyramid was a stairway toward heaven, and the earliest large pyramid was built in step form. It was the center of a religious drama showing the glorious triumph of order over chaos, of spirit over instinct, of mind over matter.

MYTHOLOGICAL DRAMA IN EGYPT

Since 1904, when Heinrich Schafer published his monograph on the mystery play of Osiris at Abydos, Egyptologists have been in dispute over the existence of drama in Egypt, and some continue to say there was none. The difficulties are definition and interpretation. There certainly were performances by masked men impersonating the gods and the legendary heroes, but those who look for a modern auditorium or a Greek amphitheatre can find nothing to call a theatre. The (masked) performers presented the mythological events that sanctioned the coronation of the king, the union of the dead king with sky and earth, and the divine second birth of the new king. The king himself played the central role at the first performance, but priests performed at the daily or annual repetition. Many Egyptologists have said that this is ritual and not drama and have called the principal performance buildings "mortuary temples" rather than theatres. In 1948, in *Kingship and the Gods*, Henry Frankfort described several forms as dramas, but before he published his *Ancient Egyptian Religion* the following year he changed his mind. He wrote, "They have been called dramatic texts; they certainly are not drama. For their purpose is to translate actuality into the unchanging form of myth." But that is exactly what mythological drama does—it translates human concepts into the abstract form of myth.

The question of dialogue and action has also been a difficulty. While some texts are clearly in dialogue form, some have extensive passages that look like monologues, songs, hymns, choruses, and narration or description. Theodor Gaster, in his study of Near-Eastern dramatic texts, *Thespis*, thought he had found not the dramas themselves but literary or choral developments based on earlier dramas. But there were certainly many scenes of action in Egyptian performances—the gods helping the king, as Horus, to mount a ladder to heaven, for instance— though some passages look like descriptions of action that may or may not have been seen by the audience. Since we do not hesitate to call the choruses in ancient Greek tragedies and the Oriental travel songs dramatic though they deal with off-stage or imagined action, and since we accept the descriptive recitations in the

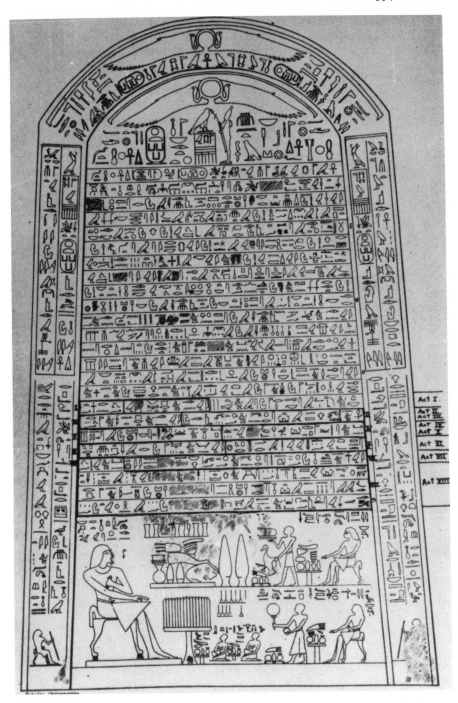

Hieroglyphics on the Ikernofret stone depicting the account of the Abydos passion play, c. 1868 B.C..

Japanese puppet theatre and the narrative songs of Bertolt Brecht as parts of the theatre, it seems logical to call the Egyptian performances drama.

A break in the academic ranks came when two Egyptologists in England, H. W. Fairman and A. M. Blackman, announced that the illustrated text engraved on the tomb walls of the Ptolemaic temple at Edfu was a play. In a series of articles published between 1935 and 1942 in the *Journal of Egyptian Archeology*, they explained their conclusions. After Professor Blackman died, Professor Fairman continued their study and in 1974 the University of California Press published his translation and arrangement of the material as *The Triumph of Horus*. He was especially encouraged about his treatment of the text after seeing two performances in England, one by the theatre group of the Padgate College of Education and the other at Cheltenham. In his "translation" Professor Fairman used several forms of verse as well as rhetorical address and choral hymns of greeting, praise, and bragging. If the definition of drama in performance is confined to the give-and-take of everyday characters, it is not surprising that the first students of Egyptian literature sought other words than drama to apply to the texts they found.

It has been known for some time that each king assigned the taxes from several cities to endow daily performances at his tomb, and there seems to be a definite distinction between the priests who performed the dramas and the regular performers of ritual worship. There are two monuments of actors where their services in the drama are recorded. In the Twelfth Dynasty, I-cher-nofret, the chief treasurer of King Sesostris III, not only recorded that he arranged the procession in search of Osiris and the decoration of the body in its ship, but states, "I struck down the enemy of Osiris who opposed the heshemet-bark." An actor in the Eighteenth Dynasty, about 1580 B.C., brags on his modest tombstone: "I was the partner of my master in all his declamations. When he was a god, I was a prince. When he killed I brought back to life." Most of the extant texts begin a speech with the hieroglyph for "says" and most passages use the first person and direct discourse. The properties used are mentioned as lifted or handled, and frequently their symbolic significance is explained. Besides the permanent structures of several levels, such specific scenic elements as mountains, cities, and gateways are mentioned, indicating a staging similar to the miniature settings of the Middle Ages in Europe.

THE PYRAMID TEXTS AND THE RESURRECTION DRAMA

The most impressive drama showing the healing of the breach of time is the pyramid resurrection drama, first performed by each new king and thereafter performed each morning at sunrise by endowed actor-priests on a special two-story platform, the King's "House of Eternity" or "House of Millions of Years," built on the east side of the pyramid. Extensive quotations from the drama are inscribed in the limestone corridors and chambers of five major pyramids and several smaller pyramids of the Fifth and Sixth Dynasties built between 2345 and 2150 B.C. The inscriptions seem like a collection of key passages from many dramas, and it is not possible to tell just which passages were used in any one performance.

In the Middle Kingdom variants of the Pyramid Texts were recorded on the coffins of both kings and rich men, and in the New Kingdom the *Book of the Dead* developed the journey of the soul as part of a drama for the resurrection of the whole populace.

The central action of the drama is the resurrection of the dead king, as Osiris, and the installation of the living king, as Horus. The resurrected god, Osiris, identified with his son Horus, joins the rising sun, comes through the gates of dawn, crosses the celestial river on the sun-bark, and is hailed in song and dance by all the gods and reaffirmed as the son and equal of Re-Atum, the Supreme Spirit. First Nut, the sky, and Geb, the earth, as primeval ancestors of the gods, reclaim the dead king: "The King is my eldest son who split open my womb, he is my beloved, with whom I am well pleased." This is followed by the speeches of the opening of the mouth spoken by the living king, as Horus, to his father. Even if some speeches calling on the King to rise could be spoken by a priest to a coffin or a statue, others certainly seem intended to be acted in character: "Wake up, wake up, O King, wake up for me! I am your son: wake up for me, for I am Horus who wakes you." The king himself addresses the supreme god Re by his secret names and reminds him that one cannot be reborn without the other. The king's resurrection as a winged spirit is celebrated: "His mother the sky bears him alive every day like Re, and he appears with him in the East, he goes to rest with him in the West, and his mother Nut is not free from him any day." The gods announce to the divine spirit Re: "Re-Atum, Unas comes to thee, an Imperishable Spirit. Thy son comes to thee. This Unas comes to thee . . . Seth and Nephthys, hurry! Announce to the gods of the South . . . Osiris and Isis, hurry! . . . to the gods of the north." And so for the guardians of the East and West. "Re-Atum, thy son comes to thee. . . . Let him ascend to thee! Enfold him in thy embrace! This is thy son of thy body eternally." He is separated from death and the netherworld and reborn as a winged spirit, a Ba.

The central action is played by the young king. Horus comes to the tomb of his father and declares: "I have come to raise thee up. I am come to kill him who killed thee." He must come to terms with his past and heal the breach before he can take up his own true role. His father was killed by the destructive element that wants to return to chaos, and he himself is damaged by the conflict, but all the forces of the universe join him on the side of order against chaos. Gods and animals help him find the scattered parts of his father and his own lost eye. As king he is part of the shining power of the dawning sun and the fertilizing power of the Nile. He is the active center of recurrent eternal life.

25

Some terms in the Pyramid Texts show that the drama was used long before any pyramids were built. The expressions "Throw off the sand from thy face" and "Remove thy earth" go back to the time before the First Dynasty, when kings were buried in primitive graves of desert soil. Phrases concerning the opening of a tomb, such as "The bricks are drawn for thee out of the great tomb," seem to date from the time of the brick tombs at Abydos in the First and Second Dynasties. There are images of crossing celestial waters on two reed floats, a very early form of boat. Such examples indicate that the resurrection drama is at least as old as the beginning of the Egyptian kingship, some time between 4000 and 3000 B.C., and may be an adaptation of earlier resurrection dramas in existence centuries before there was a king.

THE MEMPHIS CREATION DRAMA

A variant of a small part of the resurrection drama, a version that may be even older than the Pyramid Texts, was copied on stone in the eighth century B.C. by order of King Shabako, the Ethiopian Pharaoh who founded the Twenty-fifth Dy-

Incised wall drawing, in the Temple of Horus at Edfu, illustrating the arrival by boat of the Pharaoh Horus in the pyramid drama, *The Triumph of Horus*, 110 B.C.

26

nasty and revived the style and customs of the Old Kingdom. The stone was used in modern times as a nether millstone, and the middle part of the text was destroyed by grinding. It was brought to the British Museum early in the nineteenth century; no one could make sense of it until in this century the historian James H. Breasted noticed that the columns of hieroglyphs were turned toward each other just as characters face each other in the dialogue of a play. Part of the text was a narrative and philosophical introduction that probably was read or chanted in the performance. Adapted to serve as a stone memorial for Shabako, the text is only a slight rewording of an ancient drama to establish the king as son and appointed heir of the gods.

The play tells how Geb, the earth god, established Horus as king of Egypt. He first separated Horus from his brother Seth and stopped them from fighting. The dialogue is given:

Geb to Seth: Go to the place where you were born.
(The stage directions indicate that Seth moves to his city of the North).
Geb to Horus: Go to the place where your father was drowned.
(Horus moves to his city of the South).
Geb to Horus and Seth: I have separated you.

Then the narrative continues:

"But it displeased the heart of Geb that the part of Horus was equal to the part of Seth. Then Geb gave his heritage to Horus, son of his own son."

Geb to the Ennead (council of the gods): I have decreed, Horus, that you shall be my embalmer, you alone, Horus. My heritage is to this heir, Horus. My heritage is to the son of my son, Horus.

THE NILE CORONATION PLAY

In a procession down the Nile, a series of episodes derived from the Pyramid resurrection drama was performed by a new king as part of his accession and coronation. The preparation of a boat and his ceremonial journey on the Nile and receiving of gifts at several stops are dramatized as a journey of Horus to gather and restore the dismembered body of Osiris and find his own eye and so heal the breach in continuity caused by the death of the old king.

This remarkable coronation play is known from the Ramesseum Papyrus found in 1895 in a Middle Kingdom grave west of Thebes. It is the production notebook of the manager of the performance for the accession in 1970 B.C. of Sesostris I who, as king, played the god Horus. Besides crude drawings of the performance, mostly on a boat, the papyrus lists the properties, describes the actions, and explains their symbolic or dramatic meaning. It is the most detailed account of an

Hieroglyphics on the Shabako stone, eighth century B.C., depicting a Memphite drama, probably a coronation play of about 3100 B.C. Loss of hieroglyphics and black markings in the center are due to the later use of the stone as a nether millstone. *Courtesy of the Trustees of the British Museum.*

Egyptian drama, and since it contains several speeches from the Pyramid Texts of the Old Kingdom, it confirms the continued performance of that drama in the Middle Kingdom.

The main action is the giving of gifts to the king, interpreted as giving the eye to Horus to restore the damage caused in the conflict with Seth. The first episodes are concerned with the decoration of the boats and the embalming of the dead king, with a procession through the mountains and offerings including bread, water, milk, oil, and wine, as well as special incense and purple mourning garments for the dead king. Constantly, the living king is behind his father's body, and the divine spirit is behind the king. The notes indicate that the sacrifice of animals is interpreted as the dismemberment of Osiris. When Thoth says to Osiris, "I have raised Horus that he may avenge you," the notes indicate that a club is handed to Horus and he traverses a symbolic mountain. At another place the threshing of barley by having a male donkey tread on it is dramatized as the conflict of Osiris and Seth. Horus speaks as to Seth and his followers: "Do not beat my father," and to Osiris: "I have beaten those who beat you."

Thoth is the most frequent secondary character, but Geb, the primeval earth god, speaks in some episodes, as when he orders Thoth to give Horus his dismembered head. The manager's note indicates that here the heads of a goat and a goose are offered to the king. At one point a pole with cross bars used to measure the height of the Nile, called a djed-column, is ceremonially lowered into the water and raised again; in the drama this represents the children of Horus beating Seth and thrusting him under Osiris. The manager notes that the children of Osiris are played by the high priests of Heliopolis, the ancient sacred city of the united lands. At the end, Geb stops the strife, Seth is bound, and the dead king is resurrected. The two scepters and two feathers not only bring the two lands into the hands of one king but Horus grafts into his body the testicles of the dismembered Seth. The Great Ones of Upper and Lower Egypt are ordered to approach, and in the midst of protecting incense, the double crown, identified as the lost eye of Horus, is put on the king. He distributes bread and beer, symbols of the restored fertility of the land.

Sacred cities are mentioned, and masked figures of the gods take part in the incidents, but most of the playing places are given symbolic names: the Gold House, the White Chapel, the North Hall of Being and Standing, the Desert.

THE *HEB SED*, A JUBILEE REJUVENATION DRAMA

Even more is known about the performance of the Rejuvenation Drama of *Heb Sed*, since each king built a large hall or enclosed area for his jubilee and often decorated the walls with pictures of the performance. Close to Djozer's large step pyramid at Sakkara, the earliest large pyramid, are the remains of a large Heb Sed hall; on the two long sides are indications of the booths for the local gods from Upper and Lower Egypt. A number of kings of the New Kingdom built and rebuilt Heb Sed halls as part of the enormous complex at Karnak. The Heb Sed hall at Rubastes was rebuilt a number of times, notably by Rameses II and centuries later by Osorkon of the Twenty-Second Dynasty, about 844 B.C. Detailed pictures are carved on the walls of this festival hall. From Old Kingdom to New Kingdom and into Roman times, the Heb Sed was a popular festival and was important in strengthening the power of the king.

Some kings held a Heb Sed after thirty years of rule, some much earlier, and some held a second Heb Sed after an interval of a few years. It not only gave the king a symbolic burial and resurrection but reestablished him on the double throne of Upper and Lower Egypt, attended by masked representatives of the local gods of the cities, and showed him, under the direction of the supreme god, taking possession of the two lands. It began with a splendid procession, with the king, dressed like Osiris, the god of the dead, and adorned with his insignia but speaking the words of Horus as he takes his place on the double throne and reenacts his first enthronement. The spirits of Pe and Nekhen, the traditional sacred cities of the two lands, give him long life, and Thoth and other deities present him to Amon-Re.

In the private drama in the tomb, the king was greeted by the assembly of twelve gods, the main gods of the Ennead and several others. There he was given rebirth and emerged as Horus. A pair of obelisks, symbols of body and spirit, served as twin shafts to catch the light of sunrise and carry it into the tomb house as part of the resurrection. At the end the king put on a kind of kilt with a tail to do a running dance to take possession of the symbolic fields. The term *Heb Sed* means the festival of the tail.

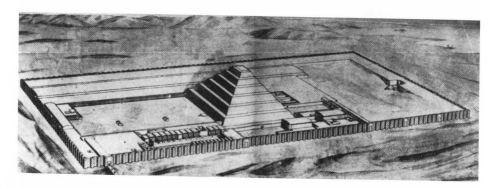

Reconstruction of the step pyramid at Sakkara, c. 2600 B.C. Drawing shows a courtyard for Heb Sed performances. *Courtesy of the Trustees of the British Museum.*

NEW KINGDOM THEATRES

About 1580 B.C. rebels from the southern part of Egypt finally drove out the Hyksos intruders and reestablished the capital at Thebes (modern Luxor). The kings of the New Kingdom chose the mountain west of the river as a symbol of the "Risen Land," the sacred link between earth and heaven, and dug their tombs into the stone of the "Valley of the Tombs of the Kings." Then on the plains between the mountain and the Nile, each king built his "House of Millions of Years," the "mortuary temples," as some Egyptologists have called them. The most striking one still exists in a good state of preservation: the theatre of the remarkable woman Hetshepsut. It is a beautiful sculptured form of two colonnades facing two large open platforms and two ramps, the final achievement of a theatre form freed from subservience to the pyramid. In the Old Kingdom, the king's House of Millions of Years, built against the pyramid, was a relatively small building of two stories, with inner colonnades and an open platform facing the rising sun. A long covered passageway from the Nile led to the open platform for the resurrection drama at sunrise. In the Middle Kingdom, the tomb pyramid was much smaller, and the platform of the theatre was built all around, enclosing the pyramid.

Since Hetshepsut had herself crowned not as Queen but as King, it was important that her coronation drama emphasize her rebirth as a son of the supreme god Amon. On the walls of the corridors of her House of Millions of Years are illustrations and some of the dialogue of her drama. First she visits the two shrines of the Two Lands. Anubis at the north shrine and Amon himself at the south shrine give her long life and declare that she is the child of the god. The play proper begins

Model of the mortuary temple of Queen Hetshepsut, Luxor, Egypt.

with Amon summoning the Ennead, including Horus and Hathor, the mother cow goddess, especially associated with Hetshepsut. Amon announces that a mighty princess will be born: "I will give for her the two lands in peace. I will give for her all lands and all countries." The scene of the conception shows Amon sitting before the Queen Mother, holding one sign of life to her mouth and the other to her hand, near the center of her body. Then Knum, the potter-god, creates the twins, the boy and his Ka or double. The frogheaded Hebet holds the sign of life to their nostrils. The birth scene is on three levels, on the framework of three beds, one on top of the other. A nurse holds the twins to be seen by the gods and goddesses, who include at the bottom level the grotesque dwarf god Bes and the pregnant hippopotamus goddess. Amon receives his daughter, presented by Hathor, embraces her, and declares her his "first born, as king to take possession of the two lands on the throne of Horus like Re." Next she is taught to walk and talk by the gods, baptized by Amon and Horus, and crowned by her father Thothmes I, who after his sons had died prepared his daughter to be king.

DRAMA AT KARNAK

After Akhenaten's short-lived attempt about 1348 B.C. to establish a new religion at his own city of El Amarna, the kings returned to Thebes and reestablished the old dramas. Although some continued to build their own Houses of Millions of Years west of the Nile, the center of dramatic activity apparently shifted to the great complex of temples on the east side of the river known as Karnak. Certainly several Heb Sed rejuvenation festivals were performed there, with elaborate courts built or rebuilt. The sacred lakes must have served for solar barks both for parts of the morning resurrection drama and for performances designed to cure illness and promote health. Passages from the old Pyramid Texts indicate that the ancient resurrection dramas were still performed, and areas intended as Birth Houses show that the nativity, especially, and probably other parts of the coronation drama, were also performed. Of special interest are the two great sacred ways which cross at right angles in the *hypostyle* hall. One leads toward the water down an avenue of ram-headed sphinxes, and on festival days a great procession carried the statue of Amon in a boat to the temple at Luxor. The other sacred way leads through the middle of the great hall, then through a series of pylons, on south to a separate enclosure around the temple of Mut. It resembles the sacred way leading into the precinct of Demeter at Eleusis near Athens and the sacred way leading into theatres at Knossos and Phaistos in Crete. Mut was the earlier, earthly wife of Amon, corresponding to Demeter, wife of Zeus and goddess of spring growth and agriculture.

32

LATER VARIATIONS OF THE DRAMAS

Once the outline of the main drama is made clear—the episodes of Isis' search for the body of Osiris and Horus' triumph over Seth and the simultaneous resurrection of the dead king and ascension or rejuvenation of the son—it is possible to recognize many separate episodes or variations of the central drama. At Abydos the *Mystery Play of Osiris* continued as an annual festival with a free-for-all battle between the attendants escorting the statue of Osiris and the opponents trying to prevent the resurrection. At Edfu the annual triumph of Horus over Seth was developed in Hellenistic times as the harpooning of a small hippopotamus made of bread and the distribution of the pieces of bread to the gods come to celebrate. Imhotep, the legendary architect and healer of the Third Dynasty, served as narrator, and there were choruses of harpooners, sailors, princesses, and women representing the two lands of Egypt.

Under the domination of the Persians, who conquered Egypt in 325 B.C., the invader is identified with Seth, now triumphant, and Thoth makes an impassioned plea to the great god Re: "See now, the miserable Seth has returned to pillage and rape, to destroy the sanctuaries and throw the temples into tumult. . . . This is a violation of your order." The divine Re reconfirms his ancient assignment of Egypt to Horus and orders Seth sent back to Asia.

Lyric aspects of drama were developed in many ways. Popular with both singers and dancers was the lament of Isis and Nephthys for Osiris. A ballet-drama of the Four Winds presented a variation of the attempt of Apophis, the jackal god, to prevent the rising of the sun. As a divine prince is coming through the doors of a pavilion, the Four Winds, played by singing dancers, try to stop the procession, but a beggar dancer captures them and forces them to their knees. As the Four Winds live forever, so, with control of their power, will the prince.

Although the mythological dramas of the Old Kingdom seem entirely serious, some comic effects appeared in dramas of the Middle Kingdom. In one version of the coffin text the scene of the birth of Horus is followed by comic bragging of the precocious child: "I am Horus the Falcon, on the battlement of One whose name is Hidden. My flight reached the horizon. I have surpassed the gods of the firmament. . . . Even the eagle cannot match my first flight."

In the New Kingdom, comic scenes were developed around the figure of Apophis, whose special duty was to prevent the sunrise. Tired of the opposition every morning, Re had sent three champions, Thoth, Horus, and a butcher-god, to battle. In a speech of the Brimmer Rhind papyrus, Thoth invites Re to come up over the horizon to see how the three have laid out Apophis. In an incident in Chapter XXX.X of the *Book of the Dead*, Apophis, hoping by guile to get to the sunrise, is taken by the gods. He tries alternately by menaces and by pitiful cries to get out of his trap. Seeing how well the gods have disposed of him, Re sets out on the lake of turquoise and the gods celebrate.

Egypt gained a remarkable stability by repeating the same dramas over and over. The pyramid drama was repeated every morning at sunrise, and at some times there must have been several going on simultaneously at different pyramids. Doubtless the first performance by the new king was well attended, but as long as the endowment lasted the plays would be performed whether anyone was watching or not. Of course, the great processions performed on annual festival days would draw the entire populace. The coronation drama, performed only once a generation, spread its episodes in sight of the entire nation, while the Heb Sed jubilees were mostly inside a large enclosed court that would hold a few thousand.

The exploration of Egyptian drama has barely begun, and many new plays may be discovered with more intimate personal content. But at this point what is most impressive is the power of tradition and continuity. Since the dramas presented the gods and the great cosmic myths that gave stability to the nation, it was important that they be performed with a minimum of change from one generation to the next.

II

The Oriental Art
of the Theatre

Geisha girls in various poses. *Illustration by Martha Sutherland.*

Introduction

No other ancient civilization is closely comparable to the Egyptian. Egypt absorbed invaders, and the influence of other peoples was minimal. But when we turn to the ancient civilizations of Asia—India, China, and Japan—we find that though each had its own history and special qualities, there were similarities in philosophy, religion, and the attitude toward art, and at times one country affected another. In their Iron Age, which began as early as 1200 B.C. and lasted in some places into the Christian era, each had small city states close enough to stimulate one another and independent enough to foster diversity.

The Iron Age drama is a religious drama, produced primarily at sacred temples and associated with great processions and festivals. Though the gods appear, they are in the background or are presented in their human forms, subject to the same loves and betrayals, hopes and guilts, as mortals. It is a more humanistic drama than Egypt's because of a change in religious outlook.

Between 600 and 450 B.C. new prophets appeared in several places, giving the old religion new directions: Zoroaster in Persia, Micah and Amos in Judea, Buddha and the prophets of Jainism in India, Confucius and Lao Tsu (the founder of Taoism) in China, and Aeschylus in Athens. These prophets shifted the emphasis from prescribed rites to the choice and responsibility of the individual. All defined God as a universal principle rather than a tribal or national champion, and offered salvation or enlightenment for the individual's advancement in wisdom and devotion.

Great empires still existed and sometimes overwhelmed the small city states. But even in the empires the citizens wanted to share in spiritual benefits. In India and China imperial rulers, who claimed celestial endorsement but did not claim to be incarnations of God, allowed the individual a great deal of freedom. It was for the painter, sculptor, and actor to show, in visible symbols, the all-too-human essence of the invisible divine. This was true even in Japan, where an authoritarian and isolationist government did not promote fanaticism in religion or greatly hamper individual artistic expression.

An important difference between the drama of the Iron Age and earlier drama is that some of the new drama is written down and can be enjoyed as literature. Since the eighteenth century the ancient Sanskrit drama of India has fascinated literary historians and poets of the West. Western poets of the twentieth century have been influenced by the poetic form of the Japanese *Noh* in translation. Sanskrit and Noh drama hold up as first-rate literature for the armchair reader. Chinese drama and Japanese *Kabuki* are also, with a slight orientation, well worth reading. But the most important fact about the ancient drama of the Asian countries is that traditional performance still exists. Kipling's soldiers were attracted by free love and temple bells in Mandalay, Gauguin by exotic color and frank nakedness in Tahiti, and Conrad's outcasts by the spicy smells of the East that helped them to forget Europe. But today the sensitive traveler can enjoy the essence of the East in its theatre, find some of its spiritual meaning, and delight in the sensuous values and the virtuoso skills in acting, song, and dance. As a living experience the drama of Asia, even the classic Indian drama of more than a thousand years ago, is available in performance by highly skilled singers and dancers.

We turn with pleasure to a continent where art is highly developed and is regarded as a basic way of knowing and worshiping the eternal. The direct relation between art and metaphysics, so characteristic of primitive art, persists in the main traditions of the sophisticated cultures of India, China, and Japan. There is no distinction between sacred and profane art.

Where science teaches a Westerner to be an uninvolved observer of the objects of nature, religion teaches an Oriental to see oneness behind all particular subjects, not through a scientific theory or a concept of abstract objects in theoretical space but through the color, fragrance, and texture of his experience in looking at nature or art or in worshiping God. Hence art is a direct way of knowing the *tao*, the unity behind all ethics and religion. Art is at once the particular and the universal, the blueness in the flower, the transcendental captured in an image.

The ideal aspect that still makes a strong appeal to the senses is defined in the classic Hindu doctrine of *yoga*, the principle by which any artist creates. The word *yoga*, cognate of the English *yoke*, is the tie that identifies the artist with the idea he wants to express. He must first contemplate his object, which may be a god or hero or a tiger, until he is identified with it and loses the self as he is possessed by the theme. In the second step, often when he is absent from the object, the image is completed in his mind in a kind of trance or mystical vision. He takes the third step by putting down in paint or words a copy not of the particular object but of his vision.

The Chinese painter traditionally made provision for the indication of the unseen, the "round the corner," "behind the mountain," the metaphysical. One important way to achieve his purpose was to leave large empty space in the midst of the landscape. As Taoism pointed out that the important part of the bowl was not the pottery but the empty bowl shaped and defined by the pottery, so a painting should have empty spaces that were not merely restful but vibrant with thought of the unseen. Oriental theatre thrives on suggesting houses that are not seen and indicating properties, horses, people, and battles by the skilled way the character reacts to the supposed objects. In Peter Shaffer's *Equus* (1973) the actors wearing horse's heads are an Oriental concept.

Art as the bridge, the yoke, between man and God was nowhere more important than in the romantic treatment of love. Though the erotic has never been absent from Western religion—as witness the interpretation of the Song of Songs as the love between Christ and the Church, the nun as the bride of Christ, and the Virgin as an object of romantic adoration—yet since the time of St. Paul most churchmen have looked askance at the erotic. But except in the views of extreme ascetics, Eastern religions emphasize love among the gods as an important part of world history. Far more than the worship of fertility common to simple cultures, the erotic symbolizes important metaphysical relations between the visible world and the invisible, earth and heaven.

Most Oriental theatres make no use of scenery, and even the Japanese Kabuki, which uses very spectacular scenery, is not hampered by it. The settings can move forward or backward, turn around, or disappear as the convenience of the acting suggests, and both the "flower path" through the audience and the forestage area permit acting that is not related to a setting. Properties are either indicated by pantomime or brought on as needed by property men who are not noticed by actors or audience.

In subject matter, also, the Oriental drama has kept much of the fairy-story quality of children's play. Heroes are idealized dream figures fighting demonic villains. Magic spells abound, and monsters and supernatural beings move in and out of the story. Tremendous difficulties are overcome to rescue the beautiful heroine from ugly, wicked, and grotesque surroundings. European poets of the Romantic age found Oriental drama, especially the Sanskrit drama, very much to their liking. Later, realistic writers tried to banish romance and fairy tales as childish and perhaps dangerous fantasy. But since Freud and Jung, we have rediscovered profound meaning in fairy tales and see that a romantic journey into childhood may be an important journey into the depths of the subconscious or into the ancestral sources of health and value.

The mask is the most conspicuous vestige of the ancient journey back to the lands of gods and ancestors. And Oriental theatres have produced magnificent masks, some as robust and elemental as the masks of the South Sea Islands, some unequaled anywhere for exquisite grace. Painted faces are only one remove from the mask, allowing the face to move and the actor to adapt a traditional pattern to his own face but setting the performance into a realm of ancient ceremonies and primitive archetypes. Shadow plays and puppet theatres, far more important in the East than in the West, are close kin to the regular theatre, and in Java and Japan actors have been influenced in their acting style by the high accomplishments of the puppets.

Yet everything about Eastern theatre is to the last degree professional. It leaves nothing to chance or the inspiration of the moment. If masks and painted faces follow age-old patterns, they are yet created with the utmost care by techniques that take years to learn. Training in dance and song lasts a lifetime. The performer often begins serious study in early childhood, and a Kabuki actor is not considered to have reached the peak in performance until he has had twenty to thirty years of professional experience.

Westerners may speak patronizingly of the simple quality of Eastern theatre. But it is far from certain that the Western naturalistic actor, who depends on summoning up the remembered experiences of his own limited past or the actor in an open-theatre performance who tries to exploit the spontaneous feelings of the moment, can create a more mature work of art or a more mature response in the audience than an actor trained in a technique that has been polished for hundreds of years.

Performance of Cambodian shadow puppets in front of a translucent screen. *Illustration by Martha Sutherland.*

40

The Theatre of India

THEATRE IN THE CLASSIC AGE

In the Bronze Age (4000 B.C.–2000 B.C.) both India and China had mythological dramas and popular performers invoking the gods in song and dance. But India produced a sophisticated drama, romantic and secular, seven or eight hundred years before a comparable drama appeared in China. The earliest Eastern drama that is fully documented was given in northern India in the classic age that lasted for more than a thousand years, beginning with the establishment of the Maurya dynasty by Chandragupta about 320 B.C. and the wide conquest of the third Mauryan king, Asoka (264 to 227 B.C.). In the fifth century A.D. the Huns from central Asia, whose invasions reached from China to Rome invaded India, and with the break-up of the Gupta kingdom the creative spirit was gone. Poets continued to write Sanskrit plays even into the fourteenth and fifteenth centuries, but after the Mohammedan conquest began in the ninth and tenth centuries the classic Sanskrit plays were no longer performed at court. Popular dramas in the several vernacular languages have been handed down orally from performer to performer to this day, and, even more important, the classic dance tradition begun in the age of the Guptas has persisted in temples and villages under both Moslem and British rule. It appears in its purest form in the *Bharanatya* performed by solo girl dancers in northern India, but also, in a modified form, in the derived classic dances of Southeast Asia from Thailand and Cambodia to Indonesia.

Long before the classic age India absorbed much of the Bronze Age civilization from Asia Minor, and then, between 1900 and 1200 B.C., the Aryans invaded from the high plains of central Asia, bringing chariots from Persia, horses from the steppes, and cows and cow goddesses from the Near East, singing of their triumphant warrior gods in the Sanskrit hymns and narratives that were later gathered together in the Vedas. But in India in the classic age the war gods of the Aryans had acquired a sense of guilt, and Intra, who had conquered demons and released pent-up rivers, had to suffer for his daring and become aware of the suffering of men.

The suffering of this world was met in different ways by the three religions developed in the classic age. The Jainists drew an appalling picture of a meaningless cycle of creation and destruction, rising and falling, striving and degenerating, through countless millions of years. The only hope for an individual was to escape from the chain of reincarnations by extreme austerity and abnegation of desire. Buddhism offered a middle way. Its devotees saw the world as unworthy but not loathsome, and though seeking escape from the meaningless round of will and desire, looked on the world with compassion. The Mahayana sect also promised a vision of the charm and jewel-like beauty of the heavenly state as an aid in spiritual contemplation—a vision that encouraged attention to music, painting, and sculpture. After Asoka, the early Mauryan king, had established his empire by bloody conquest, he was converted to Buddhism and encouraged Buddhist thought and art. But Buddhism in India soon gave way to Brahmanism, and only outside India has it been an important religion.

In Brahmanism, or Hinduism, the modification of the traditional Aryan religion of the Vedas, the ideal was the achievement of spiritual enlightenment that would transcend the shortcomings of the world. Hence Sanskrit drama is not concerned with the battles of Indra but with the gentle sorrows of separation and reunion. Neglect, forgetfulness, and blindness cause the difficulties of life, but if the truth is persistently sought, it can be brought to light. As the King in the last act of *Shakuntala* (c. 400), by Kalidasa, the greatest drama that survives from the classic age, enters into the celestial garden of contemplation and penance, he finds the beautiful wife and son he had lost through blindness and negligence, and he learns that his son is destined for great deeds as a champion and leader of his people. The King does not repudiate the world of jewels, power, and love, but he finds the world of youthful illusion transformed by a more mature spirituality.

Apparently there were mythological plays about cosmic events, such as *The Churning of the Ocean*, to produce the "ambrosia" of health, beauty, and immortality. Although the classic Sanskrit dramas are concerned with human action, the immortals and their conflicts are always in the background. The king in the last act of *Shakuntala* returns from a celestial battle with the demons, and in *The Later History of Rama*, twin boys stage a contest with supernatural weapons, probably a miniature version of the cosmic battles in the mythological dramas. The popular plays of Rama that have come down to our day in the vernacular languages include many cosmic battles and sieges.

The sacred legends of the origin of drama, recorded in the great discourse on dance and drama, the *Natyasastra* (c. 300), indicate the importance of recitation of the Vedas, but define the drama as a new form, a fifth Veda, distinct from the older Vedas. Drama was created by the gods to bring a blessing on the Silver Age. Since the Golden Age had direct contact with the gods and no sorrow or conflict, it had not needed drama, but as quarrels and jealousies raged in earth and sky, the gods saw that the many people of the lower castes had no access to the sacred lore

42

of the Vedas. Manu, whose task it was to sustain the world, was especially disheartened. Then Indra and the other gods appealed to Brahma, who created a fifth Veda that would be available to all castes, taking from each of the four existing Vedas a particular characteristic—recitation from the Rigveda, song from another, acting from a third, and *rasa*, or emotion, from the fourth.

Brahma founded the drama as an *agon* or conflict. Watching a fight between the god Krishna and two demons, he found it so fascinating that he undertook to put the essence of the postures and movements into drama. His play, *The Defeat of the Demons*, was to be the feature of a new festival for the erection of a "Banner of Indra" which would have the power to ward off demons. Since it was not appropriate for Indra to act, the play was entrusted to the divine sage Bharata and his hundred sons. Ever since then actors have been known as sons of Bharata, and the *Natyasastra* is attributed to him. He was supplied with musicians, heavenly nymphs, or *apsaras*, as dancers, and an enclosed theatre for performance.

When the demons realized that such a theatre might present an unfavorable picture of their defeat, they raised objections, but Brahma assured them that the theatre would not attack particular persons. His speech is an eloquent statement about the nature and purpose of the stage:

Why are you so displeased, my demon friends? I have created this Fifth Veda so that there

Eighteenth-century manuscript drawing of King Dushyanta with his wife Shakuntala and their son Bharata, the "All-Tamer," being driven in a royal chariot by the comic charioteer. *Courtesy the National Museum, New Delhi.*

43

would be a better mutual understanding between you and the Gods. It is not a piece of propaganda in any part. The three worlds shall be described here. There is religion for those who are religious minded, love for those that are amorous minded, knowledge for the ignorant, criticism for the learned, a delight for the Gods, and a solace for the afflicted. In short, everyone will find in drama just what he needs and what is good for him. It preaches yet delights, it is recreation yet it is reasonable, it teaches yet is broad-minded. Where else would you find reason with recreation, knowledge with attraction, and morality with beauty?

The demons were satisfied, the drama began, and Manu found courage to go on bearing the weight of the world.

The standard prologues of the classic plays used traditional religious songs, dances, dialogues, and prayers to invoke the gods. The musicians who enter to the sound of drums and begin a concert are joined by dancers. The men perform the vigorous *tandara*, the dance of Shiva as he alternately creates and destroys the world. Then the women present a more charming and voluptuous dance, the *lasya*, associated with Parvati, the spouse of Shiva in his more beneficent aspect. A ceremony of raising the mast for the banner of Indra follows, and a procession pays deference to the guardians of space at the four directions. Then the reciter gives a benediction to the god or gods of the occasion and to the patron who is presenting the play. The clown, or Vidushaka, may enter with playful repartée. The director of the company interrupts and asks the leading lady to sing a song to set the mood and announce the name of the play. Thus there is a gradual transition from religious invocation through prayer and dance to the play itself.

Hindu dance combines many traditions. After Alexander invaded India, a Greek kingdom was set up in the northwest and Gandhara sculpture shows a strong Hellenistic influence. Sometimes Hindu dance seems a combination of the free, humanistic sculpture of Greece and the precise, patterned art of the goldsmiths and jewel-makers of central Asia. Temple walls were covered with paintings and carvings of swaying, dancing heavenly beings. In Hindu art the embrace of lovers, the twining of the vine around the tree-trunk, the mathematical pattern of leaves and flowers, all signified the union of time and eternity, the visible and transcendent, the worldly and the divine.

THE AESTHETICS OF HINDU DRAMA

Central to Hindu aesthetics is the doctrine of the *rasa*, a word that seems to have meant a juice or essence and hence a flavor and is sometimes translated "mood" or "sentiment." While songs may deal with a wider list of rasas, the dramatist is expected to choose from nine traditionally suitable ones—love, heroism, sorrow, anger, mirth, horror, odium, wonder, and quiescence. As one would expect of romantic drama, love, heroism, and wonder are the most frequent rasas. Though a rasa corresponds to an emotion in real life and must seem accurate and well observed, it is known in a separate realm of the mind. The *Natyasastra* emphasizes the separation of experience from the treatment of it in art. But the artist can communicate his fresh image only if he has a tradition of shared and recognizable techniques. He creates his rasas by the use of conventional *ragas*, or melodies, *talas*, or rhythmic patterns, and *mudras*, or gestures.

Where traditional Western music is confined to two scales, major and minor, and a few suggestive moods for special occasions, Hindu music has an almost unlimited number of ragas and a large number of established moods. The composer or singer was free to invent new ragas or talas to suit his fancy, but the classic age furnished him with a number already familiar to the audience. Some ragas were associated with the time of day, some with the season, and some with particular colors, flowers, or trees.

Equally precise were the mudras. This language of gesture served with or without words as the basis for dance and drama far beyond India. With slight variations it has been handed down these two thousand years. Not only do several treatises from the classic age give exact definitions of the gestures but many paintings and sculptures show the mudras, and a thirteenth-century temple of Shiva at

Nineteenth-century painting from the Jakata Screen manuscript depicting Indo-Chinese dancing girls in the Royal Pavilion while the Royal Prince arrives in the royal chariot. *Courtesy Musée National des Arts Asiatiques, Guimet.*

45

Chidambaram is adorned with exact illustrations in sculpture of the most important mudras listed in the *Natyasastra*.

There are twenty-four head gestures, six or more glances of the eye, six movements of the brow, and four movements of the neck. There are five leaps, ten gaits, and eight motions for stamping, walking, rolling, wavering, and so on. It is said that there are as many hand gestures as there are thoughts in the mind. Of basic hand positions some traditions have names for as many as twenty-eight for the single hand and dozens for the combined hands. All the positions have names, and each is associated with color, a patron god, and a race of people, and often has a legendary act of some god or hero as its origin. Thus the flag hand, the simplest, with fingers and palm straight and thumb close against the forefinger, is said to have originated when Brahma greeted a friend with a cry of victory. It is used with different movements to bless, to direct someone to approach or go, or to describe flame, cold, heat, the wings of a bird, rain, or simple actions like cutting.

THE HINDU THEATRE

There is no clear picture of theatrical conditions in Gupta India, but piecing together many references, we suppose a great range of activities, with traveling acrobats, magicians, singers, dancers, reciters, and actors employed at temples, at homes, for weddings, or any special occasion or festival. We must imagine performances in streets, gardens, and squares as well as in courtyards of palaces and temples. Many Gupta temples, like many Asian temples today, had platforms, either open or roofed, for musicians and other performers, and some temples and palaces had splendid theatres.

The Sanskrit plays that have come down to us are addressed to a courtly audience, and we presume that they were performed only in the great temples and in the palaces of kings and rich noblemen. The prologues of the plays indicate that professional companies were hired for the occasion. The *Natyasastra* has directions for constructing three types of temporary buildings—rectangular, square, and triangular—with ascending steps for the audience to squat on. For a permanent theatre in a palace the recommended plan is a room twice as long as wide, one half devoted to the audience. The stage, say forty-eight feet square, would be further divided so that the main acting area, twenty-four feet square, would have a frame supported by two twelve-foot columns and separated from the rear stage by a curtain. Decorated cloths and walls shaped the open playing area and allowed the disclosure of arranged groups. The curtain, called "the Greek" and perhaps of Hellenistic origin, must vary in color according to the type of play—white for a love drama, yellow for a heroic play, somber for a pathetic scene, variegated for a comic, black for a tragic or horrible, red for a violent, and so on. References to gods suggest that a higher stage level was available and perhaps some means of letting an actor descend through the air from above.

The *Natyasastra* stipulates that in a theatre auditorium the pillars were to be painted different colors, to indicate where the different castes would sit. At the center was the king's box, with his wives and officials of the court seated around him in strict protocol.

The musicians, according to some accounts, played unseen, but other accounts describe the spreading of a beautiful carpet and the seating of the musicians, the drummers facing east, left of them the tambourines, a singer facing north, at his left the lute, zither, and flute players. Members of the chorus took their places at the same time, the leader in front of the singers.

Although there was nothing we would call scenery, there were some properties. The *Natyasastra* describes the making of fountains, rocks, houses, and caves of light bamboo frames and cloth so that they could be brought on easily. Mechanical horses, elephants, lions, tigers, and monsters could be pulled on by cords or made to work by actors inside.

The offstage voice had many uses. It might be impersonal, narrating what had happened or was to happen out of sight of the audience. Sometimes it made comments or gave advice or warning to those on stage. Sometimes it spoke for supernatural beings or for animals or plants, reinforcing the feeling, never absent in Hindu drama, of the closeness of the spiritual essence of all nature.

The conventions of characterization were set by characteristic movements and by dress. Usually a maiden was dressed in dark blue, and her dress and hair indicated her mental state. When Vasantesana, the heroine of *The Little Clay Cart* (c. 400), appeared on the stage, the audience knew at a glance by her dress, hair, jewelry, and the ending *-sana* of her name that she was a courtesan, though a charming, admirable, and even modest heroine. Showy jewelry made of cheap materials to imitate gold and silver and precious stones also served to indicate the status and condition of the characters. There are descriptions of masks with openings for forehead, cheeks, ears, mouth, and neck, probably used for demons, supernatural beings, and monstrous villains.

Most vivid of all conventional characters is the clownish companion of the king, the Vidushaka. The word means one who spoils or disfigures, suggesting a scandalmonger as well as one who subjects high ideals to the light of everyday reality. This pairing of hero and comic, of romance and reality, has appeared in festivals all over the world from primitive times and makes a special appeal to the creative writer, as we see in Lear and his Fool, Don Quixote and Sancho Panza, and other literary pairs. Like a lightning rod the clown deflects ill luck and irritations of daily living to himself and allows the hero to live a life untouched by petty cares. In the Buddhist morality plays he is the doubter who argues against his friend's conversion yet gives in at the end. In one of Kalidasa's plays he helps the

47

king deceive his queen and have a glimpse of a beautiful dancing girl. One hero describes him thus: "Droll in company, comforting in sorrow, and brave in facing the foe, he gives delight to my heart. Indeed he is my second self." As one who easily moves in the world of women, he can be an intermediary between hero and heroine. As a commentator, speaking the language of every day, he is a bridge between play and audience. As companion of the king, the Vidushaka is recognized as a Brahman, a member of the highest caste, but he only pretends to learning and speaks not poetic Sanskrit but the Prakrit of everyday life. In appearance he is the opposite of the hero—bald-headed, hunch-backed, dwarfish, with yellow eyes and distorted mouth. Sometimes he is described as dressed in rags and skins, but considering the emphasis on beauty in all Oriental drama, we can hardly suppose that he wore anything uglier than a few patches of silk and fur.

In treatment of time and place Hindu drama was completely free. At one moment the stage was a street, at the next a room in a house; when different seats were brought in the scene was a court ready for a trial. Yet there is compact structure in the plays, and between acts events are narrated briefly so that each act is closely related in time, action, and mood to the preceding. In this respect Hindu drama is more like modern Western theatre than like the Chinese and Japanese.

The classic Hindu drama must have been spectacular in the splendor of music, dance, mime, and moving tableaux. There were many very complex scenes of vivid action and undoubtedly many moments of dance not indicated in the text. In *Shakuntala* there are two long travel songs by King Dushanta and his attendant. At the beginning of the play the king and a charioteer are in a chariot pursuing a deer, slowly at first, jolting over rough ground, then very fast, until the king starts to shoot. A hermit suddenly stops them, reminding the king that he is on holy ground of a hermitage. At the beginning of the last act he is again in a chariot, this time a heavenly chariot flying through the air. He stops to visit one of the gods in a heavenly hermitage of penance and meditation.

The *Natyasastra* gives some details of how the actor mimes in short steps the ride in a chariot, indicating that he is holding his bow in one hand and the pole of the chariot in the other. He has learned special steps to indicate getting in and out of the chariot. He shows in mime that he is mounting an elephant by his handling of a goad, that he is riding a horse by the use of a bridle, and that he is in other kinds of conveyance by the use of a whip. Special emphasis is put on how the actor develops a characteristic gait for each character.

In Hindu drama nature and art are interwoven. Since the visible world is but an insubstantial emanation of the underlying spirit, the Brahma, all nature is alive, and it is not surprising to find in the dialogue, besides rich imagery of stars, vines, flowers, and animals, the use of the voices of animals and trees. Often at the end of the play comes a spectacular gathering, the heavens full of sacred immortals, dancing apsaras, gods, birds, beasts, and flowers.

If all life is seen as a vision, we are not surprised to find the mirror images of painting, sculpture, dream, apparitions, and the play-within-the-play. In *The Later*

History of Rama, the exposition is handled subtly by showing Rama and Sita looking at a mural painting of their past, commenting on the moments when they were
most happy. Their separation is movingly presented when a goddess allows her to
return to him invisible. Thinking she is dead, he supposes that her touch and his
awareness of her presence are only memory and imagination. At the end she is
brought back to him in a play-within-the-play performed by the apsaras, except
that she plays herself. In Hindu drama the world is not dross and violence but love
and beauty, experienced as the sorrow of separation and misunderstanding until
all can be resolved in spiritual enlightenment. Together at last, the lovers overcome the limitations and separations of finite existence in a celebration of the
glorious unity of all.

Kalidasa's *Shakuntala* is the pearl of Sanskrit literature. Through Goethe and the
nineteenth-century romantics it has had a great influence in the West, perhaps
more than any other work from the Far East, and not much less than the *Rubaiyat*
(early 12th century) and the Arabian Nights tales from the Near East. By common
consent the greatest poet and dramatist of India, Kalidasa left several poems and
two other plays besides his masterpiece. Nothing is known about him but a few
legends and references to him in the works of others.

Shakuntala presents the basic patterns of all romance: love, separation, reunion,
deep yearning, temporary difficulties, triumph, demons of evil and accident overcome by the final recognition of true worth. The settings are symbolic of the life
of imagination: an Eden of innocence, a sacred grove into which love finds its
way; the deceptive world of the court; and finally another enchanted grove, beyond the sky, where hidden treasure is revealed, where heaven bestows its blessing, and where matter is resolved into spirit.

The first act of *Shakuntala* shows the budding of love in early summer in a sacred
grove presided over by a hermit sage. The king has left his court life and wives,
hoping to find peace in the quiet of nature, but he is restless with unsatisfied longing. He finds a beautiful young girl, Shakuntala, ward of the hermit sage. She has
grown up in close harmony with nature. The King comes to Shakuntala's rescue
when a bee pursues her lips. A herd of deer is frightened by an elephant disturbed
by the king's party. The king and the maiden part with lingering backward glances.

In Acts II and III the longing of love is painful. The king cannot sleep. His
clown companion is unsympathetic and impatient with the rude life of the woods.
Messengers summon the king back to court, but the hermits ask him to protect
the hermitage from demons. He is torn between his two duties. In Act III the
king, seeking a cool bower, finds Shakuntala, also restless, being fanned by her
maids. He overhears her speak of her love and compose a song as a letter to him.
They speak their mutual love and vows and quietly part as demons cast shadows
and create terror in the evening.

In Act IV the shadows deepen. Will the king accept her as his wife? What will
her hermit father say? A visiting sage, furious at being neglected, puts a curse on
her. With her father's blessing she departs from the protecting grove of childhood

49

into the uncertainties of the adult world. The trees, plants, deer, and peacock all speak sorrowful farewells. She is like the doe, slow with the weight of her young. To the last her pet fawn tries to hold her back.

Two scenes from Kalidasa's *Shakuntala*, c. 400 A.D. *Top:* King Dushyanta sees Shakuntala for the first time. *Bottom:* Shakuntala ignores her companions to linger with King Dushyanta. *Courtesy the National Museum, New Delhi.*

Act V moves into the busy world, where hearts are hard, the ways of love devious. The hermits who escort Shakuntala to the court feel that here is "a house lapped in flames of fire" where people are "unclean and manacled and fettered as slaves." The king listens to a haunting song which half wakens his memories and longing, but when Shakuntala comes to him the curse is working and he remembers nothing. She has lost the ring her lover gave her that would remove the curse. She laments her lost innocence, but there is no returning to Eden. But if the world contains malignity, there is also a ring that can undo the curse and comic fishermen who by chance find the fish that had swallowed the ring. The king recognizes the ring and grieves for what he has lost. As he judges a case of the inheritance of an unborn heir, he thinks of the loss of his own heir.

In Act VII the king enters an enchanted grove of penance and austerity beyond the sky, where he meets his son, a boy prodigy taming a lion's cub. By a series of tests and the use of talismans, the king discovers that this is the hidden heir, and he is reunited with Shakuntala. The gods give their blessing and predict the supernatural power of the child who will rule over wide empires. Sorrow is dissolved in enlightenment; matter is transformed into spirit.

The Little Clay Cart puts more emphasis than *Shakuntala* on the worldly and comic. It may come from a later century. There is no supernatural element, and poetry is only incidental. The hero is a gentleman who has lost his money and the heroine is a charming courtesan. The traditional plot of the discovery of the lost heir to the throne is marginal and is combined with exciting episodes in streets and law courts, where thieves, servants, gamblers, cheaters, and cart drivers appear. The romance is leavened with pithy observations about justice and the ways of the world. This combination of exotic charm and skeptical social comment accounts for the success of *The Little Clay Cart* in New York in the 1920s, when it was given a charming production at the Neighborhood Playhouse. But for arousing hidden dreams, one will always turn, like Goethe, to the greatest of all romances, *Shakuntala*.

POPULAR TRADITION IN THE DRAMA OF INDIA

The theatre did not disappear with the classical Sanskrit drama. In fact, popular theatre in vernacular languages probably throve all through the Golden Age unnoticed by the literati who analyzed and imitated the classical models. Even during the Mohammedan and the British domination it continued, and today, we are told by Balwent Gargi, our best authority, that 700,000 towns and villages in India have active folk theatres. They derive from the classic theatre or from the mythological plays that antedated the known classic plays. The folk plays keep the traditional religious introduction, the conventional clown, and the combination of recitation, singing, dancing, and acting, and many folk plays keep some equivalent of the setting up of the banner of Indra to drive away demons and consecrate the grounds to a sacred purpose.

In the centuries of disorder after the breakdown of the Gupta reign and the continuing advance of the Moslem invaders, India developed many aspects of a feudal system. This was the period—900 to 1500—that saw feudalism in Europe and Japan, the blossoming of Islam, and in many countries an intensification of religious devotion. In the West, devotion centered on the Virgin Mary, then permeated the cult of the knight in love, expressed most strongly in the romances about Lancelot and Guinevere and Tristram and Isolde. The love for a beautiful woman became the symbol of love for the divine. In India the combination of the sensuous and the longing for the divine centered in the story of Krishna and Radha and the Gopis, which had great influence on all the arts, especially dance and drama.

Krishna is one of the incarnations of Vishnu, and stories of the mischievous pranks of this dark boy as he was reared by the Gopis, wives of cow-herding people, were very popular. The Gopis soon found that Krishna was more than a naughty boy. Poets sang of the night when the sound of his flute called the Gopis out to dance in the moonlight. Wilder and wilder circled the dance as Krishna multiplied his presence and teased and embraced each woman. When he left them they recognized that their sensuous longing was a yearning for the divine, that the god was immanent in every being and experience and at the same time transcendent. In time the poets picked out a particular partner for Krishna—his lovely Radha—and dancers for many centuries have danced the circular dance of the Gopis around the divine figures, usually acted by two beautifully made-up boys. Some Buddhist sects used the image of sexual union as an image of union with the divine, and some followers of the Tantric Shakti cults held rites worshiping the female and leading to sexual orgies in the temples. In the sculpture of the famous temples of Khajuraho, charming heavenly nymphs dance and sway and lead their youths to sensuous appreciation of divine unity.

Dances and dance dramas based on the love story of Krishna and Radha are found today throughout India. The sensuous Kathak dancers of northern India specialize in scenes of the story. In many temples and monasteries dance and music dramas are the chief devotional offering. In Manipur State, Krishna dramas are performed at six popular festivals each year. But the greatest development has centered in the small Braj area, Krishna's homeland, not far from Delhi. Professional companies perform the *raslilas* in the temple courtyards before devout crowds. The first part—religious devotion with prayers, songs, and dances—requires a skilled actor-singer to work the audience up to a high pitch of swaying, clapping, shouting, and singing. Most raslilas center in the dance of the Gopis and the longing of Radha and the Gopis when Krishna has left in jealousy and anger. Some are light and concern Krishna's mischievous teasing of the women. A favorite, *Ud-*

dhava, combines the love scenes with a philosophical debate. Uddhava tells the women that they should meditate on the abstract concept of God, who pulsates in every leaf, blade of grass, or grain of sand. But the women are in love with the physical image of Krishna and try in vain to contemplate the abstract. Finally the philosopher begs Krishna to return to them.

Even more spectacular are the *ramlilas*, the plays about Rama, which are especially popular in Benares and neighboring towns. The October festival is cele-

Moonlight dance of Devadasi—Indian temple priestesses with Krishna. *Illustration by Martha Sutherland.*

brated with fireworks, processions, pageants, dances, and dramas, all concerned with the stories of the *Ramayana* (c. 200 B.C.–200), especially the banishment of Rama, the abduction of Sita by demons, and her rescue with the help of the great monkey general Hanuman. There are processions at different parts of town for Sita's marriage, Rama's coronation, and especially for the triumphant return from exile, the Maharaja taking official part with his elephants. As many as 100,000 people may join in one of the demon processions. Acrobats and tumblers entertain along the way, and duels and sword fights may take place between gods and demons. The destructive goddess Kali is represented, and some wild episodes with blood, skulls, and lewdness are included. The ramlilas themselves take several forms. Some are acted fully, with innocent boys taking the main parts. Some are mimed as the stage-manager-reciter sings the story and dialogue. Some are elaborate tableaux to be disclosed when a curtain is drawn. Some actors are highly trained, while some are village performers whose only acting is in this yearly event.

Of the hundreds of folk theatres that survive today, Westerners have been most interested in Kathakali, the vigorous, colorful dance drama of Kerala, on the southwest tip of the country. It is a warrior drama of challenges and combats, reflecting the traditions of a country of chieftains and petty principalities. The most popular subjects are taken from the conflicts of Krishna and the demons, with the monkey general Hanuman playing a prominent part. Some songs and dances derive from prehistoric Dravidian sources, but some songs are taken directly from the classic Sanskrit drama. In dance, Kathakali continues a tradition of gesture very similar to the classic Baratanatyam described in the *Natyasastra*. A gesture language of more than five hundred mudras is carefully taught to the performers. Makeup is elaborate, producing almost masklike enlargements of the face.

A raised platform is used in performance, with the audience on one side or partly around three sides. A curtain is placed part way upstage, usually held by two attendants, to allow an important actor to begin his scene with only the feet and head visible and, at a climax of sound and action, to be suddenly disclosed in his full glory.

Western drama was introduced to India by the British, and there are modern theatres in the larger cities. India has active drama schools and has produced good modern dramas, most of them dealing with problems of life in India. But rather than sampling the new plays, the Westerner interested in theatre will wish to seek out performances of the strange and beautiful traditional dramas.

The Chinese Theatre

Of all Oriental theatres, the Chinese theatre as it existed before the Communist regime has had the greatest impact on the theatre of the West. Since 1912, when a play in the Chinese manner found a large audience in New York, playwrights and directors have looked to the Chinese stage as the perfect foil for Western naturalism. Even more than expressionism or the Elizabethan stage the Chinese theatre has offered a creative alternative to realism.

The traditional Chinese theatre is children's make-believe raised to a high art. There is no front curtain, no proscenium frame, no scenery, no properties. The actor struts down to the front of the stage, accompanied by lively music from an orchestra sitting on the stage in full view, to tell the audience who he is and what he intends to do. If he needs a chair, a property man, ignored by the audience, puts it in position. If he is to climb a mountain, the property man puts a chair on a table and the actor struggles up, creating mountain scenery in the imagination. He opens and closes doors that are not there and steps over an imaginary threshold. He rides a tasseled whip as a horse or strokes with an oar to indicate the movement of a boat. The magnificent costumes and the fantastic painted faces offer the sharpest contrast to the realistic stage. The Chinese stage is a symbol of freedom and the power of the imagination. The Chinese actor creates a sophisticated art rich in song, dance, and acrobatics, in characterization, but above all in a combination of voice and mime. The absence of scenery and realistic properties allows greater emphasis on mime, and the orchestra creates a rhythmic base for a wide variety of moods.

The first play given in the West in the Chinese manner, *The Yellow Jacket* (1912), was not a translation of an actual Chinese play but a compilation from several plays and stories, but the charm of the romantic plot and the comic power of the characters came through in spite of the ridicule by an audience unaccustomed to the method. The Western theatre had tried to get rid of convention, but here was theatre that was exciting because it used convention, and dramatic because it was art and not life. After its success in New York *The Yellow Jacket* was trouped for two decades in England and America by Mr. and Mrs. Charles Coburn. Reinhardt produced it in Germany and Austria, Stanislavsky in Moscow, and Benavente in Madrid.

In the 1930s the West had a chance to see real Chinese theatre when Mei Lan-fang, the greatest Chinese actor of his time and probably of all time, made several visits to the West. In 1931 he showed America that Chinese theatre had more to offer than charming simplicity and laughable naïveté. He gave a better idea of feminine grace and delicacy than any woman could give. Instead of the underacting expected in the West, he offered singing and dancing with elaborate artifice and fine technique.

In 1934 an expert professional production of a Chinese play, *Lady Precious Stream*, written and directed by a young Chinese actor and scholar, H. I. Hsiung, was enthusiastically received in London. It was equally successful in America and has been a favorite in American schools. Hsiung did not attempt song or dance but gave the poetic passages an exalted tone and a musical background and adapted the conventional gestures and movements of Chinese theatre to the range of Western actors.

Mei-Lan-fang, twentieth-century Chinese actor. *Courtesy the Billy Rose Theatre Collection. The New York Public Library at Lincoln Center. Astor, Lenox and Tilden Foundation.*

A more spectacular production of a Chinese play in the West was *Lute Song*, given in 1946 in New York in a plain prose version, with the musical-comedy actors Yul Brynner and Mary Martin singing vaguely Chinese songs. Robert Edmond Jones designed the setting and costumes freely, adapting the Chinese method.

Since the middle of this century the contact of East with West has been more direct, as expert Taiwan and Peking companies have come to the United States.

THE THEATRE IN CHINESE HISTORY

The classic Chinese theatre, though it has been gradually reshaped over the centuries, has brought down attitudes toward life and techniques from the mythological dance dramas of the Bronze Age, the ethical patterns of Confucius and Lao Tsu, and the court dramas of the T'ang and Sung Dynasties, when China was the most civilized country of the world.

Chinese civilization is almost as old as the ancient cultures of Egypt and Asia Minor. By 2000 B.C. metal craft, the wheel, and the idea of writing had spread across central Asia and had transformed the people of the lower valley of the Yellow River. By 1200 B.C. there were sizable city states and considerable development of religion and the arts. But from the beginning the religion of China was more humanistic than that of India or the Near East. The Chinese mythological dramas deal more with wise kings and emperors and noble ancestors than with powerful gods. We have sculptured representations of Fo Shi and Nu Kuo, the founding deities of the Chinese world, their fishlike tails entwined, attended by winged spirits and demons riding on griffins, phoenix, and dragons. The richly sculptured bronze urns show the square-faced masks the dancers would have worn, faces remarkably like the masks common in the Mayan sculpture of the New World. The traditional opening ceremony in the Chinese theatre, presenting the eight Buddhist immortals, may derive from very ancient dramatic forms. As in India, the banners set up for a theatrical performance notify the unfavorable demons that a dance drama is a triumph over them.

Mythological plays of the earthly activities of the immortals have continued to be popular in China, and spirits, often in animal form, may suddenly help the hero or heroine of any drama. Traditionally on the seventh day of the seventh moon is produced a play called *The Crossing of the Milky Way*, telling the ancient story of two stars, the Celestial Cowherd and the Weaving Maid, who fell in love on a sojourn on the earth and had two children. The angry Queen of Heaven called them back to the sky and created the Milky Way to keep them apart. Once a year they are in conjunction and the Cowherd is able to cross the Milky Way to the Weaving Maid on a bridge of birds' wings. The story is similar to the Indian story of the god Krishna, who, in the form of a herdsman, danced with the milk-maid Radha. As in India and Southeast Asia, there are in China many popular plays about the king of the monkeys who brings superhuman aid to mankind. For centuries one of the most popular Chinese plays has presented a girl who is really a white snake in human form, but the Chinese put the emphasis on her sorrows as she is separated by a righteous monk from the husband she loves.

China emerges into the clear light of history in the Iron Age, the first millennium B.C., at the same time as Greece. By 1100 B.C. a new people, Chou people, established a hegemony over several small kingdoms in the Yellow River valley. These people enlivened their sacred festivals with beautiful dances and dance dramas, turning the festival antics of demons and clowns into comedy and the war dances into military drama. In 716 B.C. a splendid temple was built especially for performances by choruses, dancers, and mimes.

Chinese nineteenth-century platform stage. *Illustration by C. Marks.*

Chinese drama owes even more to the great religious philosophies of the early Iron Age—Confucianism and Taoism—than to the festival dance dramas. Confucius raised Chinese thought to a high place of general law and humane ethics. The best way to worship the ancestors, Confucius taught, was to honor the family, the neighbors, and the emperor. If man had order in himself and his personal relations, the state could not fail to have harmony and order.

Confucianism teaches man how to achieve order in himself and in society. But from the simple people came the mystic, anarchic religion of private life, the "way" of Tao. Taoism taught that one should not trust a ruler, that the only rule is not to rule, and that one should never contend but get along by indirection. Tao was at first a religion of nature, with earth spirits to be invoked and demons and ghosts to be exorcised, but in the Chou age it was raised to a mature philosophy as a study of the Tao, of living in harmony with nature. It is a live-and-let-live philosophy that shows a sense of humor. Besides the high-minded Confucian heroes and corrupt villains, Chinese drama has always had amiable comic rogues.

For more than two thousand years the Chinese have combined these two philosophies—Confucianism to remind them of their duties and Taoism to remind them to be relaxed and natural. One character in a play will offer elaborate ceremonial deference, bowing and waiting for the superior to exercise his prerogative. But the other immediately begs him not to stand on ceremony and the two relax for direct sociability. On a higher level these philosophies are the basis for subtle scenes of high comedy, as the characters make complex adjustments and delicate transitions. In *Lady Precious Stream* the young soldier must reveal to his bride that he is ordered to distant duties and to establish a new relation with her. He puts his information in the form of a conundrum and gives her a chance to play a verbal game while she makes the adjustment. Later in the play, when the husband returns after many years, now a king with a new wife, the Empress of the Western Regions, the first wife must establish new relations with both him and her parents. He has just as difficult a task in helping the two women find their places in his household as First and Second Wife. A Confucian weighing of ceremonial protocol is necessary as well as a Taoist sense of tolerance and a high-comedy sense of humor. In his English adaptation, H. I. Hsiung simplified the problem by supposing that the hero has not yet married the empress and that she comes home with him to protect him with her army, then gradually accepts the fact that he is already married and agrees to become his "sister."

Instead of uniting into the one orderly nation Confucius dreamed of, the Chou city states continued their petty contentions and wars until 221 B.C. In that year, a century after Alexander ended the squabbles of the Greek cities by sweeping them into a corner of his empire, a general from the West, Shih Huang-ti, conquered the Chou states and imposed a tight military government, burning all books and trying to destroy traditions. For a short time he stirred up the leisurely Chinese to the building of innumerable palaces and the 2500-mile Great Wall. But after he died the Chinese, under the leadership of the Han family, rejected the uncongenial regime, pieced together their literary classics, and made them the basis for a national system of education and of competitive examinations for positions as governors, judges, and administrators. This system united the country and established a nation-wide pictographic writing that could be read in all the dialects. The Han emperors, expanding their realm to the south and establishing trade with Japan and many of the Pacific islands, made their thriving country, called Chung Que, or Middle Kingdom, the center of Asian civilization. The stable educational system enabled China to survive many dynastic changes, many wars, and several major invasions. It was not radically changed until the republic was established in 1921. For many centuries a favorite hero of the Chinese drama has been the ambitious young student who leaves his parents and wife in a village while he advances to a high position in the capital. In *Lute Song* the scholar-hero is very sad as he is cut off from news of home and forced to marry the prime minister's daughter. But his city wife discovers his sorrow and helps him return to rescue his family and generously takes the position of second wife as the emperor comes to reward the young man's family loyalty. The conflict between family loyalty and ambition is given a comic and melodramatic treatment in *Twice a Bride* as the young man, afraid of being ashamed of his village wife, pushes her into the river, only to discover later, to his chagrin, that the city girl he wants to marry is his village wife, luckily rescued from drowning and adopted by the governor.

When Buddhism was introduced in the Han period, the Chinese religious trinity was complete, for Confucianism, Taoism, and Buddhism complement one another and a Chinese can believe in all three. Buddhism added an emphasis on otherworldliness that was missing in Confucianism and Taoism. In dwelling on suffering, the Chinese put great emphasis on compassion and turned the pitying spirit of Buddha into a goddess of Mercy, Kuan-yin, whose presence is felt in many of the plays. Although the Chinese Buddhists, like all members of the Buddhist faith, taught that everything is transitory, they were not so ascetic as the first Buddhists in India. Instead of turning away from the world in contempt, several sects, especially the Ch'an (Zen) Buddhists, sought to experience the invisible spirit through contemplating nature and art.

There are a number of references in the Han period to Chueh-ti entertainers who presented acrobatic displays and dramatic songs and dances in the towns and at court. Reminiscent of dramas dealing with the Egyptian Horus is a serious play about a young champion come to fight the wild beast that had killed his father, which had its comic version in a Han drama about Huang (Emperor) of the East Sea, a magician, now old and a tippler and no match for the White Tiger he fights. The Chinese have always preferred the comic to the serious, the romantic and human to the mythological.

THE GOLDEN AGE OF THE ARTS: T'ANG AND SUNG CHINA

The Han dynasty came to an end in 220 A.D. and was followed by several centuries of invasions, disorder, and civil wars. San Quo, or Three Kingdom period, furnished the material for the most famous Chinese novel, *San Quo.* Many of the noisy military plays of the modern Peking Opera are dramatizations of the deeds of heroes of that novel. They stir national pride in battles with Huns, Turks, Tartars, and other invaders from the "Western Regions." They fill the stage not only with soldiers and generals but with jealous imperial concubines, plotting palace eunuchs, assassins, monks, and comedians, and present hair-raising episodes of treason, ambush, combat, and murder. The high points are the acrobatic duels danced to deafening clashes of cymbals and drums, with whirling of swords but without any real contact between the fighters. For all the fierce action, however, the most admired generals are the ones who win by craft or clever psychology. As in European medieval romances, episodes of chivalry and love are frequent. A favorite battle scene is that in *The Rainbow Pass,* in which a woman warrior realizes that her opponent is in love with her and permits herself to lose the battle.

For the second time, the anarchy of several centuries was ended by a foreign conqueror who roused the Chinese to prodigious efforts. More than five million workers were coralled under the guard of 50,000 police. Their main achievement was a great canal uniting the Yellow River and the Yangtse. But in 618 A.D. the tyrant emperor was captured, the regime collapsed, and the T'ang dynasty began an age of peace and order that lasted more than six hundred years—an Eastern Golden Age contemporary with the "Dark Ages" in Europe. Truly the center of the world, China developed a cosmopolitan culture by absorbing influences from its many provinces as well as from its neighbors, north, south, and west. To the east, Japan was just emerging from the Stone Age and eagerly borrowed everything it could from China.

Puppet plays were popular in T'ang China and may have existed since the earliest times. Apparently from Turkestan came the idea of using shadow puppets at funerals, partly, it is said, as a means of showing scenes of the life of the deceased but also as a vehicle for the soul of the deceased. Two legends of T'ang times indicate a traditional connection between shadow plays and funerals. One legend says that shadow puppets were invented when a necromancer made a shadow figure to fool the superstitious emperor who had just lost in death his favorite concubine. The other legend tells of a vizier who produced images of two court fools the emperor had ordered executed and then wanted alive again.

The traditional founder of Chinese theatre was a T'ang ruler who reigned from 847 to 859 A.D., known as the Ming Huang, or brilliant emperor. Ming Huang

61

dreamed he made a trip to the moon, where he was impressed with the singers and actors in the Palace of Jade. When he returned to earth, he founded a school in a wing of his palace known as the Pear Garden, and to this day actors are known as Children of the Pear Garden. Before he goes on stage each actor burns incense before a statue of this patron deity of the theatre. Ming Huang and his favorite concubine, Yan Kei-fei, have become legendary figures and the subject of countless poems and plays. She was known as the patroness of the performing arts and is associated with the poets Li Po and Tu Fu. It is said that, to make her beautiful phoenix eyes tremble with delight, the emperor would put on a clown costume and join the actors on the stage. Or the two would listen to his court orchestra of seven hundred members or his outdoor orchestra of a thousand musicians and singers in the Pear Garden.

The most famous play about these lovers, *The Palace of Eternal Youth*, written in 1688 by Hung Sheng, is, like *Shakuntala*, a poem of love in spring gardens, anguish and separation, and reunion on a celestial plane. It is a play of purification and spiritual enlightenment, but peculiarly Chinese in its human embodiment of celestial forces. The lady Yang Kei-fei was in her previous incarnation a dancing fairy

Typical nineteenth-century outdoor teahouse performance.
Illustration by Martha Sutherland.

of the moon. She and the emperor visit a village festival and she composes new songs for him. When he neglects his public duties, a rebel rises and insists that she be executed and her family removed from the court and that the emperor's son rule. The emperor wanders through cold rain on mountain roads longing for her, and from heaven she is equally drawn to him. The Celestial Cowherd and Weaving Maid finally permit them to meet in an eternal spring festival, where human sorrow is transcended as her heavenly songs and dances purge him of grossness but not of passionate longing. She is an embodiment of ideal beauty, not of Buddhist austerity.

T'ang drama seems to have consisted mostly of short dramatic songs and dances that presented one character at a time. In the next dynasty, the Sung, especially under the patronage of the Emperor Chen Tsung (998–1023 A.D.), plays of several acts were developed, but only one character in each act would sing.

It was under the Mongols that the drama became the popular art for the whole nation. When they conquered the northern part of the country in 1234 and the rest in 1279, the scholars and poets, thrown out of their government positions, turned to writing plays and novels, genres they had despised. Since north and south China had been divided for more than a century, the drama developed differently in the two areas. The northern drama, accompanied by the lute and other strings, stressed melody and tone, while the southern was made strongly rhythmic by the domination of drums and wooden clappers. The northern style emphasized acting and music, making its greatest appeal to the ear, while southern style, with polished movement and splendid costumes, made more appeal to the eye. Two of the greatest classics of Chinese drama, one southern, one northern, originated in the Tuan or Mongol period. Though they were adapted to later styles, they show that the Chinese classic drama had reached a full maturity by the thirteenth and fourteenth centuries, a little before Chaucer and the full development of the outdoor religious cycles in Europe, and before the first blossoming of the Japanese Noh drama.

The masterpiece of the southern style was Kao Ming's *Pi Pa Chi—The Lute* (14th century), or *Lute Song* as it was called in the New York version of 1946. It has remained a favorite and was adapted to later styles in the Ming period and in modern times.

The northern masterpiece, Wang Shih-fu's *The Romance of the Western Chamber*, which is as suitable for Western audiences as *Lute Song*, has not been streamlined for them, partly, perhaps, because it is so much like *Romeo and Juliet*, but there are three good poetic translations. With very little plot, the sixteen acts (or twenty with later continuations) develop in lyric solos and duets the changing aspects of a love affair: secret trysts, tender parting, and anguished separation. Again the hero, Chang, is a young student, but we see him not in public life but lingering on the path of dalliance. As a guest lodged in the western chamber of a monastery, he gets a glimpse of the beautiful Ying Ying, whose mother has come to arrange rites

63

for the deceased father and is lodged in an adjoining wing. Since a modest Chinese girl cannot meet a strange man, Chang has to sing of his love in cryptic phrases over the separating wall. The mother has already promised Ying Ying to a wealthy cousin; but Chang gains access to his love by a fairy-story solution. A bandit lays siege to the monastery, declaring that he will kill everyone in it unless Ying Ying is given to him. The mother announces that anyone who saves them may have the hand of the daughter. Chang writes to his sworn brother, the great general of the western army, and persuades a young novice of the monastery to run day and night to take the message that will bring a rescue party. The mother then arranges a ceremonial supper for the couple, but when she has them pledge each other as brother and sister they realize that she will not keep her promise. Each pines away at great length in song. Chang sends repeated love messages by the maid, and finally Ying Ying agrees to come to his western chamber. He sings his impatient expectation, like Juliet before the wedding night, and when she enters shyly without a word, he sings a description of their love in the delicate imagery of nature:

> Her cloud-like hair is unbound.
> She hides her shy head in the embroidered pillow.
> Why will you not turn your face to me?
>
> . . . .
>
> Now the quiet dew is falling on the fragrant earth.
> The breeze scarcely stirs on the lonely stair.
> The moonlight fills our quiet western chamber
> While the cloud envelops the tall watch tower.

The mother is furious when she learns of the meeting but is persuaded that she herself is to blame and agrees to the marriage when Chang shall return from his studies and examinations in the capital. There are tender farewells, and Ying Ying sings a delightful song instructing Chang to take care of himself in the capital. Continuations of the play express Chang's loneliness and anguish in thinking of his distant love and show a comic routing of a rival lover when Chang returns as an important government official to claim his bride.

K'UN CH'U: THE FLOWER OF MING DRAMA

After the Mongols were driven from power in 1368, the Ming dynasty restored the old traditions in politics and the arts and began a long, peaceful reign with high artistic achievements. At first the Ming emperors favored a northern style of drama, but about 1522, a little before Shakespeare, a new style was invented, based on southern patterns, which shortly won prestige and for three centuries was the national drama of China.

The new style was created by Wei Ling-fu, who found a musical basis in the folk songs of K'un Shan, his native town in the province of Kingsu, near the commercial city of Soochow. Hence the style is known as *K'un Ch'u*, or sometimes simply *Kunshan*. It became the favorite entertainment of the merchants and with them it spread all over the country.

By finding an appealing, flexible musical base and taking the best from a number of local forms, both northern and southern, Wei established a drama of national scope. While he borrowed some elements from a noisy style called *Yi-Yang*, the dominant effect was of a soft, gentle, refined style that in sad scenes melted the audience to tears. Soon some of the best poets were writing for K'un Ch'u and it won the approval of literary scholars. It became popular at court banquets, and singsong girls entertained their guests with the songs.

But poetic and musical subtleties and the inordinate length of many K'un Ch'u plays contributed to the decline of the form, which by the eighteenth century was old-fashioned. Peking Opera, invented in the late eighteenth century, used more up-to-date diction and simpler music, more melodramatic plots, and more popular effects, and soon K'un Ch'u was beloved of only a few connoisseurs. Its commercial importance was over, and the large audience that had supported K'un Ch'u for more than three centuries was gone. But the style never completely disappeared. The best actors studied K'un Ch'u as well as Peking Opera, and some actors kept performing in the old K'un Ch'u style. In the 1950s a still-flourishing Soochow company visited Peking.

In the last chapter of her book on Ming drama, Mrs. Josephine Hung points out that a large number of scenes in Peking Opera were derived from plays of Ming days and that often the older melodies were used. In the second volume of *Traditional Chinese Plays* (1909), A. C. Scott presents, with rich detail from the Peking performance, two short plays that were adapted from K'un Ch'u for the Peking public: *The Longing for Worldly Pleasure*, played by Mei Lan-fang for many years and in America in 1931, and *Fifteen Strings of Cash*, a farcical melodrama that had survived in Soochow and was presented by a Chekiang K'un Ch'u troupe in Peking in 1956.

CHING HSI, OR PEKING OPERA

Peking Opera first won national attention in 1779, when, for the celebration of the forty-fourth year of the reign of the Manchu emperor Ch'en Lung, actors from all the provinces played in the capital. Of several groups who stayed on to win over the Peking audience, the actors from Anhui were especially popular. They adapted their dialect to please the Peking public, borrowed from other styles, and again created a national style of opera known as *Ching Hsi* (capital opera), or to Westerners as Peking Opera.

There were many reasons for the popularity of Ching Hsi. If it is often noisy and melodramatic, it has colloquial language very different from the poetry and rhetoric of K'un Ch'u, and the emphasis is on the performance. While great writers of the Ming and early Ching or Manchu period were proud to write for the stage, no one knows the authors of the Ching Hsi plays.

In music the two styles are quite different. K'un Ch'u had greater variety of melodies, many of them soft and delicate. Peking Opera uses only eight melodic patterns, all familiar to actor, orchestra, and audience. Where K'un Ch'u songs are accompanied by the soft-toned bamboo flute, the characteristic accompaniment in Peking Opera is the two-string violin with its sharp wail. While in the earlier styles most characters used a natural range of voice, many characters in Ching Hsi use a strained tone, a high falsetto for the female roles and some of the young heroes and a heavy tone for the painted-face characters: generals, governors, and so on. Like the Ming drama, Peking Opera distinguished between civil and military plays but emphasized the military. For the battles, a company of acrobats is

Typical nineteenth-century Peking Opera theatre.
Illustration by C. Marks.

66

often brought in to leap and fall, killing one another over and over again. The military derring-do is accompanied by deafening noises from the orchestra, mostly percussion.

Peking Opera keeps the four types of actors and roles that had been established in Yuan or early Ming times. Each actor is trained from childhood for one of the subtypes within the fourfold classification, and rarely does he change to a different role. It was considered extraordinary that Mei Lan-fang, who played only women's parts, could excel in several types of female roles. The four types of roles, female and male, are *Tan*, or heroine, *Sheng*, or hero, *Ching*, or painted face, and *Ch'ou*, or clown. The Tan roles have several subdivisions, in which the acting varies: the modest, virtuous heroine, the flirtatious girl, the woman general, the acrobatic warrior maiden, and others. A subdivision of the Sheng is the Hsiao Sheng, or young man, the romantic lead, usually an ambitious scholar dressed in pale colors who sings many songs. The Ching, or painted-face, roles are the most startling. The actors have ornate, colorful costumes and elaborate headdresses, the hair is shaved back to give a very wide forehead, and the face is painted in a complex geometrical design. These roles are extroversive, swaggering personalities, military generals and governors, often gruff and sometimes treacherous, who scarcely sing at all but must be skilled dancers and acrobats. The colors and patterns in the Ching faces are symbolic. In general, red is for loyalty and virtue, white for cunning, blue for bold wildness, yellow for intelligence, and so on. Gold and silver indicate supernatural characters. But there are many subtle variations to suit particular characters.

The Ch'ou or clowns are also called "little painted faces," since they always display a white patch in the middle of the face and black lines around or crossing the eyes. Like the clown in many countries, the Ch'ou sometimes steps outside the play to make racy comments about the other characters. The Ch'ou actor, like the male "dame" in the traditional English Christmas pantomime, usually plays the comic old woman.

The monkey king and his many attendants, clever, supernatural helpers of mankind, combine acrobatic feats with the dignity of divine kings and the playful movements of the most mischievous of animals.

In early days the actor was apprenticed in childhood to an older actor who taught him the conventional actions and his particular role. But in the twentieth century there are schools. In the Ming dynasty and the early part of the Ching or Manchu period there were usually actresses for the female roles, but about the time Ching Hsi was established in Peking, the Manchu emperor banished actresses from the stage because of their immorality. Male actors were then trained from childhood in falsetto singing and feminine movement. Ever since the overthrow of the Manchu regime and the establishment of the republic in 1912, men are no longer trained for Tan roles, but it takes almost as long to teach a girl the mincing walk of the heroine, which must suggest the bound feet all well-born ladies used to have. The effect is helped by a shoe-legging that hides the real feet and puts the weight on minute shoes below. Every movement of hand or body must show feminine grace, whether the character is sewing with imaginary needle and thread, opening a door, or drinking tea. In the military plays a lady warrior with spear or sword must dance, in her feminine way, as intricate an acrobatic fight as her male opponent. Most exquisite of all is the lady's handling of her long sleeves. Derived from ancient styles of dress, the actor's "rippling water sleeve" is a piece of light-weight white silk one or two feet long, added as a cuff to the regular sleeve. It hangs softly far beyond the hand, and many gestures are made with the hand unseen. But with a graceful flick of the wrist the actor can throw the silk open and reveal the hand.

Movements and gestures are standardized. Each character has a special entrance walk. Manipulating the whip that indicates a horse takes long practice, and a good actor delights his audience by his grace in dismounting as much as a ballet dancer delights a Western audience with a well-executed pirouette. The action of opening an imaginary door, moving the bolt, pushing back the sliding leaves with both hands, and stepping over a six-inch imaginary threshold is not merely a device to suggest absent scenery but a dance movement by which the actor shows the character he is portraying and his own skill in movement. Sitting is done with a flourish after a complex curved approach to the chair; rowing and balancing in an imaginary boat are suggested by graceful, controlled movements. The military fights are elaborate dance numbers, but a general may have just as complex a pattern of movement in making the seven-foot-long pheasant feathers of his head-dress dance, now by shaking or turning the head, now by taking the tips of the feathers in his hands and moving them in circles before his face, or again by angrily taking the tips between his teeth. There are dozens of ways of laughing, bowing, or handling food or drink. Since many of the names of the gestures are used in the terminology of ancient dance, it may be assumed that not only the set dances but the whole style of acting was derived from dance.

Stage properties belong to the theatre and not to life; they are either functional or symbolic and always simple and beautiful. The same theatre chairs and tables, with embroidered silk covers if the characters are rich, are used for any scene of any play. The property man piles chairs on a table with a plain green cover to indicate a mountain the actor is to climb over, or any height from which he is to look out or to jump. Equally functional is the cushion the property man puts in a chair as the actor sits or on the floor as he kneels, as much for protection of the costume as for the actor's comfort.

Of the symbolic properties, the most picturesque are the horses and carriages. A horse is represented by a whip on which silk tassels hang at regular intervals. The actor can indicate leading the horse, mounting, riding with various gaits, dismounting, turning the horse over to an attendant. A spirited or angry horse or a horse that throws the rider gives the actor further chance to show his skill. Two yellow flags on which wheels are painted represent a chariot, and the actor must be carefully trained in the mime of getting in and out and scurrying between the flags. The poles of the flags may be held by an attendant who runs along back of the occupant of the chariot. Four attendants running around the stage waving black flags indicate a wind storm. Flags painted with waves indicate a flood or the sea. When a character is to commit suicide by drowning he leaps from a chair and is met by attendants carrying the wave flags, and all run off stage together. For snow one attendant whirls a banner and another shakes white bits of paper over the actors, who shiver and complain of the cold.

To indicate place, panels of symbolic scenery about a foot and a half wide and five feet high are used. The property man leans two of these, painted with pictorial symbols of mountains, against two chairs, and the scene is set. The largest portable properties are pictorial hangings, of which the most frequently used is the city gate. Two attendants hold up a bamboo pole on which is hung a cloth painted as a city gate. Defenders and guards climb on chairs and look over it. When the gate is to be opened the attendants lift the poles higher and the traveler passes under. In *Lady Precious Stream* the same curtain represents three mountain passes in succession as the Empress of the Western Regions pursues the hero in a movie-like chase sequence. For a tableau of heaven, attendants hold a similar curtain painted with clouds, while behind it is arranged on chairs and tables a tableau of a god on a throne flanked by four spirits bearing tall shields painted with symbols of clouds.

The most interesting hand properties are the many weapons—swords, javelins, spears, arrows—which become part of elaborate dances, parades, and tableaux. When the general arrives, four soldiers bearing bright-colored banners parade and dance around the stage, accompanied by the din of the orchestra. They fill the stage with the panoply of war as well as the armies of hundreds on the nineteenth-century stage or the thousands in movie processions and battles.

The classic Chinese theatre has always been a musical theatre, alternating dialogue and arias, and not only the arias but the emotional moments of dialogue and all the movements, entrances, and pantomimic actions are accompanied by a small orchestra. In this respect a Chinese play is like a nineteenth-century melodrama, in which every step, every gesture, and every turn of thought and mood are underscored by music.

The orchestra sits on the stage in sight of the audience, often at stage right, where the actor makes his entrance and gives the cue for his music. Musicians may leave or drink tea or read a newspaper when they are not busy, for the audience ignores what it is not supposed to see. Percussion is the thread that ties the performance together, setting the rhythmic patterns for the actor, while the other instruments enlarge and enrich with color. The wood blocks and drums of various sizes are the most important percussive instruments, but they are reinforced by gongs, bells, and cymbals, which are known as the military part of the orchestra.

In civil plays the strings and wind instruments predominate. They include horns, reed organs, flutes and flageolets, lutes and guitars that are plucked, and several high-pitched violins played with a bow. In some styles the violin accompanies the falsetto arias, and its small tone and narrow range are monotonous and piercing for Western ears. There are a number of styles of music that differ as much as the music of Mozart, Wagner, and Strauss, each with its own kind of melody and characteristic instrumentation. One style is known as "two flutes" because of the flutes that accompany the voice. Other styles are dominated by the castinet, drums, or cymbal, or by certain kinds of rhythms. Some are based on music associated with spring, others on the music commonly used for weddings, funerals, and other family rites. During the Manchu dynasty, perhaps because the military Manchus were less sensitive than their predecessors, a noisy style known as *pan tyn* dominated most theatres. It may have been fitting for the Manchurian plains, but indoors it is too raucous for sensitive ears and many twentieth-century actors have preferred to revive quiet styles that had been neglected.

The classic Chinese stage has been an art of the actor. Since the musicians learn the basic patterns of movement and song, they do not follow a score but watch the actor closely to adapt to his subtlest change of rhythm, ready for him to signal a beginning or a change of a song by a flick of his sleeves. An important actor will have his own violinist following in his footsteps on stage to accompany his songs. Conventional movements and hand properties not only serve to clarify the story but are vehicles by which the actor delineates character and creates emotion. Old forms and conventions do not hamper the good actor, but, by freeing him from the necessity of improvisation or hesitation, enable him to reach a high degree of perfection.

THE CHINESE THEATRE IN THE MODERN WORLD

Can a classic drama that has been the soul of China for more than a thousand years, and that was derived from roots of two thousand years before that, survive in a westernized, industrialized, and finally communized China? Into the 1950s there seemed no doubt that it could. Important Communist officials favored it, and the actors were able, by judicious selection and minor rewriting, to adapt it to the new age. But by the decade of 1964 to 1974 the young Communists seemed determined to make it disappear. Only social realism of the narrowest propaganda intent interested them.

Many of the leaders of the 1912 Republic were not interested in the classic stage and expected their drama, like their clothes, to follow the style of the West. Even Lin Yutang, who wrote brilliantly for the West about the Chinese way of life, had

70

only contempt for the native theatre. Realistic theatre Western style was gradually introduced. Students educated in Japan produced *Uncle Tom's Cabin* and *Camille*, but in 1919 a literary society began the production of more recent Western drama and the writing of new plays.

The modernization and westernization of China furnished the main theme of the new plays. After the Japanese invasion of China in 1931, the government fostered companies presenting anti-Japanese and patriotic plays, which won a considerable audience. The actors were usually not trained in classic theatre and used only a few of the conventions and effects of the old drama. Most modern plays have followed Western social realism, with situations similar to those in nineteenth-century melodrama, so that they seem nearer to Dickens than to Chekhov. The Communists developed village propaganda plays similar to the agit-prop plays in Europe in the 1930s which led to the epic drama. The Chang Kai-shek government built modern theatres for propaganda plays in Chungking, the wartime capital, and in Taiwan after it fled there in 1949.

At the same time the classic theatre borrowed from the Western style, and by the 1950s most Peking performances showed several radical changes. The platform stage was moved behind a proscenium, and often a series of plain curtains hid the scene changes and the property man. A number of scenic pieces were introduced, some of them simple suggestions of walls but many of them painted backdrops. The orchestra was moved to the wings or to the front pit. The actors still moved freely in and out of the wings and spoke and sang directly to the audience, but much of the distinctive Ching Hsi form was gone.

Some Communists denounced the age-old theatre as a product of feudal society, and others were ashamed of it because it was not Western, but some important leaders defended it as a popular diversion and a great national achievement. Everybody knew the stories. Workmen sang songs from Peking Opera, and the arias were constantly on the radio. To adorn his speeches, a politician could refer to a fund of romantic stories that everyone knew from stage performances. In 1950 a theatre school was founded for the training of performers in Peking Opera. In 1952 an all-China theatre festival brought companies from the provinces to perform their distinctive styles in the capital. The Minister of Culture defended the traditional theatre as a creation of the people, bearing the spiritual wisdom of the nation, expressing the longing of the people for land and freedom and their rebellion against tyranny. Even the supernatural drama of the Pilgrim Monkey, he pointed out, showed defiance of the Queen of Heaven. During the mobilization for the Korean War and for the crisis over the Straits of Formosa, the best classic actors were sent to the camps to raise the morale of the soldiers.

Repeatedly in the 1950s the top opera companies were sent abroad to show China's cultural achievement. They were received with great acclaim in India and Europe, and as late as 1960 in Canada. Communist leaders hoped to preseve the best of the old, cutting some scenes, rewriting others, and using the old idioms to develop new operas that were in harmony with the new ideals. Yet critics kept up the attack on the old drama, condemning it for preserving fatalism, superstitions about the supernatural, a feudal morality, gruesome murders, and discrimination against ethnic minorities. The puritans among the Communists especially objected to the erotic scenes of a young wife or maiden thinking of her absent husband and suggesting in mime her thoughts—scenes that had seemed delicate and charming to the connoisseurs. Most of all, Communists objected to the portrayal of old loyalties that had been ingrained in the Chinese character and reinforced by Confucian philosophy—loyalty to ancestors and parents, loyalty of a servant to his master, of a vassal to his lord. The basis of the drama in *Lute Song* is the triumph of family loyalties over everything—a theme very affecting to Westerners. Confucian humanism put family relations at the center of man's being, while the Communists considered society and the cause all-important.

In 1957, when the regime announced a relaxation of control and invited "a hundred flowers" to spring up, it seemed that the worst threat to the old drama was over. But in a few months attacks on the "rightists" became stronger. The actors had made considerable changes in adapting the old plays to the new ideas. When Chou Hain-fang, a contemporary of Mei Lan-fang, who was known as a leader in the gradual modernization of old traditions, was fêted in 1961 at a special performance celebrating his sixty years on the stage, he was photographed shaking hands warmly with Chou En-lai. But when he played in Shanghai in 1965 he was so bitterly attacked by the critics that he committed suicide. Red Guard youth were determined to wipe out every vestige of the older bourgeois culture, and they had strong support from Chang Ching, Mao Tse-tung's wife, when she became Cultural Adviser to the Chinese army. No one in the cities dared present a classic play, and by 1968 not even a Hong Kong bookstore offered any of the old plays for sale.

In *Folklore in the Modern World*, an article by Walter and Ruth Meserve expressed confidence in the survival of Peking Opera and other traditions, no matter what the attitude of a current government: "Yet when the propaganda of the Party has become tiring and monotonous in its frequent refrains, it has been the old plays, the old operas, the old tales of days gone past, filled with exalted emperors, flourishing generals, revenging ghosts, and the mythological rulers of the universe, to which the people have returned—with or without the sanction of the Communist Party of China. The drama is part of the enduring popular cultural heritage of China that will survive the vagaries of current censorship."

After the death of Mao Tse-tung the attitudes and activities of the Red Guard and the "Gang of Four," which included Chang Ching, were repudiated. A more tolerant, though cautious, attitude toward traditional culture replaced the fanaticism of the preceding regime. The trend of the 1980s seems to be toward the preservation of traditional art forms.

During several cultural changes in mainland China, the military government in Taiwan promoted the performance of authentic Peking Opera. Soon after the several million Chinese refugees fled to Taiwan in 1949, the Air Force, followed by the other branches of the army, set up a drama training school, partly as a project for war orphans, which trained boys and girls, beginning at the age of seven, in the singing and the acrobatic techniques of acting for Peking Opera. In 1962 and 1963 the Air Force Company played in New York for several weeks.

THE INFLUENCE OF THE CHINESE THEATRE
ON THE WESTERN THEATRE

The West devised some alternatives to realism without Oriental influence. It had its own classic theatre of ballet and opera, the examples of Greek and Elizabethan theatres, which were not realistic, and the example of painters who had broken with nineteenth-century pictorial realism. But many theatrical innovations since realism have been in the direction of Oriental theatre, and many of the innovators consciously tried to use the methods of the East, especially of China. Thornton Wilder and Bertolt Brecht strove to find Western ways to gain the freedom and power of Chinese theatre.

Our Town (1937) by Thornton Wilder, who had spent some of his boyhood in China, was the first Western play to adopt Chinese methods. Wilder had experi-

Cantonese painting on rice paper depicting a Chinese theatrical scene, 1860. *Courtesy of the Trustees of the British Museum.*

73

mented for a decade in one-act plays before he found the right method for his full-length play about the life of a New England village. Although the final product is early American in rhythm and meaning, much of the method is Chinese. While it has had few close imitations, it can be called the most revolutionary play of this century.

The two most striking techniques in *Our Town* are copied from the Chinese theatre. One is the character who addresses the audience, the Stage Manager. Wilder combines him with the Chinese property man, and as he is developed, he becomes completely Yankee. His speech has a poetic quality, but Wilder did not attempt the ornamental poetry of the Chinese. The second Chinese technique is the treatment of setting. Wilder's Stage Manager describes a town which is not represented on the stage and invokes the imagination of the audience, then playfully makes a concession to those who want scenery by having simple trellises brought in—such picturesque properties as the Chinese might have used. But they would never have dreamed of allowing the back walls of the theatre to be seen or of using a bare plank for a drugstore counter but would have had beautiful fabrics as a backing and bright paint on the properties. The scene of the men and women sitting in chairs to represent the dead in the cemetery is essentially Chinese, though the return of Emily from the graveyard to take one last look at herself and her life may have been suggested by the Japanese Noh drama. Wilder shows Confucian confidence through a view of man secure in the family, the nation, and the universe. The Chinese method, freeing the characters from realistic background, allows the timeless essence to come out clearly.

In writing his epic plays, Bertolt Brecht was strongly influenced by the Chinese theatre. He had seen Reinhardt's production of Klabund's adaptation of *The Circle of Chalk* in 1924. In 1935 he saw Mei Lan-fang in Moscow, not only playing in a theatre but demonstrating Chinese acting in a dinner jacket for a small group. Here was an actor who created a character yet looked at it from a distance and kept the audience at a distance. In Brecht's epic plays the characters acted in full light on a bare stage, with only a few indications of setting and no attempt to hide scene changes. By freedom from heavy illusionistic settings, Brecht gained the freedom of the Chinese stage to follow a fabulous story through many episodes, up mountains and down valleys, bringing in soliloquies, narration, songs, discussion, mottoes, signs, projections—anything his theme might call for.

While all Brecht's epic plays show this Chinese freedom, two based very closely on Chinese drama have become especially well known. *The Caucasian Chalk Circle* (1955) is a modern reinterpretation of the main events of *The Circle of Chalk*, set not in China but in some unspecified pre-Bolshevik land between Russia and Persia. But Brecht gives the play a different conclusion. Where the Chinese play supported the principle of legitimacy and restored the child to its true loving mother, Brecht's gruff judge, by the same text, gives the child to the peasant girl who had cared for it when the aristocratic mother had abandoned it during a peasant revolt. In his epic plays Brecht removed the characters from what is expected on the stage, and from what is usually assumed of social background, by having a story-teller introduce and comment on scenes, by bringing small groups of people across the stage to indicate the lack of social order in a revolutionary time, and, like the Chinese dramatists, by putting much of the action as well as the emotions into song. He leaves his characters a few of the Confucian humanitarian virtues. But in spite of their humanitarianism, they have one most un-Confucian quality: like the materialistic people of Russia and America, they grab what they need. Confucius would never have imagined man outside a well-established social order. Brecht's most vivid character is the peasant interim judge, Asdak, a combination of the corrupt judge and the upright governor in *The Circle of Chalk*, who takes bribes and is innocent of legal training but out of fun, anger, and perverseness, deals out a rough justice on the basis of the primitive needs of the peasants. The scenes of *The Caucasian Chalk Circle* are excellent adaptations of Chinese principles to the Western stage; the scene of Grusha crossing the perilous bridge over the mountain chasm must be mimed with the help of only a suggestion of a swaying bridge, and the scene of Grusha and her lover facing each other from opposite sides of a river was done by the Berliner Ensemble with two rows of low-standing reeds to outline the two edges of the river.

In the matter of action and gesture, Brecht again found help in the Chinese example. His characters are trying to find possible solutions to social problems, and the actors give demonstrations to make the audience think. Brecht uses a clear-cut, archetypal pattern of action and strong gestures such as primitive people might develop in an old tradition of ritual, dance, and drama.

In the 1950s John Patrick's *The Teahouse of the August Moon* popularized a few aspects of Chinese theatre. Sakini stole the show with his addresses to the audience and his aphoristic comments. The easy flow of action, with change of picturesque settings before the eyes of the audience, seemed more appropriate to the material than Wilder's Oriental methods in the New England village of *Our Town*. While there was only incidental music and a brief dance, a poetic mood of color and charm pervaded the performance.

Among the absurdists of the 1950s and 1960s there was great interest in the Orient. Jean Genet had picked up some general knowledge of Eastern theatre, but after he saw the Peking Opera performance in Paris in 1955 his work showed much more direct influence, fantastic makeup and costumes, for instance, for the General, the Bishop, and the Judge in *The Balcony* (1956); and in *The Blacks* (1958) the man playing a woman's role, the blacks playing in white-face masks, and the catafalque indicated by chairs and a cloth cover show a successful discovery of Western equivalents for Eastern devices.

The idea of playing without the illusion of romantic lighting had a great appeal in England in the 1960s and 1970s. Peter Shaffer's farce *Black Comedy* (1965) used light for supposed darkness, darkness for supposed light. Shaffer had seen in Peking Opera the power of the night fight with thieves, always played in full light with the audience imagining the darkness. The convention was even more startling when Peter Brook applied it to his productions of Shakespeare, playing the heath scenes in *Lear* in full lighting and playing that most romantic, moon-drenched play, *A Midsummer Night's Dream*, without a leaf and in full stage lights, leaving time of day and atmosphere entirely to the actors, the dialogue, and the imagination.

The Japanese Theatre

While in China traditional theatre was discarded or transformed under the early Communists, the Japanese have preserved their classic forms, helped make them available to visitors to Japan, and subsidized the visits of performing companies to the West. Since the late 1940s, Western interest in Japanese theatre has grown as visitors return with enthusiastic reports. Even before World War II Arthur Michener and Paul Green led the chorus of writers announcing that Japan, in the rejection of realism and the artistic use of poetry, music, and dance, held the secret for the future theatre of the West. The techniques of Japanese classic drama are no longer esoteric mysteries passed down secretly from father to son. Scholars and critics, Japanese and Western, have edited, studied, and translated the plays and the extensive technical and critical writings. As Western eyes became familiar with Oriental art and Western ears with Oriental music, and as Western minds were entranced by Zen Buddhism and the many other Eastern spiritual insights, it became possible not only to read and see Japanese dramas with pleasure and understanding but to present adaptations of the plays in Western theatres. Western visitors to Japan are fascinated to find thousand-year-old dances and three highly developed lyric theatres established three to five hundred years ago and still performing as living traditions.

FIVE PERIODS IN JAPANESE THEATRE HISTORY

The theatre historian divides Japanese history into five main periods, each with its characteristic forms of theatre. In the first seven centuries of the Christian era Japan emerged from the Stone Age with the help of Buddhist missionaries from Korea and China. In this early age a number of mythological dance dramas were developed that were closely related to Shinto and Buddhist festivals. The second period, called the Heian period, began in 794 A.D. with the establishment at Kyoto of the imperial court and an aristocratic society, modeled on the splendors of the Chinese culture of the T'ang and Sung dynasties, that made its own versions of Chinese poetry, dance, and drama. In the third period, from 1192 to 1603, feudal lords turned away from the Chinese-oriented court and, between battles of the civil wars, sought to build a native Japanese culture. In the fourth period, from 1603 to 1868, under the absolute control of the Tokugawa Shoguns, who shut Japan off from the rest of the world, there arose a new city culture of merchants and artisans. The fifth period, the Meiji, which began in 1868 with the overthrow of the shogunate and the restoration of the emperor, has seen the rapid introduction of Western culture. Yet older forms have been continued alongside the new, for the Japanese, though adept at borrowing from other cultures, have kept an extraordinary interest in their own traditions. Many of the primitive dance dramas persist in village festivals; the Heian court dances have been performed for the emperor for a thousand years and are now sometimes shown on public occasions. The Noh lost its rich patrons when the feudal system was abolished, but in recent decades has found a new audience. The Kabuki still flourishes in the large cities and is the main fare at the National Theatre in Tokyo. While some modern productions in Japan follow Western realism or Western operatic or other musical forms, many borrow techniques and effects from native traditional forms. The Japanese have proved to the world that it is not necessary to destroy the old while creating the new.

As in other countries, the primitive Japanese, from the beginning of community life, celebrated their relation to the gods and the seasons with masks, dances, and dramatizations of sacred events. Deer dances recalled the supernatural deer who came one year to save the rice fields from a plague of insects. When a Korean introduced a Chinese lion dance, representing a fabulous beast the Japanese had never seen, it absorbed native animal and dragon dances, and a *shishi* dancer, wearing an animal mask and a long mane, still brings a blessing to many festival processions as well as to several episodes in both *Noh* and *Kabuki* drama. In other masked dances the gods of sea and rain arrive to punish misdeeds and bring a blessing for the new year. Some dances tell the half-comic story of two primeval brothers, the Great Hunter and the Great Fisherman. When the Hunter loses his brother's fishhook, he must seek it at the bottom of the sea at the home of the dragon god, whose daughter he married. The child born of the union becomes the father of the first emperor, and the Hunter, bringing home the power to control the ebb and flow of the waters, makes his brother smear his face and hands with red and act drunken scenes for his entertainment. This tradition connects the origin of the imperial family with the beginnings of comic drama. The sacred *Kagura* dances still include a comic drunken dance of the Fisher as well as a comic dance of a man struggling with the rising waters controlled by the Hunter.

Some dances tell of the great ancestor of the Japanese people, the sun goddess, Ama No Usume, and how both dance and drama originated when she became angry and had to be lured out of her cave to bring back sunshine and happiness to the world. The eight hundred other gods gathered outside the cave, forged an iron mirror to hang on a tree, decorated the place with evergreen boughs, and turned a tub upside down for a resounding dancing stage. As one of the goddesses began to dance and take off her garments in a kind of religious strip-tease, the others laughed so loud they aroused the curiosity of the sulking sun goddess. When she opened the cave to look, she was seized, made to look at her own wintry visage in the iron mirror, and persuaded to bring spring once more to the world. The spring-rousing dance on a tub is one of the sacred Kagura dances still performed in Shinto temples and at court.

The importation of dance dramas from the continent began well before the emperor established his court at Kyoto on the model of the Chinese capital city. In 612 A.D. the Prince Regent introduced *Gigaku*, a dance form of T'ang times in China that had died out there but remained popular in Japan for some five or six centuries. Gigaku dramas are no longer danced, but more than two hundred masks have been preserved and descriptions of the characters and actions include a dancing lion, a bird, a comic old man, a young girl fighting off the old man, and a king with eight attendants all comically drunk. That the masks have Aryan features rather than Chinese, suggesting an origin in India or even the Mediterranean area, is evidence of the international influences at the splendid T'ang court and the ability of the Japanese to adopt suggestions from abroad.

Another dance drama, *Bugaku*, has come down to the twentieth century in Japan as the official dance drama of the imperial court and a few important temples. It developed a square platform stage surrounded by a balustrade but open for entrances by steps on the sides. The dances from the left side, said to come from China or India, use soft, eerie music from blown instruments. Those from the

Japanese open-air theatre of the nineteenth century. Samurai watches a Noh drama. The stage has some elements of Kabuki decoration. *Illustration by Bobbie Okerbloom.*

79

right side, said to come from Korea and Manchuria and to include some native forms, have more angular movements, accompanied by percussion, especially from a large ornamented drum. More than fifty Bugaku have been preserved. Some are standard invocations and closing numbers. Some are intended to drive away demons, some to bring health and prosperity.

The third period of Japanese theatre history was dominated by the warrior class, or *samurai*, who took control in the twelfth century. While they left the emperor on the throne as a ceremonial figurehead, they distrusted the aristocratic court with its worship of things Chinese. When the Mongols conquered China, bringing an end to the Sung dynasty, they made several unsuccessful attempts to invade Japan. The day of Japanese subservience to the Chinese was over. The feudal lords built up a strong military regime under a chieftain they called the *shogun*, and part of the time their headquarters were at Kamakura on the east coast, far from Kyoto.

The Japanese feudal system was developed in the centuries that saw the rise of feudalism in Europe, and, like Europe, Japan had several hundred years of civil wars, with one period of peace and prosperity under the Ashakaga shoguns in the

Ancient lion dance among the peonies, contemporary Kabuki theatre. *Courtesy the Japan National Tourist Organization.*

fourteenth century and the final establishment of a strong central government late in the sixteenth century. This military class, samurai under the shogun, torn by intrigue, feuds, and civil wars, beset by uncertainty and violence, turned to the arts of Zen Buddhism. The Zen emphasis on discipline appealed equally to a warrior, who must use his sword, and a priest, who wanted to transcend the burden of violence and shame.

Unlike some other sects of Buddhism, Zen did not insist on an escape from this world into a "Pure Land" or offer quick salvation by the repetition of magic prayers. Whether swordsmen, dancers, actors, or protectors and rulers of the country, Zen students believed that by a long hard discipline they could discover in this world the stillness and peace that underlies the turmoil and ever-changing appearances of existence. Besides Zen poetry, the Samurai Buddhists loved the tea ceremony, the austere Japanese garden, monochrome ink and brush painting, and the Noh theatre. Following a style originating in China, the Zen painter, with one color of ink, a few suggestive details of mists and mountains, and large empty spaces, could lead the mind into contemplation of the unseen. In the tea ceremony, by keeping the attention focused on simple traditional actions, on plain bowls and implements, one could free the mind for spiritual contemplation. The Japanese garden was carefully planned as a miniature image of the wide world, but with complexity and disorder under control. Small trees, streams, and bridges suggested casual austerity, or the rock gardens, with a few rocks or patches of moss in carefully raked sand, suggested the larger world of islands and seas, adventure and return, tension and peace.

DEVELOPMENT OF THE NOH

In the fourteenth century, the Ashakaga shoguns established an interval of peace and prosperity and at this time the Noh theatre was perfected. It was not an entirely new form but combined suggestions from many forms both courtly and popular. One of these germinal forms was *Shushi*. Spell-making Buddhist priests, clad in splendid robes, performed dramatic dances with sacred songs and chanted scriptures to the music of drums, bells, and flutes. *Okina*, the Noh drama that is always used as an opening ceremony for the New Year and other propitious occasions, may have originated with the Shushi priests as early as the twelfth century. It has no plot and includes passages that have long since lost their meaning, but it is known as a dance prayer for long life and blessing, with a divine figure and a wise man answered by a comic peasant, who performs a vigorous dance of spring planting. More is known about the colorful *Ennen*, professional performers for the Buddhist temples, who incorporated quotations from old poems and songs, sacred and profane, keeping the dignity of old traditions and creating a carefully controlled poetic tone.

A form called *Kowaka* was popular for centuries and is still performed in some isolated villages. Like the medieval ballads of Europe, it was a kind of epic tale about the heroes of the civil wars. Though written in the third person, it was recited, mimed, or danced by at least two performers. Sometimes the samurai joined the professionals in performance. The great leader Nobunaga danced the Kowaka the night before the victory of 1560 which made him Shogun and put an end to the feudal wars.

Kusemai dancers, both men and women, sang story songs in a new unconventional rhythm with a sharp drum beat that made a powerful basis for the dance. The Kusemai passages became one of the most powerful appeals of the Noh, especially in the final scene danced to the chant of the chorus.

The two immediate predecessors of the Noh were the *Dengaku* and *Saragaku*, both of which were highly developed professional performances by the twelfth century. The Dengaku was originally a harvest celebration—the word means "field music"—but after court poets and dancers had created elaborate versions with beautiful costumes the Dengaku were probably as far from the rustic celebrations as European pastoral poetry and plays were from the actual life of rude shepherds. For several centuries the great lords kept professional companies of Dengaku performers. Saragaku, or "monkey music," the great rival of Dengaku, is said to have been imported from China but was combined with native forms. Originally Saragaku were given by popular performers hired to present at temple festivals all kinds of acrobatics, juggling, and magic, as well as songs and dances. Some of the early plays were apparently satiric and grossly comic.

In 1374 the shogun Yoshimitsu, a poet and musician himself, visited a temple to see a much-talked-about Saragaku performer, Kanami, and was so entranced with both the actor and his son Zeami that he set them up as performers in his household. They brought together the various strands of theatre and created a form that united poetry, acting, singing, and dancing—the Noh. They wrote most of the plays famous in the repertory today and Zeami wrote the most important essays on the technique and aesthetic of Noh.

Zen principles underlie the Noh. The stage of plain wood is austere, and the costumes, though of bright colors, are of simple, exquisite patterns. Movements and gestures are extremely simplified. A theatre with colorful costumes, masks considered among the finest sculptures of the ages, passionate music from drums and flute, rich chanting by actors and chorus—a theatre with a feast for eye and ear—yet directs the attention to the unseen, the idea, the spirit.

In a time of peace and plenty Noh flourished as a court art for the discriminating audience around the shogun. But by the middle of the fifteenth century, at just the time when France and England had dynastic wars, Japan was devastated by a new wave of civil war, and the actors took to the road to win a popular audience at temples and festivals. They wrote plays with vigorous conflict and a wide range of realistic characters quite different from the austere theatre of Kanami and Zeami. They even wrote some Christian plays, for Jesuit missionaries after 1549 made many converts in Japan.

But gradually, in the sixteenth century, new ruling families reestablished the central authority and Noh again became the favorite theatre of the shogun and the rich *diamyos*, or vassal lords. When the Tokugawa family took over power in 1603, cut Japan off from the rest of the world, built their palace in Edo (modern Tokyo), and set up one of the world's most strict authoritarian regimes, the Noh continued to flourish as a performance theatre, but as a fixed, traditional art handed down from father to son, master to pupil. At the time when French critics established a classic age in Europe, the Noh actors selected some two hundred plays and established them as the repertory that has come down to the present. They had new masks made, eliminating all realistic or individual elements. They simplified the music to two scales, a stronger and a weaker. They refined and simplified the texts, reducing the number of characters and eliminating the more individualized lower-class characters. Plays with strong conflict were rewritten so that the climactic scenes could be played by the *sh'te*, the chief actor, alone. The secondary or *waki* roles were simplified to a standardized pilgrim-priest. A pace of performance was set that makes performances today move, it is estimated, about half as fast as fifteenth- and sixteenth-century performances. The result is to reduce even further the kind of dramatic conflict expected in the West and to emphasize a poetic mood of religious contemplation.

Japanese rural entertainments, bringing in ancestors of Noh dramas.
Illustration by Martha Sutherland.

Only for some very important occasion, like a campaign to restore a temple, were the Noh companies permitted to give public performances, setting up their stage in a large outdoor enclosure. When the Tokugawa were deprived of power in 1867, the Noh actors were left without homes, and only a few persisted in trying to find public support for an old Japanese art in a country that was turning against its traditions in order to be Western. When Japanese began to visit the West, however, they saw that opera, a traditional art of the Western aristocracy, was held in high esteem. When the Duke of Edinburgh visited Japan in 1869 and General Grant, the ex-president of the United States, in 1879, Noh performances were part of the official entertainment. The emperor showed some interest in the traditional form and attended the opening of a Noh theatre in 1881, and the dowager empress became a patron. Gradually several Noh companies set up in small theatres in the cities to make a precarious living. In the twentieth century the Japanese have realized that they can be both Japanese and citizens of the world; today Noh is part of a system of nationally protected and supported theatres.

THE MODERN NOH THEATRE

The Noh is a temple art, and the stage is a temple with a temple roof that happens to be under a modern roof and with modern seats on two sides for the convenience of modern guests. The theatre has the dignity, stillness, and intimacy of a small religious shrine. As in the Chinese and Elizabethan theatres, the stage is a platform projecting into the audience, with no front curtain and no painted scenery, presenting the actor as a three-dimensional sculptural form. As on the Chinese stage, the property man and musicians sit in back of the actors, visible all the time, and at one side a chorus of six to ten men sit on a gallery-extension of the stage, guarded by a balustrade. At the back of the stage, behind the musicians, the wooden wall is painted with a stylized pine tree, symbol of immortal life, supposed to be the sacred yogo pine tree at the Kasuga shrine at Nara. At stage right is a long extension, the *hashigakari*, which serves as a bridge from the actors' dressing room to the stage and a symbolic bridge from the other world to this. Some important scenes are played on the hashigakari, and three small pine trees, suggesting heaven, earth, and man, mark the stages of travel of the character who gradually approaches the shrine or sacred spot on the main stage. The stage floor is of highly polished Japanese cypress wood, which reflects the bright-colored costumes, and earthen jars are suspended underneath to add to the reverberation when the actor stamps the floor in vigorous dance. Steps at the front, now rarely used, are kept as a relic of the expected presentation of a gift by the feudal lord. Even in the modern indoor theatres, the hashigakari and the stage are separated from the audience by a bed of pebbles, preserving the tradition of

Two scenes illustrating contemporary Noh plays. *Top:* Dance of the Bell, showing position of musicians. *Bottom:* Relationship of the hashigakari to the main stage. *Courtesy the Japan National Tourist Organization.*

the outdoor temple and marking the aesthetic separation of the real world from the spiritual world of the play.

The Noh theatre is far more abstract and symbolic than the Chinese. Even without scenery, Chinese actors make the audience see particular places as invisible doors slide open for lover, parents, and in-laws to carry on the affairs of everyday life. But most Noh characters are gods come down, ghosts come back, dream images of warriors refighting ancient battles, distraught women reliving their memories of sons, brothers, or lovers lost long ago, or demons exposed and banished by the power of prayer. A Noh performance is a Shinto temple rite, invoking a blessing on the people and the seasons and at the same time a Buddhist journey of the soul out of the darkness of ignorance and desire into spiritual enlightenment. The Noh combines the Shinto reverence for the spirits of animals, trees, and rocks with the Taoist belief in the unity of all existence and the Buddhist belief that all men and women, animals, trees, flowers, rocks, and snow are capable of achieving Buddhahood. Hence Noh plays are rich in nature imagery, and the center of action is usually not a real house but typically a half-forgotten old shrine, a blossoming plum tree associated with some legendary event—a place for memories, phantoms, and dreams. In a Noh play there is emphasis on the transitoriness of life, and at the end, whether beauty or anguish has possessed the mind, it is gone, leaving only a sad memory.

To begin a Noh play, the three or four musicians come slowly down the hashigakari wearing ceremonial costumes: plain, long-sleeved dark robes and much brighter, stiff over-robes with wide lapels and belts. The flutist, sitting in the corner, plays the introductory music, a strange, unearthly note like a distant cry of pain. At lyric moments he accompanies the actor, giving an exact presentation of the melody, while the actor may vary from it to give nuance in his interpretation. The drummers, sitting next in the row of musicians, set a rhythmic base for the play. Many sections of the play are in free rhythms, like free verse, though some have fixed patterns. There are special patterns for the entrance travel songs, the main dialogue, and the dances. To Westerners the rhythms seem very complex, and the drummers seem to be carrying on a contest with the actors, now in the same rhythm, now in syncopation. For a majestic pattern a beat is used for each syllable, and for a faster pattern, a beat for two syllables. In the more complex passages the standard twelve-syllable line, usually divided into half lines of seven and five syllables, is coordinated with eight beats of the drums. There are many skipped beats, alternations, and syncopations, and to fit the words into the rhythmic structure requires great skill in the actor. Throughout, the drummers increase the excitement with vocal interjections between the drum beats, crying "ya" before the first and seventh beats, "ha" before the second, sixth, or seventh, and "y-yow" and "yo-oi" on odd-numbered beats for the tense moments.

Music is inseparable from the text. No one ever sings or plays the music or dances the dances without the words. There has never been the danger, constant in Western opera, that the music will hold more interest than the drama. No emphasis is placed on beauty of the singing voice. Taken rather slowly, the songs are intoned deep in the throat so that the words would not be completely clear even if the main character's face were not covered with a mask and if the medieval court language were comprehensible. The actor expects to communicate more by tone and phrase than by individual words, and the student usually has the text in his hand.

To the Western visitor the drummers may at first seem too loud, and the yelps and grunts distracting. Yet when a passage without accompaniment arrives, one is aware that the sounds have had a hypnotic power, as necessary as the orchestral sound track for a movie.

The attendant who sits at the back, near the musicians, is not quite a Chinese property man. He helps the main character change a mask or take off or loosen a costume, but he is also an understudy to the main actor, ready to prompt him or even to step into his part. The Noh properties are few and much less realistic than those on the Chinese stage.

Gesture and movement are simple and controlled. The conventional walk by gliding the foot in its two-toed sock along the polished floor, pointing the toes high until each glide is complete, is a traditional walking discipline of Buddhist meditation. The slow pace gives dignity. Aside from the actions of particular characters and the elaborate handling of the fan, the actors kneel, bow, rise, turn, and stand in conventional ways. A hand raised to the level of the eyes expresses grief, and a mother indicates digging in the grave where her son is buried by merely spreading her arms. On a battlefield there is no pursuit or attempt to escape, and no blows are given or feigned. Instead, opponents confront each other in dance with increasing inner tension, until one comes behind the other and takes his sword.

While the main event of many Noh dramas is the exorcism of a ghost or the release of a soul from the memory of an ancient wrong, the restless soul must first be brought into view in his natural self. Hence most Noh plays are written in two parts. First a wandering priest, singing a travel song, arrives at the sacred or romantic spot and finds the central character, played by the sh'te, in a debased form, old, feeble, ill or poverty-stricken. The priest is played by the waki without a mask and in simple robes. In the interval between the two parts one or more of the Kyogen actors may tell the audience about the main character. In the second part, after a build-up of drums, the curtain between the dressing room and the hashigakari is suddenly pushed out with bamboo poles, and the sh'te, in a mask and a splendid costume, comes on. He may have a vigorous dialogue with the waki, but the climax of the play is usually a solo dance by the sh'te, with the waki as spectator. The chorus chants along with the sh'te, or announces him, and as the dance becomes more vigorous may take over, both describing his actions and chanting his lines. Some of the dances in the Noh plays, especially the demon dances, are lively, though most are slow and stately, scarcely differing from one play to an-

87

other. The kimono sleeve becomes a means of expression, spread out like a bird or a ship in sail, held down like a drooping flower, or flung over the wrist, and the fan not only gives point to each movement but becomes any object required.

Masks are extremely important in setting the style. Connoisseurs try to collect them, but those belonging to the acting companies have been declared national treasures and cannot be sold. A Noh company may have as many as 120 masks and never use any one mask in more than two or three plays, since they are differentiated for the particular quality of the character. Many are designed to give a dark, melancholy look when the head is inclined and to appear cheerfully smiling when the head is held high. They are painted subtly, and some, especially the masks of deities and demons, have touches of red and gold. They give a strong impression of reality, though reality in miniature, since they are smaller than the actor's head. The delicate masks of the maidens contrast with the very full costumes. Some characters, especially the animal demons, require elaborate wigs, while other masks are finished with hats of cloth.

Costumes are less specifically related to the particular character than the masks, giving only the general effect of beauty and grandeur. The style was derived from that of the military nobility of feudal times. A simple kimono may serve for the female characters and as an undergarment for the male. The large brocade overgarments, with elaborate sleeves and skirt, may be so stiff with gold and embroidery that the character seems as wide as tall. Yet the pattern of the cloth has a kind of majestic simplicity, and the actor can make the costume shiver and flow with either delicate or vigorous dancing.

Five Noh masks. *Illustration by Martha Sutherland.*

THE NOH PROGRAM OF PLAYS

An ideal Noh program in the days of the samurai consisted of five plays from different groups, chosen to give a harmonious sequence, with appropriate comic *Kyogen* (little farces) in between. Today the usual program is two or three plays, each punctuated with a Kyogen or two. The principle of organizing a program requires a three-part sequence known as *Jo-Ha-Kyu*. The opening, the *Jo*, must be stately, solemn, and powerful. Especially appropriate here are the "god pieces" in which a god reveals himself and performs a dignified dance. The ending, the *Kyu*, must be short and fast, most often presenting a wild dance of a demon, lion, fox, or wine-dragon or monkey-monster that is usually killed or driven away. The middle, or *Ha*, the main substance of the program, contains the more delicate songs and dances or the most powerful reexamination of some violence of the past that must be faced and expiated. Here are placed the warrior plays, the "woman's pieces," and "insane pieces," and the plays about more ordinary characters.

In the warrior plays, a famous hero of the civil wars reenacts his great battles, usually in a dance against enemies conjured up in the imagination. In the first part of the play the warrior is a blind or aged man long retired to a cave or hut. But in the second part he appears in his full glory as he was many years before. Some nostalgia for the passing of youth and splendor may be expressed, but the play brings the passions and deeds of long ago to the conscious mind in order to purge the soul and prepare it for the enlightenment and release promised in Zen Buddhism. The warrior both feels the old fury and looks at it from a later time, understanding the transitoriness of all action in the light of eternity and the promise of salvation through prayer.

Atsumori by Zeami shows how a heroic battle scene could be turned into a poetic drama of Buddhist release. The story is told in the *Heiki Monogatori* (late 12th century), a collection of tales about the warriors of the Heiki clan. In the course of a battle an old warrior pins down his opponent, but when he finds a noble youth of sixteen under the helmet he decides to spare him. But the insolent boy taunts him, and when his own men come up the warrior kills the youth, promising him that he will pray for his repose. He abandons his career as warrior to become a priest. The boy's ghost returns to the spot where the fighting occurred and refights the battle with vengeful fury. When he raises his hand to strike and sees not the old warrior but the priest praying for him, he realizes how much he needs prayer. "Pray for me again, oh pray for me again," he cries as he bows his head to the ground. The exorcism is even more explicit in *Fujita*. The mother of the victim of a victorious general accuses him of the murder. When he claims that it was unavoidable, she begs him to kill her too. In the second part of the play, the dead man's ghost appears, full of hatred, to reenact the battle in dance, but he is quieted by

Noh actress Matsu Kaze showing woman's mask. Scene from *Two Sisters Gathering Buckets of Sea-water.* *Courtesy the Japan National Tourist Organization.*

Two contemporary Noh actor-dancers. *Top:* Funa-benkei. *Bottom:* Ebira. *Courtesy the Japan National Tourist Organization.*

the prayers of the general and thinks of his own need for prayer.

In the "woman's pieces" the main emphasis is on lyric dance. In *Hagoromo*, a heavenly maid dances to regain her feather robe found and held by an amazed fisherman. In other plays the spirit of the maple, the wisteria, the iris, the butterfly, or the snow may dance in the form of a young girl. Sometimes a woman is involved in the same fury of battle as a warrior. In *Tomoe*, the ghost of the sweetheart of the defeated warrior of the Genji clan returns. She had fought alongside him until he was defeated, then to give him time to commit suicide had fought off a number of enemies, and has come back to take as keepsakes his sword and robe. The play is presented as the dream of a monk who had found a peasant girl in a shrine dedicated to a warrior god. The same girl, played by the same principal actor, makes a spectacular entrance in the second part and dances the battle scene. At the end she joins in the monk's prayer for release from her shame.

Even more characteristic of Noh plays with the theme of expiation are two other plays about women facing their past. In *Sotoba Komachi*, which has appeared in some of the favorite anthologies of world drama, the priest finds, at the place where a famous girl had lived, an old woman, Sotoba in her debased form, hardly to be recognized. But in the second part she appears in her proud, youthful form, to face the time when she had destroyed a young man by demanding that he swim over to her a hundred nights before she would see him. On the ninety-ninth night he drowned. At one point she assumes the part of the young man and fully realizes both her own cruel pride and his suffering. She wins a final release and fades away.

Most touching are the mad scenes, mostly of women who have lost their sanity through some great grief—variant of the Buddhist image of man in darkness, suffering and searching. Thus the middle section plays, whether warrior, women, or frenzy plays, are concerned with suffering and release from suffering.

The opening and closing dramas are concerned with the supernatural—the invocation of the gods and the driving off of evil in the form of demons. The three-part arrangement of Jo, Ha, and Kyu is a spiritual sequence from divine blessing to expiation, enlightenment, release from suffering, and celebration of a triumph.

THE AESTHETICS OF NOH: *MONOMANE, HANA, AND YUGEN*

The creators of Noh not only perfected an important form of art, they worked out a major system of aesthetics in which reality is transformed by selective control of beautiful materials, the disciplined skill of the performer, and the invocation of the unseen spirit behind the visible image. By the ninth and tenth centuries, in the Sung dynasty, some Chinese critics, in reaction against the gaudy elegance of the T'ang dynasty, called for a simplicity that was not primitive or crude but was achieved by simplifying the rich and gorgeous, as though a colorful

Noh actress Hanagatami. Note the elaboration of the costume. *Courtesy the Japan National Tourist Organization.*

inside were covered by a plain outside. They expected a young poet to try an elaborate style first but to strive for simplicity as he matured. In the same age, artists made a cult of painting in a monochrome ink wash and using only quiet colors in ceramics.

This theory of beauty was developed by the Japanese Zen Buddhists in the concept of *yugen*. The word referred to the obscure and dark that lies under the surface, implying a depth of meaning and richness of association half-revealed. To some poets yugen was associated with the pensive mood of autumn, to others with the bright charm of beautifully dressed ladies in a garden of flowers. It might be aroused by nature when the sight of wild geese vanishing among the clouds, of a boat disappearing behind far-off islands, or of the sun sinking behind a flower-clad hill created a contemplative mood. It was equated with the perfection of the gentle manners expected of the young noble at court.

In essays which Zeami left as secret instructions for his disciples, he applied the concept of yugen to the Noh in terms of limitations and disciplines as the actor strove through the phases of his life to perfect the *hana*, or flower, of his skill. Zeami's company was famous for its *monomane*, or accurate miming of life. Zeami insisted that art is based on life, but is at the same time very different from life. That difference was created by the flowering of the actor's hana. Starting at the age of seven, the actor should practice the skills of song and dance and only later apply those skills to the three difficult character types: old people, women, and warriors. Song and dance must move the imitation away from reality toward beauty and the ideal. Zeami thought, probably reflecting his own experience, that the actor might find the years from seventeen and eighteen to twenty-four and twenty-five the most difficult, but he must persist with constant practice, for only after twenty-four or twenty-five would real achievement be possible. He must strive toward his zenith at about thirty-five and expect the real hana to emerge only at forty-four or forty-five, when his youthful charm was completely gone. Yet along with his controlled skill, the inspired actor would include some startling or even coarse element that transcended skill or analysis.

KYOGEN: COMIC INTERLUDES ON THE NOH STAGE

Between the serious Noh plays are performed little farces called *Kyogen*, or "mad words." Though they grew from the same origins as the Noh and sometimes parody the patterns of the Noh, they are not heroic and poetic but human and earthy. The stately world of ancient heroes gives way to the disordered world of ordinary people with schemes and worries. Instead of the slow intoning, there is racy colloquial speech. Except for an occasional song or travesty of serious chant, there is no music. The ghosts are replaced by very palpable servants and neigh-

Noh comic mask: Yashima.
Courtesy the Japan National Tourist Organization.

bors. The gods have descended to the streets and back rooms of real life. The thunder god misses his footing on a cloud and tumbles to the ground, and for the painful bruise the quack doctor gives a needle treatment that makes the god scream. If the serious Noh shows the height of man's aspiration and the depth of his torment and regret, the Kyogen shows the acceptance of the finite world as it is.

A few Kyogen plays are like the Noh plays of blessing, with farmers dancing and singing the joy of peace and plenty. Sometimes the Kyogen is a travesty of the Noh. Battle scenes, typical of the warrior plays, may be burlesqued. In *Dobu Kacchiri* the men recite an account of a famous battle:

What bloodshed! What confusion! Some had their chins cut off; some their heels. Confused amidst the din of cries and groans, they clapped the severed heels on their bleeding chins and the severed chins on their bleeding heels. Ah, strange sight indeed! Three or four hundred battle-scarred soldiers with beards on their heels and blisters on their chins.

Buddhism, pervasive and serious in the Noh, is treated humorously in the Kyogen. *The Bird-Catcher in Hades*, a sixteenth-century play, parodies the serious Noh play *Cormorant Fisher*. Where in the serious play the offender finds mercy because of a good deed, the offender in the Kyogen escapes hell-fire when he demonstrates his trade of cook and the king of Hades finds his roast birds irresistible. In another play, Mr. Dumtaro makes both his uptown wife and his downtown wife completely subservient when he threatens to become a Buddhist monk.

Most of the Kyogen have the usual low-comedy plots of misunderstandings. The house boy Tarokaja, or Taro, alternately cheats his master and gets him out of straits; a nephew tries to get the better of an aunt or uncle. Taro starts to beat the scarecrow in the melon patch only to discover that it is the master in disguise. He escapes beating at the end while everyone is yelling "stop him." In *Hanago* (translated as *Abstraction*), a playboy husband, in order to get away from his wife to see his sweetheart, pretends to spend the night in Zen meditation and puts his servant Taro under the meditation robe. The wife, trying to be sympathetic, discovers the servant, hides herself under the robe, and listens to the husband tell of his exploit. When in one play a blind man is ready to carry another on his back over a river, a mischievous stranger jumps on and gets a free ride, then drinks the sake poured for the other blind man and sets the two fighting. In another play a jealous blind husband ties his wife to him by his sash, but the other man runs away with the wife, leaving the husband tied to a monkey and trying to embrace it. Frantic flight is the typical end of a Kyogen, corresponding to the fading away of the spirit in the Noh.

Although Kyogen is considered an integral part of the Noh theatre, it is never played by the same actors. Most Noh companies have their own home theatres, playing occasionally at temples or other public places or even sharing programs. The Kyogen actors belong to their own two companies with their own headquarters, plays, costumes, properties, and traditions. Besides giving the comic plays, they fill certain minor roles in the Noh plays, most often merely functional servants and messengers. But in a few Noh plays the Kyogen role is that of a lively innkeeper or boatman, suggesting the rich variety of early Noh before it was crystallized in the seventeenth century.

The Western traveler in Japan is likely to get much more out of a performance of Kyogen than out of the austere Noh. When two Kyogen performers from the Omira Company spent the year 1961–62 teaching and performing at the University of Washington, they had good response from American audiences.

NOH AND WESTERN THEATRE

It is possible to see in many twentieth-century plays and dances the influence of the Noh. If *Our Town* owes its general method to the Chinese classic stage, the return of Emily from the grave to confront a significant moment of her past is like an episode in a Noh play. The gentle fading of time into eternity at the end of the play is like the Buddhist sense that everything passes away. While Martha Graham's dances owed more to the Freudian concept of the unconscious and to the myths of early Greece and early America than to anything from Japan, her creation of a character alone in a dream world or surrounded by dream figures was much like the main dance of the Noh. The portable, bone-like forms created for her dances by the Japanese-American sculptor Taamu Noguchi had the same austere function as a Noh house or boat.

In the 1960s and 1970s there were several attempts in American schools to create a Noh production. In 1964 the Institute for Advanced Study of Theatre Arts in New York brought from Japan the Noh actor Sadayo Kita to direct American actors in *Ikkaku Sennin*. In 1970 a drama about Saint Francis that imitated the Noh was written and produced at Earlham College. The author, Arthur Little, the musician, Leonard Nolvik, and the choreographer, Eleanor King, who had all studied the art of Noh in Japan, tried to keep the rhythms and some of the tones of the Noh, adapting them to the story of the Christian saint.

More important than these school productions is the work of three major artists who made a deep study of Noh and created something of their own in its spirit. The Irish poet William Butler Yeats never managed to get to Japan, but the English composer Benjamin Britten and American choreographer Jerome Robbins made their pilgrimages to Japan before creating major works in the spirit of Noh.

The discovery of Noh drama was a major event in the career of Yeats. Eager to go beyond the fairie legends and impressionist moods of the Gaelic theatre, he hoped to find some "artifice of eternity," to evoke the universal Great Mind and the spirits of the past who, he believed, peopled the air. He knew of Gordon

97

Craig's strong interest in Oriental theatre. He came under the spell of the Noh when he hired as secretary the young American poet Ezra Pound, who was preparing an edition of the translations of Noh drama left by Ernest Fenollosa. Yeats wrote a preface for the book, which appeared in 1916. From that time on, none of his plays was without some influence from the Noh, and in some he attempted to find Western equivalents, as far as he understood a theatre he had never seen. The artist Edmund Dulac made masks for him, and the Japanese dancer Michio Ito, though he had had no training in Noh, showed him the Japanese effects of simplicity and austerity. Of his new direction Yeats wrote: "My blunder has been that I did not discover in my youth that my theatre must be the ancient theatre that can be made by unrolling a carpet or marking out a place with a stick, or setting a screen against the wall."

Closest of Yeats' plays to the spirit of Noh is *The Dreaming of the Bones* (1919). A modern man, fleeing from the police because he had taken part in an Irish insurrection, climbs a high hill to the ruins of an old abbey and graveyard. A strange man and woman in masks speak of two ghosts that can never kiss or rest until someone can forgive their crime. He responds to their mood, but when he learns that they are the couple who first betrayed Ireland by bringing in the Norman conquerors, he declares that they can never be forgiven. So they drift away, unsatisfied, dancing restless forever. Yeats found no Buddhist enlightenment to bring him release from Irish conflicts, but he found a vivid dramatic way of shedding the light of poetry, dance, and song on Ireland's tragic plight.

Tragic, too, is the psychological dilemma of love in Yeats' *A Full Moon in March* (1935), probably his best play in the Noh form. The opening song of the attendant musicians presents the opposing images of crown of gold and dung of swine. When the queen is dancing with the swineherd's severed head, they sing for both the queen and the head. After the queen sinks down kissing the head, like Salome, the attendants comment on the action. Yeats is dramatizing the old ritual pattern: the new spring is born out of desecration and violence.

As Irish freedom settled into a tight bureaucracy in the 1930s, Yeats continued to use the form of the Noh to revive symbols of the Irish past as protests against the chaos of the present. *The Words upon the Window-Pane* (1934) is a prose evocation of Jonathan Swift, who speaks through a spiritualistic medium to refuse the love of Vanessa because he rejects all mankind. Yeats' last Noh play, *The Death of Cuchulain* (1939), is a bitter tale of a hero so crazed that after fighting his son and attacking the sea, he is caught in a net and killed for a few pennies. Yeats had long sought to create from mystic literature and his own dreams some vision that would reconcile Catholics with Protestants, Ireland with the wider world, the heroic tradition with modern life, the worlds of the supernatural and the unconscious with the world of daily life. The Noh drama, with its interpretation of image and spirit, of past and present, naturally had such appeal for him.

Musical use of the Noh came in the 1960s. After he had seen in Japan several performances of the Noh drama, Benjamin Britten in 1964 produced *Curlew River*

(1964) in an Anglican church in England. *Sumidagawa*, or *Sumida River*, the Noh drama, shows a distraught mother who crosses the river Sumida in search of her lost boy, to find people praying at his grave as at a shrine. When she tries to dig into the grave, the boy appears and speaks to her, then disappears in the dawn. Britten and his librettist, William Plomer, set the story in medieval England with a chorus of monks who put on half-masks and appropriate garments as they are needed to represent the characters. The high point of the vision of resurrection is the prayer of the monks, but there is no dance. The music is powerful, written mainly in the idiom of medieval chant, with only a few Japanese touches.

Finally a major dancer made his pilgrimage to Japan and created a ballet based on the spirit and some of the methods of the Noh. In the winter of 1971–72 the New York City Ballet presented *Watermill* by Jerome Robbins, to the hissing anger of the regular balletomanes who could not recognize a single movement as traditional ballet style. Without any detail directly from the Noh, Robbins created a tension and austerity like that in the Noh. Six musicians with Japanese instruments—drums, gongs, bells, and flutes—provided a sustained mood, with intervals of silence as a man slowly, ritually, came downstage and lay down to watch the stages of his own life and the changing phases of the moon against the blue sky. An exuberant boy enters and men cross the stage scattering seed. A man and a woman perform a slow insect-like mating dance. Harvesters and reapers cross, and the watching man picks up two stalks of wheat ten or twelve feet long and performs a very slow abstract dance. Leaves begin to fall, and an old crone comes out from behind a haystack. Then leaf-like or coffin-like forms rise from the floor and ascend diagonally into the sky, bringing to an impressive close this new dance drama with scenic motives in the style of Kabuki and the spiritual contemplation of the Noh.

THE KABUKI THEATRE

With the rise of several powerful shoguns in the sixteenth century, trade flourished, Portuguese and other Europeans found their way up the China Sea from India bringing goods and new techniques and ideas, and Jesuit missionaries were welcomed and made many converts. But the new international influences seemed a threat to order. Several shoguns tried to suppress the Jesuits, and in 1595 some Christians were crucified. When the first Tokugawa gained supreme power in 1603 and established himself in the castle at Edo, far from the Emperor's court at Kyoto, he set up a stable regime with strong central control and a system of secret police. He forbade any Japanese to leave the country or any traveler to return. He cut off all foreign trade except through a small colony of Dutch merchants located on an

Kabuki actor Shakkyou in a contemporary musical comedy version of Kabuki, *The Wicked Demon Glimpses at the Curse. Courtesy the Japan National Tourist Organization.*

island in the Nagasaki harbor. The strict regime did bring peace and prosperity, and commerce and the arts flourished.

The merchants were hemmed in by strict rules. They could not travel without special papers or even wear bright-colored clothes on the streets. They had no access to the culture of the aristocrats around the emperor in Kyoto or of the powerful samurai around the shogun. Only at an occasional public performance to raise money for a temple could they see a Noh play, a kind of drama too refined for their taste in any case.

The merchant class developed its own culture and welcomed a new form of theatre entertainment—Kabuki. By adding erotic suggestions to an old Buddhist dance intended as a prayer for the dead, a clever woman named Okuni developed a celebration of peace after the civil wars. She was an immediate sensation. Presently she put on a sword and man's robe and impersonated in dance some of the famous heroes of the recent wars. In one of her most popular acts a young fop dallied with the mistress of a teahouse, and she often ended with a farcical, erotic scene in a bathhouse. She added other performers, mostly women who danced as military heroes, and a few men who danced women's roles. After her lover died, she acted his returned ghost, not seeking religious release but reveling in his martial and erotic memories. Thus in its earliest form Kabuki had an element of *yatsuchi*, of clever disguise, double meaning, or sly parody. The transvestism was only one of the new devices. Audiences expected indirect reference to recent events, even in heroic scenes of the feudal wars, or perhaps a partial re-creation of a legendary hero in scenes with contemporary setting. There was not only a sporting interest in getting around the censorship of the regime but a delight in recognizing hidden meanings. The modern word *Kabuki* is written with characters meaning song-dance-skill, but the earlier word meant leaning, tilted, or contrasted, suggesting something out of the ordinary and unruly, a frolicking and flirting and showing off on a downhill primrose path. Kabuki gave a sense of defiance of restraint even in its mature manifestation, when it expressed the acceptance of the necessity of restraint.

Okuni and her followers emphasized the charms of the dancers, and many in the audience followed the lure of the actresses after the performance. The theatre was known as "pleasure-woman Kabuki." Alarmed that some of his samurai, though they were forbidden to go into the merchants' quarters, squandered their money and fought duels over the favors of the actresses, the shogun in 1629 put an end to the scandal by forbidding women to perform on the stage.

The way was open for companies of boy actors, who were already playing. Soon the good-looking young men in both male and female roles were as popular as the pleasure women had been. It was an age of the "cult of youth" when each samurai kept a page to serve him in his military life, and the attachment was often emotional and homosexual. One shogun welcomed the boys' companies at court, but there were squabbles among the samurai for the favors of the popular boys and the next shogun in 1652 put an end to boys' Kabuki.

101

The boys' companies made several contributions to the Kabuki tradition. They made adaptations from Noh, especially from the comic characterization and mime of Kyogen, and they introduced acrobatic effects. Today acrobatic scenes are so important in Kabuki that companies of acrobats are hired just to perform battle scenes, and yet the Kabuki actors, too, have acrobatic skills. The most important innovation in the boys' companies was the increase in story interest. With Okuni a program had been like a revue, with many separate acts of unrelated songs and dances, but the boys used longer sequences.

The full maturity of Kabuki was achieved in the Genroku age, the golden age of city culture that began in the late seventeenth-century, continued into the eighteenth, and, with some nineteenth-century modification, lasted until the end of the Tokugawa rule in 1868. For several years after the boys' companies were suppressed, there were no performances, but finally new companies, using only adults, were allowed. Since neither sex nor physical beauty could be emphasized, men's Kabuki turned to the skills of acting, song, and dance. The dialogue became more important, and an extended drama of several acts was developed, though the *shosa*, or short play that is primarily dance, remains one of the most popular attractions in Kabuki theatre. To the present day an eighty-year-old actor does not hesitate to perform the role of a young girl, because the audience will be interested in his skill rather than in personal charm. The *onno-gata*, men who specialized in women's roles, gave Kabuki one of its most striking elements, presenting the abstract essence of a woman by makeup and movement. It takes Westerners a little time to grow accustomed to the heavy necks and strong bodies, but actually the use of men in onno-gata roles is less outrageous than the use of skilled castrati in soprano roles so popular in Baroque opera in Europe at just the time when men's Kabuki developed.

When in the seventeenth century Noh actors simplified their plays, Kabuki moved in the opposite direction, adding complications in plot and a greater variety of characters, increasing the tensions of angry threats and violent action on stage. The same heroes of the civil wars who floated like ghosts on the Noh stage strutted noisily on the Kabuki stage with dozens of attendants and spectacular scenes of battles. *Jidaimono*, or heroic historical drama, remains one of the main types of plays in the Kabuki repertory. When a play of the Noh theatre is presented in the Kabuki version, the Noh pine tree, much enlarged, is shown on the backdrop, and musicians and members of the chorus, dozens of them, are seated on platforms that extend the whole width of the stage.

Soon after Kabuki theatre began, a variant, a domestic or social drama called *sewamono*, was developed to present contemporary characters and recent sensational events. In 1703 Chikamatsu Monzaemon started a vogue of plays about love suicides by putting on the puppet stage a play called *The Love Suicides at Sonezaki*, based on an actual event of the month before. When the play stimulated a run of double suicides the authorities made new restrictions. But the sewamono con-

102

tinued with pathetic stories of misfortune, crime, and betrayal. The loyal prostitute became a favorite heroine. Sometimes a samurai is in love with her and tries
to get money to pay for her release, but more pathetic is the poor man, victim of
misfortune and treachery, who needs her love. Especially in Kyoto and Osaka,
actors developed a pathetic style of acting called *wagoto*, or "soft stuff."

In sharp contrast was the bombastic *aragoto*, or "rough stuff," acting developed
in Edo, the military capital, by Danjuro Ichikawa the First. Danjuro became famous as a boy actor, portraying a legendary baby-Hercules, red-faced and mus-
cular, who went about with an ax over his shoulder. He had adopted the energy
and some of the gestures of the most popular figure on the Edo puppet stage, a
superman of fierce exploits who threw the other puppets around so violently they
needed frequent replacement. Danjuro's most vivid character was the "chivalrous
commoner" who defied the samurai and rescued and protected the common
people. There were actually such men who dared strut down the streets in defiance of the samurai, to the adoration of the crowds. Out of their swaggering
walk and swinging arms, Danjuro created a characteristic stage movement called
roppo, or "six directions" (in Asia, up and down are included with the four directions of the Western world).

Japanese Kabuki, eighteenth century.

Aragoto performers shout vivid, mouth-filling phrases, intensives, and expletives that have no meaning in themselves. In an age of governmental and social repression, Kabuki turned loose its soul in a gallamaufrey of vocalized gestures of defiance.

Aragoto makeup was correspondingly wild and intense. Supposedly derived from Chinese painted faces, the Japanese bold lines follow more closely the contour of the face. As in China, the colors have symbolic meaning—wide red lines under the eyes and up the temples for the handsome brave hero, blue or black and red under the eyes and around the cheeks for evil, and so on. Sometimes a flesh-colored garment is worn over the body, with red lines to outline the muscles and padding to fill them out. With thick-soled shoes and a six-foot sword, the aragoto actor could shake the heavens with his thunder. At the end of the play he might accept death or defeat, but for several acts he enabled the audience to indulge in dreams of heroic defiance.

BUNRAKU, THE PUPPET THEATRE

In the eighteenth century the *Bunraku,* or puppet theatre, threatened to put Kabuki out of existence. The Kabuki actors won out only by adopting the more elaborate scenery of Bunraku, adapting their plays, and borrowing some of their stylized movements.

At about the same time that Okuni started her performances, *joruri,* or ballad singers, began performances of stories with dialogue and soon became popular with the same city audience. The revolutionary element that raised this singing above earlier ballad singing was the *samisen,* or "three-string" musical instrument, which had found its way up the Kyushu Islands from China. Okuni used as musical accompaniment gongs from the temples and the stately flute and drums from the Noh theatre, but the more lively samisen became the characteristic instrument of the "floating world" gaiety of the Genroku era. The musician using a plectrum could strike both the strings and the sounding board, and a good samisen player could describe all dramatic moods from gaiety to sorrow, rapture to anguish, and suggest wind, hail, or soft moonlight.

Almost as soon as joruri reciters became popular, a combination was made with puppets. To the accompaniment of the samisen, the performer recited a combination of narrative and dialogue while the dolls, about one-third human size, acted out the story. The main manipulator, in rich costume, stood directly behind each doll. As more elaborate dolls were developed in the eighteenth century, two assistants, dressed in black, were added for each puppet so that the eyes, mouth, hands, and legs could be animated separately.

Contemporary operators of traditional eighteenth-century Bunraku puppets. Figure in black assists in manipulating the rods that move the arms.

The golden age of the joruri-doll theatre came in Osaka in Genroku times, at the end of the seventeenth century, with the collaboration of three superb artists—a joruri reciter, an expert puppeteer, and the greatest playwright of Japanese history, Chikamatsu Monzaemon. In 1685, he left the Kabuki actors and devoted himself to the doll theatre, for which he wrote approximately one hundred plays. Many were historical epics about superheroes. A good example is available in *The Battles of Coxinga*, the story of a refugee from the fall of Ming China in 1644 (just forty years before the play was given), who returns from Japan, where he had been in exile, with his son, a superman who rides a tiger, scatters armies, tears down castles singlehandedly, and restores the hidden Ming prince to his throne—a piece with intrigue, adventure, and musical spectacle worthy of a film epic. But the puppet plays that won the hearts of the people were those of everyday life.

When a Western traveler sees a scene from a Bunraku play at a department store or special tourist center, he usually hears a recording on a sound track and has little notion of the important part played by the reciter in a full production. At first the reciter is a distraction as he sits at the side of the stage with his samisen player, reading or chanting from a script on a stand before him, showing so much emotion in his face that he seems more important than either the puppets or the manipulators. But gradually the spectator learns to take in the reciter out of the corner of his eye while watching the puppets, and the manipulators also recede to the edge of consciousness. The moving eyes and eyebrows are at first comic but soon seem very expressive. No live actor can concentrate with the intensity of a doll watching himself slowly doing something with his tiny hands or with the big hands of the manipulators. No living actors can do as well with transformation scenes in which a man is quickly turned into an animal or a demon. Above all, puppets can contract to a very low position, rise to stand ten or twelve feet high, soar on into the air, and sweep through the skies. This lightness and freedom enables them to perform dances of superhuman dimensions.

MODERN KABUKI AND OTHER DEVELOPMENTS

In the nineteenth century sewamono was made more realistic in much the same way that European melodrama was made more realistic: the slums of cities and the local color of many other real places were put on the stage. Playwrights appeared who were able to raise the racy language of the slums to poetry and explore the depths of human feeling in sentimental scenes of the unfortunate and mistreated poor. *The Love of Izayoi and Seishin*, by Kawatake Mokuami was one of the most popular of the new realistic Kabuki plays. The strong sense of fatalism, the implication that the runaway monk and his love, the prostitute, were destined to crime and suffering because of deeds in an earlier incarnation, adds to the pathos as the two become more deeply involved in theft and murder. Scenes of repentance alternate with scenes of bold crime. The lovers at times blame fate and at times decide, like Macbeth, that they have gone so far that they may as well live up to their demonic reputation. The sad farewell as they go to their deaths together is an operatic finale.

After the Meiji restoration in 1868, when many Japanese wanted to westernize everything, a much modified Kabuki style called *Shimpa* was achieved by toning down Kabuki spectacle and using an acting style much nearer the realism of the West. It is an interesting comment on the Japanese character that the new style became another historical tradition. There are playwrights, actors, designers, and technicians who specialize in the quiet, impressionistic moods of Shimpa. Women play the women's parts, and a favorite subject is the private sorrows and adventures of geisha girls.

A very popular offshoot of Kabuki is the all-girl *Takarazaka*, started in a resort town near Osaka in 1914. It uses the most striking elements of Kabuki and adds dance and local color from festivals and folk dances. It is a revue theatre, bright with sequins and ostrich feathers, and it specializes in the marvels of modern machinery, with moving stages and elaborate lighting.

THE ACTOR AND THE STAGE

The Kabuki developed several stage forms that made it distinct from all other theatres. At first Okuni combined the simple square platform of the court dances with the temple roof and entrance bridge of the Noh stage. In the eighteenth century, several major changes produced that Kabuki stage as it survives to this day. As theatres were enlarged and more elaborate settings were built on the rear stage, the forestage was extended to bring the actor out to the audience. But that left the old bridge area much too far away for the travel-song scenes from the Noh that were still popular. The brilliant solution was to build the bridge through the audience, and today the principal entrances and exits are made through a door at the rear of the auditorium, giving the actor some of his most vivid scenes on the way to or from the main stage. This bridge or runway is called the *hanamichi*, or flower path, no one knows why, unless perhaps the fans used it to bring money and flowers to their favorite actors. Today the hanamichi has electric footlights and a trap door for sudden appearances.

Unlike the Noh theatre, the Kabuki early developed elaborate scenery, changed in full view of the audience. Light painted screens are slid on and off, painted backdrops are lifted or taken down, platforms are moved, or free-standing gates,

107

tree trunks, bridges, or boats are brought on and taken off by stage attendants. Platforms of light construction, with rollers, make it possible to show first the exterior of a house, then by removing the walls, the interior. The several stage levels permit a climactic progression for the actor. In one play, a large waterfall comes down the center of the stage, as between two houses, and empties into a pool at the front of the stage. The effect is created by means of painted cloth pulled over rollers and rounded platforms with plastic cloth rocks at the front and small wings of rock and clouds at the sides.

For a quick change of setting, the doll theatre in the eighteenth century invented the revolving stage, and it was immediately adopted by the Kabuki. Europe had developed a small revolving stage in the Renaissance, used in the *tableaux vivants* on city streets for a magic transformation, and in the court masques to present the honored guests suddenly in the center of the stage. But that device was forgotten, and the modern theatre of the West has borrowed the larger turntable from the Kabuki.

The Kabuki actor is nearly always on the forestage, separated from the background. In many plays that use patterns of Bunraku the joruri reciters and the musicians are ranged on a platform at one side of the stage, in front of part of the scenery. For certain effects the actor or dancer may make an entrance down the center of the stage standing on a rolling platform, as the regular scenery divides, moves apart, and closes after him. Or if he needs more room for a large action, part or all of the scenery, having indicated the locale of the play, may be pulled aside.

The stage attendants, called *kurombo*, or "black men," are more numerous than the black-costumed property men of the Chinese stage. Besides handling scenery and properties, they keep close attendance on the actors. In the first days of a new play, an attendant may crouch just behind the actor, following the script to prompt him. In early times the kurombo often held a candle at the end of a rod to give extra light to the actor's face. The actor often needs the help of the kurombo in taking his arm out of the kimono for a more vigorous handling of a weapon, and many changes of costume are made on stage. One of the most sensational effects in Kabuki requires the actor to assume in rapid succession a series of characters, and to shed one costume after another. To make this possible, each costume is basted together so that the kurombo, with a quick pull, loosens the seams, and the costume falls in pieces in his hands, revealing the one underneath.

Kabuki costumes are among the most colorful the stage has ever produced. There are many types of wigs for ladies, for old monks, for demons, and for characters that take the form of animals. The symbolism is more obvious than in the Noh theatre, but still a garment is a beautiful stage costume and not an attempt at realism. A fur covers the head and shoulders to indicate a fox, but the face has a conventional demon pattern and the rest of the costume is of richly patterned material. Some characters wear wooden clogs, but an actor dances in bare feet or in the soft, light-colored, bifurcated sock called a *tabi*.

Even though many realistic touches may be included, Kabuki acting is based on a lifetime of training in body and voice. Scenes and speeches are arranged for the virtuoso performer and include many set pieces such as the travel song, borrowed from the Noh, which becomes an interest in itself. Song scenes are sometimes performed as separate acts, apart from their plays. Even the plays of everyday life include many song and dance passages, and plays of the "music-gesture" type are entirely sung, with many dances, some related to the story, some incidental. Some scenes are arranged to lead up to a "narration," a set piece that could be removed from the play, the actor even emphasizing its irrelevance by beginning, "I shall now tell you the story." Sometimes when an actor performs a dance scene based on the style of the puppets, another actor dressed as the old-fashioned puppeteer pretends to be animating the human doll. Sound and action may be suspended while one actor, in the tense silence, performs a strong emotional pantomime. Or the actor may build his dance scene to a position of tension and suddenly freeze into a striking pose, called a *mi-e*, while an attendant rapidly beats two wooden clappers.

Any Kabuki play may be embellished with short or long scenes of dance. The travel scenes, so quiet and subjective in Noh, burst into elaborate processions in Kabuki, coming down the hanamichi and flowing over mountains, past gates, and through forests on the main stage.

Spring and autumn folk dances may be developed into spectacular scenes. From *Okina*, the Noh play of New Year's blessing, is taken the dance of Sambaso, the vigorous farmer from the ricefields, who for the Kabuki audience mimes such spring scenes as dressing for a wedding, riding the wedding horse, and becoming a farmer again. In the Noh version of *Dojoji* (1753) the priest invokes power to quell the demonic jealous woman who tries to destroy him and the new bell. In the Kabuki version the religious conflict is lost and a long dance is developed showing the phases of a woman's life from girl to jealous demon, with seven changes of garments and hats. The ancient lion dances are given human themes, often sentimental, showing now a young girl dancing as a lion among peonies, teased by butterflies, now a father and son between red mountain peonies and white valley peonies acting out the hopes, pride, merry companionship, and conflict as a son grows up and replaces the father.

THE DRAMA OF OBLIGATIONS

Through the Kabuki drama for nearly four centuries the Japanese turned their rebellious impulses into symbolic gestures and inner repression so successfully that there has not been a serious civil disorder since the Tokugawa rulers came to power. After Admiral Perry sailed into Tokyo harbor in 1853 with an American fleet and forced the Japanese to renew contact with the outside world, foreign influences spread fast without creating serious disturbance. When the Shogunate was abolished in 1867, the emperor, neglected for a thousand years, was restored to authority and moved from Kyoto to Edo, which was renamed Tokyo, or Western Capital. Parliamentary parties and industrialization developed before the end of the century, and a new military regime came into power in the 1930s. After the defeat in 1945, there were even greater changes. But still the Japanese have maintained public order. The psychological training of the centuries has enabled the individual to fulfill his obligations to the family and society by repressing individual impulses. The Kabuki has provided an exorcism of inner tension by dramatizing heroic self-assertion and high deeds of achievement or revenge, and at the same time channeling that assertion into renunciation and sacrifice of the self in deference to a ruler or a code.

The styles of Kabuki have combined the two aspects of submission and assertion—on the one hand, a puppet-like submission to the music and rhythm and to the techniques and traditions handed down from master to pupil, from father to son; on the other hand, in aragoto, the patterned assertion of energy, defiance, pride, and determination.

The plays show the same balance of assertion and submission, independent action and acceptance of rule and authority. *The Confrontation of the Soga Brothers*, a Genroku play traditional for the month of January, shows the two sons of a slain father bringing New Year's gifts to the court of the lord who killed him. One brother wants to take revenge immediately, but the other restrains him, since violence is not permitted on formal occasions and felicitous days. They declare their intent but must bide their time until the season later in the year when the lord agrees to meet them.

The pride and self-respect of the merchants and common citizens were dramatized symbolically in *Kagemasa's Interpellation of the Thunder*, one of the aragoto plays about the chivalrous commoner. While others are presenting armor at the birthday of the shogun's son, the loyal merchant Kagemasa presents a chest containing only a merchant's ledger and an abacus for counting. The haughty lords are contemptuous and one comes forward with a real gift, a sword. Kagemasa steps up with a defiant "Shibaraku," or "Wait a moment," and breaks the sword in two. The wicked noblemen try for years to ambush and kill Kagemasa, but he escapes. The entire play is no longer presented, but that one incident has had dozens of imitations, and "Shibaraku!" has rung down through the centuries to warn oppressive officials that they molest the common citizen at their peril.

In order to be faithful to his trust, the hero of Kabuki undergoes any amount of humiliation. He may be torn between his different obligations and have to violate even his love for his family in order to carry out the higher duty. The combination of heroism and acceptance of humiliation characterizes the *Chushingura*, or *The*

110

Forty-Seven Ronin (1748), the most loved and famous of Kabuki plays. It was based on an actual event of 1701–03 that aroused great popular response—the one event that came near shaking the stability of the Tokugawa regime. One lord had attacked and wounded a superior lord within the shogun's palace. Ordering the man to die by his own hand, the shogun declared the incident closed. But forty-seven of his devoted followers resolved to get revenge on the arrogant lord who had caused their lord's downfall. They bided their time, hiding their intentions, and in defiance of the shogun achieved their revenge. The shogun ordered them executed as criminals, but public opinion was so aroused in their behalf that he was forced to permit them an honorable death by harakiri.

More than a hundred plays were written on the subject, but one version, written in the eighteenth century by Isumo Takeda and his collaborators, has outshone the rest, dominating the Japanese drama even more than *Hamlet* has dominated the English. With extremely good acting parts, it furnishes a combination of private deed and public rule, righting a wrong in the realm without disturbing the fundamental acceptance of order. The forty-seven homeless retainers are not rebels and take no thought of themselves, enduring all kinds of humiliation and gladly paying with their lives for the arrogance of independent action.

The typical pattern of the love plots so popular in the plays of Chikamatsu has the same implication. Personal pleasures and satisfactions do not seem evil to the Japanese, who have never had what Westerners call a sense of sin; but they are always subordinate to obligations. In the plays love is shown in conflict with some obligation. The girl belongs to a disgraced family or the father orders the son to marry elsewhere. Sometimes the couple defy obligations and are united, but they always pay in the one way they can, committing suicide together. It is not a defiant gesture or a defense of individual integrity, but an acceptance of obligation.

The function of this romantic drama, as of all romantic drama, is to glorify the idealistic motivations that underlie everyday life by projecting them into the colorful panorama of ancient times and heroic deeds. As the Japanese accept the petty obligations of daily life, they feel "tangled by giri." But in the romantic drama simple loyalty to a lord or to one's fellow samurai was a glorious act.

THE KABUKI HODGEPODGE

Since Kabuki borrows from so many other traditions, it seems at first like a hodgepodge. Since the Chinese opera stage had no scenery, the Chinese property man sat quietly at the side until he was needed. But in the elaborate scenery of Kabuki the property attendant must be furtive. Dressed in black, his face covered by a hanging veil, he sneaks out from behind a wing or a tree to bring on or remove a property or to hold a black cloth in front of the escaping dead man, then dash away himself or hide behind a tree until needed again. Where the Chinese theatre played everything in full lighting and the Western theatre darkens the house and brings stage lights low for twilight and night, Kabuki mixes the methods. Some scenes are in full general lighting, then for night the stage lights are lowered and the house lights slightly lowered. Or a blue curtain for twilight or black for night is dropped over the entire setting.

Either the main Kabuki curtain or such a night curtain may be used, as in Western theatre, for a scene change. But at other times the scenery is changed before the eyes of the audience. A scene may begin with a full setting, then parts of the setting move to the side or back to make more room for the actors. For one part of the play the audience gets used to a discreet accompaniment of samisen and blocks performers vaguely seen through slits in the scenery. Then suddenly on the other side of the stage a section of the scenery opens to reveal a pair of reciters seated at their script stands and two or three samisen players. In some plays mood music of harp, massed strings, and horns, usually taped, may be added to or substituted for the native Kabuki music. At other times over the loudspeaker come expressionistic effects: remembered speeches, distorted echoes from the past, choruses of voices, or sounds of turmoil or terror.

Yet there are some principles that bring the disparate elements into a kind of unity. In contrast to Noh, with its illusive yugen, Kabuki is a popular theatre. It is environmental theatre, using multimedia to give the audience a very full experience. For all that it gives the illusion of real palaces, real spring festivals, real sorrows of poor sufferers, it is a stylized form, using the manners and customs of different classes of people not merely to build a real texture of geography and time of day, as in Western naturalism, but to enable a highly trained actor to create a superimage of mankind.

KABUKI IN THE WEST

While the bright color and vivid acting have excited the traveler, Kabuki has had far less influence on the West than has the Chinese theatre or the Noh. It was easier to invent a Western method of acting Chinese plays, and the Noh had more appeal for poets. John Masefield's *The Faithful* (1916), an adaptation of *Chushingura*, attracted attention in London and New York by its stately action in front of a few Japanese screens. The expressionists welcomed the method as another attack on realism, but no other playwright or producer followed its suggestions.

Only one occidental writer, the poet Paul Claudel, was deeply influenced by Kabuki. While he was French ambassador in Tokyo he thought Kabuki a combination of drama and music preferable to the opera of Wagner. Where Wagner submerged the actor in the music and made the voice only one strand in a complex web of orchestral sounds, Kabuki kept the actor dominant and set off the voice in contrast to the drums and samisen. The instrumental music created mood and atmosphere independently, and the voice worked against it rather than blending with it in a vague mélange.

Claudel was ahead of his time, but two of his plays with music eventually made a strong impression. *Christophe Colomb* and *Jeanne d'Arc au Bûcher* (*Joan of Arc at the Stake*) are not plays in the ordinary sense, using monologues, recitations, narratives, and choral passages that are better known to musicians than to drama audiences. *Christophe Colomb* (1928), as first set by Darius Milhaud, was produced in Germany by an opera company. Milhaud wrote new music on a more intimate scale for a stunning production by the Renaud-Barrault Company in Paris in the early 1950s. *Jeanne d'Arc au Bûcher*, with music by Arthur Honegger, first produced in Basel in 1938, was produced in America by the Philadelphia Orchestra with Vera Zorina in the role of Jeanne, and the recording aroused considerable excitement among young listeners. The play has had a number of productions in America. Without giving his play a Japanese flavor, Claudel showed how some Japanese methods could be adapted to the Western theatre. His work has been important in the development of epic theatre in the West. By the middle of the twentieth century, the methods had become part of the general trend toward freer forms of playwriting and greater use of music, poetry, and dance.

Under the direction of Earl Ernst, the University of Hawaii led in the production of Kabuki plays for American audiences. In the seventies Leonard Pronko at Pomona College produced several Kabuki dramas, and in a production of Marlowe's *The Jew of Malta* showed how Kabuki might be used in Western theatre classics.

With the opening of Japan to foreigners in the latter part of the nineteenth century, Western countries developed greater interest in Japanese arts and crafts— paintings, porcelain, screens, fabric, embroidery—and in Japanese dress, customs, and manners. Such interest appeared in theatre in Gilbert and Sullivan's *The Mikado* (1885), with its picturesque, comic charm. An English musical play *The Geisha* (1892) was in part the inspiration for Puccini's *Madame Butterfly* (1904), with its sad story and slightly exotic music. A failure at its first performance at La Scala, this became one of the most popular operas of the twentieth century. Neither *The Mikado* nor *Madame Butterfly* owed much to the Kabuki theatre, but by 1976 Stephen Sondheim (composer), John Weidman (librettist), and Harold Prince (director) were able, in *Pacific Overtures*, to make effective use of some elements from both Bunraku and Kabuki. The use of Japanese and Japanese-American actors added an aura of authenticity. Still, this was essentially another Broadway musical.

III

The Theatre
of Ancient Greece

Clytemnestra (Lee Richardson) welcomes her husband Agamemnon (Douglas Campbell) upon his victorious return from Troy in the world premiere of *The House of Atreus*, adapted by John Lewin from the *Oresteia* by Aeschylus.

115

Introduction

The theatres of the Orient were little known in the Western world before the nineteenth century. It was the Greek and Roman theatres, rediscovered and reshaped in the Renaissance in the fourteenth and fifteenth centuries, that provided the first links between ancient and modern theatre in the West.

Though Greece blossomed a little earlier than India and China and left a more extensive record, it was another creation of the Iron Age, when cheap iron, easy transport, and coinage had transformed the Bronze Age world. As in India and China, there were a number of small city states, and drama was a religious drama, produced primarily at sacred temples and associated with great processions and festivals.

But by the sixth century B.C. Athens had banished her kings and was gradually shifting power to a council of citizens. She would finally create the world's first democracy, giving a greater scope for individuality than any previous regime. The Athenians reshaped their institutions to encourage change and variety, even at the risk of losing control of order. It is not surprising that the city had a very rapid growth and a blossoming of civilization or that the Golden Age lasted for a very short time. That Greece, and hence Western Europe and America, moved faster than Eastern countries toward the liberation of the individual may be explained by a basic difference in traditional mythology. In Asian myths, according to Joseph Campbell, both the world and man are part of god, and hence man is strongest when he loses his individuality in a universal nirvana. But from Persia west, according to Campbell, god appears in mythology as separate from the world and man and hence something to challenge man and something for man to challenge. In his earliest mythology, European man had a basis for the effort to make himself and the world more worthy of a distant divinity and also for a sense of guilt if he failed. *Prometheus Bound*, one of the earliest Greek plays, shows the Titan in rebellion against the king of heaven. Where Egyptian drama and most traditional Asian drama celebrated an ancient triumph of order over the demons of chaos, Greek drama presented heroes who continued to challenge the established order of the universe. Hence the Greeks developed the genre of tragedy and prized it above comedy, and even the comic heroes of the Golden Age were enterprising individuals who set about changing the world.

The dynamic element in Athenian democracy was a middle class of growers, artisans, and traders, who gained the cooperation of the old aristocrats. The center of cultural life was not the palace or temple, as in Egypt and Asia, but the marketplace and that open marketplace of the mind, the theatre. The actors were not kings and priests but poets and artists competing in open contests for prizes. Where the Egyptian king performed at his coronation virtually the same drama his predecessors had performed for hundreds of years, and Eastern audiences have expected repetition of the same traditional dances and plays, Athenians of the fifth century saw new plays every year at their festivals. Where the heroes of most Oriental drama strive to recover an old order temporarily lost or to gain a deeper understanding of a universe that moves slowly in its own mysterious ways, Greek heroes challenge the universe and set out to hew a new order out of the rough stone of the old.

The pride and confidence of Athenians in the Golden Age grew out of two triumphant struggles—a class struggle within the country in the sixth century, culminating in the establishment of the democracy about 500 B.C., and the defeat of the invading Persian armies of 490 and 480 B.C. The class struggle came in response to a crisis of expanding population and trade. For a while overcrowding was relieved by establishing colonies in the Near East and Italy, but by the seventh century the light topsoil had been so exhausted that not even those who stayed at home could be supported by simple farming and stock raising. Athens and Sparta each made characteristic adaptations to the crisis. The Spartans enslaved their neighbors, the Messenians, then set themselves against further change, turning their state into a military camp. In contrast, the Athenians planted olive trees and grapevines that could use the subsoil and took a risk no nation had taken before by importing a large part of their grain. Soon Athens was swarming with new classes—wine and olive growers, manufacturers, potters, traders, and shippers—who challenged the authority of the old landed aristocracy. The contention led to a series of dictators, or "tyrants," each exacting more concessions from the aristocrats and extending the franchise to more of the merchants and artisans. Finally the tyrant Cleisthenes broke up the old tribes, shifted the power to a council of five hundred, and democracy was born. The dominant middle class developed the Greek emphasis on the mean as a reconciliation of extremes, an ideal that has appealed to democracies ever since as offering the greatest possible freedom to the individual.

Two of the sixth-century dictators were very wise. The Greeks attributed their great respect for law to one of them, Solon, who seemed a gentle though just ruler after the harsh edicts of Dracon. The respect for law led to the search for the laws of nature and the laws of the mind, hence to aesthetics, philosophy, and science. A Greek temple is a monument to the laws of harmony and balance, and a Greek mask shows both gods and men as human embodiments of universal forces. When Aeschylus dramatized the triumph of the small Greek nation over the invading Persian army, he had his Xerxes express astonishment that the Greeks had not run away, "especially as you say they are free and there is no one to stop them." But his Greek captive answered, "They are free, O king, but not free to do everything. For there is a master over them named Law, whom they respect more than thy servants fear thee."

Peisistratus, the tyrant at the middle of the sixth century, counteracted the dominance of the old tribes by fostering the public occasions that brought the whole city together. He had the Homeric epics collected and recited at the Pantheneum festival so that all Athenians could be proud of the ancient Greek heroes. He transformed the spring festival of Dionysus into the City Dionysia, with public money and state prestige behind it, and made a contest in tragedy the high point of the occasion. From the first festival in 534 B.C., drama played a major role in Athenian public life. Soon the last tyrant, Cleisthenes, gave the festival still greater importance by establishing a contest in *dithyrambs*, the traditional choral dances in honor of Dionysus, with each tribe entering a chorus of fifty men or boys. Since Cleisthenes had redistributed Athenians of all classes into ten tribes, the dithyramb contest each year gave some five hundred men several weeks of rehearsal and performance of complex dance-chants. A poet found not only trained performers but a sophisticated audience for the choruses of his plays.

THE DIONYSIAN FESTIVAL AND THE ORIGINS OF TRAGEDY

The first contest in tragedies occurred at the spring festival of Dionysus in 534 B.C. and was won by Thespis. So much is known. But there has been much scholarly speculation about how tragedy developed. Most theories have assumed that it derived from the spring festival. But in this century scholarly research has shown that tragedy was added to the spring festival but did not grow out of it, that there is no solid evidence that tragedy was ever Dionysian in any sense except that it was originally and regularly performed at the City Dionysia. It is confusing that actors were called priests of Dionysus and that when they organized a guild they used the name of Dionysus.

The theory of the Dionysian origin of tragedy dates from the publication of *The Birth of Tragedy* (1872) by Friedrich Nietzsche. He defined two points of view, the Apollonian and the Dionysian, one expecting art to give life logic, calm, and order, the other delighting in the wild and irrational. In tragedy, he suggested, the actors and the action expressed the Apollonian world while the chorus, originally a wild satyr chorus, expressed the Dionysian world, based on primitive depths of feeling.

An early twentieth-century theory of the invention of tragedy assumed that a chorus of men at the Dionysian spring festival were accustomed to dress as goat-like satyrs and improvise laments for the death of Dionysus and songs of revelry to celebrate his resurrection. Arion was supposedly the first poet to compose a dithyramb for this group, and train the chorus to perform it. Then one day Thespis stepped out of the chorus, or, as a messenger, reported the death of Dionysus. Thus he invented the actor and a rudimentary form of dialogue and changed a narrative-lyric choral form, with singing and dancing about something offstage and past, into a form dealing with the dramatic present. But if the dithyramb was once associated with the worship of Dionysus, it kept no trace of that connection. Moreover, it was added to the festival after tragedy was established.

Another subject of scholarly concern that has been resolved is the number of actors in the tragedies. The plays of Aeschylus can be divided into one-actor, two-actor, and three-actor plays, to fit an evolutionary sequence. In the three plays of the *Oresteia*, produced in 458 B.C., shortly before Aeschylus died in 456,

Dionysus in a ship sailing down through the Aegean Sea to Attica. *Courtesy Staatliche Antikensammlungen und Glyptothek, München.*

he followed the lead of the young Sophocles and used three actors. His two-actor plays can mostly be dated in the 470s and 460s. But *The Suppliants*, with one actor, formerly thought to be an early play, is now known to have been given in 460 B.C. It seems apparent that the number of actors depended on the requirements of the play, not on the growing ability of the dramatist to use more actors.

Months before each City Dionysia, the highest city official, who was in charge of the festival, looked over the tragedies submitted and decided which three poets

Seated *choregus* (leader of the chorus) distributing masks to actors.

121

would be granted a chorus, for the state paid the choral performers. Then by lot were chosen three *choregi*—rich men who were required to pay for the actors, costumes, masks, and music. The poets were assigned by lot to these three angels. Some choregi were so generous they all but clothed the actors in gold, but a poet might draw a niggardly one. If the poet won, his choregus was crowned and honored along with him. Competition was keen, though the first prize was only a tripod, which was usually dedicated and enshrined in a public place. To prevent bribery, the judges were chosen by lot in a complicated secret process. A few days before the festival the participants showed themselves to the public in a *proagon* in the Odeion, or large music hall, in masks and costumes. A herald read the names of the poets, performers, and plays, thus whetting the interest of the public.

The night procession at the beginning of the festival did belong to Dionysus. His statue was taken out of the city to a shrine on the road to Eleutheria, whence his worship was originally introduced into Athens, and by torchlight, amid revelry, wine-drinking, and love-making, it was brought back to the theatre to preside over the contests in the god's honor. By dawn the next day the entire free male population crowded into the theatre of Dionysus, which held at least 17,000.

Dionysian procession. Worshippers carrying a large image of Dionysus (with exaggerated phallus), followed by musicians who serenade Thespis in an ox-pulled cart. *Pen and ink drawing by Martha Sutherland from a black-figure vase in the British Museum.*

The tickets, which paid only for the repairs and upkeep of the theatre, were cheap, and anyone too poor to pay could apply for a free ticket. Probably few men brought their slaves or their wives. Though many of the plays were about ancient women who took part in public life, Athenian women had long been assigned to the home.

The first day of the festival began not with a play but with solemn ceremonies—a sacrifice on an altar and a libation before the statue of Dionysus. There were proclamations of citizens on whom crowns were bestowed, reception of delegates and tribute from the allies, and a kind of graduation ceremony for the orphans brought up by the state. Each of the ten tribes presented a dithyramb, five tribes entering choruses of fifty boys, five entering choruses of fifty men. Each poet entered four plays—three tragedies and a satyr play. Aeschylus usually wrote his tragedies as a trilogy and often included the satyr play to complete a tetralogy, but later poets presented separate plays.

SATYR PLAY AND COMEDY

The evidence indicates that the satyr play was imported from other parts of Greece and added to the tragedies at the end of the sixth century B.C. It was written by tragic writers and acted by tragic actors, never by comic. The costumes of the main characters, to judge by the vase paintings, were like tragic costumes. The formal structure of the play was like tragedy, with the same meter for the

Choir of cithara-playing satyrs. *Courtesy the Metropolitan Museum of Art, Fletcher Fund, 1925. (27.78.66)*

dialogue of the episodes and a similar freedom in meter for the choral odes. The satyr play did not burlesque the serious gods or treat the affairs of everyday people, and it was not satiric. The word *satire* did not derive from *satyr*. Apparently the satyr plays were written about the few gods and heroes associated with spring revelry, especially ones who could come back from the underworld, like Heracles or Odysseus. The chorus of boisterous and often obscene satyrs created a mood quite different from either tragedy or comedy. But knowledge of satyr plays is very limited. From Aeschylus, who was considered the best writer of this kind of play, there is none extant, and from Sophocles, only a part of a play. The only complete example is Euripides' *The Cyclops* (undated), which shows how Odysseus tricked and blinded the one-eyed Cyclops in order to escape with his men from the cave. The mythological pattern of resurrection, perhaps characteristic of satyr plays, is shown in Euripides' *Alcestis* (438 B.C.), which is classified as a tragedy though Euripides presented it as the fourth, or satyr, play. There is no boisterous chorus, but a drunken Heracles whose revelry makes a sharp contrast to the funereal mood of the household he visits. When he learns of the death of Alcestis, he goes to the underworld and brings her back.

Comedies were the main fare at the Lenaean festival, which took place earlier in the spring, but by 486 B.C. they were also regularly given state support and prizes at the City Dionysia. Sometimes several comedies were presented on one day, but usually one comedy was presented after the tragedies and satyr play. In *The Birds* (414 B.C.), a character is delighted at the idea that with wings one could slip out of the tragedies, fly home to dinner, and get back in time for the comedy.

THE THEATRE OF DIONYSUS

On the south slope of the Acropolis in Athens the theatre of Dionysus still stands with its circles of seats, its horseshoe-shaped orchestra, and some stones of the stage constructed here by the Romans. There is little left from the fifth century. The theatre opened out before the small temple of Dionysus, like a courtyard large enough for thousands of spectators, offering a wide landscape to the mountains and a glimpse of the sea. Above it, high on the Acropolis, stood the temple of Athena, the Parthenon, where the priests could make offerings; but the humble shrine of Dionysus was on an open road in reach of all. The Greeks called the theatre a *theatron*, a place to see, in contrast to the Romans, who called their gathering place an *auditorium*, a place to hear. The "things performed" were the *dramata*, whence our word drama.

Even during the fifth century this theatre was rebuilt and modified several times. We read of wooden seats collapsing and being replaced by stone, and later by marble. We are not even sure what the basic shape of the orchestra and seats was, whether there was a raised stage for the actors, or what the *skene*, the scenic background, looked like. If we think of the splendid marble buildings of Hellenistic times—that is, after Athens was swept into empire by Alexander—we visualize a large circular orchestra for the choral odes, almost surrounded by circles of seats with room for fifteen or twenty thousand people who faced a high raised stage as part of a large two- or three-story skene, framed by wings or *paraskenia* at the ends. The façade had at least three doorways on the acting level and niches with statues on the upper floors. But if we think of the necessities of the classical plays, we get a much simpler picture. For the three plays of the *Oresteia* (458 B.C.) for instance, we need the front of a palace, an altar or tomb not far from the palace door, and a large open space for the chorus to perform the odes, for actors and chorus to meet, and for Agamemnon to arrive in a horse-drawn chariot. From the chariot Agamemnon must walk on the royal robe directly into the palace without more than two or three steps. For the last play, the palace front can be first a temple of Apollo, presumably at Delphi, and then a temple of Athena at Athens. The skene must have resembled a palace and a temple, and we visualize a beautiful permanent architectural structure. When we read about machines we can easily fit most of them into the one-story palace-temple image: a crane to let a god down from the roof and an *ekkeklema*, or rolling platform, to bring out through a doorway a small tableau of what has happened offstage. But some accounts mention painting and scenes that pull and scenes that turn. And finally, in a list of Greek and Latin theatre words compiled by Pollux in the second century A.D., we find walls, tunnels, lean-tos, sheds, curtains, and devices for showing sailors at sea. It is not easy to reconcile such scenic devices with our classic vision of an unadorned marble palace. The Athenians painted many of their public buildings bright colors. Should we imagine the palace-temple, with or without scenery, as painted in bright colors or the honey-brown of the Parthenon marble or the dead white of nineteenth-century architectural drawings and plaster casts?

Athens probably did not have a round orchestra until quite late in the fifth century. Carlo Anti, an Italian scholar, insists that the early form was rectangular or trapezoidal and that only near the end of the Golden Age was it converted to round. One early theatre at Thorikos, very close to Athens, was never converted and shows its rectangular form today. The ruins of the theatre at Syracuse in Sicily, Anti insists, show the trapezoidal structure that was later rebuilt. The playing area and seats at the initiation shrine at Eleusis are rectangular, and the theatres at Knossos and Phaistos on Crete, built before 1400 B.C., show a long sacred way leading to a square with steps for seats on two sides and a raised platform at the enclosed corner either for performers or special guests.

Even the image of a stately palace-temple front is in question. It has been suggested that the prototype of the skene is not a palace front but a raised shrine for a god and that the statue of Dionysus brought back in procession the night before the festival began was placed not at the center or far edge of the orchestra, as has been guessed, but high on the shrine that became the skene. We know that the Emperor Nero, five centuries later, had his own statue (as a divinity) put into the niche of Dionysus over the central doorway in the theatre at Palmyra; that was the traditional place for the god to be honored as presiding over a festival. In Euripides' *Hippolytus* (428 B.C.) the setting is not so clearly the front of a palace as a formal entrance supporting the niches for the statues of Artemis and Aphrodite, symbols of the psychological forces that dominate the play. At the end of *The Bacchae* (c. 405 B.C.) the character of Dionysus speaks from a high level, far above suffering mortals. It would have been impressive to see the actor playing Dionysus speak from the niche that held the statue of Dionysus, or just below him. Or perhaps this is what the lexicographer Pollux meant when he said that the *periaktoi* could be used to bring on a deity; perhaps the triangular piece of scenery revolved to substitute an actor for a statue.

It has usually been assumed that the theatre began with no setting at all and that between the time of the production of *Prometheus* and the production of *Agamemnon* a skene became customary. Certainly the scene of Prometheus bound to a mountain rock by chains could not have any indication of palace or temple. But if the skene was a niche for a god or hero rather than a realistic palace front, there may have been a skene of some kind from the beginning of the drama contests, perhaps with simple, changeable indication of rocks or caves or whatever each play required. In that case no major change of setting would be necessary.

THE PERFORMANCE MASKS AND COSTUMES

Like the actors of ancient Egypt and much of Asia throughout the ages, the Greek actor wore a mask and an elaborate costume, setting him apart from ordinary people. Nearly all Egyptian masks represent the heads of animals, though the body and costume were of human form. The Greek drama was much more humanistic, and when the gods came on stage they looked like human beings. Io in *Prometheus* wears a cow mask, but she is a debased human being temporarily turned into a beast.

The mask was more than a device to help three actors play many roles and a chorus of young men to represent old men, women, or animals. It could create an atmosphere of great and awful deeds, invoking thoughts of gods and the metaphysical. If it imposed severe artistic limitations, it offered great artistic advantages. Though it did not permit subtle play of facial expression, it could create a clearer, stronger, and less ambiguous expression of grief, sorrow, triumph, or cruelty than any human face, and project that expression far beyond the few rows of spectators that see facial expression.

127

None of the masks have survived, but painters and sculptors copied them, so that we know how many of them looked. They were carefully modeled of wood, linen, cork, and plaster and painted in full color, covered the entire head, and greatly increased the actor's size. Indeed, the *oncos*, the top extension that resembled an ancient ceremonial headdress, was sometimes as high again as the face. The mask indicated immediately whether the character was god, goddess, king, queen, prophet, messenger, old hag, nurse, shepherd, or slave. There was white hair for the decrepit; gray hair for age; black hair for the tyrant; fair hair and tanned smiling face for the young lover; flaxen hair, fierce countenance, and bushy eyebrows for the young hero; and faces to denote suffering and misery. The mouth had to be large enough for the actor to speak and sing without difficulty. A few masks, especially those of comic old men and slaves, show such large, fish-like lips that we wonder if some masks gave the voice a slight support like a megaphone.

Comic and tragic masks. *Illustration by Martha Sutherland.*

The tragic costume likewise increased the size of the actor and set him apart from ordinary men. The thick-soled *cothurnus*, or boot, added several inches to the height, more for the king than for his attendants. Padding increased the size of the arms and body. A traditional long-sleeved ceremonial robe, influenced by Oriental costume, entirely hid the performer. It had elaborate ornamental designs, painted, woven, or embroidered.

The costume, like the mask, marked the difference between king and shepherd or soldier. Teiresias and other prophets wore robes of net around their whole bodies. Dionysus had his long wand, or *thyrsus*, and a characteristic hunting dress, a saffron robe with a broad flowered band; Heracles, his club and lion's skin. The unhappy, especially fugitives, dressed in white or ash-gray. A woman in distress wore a black trailing dress and a gray or yellow wrap. Special colors and garments were worn by those on the way to a wedding or festival. Euripides defied traditions of dignity and beauty by putting his distressed characters, even if they were kings, in rags, establishing a new tradition that lasted many centuries.

THE CHORUS

The chorus makes Greek tragedy seem completely different from modern drama. As we know little about the singing or chanting or the mime-dance, we can only guess at the effect of the performance. The enormous orchestra circle was there for large dance movement, and the visual element was considered as important as the words.

Since we know that the dithyramb had fifty performers, we can assume that there were fifty in the early tragic chorus. Since there are twelve distinct verbal reactions to the catastrophe in *Agamemnon*, it has been supposed that early in his career Aeschylus cut the number in the chorus to twelve. It is known that Sophocles set the number at fifteen, and Aristotle tells that there were two formal entrance arrangements of the fifteen, in three rows of five or five rows of three. But we do not know whether the chorus kept to a geometrical formation for the rest of the performance. The variety and range in the words and lines of the text suggest great freedom for the poet-choreographer in planning the presentation of the odes. When the chorus is protagonist, it is active throughout the play. But in most plays the actor or two or more actors carry the action. During these *episodes* the chorus may remain silent or may speak as a character in short speeches and in the same standard meter the actors use for dialogue. Some editors assign such speeches to one or several members of the chorus, though the texts do not indicate whether one member or the whole chorus speaks. Then at regular intervals the chorus takes over the play to perform a *stasimon*, or standing ode, while the actor goes

129

offstage or remains silent. In most plays some formal odes are shared by the actor and the chorus, though translators do not always indicate the fact. Such a formal ode is called a *kommos*. Thus a Greek play between the formal *parados*, or entrance song, and the *exodos*, or recessional song of the chorus, has a rhythmic pattern of alternating episodes and odes. There were at least three fairly distinct verse forms—a form for spoken verse, a form for song, and the complex form of the odes. Some scholars think there were special verse forms for speeches that were danced by the actor. The odes were composed in a balancing of *strophe* and *antistrophe*, usually followed by an *epode*. The word *strophe* (turn) may indicate that the first group of lines was danced in a progression in one direction and that the next group, perhaps with the same melodic pattern, progressed in a different direction. Or one half the chorus may have taken the strophe and the other half the antistrophe and all together the epode. But these are guesses. The strophe was made up of lines in pairs, the second line in each couplet using the same rhythm and meter as the first, but probably not the same melody, as that might preclude a contrast or development in meaning. Certainly there was the greatest freedom in progression from one pair of lines to the next.

The flute player led the *parados*, playing on his Phrygian double pipe the melody the chorus sang. The large lyre, or *kithara*, accompanied them, marking the rhythm with a chord plucked between the words or phrases. Greeks knew nothing about harmony or counterpoint but kept all the voices and the pipe on the same melody, which seems to have been subordinate to the meaning and words.

The chorus had a definite character in the play. When it was not the protagonist, it was usually deeply involved in the main action. In Sophocles' *Oedipus* (429 B.C.) the chorus of Theban Elders is as concerned as Oedipus in searching out the murderer of Laius and ridding the city of plague and pollution. Sometimes the chorus makes a striking contrast with the protagonist. The Sea Nymphs who

Satyr dancers and musicians. *Illustration by Martha Sutherland.*

sympathize with Prometheus in *Prometheus Bound* advise submission, but when he defies Zeus they stand by him. Sophocles' Antigone seems isolated because she is surrounded by a chorus of hostile old men, but when at last they sympathize with her and condemn Creon, the effect is all the more striking. In relation to the action, the chorus might be protagonist, participant, intermediary, prosecutor, judge, or audience. In relation to the main characters, the chorus might react, comment, attempt to intercede, advise, sympathize, or oppose.

Although the modern reader can usually visualize the action in the dialogue of the episodes, he is likely to think that the odes mark relaxation of tension. But they are more often an intensification of emotion. In Sophocles' *Electra* (c. 413 B.C.), Electra and Clytemnestra threaten each other but control their smoldering hostility. The moment they are out of sight the chorus bursts into full-throated, full-bodied expression of the hatred and horror. Many choral odes have an action of their own, sometimes an action that is a key to the whole play. Until the coming of the movies, flight and pursuit had to be reported on stage or shown only at the beginning or end of the action. But the Greek chorus could show such action in dance. When Creon, finally convinced that Antigone must be saved, rushes out to rescue her, Sophocles gives in choral dance a symbolic run—a procession to bring Dionysus to the city, a quickening of hope and joy before the news of the catastrophe. After Oedipus has confronted Teiresias and the figurative pursuit of the murderer is under way, the chorus mimes a wild pursuit of a fugitive by the Furies and the son of Zeus.

The chorus could present an equivalent on stage of the violence that takes place out of sight. In Euripides' *Hippolytus*, Phaedra rushes inside the scene building to hang herself. For a moment the chorus is transfixed with horror, then all fifteen, as they sing in unison, mime the tying of the rope around the neck and the swing from the rafters. In *The Bacchae* (c. 405 B.C.), while Agave is with bare hands beheading her lion-son out of sight on the hillside, the chorus, in the name of vengeance and Dionysus, mimes the killing by the stroke of a blade on the neck.

Instead of such a direct parallel to the offstage catastrophe, the chorus in several plays enacts a similar example, historical or mythological, that casts a special tone or meaning on the dramatic situation. The main story of *Iphigenia in Tauris* (c. 414–412 B.C.) is the escape of a brother and sister from a tyrant, but as they are escaping the chorus mimes the combat in which Apollo killed a primitive monster, rescued his sister, Artemis, and established a new religious cult.

There are even specific individual acts and dialogue in some odes. The most vivid is the treatment of Iphigenia in the first ode of *Agamemnon*, where one member of the chorus for a moment becomes Iphigenia, is raised and placed on the altar, cries out to her father and is gagged, as another member becomes Agamemnon and speaks about her. The chorus turns away from the pain, probably covering Iphigenia during the simulated sacrifice, then moves on to the narration of past events and expression of forebodings, fears, and hopes.

131

There is every evidence that the Greek playwrights throughout the fifth century thought the chorus as valuable as the actor. Although Aristotle seems to think that Euripides wrote odes that were not closely related to the episodes, that is not true of any of the plays that have come down to us. In view of our acquaintance with the many forms of story-telling in the Orient—solo and choral, narrative, lyric, and dramatic—we see what good theatre a chorus can be. In modern expressionism and in epic theatre, not to mention musical comedy, we have seen choral groups used very flexibly, now commenting on the action, now taking part, now telling the narrative past, now acting in mass, now becoming separate individuals. Brecht showed that the effect is no less theatrical when a character demonstrates to the audience in narrative, stepping in and out of the past or in and out of various characters, than when he speaks lines of a single character. The Greek chorus did not just *tell* the audience about past events; it had a dozen ways of bringing past events vividly before the audience.

In reviving Greek plays the chorus is the most difficult problem. The style of Italian opera and classical ballet is much too elegant for Greek choral song and dance. Early in this century "aesthetic dancing" was tried for the choruses with delicate girls in soft nightgowns waving their arms, draping themselves on steps or leaning on columns, moving from one soft group pose to another. They created classic dignity, but they muted shock, cruelty, or rebellion. Choral speech can give a sense of group reaction and objective comment, but to combine it with movement of speed or intensity takes endless hours of rehearsal. Some directors put their best dancers at the center and their best speakers at the edge, where their movement can be minimal. But the effect is still not as intense as the pain and outrage of tragedy require. By using primitive rhythms, Darius Milhaud achieved a good primitive excitement in his musical setting for the *Oresteia*. In the 1930s a New York production of *Mamba's Daughters* using Negro spirituals and camp-meeting movements raised the scene of a suicide to a full intensity. Using his own variation of musical comedy and religious choir music, Kurt Weill created some powerful, rather Greek-like choruses in *Lost in the Stars* (1949), Maxwell Anderson's dramatization of Alan Paton's novel *Cry, the Beloved Country.* In 1969 Richard Schechner made his own version of *The Bacchae* in *Dionysus 69*, gaining from near-nudity at least a wild physical and sexual abandon. Most producers using a chorus would want at least drums, and many feel the need for much more music, though something outside the traditional Western musical idiom.

Aeschylus: A Vision of Human Destiny

The Athenians felt that they had a destiny different from that of the barbaric peoples around them, or from that of the Egyptians and Persians with their custom-bound tyrannies. It was their destiny to create a new type of man, an athlete with handsome body and supple mind, a scientist with understanding of the laws of nature, a musician using music to harmonize the complex forces of the soul and of society, a poet to pierce the deep ways of the mind, a philosopher to interpret man's place in the universe. With a great struggle they had broken free from their own tyrannies to create a democracy. Aeschylus wrote a series of plays to show them what their struggle meant, how from the depth of suffering and sin the soul could reach new spiritual understanding, how from superstitious rites and blind compulsions a new society of free minds could rise.

One of the great historians of the world, Aeschylus had a clearer interpretation of history than his younger contemporary, the great Herodotus, and by presenting history in dramatic form he had more impact on his age. As a theologian he reshaped religion, and his plays are among the great religious scriptures of the world. As a metaphysician and philosopher he had a profound influence. Aeschylus created for his day a metaphysics of democracy, a cosmology for guiding the individual in relation to history, religion, and society.

The achievement of Aeschylus is all the more remarkable because he had to create the medium through which to express his vision. Others, as we have seen, had already put the single actor and the tragic chorus together, and official contests had encouraged experiments in tragedy for almost half a century. But from a very simple choral drama Aeschylus created one of the major artistic traditions of the world. He raised the dialogue to dignity and the choral passages to grandeur. He perfected the painted masks and tragic costumes, giving them greater size and making them more expressive of each god or hero. He was the first great musician to compose for the theatre, adding drums and trumpets for his large processions and scenes of gods and warriors. He gave the chorus richer music and more complex and varied dance movement, changing the rhythm and meter of the verse to express the most subtle nuances of thought or feeling. Besides directing movement, dance, and music and designing costumes and properties, he acted, danced, and sang his leading parts. Above all, he was a great poet who used thunderous sound effects and rich diction and imagery to create great themes and characters.

133

He was the first to unite the poetic tradition of the epic with the new lyric drama. He considered his works slices from the banquet of Homer, but in religion and philosophy and depth of human understanding he was greater than Homer, and his poetic language was in no way inferior. His dynamic vision of social change brings him nearer to our day than Homer.

Portrait bust of Aeschylus. *Negative from the Photographic Archive, Capitolini Museum, Rome.*

THE EARLY PLAYS

The earlier plays of Aeschylus, written for one or two actors and chorus, are more like operas than like modern realistic plays, rising to song at all the high points: laments, invocations, exorcisms, challenges, combats, and pursuits. Yet Aeschylus knew how to make the actor dominate. *The Persians* (472 B.C.), the earliest Greek play extant, is unusual in that it deals not with an event of the historic past but with recent events: the defeat of the invading Persian army in 480 B.C. Aeschylus, who had been one of the heroes of the battle, dramatizes not only the Greek but the Persian point of view as the Persian people gradually learn, from heralds and then from the ghost of Darius, of the terrible defeat that one man's pride and ambition has brought on their nation. The Asiatic costumes would have kept the aesthetic distance created in other tragedies by costumes of the legendary past.

The formal lyric element is well illustrated in *The Seven Against Thebes* (467 B.C.). There is no combat on stage and not even dialogue in the modern sense. The central action, the *agon*, consists of a series of seven challenges and seven answers. Eteocles speaks for himself and the other six champions protecting the city. The invading brother does not appear; the second actor, in the character of spy or messenger, describes the challenges and recites the vaunts of the seven opponents. Yet Aeschylus is able to present the *pathos* or painful choice of the hero and to give the hero's crisis a sanction in the concern of the citizens. Eteocles chooses to protect the city, though he knows that, as the cursed sons of Oedipus, both he and his brother will be killed. After the offstage catastrophe the chorus expresses its pride that he has saved the city and laments his death.

The Suppliants (c. 490 B.C.), not an early play, as was once thought, was produced in the 460s, only a few years before *The Eumenides*, the last of the *Oresteia* trilogy, which also uses the chorus as protagonist. The daughters of Danaus, having fled from Egypt pursued by their cousins, seek refuge from violence in Greek Argos, the land of their ancestress Io, as a land of reason, law, and order. After consulting with his people, the King of Argos promises them refuge. The chorus sings a blessing on the land and dances to drive out evil and pestilence. We have already noticed the ode they sing to invoke a safe end of their own flight as they dance out the flight and rescue of Io. *The Suppliants* is the first play of a trilogy, and although the other plays are lost, we can surmise the action from the well-known story. Taken by force by the cousins, who represent unreasoning desire, the maidens are so outraged that all but one of them kill their captors in the night. That one maiden comes to an understanding with her captor. The third play showed the solemn establishment of marriage and celebrated the emergence of reason and consideration, law and order, from a barbaric age of force and desire.

THE *PROMETHEIA* AND THE *ORESTEIA*

Aeschylus carried even further his optimistic vision of wisdom achieved after violence in his two great tetralogies, the *Prometheia* and the *Oresteia*. We cannot date the *Prometheia*, indeed are not sure that Aeschylus wrote it, but we know that the *Oresteia* was produced in 458 B.C., just two years before he died. The *Prometheia* projected the vision of the emergence of order out of blind chaos into the realm of the gods and Titans near the dawn of the world, when Zeus, a young god, has deposed his father Kronos and, like an early Athenian tyrant, persecutes his enemies, ravishes maidens, and is prepared to leave humanity to perish. If such blind force is left unchecked it will wipe out mankind and eventually destroy itself. If Zeus must be overthrown by another upstart rebel and that one again overthrown, there is no end to violence. Like the Hindus, many early Greeks held the idea that existence is a wheel of will and desire turning without stop and that man's only salvation is to free himself from it. But Aeschylus believed that the very order of the universe could be changed, the chain of pain and violence broken, if will would contend for intelligence. Prometheus, or Forethought, one of the deposed Titans, must contend against the upstart Zeus, not only to save mankind but to save Zeus himself, when after a cycle of 30,000 years he shall have grown wiser.

For *Prometheus Bound*, Aeschylus chose the moment of greatest conflict, when Prometheus, chained to a rock on a peak in the Caucasus, cries defiance to Zeus and is shattered by a thunderbolt and buried in the rock. But before the final *agon* Prometheus has a series of visitors who by contrast strengthen his determination: a chorus of sea nymphs bringing him pity, the comic compromiser Oceanus, god of the changing waves, and the maid Io, a pathetic victim of Zeus's tyranny, transformed into a cow and pursued by a gadfly. In spite of appeals and threats, Prometheus defies Zeus to the end:

Then let the twisting flames of forked fire be hurled upon me. Let the very air be rent by thundercrash, savage winds convulse the sky, hurricanes shake the earth from its foundations, the waves of the sea rise up and drown the stars, and let me be swept down to hell, caught in the cruel whirlpool of Necessity. . . . It does not make me tremble!

We have only the speeches in the manuscript and do not know how the ending was staged. If the play was produced before a permanent scene house was built, perhaps the rock with Prometheus chained to it was pulled over the embankment at the end of the orchestra and disappeared from sight. More likely the chorus expressed their terror in wordless dance and suggested the violence of storm as they fled, while Prometheus sank between the rocks.

To the last Prometheus cried out against the injustice of the universe: "O Holy Mother Earth, O air and sun behold me. I am wronged." Here is the heroic mode of tragedy. The hero takes an independent stand, separates himself from the universe, faces his suffering, and, like Lear in the storm, cries "Oh! Oh! 'Tis foul!"

From the quotations and references that have survived we can reconstruct the final play of the *Prometheia*, *Prometheus Unbound*. In the thousands of years that have passed both Prometheus and Zeus have changed: Zeus is more wise and Prometheus is more humble. Zeus is about to send Heracles to help mankind clear the earth of the primeval monsters, and he orders him to shoot the eagle that has been endlessly tearing at the liver of Prometheus. Prometheus' mother, Goddess of Earth, and Athena, Goddess of Wisdom, finally reconcile Zeus and Prometheus and bring a new order of peace and wisdom to the world.

Of the other great tetralogy, the *Oresteia*, we have all three tragedies—the only trilogy that has come down to us—though the satyr play is lost. The *Oresteia* is the earthly counterpart of the *Prometheus*, tracing in human affairs the same emergence of wisdom, order, and harmony out of primitive violence. Against a background of conflict between the new gods and the old fates, in the aftermath of the Trojan War, is played a bloody story of royal murder, matricide, and tribal vengeance that has no end until Athena comes down to Athens to establish a new order of lawful society.

As a double murder story the Oresteia trilogy is strong, with vague forebodings, gradual build-up to climaxes, terror when a murder is being committed offstage, then a sense of relief and freedom that is ironic, since the next act of vengeance is always waiting. But the murders are only the most vivid strands in a complex web of images, musical patterns, ironic contrasts, forebodings, memories of past sins and terrors, and philosophical and religious reflections. The musical pattern of the entire trilogy, with ironic hope leading to a new crisis, is repeated many times in the smaller units. In the opening scene of *Agamemnon* the watchman on the roof turns from mournful prayer to dances and shouts of joy when he sees the signal that means that Troy has fallen, but the joy is quickly quenched when he thinks of the evil in the house. The same pattern of a joyful crescendo quenched in alarm and foreboding is used by the chorus. When they see the altar fires lighted by Clytemnestra they sing of the glorious beginning of the Trojan expedition, but as they reenact the father's sacrifice of his daughter Iphigenia, which they make into a kind of flashback with one member of the chorus as Iphigenia on the altar and one as Agamemnon, they are plunged into premonitions of calamity. The Herald's speech and most episodes and odes follow the same pattern of rising hope doomed to despair. There seems no escape, though many of the characters and the chorus repeatedly pray for relief and peace. But as with other trilogies of Aeschylus, the ending solves the private problem by a new political and religious order.

Aeschylus constantly enlarges his scope by wider reference and comparison, often with sharp irony. Clytemnestra's prayer that the Greeks may not violate the sacred shrines and altars of Troy comes just before the Herald brags that the

Greeks destroyed everything, and the chorus then sings the second stasimon about the god's punishment for the violation of sacred things. The prayers of the chorus that they be not a "sacker of cities" or a captive are ironic preparation for the arrival of Agamemnon bringing the captive Cassandra with him.

Agamemnon's entrance with great pomp must have seemed to the Greek audience an omen of disaster, for they believed that *hubris*, or pompous pride, was the greatest possible offense against the gods. But Aeschylus gives a deeper meaning to the fate of Agamemnon. He has his chorus sing of Helen's violation of the sacred marriage bond and the desolation she brought to Troy. This is a vivid preparation for the actions of Clytemnestra, Helen's sister, already guilty of violating the marriage bond and plotting destruction for Agamemnon. The chorus, using Helen as an example, disagrees with the old doctrine that prosperity brings misery and insists that not prosperity but sin causes ill in the world. Just before the entrance of Agamemnon, the man who inherits a family curse and, according to tribal laws, passes on to his son a duty of vengeance, the chorus announces a new concept of inheritance and fate; the spirit of deep night that broods in the house is the sin that breeds sin, but the chorus looks forward to a justice that finds a dwelling for the pure in heart—a prophecy fulfilled in the last play, *The Eumenides*.

The magnificent *kommos* of Cassandra—the ecstatic death song she dances with the chorus—is so filled with images of past vengeance and of the violence about to occur that, like the choral odes, it reinforces the theme of present vengeance

Modern interpretation of Clytemnestra welcoming Agamemnon home. *Illustration by Martha Sutherland.*

138

and yet calls for an end to such vengeance. Prophetess that she is, Cassandra can see only the long chain of sins behind and the bloody death that stares her in the face. But after she has entered the house and just before her piercing scream following the murder, the chorus chants the central question of the trilogy. If such a man as Agamemnon, honored by the gods, must be struck down to pay for the past, if bloody deed endlessly demands bloody deed in payment, then what meaning is there in any man's life?

The verbal and visual imagery often clarifies an issue. Clytemnestra is compared to a lioness, couching with the wolf to slay the lion. In the second play she is a snake that has strangled an eagle and left its nestlings to starve. Orestes is a flying fawn pursued by hell-hounds. The net is such an important figure that it serves as a unifying image for the whole trilogy. Clytemnestra throws a net to trap Agamemnon in his bath; Zeus throws a net over Troy; the chorus is caught in a net of fate; the Eumenides weave a net of blind rights from which Orestes must escape. The red robe Agamemnon walks on at his first entrance appears again over his body at the end of the first play; then at the end of the next play over Clytemnestra's body, and at the end of the trilogy in the happy procession welcoming the Eumenides to their new home.

Much of the ironic imagery is related to the ritual aspects of the trilogy. The killing of Agamemnon is described as a sacrifice. Cassandra sees herself as a sacrificial victim. Clytemnestra, standing over the dead bodies, describes the sacrificial blow as a drink-offering to Hades, deliverer of the dead. She uses age-old images of spring and renewed fertility—the spurt of blood, the drops of deathly dew that made her feel like a cornfield rejoicing at the flow of heavenly moisture. The title of the second play, *The Libation Bearers*, suggests not only the pouring of libations at the beginning but the pouring of Clytemnestra's blood at the end. An invocation at the tomb of Agamemnon brings his spirit to life, and the two children sacrifice their mother as a duty to his tomb. Clytemnestra's ghost chants an invocation to waken the sleeping Furies, who chant and dance magic incantations, calling on the old powers of darkness and night. In the third play, *The Eumenides*, Apollo, the god of light, brings in images of light, hope, and understanding; a new kind of legal ritual, trial by jury, is established, and Athena, with praise for Persuasion, a new kind of magic, transforms the Furies into benevolent deities. An age-old ritual, the procession, concludes the trilogy, joyfully bringing into the city the Furies, transformed into blessed beings.

The Eumenides shows Orestes fleeing from his deed, pursued by the Furies. The first conflict is between the Furies, who represent blind Necessity, which is older than Zeus, and Apollo, the representative of Zeus. On the social and historical level the Furies represent the primitive tribal order in which descent was usually traced through the mother. They denounce the "younger gods" who would interfere with their duty to avenge the death of Orestes' mother. But Apollo, who represents the sixth-century aristocratic social order, based on paternity, defies them.

He argues that as the son does not inherit from the mother but only from the father, Orestes had the greater duty to avenge his father.

It remains for Athena, the greatest of Zeus' children, to bring a solution by establishing a new order—trial by jury. The exemplar of moderation and restraint, goddess of public speaking and persuasion, the very soul of the new democratic life of Athens, Athena is able to persuade the Furies to act as benevolent guardians of the new Athens. The Greeks did not believe that dark, irrational forces could be driven out or ignored; they believed that art and persuasion could transform them. The idea of a court to settle disputes is one of the fundamental ideas of civilization. It is the foundation of law and order, demanding a public hearing, advice of experts in considering the application of general laws, and judgment by one's peers. It is basic to Freudian psychology, bringing out the hidden impulses to objective view. It is basic to science, which, like all civilization, is advanced as individual insights are brought into open inquiry to be tried, checked, and improved.

Southern Italian crater vase depicting the first scene from Aeschylus' *Eumenides. Courtesy of the Trustees of the British Museum.*

Sophocles: Humanist of the Golden Age

For half a century, between the glorious Persian Wars and the disastrous war with Sparta, Athenian civilization blossomed. As the military defender of all the Greeks, the city gathered tribute from a confederation of city states and spent much of it in public works, enlarging and beautifying the city. New jobs and cultural fame attracted artists, craftsmen, and merchants. The problems of tribe and class and public institutions had been solved; the problems of relation to the wider world had not become acute. For a golden moment man had a chance to emerge as an individual. Would he face the responsibility and pay the tragic price often exacted for being an individual?

The Golden Age of Greece was best expressed not in the accomplishments of its leader Pericles, who rebuilt Athens in marble and fostered a democracy so wonderful that the Athenians wanted to expand it into an empire, or in the statues of Phidias that adorned the splendid new temples and public buildings, but in the person and plays of Sophocles. Sophocles the happy, the serene, the golden, seemed to his own age and to posterity the perfect expression of Athenian civilization.

It was his good fortune to be a boy at the most heroic moments of Grecian history when the Persians were twice driven back. He was one of the boys chosen as most talented in music and dance to celebrate the final victory over the Persians. As a young man he saw Athens rebuilt and its institutions flourish. He was handsome, rich, talented, a painter, musician, actor, director, playwright, poet, military general, priest, government official, friend of poets and princes, and darling of the populace. With age his great talents remained undimmed, and at nearly ninety he wrote one of his finest plays. Happy even in his death, he died just before his beloved Athens was defeated by Sparta and the Golden Age was brought to an end.

Sophocles is the epitome of classic Greece because of the depth and maturity of his insight, which was based on a tragic view of life. Tragedy faces the weakness, evil, and defeat in the world, as well as the splendor, heroism, and grandeur of mankind; it faces also the helplessness of man before fate, his dependence on the gods, and yet his responsibility for his own choice. Sophocles' plays most fully express the classic age because, as Matthew Arnold put it, he "saw life steadily and saw it whole."

141

Portrait head of Sophocles. *Courtesy Alinari/Art Resource, N.Y.*

Where Aeschylus showed the extended development of history in a trilogy or tetralogy, Sophocles took as his unit the single play. Although he could write magnificently for the chorus and give his actors music for their high points, he was the first man to develop fully the dramatic tension of scenes in dialogue. We think of Sophocles when we think of humanism, of the phrase "Man is the measure." With him, theology, philosophy, poetry, music, and drama are the means of understanding the responsibilities and values of being human.

His most heroic character is Antigone. When she marches to her burial cave, she is terrified, but she knows that as a human being she must choose and choose love rather than hate.

Sophocles' Electra is a human being—not like Aeschylus' Electra, the impersonal instrument of religious vengeance, the priestess who brings Orestes back by her invocation at her father's tomb. Sophocles shows the deeper psychological forces working through the personality. He includes prayers and libations, but he leaves the tomb of Agamemnon offstage. It is Electra's personal view of duty to her murdered father that matters. She feels completely alone, and her choice is an individual one, though based on her character as a human being.

I have no choice: what alternative for one who sees the evil? And I see it, night and day I see it, not diminishing, growing. My own mother hates me, I live with my father's killers and obey them; from them I receive the means of life, or perish. And that life: do you suppose it is sweet to me to have to see Aegisthus in my father's seat, wearing my father's clothes, pouring libations at the hearth where he brought my father down? When I see the final insolence accomplished: in my mother's bed (if I must call her mother) my father's killer?

Clytemnestra, the mother, is just as womanly. She is sick of her memories, weary of contending with Electra, unable to hate her son but terrified of his return. Here are individuals recognizable today as they were twenty-five hundred years ago.

Sophocles begins *Philoctetes* (409 B.C.) with the hero abandoned on a desert isle, suffering from a repulsive, incurable wound, bitterly accepting his separation from mankind. He realizes the treachery of those who ask for his help in the Trojan War, and the futility of that war. Yet at the end, with the approval of his patron god, he casts his lot with his fellow men. Recognizing fully the depravity man is capable of, Sophocles was still committed to mankind.

Beyond all other qualities, it is the philosophical and religious meaning of his major figures that places Sophocles in the first rank of dramatic, literary, and religious writers. *Antigone* and *Oedipus Rex* are two of the world's great scriptures.

ANTIGONE

Antigone is the great example of conscious choice. She knows herself, the alternatives, the choice that is necessary if she is to fulfill her being. She knows that she must put the laws of the gods above the laws of man and that there are realms where Creon's hatred for the dead brother no longer has meaning. "It is my nature to join in love, not hate," she sings.

In the first part of the play Creon is only the antagonist, but before the end he too becomes a tragic figure. He is stern, self-righteous, outraged that a member of his family should disobey his public proclamation, accusing others of his own faults—pride, stubbornness, and family disloyalty. When both his citizens and Teiresias tell him he is wrong, he relents and tries to undo his action. But he is too late. Antigone and his son are dead, and his wife kills herself. At last he becomes human. Out of suffering comes wisdom.

The choral passages present a series of symbolic actions that indirectly, and often ironically, build the religious sanction for Antigone's case, even when they seem to support Creon. After Antigone announces her determination to violate Creon's order, the chorus enters with a victory march to prepare for Creon's royal entry. The victory march functions on two symbolic levels. The chorus reenacts the recent attack on the city that led to the death of Antigone's two brothers, thus celebrating the victory of civic law and order. But on the level of divine order the chorus sings of the part Zeus takes in the battle. Hating the sound of bragging tongues, he smites the man who has climbed the walls to shout his triumph. Although this choral ode seems to reinforce Creon, the symbolic implication prepares us for a similar smiting of Creon. The words would indicate that the audience saw the action of smiting in the movements of the chorus.

In the last stasimon the chorus of old men reenacts a procession to bring Dionysus into the city from afar, giving the audience the visual and emotional equivalent of Creon's run to the cave in which Antigone has been sealed, and at the same time providing the quickening of hope and joy needed before the revelation of the catastrophe.

OEDIPUS REX

Where Antigone is fully conscious of what she is doing and why, Oedipus is the great example of unconscious tragic figure. He only gradually learns what he has done and who he is. More than in any other play the suffering raises the question of why—and each generation, each person, finds a special answer.

To the Romantic critics of the nineteenth century, *Oedipus* seemed a tragedy of fate, for they wanted to blame man's sorrows entirely on the gods. To the scientific naturalists of the late nineteenth century, who thought the universe cruel, relentless, and inscrutable, Oedipus seemed another example of a man caught by environment and heredity. On the other hand, those who subscribe to a simple, clear-cut morality find in Aristotle's concept of the tragic flaw a way to make Oedipus guilty of pride and rage. The chorus clearly thinks him impious in his attempts to disregard the oracle. But the accusation of impiety merely makes the gods appear impersonal and cruel in allowing such predictions to determine man's fate. Taking a Marxian view of the weakness of all democracies, the critic George Thomson finds in the ironies of the play a sense of the inherent contradictions of Athenian life, as the democracy, whose hopes were celebrated in Aeschylus' *Eumenides*, had been corrupted by plutocracy, expansion of the empire, and conflict with Sparta.

But the play appeals to the twentieth century not as a picture of man against a cold fate or as an echo of political contradictions, but primarily as a psychological myth of a man searching for his own identity and then facing responsibility for his own acts. Oedipus, relentlessly probing the past until self-knowledge destroys him, becomes a modern hero.

On the surface, *Oedipus* is a brilliantly organized "who-dun-it" about a detective interrogating a series of witnesses to locate the murderer. The audience knows the detective himself is the murderer. The play moves rapidly through a series of episodes, each with its own conflict, reversal, and surprise. All lead by ironic contrast to the great climax when Oedipus sees who he is and rushes out to blind himself. The imagery of eyes, blindness, and insight is woven into both action and words. Blind Teiresias sees the whole situation while Oedipus, who was able to answer the riddle of the Sphinx, cannot see himself and gains insight only when blinded.

Oedipus did not even know his father and hence did not have an "Oedipus complex." The term was derived not from the play but from the general story of a man who killed his father and married his mother. But Sophocles, in the structure of the play and especially in Jocasta's attempt to escape, anticipates the basic pattern of a psychoanalysis. Like a typical patient, Oedipus meets a new crisis, his old abilities fail, there is a blight and barrenness that indicate a hidden guilt long glossed over. He goes to an impersonal wise man for advice, and Teiresias makes a full diagnosis. But Oedipus' reaction is anger; he is not ready to face himself. Next he projects his own guilt on others, accusing the prophet and then his brother-in-law of plotting his death. Jocasta, attempting to relieve his intolerable fear by proving that oracles are worthless and the world meaningless, presents the pleasure principle, discrediting the super-ego. For a short time Oedipus is free from fear, rejoicing at news of the death of his foster-father, relieved of an ambiguous emotional tie. When he finally sees the truth, he turns his aggression on himself. When the destructive fit is over he takes full responsibility for what he has done.

He apologizes to Creon and takes a new course, with a sense of harmony with himself and with the gods. He has found his identity.

When Oedipus comes on stage after blinding himself, he not only expresses anguish and speaks a pitiful farewell to his two small daughters, but reexamines his deeds and responsibilities. At first he curses the day he was born and the predictions before his birth that had seemed to control his fate. But when the chorus blames Apollo, the god behind the oracle, he says, "Apollo spoke the word, but mine was the hand that did the deed." At no point did the gods force men. It was Laius who sent the child to the mountain, a shepherd who brought him down. It was Oedipus himself who left his foster parents, who killed the man where three roads cross, who married the queen. It is the man Oedipus who then starts a new life, who finds his identity.

A Roman terra-cotta relief depicting a scene from a tragic play. *Courtesy Alinari/Art Resource, N.Y.*

Again, it is the chorus that brings into view the subconscious forces underlying the action. In the parados, the chorus rushes on stage with anxiety, dancing out the suspense about the words of the oracle. It invokes Athena, Artemis, and Apollo, three gods who can avert fate, and laments the plague on the city. Then it calls on Zeus to drive Ares, the god of destruction, back into the sea. The words suggest that it performs vigorous actions of driving out demons. At the same time the exorcism is a symbol of the efforts of Oedipus to drive pollution from the city. The symbolic combat in the chorus prepares for the dramatic combat between Teiresias, the man of god, and Oedipus.

When Oedipus is tracking down the murderer of Laius and searching for his own identity, the chorus mimes a wild pursuit of a fugitive by the Furies and the son of Zeus. It suspends judgment and reaffirms loyalty to Oedipus, yet the actions have created terror that belies the words.

In the next stasimon, the chorus counteracts the implications of the preceding episode. Jocasta has bragged that the oracle had been circumvented. Reaffirming not so much the specific oracle as respect for all sacred things, the chorus mimes the fate of the arrogant tyrant who, reckless of the gods, climbs to the top and is cast headlong down.

The ode at the catastrophe, when Oedipus rushes out to blind himself, repeats in musical terms the basic *peripeteia*, or reversal, of the play. It celebrates the glory, importance, and honor of Oedipus, then carries the audience to his fall and marks the conclusion that at last the fugitive has been caught.

THE LAST PLAY

At ninety Sophocles died, leaving a strange and wonderful play, *Oedipus at Colonus*, as his farewell to earth and as a benediction on Athens. In the grove sacred to the Eumenides, it is not history and the gods that bring a blessing on Athens as in Aeschylus' *Eumenides*, but an exiled old man about to die who has finally made his peace with life—the Oedipus whose ruin Sophocles had dramatized many years before. Attended by his loving daughters, the old man washes his hands of the selfish demands of his brother-in-law, casts off with a curse his war-ready son, and finds sanctuary and peace in the justice and mercy of Athens. In Theseus, mythical founder of Athens, he finds at last a father he does not want to kill. In the sacred grove, not in his own family, he finds that he can penetrate the tribal taboos and find communion with the maternal wisdom of the race. The chorus of weak old men chants the famous ode on the evils of man's life, like a rock in the wild north sea fronting the rude assault of the billows of adversity, and on unfriended old age, worst ill of all; hence "the greatest boon is not to be; but, life begun, soonest to end is best." But Oedipus, free of his pollution and submissive

147

to the will of the gods, is at last a blessing to Athens, happy in his mystic acceptance of death.

Making his final comment on life, Sophocles shows that Oedipus finds peace in submission and humility, but the dramatist does not forget the horrible end waiting for the war-ready son, the terrible price the daughter is to pay for choosing the good, or the blind loneliness of the wandering old man.

Alexis Minotis as the blind Oedipus in Sophocles' *Oedipus at Colonus*, at Epidarus, summer 1959.

Euripides: Poet of the Agony of Athens

In less than a century the Golden Age of Athens was over, dissipated in the long-drawn-out Peloponnesian War. When Athens had been burned in the Persian War, the victorious Athenians had rebuilt the city with a new vision. But by the end of the fifth century, defeat in the war with Sparta was only a climax to inner collapse. Trade, technology, and widening communication made all the Greek cities more interdependent. The Athenians had turned the confederation formed to fight Persia into a permanent league, but the "allies," given no share in Athenian democracy, revolted repeatedly. Pericles realized before he died that the empire he had worked to create was no longer a league led by Athens but a despotism. But Sparta had already organized a rival league and Athens could not return to a simple democracy without risking subjection or annihilation.

Cleon, who followed Pericles, publicly proclaimed, "A democracy cannot govern an empire." The war dragged on; the war party tried to extend its despotism even to Sicily but suffered disastrous defeat, and Sparta won a final victory. In a burst of self-accusation, the Athenians destroyed Socrates as a scapegoat. But the victorious Spartans failed just as dismally to create a nation. Finally the Macedonians under Alexander easily took the divided Greek cities, borrowed their technology, and united the eastern world in a commercial empire. For more than two thousand years, under Alexander, under Romans, and then Turks, Athens remained a small town in the empires of other peoples.

Not only war but other disruptive influences weakened fifth-century Athens. With the increasing specialization of a growing city and the influence of immigrants and visitors from afar, Athenian life became varied and individualistic. Scientists and philosophers questioned the old ways of thinking. During the war, farmers and villagers had to take refuge within the city walls and watch their homes destroyed. The plague broke out, and bodies piled up faster than they could be burned. The survivors turned to pillaging or riotous living. Athenian generosity and nobility of character broke down. Faltering allies were massacred as readily as the enemy. This was indeed the agony of Athens.

Three of the world's greatest writers—a philosophical historian, a smart young comedian, and an old, unpopular tragic poet—reacted in very different ways to the agony; and the aging Sophocles added a fourth voice. Thucydides was cashiered out of the army early in the war with Sparta and sat quietly in another city writing objectively as he watched the Athenians bring on their own defeat. Young Aristophanes lashed out with violent satire, calling on the Athenians to throw out the dictator, the rich generals, and the war party, make common cause with the

Portrait bust of Euripides.

enemy, and reestablish peace. He wanted to tear down Socrates' house and tie Euripides to the stake. But the tragic poet Euripides gave a deeper, more symbolic expression to the agony of Athens than either of these men.

THE YOUNG ICONOCLAST

From the beginning Euripides had shocked his contemporaries by his new ideas, attitudes, and techniques. In showing up the foolishness and cruelty of some traditional beliefs and the provincial narrowness of the Greeks, he seemed to be attacking the very gods.

Euripides had begun to write by 455 B.C. but did not win his first victory in the festival contests until 441. Of the four plays he produced in 438 B.C., three concerned non-Greeks and all made artistic innovations. In *The Cretan Woman*, now lost, a Greek sailor brings to Athens a Cretan princess condemned to death in her own country because she loved a common soldier. Euripides wrote love songs for the girl that were quoted as shocking long after he was dead. He defended the right of an individual to choose and celebrated Athens as a refuge for the persecuted of all countries. The next play, *Telephus*, also lost, was famous for its presentation of a king in rags—the first of Euripides' many realistic innovations.

Only the last of these four plays of 438 is extant. Instead of the usual kind of satyr play, Euripides wrote in *Alcestis* a charming romance with the dignity of tragedy and the drunken revelry of a satyr play. It begins with a quarrel between Apollo and Death, prefiguring the greater combat with Death that is to come. The funeral of Alcestis, the noble wife who gives her life that her husband may live, is interrupted by the arrival of one of the favorite revelers of satyr plays, the drunkard Heracles. When Heracles discovers the real situation and goes off to grapple with Death for the soul of Alcestis, Euripides shifts to the human plane and writes a scene of psychological struggle. In accusing his father of selfishness in letting Alcestis die instead of dying for her, Admetus, the husband, really indicts himself. The father's bitterness makes an ironic counterpoint to the raging of the son. Only when Admetus is completely humbled, realizing that he has lost all honor, is his redemption possible. The wife is returned to her reborn husband. But she is veiled, and Admetus is forced to disregard his promises to his dying wife and obey the gods' order to take this lady into his house. The play ends happily with his discovery that she is Alcestis.

Euripides' most famous play, *Medea* (431 B.C.), is again concerned with the shortcomings of a husband. Jason is trying to discard a wife who will not quietly accept ingratitude and injustice. Medea rejoices to hear every detail of the death she has cunningly planned for her husband's new bride and the bride's father, who are caught in the searing flames of a magic dress and a wreath of gold. Then, in torture and self-loathing, she rushes off to stab her children. In the year the war with Sparta began Euripides dared to show that this dark sorceress from the land of Colchis was not so contemptible as the Greek husband who had accepted her love as long as he could gain by it, then tossed her aside. The play ends with Medea flying away in a chariot drawn by dragons, a triumphant superhuman force, no longer an earthly individual.

In *Hippolytus* (428 B.C.), Euripides wrote an almost Sophoclean play based on the Greek idea of balance. As the play opens Aphrodite and Artemis make clear Hippolytus' dangerous unbalance in his single devotion to athletics, and Love determines to get revenge. Phaedra, the tormented heroine, is so shamed by her guilty passion for her stepson Hippolytus and so outraged by his rejection that in her suicide she makes it appear that he had made the guilty advances, and her husband brings about the death of his son. The father, understanding neither the austerity of his son nor the shameful passion of his young wife, suffers most. Euripides seems to ask, Will mankind be destroyed by the irreconcilable forces of the universe? Is there no solace but the dignity of choice, the splendor of suffering, and divine compassion for pain?

THE WAR PLAYS

When the war with Sparta began, Euripides expressed his compassion symbolically through plays about ancient heroes: King Theseus, the traditional founder of Athens, and Heracles, the sacred ancestor of the Spartans. In *The Suppliant Women* (421 B.C.), Theseus goes to the battlefields and takes the dead bodies in his arms and washes them. In *Heracles* (c. 422 B.C.) Theseus reaches out to embrace his friend, the polluted Heracles, who, made blind and mad by the gods, has killed his own children. Theseus persuades him not to commit suicide but to come to Athens and continue his tasks as a friend of the oppressed. In *The Children of Heracles* (c. 425–422 B.C.), the Athenians give sanctuary to the refugee children, capture the tyrant who threatens them, then offer to free him. But Heracles' mother kills him, saving the Athenians from guilt for his blood.

A more complex wish-dream was dramatized in *Andromache* (c. 426 B.C.). Old grandfather Peleus is able to rescue the Trojan princess Andromache from her jealous Spartan captor, who then suffers an agony of remorse and shame for threatening her. But there is no shame at Delphi. The priests there were openly supporting Sparta in the current war, and Euripides has Peleus' son impiously slain at the Delphian temple. The goddess Thetis, once the wife of Peleus, bids him bury his dead and join her in a land of no death or sorrow.

But the idealism and patriotism of Euripides gave way in several plays to bitterness, irony, and fury. As the war party at home became more tyrannical, Eu-

Fourth-century vase painting illustrating various aspects of Euripides' *Medea. Courtesy Staatliche Antikensammlungen und Glyptothek, München.*

153

ripides saw his two great teachers, Anaxagoras and Protagoras, so persecuted that they fled for their lives. The younger liberal thinker Socrates, who so admired Euripides that some accused him of helping write the plays, was attacked repeatedly by Aristophanes and others, and was finally put to death in the agony of recrimination that followed the defeat by Sparta.

Hecuba is an expression of retaliation. Again the characters are Trojan heroes, who, as former enemies of Greece, could be viewed more objectively than the heroes nearer home. The action takes place on the Thracian seacoast opposite Troy as Agamemnon and the Greeks, on their way home, stop to sacrifice Hecuba's daughter Polyxena to Achilles; but the play opens with a speech by the ghost of Hecuba's murdered son—a prologue device that was to have a long life after the Roman dramatist Seneca handed it on to the Elizabethans. In the first episode Polyxena goes to her death, a willing victim of war, and Queen Hecuba masters her sorrow in dignity. But when she receives the body of her son, also, and learns that he has been murdered for gold, she lures the treacherous king into her tent, where she and her women blind him and kill his children. When Agamemnon rules that he was justly punished, the traitor turns on the judge and tells him the terrible future awaiting him.

In *Ion* (417 B.C.), mother and son, not knowing that they are related, try to kill each other. When they find out who they are, they turn against the god Apollo, who had seduced the mother and by lying had caused confusion and anguish. Here is more than an attack on the Delphic oracle of Apollo. In choosing as central character an unhappy temple foundling who does not want to go to Athens with his strife-torn parents, Euripides turns against Athens itself, no longer a place of order and harmony.

In his *Electra*, Euripides is more interested in human relationships and feelings than Aeschylus and Sophocles were in their versions of the story. Electra is a degraded girl in dirty rags. Her peasant husband welcomes the unknown Orestes, and Agamemnon's old servant helps her recognize him. Euripides brings Clytemnestra on stage so that the deed the children are planning may seem more monstrous. When Orestes falters, Electra drives him on to the murder. But these children are not the abstractions of Aeschylus. Once the murder is done they see themselves with loathing. Orestes remembers his mother's pitiful appeal as he killed her. The voice of heaven speaks in the twin gods, half-brothers of Clytemnestra and Helen, who declare the crime wrong but express pity for two suffering mortals, separating to go their lonely, remorseful ways. When Eugene O'Neill came to write his version of *Electra* in *Mourning Becomes Electra* (1931), his model was Euripides' play, with a neurotic girl, hatred between daughter and mother, self-loathing, and grim acceptance of punishment.

Five years after his production of *Electra*, just before he left Athens never to return, Euripides wrote a play called *Orestes*, a dream fantasy of guilt and hatred. The mad Orestes and Electra are surrounded, expecting the populace to stone them to death. Partly for a sadistic vengeance on Helen, the Spartan woman who started the Trojan War, partly to force Menelaus to help them, they kill Helen and lure her daughter to the roof, where Orestes holds a knife to her throat, and they threaten to burn the house down to prevent the Spartans from getting it. But suddenly Apollo arrives above as a *deus ex machina* and commands peace. Helen has been rescued and will take her place in the skies, Electra will marry their one faithful friend, and Orestes will receive purgation in Athens. Perhaps Euripides used an absurd happy ending because he now felt too deeply for either dignified resignation or tears.

Once in the course of the war with Sparta Euripides rose above ironic bitterness. *Trojan Women* (415 B.C.) is one of the great dramas of the world and the most compelling condemnation of war in all literature. The play came at a critical moment in the war—just after the reduction of the population of Melos and just before the Sicilian expedition, two of the most unwarranted actions of the Athenian war party. Early in the war, when an island, an unwilling member of the empire, had revolted, the Athenians were so furious they voted to have the men put to death and the women and children made slaves, and sent a ship to deliver the order to their general; but shortly afterward they rescinded the order. By 416 B.C., however, the Athenians had lost all scruples. When the little island of Melos, of no military importance and inhabited by only a few hundred poor farmers, wanted to remain neutral, Athens put to death the grown men and made slaves of the women and children and sent five hundred colonists to repopulate the island as their own. Thucydides wrote twenty-six chapters of his history describing this incident as the prime example of the way the Athenians were heading for their own great catastrophe.

The next spring Euripides produced his *Trojan Women*, retelling the story of the most glorious military exploit of Greek history, the conquest of Troy, from the human side. The movement of the play is a slow march of desolation—the departure of the women from the burning city of Troy. There is no counter action, opposition, suspense, or reversal. Yet through changes of mood the play has great contrast and variety. As Poseidon, god of the sea, takes farewell of his beloved Troy, Athena asks him to bring destruction to the Greeks on their voyage home. She has broken with her favorites because in pride and arrogance they have lost all reverence for the gods. Cassandra, who has found that she is destined for the bed of Agamemnon and sees the bloody fate that awaits them both, dances on stage with a torch, singing in bitter irony a glad hymeneal. The chorus completes this ironic climax with a processional ode expressing joyful acceptance of the Grecian trick of having the horse brought within the Trojan walls. But the joy is cut short by a vivid description of the Greeks' ruthless slaughter of the Trojans. Andromache, Hector's wife, shows a dignified grief, but she is broken when the Greeks take her child away to throw him from the walls. The chorus casts the splendor of poetry over the suffering by a song about another child of Troy,

Ganymede, stolen away to be a cup-bearer to the king of heaven. To Hecuba is brought on Hector's shield the broken body of her grandchild. Here is Homer's glamorous story reduced to human size. As the play ended, the Athenian audience could look toward the sea where their ships were ready to sail for Sicily—never to come home again.

TWO ENIGMATIC PLAYS

Near the end of his life, Euripides, in exile in Macedonia, wrote two magnificent but puzzling plays. The hater of war wrote what seems an acceptance of war as noble and glorious, and the man who had attacked religious doctrines wrote a religious drama showing the triumph of a god and his devotees over a cold rationalist. Yet both plays are so complex and ironical that some think they are only more subtle attacks on patriotism, military glory, and religious fanaticism.

In *Iphigenia in Aulis*, first Agamemnon, then Menelaus, tries to prevent the sacrifice of Iphigenia. When Clytemnestra arrives expecting a wedding, she denounces Agamemnon. When Achilles in his turn tries to stop the sacrifice he is almost killed by his own soldiers. The machine of war cannot be stopped. Iphigenia herself finally chooses death, for the glory of saving Greece. The ode of praise is interrupted by a messenger telling that Iphigenia was spirited away by a goddess who left a hind in her place. Agamemnon tries to cheer his skeptical wife and is off to the war amidst the shouts of the chorus telling him to bring back booty from captured Troy. Is the play really an acceptance of war as painful but glorious? Is it an ironical exposure of Agamemnon, who may have fabricated the story of the hind to placate his wife? The play was said to have been left unfinished and produced by Euripides' son. Perhaps the substitution of the hind was not Euripides' idea.

More baffling is Euripides' last play, *The Bacchae* (408 B.C.), a study of religious ecstasy. Through most of the play Dionysus is a splendid leader, inspiring the chorus, in the most beautiful poetry Euripides ever wrote, to celebrate all the joys of mankind. Pentheus, who opposes Dionysus, is first shown as a stiff-necked, unreasonable puritan and later as a hypocritical fool, dressing up as a woman in order to spy on the revels he pretends to condemn. Then comes the murder of Pentheus, left offstage of course but brought before the audience in the mime-dance of the chorus, joyfully smiting its imaginary victim. The messenger tells how the women, led by Agave, Pentheus' mother, tore Pentheus apart, thinking him a lion. The chorus brings on the still-intoxicated mother, proudly holding high the head. Gradually the chorus and her old father make her look at the bloody head in her hands and realize that she has killed her own son. Now Dionysus enters at the top of the skene and orders Agave and her father to wander over the face of the earth. When asked if a god should behave as the worst of men, he answers that Zeus willed it long ago. This is a disturbing and contradictory play, thrilling in its poetry, song, and dance, overwhelming in its violence, but leaving the audience with a feeling of compassion.

Euripides became extremely popular after his death, when general taste caught up with his strange melodies, poetic idiom, and sensational stage effects. His compassion for anger, bafflement, and pain was even more needed under the military domination of Athens by Sparta, then by Alexander, and then by Rome. His psychological analyses and lyric splendor stood out more clearly with repeated performance. Three legends, collected by Plutarch, were completely credible to the ancients. According to one, the Athenian soldiers taken prisoner after the di-

Campanion vase painting depicting Orestes and Phylades meeting Iphigenia in *Iphigenia in Tauris*. Courtesy *Musée du Louvre*.

sastrous expedition to Syracuse owed their lives to the fact that they could recite passages from Euripides. Another legend was that a Greek vessel pursued by pirates was at first refused haven in a Sicilian port, then welcomed when it was learned that some on board could recite passages from his plays. The third told that after Athens was defeated the Spartan generals gathered in council to consider destroying the city and making slaves of the inhabitants. But at their banquet a Phocian entertainer sang the first chorus of *Electra,* and the generals realized that it was unthinkable to destroy a city that had produced such a great man.

Marble relief of Euripides seated as a representative of tragedy conversing with a personification of the stage.

Aristophanes: "Old Comedy"

Aristophanes was too young to have known the heroic, democratic Athens of Aeschylus' day, but he knew that the greedy profiteers and ranting demogogues of wartime Athens had destroyed the ideal. He created a type of comedy that is at once the most vigorous satire and the most robust fun. To indignation at the corruption of his age and a high-minded call to return to the virtue of earlier days, he added grotesque exaggeration and a biting irony that set his characters in a fantasy world of broad laughter. No other comic writer has shown so wide a range—from delicate song to the strongest invective, from philosophical and political discussions to the wildest horseplay, from combats of wit to spectacular choral dances, from profound prayer to unrestrained obscenity, from gods to citizens, monsters, and animals. Though this comedy was planned for one particular audience at one particular moment, with a little knowledge and imagination the reader can be caught up in the zest and turbulence of the world's first democracy.

How Aristophanes was related to earlier comedy we can only conjecture. While tragedy was invented in one city in the sixth century B.C., comedy had existed for many centuries in many parts of the world. Certainly there were village farces all over the Greek world in the centuries before the Golden Age, and they continued long after.

In 487 B.C. a contest in comedy was given an official position at the City Dionysia, with state support and prizes. That was a half-century after the contest in tragedy was established and about a half-century before Aristophanes began writing. We owe our knowledge of his opinions to that curious phenomenon the *parabasis*. Following an old custom, Aristophanes interrupts the play near the middle to have his chorus speak directly to the audience. Besides making an appeal for the prize, they may appeal for a good reception from the audience or make any other comment. In the parabasis of *The Peace* (421 B.C.), Aristophanes brags that he has driven off the boards the petty rivals who tried to make comedy of rags and lice, of a hungry Hercules and slaves weeping from beatings. Instead of such wearisome ineptitudes and low buffooneries, our poet, so the chorus declares, has built a great art, like a palace with high towers, constructed of fine phrases, great thoughts, and jokes not of the marketplace. In the parabasis of *The Clouds* (423 B.C.) Aristophanes calls attention to the modest demeanor of his muse of comedy, brag-

159

Portrait bust of Aristophanes.

ging of not showing the phallus, or dancing the *cordax*. Actually the cordax, a whirling, kicking dance that might be licentious and was always fast, was one of many dances that Aristophanes used for both choruses and actors.

Athenian comedy went far beyond the song and dance and short skits of the village comedians. The double chorus of twenty-four and the fantastic animal characters indicate that music, dance, and spectacle had already been well developed before Aristophanes came on the scene. A Greek treatise on comedy, translated by Lane Cooper and attributed by him to Aristotle, indicates that some complexity of irony and satire had developed even before Aristophanes. The treatise distinguished three types of clowns: the buffoon, the *eiron* (the ironical character who feigns simplicity or stupidity in order to show up his opponent), and the impostor.

A serious attempt was made by Francis Cornford to show that many of the characters and plots of Aristophanes are derived from a supposed spring ritual. But whatever it may borrow from earlier feast or farce, a play of Aristophanes is far more than a celebration of spring, a temporary return to the misrule of chaos or anything else that may be found in traditional festivals. It is a theatrical entertainment that in the midst of song, dance, and fantastic characters diagnoses the spiritual health of the city of Athens and prescribes specific steps for its cure.

A VISION OF DEMOCRACY

Aristophanes had a vision of a workable democracy, and he showed a series of little-man heroes determined to drive out corruption and make the democracy work. He was not the conservative or reactionary that some modern critics have supposed. True, his heroes praise the good old rural virtues as superior to the loose living in town and ridicule new fads in education, law, and literature. But Aristophanes does not ridicule anything because it is new but only if it seems foolish, faddish, and dangerous for the public or private good. He has been called the last Greek with a sense of the individual, but he sees his individual constantly embroiled in public affairs.

The earliest play we have of Aristophanes, and one of his funniest, is *The Acharnians* (425 B.C.). The little hero, Dicaeopolis ("Honest Citizen"), sick and tired of ten years of the war with Sparta and frustrated that he has been unable to go out to the fields to celebrate the early spring rites, comes into the assembly demanding that a truce be made. Getting no results through regular channels, he sends an emissary to the enemy and secures a private truce. He fights off the chorus of super-patriots by trickery and sets up a market for scarce and forbidden goods. When an informer tries to denounce him, he wraps up the informer in a shipping box, like a breakable vase, and ships him off to a distant isle. The play ends in a

161

musical finale, with Dicaeopolis starting to celebrate the festival, drinking wine, a flute-girl on each arm, exchanging antiphonal cries with a general coming back from battle crestfallen, hungry, and covered with mud.

In *Lysistrata* (411 B.C.) a young woman, tired of waiting for her husband to come back from an endless war, stirs the other women to declare a sex strike. In a famous tease scene, one wife, after slowly undressing to get in bed with her husband, runs out six times to get something else—a mattress, a pillow, some perfume, and so on—and finally leaves him in an agony of desire.

After more years of war Aristophanes wrote *The Peace*, showing a hero determined to find peace if he has to go to another planet. Even the gods have deserted the warring earth in disgust. War has Peace in a deep pit and, with local herbs, is grinding up each Grecian city state into hash. The little man manages to cajole others into helping him rescue Peace and bring her back to earth.

The most amazing achievement of the little citizen is to stir up Demos, the manager of the public realm, to bring to trial, sentence, and depose the actual current wartime dictator, Cleon. *The Knights* (424 B.C.) is the most controversial of Aristophanes' plays because it has the most direct attack in the most vigorous in-

Black-figure vase depicting a chorus of knights disguised as horses, sixth century B.C. *Courtesy Staatliche Museen zu Berlin-DDR, Antikensammlung.*

vective. While the name Cleon is not used, the dictator is called the Paphlagonian leather-tanner—a transparent subterfuge.

In *The Wasps* (422 B.C.) the little hero finds corruption in his own family. His father is so enamored of the pay for serving on juries and the power of controlling other people's fate in the law courts that he is a natural dupe of the war party. The son tries to shut the father up at home, but the old reprobate uses every ingenious trick to try to get out. Finally the son makes him happy by setting up a court at home to try a dog for stealing a cheese.

In *The Frogs* (405 B.C.) the little man is Dionysus, descending into Hades to fetch back Sophocles or Euripides, who had both died recently. He thinks he will bring back the more popular Euripides, but after a contest between Aeschylus and Euripides he decides that Euripides, in writing about sensational popular subjects, had been one of the main causes for the decay of Athens, and he chooses to resurrect Aeschylus, dead more than fifty years, to give Athens healthy heroes of the old style. The comparisons and analyses of the three dramatists are the most extensive literary criticism from the ancient world. While Aristophanes prefers Aeschylus, he is remarkably fair in giving each man his due. Euripides defends his everyday diction, realistic characters, and emotional situations as more relevant than the heroic style to a democratic public.

The Clouds (423 B.C.) is a more detailed analysis of the corruption of Athens, attacking especially the separation of logic from truth, of values from religion, of ethics from theology, and the willingness of debaters to undertake to make either side seem the better. The hero is an old man from the country who has married a city wife and has a son given to horse racing and other expensive vices of the town. He hopes to use the "new thought" to get out of paying his debts, so enrolls in the school of Socrates. To learn abstract thinking he lies down on a thinking rug. But all he can think about is the bugs in the rug. So he makes the son take lessons. The son learns the new thought so well that he not only outwits the creditors, he proves by logic that he has the right to beat his father. When he proposes to beat his mother as well, the father loses patience and with his slaves attacks and burns down the "thinkery" of Socrates. He claims that Socrates had corrupted the youth by encouraging idle speculation and disrespect for the gods.

Twenty-five years after the play was produced, in the hysteria that followed their defeat, the Athenians turned on Socrates as a corrupter of youth and condemned him. He refused exile and drank the hemlock. In the Western world he has become a martyr as the great questioner, the father of the scientific spirit. Defenders of Socrates say it was the Sophists who held such doctrines as are satirized in the play. Others say that Aristophanes cannot be held responsible for what the Athenians did a quarter of a century later and that, in any case, it was not Socrates in the play but the petty citizen who demanded dishonest results from learning.

The remarkable thing about Aristophanes' vision of democracy at work is that it is based on a full recognition of the limitations of human nature. He does not believe with Plato and Aristotle that if people are shown what is ideal and good they will embrace it. He sees man as selfish, petty, earthy, full of greed. His heroes are no better than their neighbors. They are little everyday citizens who see that corruption in public affairs interferes with their private needs. These average citizens get something done. They prod, push, cajole, bribe, and shame their fellow citizens to work together for some public objective. They build a working democracy out of the same coarse citizens they themselves are.

This realistic view of man's limitations seems a justification for the frank treatment of all the functions of the body. Early twentieth-century readers who reveled in the obscenity of Aristophanes related it to the fertility rites of spring, pointing to the phallus regularly worn by early comic actors, even when playing female roles. Aristophanes is no longer especially shocking, and the frankness often seems artistically appropriate. What better image of the filth of public corruption than the scene at the opening of *The Peace* of the little citizen mounting a monstrous dung beetle, worried lest someone going to the privy or breaking wind might distract his steed? The erections of the men, doubtless artificial and grotesque, are essential to the action of *Lysistrata,* and the repeated double meaning of the wool the wife wants to spread on the bed is part of the imagery of home and sex. The frankness is part of Aristophanes' view that society must be run by citizens who are not motivated by high ideals of public duty but see that even their lowest desires are best served by good public order.

As Athens moved down the road toward destruction and defeat, Aristophanes turned in new directions. The later plays seem further and further removed from reality. *The Ecclesiazusae,* or *The Women at the Congress* (392 B.C.), shows helpless men, resigned to seeing the women take over and establish a communist regime. Everything else had been tried. The ruling women get bogged down in trivial if comic women's problems of equality. The last play, *Plutus* (388 B.C.), is not a satire at all but an allegory in which the distribution of wealth is corrected when the blind god of wealth is given his sight. One play written even before the final defeat of Athens, *The Birds,* has some of the vigor of imagination of the earlier plays and is sometimes considered Aristophanes' masterpiece. A dramatization of escape, it becomes a disturbing picture of the human condition that has strong appeal for the twentieth century. Two Athenians, disgusted with the times, leave the earth and fly up in the air to join the birds. Aristophanes writes some of his finest delicate poetry describing the beauty, freedom, and delight of life on the wing. The Athenians persuade the birds to build a new city by promising them they can rule the universe if they starve the gods by withholding offerings. The birds take over, and one of the adventurers from Athens marries a goddess and has himself hailed as a feathered god. They have merely rebuilt Athens on a much larger scale. There has been no escape, though they seem happy. William Arrowsmith finds the key to the play in the word *polyprogmosyne,* the force of ambition that drives the Athenians. It had transformed the peaceful, rural Athens that Aristophanes ideal-

164

izes; it led to the empire and the war that destroyed the democracy. In this view the play, as funny as it is in detail, as outrageous in its puns, as boundless in its reduction of all meaning to nonsense, becomes a sad, even tragic, vision.

THE COMIC METHODS OF ARISTOPHANES

The chorus dressed as animals is an old tradition in Greece. Early vase paintings show comic choruses of cocks, ostriches, and men riding dolphins and horses. The fifth century saw comic choruses of sorcerers, poets, juries, Amazons, seasons, dreams, ships, towers, clouds, birds, wasps, frogs, fishes, bees, and goats. Besides color and spectacle and the excuse for songs and dances in character, the animal disguises suggest a travesty of the human world. To animals were added monsters, grotesque gods and demons, allegorical figures, and images of dream journeys and magic transformations. Ceremonial events of the age of mythology abound and are usually burlesqued. The form of Aristophanic comedy is very free. As in a dream or a surrealist nightmare, characters and actions can change form or be in several worlds at the same time. It is in the spirit of Aristophanes that some action in *Hair,* the long-running fantasy of protest at the Vietnam war, was at one and the same time before a draft board, in Vietnam, and with Custer fighting the Indians.

The reader of the script may miss the hilarious effects of putting a character in a ridiculous position. Not until seeing the two ruthless connivers, banker and real estate dealer, teetering and swinging in the bucket of a crane in Maxwell Anderson's *High Tor* (1937), does one realize how funny Socrates must have been swinging precariously in a basket, saying, "I walk upon the air and look down upon the sun from a superior standpoint." When Dicaeopolis in *The Acharnians* (425 B.C.) comes begging for ragged clothes to give him a pathetic appearance, Euripides is wheeled out perched on a ladder in his favorite writing position, surrounded by the tokens of his pathetic characters.

Aristophanes often gives his plot an ironic turn that carries the situation to an outrageous extreme. In *The Women at the Congress* (392 B.C.), the young man can't kiss his girl because, by the new feminine laws, an older, uglier woman has first claim. As he is steeling himself for the crone's embrace, a still older and uglier harridan arrives to claim him. In *The Knights* (424 B.C.), a logical opponent for the corrupt dictator Cleon would be an ideal ruler. But Aristophanes provides him with a contestant who is a professional sausage seller, to demonstrate that Cleon is not even a competent liar and charlatan.

Perhaps the most characteristic comic device is to equate the large, abstract idea with something small and familiar. In *The Acharnians,* Dicaeopolis, determined to make a truce with the enemy, sends for samples. When he is handed the five-

Black-figure vase depicting Aristophanic choruses. *Top:* Warriors riding dolphins. *Bottom:* The other side of the vase—Warriors riding ostriches.. *Gift of the Heirs of Henry Adams. Courtesy of Museum of Fine Arts, Boston.*

166

year vintage peace and tastes it, he comments, "Pugh . . . it smells of pitch and shipyards." He tries the ten-year vintage peace but cries, "Ugh. This has the stink of top-level conferences. It's turned sour, just like our allies." The thirty-year vintage peace he finds delicious, and he begins his spring festival with a toast to the gods of peace and wine. In *Lysistrata*, sex is equated in dozens of ways with war and political quarrels. The two sides quarrel over who gets the bay and two legs of Megara. The American musical *Of Thee I Sing* (1931) uses many Aristophanic equations. The presidential election is in turn a beauty contest, a theatrical production, a wrestling match, and a consolation prize. The judges of the Supreme Court hop into a football huddle with cheerleader yells and barber-shop harmony, to pronounce on the sex of the president's baby.

ECHOES OF OLD COMEDY

The Athenian audience had a rare combination of concern over political and intellectual problems, a belief that criticism and ridicule were healthy, and a will-

Terra-cotta statuettes of a group of Middle Comedy actors. *The Metropolitan Museum of Art, Rogers Fund, 1913. (13.225.13, 18, 19, 24, 27, and 28) All rights reserved.*

ingness to look at several sides of an issue with a sense of humor. Of course the people who were exposed did not like it. As part of Greek religious festivals the plays had some freedom from governmental control, but after the performance of *The Knights*, Cleon did bring Aristophanes to court, and he may have been fined. In his next play Aristophanes rejoices that as they are at the Lenaea, the early spring festival, Cleon cannot accuse him of treason before the visitors and allies that flock to the major festival, the City Dionysia.

In the Hellenistic age following Alexander's conquests, the critics in the city of Alexandria, who used the terms Old Comedy for Aristophanes and New Comedy for Menander and his contemporaries, congratulated themselves that their New Comedy was idealistic and its satire free from reference to particular people and events. In the late Middle Ages in France, young men, especially law students and law clerks, organized clubs to put on satiric sketches and dramas called *sotties*, about important men and ideas of the day. With the Renaissance the taste turned again, and Ben Jonson and Lope de Vega agreed that Old Comedy, in commenting on particular men, was cruel. Shakespeare has his Jaques in *As You Like It* defend his satire as so general that no individual has to feel that he is pointed out.

Scene from the Norman Bel-Geddes production of *Lysistrata*, in Philadelphia, 1928. *Courtesy of Norman Bel-Geddes.*

In the eighteenth century, under a German king and a very unpopular prime minister, London went wild about the indirect comment on public figures in John Gay's *The Beggar's Opera* (1728), and for several years a young author, Henry Fielding, wrote musical extravaganzas that had some Aristophanic satire. But in 1737 the government put an end to that freedom with a strong censorship that lasted more than a hundred years. Fielding gave up dramatic satire and turned to the novel.

A drive to show up the failings of practically everyone possessed Aristophanes. The same drive can be seen in such different people as Molière and Charlie Chaplin. Though he used New Comedy plots rather than extravaganza, Molière was not content to satirize doctors and social fads. His picture of a religious hypocrite hit too close, and the bishop had *Tartuffe* (1664) closed. The young libertines who had applauded that play were appalled to find themselves ridiculed in the next one, *Don Juan* (1819–1824). Charlie Chaplin angered his rich friends by satirizing a business tyrant and mechanized factories in *Modern Times* (1936), then embarrassed diplomats by satirizing Hitler and Mussolini in a magnificent Aristophanic fantasy, *The Great Dictator* (1940). The little Jewish barber who defied Hitler is a true descendant of Aristophanes' plucky little citizens.

In the nineteenth century the Victorian public, long before they could tolerate Ibsen and the direct criticism of their society in naturalistic drama, relaxed enough to enjoy a gentle teasing about public problems and fads. Gilbert and Sullivan furnished that playful criticism, with romantic plots and lilting tunes. Edith Hamilton and others have compared these operettas with Aristophanes' plays for wit, spectacle, and travesty. If *Of Thee I Sing* (1931) seems the most imaginative American example of Aristophanic musical drama, there is more direct satire in the picture of a race bigot, Senator Bilboard Rawkins of Missetucky in *Finian's Rainbow* (1947).

IV

The Theatre
Of Ancient Rome

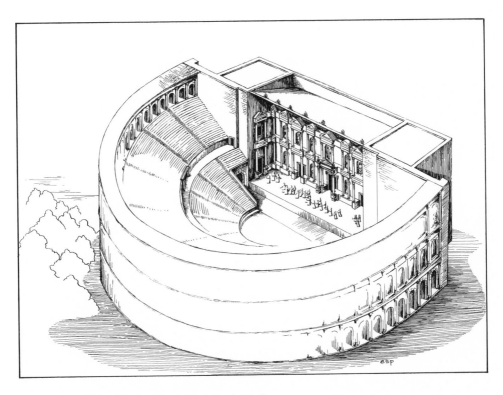

An ancient Roman theatre. *Illustration by Ethelyn Pauley.*

Introduction:
"New" Comedy in Athens and Rome

Before Rome could establish her empire and create a theatre, Athens became part of the Hellenistic empires that followed the conquest of Alexander. In
338 B.C., just fifty years after Aristophanes died, Alexander of Macedon, a pupil
of Aristotle, swept over Athens on his way to conquer Asia Minor, Egypt, and
part of India. For the first time, most of the known world was united under a central government, with Greek institutions and Greek as the international language
and Athenian comedy as its entertainment. Even when it split into three after Alexander's death, the empire laid the basis for a great expansion of trade and for
large new cosmopolitan cities. Antioch in Asia Minor grew to fabulous size, and
Alexandria, the new capital of the Ptolemies in Egypt, became a city of 800,000
in sixty years. Athens, now a tourist town, was also a college town educating
young men for the new commercial age; both emperors and merchants wanted
Athens-trained clerks. The "New" Athenian comedy furnished just the sophistication, realistic characterization, and relaxation that the merchants and their
clerks wanted.

Old Comedy, the magnificent comedy of Aristophanes, died with the Golden
Age of Athens. Only free men could write it, only citizens of a great republic could like it. The middle class audience expected a realistic picture of everyday affairs in a carefully plotted, consistent story. Gone was concern with philosophical ideas.

Comedy became completely institutionalized. From year to year and city to
city, plots, characters, and actors were almost interchangeable. The individualism
which Pericles had praised in his famous funeral oration as the great achievement
of Athens was no longer prized. Now people read the "characters" of Theophrastus—vivid thumbnail sketches of character types. At the theatre they watched a
succession of the miserly fathers, henpecked husbands, love-sick youths, and
clever slaves of Menander, himself a pupil of Theophrastus.

Among the writers of New Comedy, Menander won the highest praise from his
contemporaries. Born in 342 B.C., that is, about a hundred years after Aristophanes, he was nineteen when Alexander died. New Comedy became popular in the

173

Portrait bust of Menander. *Catherine Page Perkins Fund. Courtesy Museum of Fine Arts, Boston.*

new cities and especially in Alexandria. Cultivated gentlemen loved to have Menander's plays read aloud after dinner. The erotic themes were admirable for those who would rise from table and join their wives. Menander combined a high moral tone with tolerance for the escapades of the old men, the wiles of the young, and the tricks of the slaves. The mistakes and anxieties were always resolved in a happy ending. There was sentiment and even a gentle melancholy. The literary style was impeccable.

It has been difficult to get a just picture of Menander since none of his plays survived the fall of Rome or the Mohammedan invasion in Egypt. A badly damaged papyrus found in Egypt in 1905 contained sizable fragments of four plays and a small fragment of a fifth. They showed some subtlety of characterization and polish of style but did not seem very comic. Finally in the 1950s a complete play of Menander, *The Grouch* (317 B.C.), came into the hands of a Swiss bookdealer who published it without disclosing how he obtained it. In Lionel's Casson's translation, *The Grouch* is a rather good play, one that differs in several respects from the plays of Plautus and Terence, based though they are on Menander or his contemporaries.

Marble relief of Menander seated at a table holding the mask of a youth. On the table beside him are masks of a young woman and an old man. At the right is Menander's woman Glykera, or the personification of Skene. *Alinari/Art Resource, N.Y.*

Costumes for Menander's plays and other New Comedy, though based on ordinary street dress, made the stock characters distinguishable. The rustic, with his leathern tunic and his wallet and staff, was different from the citizen. The courtesan wore brilliant, variegated dress, embroidered mantle, and golden ribbons. The youth was different in mask and costume from the bald-headed, pinch-faced, pot-bellied, old man. The soldier, the parasite, the cook, the bawd, the courtesan's maid—all had masks and costumes which the audience recognized immediately. The slaves were comic figures with scruffy red hair, wide mouth, big nose, flabby or shredded ears, padded stomach and buttocks, and misshapen phallus.

The Hellenistic theatres, whose remains are to be found all over Asia Minor, were larger than the Greek theatres of the classic age. The stage was high, sometimes ten or even twelve feet above the old level of the orchestra, and the skene rose to at least two stories of stone structure with splendid columns usually standing out from the stone wall. Behind the columns were doorways on the stage level and niches for the statues of gods and heroes on the upper levels. At the ends of the skene were *paraskenia* brought forward to enclose the stage, doubtless with entrances of their own to supplement the three on the main façade. In contrast to the modest structure of classic times, the skene was something more than a hundred feet long, longer than the orchestra was wide.

In *The Grouch* the chorus apparently performed its entr'acte on the same stage as the actors. We assume that the tragic chorus was no longer important, but whether it played on the stage or in the old orchestra is not known. We may well ask why such a large orchestra was retained if it was not used for performance. In some of the theatres of Asia Minor the skene extends into part of the circle, but the beautiful fourth-century theatre at Epidaurus, the best-preserved theatre in Greece, has a complete circular orchestra. With perfect acoustics, the theatre serves well for twentieth-century revivals of tragedy.

Village Farces in Italy

When Rome came to dominate the world, it had not only the tragedy and the sophisticated New Comedy of Athens as models for theatrical entertainment but several robust village traditions to imitate. Certainly by the sixth century B.C. and probably long before, comedians were entertaining with songs, dances, monologues, and little plays throughout the towns and villages of the Mediterranean world. In the Greek settlements of southern Italy and Sicily such popular entertainments developed. Many were connected with Dionysian revelry, and the phallus was the badge of comedy. Two especially lively groups—the *Phlyakes* and the actors of Atellan farces—made a strong impression in Rome.

The Phlyakes, or Gossips, set up their platform in village squares, festival precincts, and, after the Greek theatre was built in Syracuse, apparently in front of the large Hellenistic proscenium. At the ends of the platform were doors with projecting roofs, and in back of the platform a façade with, sometimes at least, an open gallery above. The actors played on the ground, on a stairway to the platform, on the main platform, on the upper gallery, or climbing up ledges, brackets, and gables on the façade.

None of the Phlyakes' plays is extant, but vases show scenes of the actors. In one scene the greedy Heracles has snatched the sacrificial offering from under the nose of Zeus, who threatens him with a thunderbolt. In another, Apollo has fled to the roof of his temple, but Heracles pursues him still and he must fall into the basin of holy water and lose his bow to Iolaos, who is waiting to snatch it. Another favorite scene shows Hera caught in a magic throne, sent her in revenge by her son, Hephaistos, for throwing him from Olympus and laming him.

Besides mythological farces, there were plays about everyday people. Many contrasting pairs appear: father and son, husband and shrewish wife, rustic dupe and clever trader, slave and flute-girl. The typical costume is a short sleeveless jacket, but under that, nudity is grotesquely imitated. Tights do not fit, and many characters have large padded stomach and buttocks. The phallus is huge and sometimes seems attached to the jacket rather than the body. Often a button imitates the belly button. In one picture the button is hanging by a thread.

The other local comedy that had a great vogue was the Atellan farce. Atella, an actual town south of Rome in Campania, was already a byword for absurd customs and gawky appearance and behavior. Though derived from the same traditions as the plays of the Phlyakes, the Atellan farce developed a more fixed set of characters, who usually bore the same name from one play to another.

The usual Atellan group consisted of two old men and two slaves or louts, with an occasional braggart and glutton and one or two women to fill out the story. The first old man was Pappus, a decrepit simpleton, big-bellied and miserly, the butt of all the intrigues and pranks, the ancestor of Pantalone of the commedia

Southern Italian Phlyakes vase depicting Dionysus and Dancing Phlyakes, fifth century B.C. *Courtesy of the Trustees of the British Museum.*

178

dell'arte. His companion was Dossenus, a hunch-backed clown, the antecedent of the learned Doctor from Bologna in the commedia. (The central figure was usually Maccus, the wanton, dissolute hero, a stupid country lout who is in trouble most of the time but has his moments of triumph. He had a hump on his back, a flat, close-shaven head, a large beaked nose, and protruding ears. Titles of plays indicate the repeated fun of putting this Mack in new situations—"Mack in the Army," "Mack in a Convent," "Mack the Bartender.") He is the antecedent of Pulcinella in the commedia and of the English Punch. Mack's companion, Buccus or Bucco, in contrast, was a loud, arrogant talker.

(Atellan farce was introduced to Rome about the time the actor and playwright Plautus arrived in the city (that is, about 200 B.C.), and we would surmise from Plautus' nickname, Maccius, that he gained fame in the part of Maccus, or Mack. Certainly the genre had a strong influence on his plays. Apparently Atellan farce was primarily an actors' theatre, written and rewritten as the actors went along. But in the first century B.C. literary authors wrote a number of plays in this rustic style. Livy says that young aristocrats of the empire delighted in impersonating the characters, and apparently soldiers as well, for masks have been found as far away as the Rhine.

Southern Italian Phlyakes vase depicting the old man Cheiron being pushed and pulled up onto the Phlyakes' stage, fifth century B.C. *Courtesy of the Trustees of the British Museum.*

179

Plautus and Plautine Farce

Rome entered the Mediterranean scene late in the third century B.C., about a hundred years after Alexander. Within a half-century the illiterate farmers and soldiers of Rome became masters of all Italy, conquering the Umbrians to the north and the Greek colonies to the south. They set ships on the sea and challenged the Carthaginians, who had dominated the trade of the western Mediterranean. When they wrested the thriving Greek cities of Sicily from Carthage, they came suddenly into contact with the architecture, sculpture, and painting as well as the food, wine, song, dance, and drama of an old, sophisticated civilization. They brought back to Rome not only wealth but new tastes and many educated Greek slaves to prepare their banquets, to sing and dance for them, and, through translation and adaptation, to give them a literature and drama ready-made. One of the slaves, Lucius, gathered actors and stagehands and in 240 B.C. put on at the annual Roman Games a Greek comedy and a Greek tragedy in Latin. Soon, the Roman playwright Naevius caught the popular fancy by combining the stock characters and careful plots of the Greek New Comedy with some of the farcical action, clowning, and singing and dancing of the Phlyakes and the actors of Atellan farce.

To this thriving, expanding Rome came a young Umbrian from the north to make his fortune. We know him by his stage name, Plautus. Soon he made enough money as an actor to try a venture as a sea merchant. But that failed, and when he got back to Rome it was off to the army for everyone. Hannibal had brought an African army by elephants and cavalry through Spain and in the spring of 218 B.C. had already crossed the Alps into northern Italy. One Roman army after another went down before him until he came to the very gates of Rome. Only after a desperate struggle did Rome finally drive Hannibal out and put an end to the threat of Carthage. After the first danger was over and the soldiers and uprooted peoples in Rome began to relax, a wave of gaiety and pleasure-seeking swept the city. Roman comedy found its first great audiences, and Plautus was kept busy for the rest of his life writing farces that competed in popularity with chariot races, acrobats, and wild-beast shows.

In 200 B.C. the Roman armies turned eastward toward the three empires left by Alexander. Egypt joined as an ally, and thus Alexandria, the cosmopolitan, Greek-

180

speaking capital of Egypt, became a colony of Rome. Macedonia was soon defeated, and when in 196 B.C. the Greek cities were liberated by Roman soldiers, Roman interest in Greek culture increased enormously. Syria was next, and as news came back to Rome of the armies in Asia Minor, Plautus produced plays supposedly set in the newly talked-of cities. After the battle of Magnesia in 190, Rome stood the undisputed mistress of the world.

Plautus was born about 254 or 253 B.C. and died in 184. His life in the theatre coincided with Rome's rise to imperial power. His audience included not only rich merchants, successful adventurers, and the restless, pleasure-hunting populace but the soldiers—fresh recruits or seasoned troops in Rome between campaigns or returned from the wars triumphant and rich. Gone were the restrictions of the days of Hannibal, and everyone was ready for a lark. The Greek plays offered elegance, urbanity, and sophistication, with courtesans, banquets, and revelry. Plautus managed to keep the urbanity and combine with it the songs, robust action, and racy characters of the village farces, so that the audience could feel very Greek and very Roman at the same time. Through all the mischief and scheming shone the solid Roman virtues. The home was sacred, wives were loyal and noble. The frisky old man rarely got more than a kiss or two before his wife dragged him

Terra-cotta of a comic scene illustrating the New Comedy of Terence.

181

Two seated slaves, New Comedy types. *Courtesy of the Trustees of the British Museum.*

home or his son claimed the girl. The son was usually seriously in love, wanting the girl as his only mistress, and if she turned out to be a free-born citizen, he was delighted to marry her. Yet during the lark the stage teemed with as vivid a set of rascals as Rabelais, Hogarth, or Dickens knew.

For the tired businessman a performance of a play of Plautus was like a new year's festival, when all the restraints of the rest of the year were removed. The stage in *The Menaechmi* (186 B.C.) becomes a visual symbol of the two ways of life. On one side is the home and on the other the house of the prostitute Erotium. The husband rushes out of the home cursing his wife for always watching him and announces that he has stolen a dress from her and is going right over to give it to Erotium and have dinner with her. "Now you'll keep your spying eyes off your husband, if you're wise," he says; and he asks all the philandering husbands in the audience to applaud his bravery. Roman morality was always in the background, but the Athens of the costumes and story brought promises of freedom and a sense of adventure.

The young lover was the center of interest; the audience could see themselves in him as he pursued the charming young girl. The slave might mock the lover but went to work to get the money or thwart the rival. When the plot involved a pimp, slave-owner, or professional soldier, he would be cheated of his money and the girl and sometimes beaten. The young man's sweetheart was usually a lost girl, born of good family but, in the course of wars and shipwrecks, fallen into slavery or into the hands of bawds or pimps. Now she was an appealing figure as she was about to be sold, bartered, or rented by the year to a foreign soldier.

Many of Plautus' characters reflect the new age of luxury, sensuality, and cynicism. The parasite, always hungry, haunts the marketplace in hope of an invitation to dinner. Apparently Plautus and his citizen audience, happy to be home from the campaigns, despised the professional soldier. He appears on the stage as a swearing braggart. He thinks he is adored by the ladies and falls an easy prey to the tricks of the clever slave. Prominent among the female characters are cruel bawds and gold-digging courtesans, who have no mercy on the young lover who has already spent all his money. Two plays were written about courtesans. They are charming in *Bacchides* (189 B.C.), but in *Truculentus* (186 B.C.) they ruthlessly cheat in turn the young lover, a country lout, and a soldier. The cynical tone of the play is intensified by the surly oaths and wisecracks of the slave Truculentus.

Most important of the Plautine characters are the clever slaves who were described as "pot-bellied, with lantern jaws and hair as red as flame." They lie, cheat, and plot to get the girl for the young lover, and they take the beatings when the scheme is found out. Their ingenuity is a constant delight, and they brag of their exploits when they triumph and make sport of their woe when they fail. After a defeat they are ready to start all over again. They embody the tough persistence of the clowns of all ages, reassuring the audience of the vitality of the human race. The servant in *Casina* says to his master, "You don't like the sight of me, but I'll live

on!" From Plautus' slaves to Molière's valets and Beaumarchais's Figaro, these inde-
structible clowns do live on.

Plautus followed the popular village traditions and used song freely. Of the extant plays only one, *Miles Gloriosus* (205 B.C.), has no song, while nearly half of
Casina (184 B.C.) was set to music, and a considerable part of most of the other
plays was sung. On his first entrance a character might tell in song of his distress-
ing situation, and a running slave usually expressed his breathless haste in song.
Plautus rarely had an actor go directly from song to realistic dialogue but gave him
a transitional passage in the recitative style between song and speech. Duets of
two persons singing alternately were used to express anything from the ribald
name-calling of two slaves to the woes of two old men or the sorrow of two forsaken girls. Some plays had elaborate sequences and song for large groups. *Persa*
(186 B.C.) ends with a lavish banquet, the toasts and gaiety and dancing of the
trio who have triumphed set off by the musical groans and curses of the pimp they
are mocking and beating.

None of the melodies are extant, but the lively lyrics, with rhyme and alliteration and assonance (effects rarely used by other writers in the ancient world), indicate that song must have added greatly to the vividness of the play. We can imagine the Roman audience repeating for months afterward the refrain the wife in
Asinaria (207 B.C.) sings when she finds her husband reclining at a banquet and
fondling his son's mistress: "Surge amator, I domum"—"Get up, you fine lover,
now head for home."

Plautine farce was the greatest contribution of Rome to the theatre of later
times. A large part of our popular entertainment still follows the basic techniques
brought together by Plautus. Farce presents an image of everyday reality that is
yet removed from reality by a false situation that will be cleared up at the end, and
by farcical treatment. Where Aristophanes dealt with public heroes, mythological
monsters, or abstract ideas, Plautus dealt with the basic relationships of everyday
family life. Where village comedies presented in song and dance topsy-turvy images of clowns ruling the heavens or the institutions of the world, Plautus subordinated clowning, song, and comic effects to the plot.

The short-sighted absorption of the characters is one of the pleasures of Plautine farce. For with few exceptions farce plots are clear to the audience from the
beginning. The scheming character is shown putting on a disguise, telling a lie, or
making a mistake. Identical twins are never confusing to the audience but only to
the other characters. In *Amphitryon* (186 B.C.) when Plautus sets up his situation of
Jupiter and Mercury coming to earth in the form of a general and his servant, he
has Mercury tell the audience they can always know him from his duplicate by the
button on his cap. The pleasure of the Roman audience was not the suspense of
melodrama but the comic irony of knowing what most of the characters in the
play did not.

Plautine farce requires of the actors speed and intensity. But even more impor-

185

tant are such mechanical plot patterns as repetition and reversal. In *Miles Gloriosus* the slave fools money out of two old men in succession, but in *Psudolus* (191 B.C.) he brags that he can fool the same man twice and does it. In *Bacchides* one fooling is no sooner finished than the young man, thinking his girl loves his friend, gives back to the father the money that had been extracted from him. When he discovers his mistake the slave has to start all over again to fool a father freshly warned. Reversal makes a break in the pattern of repetition. Roman citizens were familiar with this element from the New Year's festival, in which men dressed as women, masters as slaves. In Plautine farce reversal shows the joy of the worm that turns. The two triumphant slaves at the end of Plautus' *Asinaria* make the girl kiss them, and the lover carry each of them on his back.

Plautine farce is designed for relaxation, but in achieving this end it creates a social, political, and philosophical view of the world. The social strategy in farce is evasion—to avoid a confrontation or to delay it or mitigate the rage expected if everything is brought out in the open. One scheme after another must be tried. For the average citizen as well as for the characters in farce, it is important to get some moments of private life. This means accepting a world of public rules but at a few points evading or bending the rules. Though they make a display of anger, fathers and other figures of authority may prove kind and forgiving in the end. Moreover, both parents and policemen are limited in their knowledge and often inefficient or downright stupid, and that is salvation for the miscreants of farce, who evade and fool them. The higher religions and sciences seek the large scheme of order in the universe, but in the cosmos of Plautus and of most farce since his time, there is chaos in the very nature of things. Farce presents the chaos in everyday life—a world of accidents, surprises, interruptions, and miscalculations. But the accidents help as often as they hinder. The political order in farce is limited anarchy. On a philosophical level farce annihilates time. It is good to see that time must have a stop. The week comes to the weekend and the season has its close. In one way or another everything that is started is finished. Farce assures the audience that daily activities are finite and each has its end. Through tragedy we embrace the infinite, through farce the finite.

The Comedy of Terence

Shortly after Plautus died, when the triumph of Rome was still fresh, there appeared in the city a cocky young playwright, Terence (190–159 B.C.). He was a literary man who wanted to use the theatre but despised its vulgar audience. He complained that he could not hold the clamorous crowd or compete with boxers and rope dancers. Where Plautus had vigor, Terence offered polish. Yet he was not a writer of closet drama. His plays were produced, and in the long run he has had nearly as great an influence on the theatre as Plautus.

If Terence could not find a large audience in the noisy theatres of Rome, he did find a small coterie of aristocrats interested in the Greek world, and he was proud to please them with his Latin adaptations of Menander or one of his contemporaries. A dark, handsome slave boy, Terence had been brought from conquered Carthage and sold to a Roman senator who had given him an education and his freedom. Starting before he was twenty, he produced six plays in about ten years, carefully polishing them for style and characterization, reading them to his coterie of friends. With their help he set out to visit his beloved Greece but was never heard from again, lost when he was scarcely in his thirties.

What Terence failed to gain in the current theatre he won in the esteem of history. Cicero and Horace gave him high praise, and he was considered a model for a pure Latin style by the Romans of the Empire, the monks of the Middle Ages, and the schoolmasters of the Renaissance. It is estimated that more than half of the books printed in the sixteenth century were copies of the plays of Terence to be used as Latin textbooks in grammar schools. From the Renaissance into the nineteenth century, a European playwright knew that his audience was familiar with all the plays of Terence and some of Plautus. Borrowings from Terence are to be found in Shakespeare, Ben Jonson, Molière, Sheridan, and lesser writers. Modern comedy was founded on classic comedy, and for the most part classic comedy meant Terence.

In Terence's plays the Romans saw a vision of a new age of wider freedom emerging out of a time of strict discipline, a situation that has repeated itself many times. In his plays fathers who grew up in straitened circumstances and strict family discipline on the farm are now living with more affluence in town. With dismay they watch their sons going to wild parties, keeping mistresses, and living extravagantly. They know that if they impose too strict a discipline, the son can lie or run away. If they are understanding and gentle, they may eventually win confidence, but in the meantime there may be babies and other complications before all can be set right. A play of Terence, like all New Comedy, has a happy ending and reassures both old and young that once the short period of wildness is over, the adventurous youth will settle down to marriage and a respectable life. In the meantime the severe fathers are reminded that they once had the same impulses and indeed often still try a little adventure into irresponsible adolescence.

The imaginary Athens in which Terence set his plays is kinder than the world of Plautus. The intriguing slaves have tender feelings of their own. Cruel actions are usually left offstage. Or they may be dismissed as traditional plot devices for creating a difficulty that turns out to be no difficulty. In *The Self-Tormentor* (163 B.C.) the girl was exposed to the elements as an infant by order of her father but was saved by the old woman who was supposed to put her out to die. Now she is welcomed into the family. The courtesans have hearts of gold; Thais, the noble courtesan in *The Eunuch* (161 B.C.), goes out of her way to clear the young man of his family's suspicion. And the young man of a Terence play is often shy and insecure rather than willful. This warmth and affection was to be rediscovered by the sentimental writers of the eighteenth century, and Richard Steele's *The Conscious Lovers* (1720) is an adaptation of Terence's *The Girl of Andros* (166 B.C.). With Terence the sentiment is part of a broad faith in mankind expressed by one of his characters in these words: "Homo sum: humani nil a me alienum puto"—"I am a man: nothing human can be alien to me."

Terence laid the foundation of the form called high comedy for later writers like Molière, Congreve, and Sheridan. While there are many examples of farcical deception in Terence, such as lying to gain money or time, the deception is sometimes more subtle and complex. There are delicate relationships, as in *The Self-Tormentor*, where the baffled father drives his son out in anger but is then so tormented by guilt that he will deny him nothing. His more sophisticated brother warns him against both extremes and advises a middle road. At the opening of *The Eunuch* (161 B.C.) the young man Phaedria says to his mistress, "Oh Thais, Thais. Would that you and I did love equally, and went at an even pace; so that either what you've done might trouble you as much as it has troubled me, or that I might concern myself as little as you do." His cynical adviser has just warned him of the difficulty: "For love, you know, is strangely whimsical; containing affronts, jealousies, jars, parlays, wars, then peace again. Now, for you to ask advice on the rules of love, is no better than to ask advice on the rules of madness." Many centuries later in Congreve's *The Way of the World* (1700), Mirabell feels the same exasperation with his Millamant.

Of the greatest influence on later drama was Terence's last play, *The Brothers* (160 B.C.). The plot, which Terence had taken from Aristophanes, appears centuries later in Molière's *The School for Husbands* (1661) and Sheridan's *School for Scandal* (1777). In farcical intrigue, Plautus provided the better model for later ages, but in subtle surprises of character, Terence provided a worthy foundation for modern high comedy.

The Theatre of Imperial Rome

SENECA AND TRAGEDY

Comedy was the important theatrical form of late republican and early imperial times. But in the first century of the Christian era, when Rome was at the height of its power, Seneca wrote tragedies of which ten have survived. He turned to the Greek dramatists of the sixth and fifth centuries B.C. for his material, but his works were not mere translations; they were infused with Seneca's own Stoic personality and with his sense of the corruption and violence of his own surroundings. Theatre historians have supposed that Seneca's tragedies were not intended for presentation by actors on a stage but for recitation to a select aristocratic audience, one speaker giving the speeches of several characters, with perhaps occasional assistance from another reciter in the dialogue of thrust and parry called *stichomythea*, and from a chorus. The tragedies as presented seem to have been very like, if not identical with, a new theatrical form called *monodrama* that was popular at the time. The emperor Nero, to whom Seneca had been tutor, liked to act tragic roles, presenting, apparently, solo versions of *Oedipus Blinded*, *Orestes the Matricide*, and *Hercules Mad*.

Renaissance playwrights and audiences were fascinated by Seneca, and his Latin drama, more accessible than ancient Greek tragedy, was the model for serious writers long into the seventeenth century. Thomas Kyd, Marlowe, Shakespeare, and Lope de Vega already knew how to create turbulent action on the stage, acting that Seneca's characters only reported and then analyzed. When to their plots of action they added Seneca's gloomy mood, his stoic acceptance of a world of evil, his long meditations on the ironies of life and death, his characters crying out their hatred and defiance in the most bombastic rhetoric, they had a model for creating the lurid atmosphere they wanted. Seneca's *Thyestes* even showed them how to use an outraged ghost to start the play with a call for revenge. Nineteenth-century critics were sure that Seneca's plays could not be performed successfully. But in the 1960s and 1970s both London and Paris showed a new interest in Seneca's plays. In a production of Seneca's *Oedipus* at the National Theatre in London in 1968, John Gielgud and Irene Worth showed that the long solo speeches could be quite powerful.

190

MIME AND PANTOMIME

Besides the tragic monodrama and Seneca's special development of that form, two forms of popular theatre in imperial Rome are of special interest in the twentieth century. Both were developed as arts of performance. The mime as a solo entertainer is older than recorded history; there is mention by the sixth century B.C. of individuals and small groups that had been playing in various parts of the Greek world, and in Rome, of course, there were mimes long before Plautus. But in imperial Rome the lively mime, with his clownish figure, quick wit, and song and dance, was extremely popular, holding his own against the competition of acrobats, jugglers, and rope dancers. In earlier Rome the mime play had often been an entr'acte or an afterpiece in other entertainment, sometimes performed in front of the stage on the ground level, but, by the time of the Caesars, it was often

Ivory statuette of a tragic Roman actor. The figure is only two inches high; the objects at the bottom of the figure are pegs to fit the statuette into a base. *Courtesy VILLE DE PARIS, Musée du Petit Palais, Paris.*

191

a principal feature and took over the main stage. Sometimes there was a large company—one mime group had sixty performers—but usually there was a single virtuoso with a few assistants.

Some mimes performed without masks, and in some records painted faces and facial expressions are mentioned, but most performers were masked. At the time of Julius Caesar a Syrian slave, Syrus, became famous not only for his grace of body and voice but for his moral aphorisms. Some mimes were famous for imitating prominent men of the day or for epigrammatic comments on current events, but none ventured as far as Aristophanes had gone in criticizing their rulers. Most of the subject matter was like that in Plautine farce. Sometimes a mime played a romantic role of strange adventures and escapes from danger. One mime play told the story of a runaway slave who became a famous robber until he was caught and crucified, and a condemned criminal was used in the role and real blood shed. The few texts of mime plays written by literary people are lively, realistic monologues about everyday life.

Never as popular as mime, pantomime appealed to the cultivated court circles. Curiously, it seems to be a descendant of Greek tragedy. A chorus chanted the description and the words supposed spoken, while a single dancer or a small group showed the action; hence our word "pantomime" for movement without words. Many pantomimes dealt with mythological subjects. For the story of the adultery of Mars and Venus, the dancer showed first Apollo, the sun, discovering the couple, then Vulcan, Venus' husband, catching them in a net, then each of several other gods coming to watch and laugh, and finally Venus embarrassed and Mars beseeching. In presenting the story of *The Bacchae*, one dancer made the audience see first Bacchus as an ecstatic youth leading the Maenads, then the feeble jigging of old Cadmus, then the spy who watched and recounted the revels from the greenwood tree, and finally Agave, triumphant and mad, carrying the bloody head of her son.

Both the mime and the pantomime were condemned by the Christian fathers. Mimes had satirized baptism and other sacraments, and Christians had not developed tolerance or a sense of humor. The Church fathers wrote that both nudity and sexual intercourse were shown on the stage, and the Victorians took them literally. But since nudity and sex can be represented in many ways, it is not certain that mimes and pantomimes were any more erotic than comedies and ballets of the twentieth century. In the sixth century A.D. one writer, Choricius, answered the attack on the stage, insisting that only a few of the mimes showed fools or low acts, that the actor must not be called immoral because he played immoral roles, that it was the duty of art to include all of life, that those who do evil should be blamed, not the actors who reflect it, and that laughter is a gift of God that distinguishes man from the brutes.

But during the sixth century the Christians and the Barbarians between them put an end to public performance. The mimes apparently performed for a while at weddings and private parties, but not openly. Then for the next half-millennium, when Europe had lost most tokens of civilization and returned to a very elementary economy, there were still wandering performers. It is possible that among the traveling jugglers, dancers, and minstrels a few kept some of the characters and comic scenes of the ancient world.

Theatre Structures in Rome

Plautus and Terence appeared when Rome was a vigorous republic just building its empire by conquest. The theatres they wrote for were temporary wooden structures put up for holiday games and entertainments. These buildings must have been almost as simple as the Phlyakes village stages, though combined with some features of the Hellenistic theatre. In back of the platform was a two-story *scena* with two or more doors. We do not know what kind of benches were provided for the audience, though there are several references in the plays to seats. Audiences were noisy. The prologues must fight for order and attention, warning the ladies not to chatter, nurses not to bring squalling children to the theatre, and prostitutes to keep off the stage itself.

Plays were but one of many entertainments offered free to the restless Roman public. A holiday was a time of diversion, with games, sports, and spectacles. The theatre, as one of the luxuries borrowed from the Greeks, was opposed by the older conservative citizens, and several times the Senate had a theatre building torn down; they even passed a law forbidding the audience to sit during a play, apparently hoping to discourage playgoing by making it uncomfortable. Yet the government paid the bill, except when a rich man, currying favor with the public, might take over. A general returning in triumph would offer all kinds of attractions for many days. No politician or official could hold the favor of the crowd unless he provided free entertainment.

Besides buildings in which plays were performed, and sometimes other kinds of entertainment, there were arenas or amphitheatres for sports. The oldest, the Circus Maximus, dated from the sixth century B.C. It was rebuilt a number of times as the empire grew and Rome became a large city. Besides chariot races, the amphitheatres housed many other forms of contests. Gladiatorial combats to the death were popular from the time of the war with Hannibal, when prisoners were set to hack one another to pieces instead of being executed. When that war ended, the holiday for games lasted less than a week, with one day for theatrical performances. By the time of Augustus, the first Roman emperor (27 B.C.–14 A.D.), there were sixty days of games at various times of the year. In 80 A.D., when Titus dedicated a new Colosseum, which seated nearly a hundred thousand, the games lasted a hundred days, and thousands of wild animals from far countries were

194

added to thousands of domestic animals to provide an almost continuous spectacle of combat and bloody destruction. A large scenic structure representing hills and groves was set up in the center of the Colosseum to show a condemned criminal dressed as Orpheus torn to pieces by bears. In Nero's time (37–68 A.D.) a spectacular game of "house on fire" was presented. A house with rich furnishing was burned as actors rushed in, knowing they could have anything they dared rescue. The chariot races were dangerous games with the chance of blood and death as part of the thrill. At times lakes were used for sea battles, or the theatres and amphitheatres were flooded to show the pursuit, capture, and often the burning of ships in battle. Even the Dionysian theatre at Athens was rebuilt for flooding for sea battles. By the time of the fall of Rome (376 A.D.) there were one hundred and seventy-five days of games and combat each year, with dramatic shows of some kind for a hundred days.

The imperial theatre structures date from the time of Caesar and Pompey, in the last century B.C., when several permanent theatres of stone were built. The first, in 55 B.C., came to the public through the courtesy of Pompey. In order to circumvent objection to the theatre, a temple to Venus was built so that the tiers of seats could be called steps leading up to the temple. Not to be outdone, Julius Caesar had a double theatre built, with one auditorium that could be revolved and join the other to form a large amphitheatre for gladiatorial combats and races. Later many cities built both a circus-amphitheatre, or *circus*, and a theatre of the Roman type. Sometimes a long racetrack was added as a third structure in the complex. While the theatre was often used for the more spectacular shows—combats and even sea battles—its main purpose was for the occasional performance of literary comedies and tragedies and the more frequent performance of the classical mimes and the ballet-like pantomimes.

During the half-millennium of imperial Rome, this new style of theatre structure spread from Asia Minor to North Africa, from Britain to Spain. Systematic engineers that they were, the Romans took most of the features of the classic Greek and Hellenistic theatres and organized them into one continuous unified building. They joined the auditorium to the stage by moving the stage structure up to the center of the orchestra circle, thus making the auditorium a perfect half-circle. They enlarged the Hellenistic scene building, often to three or more stories, and sometimes built a sloping roof over the stage which would have helped reflect sound to the audience. In order to complete the building and ensure good acoustics, the Renaissance architect Vitruvius tells us, a colonnade and wall was built around the back of the last rows of seats, to come to the same height as the stage house. The space over the audience, too wide to roof, could be covered by an awning. Painted notices found at Pompeii promise the audience not only awnings to shield them from the sun but showers of perfumed water to temper the sultry air.

The stage itself was only about five feet above the half-circle or the orchestra, where senators sometimes sat to watch the performance. In back of the very wide stage was the elaborate *frons scenae*, decorated with permanent columns, statues, niches, and pediments; yet it also had room for both the *scena ductilis*, or painted panel, that could be drawn aside to open up an elaborate niche or inner stage, and the *scena versatilis*, the old *periaktoi*, or triangular prisms, of the later Greek theatre. In the best-preserved Roman theatre at Orange in southern France, the large bases of the columns would furnish excellent hiding places for the many scenes where one character speaks or overhears without being seen by the other characters. At the back of the bases are small doorways out of sight of the audience, available for quick entrances and exits.

The Roman stage had both a front and a back curtain, apparently borrowed from the portable booth theatres of the traveling troupes. At least in preimperial times, mimes and other entertainers set up their platforms on the ground level in front of the stage and used both an *aulaeum* at the front that fell into a slot when the play began and was raised at the end of the performance and a *siparium*, or back curtain, for entrances and exits and hiding places. Both Ovid and Virgil speak of embroidered figures on the aulaeum that seemed to stand on the stage when the

A general view of the Roman theatre at Orange.

196

The small theatre at Pompeii, 80 B.C.

An outside facade of the auditorium side of the Theatre of Marcellus, 11 B.C. *Courtesy Archeological Library, Dept. of Archeology, University of Rome.*

curtain was raised at the end of the performance. The siparium could be either a curtain or a screen to be folded. In the ancient world indoor action was either spoken about and not shown, or banquet tables and dressing tables were brought out in front of the scenic screen. In later imperial times the modern form of curtain was introduced—raised at the beginning and let down at the end.

The effect of the enormous scena was on the one hand to dwarf the actors—but on the other hand to concentrate the attention on the immediate story by shutting off all celestial or cosmic distractions. While Greek theatres in both Greece and Sicily were located with magnificent views, inviting thoughts of the gods of sky, mountain, and sea, the Romans wanted no such thoughts. The ruins of the theatre at Taormina in Sicily show the difference. The Roman brick wall that cut off the view has now crumbled enough to allow glimpses of the sea and seacoast far below.

Even if the theatres had not been closed by the Christians, they would not have survived the collapse of the economy after the fall of Rome. For a thousand years the enormous theatre structures and amphitheatres served as quarries for building stone or were shaken by earthquakes, flaked by frost and rain, or covered with dust. The best preserved are in Asia Minor, northern Africa, and southern France. In Rome itself only the great Colosseum and the circular outer walls of the Theatre of Marcellus are to be seen. The Marcellus was gutted and rebuilt as a palace for a Renaissance prince. In Athens the Roman theatre of Herodias Atticus on the slope of the Acropolis, just west of the Theatre of Dionysus, is used for concerts and revivals of ancient plays. In Cornwall several grass-covered rounds, relics of Roman amphitheatres, served for village sports and for the great Cornish cycles of medieval religious plays.

V

Medieval Drama

A dramatized scene from *The Conquest of Jerusalem*, a popular chivalric romance. Redrawn from *The Chroniques de Charles V. Illustration by Martha Sutherland.*

Introduction

SOCIETY AND THEATRE IN THE MIDDLE AGES

In theatre history the period of the Middle Ages dates from the fall of the Roman Empire as Germanic hordes swept over Europe destroying the cities. The invaders were soon converted to Christianity, but what remains of theatre the barbarians had spared, the Church Fathers destroyed. From the sixth to the sixteenth century, Europe had no professional companies putting on written plays in theatre buildings for regular audiences. The only theatrical entertainment was by village entertainers and wandering minstrels. Gradually each social class began to adorn its festivals with theatrical elements.

The Middle Ages came to an end in the sixteenth century as festival drama—amateur, processional, occasional—gave way to the professional theatre. The Renaissance theatres took over many aspects of the medieval even as they followed new principles. In the nineteenth century various medieval theatres were studied as stumblings toward the illusion and realism of the modern theatre, and plays were read as "pre-Shakespearean drama." Today we return to the medieval theatres not only for suggestions in our own struggle with realism and illusion but because we can respond to them as splendid achievements in their own right.

MEDIEVAL THEATRES IN THREE PERIODS

We can divide the thousand years from the fall of Rome to the Renaissance into three periods with different kinds of theatres. From the fifth to the tenth century, with wave after wave of invading peoples, the only performers were attendants in religious processions and such simple entertainers as have always been known in villages around the world. In the Romanesque age of the tenth, eleventh, and twelfth centuries, the monks developed a magnificent religious art in church buildings, stained glass, sculpture, and church drama, while the feudal lords began to ornament their tournaments and banquets with music, poetry, and drama.

In the Gothic period from the thirteenth to the sixteenth century, the cities took the lead and the city bourgeoisie financed spectacular forms of theatre.

The early churchmen disapproved of the sensuality and pagan mythology of the serious Roman pantomimes and of the plots of deception and sexuality in the comedies. Moreover the mimes made the fatal mistake of deriding Christian rites. Baptism seemed especially ridiculous, but Christians cherished legends of actors who found that their mock baptism was real and were martyred rather than renounce their new faith. The Byzantine empress Theodosia had been a mime but of course had given up her wicked life when she became the consort of a Christian emperor. Not only in the Middle Ages but for centuries afterward actors were considered vagabonds and outcasts, and both Shakespeare and Molière had to be registered servants of the king in order to have a minimum protection in the law. Drama might have been reborn much earlier had the church not been so bitterly opposed to it.

Soon the empty theatre buildings, too large to be removed, gathered dust or were quarries of pre-cut building stone. A few copies of the plays of Terence were kept by the monks as examples of good colloquial Latin style, but though the monks admired the language they were reluctant to teach from pagan comedies. In the tenth century, Hrosvitha, abbess of Gandersheim, undertook to provide plays with a good Latin style devoted to Christian subjects. Though playable in form, these works may or may not have had an occasional performance in the monasteries; there is no direct evidence. For the modern reader it is amazing that Hrosvitha's Christian subjects, which she thought more suitable for young monks and nuns than Terence's worldly plots, show Christian men going to houses of prostitution to rescue or convert the girls, and an emperor, thinking he is winning a Christian girl's favors, farcically embracing the kitchen pots and pans.

That performances similar to the old Roman mime survived at weddings is indicated by the repeated warnings to priests to leave before the mime performed. Numerous denunciations by churchmen indicate that entertainers persisted in spite of official attack, but they do not tell what kind of performances were given. Especially in northern Europe, honored minstrels recited the deeds of knights and heroes. But from these isolated performers later medieval theatres took only their loose organization, direct address to the audience, and processional forms. The theatre, like the civilization of Greece and Rome, had to die in order to be born again in western Europe.

The invasions left two Christian outposts undamaged: the ancient Christian city of Byzantium or Constantinople, too distant for direct influence, and at the opposite corner of Europe, Ireland. Gradually the Irish monks brought Christianity and primitive art back to Europe.

The half millennium from the fall of Rome to the recovery of the west provided a new motivation that has made western civilization different from all others. A yearning for the ideal, the absolute, became a source of power. Monasteries offered a haven for prayer and contemplation of heaven. The longing for the unchanging world of eternity is expressed in St. Augustine's passionate cry, "How did I burn then, my God, how did I burn to remount from earthly things to Thee." To replace the fallible "eternal city" of Rome, Augustine saw in his mind the infallible "City of God." In the sixth century St. Gregory as Pope instituted a reform of the music of the church that established a universal standard of plainsong or Gregorian chant. When Charlemagne had himself crowned Emperor in 800 A.D. he was doing more than restoring a lost order, he was creating an ideal, a "Holy Roman Empire." The language reforms he instigated separated an ideal changeless Latin, a holy language, from the changing local dialects. Through the rest of the Middle Ages Europeans had two languages: a local worldly language of everyday things and an international sacred language of religion and learning.

THE ROMANESQUE AGE (1000 TO 1250)

By the year 1000 a new political and social organization had evolved in western Europe. When there was no manufacture or trade but only men and land, the farmer would trade himself for land, by *hommage* becoming the *homme* or man of his powerful neighbor, receiving his land as a fief. The neighbor in turn was the man of a higher lord and so part of a complex hierarchical order that was stable because each man inherited with his rank the control of the land and men of his father. This political system, called feudalism, persisted through the second and third periods of the Middle Ages.

In the ninth and tenth centuries, when feudalism was becoming established, all the arts showed the beginnings of new forms, which received further development in the eleventh and twelfth centuries, creating the style known as Romanesque. Architecture broke up the solid walls of the Roman basilica to support the roof on a long row of columns, which, with rounded Romanesque arches, escorted the procession down the nave to the altar. A new form of wall, pierced by brilliant stained-glass windows, made the earlier massive wall obsolete. In the eleventh and twelfth centuries, a new principle of verse, based on rhyme, began to replace classic Latin verse and Anglo-Saxon verse based on alliteration. A new form of music, polyphony, wove several voices together in a form comparable to the stratification of ranks in the feudal hierarchy. Polyphonic music, with one voice answering another at a different pitch, lent itself very well to a new church drama. The new music and new drama both received a rich development in the eleventh and twelfth centuries.

THE GOTHIC AGE (1250 TO 1550)

The third phase, from the middle of the thirteenth century to the middle of the sixteenth, grew out of the second as naturally as the pointed Gothic arch derived from the rounded Romanesque. Yet there were major shifts in emphasis. Not only were the Gothic cathedrals much higher than the Romanesque, but sculpture, stained glass, and painting became much more realistic and detailed.

Towns and cities took the lead in new cultural developments. Romanesque Europe had been a rural world with only monastery and castle to break the even landscape. The baker and blacksmith had their shops within the castle, and only gradually did the craftsmen build villages outside the lord's walls. Following the last invasion, that of the Vikings, or Northmen or Normans, in the tenth century, London and Paris grew up as administrative centers where the Normans had been stopped; in 1066 the Normans conquered England and united that country with Normandy and western France. As trade and manufacture revived, the cities became wealthier, and the city hall and guildhall of the Gothic period rivaled palace and cathedral in splendor. By the fifteenth century the new pageant dramas of the bourgeois citizens far outshone the church drama. Cities were never a real part of the feudal system, and in their struggle for independence from the local lord they often found an ally in the king. Hence the merchants, in processions and plays, celebrated their direct devotion to the church and the king.

The impact of the Crusades and the Black Death increased the independence of the towns. When the Turks took Jerusalem in 1070 and advanced within sight of Constantinople, the West was roused by stories of persecution and desecration to a series of Crusades, and the feudal lords found a new role as protectors of Christian Europe. By trading more civic independence to the merchants and bankers in return for supplies, the Crusaders unintentionally strengthened the power of the cities and the trading class.

In 1348 the Black Death, a virulent epidemic of bubonic plague, swept over Europe, killing a third to a half of the population. For three centuries recurrences were frequent. The effect both on the mood of the people and on practical affairs was enormous. Laborers who survived found that they could break their feudal ties, leave their fiefs, and even become free men in town or city. The presence of disease, death, and uncertainty deepened the strain of the grotesque and macabre that was already present in the medieval imagination. It is not surprising that medieval comedy passed on to the Elizabethan drama demonic notes very different from the tone of Greek and Roman comedy. Add to the deep emotional disturbance the political disorder of a fourteenth century that saw two competing popes, one in Rome and one in Avignon, two emperors in Germany, a raging feud in Florence, and dynastic wars in France and England, and we understand the weakening of respect for feudal authority and the increasing taste for satire.

More important than social and economic changes was the change that had taken place in philosophy since the beginning of church drama. The basic philosophy of the early Middle Ages had been what was called "Realism"—the belief that the only real things were the timeless ideas of God and that the visible world was only a shadow of ideal reality, a belief that coincides with what is known as Platonic idealism. But in the fourteenth and fifteenth centuries the prevailing philosophy, called "Nominalism," held that the visible particularities of the world are real and that general ideas were only names. Nominalism laid the basis for a very different kind of religious theatre.

In all aspects of art we can see the new emphasis on the individual in a particular local setting. One example is the use of the vernacular in poetry and drama. In the closing years of the thirteenth century Dante decided to write his *La Vita Nuova* not in Latin but in the spoken language of the Italian people. Chaucer used the English language rather than the French of the court or the Latin of the learned world. He was a man of the new cities, holding a city position. His Canterbury pilgrims are, for the most part, not concerned with divine abstractions but deeply absorbed in the world around them. In the fourteenth century the Italian painter Giotto placed his saints not against an eternal background of gold but in particular Tuscan towns, where they even mix with common men of the streets and beggars on crutches. In Strasbourg Cathedral the sculptor carved his *Foolish Virgins* not in a timeless row of separate statues in Romanesque arches but interrelated in a scene, like actors in a play. Even musicians were learning to give older forms a worldly animation. They delighted in adding to a Latin religious song one or several other voices singing a poem of love or spring in the popular language to a lively melody. A papal bull of 1324 attacked such music. Whereas church drama had centered in the joyful miracles of the Nativity and the Resurrection, the Gothic cycles of mystery plays added the terrifying subjects of the Fall, the Crucifixion, and Doomsday and showed the martyrdom of the saints in gruesome detail.

A new religious impulse in the Gothic period brought another change. Monasteries of the early Middle Ages had become rich as their worldly activities had increased. In the thirteenth century St. Francis gave religion a new direction, calling for poverty but not for withdrawal from active life. His followers, the several orders of Friars, built their institutions in towns and devoted themselves to the sick, the poor, and the sinful. They begged on the streets and developed a vivid style of public preaching on street corners and at crossroads, with satiric descriptions of worldly sins.

Church architecture and decoration showed significant change. Cathedrals became even higher and more magnificent, trying to match the infinite reach of God. In the thirteenth and fourteenth centuries, as Henry Adams points out in *Mont St. Michel and Chartres*, the churches were filled with hundreds of diverse figures, saints mingling with scenes of daily life and with portraits and heraldic shields of donors.

Gothic churches expressed the highest aspirations man has ever put into his art, flinging their thin piers of stone toward the heavens so dangerously high that some of the buildings collapsed even before they were finished. According to Henry Adams, the broken arch expressed man's finite idea of space; the spire pointed to unity beyond space; the thrust of the vaults told of the unsatisfied effort of man to rival the energy, intelligence, and purpose of God. Such a twelfth–thirteenth-century cathedral as Chartres expresses the power and charm of Mary the Queen of Heaven, and Christ appears as a triumphant hope. But in the very late Gothic parts of the cathedral fear and terror appear, with Christ as the stern Doomsday judge and sharp-clawed devils dragging souls to the tortures of hell.

The philosophical scheme of Thomas Aquinas in the thirteenth century demonstrated the unity of the universe by creating a balance between time and eternity, body and soul, visible substance and abstract form, particular instance and undifferentiated deity—a balance as daring as the balance of thrust and weight in a Gothic cathedral. Without losing that balance the thirteenth-century cathedral achieved unity out of extreme complexity: its countless columns, arches, piers, towers, vaults; its combination of stone and glass; its thousands of figures in sculpture, glass, and living actors. The unity in design derived from unity of meaning: the salvation of man through the Incarnation and the Resurrection. That meaning was present in the architect's ground plan of the cross, in the ambulatory procession around the altar, in every figure of stone or glass. The thirteenth century achieved a difficult balance between Realism and Nominalism, between the divine soul and worldly detail.

MEDIEVAL THEATRES IN THE CLASS STRUCTURE

Except for the dramatized banquets and masked balls of the nobility, where the space of the palace hall was limited, medieval dramas were presented for the widest possible public and without charge. They celebrated the united devotion of all classes—villagers, churchmen, merchants, nobility—to a common political and social order. The villagers made a cermonial visit to the manor house at Christmas time to bring a blessing on the lord's house and performed carols and morris, or sword dances, and a mummers play about St. George and his battle with a Turkish knight. In a similar public spirit, the monks, and later the parish priests, offered to nobility and townsmen dramatizations of their most sacred services, those in celebration of the Resurrection, the Nativity, and the acts of the saints. The merchants of the Gothic cities made one contribution to the social order by showing their devotion to the church at the regular Midsummer Fair, when they produced and paid for religious processions and long cycles of religious plays. The other occasion dramatized by the city merchants was the official visit of a new king or bishop. The nobility dramatized both a private occasion, the banquet or masked ball, and a public occasion, the tournament. Morality plays, as dramatizations of the sermons of the parsons and preaching friars and the lessons of the new humanist schoolteachers, partly fit into this analysis by class. Each of the seven types of theatre was shaped to serve the special festival occasion of the class that produced it, and to serve as a pledge of loyalty to the commonweal.

MEDIEVAL COMEDY

Christianity and the ideal of chivalry led to forms of comedy in western Europe that differ considerably from the satire of Aristophanes or the harsh laughter of Plautus. In Christian Europe even farce is more gentle. While village entertainment in the Middle Ages, as in all ages, was mostly comic, upper-class entertainment included comedy as a subordinate though integral part of serious theatre. Indeed the classic distinction between comedy and tragedy was lost, and Dante called his long serious poem *The Divine Comedy* (1308–1321) because it ended happily in paradise.

Besides the comedy of simple joy, we can find four distinct kinds of comedy in religious drama, indicated delicately in church drama but given vigorous expression in the vernacular drama of the outdoor productions of the merchants. The most elemental kind is the comic deflation of evil. When proud Lucifer tries to climb on God's throne, God sends him tumbling in comic confusion, cackling and wailing. A second kind of comic scene isolates the good in the midst of the evil of the unredeemed world. Grotesque and demonic are the mocking torturers who, like a squad of cruel bullies, torture Christ.

The most distinctive kind of medieval comedy might be called the benediction of the lowly. It invites laughter at humble men—Noah, Joseph, the Shepherds—for their amazement and incredulity when confronted with the divine, but they become humble attendants in the service of the Lord. The burlesque of the sacred service, a boy bishop taking charge and the choir ending each verse with the braying of an ass, was justified not only as a commemoration of the humble Child and ass of the Flight to Egypt but as an example of the idea borrowed from the Psalms for the Magnificat of the Mass: "They have brought low the mighty and exalted the humble." A half century ago the only episode in medieval drama that impressed critics was the *Second Shepherds' Play* (14th century) of the Towneley cycle of mystery plays. The episode of the Shepherds' discovery of the stolen sheep hidden in the cradle of Mak's newborn child pleased them as realism and good plotting. But today we see the episode as a variant of the discovery of the

Christ Child in his cradle and as another example of the forgiveness and benediction of the humble.

Another kind of comedy was provided by the fool or jester essential to every medieval and Renaissance court, bringing childlike innocence as well as sophisticated skepticism to an aristocratic society. Close to the King who symbolized the central order, the fool was an amusing reminder of the disorder of the periphery as well as a startling reminder of other orders beyond the border of the realm and the borders of agreed-on sanity. In all forms of drama, dialogue was secondary to self-introductions, explanatory speeches, poems, and orations.

Medieval space was defined by the procession as it moved from one place to another. Hence space and scene were related as on an illustrated map, each place indicated by a miniature but complete mountain, castle, or city, and each scene separated from the next by a foreshortened road or empty space. This undefined playing area, called *platea* or place, remained basic in medieval performance. When a located scene was established the character could identify himself with the scene, start from it or come out of it, and move into the wider platea to meet characters from other scenes. The illustrated map came to life by the use of a simultaneous or multiple setting, that is, a setting with several separate scenic units visible at the same time. The word "mansion" is used to indicate any medieval scenic unit, whether a miniature house, castle, gate, or archway. Only in the late Middle Ages and early Renaissance did the processional, simultaneous combination of miniature mansions connected by undefined acting space give way to larger scenic forms.

Medieval costuming was primarily a partial adaptation of contemporary costume. In *A Midsummer Night's Dream* Shakespeare is exaggerating for satire, but Bottom and his crew see costumes and properties in the medieval way, as adaptations of available materials, with an emblematic costume of lime and stone to indicate wall, and the actor clearly recognized inside the partial disguise of Pyramus and Lion.

The Mummers Play of the Villagers:
A Christmas Blessing on the House

The village St. George plays, like carols and morris and sword dances, were the gift the villagers brought to the lord of the manor at Christmas, a pledge of loyalty, a blessing on the house. The mummers invited themselves into the nobleman's party, and the lord was expected to offer cakes and ale or beer, not "small beer" either, as their playful song insisted, but his best. When their visit ended, the mummers made a collection of money for their own celebration.

Since the earliest extant examples of the mummers play were first written down in the nineteenth and twentieth centuries, we can only surmise that the drama took form in the time of the Crusades. The central event is a combat between St. George (or King George) and the Turkish Knight in which one is killed and then resurrected by a comic doctor. By the late Middle Ages the popular imagination had settled on seven champions of Christendom, of whom St. George of England, St. Denis of France, and St. Patrick of Ireland are most familiar to us, and several or all seven might take part in the challenge and combat. Other favorites were Bold Slasher and the Black Prince of Paradise, but over the centuries many other figures crowded in: Cromwell, George IV, who challenged "you American dog," and Bonaparte, "just come from Thumberloo." The comic doctor who brings the knight back to life may be a clownish descendant of a priest who presided over a pagan spring rite of combat, death, and resurrection. If that conjecture is correct, the St. George play is the oldest drama of Europe, with annual performance for more than 1500 years. St. George lost his dragon long ago, but some lines of Bold Slasher may indicate that the earlier opponent had the metal head and body of a dragon. It is tempting to guess that we have the relics of a very primitive theatre.

The mummers play had many self-introductions and monologues and very little dramatic dialogue and action. There was not even a set cast. As long as there were two champions to fight each other and a doctor to bring the slain to life again, the cast could be enlarged or diminished as a larger or smaller number of performers wanted to play. Yet most of the mummers plays show three distinct parts and some order and sequence in each part.

First comes the Entry or presentation. The presenter is often Old Father Christmas, but sometimes the fool or clown or simply Number One. The presenter or

Miniatures from *Roman de Fauvel* depicting two scenes of medieval mumming and disguising. *Phot. Bibl. Nat. Paris.*

his clown may have a broom to clear a space for the play. Sometimes all the players troop in for a promenade before the presenter calls on each one to introduce himself. The middle part is the real drama: the combat and revival, the champions introducing themselves with high-sounding "vaunts." This is not dialogue but a competition, both characters playing to the audience. After either the Christian knight or the Turk is killed, Old Father Christmas or another knight laments, "You have killed my only son," and calls for a doctor. The doctor, asked for his qualifications, brags of his travels and his cures: "Italy, pittaly, France and Spain. Into the pantry and back again." The doctor rides a hobby horse or a stick horse with a carved head. There may be a full dramatic episode as the doctor's saucy boy, Jack Finney, refuses to obey orders and has to be threatened. But this is repetition of formula rather than true dramatic dialogue. The cure may be a pill or a magic elixir or a mock operation or pulling a six-inch tooth. If the extraction seems difficult, the doctor asks Jack Finney to get him a good horse or the best man on his team. Jack brings forward one of the players or someone from the audience, but the doctor wants another helper, and so on until a half dozen people are lined up to help the doctor pull. As a long strand of sausage is extracted from the slain man, the doctor and his helpers fall. The players laugh at themselves and there is a large element of spontaneity and audience participation.

The third part of the play was the *quête* or collection of money, with a new set of characters to introduce themselves. Typical here is the dumb boy: "In come I that haven't come yet, with my big head and my little wit." Here also is Old Beelzebub, or Old Hind-Before, a specialist in topsy-turvydom who beats a clapper on a tub to drum up contributions, while he recites his gallimaufry of surrealist images: "I saw a great big, little bitty red house all painted green. . . . I knocked on the door and the maid fell out. I saw a bark and he dogged at me."

Little as is known about the mummers play, it is clear that it left its mark on later, more sophisticated drama.

Church Drama:
The Feast Days of the Church

If the village mummers play in some pagan form may have been older, the drama of the Christian church was the first new dramatic form of western Europe.

The church drama began about 900 A.D. in the midst of the creative activity that followed the "Carolingian renaissance" (Charlemagne's time) and lasted until the greater Renaissance in the sixteenth century. Like the Egyptian drama, it celebrated the coming of deity into the world and the triumph of eternal life over death. It began not with gods but with human beings making the joyful discovery of the marvels of the Nativity and the Resurrection.

The Christian church was the special path to salvation, a gateway between the world and eternal life. At times of procession the sacred images were brought out of the sanctuary and carried around the town, but more important were the daily services as the priests, the choir, and the whole congregation made a procession down the long nave, symbol of this world, to the chancel, symbol of eternal life. In the chancel the procession was met by the priest at the altar. While primarily a communion table for the reenactment of the Last Supper, the altar became a symbol of the Crucifixion, of Christ's sacrifice and the gift of his body and blood. It was usually built over the grave or relic of a saint and hence was also a sepulchre, and as the symbol of the sepulchre of Christ it was the center of the first church drama.

For the first thousand years of Christianity the priest stood behind the altar facing the congregation, but at the period we are describing the relationship was changed and the priest became a transitional figure, facing the same way as the congregation, representing them as he took his communion. While early Christianity had had considerable conflict over the use of images, those who loved pictures and statues had won out by the Romanesque period, and the backing of the altar, the *reredos*, was covered with paintings or carvings connected with the Crucifixion. At the archway separating the nave from the chancel were symbols of Doomsday, and in the later Middle Ages an elaborate choir screen, called the *rood* screen, was placed here with open arches for processions to pass through. The screen often supported a loft for a heavenly choir, and high above it was suspended a statue of Christ on the cross, with Mary and John below him. Priests could imagine themselves as the Marys discovering the empty tomb or as the

Miniature of the Annunciation from the *Passione* of Marcade.

214

shepherds bringing gifts to the crèche and the newborn child. It was just a step from symbolic commemoration to drama.

DRAMATIC ELEMENTS IN THE LITURGICAL YEAR

Those who think that only under rare conditions is drama invented look for influence from outside the church. But many authorities argue very convincingly that the church service already contained the elements of drama in dialogue, antiphonal response, impersonation, and symbolic representation a sacred history.

The liturgical year organized man's salvation in a great rhythmic sequence, punctuated by many saints' days and building up through two long periods of fast, Advent and Lent, to the triumphant feasts of the Nativity and the Resurrection. Beginning with the Nativity, the twelve days of Christmas commemorated the Flight to Egypt and the Slaughter of the Innocents, as well as the joyful adoration of shepherds and kings. Holy Week commemorated the events from the triumphal re-entry of Christ into Jerusalem on Palm Sunday to the Last Supper on Thursday, the Crucifixion on Good Friday, and the discovery of the empty tomb on Easter morning. As early as the time of Pope Gregory the Great in the sixth century, the church prepared for Easter by interpreting the seven Sundays before Holy Week, beginning with Septuagesima Sunday, as symbolic not only of the seven days of creation but of the seven ages of the world. A different age was emphasized each Sunday in the reading and lessons, beginning with the creation of the world and the fall of Adam and proceeding to the ages of Noah, Abraham, Moses, David, and on to Christ. In Advent the lessons emphasized the conflict between Christ and Antichrist and the Last Judgment or Doomsday. Through a great proliferation of art in the Romanesque age, this history was depicted lavishly in mosaics, carvings, stained glass, and paintings. The time was ripe to bring the mosaics and statues to life. Christians coming before the symbolic sepulchre of Christ were now met by living angels who told them to announce the Resurrection to the world and to lead the choir in the *Te Deum laudamus*.

Even before the Romanesque age many elements in the liturgy were semi-dramatic. From early centuries Palm Sunday had been marked by a processional reenactment of the triumphal re-entry into Jerusalem, and in many western European churches a wooden donkey with a wooden figure of Christ was rolled on wheels to lead the procession. At a dramatic moment in the service of Pentecost, when the account of the gathering of the apostles was read, a dove was let down by a cord from the top of the church to symbolize the descent of the Holy Spirit. When a new church was dedicated, an element of drama was introduced in the act of driving out the Devil. As the procession of priests headed by the bishop approached the closed front doors from the outside, they recited the lines from the

215

psalm "Lift up the gates," and they were answered from within by a priest who expressed the Devil's defiance with the challenge "Who is the King of Glory?" As the doors were opened, the cleric speaking for the Devil escaped by the rear door. Many of the psalms were recited antiphonally with question and answer, statement and response, and the practice was extended to many other parts of the service, two priests taking verses alternately or one, two, or four "cantors" being answered antiphonally by the choir.

In the ninth and tenth centuries Amalarius of Metz had great influence in extending the element of symbolism. His *Liber Officialis* demanded very full role-playing in the imagination and in the action of both the ministrants and the congregation. Some of his interpretations involved abstract symbolism, as when he stated that the mixing of the wine and water should bring to mind not only the Incarnation and Crucifixion but the union of Christ with the people. At times the symbolism went even further toward drama. When the priest represented Christ praying in the Garden of Olives, the deacons were to stand apart representing the disciples asleep. At the moment commemorating Christ on the cross, the subdeacons, representing the women who stayed with him, were to stand with heads bowed, but at the moment when Christ was dead and they knew that his enemies could do no more, they were to lift their heads as though in adoration. The last elevation of the Host meant to Amalarius not the Crucifixion but the Deposition and Entombment, and he states that the archdeacon must represent Joseph, while the subdeacons were to represent the Marys who bring ointments to the altar as the tomb. Critics complained that since a passage in the Offertory had been interpreted by Amalarius as a reference to Job oppressed by sickness, the celebrant repeated the lines in the manner of one who is sick. Others complained of singing suggestive of feminine voices, of sighs, sudden dramatic silences, vocal imitations of the agonies of the suffering and the dying, and of priests who "contort the whole body with histrionic gestures." One attacked "theatrical mannerisms and stage music" due to the bad influence of Amalarius.

Good Friday became especially dramatic. The cross, with its image of the body of Christ, was carried in a funeral procession and placed in a sepulchre. Often the cross contained, in a receptacle, a Host that had been presanctified. Clearly the participants thought of themselves as adoring and burying the actual body of Christ. The Mass of the Easter Vigil, an important service in early Christian centuries, had several symbolic enactments of the Resurrection. Throughout the Middle Ages the Easter Mass was the time for the baptism of adults, and the baptismal font, usually in a separate building, or baptistery, as at Florence, was a symbol of the tomb. On Saturday of Holy Week a large Paschal candle, symbol of Christ's body, was carried in procession to the font, and its light was extinguished by immersion in the water. At Vespers, as those to be baptized came to the altar in the church, the archdeacon began a chant, "Jesus whom you seek is not here; he has risen. . . . Remember what he said to you in Galilee." Then they filed out of the church as though searching for Christ. As they came to the font in the Baptistery, a second deacon invited them to "come and see the place where Christ was placed." They joined in an anthem of praise, and the deacon dismissed them with the words from the Gospel, "Go quickly. Announce to the disciples that the Lord is risen." At the Vigil Mass at midnight, baptism became a symbol of death, burial, and resurrection, each person emerging from the water as a newborn child from Christ's tomb. As the Crucifixion had been marked by the extinction of lights, the Resurrection was marked by the relighting or sudden uncovering of lights.

THE TWO *QUEM QUAERITIS*:
DRAMAS OF EASTER AND CHRISTMAS

In the ninth century new responses and antiphone and lyric passages known as tropes were added to the liturgy. Tropes were used for three important Easter services: the Depositio, the Elevatio, and the Visitatio. We have already noted the Deposition, the procession bearing the cross and putting it into a place prepared on the altar as a sepulchre. Since no one in Palestine saw the actual escape from the tomb, the Elevatio was not developed liturgically, the priests silently taking the buried cross from the sepulchre. But the Visitatio, the full realization of the Resurrection, produced more dramatic action.

More than a dozen examples of the short Visitatio play can be dated from the tenth century, and it is believed to have developed in the ninth century. In all, more than four hundred examples have been collected dating from the tenth to the sixteenth century, indicating that, with slight variations, it was played all over Europe for six centuries, long after more elaborate plays in Latin had been created at particular churches and long after the outdoor cycles of religious plays had reached their spectacular development.

The *Quem Quaeritis* is a short introduction to one of several anthems that express the joy of the Resurrection. In order to increase the sense of participation in that joy, three priests placed cloths over their heads and became the three Marys who discovered the empty sepulchre. Dialogue between the angels at the tomb and the Marys was follows:

> Quem quaeritis in sepulchre, o Christicole?
> Ihesum Nazareum crucifixum, o Celicole.
> Non est hic, surrexit sicut ipse dixit; ite
> > Nunciate quia surrexit.

Karl Young, who crowned a life's work with a full edition of the hundreds of examples of medieval church drama, undertook to trace the steps by which this little drama was developed, hoping to find a continuous evolution from the simple to the complex. His earliest example is from a tenth-century manuscript in the monastery of St. Gall in Switzerland, where the play is attached to the Introit (opening) of the Mass of Easter morning. St. Gall was a center of new developments in music and poetry, and the monk Tutilo, a poet and musician, wrote many tropes. He cannot be credited with the first church drama, however, since there is also an excellent tenth-century example from St. Martial of Limoges. The later examples show the *Quem Quaeritis* as part not of the Easter Mass but of Easter matins. A detailed description of the performance at matins is given in the *Regularis Concordia*, or "summary of rules," written in the tenth century at Winchester by St. Ethelwold for the guidance of Benedictine monasteries in England. The celebration of the joy of the Resurrection is preceded by chanted responses and sung anthems and leads up to either the processional *Resurrexi, et adhuc tecum sum* of the Introit or the joyous anthem *Te Deum laudamus*. In a frequent variant of this brief drama, the Marys meet the disciples Peter and John, who race to the tomb, and then they, instead of the Marys, turn to announce the happy discovery and the two or all five lead the choir in the *Te Deum*. The race of Peter and John introduced a note of comedy. When the Marys stopped at the counter of the spice merchant, a new character was introduced at the margin of the miraculous events who was later to provide more comedy by his trading and bragging.

In the same form as the Easter play, a little Christmas play was developed about the shepherds' visit to the manger. In some churches, in the Christmas Mass or more frequently at the end of matins, the midwives who in medieval lore attended on Mary said, "Quem quaeritis in praesepe, Pastores, dicite?" The shepherds answered as the Marys did at Easter and were told to go to announce the happy news; then they led the choir in the anthem *Puer natus est*. The earlier versions indicate not living actors for Mary and Joseph but the same kind of cloth and wood or plaster figures that have been popular for Nativity crèches from early Christian times to the present. Not until the twelfth century, when the altar had an elaborate reredos and the priests said the Mass with their backs to the congregation, were the people given several levels of representation: a choir singing for the congregation, priests performing a symbolic ritual based on past events, and priests acting the roles not only of the Marys and shepherds but of the holy characters as well.

The Christmas plays were expanded more than the Easter plays. In various combinations the group of plays contained the Annunciation, the Visitation with Elizabeth, the Nativity, and Adoration of the Shepherds and of the Kings, the Raging of Herod, the Flight to Egypt, and the Slaughter of the Innocents. Sometimes a single episode was dramatized for the particular day when its subject was celebrated—the coming of the Magi on Epiphany, for instance, when the priest-actors brought offerings to the altar and while still dressed as Magi performed the rest of the ceremony and led the choir in the anthem.

218

Besides the Easter and Christmas plays, a series of Old Testament plays developed in the church. Some were given during the weeks between Epiphany and Easter, when the seven ages of the patriarchs were the subject of the readings for each day. Closely related to the liturgy are plays about Adam's expulsion

The Three Marys at the Sepulchre. Twelfth-century manuscript from the St. Gall *Liber Responsalis*. *Courtesy the Stiftsbibliothek, St. Gallen.*

219

Block print from *Le Mystere du viel Testament* depicting the creation of Adam and Eve. *Phot. Bibl. Nat. Paris.*

from Paradise and about Cain and Abel. Other Old Testament plays grew up in connection with the Processions of Prophets that formed part of the Christmas series. On matins of Christmas day it was customary to read a sermon in which a preacher quotes to the Jews the testimony of a series of prophets who had predicted Christ, mostly from the Old Testament but including Virgil and the Sybil, who had brought prophetic books to Rome. The sermon could be dramatized by having each Prophet come forward when he was called and speak his own prophecy. The next step was to make a little drama for some of the prophets, and there are examples that present the subjects of Simeon and the Child Jesus, of Balaam riding the ass which stopped at the sight of an angel, and of Nebuchadnezzar, who saw in the fiery furnace the fourth figure "like the son of God."

From the beginning, church drama was processional, and the processional form continued throughout the Middle Ages and had a great influence on the Elizabethan stage. The Marys were first seen in an unlocalized place on their way to the tomb. At first the regular altar was used as the tomb, but the Easter services were so important that in a number of churches an Easter sepulchre was built north of the main altar. When the Marys stopped to buy unguents, another altar or a counter was needed, and the pattern of simultaneous staging was established, with two separate mansions for particular places shown simultaneously and not far apart in the church, though they represented localities not in sight of each other, and a neutral *platea*, or playing place, not necessarily connected with any locality. For the Christmas *Quem Quaeritis* the shepherds were in the open, not requiring a structure for a mansion, while the crèche was shown on the altar or near it. Some high place in the church, a pulpit or the clerestory above the lower arches, would serve for the angels. On the rood screen, besides the figure of Christ on the cross, was a gallery for a heavenly choir. For Herod's throne one of the imposing seats of the church was used.

LONGER PLAYS IN THE LITURGICAL TRADITION

Besides the standard short church dramas regularly performed as part of the liturgical year, monastic libraries have a number of longer plays that were apparently written for unique special occasions. Some scholars tried to find in these longer plays a gradual transition from short Latin church drama to the long vernacular outdoor cycles that in the fifteenth and sixteenth centuries might last many days. But there are complex and subtle plays in the vernacular in the twelfth century and traditional plays in Latin in the sixteenth, and there is no discoverable sequence from chancel plays to plays that used the nave, plays at the front porch, or plays in the open square. Certainly the drama did not move out of the church either gradually or suddenly.

The longer plays show the skill of the dramatist in using processional movement, pantomime, and song to create lyric and dramatic intensities quite different
from realism. One of the most vivid plays is the *Mystère d'Adam*, performed with
a few raised platforms against the porch of the church. Most of the speeches are
in a Norman French of either Normandy or England, yet the play was written in
the twelfth century and used the choir and the regular liturgical sequences for
Septuagesima Sunday. That Sunday, seven weeks before Easter, was the time to
commemorate the First Age, the Creation, and the Fall of Adam.

The *Mystère d'Adam* is interesting for the psychological pictures of Eve, Adam,
and the Serpent, for the conventions of the simultaneous stage, and for the techniques of pantomime and dialogue. The actor representing God, called the *Figura*,
arrives and departs by the church door. At least three separate mansions or playing areas were provided for the *Mystère d'Adam*: Paradise on the highest platform, a
neutral area or platea, and Hell. The description of paradise in E. K. Chambers'
translation reads:

A Paradise is to be made in a raised spot, with curtains and cloths of silk hung round it at
such a height that persons in the Paradise may be visible from the shoulders upwards.
Fragrant flowers and leaves are to be set round about, and divers trees put therein with
hanging fruit, so as to give the likeness of a most delicate spot.

Next comes a description of the costumes, and the author as director indicates just
how he wants his inexperienced actors to be trained. The episodes with speeches
are brief, but the group pantomime is extensive, amounting almost to a ballet:
"The demons are to run about the stage with suitable gestures, approaching the
Paradise from time to time and pointing out the forbidden fruit to Eve, as though
persuading her to eat it."

When the Devil is discouraged in tempting Adam, he returns to hell for a conference; then after making a sally into the audience he approaches paradise on
Eve's side and tries his insinuating manner on her. When Adam and Eve are driven
out of paradise they till the soil and sow corn. While they rest in sorrow the devils
plant thorns and thistles, until the devils are dragged off to hell in chains and
fetters to the clatter of pots and kettles.

Henry Adams uses the Eve of the play, along with Eleanor of Aquitaine, as an
example of the increasing power in the twelfth century of enterprising, intelligent
women. The serpent recognizes that Adam is an oaf beside this charming woman.

Also from the twelfth century an *Antichrist*, known in a manuscript from Tegern-
see in Germany, stands out from the routine church drama by the debate between
the Church and Heathendom and Jewry and by its indirect reflection of the conflicts at the court of the Emperor of Germany. The church drama was rarely so
political. In the thirteenth-century manuscript that contains the famous collection
of Latin lyrics on life, love, and spring called the *Carmina Burana* is a long play
about Christ's suffering and death, probably produced at the Benedictbeuern mon-

astery. How elaborate symbolism and lyric passages can transform an ordinary church drama of Christmas time is shown in the *Slaughter of the Innocents* of a thirteenth-century manuscript from the monastery of St. Benoit-sur-Loire at Fleury. Mary H. Marshall gives a careful analysis of this complex play. The episodes of Herod's Wrath and the Flight into Egypt are interwoven with an elaborate singing procession of the Lamb in which the children to be slain are equated with the army of virgin saints about the throne of the Lamb in the Apocalypse. Herod orders the singing children to be killed, and Rachel and the other mothers express their grief in song. An angel from above calls on the children to arise, and they sing anthems welcoming the return of the Holy Family from Egypt, ending with the *Te Deum*.

The study of medieval church drama changed radically in the 1950s and 1960s with the revival of the Christmas plays *The Play of Herod* from St. Benoit-sur-Loire at Fleury and *The Play of Daniel* from Beauvais. *The Play of Daniel* gets its greatest excitement from processions, choruses, and set speeches. The expository introduction is presented by a chorus of Princes. The arrival of the King is celebrated by a spectacular procession of the Satraps parading the rich vessels brought to Babylon from conquered Jerusalem. A group of Astrologers chant together but fail to explain the handwriting on the wall. Processions of the Queen and of the Princes bring on Daniel. As one King is dethroned, another great procession brings on the new King, Darius. The praise of Daniel leads to a procession to celebrate Christmas, as the King seats Daniel on a throne of honor. The jealous Advisors find a decree that Daniel has violated and have him thrown into the lions' den. The Angel rescues him and restores him to his place of honor just in time for him to predict the birth of Christ and for an Angel to appear to announce that Christ is indeed born. The choir sings the *Te Deum*.

These plays and a dozen others written for special occasions are church dramas because they were usually written by clerics and played by clerics or students, using church choirs and passages from the Latin liturgy. Many are in Latin, sometimes with speeches in the vernacular. Some are entirely sung, and others are a mixture of liturgical song and speech. Many seem to have been performed in churches or in a churchyard or the classroom or refectory of a monastery. They expanded the scope of the church drama far beyond the dignified if joyous annual liturgical plays the priests expected to put on.

The Religious Cycles
of the Merchant Guilds

By the fourteenth century, interest for the theatre historian shifts from the church to the streets, where the cycles of religious plays (called mystery plays) and the royal entries, celebrating the visit of a ruler to a city or town, were developing. These new forms of drama, both sponsored by the rising guilds of merchants and craftsmen under the "city corporation," used the same stories, characters, and doctrine of salvation developed in the church. But the new outdoor drama owed more in subject matter to the non-dramatic versions of sacred story than to the liturgical drama, and its patterns of production derived from outdoor sacred processions. It was a new form of theatre, spoken, not sung or chanted, in the vernacular. Though it might be written by a cleric, it was produced by the merchants, not the clergy, for a different occasion and audience and it was presented differently. It expressed the devotion of the city to God and His church and provided religious sanction for the merchant guilds.

FROM MIDSUMMER PROCESSION TO MYSTERY CYCLE

At some time in the summer almost every city of Europe, and even many small towns, held a festival that combined a trading fair and a religious procession. The

Six Pageant wagons from Louvan: Appearance of the Virgin, Assumption of the Virgin, Nine Choirs of Angels, Expulsion from Paradise, Tree of Jesse, Nativity. *Illustration by Martha Sutherland.*

Expulsion from Paradise   Tree of Jesse   Nativity

224

procession was expanded in some cities and towns to include a cycle of mystery plays. The merchant guilds hired carpenters, sculptors, and painters to prepare floats and pageant wagons, and clerics, directors, actors, and backstage specialists to add drama, either along the way or in the great square when the procession was over.

Many citizens made money feeding and housing the crowd that gathered for three days or a week or sometimes several weeks. The merchants sold their goods to the farmers, village storekeepers came to do their major buying for the year, and peddlers and craftsmen brought goods from afar. There was incidental entertainment by street singers, jugglers, acrobats, clowns, dancers, fire-eaters, and keepers of trained dogs or goats. There were quacks, palmers, pilgrims, gypsies, Jews, beggars, and mountebanks, for many kinds of people were on the roads in the late Middle Ages. Some were wandering scholars, expecting later to go into orders but traveling from one university to another in search of a congenial lecturer and begging here and working there.

In England, Beverly produced the procession and mystery plays on St. Mark's Day, and Lincoln on St. Anne's Day, while Woodkirk chose the Feast of the Assumption in August. At Louvain in France the great fair and procession took place on the first Sunday in September, near the birthday of the Virgin, and the procession was organized around her. The city and church officials led, accompanied by torches and musicians. Then came the sacred image of the Virgin taken from her chapel in the cathedral. Later came not the usual prophets of Christ but, walking or on horseback, thirty-four women of the Old Testament, each wearing some symbol of a particular quality of the Virgin and carrying a banderole with the name of the quality or a characteristic quotation. Beautiful illustrations of this procession have been preserved, telling much of what we know of the appearance of "pageant wagons" that carried the figures and scenes. They show elaborate architectural canopies framing tableaux of the Garden of Eden, the Annunciation, the Presentation in the Temple, the Nativity, the Resurrection, Pentecost, the Assumption, and the Nine Choirs of Angels. Chester had several festivals. Its midsummer fair and show was on St. John's Day, June 24, and its cycle of mystery

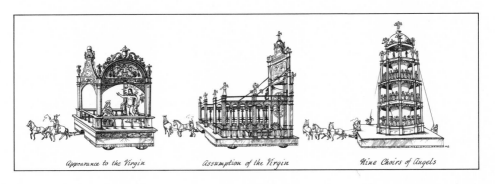

Appearance to the Virgin   Assumption of the Virgin   Nine Choirs of Angels

plays at Whitsuntide, the week beginning with Whitsunday, the seventh Sunday after Easter. But from the fourteenth century the favorite occasion for a procession was Corpus Christi, the Thursday after the eighth Sunday after Easter, and Corpus Christi was the most important day for the great cycles of plays.

A new festival in the Middle Ages, Corpus Christi gradually became the focus of the religious devotion of the rising merchant class. Following a revelation of Sister Juliana of Liege, the Pope in 1204 gave endorsement for a procession to carry the Holy Eucharist, symbol of Christ's body and hence of salvation, through the streets, stopping at various stations to bless the houses, fields, and people. The original procession was not dramatic, but since the Eucharist was a symbol of the whole scheme of salvation and the prayers and readings covered the events already long illustrated in church sculpture, stained glass, and liturgical drama, the procession soon became a moving picture book of scenic emblems, pageant wagons, and actors representing the characters of sacred history. The procession was a splendid show and whetted the interest of the audience in a drama to be performed in a large field or public square later that day or the following day. For the elaborate procession on St. John's Day at Florence the *edifizii* were carried in the procession and set down finally in the Piazza della Signoria, where a cycle of plays was presented that covered sacred history from the Fall of Lucifer to the Last Judgment.

Words could be added during the procession. For the Procession of the Holy Blood which still occurs at Bruges, short phrases are repeated every block of two. The York cycle of mystery plays is the classic example of the complete integration

Devout carrying the figure of the Madonna. Detail from a drawing of the Louvain Procession of Our Lady, c. 1594. *Courtesy Harvard College Library.*

of procession and drama, with forty-eight or more wagons moving through the streets and forty-eight separate plays performed at more than a dozen places around the city. When Queen Margaret watched the cycle at Coventry, it was so dark before the last play that Doomsday could not be performed. Her welcome may have disrupted the schedule, and perhaps in other years the whole cycle was completed in one day. It was formerly thought that the pageant wagon processional was the standard English model, but it is now known that more English cycles were produced in other forms than in the processional pattern.

In any civic procession each guild could carry a coat of arms in tableau or pageant wagon. The Norwich Grocers, for instance, used as their emblem a tree festooned with fruit and spicery. When plays were presented, each pageant wagon was assigned to an appropriate guild. In a procession for Plough Monday, the Mariners and Pilots of Hull carried a ship and presented a play about Noah. In the summer procession at York the Building of the Ark was assigned to the Shipwrights and the Flood to the Fishers and Mariners. The Goldsmiths produced the episode of the Magi, who brought rich gifts in jeweled vessels, and the Bakers, the Last Supper. The Thatchers were given the Nativity, an appropriate assignment since in medieval art a thatched roof was regularly shown over the manger. The Plasterers made the world fresh created, with miniature birds, beasts, fish, and trees, and the Upholsterers built the pageant with a bed to be used in representing the dream of Pilate's wife.

The cycles covered so much material that they were extended to enormous length. The cycle of forty-eight plays at York, performed in a single day, began at four-thirty in the morning. At Chester twenty-five plays were spread over three days. The London cycle lasted three, four, or seven days. The great *Mystère de la Passion* of Arnoul Greban, choirmaster of Notre Dame in Paris, extended to thirty-five thousand verses, required 220 characters, and took four days in performance. In the sixteenth century, cycles were written which required a month to present, but such outsize dramas had only a few performances.

Of the many cycles, very few manuscripts are extant: only four complete cycles from England and several more than that from France, besides a few isolated plays. Two from the Coventry manuscript were published before it was burned in 1879. Two cycles and a rewrite of one of them are preserved in the Cornish language. Of the English manuscripts only two are identified with particular cities, those of Chester and York. The manuscript that belonged to the Towneley family is in the Midland dialect, and scholars guess that it came from the town of Wakefield. Another manuscript is puzzling because it is called *Ludus Coventriae* (c. 1400–1450), which seems to have been a general term for mystery plays, and this manuscript is a compilation of plays from several sources that differ in quality and method of staging. From France long mystery plays by three fifteenth-century writers are extant, as well as a *Mystery of the Old Testament*, a cycle of *Acts of the Apostles*, and an enormous collection of *Miracles of the Virgin*. Classified as cycles of

227

the Gothic cities, also, are several saints' plays and long morality plays: the *Mary Magdalen* (c. 1480–1520) and *The Castle of Perseverance* of England and *L'Omme pecheur*, or *Sinning Mankind*, of France.

Painters were greatly influenced by dramatic performances both in the church and in the streets, but only a few illustrations show exactly what the plays looked like. Curiously enough, there is not a single picture of a pageant wagon from England, where this method of performance was most popular, and we must rely on illustrations of pageant wagons from the continent.

There is no good single term for these great cycles of religious plays. The most frequent Latin term was *representatio*, and from that the Italians derived *rappresentazione*. At the end of the Middle Ages the English most often used the term "miracle play" and the French, *mystère*, from which the English term mystery was derived. Some scholars have tried to restrict the term "mystery play" to biblical plays and to use "miracle play" for the saints' plays, but the distinction is no longer generally accepted. Modern descendants of the medieval religious plays at Oberammergau, Freiburg, and Elche in Spain, and in the Black Hills of South Dakota

Corpus Domini procession in connection with the festival of San Giovanni, Florence. The Saint's relics are carried under a canopy from the duomo to the baptistery, and after a long procession through the city the relics are returned to the duomo. *Courtesy Orville K. Larson.*

228

are called passion plays, though they include more than the scenes of Christ's "passion."

THE SCOPE OF THE MYSTERY CYCLES

The mystery play had the grandest subject any drama has ever had: the salvation of mankind. The entire range of philosophical and religious speculation—the nature of the universe, the forces of good and evil, why suffering is permitted, the path of salvation, and the destiny of man and God—is contained in the cycles.

It is hard to estimate the value of the whole drama. We are put off by the conventional language, the short verses and glib rhymes; we smile at the simple character motivation and the conventions of time and place. We are shocked at the bloody realism of deaths and martyrdoms and amazed at the juxtaposition of piety and comic realism. We are aware of how far the execution falls short of the magnificent subject. But we do not know how the music, the setting, and the pageantry of the procession may have lifted the performance into a higher realm. We do not know to what extent traditions derived from skilled chanting, and movement in the church may have enabled local people to rise to powerful stylized acting. Of the three great artistic embodiments of the medieval vision of human salvation—the Gothic cathedrals, *The Divine Comedy,* and the mysteries—we rank the plays as inferior to the other two, but in performance the drama may have been no less impressive than the cathedrals or the poem.

The many incidents of the mystery cycles may be divided into five or six main sections. God creates the world and Adam and Eve, but he is scarcely out of his high throne to walk the earth when Lucifer climbs into the throne and calls on all creatures to worship him. After God casts him down, Lucifer is degraded into a comic demon, but his pride remains and his "mansion," or scenic structure, the hell-mouth, is as large and brightly colored as the Lord's Heaven.

When the Devil tempts Adam and Eve the audience shudders, for God's scenic heaven is very near. Adam puts the blame on Eve. Eve puts the blame on the serpent, and the serpent blames his own nature. God's judgment is given, and the angel with a flaming sword drives Adam and Eve out of Paradise. He turns on the serpent: "Thou wicked worm full of pride, foul envy sit by thy side. Upon thy gut thou shalt glide . . . till a maiden in middle-earth be born. . . ." Adam and Eve take up the burden of human life in a world the Devil has sown with tares. Sorrow and pain, repentance and shame are their lot, but there is God's promise of future salvation.

The second group of plays is a series of episodes from the Old Testament in which God tests mankind. Cain kills Abel, and murder and responsibility enter

229

man's life. The episode of Noah's Ark echoes age-old myths of escape by water. Angry at the sins of mankind, God speaks from a tower or from an opening in the roof of the Ark and sets Noah his task. There is anxiety as days go by and Noah's plummet cannot measure the depth of the sea. There is suspense as the raven and dove are sent out on trick wires. But at the end a simple, pious Noah gives thanks, and a chastened family takes up its life on land again.

Abraham and Isaac create a scene of pathos. Isaac serves as a prefiguration of the sacrifice of Christ, but the incident is also a test of Abraham's obedience. The journey of father and son toward the mountain, one in sorrow, the other puzzled and wishing to console his father, is one of the most touching moments in the drama.

Often included in a cycle is a dramatization of the prophets who foretold the coming of Christ. The incident of Balaam, with the ass who was stopped by the angel, set in comic contrast to the prophet's refusal to obey a wicked king and his promise of a Savior, was a popular scene.

The third group of plays presents the scenes of the Nativity. The Annunciation was a moment of lyric intensity, with the *Ave Maria* expanded and the angel let down from a high heaven by an ingenious crane. Mary's tender submission contrasts with the half-comic frustration of the old Joseph. He keeps asking Mary who has got her with child and reproaching the maids for neglecting to watch

Reconstruction by George R. Kernodle of a pageant wagon of God creating the Earth. *Illustration by Martha Sutherland.*

her. He warns the men in the audience what will happen if they marry young wives. When he lies down in the field to sleep and the angel comes to tell him the truth, never was troubled man more happily relieved.

The Nativity itself was usually supposed behind the curtain, to be opened as Joseph returned or as the Shepherds arrived. But in the York cycle, Mary describes the birth in an ecstatic lyric. Joseph kneels to adore the child, and the ox and the ass low as they recognize their lord.

The shepherds in the English cycles were not Palestinians but Hanken, Harvey, and Tudde, Tibb's son, who tease one another on the hills near Chester and wrestle with their boy Trowle. When they hear the angel sing the *Gloria in excelsis,* they try to repeat the song, and argue whether he said "glory glo" or "glory glee." Since this play was put on by the Painters and the Glassworkers, the audience must have been amused that one of the glazier-actors insisted that "much he spake of glass." In France, Italy, and Germany the shepherds were also given local names and qualities. Sometimes they created a tender pastoral mood; sometimes they were satirical; often they were comic adolescents. In the famous English *Second Shepherds' Play* they engage in an elaborate plot. But before Mary and the Christ Child they are loyal adorers. They give whatever they have: a bottle without a stopper, a cup, a pair of mittens, a ball, a pipe to play tunes on, an old horn spoon that will hold forty peas.

The Adoration of the Magi would be a dull repetition of the scene of the shepherds if it were not for the wonderful Herod. He growls and snorts and screams and yells. He makes his learned councilors run to look up old prophets' predictions. He puts on a suave countenance to deceive the Three Kings, but when he learns that they have escaped he turns loose with "Out! Out! Harrow!" and swears by his great god Mahound (Mahomet) and even runs raging among the audience. Shakespeare thought of him as the prime example of unrestrained acting and gave us the phrase "to out-Herod Herod."

The angel hurries the Holy Family off to Egypt to escape Herod's slaughter of the innocents as the soldiers destroy several children, often with realistic dummies and real blood. In the Coventry pageant of the Shearmen and Taylors, the mothers sing a lullaby to the babes, then when the soldiers arrive, fight back with spoon, pot, and pan. Comic vitality prevails for a moment; then the women lose and all is desolation. In the Chester cycle one of the babes is the son of Herod, and the mangled body is taken to the father as a fitting return for his cruelty. The raging king, feeling his arms and legs rotting, dies and is carried off to hell by the Devil. Then the angel brings the news to Joseph that he may return to Judea in peace.

The fourth act of this great drama is the Passion, the Crucifixion, and Resurrection. Starting with the entry into Jerusalem on Palm Sunday, the action jumps to the Last Supper and the Betrayal. On long platforms, where the Council of the Jews and the Last Supper could be shown simultaneously, there was dramatic in-

teraction, with Judas going back and forth from one group to the other. The series of trials made vivid drama. Scenes of torturers prodding Christ alternated
with scenes of the faithful, especially Mary and the disciples. Comic scenes were
developed from the making of the nails for the Crucifixion and the casting of dice
for Christ's garments. In the Harrowing of Hell, Christ was like a great medieval
knight laying siege and storming the castle of death. Adam and Eve and John the
Baptist led the procession of souls out of Limbo as the devils set up a tremendous
howl because their gate had been torn down, then redoubled their resolution to
capture more souls to make up for those lost. This section of the plays sometimes
led to spectacular scenes of the Ascension, the Descent of the Holy Spirit at Pentecost, or the appearance of Antichrist.

The final scene of the drama is the end of the world, Doomsday. The Last Judgment was a favorite subject for painting in medieval churches and sometimes
dominated a wall or a church as completely as Michelangelo's great Doomsday
painting does the Sistine Chapel. In the drama God sat on a high throne on a
rainbow while the world burned at his feet. When the graves opened, souls
dressed in white were escorted to the gates of paradise while those in black were
dragged by orange-and-black howling devils into the flaming jaws of hell. A heavenly choir sang for the blessed, while the noise of chains and groans and pots and
pans, with the hiss of steam and crackle of fire, welcomed the damned. Sometimes
a Doomsday procession included all the classes, with a saved pope, emperor,
king, queen, judge, and merchant balancing similar figures in the procession of
the damned.

In mood the plays have almost as wide a range as in time and space. The tender
alternates with the brutal, enraptured adoration with lashing satire, spectacle with
magic or broad comedy. In the Towneley cycle, soldiers, lawyers, tax-collectors,
and bailiffs are satirized. The Towneley shepherds make sharp jibes at the rich and
at marriage and women, but they melt into adoration before the babe and mother
in the manger. The poetry of the Crucifixion includes taunts of the torturers as
they stretch the limbs and drive the nails, or such high rhetoric as that in the
French *Passion* of Jean Michel:

Mary. May your death be brief and easy.
Jesus. I shall die a death most bitter.
Mary. May it then be far away.
Jesus. In the midst of all my friends.

. . . .

Mary. May it be under earth and silent.
Jesus. I must hang high up on the cross.
Mary. Wait until you are an old man.
Jesus. In the very bloom of youth.

The marvels of the mystery plays were reinforced with startling scenic effects.
In the York Transfiguration Jesus appears suddenly on a mountain "between Moses

and Elias in a blinding light." With tremendous sound a cloud descends, bringing the Father to speak to the disciples. Then all magically disappear, leaving Jesus standing alone. The *Ludus Coventriae* presented an extraordinary tableau for the Annunciation, with the Trinity descending by a machine, three solid light beams connecting the Father with the Son, the Son with the Holy Ghost, and the Holy Ghost with the bosom of Mary.

Violence and bloody action were shown with a realism that no modern audience could take. Blood covered Christ's face from the crown of thorns. The torturers seemed to drive the nails through his feet and hands. Blood ran down the lance that pierced his side. More than once an actor playing Christ or Judas fainted during the hours of hanging and had to be taken down and revived. The slaughter of the innocents, the beheading of John the Baptist, and the martyrdom of the saints were shown by trick limbs, heads, and bodies smeared with animal blood. When Judas hanged himself, the story goes, his stomach burst and his bowels hung out. This was actually shown through the use of the intestines of an animal. Some authors added grim humor to the scene by the antics of devils unable to pull his soul through a mouth that had kissed Jesus and tearing his stomach to get it. For the martyrdom of one saint, we are told, it was not enough to burn a false body in real fire, some animal bones and intestines were included to make the proper stench.

The duplication of motifs is a reminder of the principle of prefiguration. The sacrifice of Isaac was a prefiguration of the sacrifice of Christ; Jonah's three days in the whale, of Christ's three days in the tomb. In the York cycle Isaac is made thirty years old to emphasize the parallel. We are also reminded of the fascination with numbers in the Middle Ages; the three petals of the fleur-de-lis made a symbol of the Trinity.

An explanation of the extraordinary contrasts of comic, violent, marvelous, realistic, spectacular, domestic, satiric, and devotional, of blood, prayer, music, color, and magic, lies in the interweaving of the human and the divine, the temporal and the eternal, the flesh and the spirit. The philosophy is Nominalism. Writer, painter, and actor are completely absorbed in the reality of each detail as they come to it. Their methods are in marked contrast to those in the church drama. In the outdoor cycles everything is particular and local; God walks the earth or looks out from his canvas clouds with a human face painted with gilt; the devils send real smoke from their bright-colored hell. The detail is earthy because the divine drama is worked out on earth and through man. It is contemporary and local because the men and women of the audience are caught up in God's plan as fully as the disciples in Judea.

Expository characters explain the relation of each event to the entire scheme. God speaks to the audience or to the characters. The Devil comments and sends his emissaries to interfere. Moses starts toward the burning bush, but God stops him, reminding him that he must take off his shoes to walk on holy ground. Nearly every play begins with a poetic address to the audience, explaining who the character is or asking God for instruction, usually summarizing the action that has gone before and that which is to come. Sometimes there is an expositor—Contemplation is a favorite name—who tells the audience the meaning of the events. Isaiah, the most important of the prophets who foretold the coming of Christ, may speak a Prologue to explain the Annunciation and Nativity.

Allegorical characters, as messengers from the other world, frequently show the eternal aspect of an event. When Adam and Eve are expelled in the Norwich play, they are taken over by the characters Dolor and Misery. In the *Passion* by Arnoul Greban, Lucifer sends Despair to work on Judas because only if he despairs of forgiveness is he truly lost.

The most elaborate allegory is the debate of the Four Daughters of God: Truth, Mercy, Justice, and Peace. In the *Ludus Coventriae* it begins the group of plays concerned with the Annunciation and Conception. Contemplatio is Prologue, reviewing the story of man's damnation and praying for mercy. The Virtues speak for the patriarchs and prophets and cry God's mercy to restore mankind. Truth argues that man deserves unending pain, but Mercy pleads for him. Justice condemns the presumption of man, while Peace asks for reconciliation. The debate is taken up by the Trinity, and the Son prepares to be born as man. Gabriel goes directly from the Holy Ghost to Mary.

In the French cycle *Mystère du viel Testament*, the Four Daughters give a continuous comment as a divine counterpart of the drama on earth. After the disobedience of Adam and Eve, Justice and Mercy hold a debate, and they are heard again when Cain kills Abel. Noah is saved through the plea of Mercy. She weeps when Joseph is sold into slavery, but God points out that Joseph prefigures the torture of Jesus, whose innocent blood will also be sold. The high point is the miraculous birth of Isaac and his sacrifice. God is disturbed at the wickedness of the five cities of Sodom. After a scene of depravity, Justice cries out, "Vengeance, vengeance, vengeance," and God sends the angel, whom he addresses as "my son Jesus," to promise that if ten just men can be found mankind will be saved. A spectacular scene of fire and destruction is followed by the birth and adoration of Isaac, which God plans as a prefiguration of himself and Christ. The divine figures watch with agony the scenes of the human father and son. At the crucial moment Mercy persuades God to relent and send the angel to save Isaac.

Another way of linking the particular and the eternal was to relate biblical events to the liturgy of the church. As three-year-old Mary climbs the fifteen steps of the temple, she recites the fifteen verses of a popular devotional litany for Mary. Mary recites a Latin devotional psalm which Anne, Mary's mother, repeats verse by verse in English. Christ at the Last Supper gives his disciples communion with his blood and body, and in the agony in the Garden the angel comes down from the mountain to bring him a chalice to drink as a last sacrament. Choirs sang and familiar antiphons and sequences were borrowed from the liturgy. Many scenes popular in stained glass and painting were emphasized for their tableau effect. The procession from the cross to the tomb was so planned as to allow Mary to sing a lament with Christ in her lap in the position of the popular "Pieta."

The extreme contrasts were parts of a method that interwove the shadow with the substance, the idea with the example, the type with the particular, the divine with the human, the eternal with the immediate, in the great plan of God's creation and salvation of man.

THE STAGING OF THE MYSTERY CYCLES

Born of processions, the cycles kept the processional staging; that is, the actors moved from one position to another, playing now in the open, now in front of, now partly on or in, one or several scenic structures. From earliest times a religious procession carried a number of portable symbolic units—throne, temple, tower, mountain, ship, or tree—which served as tokens of certain characters or places, and such scenic nuclei are spread along ancient carved and painted friezes. In the medieval outdoor processional drama, scenic elements were built with more elaborate detail but were still merely centers of action. All the scenic elements were separate, and two or several dozens of them might be in sight at the same time in the arrangement known as simultaneous or multiple setting or staging.

The most common name for these scenic elements is the French word *mansion*. A tree, throne, mountain, or the column from which the cock crowed for Peter's betrayal was as much a mansion as a castle, house, or temple. Each mansion served to locate but not to limit the scene. The characters acted all around it and were supposed at the place it identified; or if they ignored it they could be supposed far away. Another mansion might be only a ten or twenty feet away yet be supposed many miles distant.

MANSIONS ON PAGEANT WAGONS

The English method of putting one or two mansions on a wagon and playing each episode in a number of places around the town was the most picturesque way of staging the mysteries. In York the city corporation supervised arrangements. Many important people wanted to have performances before their houses or shops, but the city rented the right to performance and limited the number of places. Windows or raised pavilions could be rented so that the rich might see over the standing crowds. In different years there were twelve, fourteen, or even sixteen places of performance. A banner of the city was set the night before at each place, and the wagons displayed the arms of the city.

At York the cycle was divided into forty-eight (some years fifty or fifty-one) episodes and called for more than forty-eight wagons. Since three plays were required for the events of the Creation, there must be three wagons and three actors playing the part of God. Four plays showed different parts of the story of Adam and Eve, requiring four wagons of the Garden of Eden and presumably four casts of the three main characters. At least twenty plays included the adult Jesus as a character, requiring, we suppose, twenty actors. It is hard to see how there could have been any doubling, but there must have been some since one city regulation prescribed that no actor be required to play more than twice.

At Coventry there were only ten plays, of which the pageant of the shearmen and taylors has survived and is frequently played today. It used only one wagon even though it included the Annunciation, the Journey to Bethlehem, the Nativity, the Adoration of the Shepherds, the scene of Herod, the Adoration of the Magi, and the Slaughter of the Innocents. Only the crèche was carried on the wagon, the other scenes being played on a bare wagon or on the open street. The directions read, "Herod rages in the pageant and in the street also."

Because one man wrote in the seventeenth century that the wagons were two stories high and that the lower story was covered with cloth and used as a dressing room, some students have supposed that all pageant wagons had this arrangement. Now it is certain that very few actors made a change of costume, so that few wagons would need a dressing room; there is also evidence that the cloth for the lower part of the wagon merely covered the space from the wagon floor to the ground, including the wheels; and it is certain that there were many kinds of pageant wagons.

It might seem that the pageant wagons were small, since in several English cities each was pulled by six or eight men. But in some cities two to four horses were used. It might be supposed that only small scenes would be moved over the cobblestones and mud, along narrow streets where filth was drained down the center and dung-heaps were piled beside the house doors, streets so narrow that the projecting upper stories of houses sometimes almost met; yet evidence indicates very large scenic buildings. One seventeenth-century writer recalled the "Theaters for the several scenes, very large and high, placed upon wheels." Though there is not a single picture from England, the drawings of the wagons in a procession at Louvain, a city whose streets were not exceptionally wide, show far larger structures than scholars had supposed. The wagon of the Tree of Jesse supports a wrought-iron tree on whose branches stand thirty small children as kings and at the top a small actress for the Virgin. The wagon of the Assumption of the Virgin carries at least sixteen people in a colonnade more than twice their height. The figure of the Virgin in a Glory (a circular frame, often elaborately decorated and lighted, enclosing a divine figure as in a halo) is being raised by ropes and pulleys to an upper stage, where a picture of the Trinity stands in a panel rising, it would seem, twenty or thirty feet. In a tall open tower dozens of singers representing the choirs of angels appear on three of the five stories. No wonder two men walk beside each wagon holding guide ropes fastened to the top, to keep the structure from toppling over as the three or more horses draw it along the streets.

The actors of the mysteries played both on the wagon and in the street, sometimes starting the play on foot before the pageant wagon arrived. In the York play, Mary and Joseph were walking and talking of what they had seen at Jerusalem when they missed Jesus and turned back. Shortly the wagon with the temple appeared, showing Christ with the doctors. Joseph and Mary re-entered, weary after looking for three days, and saw the temple at a distance. In the York Adoration, the shepherds walked alone until they saw a marvelous sight and heard the angels; then they started toward the wagon, saying, "Here is the burg there we should be." The wagon held an inanimate tableau, with living actors depicting shepherds and angels. In the Coventry pageant of the Shearmen and Taylors, Herod and the Magi arrived on horseback.

Sometimes two mansions were placed on one wagon. The Chester Fall of Lucifer had both God's chair and a dungeon or "pitt of hell," and Simon's house was shown alongside a castle of the city of Jerusalem large enough for Jesus to enter and overthrow the moneylenders' tables. In the York Entry into Jerusalem Jesus rode an ass toward "yon castle," and Zaccheus climbed on a tree to see without being seen. Jesus dismounted and let Peter take the ass away. The citizens of Jerusalem welcomed him, but it is not clear that he ever entered the castle-city. Two wagons were used in the York play of the Three Kings. The Kings started the play on foot; then the wagon of Herod pulled up, or they turned to it, and they saw a wagon with the Bethlehem stable beyond—"Sir, here is Jerusalem . . . and beyond is Bedlam." Herod, on the Jerusalem wagon, sent the Kings on "To Bedlam, it is but here at hand." As Herod's wagon moved out of sight, the Kings saw the star and approached the Bethlehem wagon. Apparently the tableau of Mary and the Child was not visible until a maiden disclosed it by drawing a curtain.

Sometimes a flat wagon with no mansion, a "forepageant," was drawn up alongside the main wagon to give a free acting area. In the Coventry Purification, Joseph and Mary came out of the temple "into the forepageant." That structure must have been very useful for the York Doom, since the main scene would crowd the principal wagon. God descended from a very high "Trinity House" to his Judgment seat, where he sat on a rainbow surrounded by revolving circles of clouds and angels' heads, his feet apparently resting on the burning world (a barrel of burning tar, to be replaced several times during the day). The forepageant held the graves, the trap doors through which the souls rose to be judged, and there was still room on the main pageant for doors to heaven and hell. This, like several other shows, suggests that the scenes were visible from three sides but not all the way round.

MANSIONS IN A ROUND

The simplest method of using mansions in a production was to place them around the outside of a city square or a round playing area. An outdoor cycle required twenty to sixty structures.

Drawings from Donaueschingen in Austria and Lucerne in Switzerland show where the mansions were placed for performance in a city market square. The plan for Donaueschingen is divided into three parts. In the lower part are Hell and the Mount of Olives. In the middle part are the seats of Herod, Pilate, Caiaphas, Annas, and the Last Supper, while the uppermost part holds the crosses of the Crucifixion, the Sepulchre, and Heaven. For the two-day Lucerne play the many mansions were set against the houses on all four sides of the square and a few in the center.

Many cities found a better solution by building a small round amphitheatre with an open playing area in the center for most of the action. Especially in Cornwall, the remains of old Roman amphitheatres were used. One had a flat center more than a hundred feet in diameter (the *platea*) and at the outside a parapet ten or twelve feet high. The audience stood in the platea or was seated on the sides of the parapet. The several mansions were built at the top of the parapet, that is, in back of the audience. Each of the main characters had a mansion, and when he appeared he followed the stage direction "Pompabit"—to parade or make a show. The audience could turn and watch him. He usually had a self-introduction, much like the characters in the Mummers plays, and there might be a little action at his mansion, which often had a platform or porch. But for the main scenes he came through the audience to the platea, where all kinds of action took place. Troops of horsemen arrived; a ship sailed in a ditch, probably with actual water; crosses were erected for the Crucifixion, and graves opened for Doomsday. Often a kind of temple stood in the platea to serve for the Last Supper as well as several other scenes needing the definition of a structure.

At the center of the round area for the English morality play *The Castle of Perseverance* stood a tower, apparently open on the first story, allowing action within to be seen from all sides. The Virtues defending the castle appeared at the top of the tower and leaned over a parapet. According to the ground plan, the whole area was bounded by a circular ditch, "or else that it be strongly barred all about," and around the circle (either outside or inside the ditch) were five mansions for the main characters, God at the east, Mundus west, Care south, Beliel north, and Covetise northeast. Earlier scholars have supposed that the purpose of the ditch was to separate the audience from the platea, but they have misread the text. The audience was within the area bounded by the ditch, which Richard Southern believes served to keep out those who had not paid. Whether the mansions were inside the ditch or outside, the characters who had mansions began by making an appearance and then coming through the audience to the central platea.

A beautiful fifteenth-century miniature by the famous painter Jean Fouquet illustrates just such an arena theatre. At the center is a scene of the martyrdom of Saint Appolonia. In the midst of the action stands the director, in full sight of the audience, holding his prompt book and guiding the action with a long baton. At the far side the fool is pulling himself together after a whipping. Six mansions are shown at the outside, raised above the heads of the audience on high poles, with ladders for the characters to come down to act in the platea. At the left is a choir of angels; next come musicians playing a pipe organ and horns and trumpet. The throne mansion has a front curtain, but the throne is empty since the king is in the platea. The next two mansions probably house important spectators. At the right is hell-mouth, the usual monster's head with two stories. Most of the audience is standing around the platea. This differs from the English and Cornish rounds only in that the mansions form a continuous structure around the playing circle.

MANSIONS ON A PLATFORM

The method of using the mansions most popular in France but known also in England, Germany, Italy, and Spain was to put them side by side along a platform. Grandstands could be built for most of the audience, with boxes, to hold important people above the crowd.

Such platforms were usually from a hundred to a hundred and fifty feet long and perhaps thirty feet deep. Heaven with its gilded gateway was always at one end, "the right hand of God" (the left of the audience), and Hell at the other end. God's throne was usually on an upper level surrounded by a Glory of two or three concentric bands which revolved, carrying lights and wooden angels. Often God was accompanied by the Four Daughters, and usually a choir of angels celebrated his acts. A crane was necessary to let down Gabriel for the Annunciation, and sometimes God himself came down by a machine, also called a Glory. Some towns built a crane large enough to let down the whole group of Satan and the other rebel angels from heaven.

Hell was not only the mouth of a monster but also a fortress, which Sir Beelzebub in the Towneley cycle organizes for a siege by barring the gates and setting defenders on the walls. The jaws of hell flapped after each entrance by means of a rope and pulley, and inside could be seen devils throwing souls into a cauldron while other devils blew up the fire with bellows. Such real fire and smoke must have required masonry rather than the wood, canvas, and plaster of the other

Miniature from Etienne Chevalier's *Book of Hours* depicting The Martyrdom of Saint Appolonia.
Courtesy Musée Conde, Chantilly.

Miniature of the director of the Passion of Valenciennes, 1545. *Phot. Bibl. Nat. Paris.*

mansions. Some plays call for as many as seventeen mansions between heaven and hell, though probably the same throne mansion, open temple, or mountain was often used for different scenes. Next to heaven was the earthly paradise, where Adam and Eve appeared amidst picturesque trees hung with flowers and fruits, and next to hell was limbo, a prison fortress where the souls of the unbaptized awaited the coming of Christ. Between paradise and limbo there was no set order, but a temple, a throne mansion, a tower for Satan to show Christ the world, a mountain for Abraham and Isaac and for Gethsemane (provided with a device for an angel to be let down), a cave for the burial of Christ, and often a sea with real water and a real ship were standard mansions. Sometimes a mansion was covered for one scene with a painted curtain which was removed for a different scene. Often a mansion was closed by a curtain until its characters were to enter the action.

The great advantage of the multiple stage, whether on a platform or in a round, was that it permitted almost as much interweaving of parallel actions as the movies do, and some breadth of action not possible even on the widest screen. The Nativity scenes of the Greban *Passion* interwove action in heaven, hell, and a number of places on earth. Immediately after Mercy in heaven pleads for man's salvation, from the prison of Limbo at the other end of the platform come the cries of

View of a medieval staging for a passion play, Cologne, 1581. *Courtesy of the Board of Trustees of the Victoria and Albert Museum.*

242

Medieval staging for a passion play, Valenciennes, 1545. *Phot. Bibl. Nat. Paris.*

Medieval staging for a passion play, Lucerne, 1597. *Zentralbibliothek Lucerne, Bürgerbibliothek. Property of Korporationsgemeinde Lucerne.*

243

Adam and Eve, Isaiah, and the other patriarchs for a Savior to release them. Gabriel is sent to earth for the Annunciation and returns to heaven to report. The song of the angels is answered immediately by the hellish singing of the devils. The Journey to Bethlehem is initiated when Cirinus, ruler of Judea, orders a census of all subjects of Caesar. The Nativity is interwoven with scenes of the angels appearing to the shepherds on a hillside before they come to adore the Child. The Magi are related to Herod and the crèche and the angels and have a drinking scene of their own. The Slaughter of the Innocents is cut in with the Flight to Egypt, the burning of idols before the Christ Child, the suicide of Herod, and devils carrying him off to hell.

The Passion scenes of the *Ludus Coventriae,* though apparently not the plays of the rest of the manuscript, have a similar wide panorama. Action that took place over several days and at many places around Jerusalem is compacted into a continuous series of scenes. There is extraordinary economy in the simultaneous staging as the attention moves without a pause from one scene to the next.

Entries and Street Theatres:
The Merchants' Welcome to the King

The most splendid civic event in the Gothic period was the king's visit, soon after his coronation, to the major cities of the realm. For the merchants, the Royal Entry was more important than the coronation, and they dramatized the event with an even greater expenditure of money and creative energy than they poured out for the great religious dramas. The tableaux and street theatres which they paid for were important sources of livelihood for architects, artists, and artisans, as well as for dramatists and actors. Rarely did men with artistic ability get a chance to redecorate an old pageant wagon or rewrite a religious play, but when the king was coming not only were new orations, themes, and dialogue required but new tableaux were built, up-to-date in style and as lavish as the city could afford.

The city had to be refurbished, and gates, streets, fountains, and public buildings had to be made to speak with banners, music, painting, oratory, and drama. For the king must be reminded of the history of the town and particularly of the fact that his ancestors had granted charters with important rights and privileges. He must also be told in tableaux and little plays of the immediate problems of the city.

STREET SHOWS FOR THE KING

From the outer gate to the city hall the king might pause at as many as twenty scenic devices. Although some were only heraldic or allegorical decorations, most were entire street theatres with elaborate *tableaux vivants*, either on triumphal arches above the street or on structures at the side of the street, against a public building, or in the public square. Music was usually played as the king approached, and many devices were arranged with doors to open like a box or with a curtain to be pulled to disclose the tableau. Sometimes a maiden descended from a heaven of clouds high on the first gate or triumphal arch to present a gift to the king. Sometimes living actors moved in pantomime, and sometimes they amazed the king by

245

holding still without batting an eye while a prologue-orator explained the tableau. The architect or painter often depended for explanation on words written in a cartouche on the frame of the picture, but occasionally he tried the device of the banderole, putting into the hands of each actor a scroll on which was written the motto or short speech by which the character was recognized. But more often short plays or even little operas were given. Most of the structures were wooden frames covered with cloth and painted. Many wood-carvers were needed for the decorative detail, and sometimes lead and glass workers. The Antwerp reception of Philip II in 1549 required 895 carpenters, 236 painters, 16 wood carvers, and about 500 other workers over a period of several months. In the performance appeared 137 actors, not counting those in the shows of the foreign merchants. Throughout the period women played women's roles, in contrast to the use of boy actors in religious drama. If the entry took place at night, torches and lamps were lit to show up the hanging cloths, silk costumes, and jewels.

For themes of the *tableaux vivants* the designers drew on the entire range of literary, artistic, and popular lore. As in painting and literature, a gradual change occurred from the dominance in the fourteenth century of religious subjects to the popularity in the sixteenth of classical mythology and romantic history. Earthly kings were placed in the same scenic thrones used by the King of Heaven, and nymphs and goddesses found their way among the religious virtues in the same "antique" costumes. The principle of prefiguration was even more popular in the street shows than in the mystery cycles. In 1515 the city of Bruges tried to impress Charles V with the importance of its charter by showing one tableau of an early Count of Flanders granting privileges to the city paired with another of Moses bringing the Tables of the Law down from Mount Sinai. When the English princess Margaret of York entered Bruges in 1468 to marry the Duke of Burgundy, the *tableaux vivants* showed scenes of famous marriages: Adam and Eve, the marriage of Esther, the marriage at Cana, and the Song of Solomon. When Charles V, having decided to abdicate, took his son Philip in 1548 to be received as ruler in all the important cities of Italy and the Low Countries, history was combed for examples of other rulers who had turned over the state to a young son. Most of the cities also presented an arcade of the famous Philips of history. A tableau of Saint Catherine welcomed to London both Queen Catherine in 1421 and Katherine of Aragon in 1501. Anne of Brittany found not only the Queen of Sheba but the five Annes of the Old Testament waiting in tableaux to receive her in Paris in 1504.

Besides such historical enhancement of the ruler, the tableaux might present the needs and hopes of the city. To gain forgiveness for a recent revolt against the Duke of Burgundy, the citizens of Bruges in 1440 sent the city fathers to meet him with bared heads and feet. But they reinforced their appeal with a series of tableaux of ancient rulers who showed clemency to their erring subjects. Again in 1515 the city of Bruges needed special consideration. For several decades the river to the sea had been silting up, and Bruges, once the richest city in the world, saw its business firms move, one by one, to Antwerp. When the young prince Charles V, grandson of the emperor and heir of the Netherlands and Spain, came to be in-

A scene from Charles VIII's entry into Bruges in 1515, Charles receiving the Alderman of Bruges, *Illustration by Martha Sutherland.*

247

A garden of animals from Charles VIII's entry into Bruges in 1515. *Phot. Bibl. Nat. Paris.*

King Solomon and his court from Charles VIII's entry into Bruges in 1515. *Phot. Bibl. Nat. Paris.*

249

stalled in his provinces, Bruges showed him in tableaux the glorious history of the city and the honors and privileges granted by the earlier counts of Flanders. One allegorical tableau represented Riches standing behind the Graces and the Arts. Then the prince came before two scenes that went to the heart of the situation. The first showed a despairing lady named Bruges being deserted by Business and Merchandise, and the next showed Law and Religion forcibly preventing the desertion.

Religious conflicts in the sixteenth century, especially in the Low Countries and Britain, made it very important that the ruler have the right opinions. The chronicler gives a touching description of the young Queen Elizabeth of England receiving from a *tableau vivant* a book marked "Truth." Edinburgh gave Mary a sincere welcome on her return from France in 1561 but wanted to make clear that the Catholicism of France was hated. As a warning of the vengeance of God on idolaters, a tableau was presented of Korah, Dothan, and Ibiram destroyed while offering strange fire upon an altar. In Flanders the shows presented now Heresy stamped out, now Inquisition with a bloody face, according to whether Catholics or Protestants were in control. Brussels in 1577 welcomed William of Orange, the Protestant, with scenes of David, Moses, and Joseph saving the people. The following year, when the Catholic nobles brought in Archduke Matthias of Austria, he was greeted by shows of Scipio Africanus and of Quintus Curtius plunging into the yawning abyss to save the people from pestilence.

In providing street shows on festival occasions the city merchants made their greatest contribution to the harmony of the realm. The shows were also important in the education of the people, revealing a strong sense of man's place in a rich and romantic social order and of his place in history, using the past as a storehouse of examples to enhance present events. Like the great religious cycles, they gave a sense of divine order; for the show façade related the heavenly king and the earthly king, and many tableaux included a representative of the common people. They showed allegorical figures of royalty controlling civil war and disorder, stamping out error and rebellion, but also royalty listening to Wisdom, Piety, Prudence, Magnanimity, Justice, and Clemency.

SCENIC DEVICES IN THE STREET SHOWS

The Royal Entry kept some aspects of the traditional procession, with the king, in effect, putting on a show for the people as the city fathers, with musicians, ceremonially marched outside the town to meet him and escort him in. But in his entry the king was as much audience as performer, and the street tableaux developed large architectural forms more complex than the tableaux used in the earlier processions. The procession, like the frieze, was a time art, the eye moving along a series of items in time, never stopping long enough to organize any number of people or scenic details in space. But in the Royal Entries the king did pause for a moment at each show. For the first time in Europe, processional time was halted. The street shows gave an opportunity for development of more complex forms of staging and prepared the way for the even more complex staging of the Renaissance.

All the simple traditional scenic forms of the procession—tree, throne, mountain, cave, fountain, canopy, chariot, boat, and others—appeared among the street tableaux. Sometimes they identified the place where the characters were supposed to be, but more often they were symbolic emblems with traditional meanings. A garden could be represented by a tree, a gate, a hedge, or a fountain, but in any form it was a symbol of the flourishing realm rather than a real garden. So with the mountain. The scenic devices were emblems to be decorated, ornamental containers for actors and tableaux rather than real scenic background for a story or play.

As might be expected of such symbolic emblems, two or more were often combined. Realistic appropriateness was disregarded. A tree might be placed on top of a mountain or a mountain on top of a tree, a ship might rest on a mountain or on top of an arch, and a throne might be set into a castle, ship, cave, tree, or rose. Any symbol could be built of gold or leaves and decorated with tapestries, banners, and shields.

But far more important in the street tableaux than the traditional devices of the procession were five elaborate scenic forms too large to be easily carried in procession, forms that became the basis for several of the new theatres of the Renaissance: castle, pavilion, arcade screen, triumphal arch, and a conventionalized complex façade.

The castle, the most frequently used form, contributed some of the main patterns to the Elizabethan stage and to the early proscenium arch. It appeared everywhere in art, social ritual, pageantry, and allegorical fancy. Crowns, thrones, dishes, and even tombs were made in the form of castles. Daily life of the aristocracy centered in the castle, and to the lower classes the castle was a symbol of their sovereign, and its walls were their protection in time of war.

In medieval religious plays Jerusalem was regularly represented by a castle, and the city of Emmans was a castle with an open arch large enough to show the evening meal of the disciples. Hell was a combination of a monster's mouth and a castle to be assaulted by Christ. Even when a castle represented a known city gate or a kingdom, it might be covered with flowers or decorated with tapestries, banners, and shields. Sometimes it was a single tower, but the more usual form was a façade of two towers framing a two-story panel between. The central arch could

Tableau vivant for the entry of Prince Ernest of Austria into Antwerp, 1594.

be opened to show a tableau within, or, treated as a niche, it might become a background for a throne or tableau on the forestage. Sometimes a throne-canopy with its roof and two forward columns was added to the castle. An upper story above the arch and windows in the side towers could be used for other tableaux or for allegorical figures related to the main theme of the show. The top was especially the place for heaven and heavenly musicians. When Katherine of Aragon arrived in London in 1501 to marry Prince Arthur, the top of a street castle held an ingenious revolving astrological device, with the angel Raphael (the symbol of marriage), sitting in a pinnacle above and three famous astronomers on a canopied bench below. Sometimes a heavenly throne held the character of Honor high on the front of the castle while on the forestage a figure representing the king was surrounded by attendants and royal virtues.

The formal pavilion—a canopy supported by four columns—might be used alone to frame a single figure or a group, or it might be hung with a curtain that made it represent an interior. Often it was simply a two-column canopy over a throne projecting from a castle or an arcade screen.

The arcade screen was most useful to present a row of portrait figures such as the prophets or the famous Philips, each in a separate arch, or to frame a small tableau in each opening. In a gallery at the top might be placed angels or other musicians, or a heavenly throne for the Trinity or an allegorical figure, especially the character Honor. Below in the arches or on a forestage, as in the castle, an actor-king and attendants might appear.

The fourth of the great structures in the street theatres was the triumphal arch. Based not only on the Roman triumphal arch but on the gate of the medieval walled city, it displayed coats of arms and shields and sometimes had castle towers and turrets and a gallery for musicians and a welcoming orator. Many times actual city gates were decorated with torches, banners, arms, shields, tapestries, paintings, and inscriptions. Temporary structures could be opened for *tableaux vivants*, decorated with green boughs and flowers, or transformed into a rock, cave, sea, ship, or temple.

Royal entries with street theatres that used all the traditional devices continued beyond the medieval period. Magnificent triumphal arches were built in London in 1604 for the entry of James I. All had living figures, and most had both a gallery for musicians and a speakers' gallery, from which speeches written by Thomas Middleton, Ben Jonson, and other prominent authors were delivered. All were complex façades looking a little like castles but combining in one unified architectural structure the separate thrones, niches, galleries, pavilions, paintings, curtains, miniature scenic emblems, and *tableaux vivants* of other street theatres. The first one, in Fechurch Street, was called "Truscan," but the classic columns were incidental to the elaborate theatre façade. The "forehead" or "battlement" of the edifice was a medieval town-canopy, a three-dimensional model of the whole city, showing the most prominent houses, towers, and steeples. In panels inscribed "Londinium" and "Camera Regia" were three levels for living characters. In the central panel sat Monarchia Britannica with Divine Wisdom at her feet and the six Civic Virtues around her in separate niches. Two open arches spanned the street, and a central panel between them held three niches, the largest for a speaker, Genius of the City. On the lowest level, in a pavilion projecting forward beyond the rest of the façade, was the other speaker, Thamesis, leaning on a gourd, symbol of the flowing river.

The last form of the street theatres, the façade, was a distillation of the basic patterns of castle, arcade, and triumphal arch. By the sixteenth century a conventionalized composite façade structure had absorbed the patterns and symbolism of all the other devices. It might show three or five arches and a heavenly throne, all borrowed from the arcade screen. It might keep the two-tower-plus-central-panel pattern and a serve as a castle. Placed at the side of a street, it still looked like a show triumphal arch. With a throne set against its central panel it was a throne-tableau. With the central panel opened up it was a proscenium arch. With the side doors and upper stage also opened it was a composite frame for a group of tableaux and a model for the Flemish and Elizabethan stages. It might be decorated with tapestries, paintings, banners, and shields, and lighted by torches and cressets. At the top might be singing angels and other musicians and clouds or astrological symbols of the sky and a heavenly throne. The designer could build into it trees, caves, tents, mountains, a garden gateway, a fountain, and even a ship, and still its columns, arches, and architectural canopy unified it as one show façade. More and more the older, realistic details—castle stones and battlements, heavenly clouds, a ship's sails, tiles of a roof, leaves of an arbor—were dominated by architectural design. But in the eyes of the spectators the street façade was a decorated device ready to disclose a dancer or orator or to present romantic tableaux while at the same time it was itself an impressive show.

The street shows made great advances in theatre forms. Before the end of the fifteenth century they introduced elaborate machines: descending angels, rising trees, opening clouds and mountains, turning globes, and revolving stages. They developed elaborate architectural façades with platforms, curtains, inner stages, upper stages, and galleries. They made the transition from the separate early medieval scenic emblems to more abstract architectural symbols. Above all they taught the citizens to respond to poetry, oratory, drama, art, and architecture, all united in the service of great national and historical themes.

The Tournament:
The Public Drama of the Nobility

In the tournament the nobility of Europe not only offered a spectacular show, they dramatized themselves as the defenders of the realm, the champions of Christianity against the infidel, and the embodiment of the highest ideals of chivalry. No public celebration was considered complete without a tournament.

In the early years of feudalism the knight was a rough fighting man constantly at war for protection of his lord or for his own gain, and the tournament was his game for training and for proving his skill. The church was opposed, and kings, wanting neither to lose men nor to risk conspiracy, discouraged the sport.

With the Crusades the church found a dedication for fighting men. In 1095 Pope Urban roused the chivalry of Europe for the First Crusade to rescue the Holy Land from the Saracens, promising that "now they may become knights who hitherto existed as robbers." Fighting for private gain became less widespread. It is true that in one crusade Richard Coeur de Lion, King of England, was long held in a German prison for ransom, and in another the Venetians persuaded the Crusaders to sack the Christian city of Constantinople, their rival in trade, rather than the cities of the infidels. But in spite of many lapses from true chivalry, the age had a high ideal. The ceremonies of creating knights were religious, including purification, fasts, prayers and vigils, confession, a Mass, a sermon, the blessing of the sword at the altar, and the taking of solemn religious vows. Churchmen sanctioned the institution and called on the true knight to defend the church, uphold the faith, venerate priesthood, protect the poor from injury, and pacify the country. If *The Song of Roland* (c. 1100), the story of the devotion of Roland to his lord, Charlemagne, and his friend Oliver, in the wars against the Moors, expresses the feudal ideal of loyalty, the tales of Sir Galahad the Pure and the search for the Holy Grail express the equally strong ideal of religious devotion.

In the time of the early Crusades, the Romanesque period, the church itself was both militant and idealistic. Henry Adams suggests that the best symbol of the age is the Abbey of Mont St. Michel, standing tall like a sword at the edge of the land, dedicated to the warrior archangel, Michael. The age which follows (the Gothic period), Adams suggests, is symbolized by the Cathedral of Chartres, dedicated to the Virgin, and between the two churches he finds the transformation of a civilization—one of the most profound changes of sentiment in all history, for be-

255

tween the eleventh and the thirteenth century the worship of woman came into the world. The adoration of the Virgin transformed the church, and the Court of Love—a cult developed by the troubadours and noble ladies—transformed poetry, art, and man's feelings and motivations. In the tournament, rules had been established which made the fighting less dangerous, and chivalry and the court of love provided ideal worlds of history and poetry. When the tournament was dramatized in the fourteenth, fifteenth, and sixteenth centuries, it was more than a demonstration of feudal and crusading loyalties; it was dedicated to and presided over by a beautiful lady, with the knight in love as the central figure.

THE KNIGHT AND THE COURT OF LOVE

The new ideal of love dominates not only the tournament and the masque but all drama from Shakespeare and Racine to Ibsen and Anouilh and the popular romances of Hollywood. The passion of love, with the exaltation of woman and the complete transformation of the lover, was a creation of the Western world.

Courtly love originated in Provence and was brought north by a remarkable woman, Eleanor of Aquitaine, granddaughter of a noble troubadour, who was queen of France for fifteen years, then queen in England and the English portions of France for some fifty more. At the court of her daughter Marie, Countess of Champagne, Chretièn de Troyes put the religion of love into a new version of *Lancelot*. Lancelot, a humble vassal of his Guinevere, undergoes severe hardships and debasement in obeying her orders, even riding in a criminal's cart and suffering derision as a coward in a tournament. When he wins her, he is a worshiper kneeling before her bed to adore her and genuflecting as he leaves. By the thirteenth century, lyric poetry, romances, and tournaments were permeated with the new sentiment. *The Song of Roland* was the last great poem without a heroine.

In search of origins, scholars find elements of the cult in Plato's concept of love, in the merry sensuality of Ovid's *Metamorphoses* (8 A.D.), and in love poetry of the Arabs, but none of these sources explains the central passion. Ezra Pound suggests that southern France, less disturbed by the Germanic invasions than other parts of Europe, had retained elements of the ancient Hellenic cults of ecstasy and the mystic sense of divinity in spring growth and the rites of May. He points out that monasteries and nunneries were not completely ascetic but transformed the appeal of the senses into the poetic adoration of Christ the Bridegroom for the nuns and the charms of Our Lady for the monks. Denis de Rougement, a twentieth-century writer, is sure that courtly love was an expression of the mysticism of the Cathars, a religious group within Christianity that derived from near Eastern sources and flourished in a region near that of the troubadours. Regarding the material world as evil, they advocated physical chastity and considered love an ardent yearning for union on a spiritual plane that could be realized only beyond death.

Henry Adams pictures the great feudal lady managing her household for months at a time when her husband was absent on Crusades or wars or at tournaments, with few women but a large number of men: pages sent by their parents to be educated for knighthood, young men about to become knights, and young knights who, lacking estates of their own or a military project, were hangers-on of the castle. Her main task was to teach her men manners. Worship of women and courtesy to all people were important ideals in that civilizing process. With the help of the troubadours with their love lyrics and metrical romances, she set up a game called a "court of love" to decide the suitable punishments and rewards of lovers and the precedents and rules for the behavior of the knight in love. Whether or not there is a causal relationship between the cult of the Virgin and courtly love, they appeared almost simultaneously and developed in the same direction.

The cult of romantic passion defied feudal and Christian concepts. It was frankly adulterous; the knight was expected to fall in love with another man's wife. In the feudal system, marriages were regularly made for family advantages, with no consideration of personal choice. The church condoned innocent sexuality in marriage but condemned passion as a sin under any circumstances. But the new ideal made passion the source of all hope, virtue, courtesy, and nobility, the source of great suffering but also of happiness and all values in this world. Since love was illicit it must be secret. Poetry and art expressed through symbols and allegories the feelings that could not be spoken directly. In a feudal and religious world that made no provision for choice and spontaneity, the cult of love gave the individual a great sense of release.

In exalting the woman and making the man give up everything in the service of love, the cult shifted the emphasis in sex from possession to the idealized pursuit, still recognized in our term "courtship." The lover preferred delay; he wanted the woman to be difficult and rejoiced in the long series of tasks she set him. For all the sensuous imagery and the initial emphasis on adultery, the Court of Love is one of Europe's great attempts to turn attention from the physical to a spiritual, idealized relationship between a man and a woman.

Courtly love left a long and amazing heritage. Even in its own day it was travestied as too extravagant and ideal, and stories and plays showed the would-be lover getting caught by the husband or being ruled by a woman who did not possess the qualities of true chivalry. In the period of the Renaissance that succeeded the Middle Ages, Shakespeare's *The Taming of the Shrew* suggests that more robust relationships between men and women will find their place. By the 1590's Shakespeare's *Romeo and Juliet* and Spenser's *Faerie Queene* had reconciled romantic love and marriage. The medieval courtly romances assumed that the knight in love would be a great soldier fighting for his king or his church, but these feudal demands often went against spontaneous choice in love, and by the seventeenth century (the Baroque period) the conflict of love and honor became the basic theme for many plays.

A powerful dynamic force was created in western Europe that persisted, in modified form, in the Renaissance and down to the present. That force stirred the heart of the knight at the tournament.

THE DRAMATIC TOURNAMENT

In the fourteenth and fifteenth centuries and on into the late sixteenth century (for medieval practices did not cease abruptly at a fixed date), the tournament was not only a game, with weapons blunted and danger circumscribed by rules, but a drama, with setting, story, impersonation, and costume and a standard form of auditorium that had considerable influence on the modern theatre. The individual combats were still exciting, but the fighting was almost incidental to the pageantry, with processional entries and parades, music, dance, oratory, and poetry. Now the knight had both the Court of Love and the many romances of chivalry in poetry or prose to define his character and to furnish him glamorized roles to play. Many tournaments presented the characters of King Arthur's Round Table or the heroes of Charlemagne's time or of the Crusades, though even such nonmilitary figures as shepherds and monks might appear.

The tournament field was a showplace where the knight might prove his worthiness before his lord and his lady-love. At the south side of the field stood the pavilions of the lord of the day and the ladies of honor (often combined into one pavilion), the home base where the knight presented himself and offered his services and where he came at the end for recognition of his triumph, though the actual giving of prizes usually took place indoors at the banquet that followed. Sometimes the pavilion was part of the dramatic setting, a thatched cottage, for instance, for a tournament with a pastoral story. Nearby stood another scenic structure, sometimes a castle, sometimes an enchanted fountain, tree, or grotto, where the knight touched with his lance one of several shields to indicate which course he would enter. Around the field were erected various doors, castle gates, bridgeheads, and narrow passes where the knight was challenged and had to overcome obstacles. His final goal was a castle where a lady was held captive, or a magic stone in a secret wood where a prince or a sword was bound by the enchantment of a wicked magician. Each knight fought with his actual prowess, and except when the final pass had to be won by the guest of honor, no one knew who would win each encounter.

The tournament often began with an Entry to present the whole cast to the audience in a striking way. When there was a story framework for the event, the

Entry was usually planned as part of the same story, but it might be developed separately with its own music, pageantry, and impersonation of historical or fictional characters. Froissart records the charming entry to the jousts in London in 1390 of sixty ladies mounted on palfreys, each leading a knight by a silver chain. The knights were richly dressed, with retinues that wore their heraldic colors or special insignia. Bizarre costumes were often used in making a "gallant appearance." In 1561 for the tournament celebrating the marriage of William of Orange and Anne of Saxony at Leipzig, the costumes included those of Tartars, pilgrims, fools, hunting monks, and Netherlands cuirassiers, and each group had a band of musicians in similar garb. At a tournament given at Kassel in 1596 by the Landgrave of Hessen for the visit of the Duke d'Alencon, the Seven Deadly Sins, the Nine Muses, the Four Cardinal Virtues, and other figures appeared in procession before the tilting. At one of the series of jousts celebrating the marriage of Margaret of York and the Duke of Burgundy, the Comte de Roussy made his entry in a very spectacular way. First came a dwarf with a key, and behind him a castle on wheels with four towers and a gate that would open and close. When they reached the royal gallery, the dwarf opened the gate and revealed the Count mounted within.

In the sixteenth century, pageant cars, like those used in processions and in maskings in the great hall, made part of the Entry. At a tournament honoring Catherine de Medici and her daughter appeared a chariot with cloths of gold and clouds, drawn by four white hackneys. High on the car sat the goddess Venus, and below, children dressed like Mercury sang. Another car held Cupid with more "Mercuries," who as the car went about the field delivered favors to the ladies.

When so much importance was attached to the spectacular entrance, each knight was put to it to find a theme, an *impresa* or motto, or a device that would attract attention. Fantastic devices appeared both in actual tournaments and in the fictitious combats in imaginative literature. In the *Arcadia*, Sidney has one knight and his horse hidden in a great figure representing the phoenix until the figure is burned on the field, allowing the knight to rise, as it were, from the ashes. The "unknown knight," usually in black armor, the "humble knight" in poor armor, or the "wild knight," decorated with greenery, was a romantic figure both on the field and in literature.

The peak of dramatization of the tournament was reached in the *Scharmützel*, the scrimmage, staged at Binche by Marie of Hungary, Protector of the Netherlands, when the Emperor Charles V came to install his son Philip of Spain as the new ruler. The cartel read before the Emperor related the terrible deeds of Norabroch, a black magician who held many captives in his enchanted castle. Hidden in clouds on the Isla Venturosa, the castle was approached by three passes guarded by three knights called the Red Gryphon, the Black Eagle, and the Golden Lion, with whom all knights who sought to reach the castle must fight. La Reina Fadada, a humane princess, had provided on the island long ago a stone in which was embedded a sword of great virtue. The knight who could remove it would make an end of the enchantment and rescue the prisoners.

259

Next day the knights gathered on the field under assumed names: Knight of the Blue Shield, Knight Without Hope, Knight of Death, and so on. Each knight in turn, even if he won the first pass, was defeated at one of the later passes and was led prisoner to Castle Tenebroso. But at last the Knight Aventurero overcame the Golden Lion at the third pass. "Already the sun had set," the chronicler continues, "night was approaching, and the heaven was covered with many thick clouds. And now in the Castle Tenebroso were frightful sounds, by which one knew that this man was the venturesome knight who should put an end to the strange adventures. Spectators jumped the barriers and climbed trees to see more clearly. When the Knight Aventurero had drawn out the sword, there was the roll of thunder and the cloud of painted cloth lifted from the castle. When the gate was forced, the knights who had been imprisoned rose as if from sleep. The conqueror freed them, and Norabroch was punished by being bound forever to an enchanted chair. The successful knight was of course the new ruler, Philip of Spain.

TOURNAMENT FIELD AS THEATRE

The tournament field was a form of theatre. Sometimes it was set up in one of the large rounds that replaced or imitated the ancient Roman amphitheatre, but any large place would serve: a wide place in a street, an open square, or a playfield near the castle. The king as host paid the bill, though the city officials might manage the construction.

There is a detailed description of the structure built in the Westminster Palace grounds in 1501 for the marriage of Katherine of Aragon to Prince Arthur. Walls were built "in circuit of the field of war," then "by and upon the walls" double stages, wide and sturdy, for the common people. On the south side was a high pavilion, the right side of which was decorated with hangings and cushions of gold for the king and his lords, and the left part for the queen and her ladies. From these pavilions stairs led down to the place of tourney for the use of messengers. On the north side, opposite the royal parties, were similar pavilions decorated with red silk for the mayor, aldermen, and officials of the guilds. The marshals and judges had a place below the royal boxes.

The two-story pavilions for royalty on the south and for civic officials on the north, high above the pit of action, set a pattern for the galleries one above the other in the Elizabethan and Italian theatres of the sixteenth century. The Elizabethan bear-baiting pit, important as one model for the Elizabethan stage, was a miniature tournament field, with two or three galleries above the pit.

In the sixteenth century the dramatic aspects of the tournament far outshone the fighting. Kings rarely led their armies any more and hence did not need the training in horsemanship. Henry VIII of England was very fond of both indoor jousts and tournaments. But when Henry II of France died in 1559 after a splinter of a lance had pierced his eye, the rules were changed to reduce the danger still further. Some tournaments were held in the seventeenth century, but the operatic posing of the aristocracy was better expressed in other dramatic entertainment. The horse ballet and the "carrousel," a ball game somewhat like polo played on horseback, were popular. The players often entered in costume in dramatic character. We have the magnificent costume designs of the great carrousel of Louis XIV, who was ever after known as the Sun King because he appeared in this carrousel dressed as Apollo.

Reconstruction of a medieval jousting tournament. *Illustration by Martha Sutherland.*

Banquetings and Early Masques:
The Private Drama of the Nobility

The nobles dramatized their private occasions as richly as their tournaments. At picnics, banquets, and balls they acted out, with the help of professional singers, dancers, painters, and poets, their vision of the high ideals of the courtier's life. And as with the tournaments, these forms of entertainment became more and more elaborate and dramatic. Even casual daytime outdoor occasions might be dramatized. Henry VIII and his courtiers dressed in character for a picnic in the park. Elizabeth I, on her Progresses, could scarce get to the castle she was to visit without seeing a nymph appear from behind a tree to sing or ask her decision in a *débat* between two rustics, or having someone lead her to a lake where legendary figures made music on islands or read a poem or put on a little play.

BANQUETINGS

Between the many courses of a long banquet, it was the custom to introduce diversions called in French *entremets*, in Italian *intermezzi*, and in Spanish *entremeses*. The wandering minstrel or a poet or painter attached to the noble household might plan a series of entremets to reinforce a single theme. The promotion of a new Crusade was the theme of one of the most famous of all medieval banquets: the Feast of the Pheasant given at Lille in 1453, soon after the news of the capture of Constantinople by the Turks. The Duke of Burgundy, one of the most lavish rulers in Europe, assembled the Knights of the Golden Fleece from many countries for a series of tourneys and banquets that lasted for weeks, reaching a climax in a banquet given by his nephew, the Duke of Cleves. The food was let down from the ceiling in spectacular carriages, and on tables around the room were scenic caves and forests with savage men and heraldic devices and miniature scenes. As in the Royal Entries, many of these celebrated the historic role and deeds of the family. Other devices were brought on by characters who sang or spoke. The climax of the banquet came when a Friar seated on a dromedary led by a giant came out of a miniature church to the Duke's table and told how the church was

262

being trampled by its enemies. Then a Herald, dressed in a Golden Fleece, entered with a pheasant, roasted and adorned, and announced that such a dish was appropriate for making vows. In the excitement of such a splendid occasion, challenged by both religion and chivalry, what knight would refuse to make his vow? The vow proved to be a dramatic gesture for a crusade that never took place. In this kind of medieval drama the guests expected to be participants, not an audience for a play.

EARLY MASQUES

The social dance had an even more important development than the banquet when royalty, nobles, and knights discovered that they could act glamorous roles, supported by professional entertainers. In the fourteenth century in England, a "disguising" was an actual visit by citizens calling on their town mayor or their noble lord at his Christmas or other midwinter feast. It was an upper-class version of the ceremonial visit of the village mummers to the lord of the manor, except that the citizens had no traditional play and expected to remain silent ("mum") as they made the host play "mumchance" with loaded dice and seem to win the gifts the visitors had brought. In 1377, when the quarrel between Richard II and the city of London was settled, 130 citizens rode through the streets with visors on their faces, accompanied by minstrels, and called on the king with gifts of gold. Among the disguises were those of an emperor, a pope, and twenty-four cardinals. The visitors stayed to dance, the citizens and the royal party dancing on separate sides of the hall.

In the fifteenth century the disguising still remained mum, but the Entry of the presenter or herald was dramatized. John Lydgate wrote a number of Entries for disguisings, with introductory speeches to provide a fictional excuse for the visit, sometimes a debate to be decided by the noble host, playing an image of his role as judge and ruler. In the sixteenth century the presentation of the disguisings was expanded with fantastic scenic adornment. One of the most elaborate entertainments was devised as a prologue for a ball when Katherine of Aragon was welcomed to England in 1501—another example of the development of a medieval form in the period of the Renaissance. When the king and queen had taken seats under the Cloth of Estate the disguising entered with three large pageant wagons: castle, ship, and mountain. The castle was drawn by a gold lion, a silver lion, a hart, and an ibex, with two men in each beast. Four young girls in the four turrets of the castle sang as the pageant advanced, with eight beautiful ladies in disguise looking out the windows of the castle. The second wagon held a ship with mariners, and in it a fair lady dressed as Princess of Spain. The third pageant, a great Hill, contained eight knights who assaulted the castle, won the ladies, and danced set dances with them. After the pageants and the performers left, the royal party danced.

The full dramatization of the masked ball combined the medieval form of masked visitors entering a nobleman's house to present a carefully prepared entertainment with the new idea that the maskers would be the noblemen themselves—some-

Entry of a group of grotesque dancers during a medieval banquet.

264

times the king and queen—who would arrive or be disclosed in some scenic device and present a play with the help of professional actors, singers, and dancers.

The practice of having masked aristocrats enter and dance seems to have originated in Italy. Nobles liked to go about the streets and into one another's houses in disguise, and especially from the Medici circle in Florence many songs and poems of these *maschere* have been preserved. At the English court in 1512, after Henry VIII became king, the maskers created quite a stir when they asked the ladies to dance with them "after the manner of Italy." A short time later a party was held in which a group of lords entered and chose partners and stepped into an adjoining room and put on masking apparel (great robes of Venetian fashion and faces with beards of gold) and came back to dance with the ladies. At the end the queen plucked off the king's visor, the other ladies doing the same with their partners, and when all were discovered they went in to a feast. To achieve complete dramatization it was only necessary to have professional songs, dances, and scenery serve for the Entry of the royal maskers as they pretended to be strangers from afar putting on a show before asking the seated guests to join them in the dance. Such a combination of the professional and the social was popular at court affairs throughout the sixteenth century.

The medieval arrangement of separate mansions about the hall for a masque persisted throughout the sixteenth century, even after the perspective stage uniting all the mansions in one scene had been developed in Italy. But this new form was finally adopted by the aristocrats of western Europe for their dramatized balls, in England in 1607 and in France in 1610. The spectacular perspective stage instilled new life into the masque as both French and English kings spent fantastic sums to strengthen the prestige of the monarchy against threats of civil war.

The Morality Play

Preachers and schoolteachers, the chief sponsors of moralities, were not large coherent classes like village peasants, clerics, merchants, or noblemen, and they only occasionally offered their plays to the other classes. Still, the morality was an important form of medieval drama, with its own special characteristics.

THE MORALITY AS DRAMATIC ALLEGORY

Allegory is a very old form. It makes a theme explicit from the beginning. In Euripides' *Hippolytus* the goddesses Aphrodite and Artemis are personifications of sexual desire and dedicated austerity, the two options contending for control of the hero. At the beginning of *Alcestis* the characters Death and Apollo bargain over the life of Admetus. The influential Christian epic, Prudentius' *Psychomachia* (c. 400 A.D.), was widely read, and the battle of virtues and vices that it portrays was familiar to most people throughout the Middle Ages.

There were a number of allegorical characters in the guild cycles, but they were incidental: the character Death walking silently in front of Herod, or Dolor and Misery taking over Adam and Eve at the expulsion from Paradise. The Debate of the Four Daughters of God—Truth, Justice, Mercy, and Peace—at the beginning of some cycles, was a short morality play showing the rationale of God's decision to listen to Mercy and send His son to save mankind. The terminal cycle episode, Doomsday or the Last Judgment, was a kind of morality play, with sharp conflict of good and evil and a dancelike procession of damned souls, each one often representing a sin or a general social type. After the failure of the expected millennium to arrive in 1000 A.D., the image of doom was more commonly seen as an allegory of an experience in the soul than as a literal happening to be expected.

In the morality play the late medieval mind found an alternative to the mystery cycles, which, by the sixteenth century, were awesome but unwieldy relics of the past. The subject matter of the morality was still man's salvation from sin and death, but, freed from the historical episodes of the life of Christ, it presented

266

this salvation as an immediate crisis in man's soul. While the mystery cycles were repeated with little change year after year, the morality was a dynamic form that encouraged variation and originality. Playwrights experimented with long plays and short, religious and secular, comic and serious. They brought in a variety of characters, used soliloquy, debate, song and dance, or any other solo or group form of entertainment, or even centered the play on one strong character responding to a sequence of good and evil influences.

RELIGIOUS MORALITIES

The fifteenth century produced a number of morality plays that were almost as long as the mystery cycles, but most of them have been lost. In the city of York a morality, the Paternoster play, was given at intervals instead of the mystery cycle and apparently on wagons drawn about the city, just as for the cycle. Each of the petitions in the Lord's Prayer was paired with one of the Seven Deadly Sins, and there seem to have been episodes illustrating all the subdivisions of the seven sins. *The Castle of Perseverance*, which was written about 1425 for performance in the round, has been described. All the main themes of the later moralities are contained in this long play of some 3,650 lines about Youth as he is tempted and falls into the hands of Lust and Folly, with a castle besieged by the Vices and defended by the Virtues.

The coming of Death, only one part of *The Castle of Perseverence*, became the whole play of *Everyman*. As the only totally serious morality, it is not typical, but it stands out as much the best of all the morality plays. Both a Dutch and an English version are known, and while it is uncertain which was the original and which the translation, some evidence seems to give the Dutch *Eickerlijk* (c. 1495) priority. One of the great achievements of the morality was to create one strong central character and let everything seem to happen inside his soul. The vices and virtues attacking and defending a castle may be an image of man fortifying himself against temptation, but it is more powerful to make the vices and virtues images of an inner conflict and inner discovery. Then the central character is not a dry abstraction but an image for all men, a container of all abstractions, an Everyman. *Everyman* maintains its powerful appeal through the centuries because each person can identify with its central character, called by Death to render an account of his life.

For all its terror, the play is remarkably cheerful and sane. At first Everyman is shocked to realize how undependable are the things of this world. Fellowship, Kindred, and Goods, who had promised eternal devotion, desert him, but Everyman works out his way to salvation through means of this earth. His Good Deeds, though too weak to stand, can call Knowledge, who brings him to the sacraments of confession, contrition, and penance. Strength, Five Wits, and Beauty are fellow travelers, though they must drop out in weakness before the end. As Everyman speaks the simple words of the Bible, "Into thy hands I commit my spirit," the Angel welcomes him to heaven.

The play has no trace of the grotesque or demonic or, except for the awesome figure of Death, the macabre. It is not like the paintings of Hieronymus Bosch, filled with tortured, grotesque faces or half-animal monsters. Rather it has the noble dignity of a painting of Van Eyck. The Dutchman or Englishman who wrote *Everyman* (c. 1495) in a very disturbed period found means in this world for transcending this world. Above all, the main character has such power and dignity that he goes far to redeem man's limitations.

In a modern version by Hugo von Hofmannsthal, *Everyman*, produced by Max Reinhardt, became the dramatic feature of the Salzburg Festival for a decade. Many who saw it in the twenties and thirties found it the most impressive religious theatre experience of a lifetime. Played at a long banquet table in front of the baroque cathedral, it made theatrical use of the surroundings. Processions came out of the church, and bands of dancers and revelers came through the audience. The voice of Death calling "Jedermann!" ("Everyman!") came first from under the table. The banquet resumed after a moment's pause, then another voice called from high on the cathedral, then from several places on the buildings in back of the audience, and finally an eerie "Jedermann!" came from the castle on the peak of the mountain across the river.

COMIC MORALITIES

To read the earliest comic morality, *Mankind*, of about 1468–71, is to plunge into the tumultuous disorder of the later medieval imagination. With corruption everywhere, parish priests and preaching friars won popular audiences by describing the wickedness of the world, sometimes describing it so vividly as to make it alluring. So it happened with the comic satire of the morality plays: the more vividly the sins were portrayed, the more entertaining the plays became.

By conventional expectations, *Mankind* is not really a play at all. The conflict between Mercy and the Vices and the Devil is kept in the background much of the time, while the foreground is a series of popular entertainments—solos, duets, songs and dances—nearly all addressed to the audience. Even as the characters threaten or mock each other they speak more directly to the audience than to the other characters. They must catch the attention of a free and easy crowd gathered in the great hall of a nobleman or of merchants in their guild hall settling down for an entertaining interlude after a banquet. We are not to imagine the action with scenic mansions but rather before the two doors of the architectural screen at the end of the hall. The performers even plant seed in a field on the floor of the hall.

The Vice, the most original creation of the comic morality, stole the show when he added to his role as devilish schemer and tempter of mankind the japes, songs, and monologues of the popular minstrels and other entertainers. Like Lucifer in the mysteries, he is the cause of trouble, the ruler who sets his assistants, the particular vices, to work. He is supposedly the son of the devil, but he often rails at and even beats his dad. He is a roarer who enters with a "ho, ho, ho" or a "ha, ha, ha" and quarrels with all the other characters. He is expected to swear, tear, and blaspheme both Heaven and Earth. In several plays of the sixteenth century a much subdued descendant of the Vice appears. There are few reflections of the morality Vice in Elizabethan comedy, though other clowns, jesters, and buffoons were copied. But we do find the pattern of the Vice in some of the villains of serious plays. Iago, in his compulsion to cause trouble, his ingenuity, his relish in his power, is more credibly explained by his relationship to the Vice than by any concept of psychological motivation.

POLITICAL MORALITIES

Not a crisis of the soul but the education of a ruler was the concern of the political morality. The new idea of kingship that developed in the fifteenth century was that a monarch should rule his country directly—not through feudal knights but with the help of trained administrators and an advisory council. From 1485, when Henry VII defeated Richard III and brought an end to the long civil War of the Roses, it was the policy of the Tudors to build a strong central government and control the barons. Both Henry VII and Henry VIII gave responsibility to a number of able advisors who were not from the old baronial families. The earliest English romantic play, written and produced at a nobleman's banquet in the 1490s, is Henry Medwall's *Fulgens and Lucrece*, a dramatized debate, between a nobleman and a cultivated common man paying suit to a noble young lady, that demonstrates that true noblesse is more important than feudal rank. Though the example from classical literature provides a slight variation from the morality formula, the characters are little more than abstract representatives of their qualities. The play shows the concern with the character of the uneducated counselor who, as advisor to the king, could be more important than a feudal baron.

In the hope of influencing the king in his major policies, a number of men of wealth and power in England had morality plays produced to show how a king keeps public order and prevents civil war, and to dramatize the conflict between wise counselors and ambitious flatterers. *Magnificence* was written by John Skelton,

Miniature from *The Passion of Marcodi* depicting medieval devil "vices."

poet laureate, who had been tutor to Henry VIII before he came to the throne. It was apparently produced before the king early in the reign, about 1516 or 1518, to admonish the young king, who, unlike his over-parsimonious father, Henry VII, was inclined to extravagance, and, under the influence of Cardinal Wolsey, became involved in war on the continent that threatened to bankrupt the nation. *Magnificence* gives only a friendly warning, not naming Wolsey but showing a royal character, Magnificence, lured away from Measure by Fansy disguised as Largesse. Magnificence is abandoned by Fansy, beaten and stripped of his rich apparel by Adversity. Then Poverty wraps him in an old coverlet and he goes out to beg food. The disguised clowns, Myschefe and Despair, so taunt him that he attempts suicide. But Goodhope takes the sword from him and Redresse brings him back to Perseverance and his former fine state. Revived in 1963, the play was impressive in its royal spectacle and heraldic splendor.

An even greater success in revival was the Scottish political morality *Ane Satyre of the Thrie Estaites*. Acted in the old Assembly Hall of the Presbyterian Church, under the direction of Tyrone Guthrie, it was the hit of the Edinburgh Festival of 1948. The original play by Sir David Lindsay, a Scottish nobleman and diplomat, was produced before the king in Scotland in 1540 and then again in 1552 and 1554.

In the first part of *Ane Satyre* the king is led to a bower of sensuality by his courtier Wantonness and by the smooth rationalizer Sandy Solace. The king lets Chastity and Verity be put in the stocks until Divine Correction wakes him and drives out Sensuality. The king is permitted "honest pastimes," but with Good Counsel and Diligence he summons the Three Estates to consider a general reform.

The second part of the play is a political Judgment Day as vivid as the Doomsday plays of the cycles. A pauper demands justice, saying that his lord has taken his horse and that when his father, mother, and wife died the Vicar took his three cows as a funeral fee. A fast-talking Pardoner cheats him out of his last coin. The Three Estates—the Nobility, the Clergy, and the Commons—seem unable to drive out corruption. But Divine Correction makes them listen to John Commonwealth, who points out the sins of merchant, nobleman, and bishop. Suddenly everyone confesses, as in a dream of perfect justice, but the confessions turn into a riot of general accusations. Flattery brags that he always escapes punishment. The Prioress, defrocked and flaunting a bright-colored dress, curses the friends who would not let her marry but compelled her to be a nun. The Herald dismisses the audience as he starts the minstrels in a dance tune while he goes for a drink.

Out of the satire that shows both anger and amusement at the corruption of the world, the adapter and the director fashioned a play that seemed very live to the twentieth century.

A political morality play that interested the nineteenth century was Bishop John Bale's *King John*, written about 1540 but known to us in a later revision. It is a strong, humorless attack on the pope and Catholicism, with such characters as England, Clergy, Sedition, Civil Order, Private Wealth, and so on. But when a

271

poor widow wants to complain to authority that Clergy, Pope, Monks, and Nuns are robbing her, it is not to an abstraction she appeals but to King John, the twelfth-century English king who had defied the pope. It soon becomes clear that the widow is England, and though Stephen Langton and Cardinal Pandulphus appear, two actual people involved in John's conflict with Rome, the play progresses almost completely as a moral allegory.

When in 1561–62 Lawyers of the Inner Temple wanted to warn their country of the dangers of civil war if Queen Elizabeth did not settle the problem of who was to succeed her, they produced, first in their own great hall and then in the queen's palace of Whitehall, a striking drama called *Gorboduc,* showing the tragic results of the decision of an ancient British king, Gorboduc, to divide his kingdom between his two sons. One son kills the other; then their mother kills him, and the people kill the survivors and break into civil war. The play follows the pattern of a morality play, with a good counselor to point the final moral. But the inexperienced playwrights, Thomas Sackville and Thomas Norton, gave little attention to characterization and motivation. This and other early attempts at tragedy, written by literary men, were not capable of interesting a general audience.

SCHOOL MORALITIES

School moralities, like the political moralities, belong in time largely to the Renaissance, though they follow medieval patterns. They were a product of the new humanistic education, which began in Italy by the middle of the fifteenth century and appeared in France and England at the end of the fifteenth and early in the sixteenth century. Plays were written for student performance almost since the founding of the new grammar schools. Developed by humanist schoolteachers to show patrons and parents the nature of the new education and the proper discipline for the student, these short plays usually followed the three-part plot of the religious morality: Youth being instructed by a Good Counselor, then dallying pleasantly with Honest Recreation, tempted into tavern revelry by Idleness, then shown to be a fool and led back to Diligence. One of the earliest school moralities in England is John Rastell's *Four Elements* of about 1509–1517. In the first part the youth Humanity is lectured in geography: the round earth and the exciting new-found lands beyond the Atlantic. But he is lured away by Sensual Appetite.

Lessons of manners and diet are taught in a lively morality called *Condemnation de Banquet,* written for his students by a French schoolmaster, Nicolas de le Chesnays, and printed at Paris in 1507. Diner, Souper, and Banquet are beset by Good Company, Gourmandise, and Pass-Time, then by a troop of ills: Colic, Gout, Jaundice, Apoplexy, and Dropsy. A court trial is run by Hippocrates and Galen, and

272

Dame Experience deals with conflicts common to all ages: difficulties between parents and children.

By the middle of the sixteenth century school plays were influenced by the classic revival, and the morality pattern gave way to the interplay of farcical action suggested by Plautus and Terence. But two examples, *Ralph Roister Doister* of about 1553 and *Gammer Gurton's Needle* of a decade later, although planned in classic five-act form, used native material and English, not Roman, characters.

THE END OF THE MIDDLE AGES

As the Renaissance spread throughout Europe in the sixteenth and seventeenth centuries, the forms of medieval theatre disappeared or faded into the civic pageantry or village entertainment of their origin. None of the medieval dramas were plays in the modern sense: characterization and plot were minimal. The tournament had a fictional plot and dramatic characters, but the main activity was fighting. The "guests" at the masque entered in character and performed a short play, but their main interest was in the several hours of unstructured social dancing. The mummers were only partly in character, and almost all their activity was solo entertainment. In the church drama the words were subordinate to the music and spectacular processions. Even the mystery cycles, for all their many scenes of dramatic confrontation, were visual tableaux, processions, and solo entertainment rather than plays. The moralities moved toward new developments under the influence of humanism. By the sixteenth century new alternatives to the medieval forms had developed. Small professional companies, followers of the old wandering minstrels, offered casual entertainment to be chosen by anyone who could pay. For the first time in Europe since the fall of Rome a play became a complete experience in itself.

VI

The Renaissance Theatre

David Garrick and Hannah Pritchard in *Macbeth*, 1744. *Courtesy of the Trustees of the British Museum.*

275

Introduction

The name "Renaissance" was chosen by the people who created it, who thought they were resurrecting and bringing to a new birth the ancient civilization that had been destroyed by the invasion of the Goths, the German "barbarians of the north." With the rebirth came light to liberate mankind from the bonds of feudalism, the rule of craft guilds, the restraint of trade, the hair-splitting arguments of theologians. Walls crumbled—castle walls, city walls, mental walls. As early as the middle of the fourteenth century, several scholars and artists in Italy saw the possibility of a new era that would focus attention on man himself and his activities in this world rather than on his efforts to attain heavenly bliss. The fourteenth-century poet Petrarch devoted himself to the study and revival of ancient poetry.

INFLUENCE OF THE ANCIENTS

By the end of the fifteenth century and the beginning of the sixteenth, the interest in Greek and Roman antiquities had become a mania. Architects measured the ruins of old Roman buildings. Scholars searched monastic and castle bookshelves and found many manuscripts lost or forgotten, among them hitherto unknown plays of the Roman dramatist Plautus and Aristotle's *Poetics*, dealing with the different dramatic genres. The Latin treatise on building a theatre in one chapter of Vitruvius' *Ten Books on Architecture* (1486) was an important influence.

Systematic production of ancient plays began in both Ferrara and Rome in 1486. The academic tradition of play production was begun in Rome under the direction of Pomponius Laetus, head of the Platonic Academy and a famous humanist teacher of rhetoric. He produced the Latin classics and for setting used a simplified façade of arches, similar to the arcade screen of the *tableaux vivants* of the Royal Entries. Many students from all over Europe who had come to Italy to study rhetoric carried back information about performance of the classics. In Ferrara, Duke Ercole d'Este began his spectacular court productions with Plautus translated into Italian by the court poet. Probably from this beginning, perspective scenery was used in the court theatres. Certainly by 1508, when Ariosto's *Caesaria* was created, the court theatres used perspective scenery, and hence their productions can be called the beginnings of the modern theatre.

The idea of a theatre, outdoors or in a palace-ballroom, designed for an audience to see and hear a play, was derived from Renaissance study of the ancients. When in 1561 the Antwerp merchants in their poetry club, the Rederykerkamer, built a stage decorated with classical columns for a drama festival, they felt that they had lured the Muses from Athens to their city. When in 1576 James Burbage built the first Elizabethan playhouse in London, he called it by the Greek and Roman name, The Theatre. Likewise the idea of a drama as a complete, independent aesthetic experience, to be seen and heard by individuals who have gone to the theatre for that purpose, appears in the Renaissance for the first time since the fall of Rome. Henceforth a play is not a miscellany of songs, dances, japes, and skits, an interlude to entertain between courses of a banquet, an Easter or Christmas celebration, a tournament or masked ball with a dramatized beginning and ending or a day-long procession of religious history. A play is a play is a play.

HUMANISM: GUIDING SPIRIT OF THE RENAISSANCE

But the spirit of the Renaissance went far beyond the new classic styles of architecture, beyond the comedies, tragedies, and pastoral plays produced in an "antique" style. Humanism, the guiding philosophy of the Renaissance, stimulated exploration and creative thought in many fields, both scientific and aesthetic. In

Wood block by Mattia Paga, 1556–69, depicting a Palm Sunday procession in the Piazza San Marco, Venice, led by Il Serenissimo. *Courtesy Museo Correr, Venice.*

fact, the humanists believed that science and aesthetics need not go in different directions. Extremes were reconciled in a higher unity: philosophy and religion, art and mathematics were one. Many painters sought strict mathematical rules for perspective, and expected to adapt the rules to the stage. Other painters seemed to reconcile heaven and earth intuitively by painting sacred characters shining with heavenly grace yet walking on real streets before real houses, with real bodies under their real clothing. In Fra Angelico's *Last Judgment* the monks arriving in heaven embrace charming angels who teach them a circle dance in an Elysian garden.

In the next generation, at the end of the fifteenth century and the first quarter of the sixteenth, the creative and intellectual giants of the Renaissance arrived: Erasmus, Michelangelo, Raphael, Leonardo da Vinci, Botticelli. The expanding freedom, with a new sense of purpose, unity, and order, stimulated creative minds.

Erasmus of Rotterdam was the most influential of the philosophers and educators who defined the goals of humanism. Starting out as a penniless bastard child, he became one of the greatest scholars of all time, the intellectual leader of all Europe, the philosopher of humanism—a humanism that, while dealing with man in this world, saw him always in relation to divine love. While he worked for church reform and was claimed by the Lutherans, he refused to join the Reformation battle on either side but stayed at his task of organizing and reconciling all branches of the wisdom of the past. His most famous work, *Praise of Folly* (1509), was not a philosophical discourse but an imaginary monologue spoken by the character Folly. Everything important in life is based on Folly. She revels in the ironic contrast between wisdom and pleasure. At the end Erasmus brings his ideas together in a vision of childlike simplicity, approved by Socrates and St. Paul and Christ Himself.

Contemporary with Erasmus there was Leonardo da Vinci, painter, engineer,

279

scientist, inventor—what could he not do?—speculating on the dynamics of theatre machines and the rules of perspective, where art and mathematics are one. There was Raphael, happy companion of humanist popes, equally adept at painting large murals showing a synthesis of Greek and Christian philosophy or designing stately stage settings and painting witty front curtains for productions at the Vatican. Of equal or greater genius was the brooding, dark Michelangelo. Pope Julius II had the old Gothic church of St. Peter's torn down because it was ugly and asked Michelangelo to replace it with a divine palace. Already Michelangelo had carved the nude David in white marble, such a strong, idealized body that to consider it sensual would be an impertinence. It is told of Michelangelo and Julius II that they sat in a marble quarry dreaming of a huge tomb that would capture the beauty of the struggle of man toward perfection. The tomb was never finished. The statue of Moses now in Santa Maria Maggiore in Rome and the bound slaves struggling to emerge from rough marble columns, now in the Accademia in Florence, were intended for that tomb. Michelangelo painted the Sistine Chapel ceiling, with hundreds of scenes and characters connected with the Creation, the Ex-

Pastoral scene presenting the Renaissance humanist from *Il Trionfo Della Pieta*, 1658. *Courtesy Graphische Sammlung Albertina, Vienna.*

Il Cortile Del Belvedere of the Vatican, the site of a sixteenth-century spectacle before the Basilica was remodeled by Italian artists and architects to its present condition.

pulsion from Eden, the Flood, and the Degradation of Noah. The worshiper enters the chapel under scenes of the fallen state of man and moves in reverse order through the scenes of Eden, to approach the altar under the scene of God as an abstract whirl beginning the creation.

Men of all ages are concerned with unity, but in few ages have they so consciously and ardently sought it as in the Renaissance. A comparison of Shakespeare's *King Lear* (c. 1610), perhaps the greatest and most complex play ever performed at one sitting, with the even longer forms of the Middle Ages—say *The Canterbury Tales* and the York cycle of plays—shows the superiority of Renaissance unity. Chaucer's package of separate tales is tied together by an enclosing scheme that presents the tellers of the tales and their comments on one another's stories in a very loose organization. The mystery play cycles were equally loose in structure: *King Lear* has a comparable scope and complexity, but the plots, characters, and themes are closely integrated to create a truly unified work.

The new "humanist" education was based on a wide knowledge of the classics, including drama and poetry as well as history, biography, and moral and political discourse. It was a "liberal" education, to liberate the individual from prejudices. The new man of the Renaissance was not to be trained for contemplation or the repetition of prayers, or for winning tournaments or fighting crusades. At court his native gifts were to be perfected not only through books but through sports, dancing, poetry, and music. By his wit, wisdom, and graceful discourse he should so win the confidence of his prince that he could always tell him the truth and help him avoid mistakes. The Renaissance man was to be a well-rounded individual, devoted to God and his prince, striving for perfection in his own character and justice in the state. The Renaissance brought in a new concept of man as a courtier, and produced the governor and magistrate; of man as a creator, and produced the artist; of man as observer, measurer, and controller of nature, and produced the scientist. The metaphysical basis for this ideal was the cosmic scheme of the Neoplatonists. Neoplatonism was most clearly expressed by the Platonic Academy, a group of scholars, poets, and philosophers who from the 1470s gathered around Lorenzo de Medici in Florence. The cosmos was compared to a ladder, with levels one above the other. At the lowest level is pure matter, above matter is the vegetable realm, and above that are the animals. Man, at the center, shares matter with those below him and spirit with those above. But reason, the connecting link, is man's alone. Above man are the angels, archangels, and principalities, and so on up to God. God is the active form of love, trying to draw everything upward. Man is free to move up or down, becoming like an angel or like a beast.

COURT AND TOWN

Where the macrocosm of a Neoplatonic ladder shows man's metaphysical position at the center, drawn upward toward divine love, the corresponding microcosm shows his central position in the state, drawn upward toward the idealized image of the ruler, whether he was called emperor, king, or duke. The new liberated man, who had left the feudal castle for the city, had ceased to be a vassal of a lord and had become a citizen directly under the prince.

The city had never had a comfortable position in the feudal system, and whenever possible it established the privilege of being a "free town," outside the authority of any feudal lord. In the conflict between king and barons in the fifteenth century, the cities found themselves natural allies of the king. This partnership became more meaningful toward the end of the fifteenth century as three countries of western Europe emerged as conscious "nations" under a strong central government. In 1477 the French king defeated the rebellious Burgundians and united all of France. In 1485 Henry Tudor put an end to the War of the Roses by defeating Richard III and, as Henry VII, established the strong Tudor dynasty. In 1492 Ferdinand and Isabella drove the Moors out of Granada and united all of Spain. Under the protection of the kings, the capital cities of Paris, London, and Madrid burst out of their medieval walls and institutions and offered citizens a new way of

Hall of the Five Hundred, Palazzio Vecchio, Florence, site of an early humanist theatrical activity.

life. Italy had no king and was not united until the nineteenth century. In the Renaissance each little "country" in Italy had its powerful duke. While the feudal system did not yet disappear—indeed the "Old Regime" was the main target of the French Revolution in the eighteenth century—yet in everyday relations Renaissance people thought of themselves as citizens of a nation under a king or prince.

In function prince and subject operated as two sides of a partnership, and this partnership gave shape to the modern theatre, created in the Renaissance by court and town. The theatre auditorium, with rows of seats facing a stage that has a proscenium frame and a painted picture of wings and backdrop organized by perspective, was created by professional architects at the ducal courts of Italy, usually in a long ballroom or sometimes in an unroofed courtyard. The other part of the modern theatre tradition—professional acting companies with professional playwrights—was created in the expanding capital cities of Paris, London, and Madrid.

Even from the beginning, the commerical theatres of London depended partly on the court. As capitalistic enterprises they offered their merchandise to the public, but what really put the season over was an invitation to play at court for Christmas and other festive occasions. Since the sixteenth century the theatre has been partly subsidized by the establishment, either by hereditary ruler or rich merchants.

Five fancy dress costumes skillfully designed by Georgio Vasari for a Medician court festival, Florence, 1549.

The Pastoral

In Greece three kinds of plays had been produced by competing playwrights: comedy, tragedy, and the satyr play. Following Vitruvius, Sebastiano Serlio in the sixteenth century described the same three kinds of plays but made the distinction between comedy and tragedy a matter of social class and expressed a concept of "satyric" quite different from the Greek. Tragedy, he asserted, had as characters kings and great public figures, whereas comedy presented private citizens, and he described his "tragic scene" and "comic scene" accordingly, but in his designs the comic scenes are as elegant as the tragic. He could not resist the Renaissance love of splendor.

Renaissance comedies and tragedies themselves, though supposedly following classic examples, differed radically from the Greek. In tragedy the Roman Seneca was the model, and in comedy the Romans Plautus and Terence.

For Serlio, satyric plays were those in which the characters were rustics. But his "rustic" scene was made of silk. "O immortal God:" he wrote, "what wonder it was to see so many trees and fruits, so many herbs and diverse flowers, all made from the finest silk of the most beautiful colors, the cliffs and rocks covered with diverse sea shells, with snails and other animals, with coral branches of many colors. . . . the superb costumes of some shepherds made of rich cloth of gold and silk, furred with the finest skins of wild animals. . . . I could also describe some shepherdesses whose costumes put avarice to shame."

It is clear that Serlio has in mind neither the Greek satyr play nor a play that satirizes people or manners, but the Renaissance pastoral play. This genre shows idealized shepherds scantily clad or dressed in silk, gathered in landscapes of woods and cool glades to sing the joys and sorrows of the simple life. It was a special genre, creating the anxiety of tragedy and showing the escape from danger and the happy ending of comedy.

The pastoral was a favorite form in the Renaissance. Long before our day the pastoral tradition was frozen into pink and blue Dresden china shepherds and shepherdesses. In the middle of the seventeenth century John Milton was able to use the pastoral formula in *Lycidas* (1637), his elegy for a friend. But after the French Revolution and the settling of America, the pastoral seemed as outmoded as the powdered wig. In the Renaissance and for three hundred years, however, the pastoral was an image of the Golden Age, the pagan world of Greece, of tragedy, of the world of imagination, poetry, and love.

ORIGIN AND DEVELOPMENT OF THE PASTORAL

The tradition of pastoral poetry and drama was created in the third century before Christ in the city of Alexandria. The poet Theocritus and his friends had come from Sicily to the city of the Ptolemies to make their fortunes. As they walked the hot, dusty streets and contended with the mobs gathered from three continents, they dreamed of cool shade and crystal brooks and the springtime they had known years before in Sicily, of simple shepherds tending their flocks, gathering for midday sociability in the shade or singing and dancing at a festival of the earth god Pan. Inspired by these romanticized memories, they wrote nostalgic poems of rural life that were charming and sad.

About the time of Christ, in the imperial city of Rome, another poet, Virgil, took up the pastoral tradition and set his shepherds in Arcadia. Virgil did not know the real Arcadia in Greece, a rocky, barren region. His Arcadia was purely imaginary, but all the more poetically useful.

The essence of the pastoral, whether in poetry, prose fiction, or drama, was freedom, an escape from duty, morality, demands of the superego, to a simple

The pastoral scene, "Aminta" Amsterdam, 1678.

The pastoral scene, "Il Pastor Fido" Venice, 1602.

life close to nature, in a land of eternal spring, where wants were simple and work easy, leaving time for festivals of singing, dancing, and poetry. There was time, too, for dalliance in love. The ode at the end of the first act of Tasso's *Aminta* (1571), a typical pastoral play, praised this Golden Age before "spontaneity was destroyed by the tyrant, that idol of deceit and hypocrisy, by the mad crowd afterwards called 'honour'." Nudity is sometimes an element in pastoral poetry and the pastoral prose tale, but apparently it was never brought on the stage. In *Aminta* there is a vivid narration by a minor character of how the satyr tied the naked Sylvia to a tree by hair, hands, and feet, and of Aminta's embarrassed rescue of his love, but the scene is not shown to the audience.

The pastoral had its own ways of imitating nudity. The "antique" jacket of the shepherds, based on the tunic and armour of the Roman soldier, was made to look form-fitting, with strong indications of pectoral muscles, a built-in navel, and often nipples of the breasts. The brief skirt suggested hanging strips of leather in the soldier's tunic. In the space between the skirt and the boots the knees and much of the legs seem in the illustrations to be nude. The nymph costume was even more an image of freedom. The Renaissance audience, usually the court, sat rigid, men and women held in by stiff corsets, often with a front panel of unbending metal. Materials were heavy and colors usually dark. But on the stage, among trees with silk leaves, the shepherd swain and his shepherdess nymph appeared in costumes of a Golden Age. The nymph wore a draped silk costume, often diaphanous and flowing, showing the curves of the uncorseted female body. A slit in

Five variants of the nymph-shepherdess costume. *From the left:* Fra Angelico's angel, Botticelli's attendant to Venus, Victory or Majesty, abstract image of Freedom, an allegory of Fame. *Illustration by Martha Sutherland.*

288

the skirt might give glimpses of ankle and calf, and sometimes the bottom of the skirt had been lifted and fastened by a brooch at the waist, showing the entire length of the leg. Sometimes the sleeves were starched and tied at intervals to stand out as puffs, but the rest of the costume flowed with the movement of the body.

The relation of the pastoral to the nude is clear in Botticelli's painting *The Birth of Venus*. At the center, the nude figure of the goddess is coming to shore from her birth in the sea. Meeting her are her mortal attendant nymphs in charming pastoral costumes of light, flowing material, decorated with a pattern of spring leaves. One of them is offering a veil to Venus.

There were no rules in Arcadia, no marriages, no family interests, but only the freedom of love, yet love involved another person who was free to respond or not to respond. While many lucky lovers found joy in equal love, the swain might frighten a shy maid and she might foreswear all suitors and embrace chastity among the devotees of Diana. Much of the action of the Renaissance pastoral play is concerned with the threat from two extremes: on the one side the shaggy, grinning satyr, with goat horns, beard, and hooves, and on the other side the shy girl fleeing from an unwanted suitor.

If these are the melodramatics of pastoral plots, the power of love to effect a transformation is the deeper theme. The characters are brought into danger of their lives, then suddenly comes a turn in the plot to effect a happy ending. The transformation is Neoplatonic, showing that divine love draws everything upward to its own perfection. In *Aminta*, Sylvia, the disdainful shepherdess, is finally transformed by pity, but not easily. Even when Aminta rescues her, she is angry because he has seen her naked and has touched her hand in releasing her. Only when she is told that she was the cause of his suicide does she feel pity.

Aminta and the many other pastoral dramas like it will never be seen on a twentieth-century stage. But any tourist may see in Versailles the exquisite sheepfold in a hidden corner of the park, a reminder of the time when Marie Antoinette and her ladies, dressed in silks, with bows and ribbons on their crooks, played at being dairymaids or shepherdesses in an idyllic pastoral world that could still be imagined in the eighteenth century.

Stages in the Renaissance

In the creation of the modern theatre there were at least four ways in which the medieval stage of separate mansions was reshaped. All achieved some unity through various combinations of illusionistic devices and formal architecture. The simplest of the new stages was the formal stage, exemplified by the Terence, or academic, stage in Italy and elsewhere, the similar stage used by the Jesuit Order, and the formal Rederyker stages in the Low Countries. The Hôtel de Bourgogne in Paris developed a simple form of stage that was more illusionistic than formal. A more complex development was the perspective stage.

THE TERENCE STAGE

In Rome and Ferrara where regular performances of ancient plays began, different approaches were used in recreating an ancient theatre. Those used in Rome led to the development of the "Terence stage," a formal, nonillusionistic setting. Those in Ferrara led to the development of the illusionistic perspective stage.

The Roman revivals in Latin began with Seneca's tragedy *Hippolytus*, but most revivals were of the comedies of Plautus and Terence. As the text of Vitruvius and the remains of Roman theatres suggested to Renaissance producers, the pattern of the ancient theatre called for a formal architectural backing with five doorways opening onto an open playing area. In the revivals each doorway in this arcade screen was usually assigned to a different character and often his name was printed over the doorway. The formality of the arcade screen appealed to the classic taste and was easy to fit into the budget of schools and academies. The idea of a screen such as was used in *Hippolytus* was spread over Europe by the many students who came to study rhetoric with Pomponius Laetus, and also by the many illustrated editions of the plays of Plautus and Terence, especially the edition of Terence of 1493 at Lyons. This influential publication had as editor Sulpitius Verelanus, editor of Vitruvius and a man familiar with the traditions of Ferrara and Rome. Of all the books printed and sold in Europe in the fifteenth and sixteenth centuries, more

Frontispiece to *Terence des Ducs* miniature in L'Arsenal, MS Fr 664. *Phot. Bibl. Nat. Paris.*

291

A 1496 Terence woodcut illustrating a Terence play. The upper half shows the opening scene of *Heautontimoroumenos*.

than half, it is estimated, were Latin texts of Terence. There were more than five hundred printings of some or all of Terence's plays. So the Terence stage seemed to demonstrate the very essence of the ancient world. In an illustration for a play of Plautus in an edition of 1510, painted landscapes are shown in back of the arches. In other productions a curtain in the arcade could be opened to reveal a painted setting or other indication of interiors.

The best description of the arcade in production is the account of a student performance of Terence's *Poenulus* in Rome in 1513. The stage was about a hundred feet wide, twenty-four feet deep, and eight feet above the floor. At the back of the stage was a decorated arcade screen divided into five sections by columns with gilded bases and capitals, each section framing a doorway covered with curtains of gold cloth. Above was a frieze of beautiful paintings and a gilded cornice. At the ends of the screen were great towers with doors, one marked *via ad forum*. These castle towers soon disappeared from the Terence tradition but left their impact on the proscenium.

THE JESUIT STAGE

The Jesuits, leaders in the Counter-Reformation in the 1540s, established schools and colleges all over Catholic Europe. In their emphasis on play production, the purpose was not only to train the youths but also to impress an audience with the history of the church and the power of the faith. Most of their productions were new historical plays.

Through the tradition of the Passion Play at Oberammergau, the form of the Jesuit stage has come down to our day. The earlier text of the Passion Play, which followed medieval tradition, was revised in 1662 and again in 1750 to make use of the principles of Jesuit staging. A large central stage is flanked by small curtained stages and by formal entrance ways at the sides.

THE TEATRO OLIMPICO

The crowning glory of the Terence school tradition was achieved in Italy in the 1580s in the magnificent Teatro Olimpico, which still survives in excellent condition. The pride of Europe in its century, it was typical of neither school nor court theatre but borrowed from both: an arcade screen from one and perspective settings from the other. The architect Palladio planned the building for the meetings of the Olimpian Academy and their revivals of ancient plays. It was begun in

293

1580, but the architect died soon after, leaving his son to finish it in 1584. The perspective street scenes behind each doorway, the most striking feature, were added by Scamozzi.

The façade of the forestage is splendidly decorated with columns, cornices, niches, and statues. It has no resemblance to a row of houses, but it served to suggest a city scene for the magnificent production of *Oedipus* that opened the theatre in 1585. After a build-up of drums, trumpets, fireworks, and cannon, the curtain that had covered the entire stage fell suddenly. From the inner street perspectives came music and voices singing the hymns and prayers for deliverance from the plague in the city of Thebes. The choruses astounded the spectators by changing from one exact formation to another, each member of the group locating his position by the elaborate pattern of tiles painted on the floor.

The Teatro Olimpico was not dominated by a royal box. Instead, as was appropriate for a club of equals, the amphitheatre, a flattened semicircle, gave each member a view down at least one of the perspective streets.

Behind each archway Scamozzi placed a perspective street scene. Like the front façade, the perspective settings were built of wood and plaster and painted. Some

Wood block illustrating scenes from Curtio Gonzaga's *Gli Inganni*, Venice, 1592.

of the plaster has crumbled, but the settings still give a good impression of real streets.

Fascinating as the Teatro Olimpico is, its historical importance has been exaggerated. Scholars are now convinced that it was an oddity, having no significant influence on the development of later theatres. Completely unfounded is the theory that the Teatro Olimpico is the ancestor of the proscenium frame. In the early 1920s Sheldon Cheney studied the three earliest theatres that have come down to us and noticed that the published designs of Serlio showed no proscenium. Ignoring the evidence from theatres that no longer exist, he proposed these theories: that the Teatro Olimpico of 1580–85, in the central Roman doorway of the arcade, marked the beginning of the proscenium frame; that the little ducal theatre of Sabbioneta, built by Scamozzi in 1588, expanded the frame with one larger archway in the formal forestage; and that the Teatro Farnese of Parma, begun in 1618, was the achievement of the goal to which the two earlier attempts had pointed. Cheney's theory, published first in *Theatre Arts Magazine* and again in his book *The Theatre*, has been repeated by most writers on the subject ever since. No one noticed that Cheney himself published an engraving of a complete pros-

Wood block illustrating street scenes from Mantoua, Italy.

cenium that is dated 1560, twenty years before the Olimpico was started. We now know that a proscenium frame, either flat or divided into separate parts set at different depths, dates from the fourteenth century in the puppet shows and street theatres, and in the Italian court theatres from the first perspective settings at the beginning of the sixteenth century.

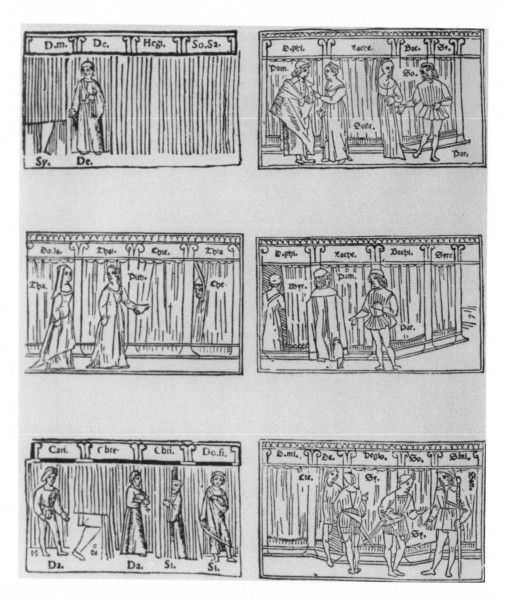

Series of woodcuts of scenes from Terentian Comedies, Venice, 1515, illustrating the Arcade Façade.

296

THE REDERYKER STAGE

A splendid variant of the Terence formal backing—a two-story façade of formal openings—was devised for the poems, tableaux, and plays presented at the annual festival competitions of the Rederyker Kamers, or Chambers of Rhetoric, of the Low Countries.

While some of the activities of the Renaissance increased the independence of the liberated individual, most cities, guilds, and academies offered highly organized corporate activities. The Rederykers created by rules and established models, and nowhere was there more citizen participation in poetry and drama than in the Low Countries. By the end of the fifteenth century every town of any size in the Flemish and Dutch provinces had its Rederyker Kamer, and often several.

The high point of the year was the annual competitive festival, the *landjuweel* (jewel [or prize] of the land). One society would invite ten to twenty societies from neighboring towns, and the contests might last a month. There were prizes for poems, songs, farce, processions, and other categories, but the most important competition was in drama. For the greater part of two centuries, until writers in the seventeenth century turned to classic subjects, the principal dramas of the Rederykers were the *spelen van sinne*, a combination of morality play and visual tableaux.

Each of the competing societies at a landjuweel gave a play in answer to a question about an agreed-on topic or *sinne*. The landjuweel at Antwerp in 1496 had the religious topic "What was the greatest miracle that God wrought for the saving of mankind?" The prize-winning *spel* was "The taking on of human nature," while another society chose the answer "The making of peace between father and son." At Ghent in 1539 the topic was still religious: "What should a dying man put his faith in?" The dramatized sermons were so earnest that it is hard to see why the authorities were alarmed. But only twenty years before, Luther had begun his attacks on church practice, and many church doctrines were in dispute. Soon plays with classic characters replaced religious dramas, and tableaux of Apollo and the Seven Liberal Arts replaced those of the Trinity or of Christ and the Saints.

In 1561 the authorities of Antwerp permitted the Violet Society of that town to hold a landjuweel based on a Renaissance topic, "What can best awaken man to the liberal arts?" The first prize went to the society whose play answered "Praise, honor, and renown" and the second prize was given for the answer, "The hope of eternal worldly and heavenly glory."

For the two spendid landjuweels of Ghent in 1539 and Antwerp in 1561, we have, besides the plays themselves, detailed descriptions and clear illustrations. The façade built as a backing for the Ghent contest was like the abstract outline of a show-castle, with two two-story towers framing a central pavilion. Both the lower and the upper pavilion came forward in a curved front and allowed quite sizeable tableaux to be disclosed by the opening of a curtain.

The main dialogue of the spelen van sinne was a teaching lesson, with Man, Mankind, or Youth as learner, and one or several characters such as Spiritual Understanding as teacher. Sometimes the comic vices, Contempt of Reason and Scorn of the Arts, or the like, tried to lead Youth astray.

It is not surprising that, at a time of the flowering of Flemish art, the visual part of the Rederyker performance was no less important than the dialogue. The *figueren*—pictures, or tableaux with actors and scenes as symbols—were the high points of the play. The allegorical characters, coming onto the forestage, would present in dialogue an answer to the question of the day. Then they would bring on or disclose an impressive scene as illustration, comment, or proof. Some figueren were painted cloths; some apparently had actors who moved in silent pantomime; in some scenes characters in the figueren replied to the characters on the forestage. Some figueren were entire scenes with dialogue and action and might be brought out on the forestage with such portable units as a shop, tent, tavern front, or arbor. The climax of the play was often a spectacular figuere of the Day of

Renaissance stage Teatro Farnese, Parma, 1618. *By courtesy of the Board of Trustees of the Victoria and Albert Museum.*

Two Renaissance stages. *Above:* The Teatro Olimpico, Vicenza, 1585. *Below:* The Schouwburg, Amsterdam, 1658. *From C. Walter Hodges,* The Globe Restored.

DE SCHOUBURGH van binnen
op 't Tooneel aen te sien

Glory: Christ, with the Saints or the Virtues, holding the figures of Sin, Death, and Hell under his feet. Or the entire scene of Judgment Day was spread over the doors, windows, and upper galleries of the two- or three-story façade.

But the most important function of the façade was to serve as a throne of honor, where Wisdom with the Nine Muses or Apollo and the Seven Liberal Arts gave immediate heavenly endorsement. As a goddess from the heavenly throne of honor, Lady Rhetoric might be let down by a theatre machine to give the prizes.

When we find in the Rederyker stage scenic emblems that can symbolize at once a Castle of Trust and a House of Hardship, an arcade of honor, an enthroned leader backed by a heavenly throne, a hierarchy of divine figures, with heaven endorsing Lady Rhetoric as she descends in a cloud machine to give prizes to her votaries, we are dealing with scenic meaning that goes far beyond the implications of the simple, formal Terence stage.

THE PERSPECTIVE STAGE

Important as the Terence stage and its variants were in the development of the modern theatre, the perspective stage ultimately had a much greater influence. On the perspective stage, a picture stage, drama was a space art. The medieval drama, in procession or on a platform stage, was a time art. As in a frieze, the eye ran along from one point in the story to another, from a throne to a tree, to a ship on wheels, never stopping long enough to allow the scenery to present a single place in depth. The medieval audience was a crowd that surrounded the action and followed it from one mansion to another. With the prince or duke at the center of the auditorium (the palace ballroom) on a dais with his special guests, the actors played on an arc facing him, and the scenery formed a larger arc enclosing the actor.

In building a temporary stage at one end of his ballroom, the Renaissance prince thought he was reviving the Roman *cavea*, with its semicircle of rising tiers of seats. But the prominent royal box was something unknown to ancient Rome. Not until the seventeenth century was the auditorium enlarged to accommodate balconies, which had been used only for outdoor entertainments on tournament fields, in innyards, and the like.

The perspective picture controlling space in depth was worked out by the painters more than a half-century before it was put on the stage. Even in the fourteenth century, before the basic principles of optics were understood, before eye-point, picture plane, and vanishing point were clearly defined, painters used architectural elements from the four sides of the picture with converging diagonal lines to indicate depth toward the middle of the picture. At each side a house would be shown with one wall flat to the front and one wall in diagonal lines indicating depth toward the center of the picture. The top was also shaped toward the center by the lines of the roofs of the houses or, in an interior scene, by perspective lines in a coffered ceiling. Thus the four sides gave an effect of "seeing through" a picture plane, hence the word "per-spective."

If a smaller arch or arcade was placed behind the first one, space was defined more precisely. A more daring device was to open up the second archway to show a second space and then a third archway, and so on, so that an arch or arcade might give the effect of increasing depth beyond easy count. It was even more effective to show a house with an arcade of several receding arches on the side next to the center street. The best device was to duplicate the entire house and show a street of narrow houses leading far back into the picture; and that was the basic method of the stage. Stage wings, set in two rows going toward the vanishing point, provided the stage pattern that lasted until it was modified by the space stages and spot and cyclorama lighting of this century.

In creating a perspective picture stage, the artist had several problems that he had not met with painting on a flat board or wall. Great depth was required on a stage where space was very limited. Lacking room for a dozen or more houses at the sides of the stage picture, the artist compromised by building several houses in three dimensions on each side of the stage and placing beyond them a flat shutter on which he painted more houses and streets to get his full depth. Or he might paint on the shutter a triumphal arch, arcade, or prominent building to give a splendid monumental end to the street. A stage with receding side houses required a floor that sloped upward to the backdrop, and the actor had to learn to move naturally on an incline. To the basic pattern of sloping floor, side houses, and back shutter, ingenious stage architects added ever more elaborate three-dimensional detail.

The front of the stage posed another problem. The stage architect began with the idea of a forestage and selected a place for a formal framing element behind which he might begin his illusionistic scenery. The result was a proscenium frame and an "apron," and in many places the apron persisted until the nineteenth century when all the picture space was pushed back behind one simple proscenium frame. In the Renaissance the proscenium was usually treated as a setting itself and showed some of the features of the castles, city gates, triumphal arches, canopies, and side doors of medieval settings. It often had considerable depth, shaping a forestage in front of the perspective setting on the sloping floor.

In the early examples of perspective setting, no curtain was used, but by the early sixteenth century, a curtain was the usual accompaniment of a perspective stage picture.

Contemporary accounts leave no doubt of the effectiveness of the stage architect's work. An eye witness describes the setting for *Cassaria* in Ferrara in 1508, the first occasion for which we can be certain that perspective scenery was used, though there is little doubt that it appeared earlier:

But what has been best in all these festivities and representations has been the scenery in which they have been played, which Master Peregrino, the Duke's painter has made. It has been a view in perspective of a town with houses, churches, belfries, and gardens, such as one could never tire of looking at it, because of the different things that are there, all most cleverly designed and executed. I suppose that this will not be destroyed, but that they will preserve it to use on other occasions.

According to Baldassore Castiglione, an Italian diplomat residing in Urbino, the production in Urbino in 1513 of *La Calandria* by Cardinal Bibbiena used more three-dimensional detail. This scene was framed by a proscenium in the form of two towers to create the illusion of a city gate and a portion of the city wall, as though the audience were outside the city looking at the street through the gate. When the same play was produced in Rome before the pope, it had magnificent scenery by the architect Peruzzi. Vasari is full of praise for the architect:

Nor is it possible to imagine how he found room, in space so limited, for so many streets, so many palaces, and so many bizarre temples, loggie, and various kinds of cornices, all so well executed that it seemed that they were not counterfeited but absolutely real, and that

Design for a tragic scene by Bramante of Urbino, 1495. *Courtesy Kupferstichkabinett der Staatl. Museen Preussischer Kulturbesitz, Berlin.*

302

Street scene drawn in manuscript of *La Betia*, a comedy by Angelo Beolco, Callea II Ruzzanta. *Courtesy Biblioteca Nazionale Marciana.*

Street scene by Aristotle San Gallo, 1535. *The Pierpont Morgan Library, New York. 1982. 75:600 attributed to Aristotileda San Gallo.*

303

the piazza was not a little thing, and merely painted, but real and very large. He designed, also, the chandeliers and the lights within, which illuminated the scene.

The development of stage perspective had a significance greater than anyone realized at the time. Since creating a perspective stage picture involved close observation and measurement of the immediate world and the formulation and application of precise mathematical principles, it was the first step toward a scientific art of play production and an important move toward the scientific foundation established by Galileo and Francis Bacon in the late sixteenth century.

The first designs for stage perspective were published in Books I and II of Serlio's *Architecture*, brought out in 1545 in Paris, where Serlio had been called to work on the palaces of the Louvre and Fountainebleau. One of the functions of an architect was to build stages and amphitheatres in the great hall of the palace for plays and spectacles. Serlio thought them the crowning achievement of an architect.

Three scenes by Sebastiano Serlio from *Architettura*, Venezia, 1552: Tragic (*below*), Rustic (*top of page 305*), and Comic (*bottom of page 305*).

We have noted Serlio's comments on the comic, tragic, and satyric scenes as he understood and designed them. His comic scene has Gothic arches, suggesting the Venice of his day, and his tragic scene, the stately columns and arches of the Renaissance idea of ancient architecture. Comedy was set and costumed as contemporary, and characters in tragedy, as well as the gods and heroes of the *intermezzi*, were costumed in the Renaissance version of "antique." But Serlio's comic scene is just as stately as the tragic, and most of the other designs of the Renaissance show no interest in the "low" mood that the classic theory implied. All settings for court plays were expected to be a splendid image of man's active life in this world.

For lighting, Serlio painted shadows on wings and backdrop, hung chandeliers above, and set "leaning lights" at the front of the stage for the actors. The lights that really interested him were created by cutting dozens of round, square, and diamond-shaped holes in the scenery and setting in them bottles of colored liquid with lamps behind, so that his city might sparkle as with jewels.

Serlio provides a detailed prospectus for the kind of stage that would soon become common in all of Europe and that would last, with some modifications, until the twentieth century.

Sebastiano Serlio's design for the Piazzetta San Marco, Venice, c. 1532.

306

Popular Theatre in the Renaissance

An account of Renaissance stages must include a description of the Hôtel de Bourgogne in Paris, a very different theatre because the audience paid admission and because the stage was not primarily formal or perspective but illusionistic. But this commercial theatre can be better understood after we have traced the development of professionalism in the theatre and have looked at some plays and performances that belong in a popular tradition rather than in the aristocratic, scholarly, classical tradition. Usually performed by traveling troupes, these farces and interludes developed from such miscellaneous sources as village farces, comic moralities, school moralities and debates, and other popular entertainment.

FARCES AND INTERLUDES

The village farces, like the Atellan farces of Rome, created a rustic world of simplicity that was rough, bawdy, and uninhibited. They express the "gaulois" spirit, in contrast to the "courtois" spirit of the romances of knights and ladies. A typical plot shows the slow-witted man of the country being cheated by a clever man of the city or a wife and her lover cheating the stupid hen-pecked husband. If the worm turned, audiences delighted to see the exploiter bested by the victim. A good example is the French farce *Maître Pierre Pathelin*, many times revised through several centuries. In this farce the lawyer gets the slow judge confused by two lawsuits, and teaches the sheep-thief, his client, to get released by answering nothing but "baa, baa."

Village farces were popular in Germany for the festival of Fastnacht, or Shrove Tuesday. Nuremberg was famous for a variety of entertainment, some in spectacular pageant wagons drawn through the streets, some on the kind of improvised platform used by the earliest traveling mountebanks. Toward the middle of the sixteenth century a small professional company set up a stage in the Martha Church to produce the plays of Hans Sachs, a poet and musician celebrated in Wagner's *Die Meistersinger von Nuremberg* (1868).

One of the interludes of the English writer John Heywood called *The Four P's* (c. 1520) presents a genial contest of four professional charlatans. A pardoner, a potecary, and a palmer engage in a competition to see which can tell the greatest lie, with the tolerant peddler as judge. The palmer offers to sell such sacred relics as the jawbone of All Hallows, the big toe of the Trinity, and the buttock-bone of Pentecost, but he wins the contest by announcing that he has never seen a woman out of patience.

A story of deception of the gullible, to be classified rather as a play than as an interlude, is *The Mandragola* (c. 1520) by the Italian Machiavelli, better known for his political treatise *The Prince* (1513). In this play a young seducer persuades the husband that mandragora (mandrake) will make his young wife bear a child but will kill the first man who lies with her. The scenes of the husband and the mother begging the wife to welcome as a lover the young man they kidnap from the street (the seducer of course) have a mock-heroic irony that anticipates Ben Jonson's *Volpone* (c. 1606) of nearly a century later. At the end the old man will have his baby and the young man will have one room in the house where he can be welcomed like one of the family.

PATHELIN CHEZ LE DRAPIER. PATHELIN CONTREFAISANT LE MALADE.

Two wood block scenes from *Pierre Pathelin*.

More is known about writers of interludes in Portugal and Spain than in any other countries, and one can follow their careers as they added new elements to this short form and became professional playwrights.

At the end of the sixteenth century Cervantes used the old theme of peasant gullibility in his *entremeses*, but, as would be expected of the author of *Don Quixote* (1605, 1613), he makes his gulls uncertain of what is illusion and what is reality. His *Cave of Salamanca* (1615) shows a clever wandering scholar who saves the reputation of his hostess and her friend, who must hastily conceal their lovers, a sacristan and a barber, from the husband. The scholar offers to show the husband a magic trick he learned in the famous cave and to make devils, in the forms of a sacristan and a barber, appear and bring a basket of food and drink. The husband's suspicions are quieted and they all go in to the feast.

The staging of interludes by traveling troupes had to be very simple. In the great hall of some nobleman the players might make use of the two doors of the screen and play in the center with the audience all around them. Or they might put up a platform and hang a curtain. If they wrote something especially for the nobleman's celebration, he might have some elaborate scenic structures built. If they played in an innyard or at a holiday fair they might set up a regular mountebank platform with a curtain hung to provide entrances from a dressing room.

PROFESSIONALISM IN THE THEATRE

In the ducal courts of Italy each production was a separate occasion for which actors were assembled and an audience was invited. Only when professional companies were established in their own buildings was continuity in the theatre assured and development of the modern theatre made possible. Such professional urban companies, with their own buildings and playwrights, developed gradually in that prosperous period of nearly a century after the establishment of strong central government in France, England, and Spain.

Italy produced a professional theatre, the *commedia dell' arte*, but since there was no central government in Italy and no capital city, it lacked a base and became famous only as a traveling theatre, playing in cities and towns all over western Europe.

The first professional secular theatre in Europe was the Hôtel de Bourgogne, established in Paris in 1548. In London, actors under the patronage of the Earl of Leicester had a company strong enough and an audience ready for James Burbage to build The Theatre in 1576. Madrid followed in 1579 with the Corral del Principe, a theatre built in a courtyard, and in 1582 with the Corral de la Cruz.

It had taken decades of hard work for players to create acting companies, audiences, and playwrights for a repertory of plays to be given in one location. In the later Middle Ages entertainers occasionally formed traveling troupes of three or four, sometimes playing for a town council or collecting pennies at an innyard or a crossroads. Before the end of the fifteenth century there were many wandering entertainers, some groups large enough to give interludes or short plays. The players arriving at Elsinore in Shakespeare's *Hamlet* are traveling professionals finding an annual welcome in a king's castle. Village performers, as in the mummers plays, were amateur volunteers, hoping by one or several performances to collect money for a feast. Sometimes a city sponsored a local group of players or welcomed a troupe endorsed by a neighboring town or nobleman, often insisting on seeing the show in order to censor objectionable words or ideas. Yet for most of the sixteenth and seventeenth centuries, especially in Protestant countries, the town mayors and aldermen were enemies of the players, and but for some powerful patron—kings and noblemen in England and the hospitals that shared in the theatre receipts in Spain—the towns might have suppressed the professional theatre as soon as it started.

In the Renaissance, players, like merchants, tried to create an independent position, selling a commodity in a society gradually changing from feudalism to capitalism. The best solution was a combination of royal protection and regular playing for the paying public. Kings and noblemen, though willing patrons, were rarely able to pay for more than a few performances a year, but by taking on the players as their liveried servants, they could protect them from arrest as vagabonds and keep a measure of control. Noblemen who had their own players could agree with the old-fashioned town officials to arrest all unattached rogues.

Richard III of England was the first king known to have had his own troupe of actor-singers. At one time Henry VII had four troupes, and Henry VIII kept two troupes of four players each to act as heralds and orators for tourneys and public shows or present songs and interludes at banquets. After the middle of the sixteenth century the number of full companies increased rapidly in all European countries. Actors with the protection of a lord became independent commercial companies, traveling part of the year but playing in their own theatres for a long season. In defending them, court officials in London used one argument repeatedly: the licensed and recognized companies who were to play before the court at the Christmas season must have some place to practice their craft and make their living the rest of the year.

Thus, from performing short farcical interludes or satiric moralities the professional players gradually developed an audience ready to watch a play of two hours or longer. Interludes of song and dance might still be given between the acts and a lively jig as an afterpiece. But the new ideal was a play with song, satire, and comic byplay subordinate to the main action, with the virtuoso display of the actor subordinate to the dramatic conflict—a play giving the audience, through romantic stories and examples from the past, both a moral lesson and entertain-

310

ment. When that ideal worked in London or Madrid, it produced an aesthetic pleasure that made all medieval forms of theatre seem trivial.

A COMMERCIAL THEATRE IN PARIS:
THE HÔTEL DE BOURGOGNE

Built in 1548 by the Confrérie de la Passion, in the grounds of the old town-house of the Dukes of Burgundy, the Hôtel de Bourgogne inherited a long tradition of theatrical performance. Since 1402 the Confrérie had been performing medieval cycle plays for profit at the Hôpital de la Trinité in Paris. When in 1548 the French parliament, following the lead of the Council of Trent, forbade the performance of religious plays, it unwittingly stimulated the performance of secular plays. The Confrérie de la Passion gave performances of nonreligious plays in their new location or, in the 1590s, rented the property to theatrical troupes.

At the Hôtel de Bourgogne an adaptation of the medieval simultaneous stage was used. Whereas the medieval platform was often a hundred feet long, the Confrérie now had a stage only twenty-five feet wide. Into this space were crowded five, sometimes six, mansions, usually representing as many different places. As on the medieval stage, the actor's entrance from a mansion identified the place, but on the crowded Hôtel de Bourgogne stage he often acted closer to the other mansions than to the one he had entered from. The naïve audience liked a story of great variety and was delighted to be in Naples at one moment and then, after a few strokes on the violins, across the seas in a distant country. Or the mansions might be changed, a cloth suddenly removed, a curtain opened, or part of a mansion turned to show the inside of a cave. Ghosts might come from smoking caves, devils fly through the air, or a god descend from heaven with thunder and exploding firecrackers. Magicians and supernatural characters could make sudden changes in people or scenery. Spectacle became more and more indispensable.

In the 1550s during the reign of Catherine de Medici, a rebirth of French poetry occurred, and some of the new writers wrote tragedies and comedies based on classic principles that were performed in colleges and palaces and even by commercial players. But the religious wars of the 1570s and 1580s interrupted this French renaissance. After peace was achieved, Henry IV of Navarre presided over a court totally lacking in culture.

Performances at the Hôtel de Bourgogne were geared to the taste of the time. Broad farces won an audience of soldiers, lackeys, pickpockets, thieves, and whores. Admission prices were low. The King's Guard, called the Mousquetaires, and the lackeys following their masters expected to force their way in without paying. There were fights at the door as well as in the pit. The crowd stood on a flat floor struggling to get a glimpse of the stage, eating, spitting, quarreling,

311

noisily answering back to the actors as well as to each other. Sometimes an over-dressed duke might enter, interrupt the play, and noisily demand that a seat be brought for him on the stage itself. Cultivated people had no part in the popular theatre.

A number of traveling companies had rented the Hôtel de Bourgogne in the 1590s, but none had made a go of it until Valleran LeComte, who already called his troupe Les Comédiens du Roi, leased the theatre and made Paris his headquarters. It was about 1598 that he engaged Alexandre Hardy as playwright. Hardy won the city audience by giving them violence, coarseness, obscenity, and semi-nudity in love scenes. His plays were full of action, with many short episodes and

Great door of the Hôtel de Bourgogne: "Al Comedie des Comediens," 1635. *Phot. Bibl. Nat. Paris.*

frequent surprises and turns of plot. Nothing was left to the imagination or reported by messenger. There were battles and killings with plenty of gore. Heads were cut off, bodies cut up, eyes gouged out. Sometimes carnage filled the stage. For such a restless, noisy audience, everything had to be made clear by repeated explanations. There were some long speeches of soaring rhetoric, building up to the quick give and take in defiance of an enemy or encouragement of an ally. The simple moral was driven home like a battle cry. Countless spectacular effects were added to every performance.

Interior drawing of the Hôtel de Bourgogne by A. Bosse. *Phot. Bibl. Nat. Paris.*

313

Reconstruction by Pierre Sonrel illustrating the decor by Laurent Manelot for *Les Ménechmes* by Rotrov. Hôtel del Bourgogne, 1646. *Phot. Bibl. Nat. Paris.*

314

Hardy was never able to bring more sophisticated people to the theatre. It remained for a later generation to combine the audiences of town and court, and by that time the critics had expressed such contempt for the popular theatre and built up such prestige for the classic form that the older kind of theatre, represented by the Hôtel de Bourgogne, had no chance with the new guardians of culture.

Not only in Paris but in London and Madrid the commercial theatre, with professional actors, won out.

The Commercial Theatre in England

The new individual of the Renaissance found himself almost completely free in the London of Queen Elizabeth. A new audience was reflected in a new form of stage and a new kind of acting company, and Marlowe, Shakespeare, and others gave the theatre some of the most magnificent dramas the world has ever known.

London was an exciting place. A stream of new people poured in. From farms and villages, from the colleges, from the homes of the country gentry and noble families came ambitious youths, eager to make their fortunes, get positions at court, or make a name as poets. The monastic orders had been destroyed by Henry VIII and monks and friars set adrift. The guilds were still powerful and offered security to the apprentice who was willing to work for years as a jour-

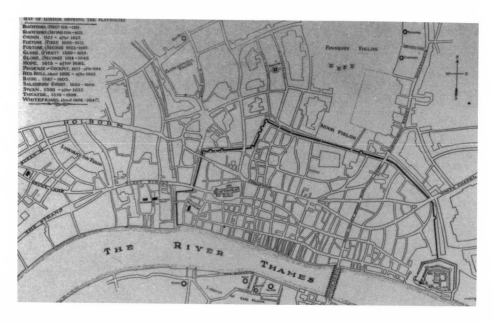

Map of London showing playhouses erected before 1640.

316

neyman, but new capitalist managers were getting richer than any master crafts-man in a guild shop could dream of being. The royal court was now more impor-tant than the old feudal lords, who themselves began to spend more time in London and to build palaces there. An able young man had a chance to rise rap-idly in their service.

But these new merchants and half-resident nobles were ready for more than rich clothes and jewels. Besides sermons, they read books of travel and history and even discussed sonnets and romances and plays—and they went to the the-atre. The law students put on masques in their own Inns of Court and were devotees of the public theatre. University graduates discussed the latest poem, satirical pamphlet, or play and made fun of pious country people who knew nothing of wit, classical learning, and city manners—and they went to the theatre. Soldiers and apprentices also flocked to the theatre. Even the day laborer, when he could get away of an afternoon, and women of all classes and disposition found places.

The auditorium of the Elizabethan playhouse was one of the most successful ever devised for getting a large, miscellaneous group of people close to the action. It consisted of an open pit, where the groundlings stood, surrounded by the stage

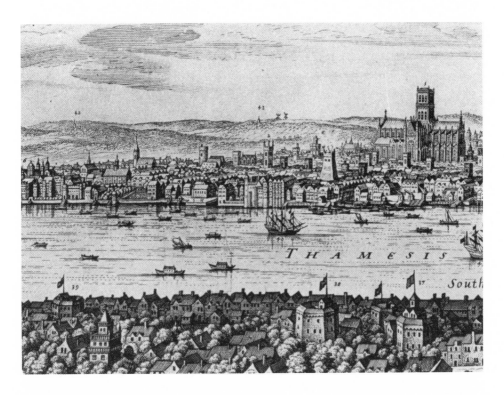

Section of Merian's view of London, 1638, showing The Swan (39), Beergarden (38), and Globe (37). *By permission of the Folger Shakespeare Library.*

317

and three rows of galleries where spectators were seated. The tournament fields had established a pattern of a pit surrounded by wooden boxes one or two stories high. But a more immediate ancestor was the innyard, used by players in London since the 1540s and even earlier by strolling players outside of London. In many inns an open court was surrounded by the galleries that led to the guest rooms. When players performed in the courtyard, haulers and drivers could come out of the stables and townsmen out of the tavern on the ground floor, while the guests sat in the galleries. With three galleries, the Elizabethan theatre could seat more than a thousand—perhaps 1500—without removing the most distant spectator more than thirty or forty feet from the main acting area—about as far as the fourth row in the orchestra of our modern, smaller theatres. On occasion more than eight hundred persons might be crowded into the pit, making a total of over two thousand.

THE DESIGN OF THE ELIZABETHAN STAGE

The Elizabethan (or Shakespearean) stage was formal rather than illusionistic. At the back of a platform stage that extended into the auditorium so that the acting space was partly enclosed by the spectator galleries was a complex two-story screen of arches and niches—a symbolic structure. On the platform stage in front of it, realistic properties might be placed. But there was no front curtain, no proscenium frame, no painted scenery, no pretense of creating an illusion of actual place. The splendid façade at the back of the open platform presented at least six openings, either for entrances and exits or for small scenes to be disclosed in doorways behind curtains. At the stage level of the façade were two doorways and an inner stage, and on the upper level were balconies and windows. If it was necessary for the audience to know an exact place, the playwright had some character say, "This is the forest of Arden," or "What country, friends, is this?—This is Illyria, Lady," or "What wood is this before us?—The wood of Birnam." The most commonly accepted picture of the Elizabethan stage is a bare platform strewn with rushes, with a penthouse roof supported by two splendid columns and backed by an architectural façade, or "tiring house" (where the actors changed their attire). The basic pattern of the Elizabethan stage façade was apparently derived from the throne pavilion, the arches, and the inner and upper stages of the street shows erected on civic occasions. It was left to the audience to turn that background into field, forest, cave, mountain, house front, room, castle, or city gate.

318

ORIGINS OF THE ELIZABETHAN STAGE

Much scholarly effort has been expended in tracing the origins of the Elizabethan stage. Some have related it to the innyard, to the medieval religious stage, to the screens in the great halls, to the court settings. But no one early stage can explain satisfactorily the complexity of the Elizabethan. The closest ancestor turns out to be the *tableaux vivants* of the street theatres, but its full line extends back to Hellenistic art and the Greek theatres, for the Greek stage background made such an impression that artists, sculptors, and architects used its forms and conventions and brought several of the patterns into the stream of western art.

From the Hellenistic stage the Elizabethan stage inherited a complex two-story screen of arches and niches. In the Middle Ages that complex screen became a vision of the Judgment Day, with Christ in the heavenly throne sitting on a rainbow and surrounded by choiring angels and saints. Below were hell-mouth at one side, the opening graves of earth in the center, and the gate of heaven at the other side. A variant was the choir screen of the medieval church, with its three or more arches and its gallery above for singers and for statues of Christ on the cross with the attending Mary and John.

Pen and ink drawing of a typical English Innyard, c. 1600. *Phot. Bibl. Nat. Paris.*

319

In the Elizabethan theatre that screen was combined with the castle. In medieval art and heraldry and in the street theatres the castle usually had two side towers framing a central two-story panel. Musicians and sometimes ancestors or allegorical figures looked out of the top gallery and upper arches and windows. Sometimes the center panel had a large arch, but often it had a niche for a throne, which might be topped by a canopy with two columns to support it. The canopy too had its heavens for angels, musicians, and symbols of the skies. At other times the throne-canopy was combined with the arcade screen. All three symbols were combined in the Elizabethan stage façade. Another major showpiece, the triumphal arch, belongs to the ancestry of the Elizabethan stage. The arch, too, was a castle and brought with it a pattern of central arch, side doors, upper stage, heavenly musicians, and many decorations of shields, banners, tapestries, paintings, and allegorical statues. But even the minor showpieces made contributions: the tomb and altar contributed patterns of two and three stories, or earthly and heavenly figures set in a façade of columns and canopy. So the Elizabethan stage was a composite, and particularly a combination of all the main patterns of the tableaux vivants, together with the decorations and the atmosphere of royal pomp, civic pride, romantic stories of ancient deeds, allegorical reminders of great themes, and the solemn excitement of civic pageantry.

Looked at in this way, the penthouse was not merely a roof to protect the actors from rain but a canopy over a throne, a ciborium over an altar, a baldecchino framing a living statue. It was itself a symbol. Its regular name was the heavens, and it bore stars and moons and astronomical symbols of the sky. The formal side doors were not mere convenient entrances or realistic doors. They were the side gates to the two flanking towers of a castle; they were the side arches of a choir screen, the side arches of a triumphal arch. The central opening was not a mere inner stage but a city gate through which triumphal processions might enter; it was a decorative frame for tableaux. The upper stage was no terrace or gallery: it was the battlements of a castle, the gallery for musicians and minstrels, the rostrum for an orator, the observation booth for allegorical figures and observers. The third opening was not merely a top gallery: it was the turret of a castle, the crow's nest of a ship, a heavenly throne.

WAYS OF USING THE ELIZABETHAN STAGE

The Elizabethan stage was flexible and could be used in a number of ways. Consistency of treatment was not required by the theatre management or by the audience. The stage was a platform, much like the mountebank stage, holding the actor high and thrusting him out in the midst of the spectators. The English

320

scholar C. Walter Hodges believes that it was head high from the ground, allowing full space for traps and hell effects to be worked from below. The actor could make a whisper heard and a raised eyebrow seen, and he had a platform and space and sky to show the pomp of audacious deeds. He could make an aside audible since he was only three feet from some groundlings and a dozen feet from spectators seated in a gallery.

Writing for action on an open platform, the playwright must plan to begin his scenes with one or two people and gradually add more until the stage was full, and at the end he must take his people off a few at a time and provide some action for those left on stage. When a character was to die on stage, a processional had to be planned to carry the body out. When it came off well, that funeral procession, with cannons and drums and sometimes trumpets, could be very effective, as it still is at the end of *Hamlet*. But of course if everything did not go smoothly it could be the occasion of hysterical laughter. The story was told of one famous Elizabethan actor named Fowler who "at the end of the Fourth Act he laid so heavily about him, that some mutes who stood for soldiers fell down as they were dead ere he had touched their trembling targets: so he brandished his sword and made his exit; which they perceiving, crawled into the tiring house, at which Fowler grew angry and told 'em 'Dogs you should have laine there till you had been fetcht off,' and so they crawled out again: which gave the people such an occasion of laughter, they cried, 'that again, that again, that again'."

But the Elizabethan stage could be used in much the same way as curtain stages were used. On the Spanish stage curtains could cover all the background or be drawn aside to disclose many different doors, niches, and balcony scenes. There is no evidence that the Elizabethan stage was ever covered entirely with curtains, though there are a few puzzling references to a countenance dark as the black curtains hung around a stage for tragedy. Was such use of curtains standard, or was it only occasional? It is strange that there is so little documentary evidence of what would have been a striking effect.

In some scenes the background of the stage was used as if it were a single mansion or group of mansions as on a medieval stage. We have seen that, by the medieval convention, actors could walk out onto the *platea*, or open playing area, and be supposed within the place identified by the mansion. On the Elizabethan stage the inner stage could be identified as a room, and the characters could walk out onto the forestage and still be supposed in that room. Sometimes a bed was pushed out so that the character could be more easily heard and seen. Sometimes different parts of the stage represented different places, as in the medieval use of simultaneous staging with a number of mansions. Sometimes the multiple convention was made more explicit when sizable scenic devices were set up, whether as part of the façade or as freestanding structures.

The stage might also be used for a procession, creating an effect like many medieval performances. Actors might bring properties with them, set them up and

Tableau vivant for the entry of Francis of Annon, Duke of Brabant. Antwerp, 1582. *By courtesy of the Board of Trustees of the Victoria and Albert Museum.*

The Flemish Arch. The Triumph of James I, London, 1604.
By courtesy of the Board of Trustees of the Victoria and Albert Museum.

play a scene, and then move off in procession. Not only were tables and chairs brought on, but a great many elaborate properties: thrones, shopfronts, beds, chariots, trees, arbors, tents, rocks, caves, wells, mossbanks, biers, barriers, bars, walls, gallows, and even hell-mouth. Except for the arcade screen and castle and triumphal arch, which were absorbed in the façade, the Elizabethans used all the temporary scenic mansions that were known in the Middle Ages. Some of these properties may have been conventionalized and miniature editions of the real, but mostly they were substantial. When in *Much Ado About Nothing* (1598–1599) Benedict and then Beatrice hides in an arbor, we must suppose that a beautiful arbor with seat, trellis, and vines was used. We have a picture of the portable arbor on which Hieronimo's son was hanged in Thomas Kyd's *The Spanish Tragedy* (1587). Rocks, wells, and mossbanks could add a picturesque outdoor effect. For battle scenes portable tents could be brought up as part of a procession. The last act of Shakespeare's *Richard III* makes beautiful use of tents.

An important way of using the Elizabethan stage was to suppose it a real place. If the scene were supposed outdoors in front of a house, there were the upper

Reconstruction of Elizabethan theatre by Orville K. Larson, incorporating elements of tableaux vivants and entry arches.

windows and upper-story gallery from which people could speak as from a real house. Although E. K. Chambers is plainly wrong in supposing that all scenes were thought of realistically, yet a large number of them were so regarded, and much of the time when a new set of characters entered, the audience soon realized where they were and saw all parts of the stage as fitting the conditions of that place. Within the basic convention, this was one kind of realism.

But many scenes were presented not as realistic but by the conventions of the tableaux vivants of the street theatres. The façade was decorated like a symbolic tableau, with marble columns, shields and streaming banners, tapestries and paintings, clouds, heavenly thrones, and astrological symbols. Some of the battle and siege scenes, so frequent in Elizabethan plays, may have looked fairly realistic, with defenders shouting defiance from the city walls and attackers climbing up and capturing the battlements, then opening the central gates for a triumphal entry. But often the symbolic pageantry was more important than the realism. For instance, in Thomas Heywood's *The Four Prentices of London* (1600), the English adventurers arrive before the city of Jerusalem, marked by the standard and crown of the sophy. They climb the wall, "beat the Pagans, take away the crowns on their heads, and in the stead hang up the contrary shields, and bring away the ensigns

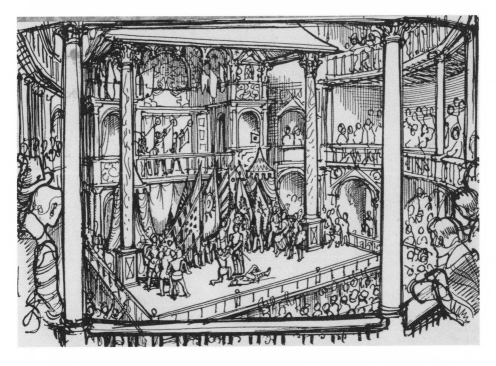

Performance of Shakespeare's *Richard III* seen in the Elizabethan public theatre. *A drawing from C. Walter Hodges,* Shakespeare and the Players.

flourishing them, several ways." Later they scale the façade as a tower and put a cross on the wall. Just as symbolic is Act V, Scene 5, of *Macbeth*. It begins with the entrance of Macbeth and soldiers "with drums and colors," and Macbeth gives the order "Hang out our banners on the outward walls." Surely the soldiers did not go out of sight to hang the banners. The scene is a symbolic tableau of Macbeth's

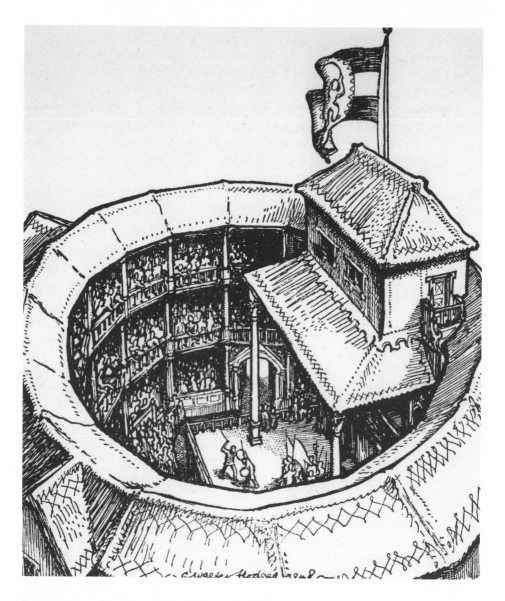

Reconstruction of an Elizabethan theatre by C. Walter Hodges.

castle, with Macbeth asserting his dominance, gathering his defenses, and getting set for a siege. The opposing forces could come on with their own flags and march across the forestage and the audience would understand that they were still some distance away from Macbeth's castle. Macbeth's banners would stay in sight decorating the castle until the very last speeches, when the castle is in the hands of new forces and all the thanes kneel before Malcolm as the new king—a castle tableau still, perhaps with some added insignes and flags.

The façade still kept a number of the combinations of scenic symbols from which it was derived. Time after time in the plays, scenes before castles are followed by coronations. The ending of *Macbeth*, while not a coronation, is a tableau of fealty to the new king, especially appropriate before the castle he has just captured. In Marlowe's play, Tamburlaine sets up a banquet in front of the castle-city he has just captured, and in the same scene crowns his followers as subsidiary kings.

At times the heavenly throne, that opening on the third level of the façade, above the upper stage, was used in ways very similar to the use of allegorical thrones of honor in the tableaux vivants. In *The Spanish Tragedy*, Revenge watches the whole play, as does the Ghost of Andrugio in John Marston's *Antonia and Mellida* (1599). Oseas the Prophet is seated in a heavenly throne to make moral comments on the action in *A Looking Glass for London and England* (1590).

Another combination of tableaux that influenced the playwrights was the altar and the tomb. The fourth act of *Much Ado About Nothing* takes place before an altar for an elaborate wedding scene. A few scenes later the bridegroom and his friends gather before the tomb of the bride, supposed dead. The same family shields and colors would have served for both.

Sometimes the Elizabethan stage was used as a theatre machine, with quite different scenes presented at the same time, or next to each other, without any of the realistic or tableau conventions. The most striking of these scenes were dreams, thoughts, and magic apparitions. But the playwright could juxtapose different scenes of any kind and use the complex structure of forestage and six or seven openings in the façade. In Thomas Heywood's *A Woman Killed with Kindness* (1603) an unwelcome thought is visualized for the audience, like a vision scene in a modern expressionistic play. As Wendell is thinking of his desire for Mistress Frankford and his respect for her husband, he sees, above him on the balcony, the couple happy together with their son. In other ways the stage had the freedom of a movie. Hilltop and valley could be shown at the same time with upper stage and forestage. Different parts of a ship or scenes from different ships could be shown side by side; and the different parts of a battlefield, with a surge of many soldiers interspersed with close-up scenes of the leaders, could give a kaleidoscopic impression of complex action.

AUDIENCE AND THEATRES

The audience of the Elizabethan theatre was one of the most amazing in history. For more than three decades it was a cross section of London. People of all classes came together, united by the vision they found in the drama of history, of London, of themselves. The "stinkards" stood on the stone floor of the pit. At one time they could get in for one penny, and they never had to pay more than two— about the cost of a beer or a cheap meal, and only a third of the cost of a pipeful of tobacco. The richer merchants paid another penny and sat in the galleries, while the lords paid more and sat in the luxurious lords' rooms overlooking the stage. In some theatres the fashionable, overdressed dandy paid for a stool on the stage or sat or lay on the rushes of the stage floor. But all classes were united by the vision on the stage of great individuals who were a part of history, of a great realm, of a terrifying destiny. Like themselves, the heroes on that stage stood free, barely emerged from the cocoon of an older order, asserting themselves to the utmost, though uncertain of what might be the responsibilities, the consequences, of their freedom. The very form of the stage was an expression of the situation of the Elizabethan spectators. The actor stepped forth free to act on a bare, open platform, but his freedom was calculated in relation to an architectural background that was a symbol of religious and political order.

Many Elizabethans disapproved of a democratic institution that cut across old social distinctions. One outraged man declared that now "every lewd person thinketh himself, for his penny, worthy of the chief and most commodious place without respect of any other." After writing for such an audience for more than a decade, Thomas Dekker was still amazed that the theatre would allow "a stool as well to the farmer's son as to your rich lawyer, that your stinkard has the self-same liberty to be there in his tobacco fumes as your sweet courtier hath," that players were glad to play three hours for two pence to the basest stinkard in London.

Strong opposition to such an audience and such a theatre came from several sources. Preachers protested the interference with church-going, and bear-baiters protested the competition, and some attempt was made to limit the times when the theatres were open in order to leave Sunday for the preachers and Thursdays for the bear fights. The danger of riots in public gatherings and the danger of spreading the plague were used as excuses by enemies of the theatres. The plague, at least, was a real danger, and the theatres were closed, sometimes for a year at a time, when it was more deadly than usual. Then the players took to the towns and villages to survive.

The constant enemies of the theatre were the Puritans who fought the stage with every means at their disposal. The Puritans never tired of denouncing the motley gathering in the playhouse. Were there not cutpurses and prostitutes in the audience? Did not the theatres prevent large numbers of people from spending money in the city? Did they not draw apprentices and servants away from their work? One official protest branded the theatres "the ordinary places for vagrant persons, masterless men, thieves, horse stealers, whoremongers, coney-catchers, contrivers of treasons, and other idle and dangerous persons to meet together. They maintain idleness in such persons as have no vocation and draw apprentices and other servants from their ordinary work and all sorts of people from the resort unto sermons, and other Christian exercises to the great hindrance of trades and profanation of religion."

But the efforts of the acting companies to survive under heavy opposition ended in a triumph that lasted for several decades. In 1570 James Burbage built the first playhouse in London, The Theatre, and two years later The Curtain was opened. Both theatres were in Shoreditch, an expanding new area in the northeast of London, next to a popular park and drill field and near a busy road into London. But in 1590 Burbage's son Richard, the leading actor in the Lord Chamberlain's company, in which Shakespeare was an actor and shareholder, had a dispute over renewal of the lease for The Theatre, and in 1599 he and his brother and their workmen tore down the building, carried the timbers across the Thames to the area on the South Bank called Bankside in Southwark, where the bear-baiting pits were located, outside the authority of the city of London, and built The Globe. Other theatres, notably The Rose and The Swan, both smaller than The Globe, were built in Southwark, and for the rest of the reign of Elizabeth, the reign of James I, and most of the reign of Charles I the theatres outside London city throve. But the Puritans who controlled the city council of London had forced the theatres outside the city, and in 1642, when Cromwell's army was waging war on the Royalists, they closed all the theatres. Except for a few surreptitious performances, no theatrical entertainment was available until the Restoration of the monarchy in 1660.

In the struggle for survival, Elizabethan acting companies had early found an ally in the court. In the 1570s Elizabeth's court ruled that all players were vagabonds *unless* they were in the service of some high lord responsible for them. Henceforth each company of actors attached itself to a patron, a powerful nobleman, a high official of the government, or, as the central government became stronger, to a member of the royal family. Thus the company of which Shakespeare was a member was known as the Lord Chamberlain's Men, later as the King's Men. A sponsored company could of course play at the patron's court, and a company was often invited to play at Elizabeth's court for Christmas or other festivities, but for year-round employment it must depend not only on playing in a public theatre but on an occasional tour through the country.

Besides playing at court, some companies managed to perform elsewhere inside the city in spite of the Puritans and their laws: they built "private houses" in spots that had immunity from city regulations. The religious order of Blackfriars had been disbanded by Henry VIII, but the site of the building was still exempt from city laws. Several children's companies played at Blackfriars, and in 1608 the King's Men (with Burbage and Shakespeare) took it over for their winter location.

The audience of the public theatres in Shakespeare's day was lively and unruly. Ben Johnson railed at both the groundlings—"rude barbarous crew . . . no brains . . . hiss anything that mounts above their *grounded* capacities"—and the capricious gallants who "will approve nothing, be it never so conceited or elaborate, but sit making faces, and spitting and cry 'Filthy! Filthy!!'" Shakespeare's Hamlet takes a crack at the groundlings who "are capable of nothing but inexplicable dumb-shows and noise" and people like Polonius who, unless they see "a tale of bawdy, go to sleep." The students and apprentices, especially, were often noisy and demanding. One man remembered the holidays, especially Shrovetide, when sailors, watermen, shoemakers, butchers, and apprentices filled the house and insisted that, no matter what play had been announced in the posted bills, the players must act what the audience wanted.

MISUNDERSTANDING AND UNDERSTANDING

When the Puritans closed the London theatres in 1642, most of the buildings were torn down or converted to other uses. There was no theatre in the Commonwealth under Cromwell. After the restoration of the monarchy in 1660 the first company played in an old London theatre but only until its new house could be built; for a new era was beginning. Italian and French theatres had long used perspective scenery, and the English court masques also. No one regretted the death of the old type of stage and theatre, and no one made a sketch or wrote a detailed description. The Restoration had only contempt for the little that was half-remembered about the Elizabethan stage: a pit without seats, a plain stage platform covered with rushes, a simple playhouse with no painted settings, no scenery. This was the first step in falsifying the Elizabethan theatre.

The second step was to edit Shakespeare's plays in such a way as to adapt them to the new kind of staging—a process that in most editions still stands between the reader and a fresh visualization of the original staging. In 1709 Nicholas Rowe brought out an edition of Shakespeare with the scenes marked by localities, much as he saw them produced in the painted settings of his day. Where Shakespeare merely wrote "exeunt" for one group of actors and "enter" for the next, each new scene was now given a location: "a street," "a church," "a room in Leonato's house," "another part of the forest," etc. Shakespeare may never have thought specifically where some scenes were, but all were now tied down.

In 1790 Edmund Malone, the first scholar to apply the historical method to Shakespeare, published *Plays and Poems of Shakespeare*. Realizing that actors had played in the innyards of London and other cities and towns for more than a decade before the first theatre was built, and occasionally all through the period, Malone supposed that the main model for the theatre was the innyard. We have introduced the innyard as one probable model for the auditorium of the Elizabethan theatre. The question is whether Burbage, in building The Theatre, kept a simple platform such as would be used for performance in a courtyard and merely added entrance doors at the sides of the inner stage and perhaps windows over the doors and a penthouse roof to protect the actors from a sudden shower. Most theatre historians are now convinced that there was a much more elaborate and symbolic façade.

The next important theory appeared in Germany near the end of the nineteenth century: the alternation theory. Seeing that some of Shakespeare's scenes seem to require a full setting and make use of properties, while others involve only a few people and could be played on the forestage in front of a curtain, German scholars evolved the theory that the Elizabethans regularly wrote their plays to alternate large scenes on the inner stage with unlocalized scenes on the forestage while the curtain was closed to permit the setting up of the next scene on the inner stage. But more thorough study soon revealed that many times two scenes with large properties came together without a curtain to cover the change. Plainly there were many changes before the eyes of the audience. It is certain that some tableaux, as of Faustus in his study surrounded by his books and astronomical instruments, were arranged behind a curtain and disclosed as a picture. But it is also certain that thrones, banquets, wells, mossbanks, trees, and other large properties were brought onto the apron in plain view.

A new historical approach was begun in 1905 by an American, George F. Reynolds, who came to the conclusion that the Elizabethan stage reflected many practices of the simultaneous stage of the Middle Ages. He was particularly interested in those times when a throne or a large tree was brought on for one scene and evidently left on during an entirely different scene, to be used again later. Emphasis was shifted from the bare platform or arranged inner stage to the convention of medieval staging and elaborate properties on the forestage. In 1908 William Archer suggested as an origin of the Elizabethan stage the screens of the great halls. In private palaces and in schools and colleges and such great buildings as the London lawyers' Inns of Court, the common room had a large screen at one end, with two formal doors and a minstrel's gallery that could serve as an upper stage. So many historians have imagined the Elizabethan stage as a Gothic structure of beam and plaster in shades of tan and brown that Archer's suggestion of a rich architectural background was lost for a long time.

Every previous historical approach was overshadowed by the publication in 1923 of E. K. Chambers' study, in four volumes, *The Elizabethan Stage*. Chambers was convinced that he had discovered the *one* way that Elizabethan plays were staged: by successive staging. Whenever a group of actors entered and established the scene as one place—a courtyard or palace room or woods or field—then all the stage was that place until the end of the scene.

After playing in the round had become familiar in the 1930s, Leslie Hotson developed the theory that the Elizabethan stage was really theatre-in-the-round, with audience on four sides. Another of his conclusions about the Elizabethan theatre was that masked "stage keepers," like property men in the Oriental theatre, were always on stage to arrange properties, pull curtains, and wait on spectators who had seats on the stage.

The Blackfriars' theatre, restoration by G. Topham Forrest, 1922.

332

The most radical new development has come from the comparative study of all forms of the Renaissance theatre not only in England but on the continent. In 1944, I advanced the theory that the Elizabethan stage must be viewed in relation not to any one form of the stage but to the whole tradition of medieval and Renaissance art. I called my book *From Art to Theatre* (1944) and traced the development in medieval art and sculpture, in stained glass, carved tombs, tapestries and paintings, of the conventions of relating characters to an architectural façade that combined several of the scenic symbols known in processions and in frieze forms of art since before the dawn of history. The immediate transitional form between art and theatre was the tableaux vivants of the street theatres, already examined. When the Elizabethan stage is seen in that context, it appears not at all as a plain, negative background but as a rich showpiece, splendid in appearance and suggesting all the pomp of a royal welcome, the splendor of tableaux of old battles, famous heroes, and legendary loves.

The wider comparative approach was brought to full expression in 1953 in *The Globe Restored* by C. Walter Hodges. He reviews and publishes all the pertinent visual evidence and presents a score of splendid drawings. He points out that the basic form of the Elizabethan stage was still the form of the oldest and most widespread kind of stage—the mountebank stage, with an open platform and a booth at the back for dressing and making entrances.

PICTORIAL EVIDENCE

Two pictures of the interior of a theatre that may be representations of an Elizabethan theatre have been found, but neither can be accepted as absolutely authentic by the careful Shakespearean scholar. In 1888 there was found in a Commonplace Book in the library of the University of Utrecht, Holland, a drawing labeled as the interior of The Swan Theatre. The drawing was made by a man who was never in England, though he made his drawing as a copy of one a friend had made on his return from England. One cannot know how careful he was in making his copy and whether he omitted some details. The sketch looks as if its original might have been made during a rehearsal, since there are no spectators in the galleries. It disagrees in several respects with conclusions about Elizabethan theatres that had been reached by careful scholars. While there are two entrance doorways on the stage, there is no sign of a third entrance or of an inner stage. Was the Swan unlike other Elizabethan stages in having no inner stage? To complicate the problem, several scholars in the early twentieth century decided, on other evidence, that if there was an inner stage on any public theatre, it was only a small space where a curtain could be drawn aside to reveal a tableau or very short scene.

333

Johannes de Witt's sketch of the Swan Theatre.

334

In the *New York Review of Books* for May 26, 1966, appeared an article, "New Light on the Globe Theatre," by Frances A. Yates. In studying books on the art of memory, she had found a book by an Englishman, Robert Fludd, written in Latin and published in Germany in 1619. A section of the book was devoted to memory devices, and, as an example, Fludd tells his readers to think of an actual building, say a theatre, then in their minds put the five things they are trying to memorize into the five openings of the theatre. There is an engraving of a theatre, made by an engraver who had not been in England. Did Fludd send or bring a sketch (now lost) from England for the engraver to use? On the double bow window above the central section of the stage is printed as a title *Theatrum orbi*.

AUTHENTIC RECONSTRUCTIONS

In the nineteenth and twentieth centuries a number of supposedly Elizabethan theatres have been built, usually for production of Shakespeare's plays. But two recent projects on a large scale involving reconstruction of The Globe Theatre are of special interest. In the late 1960s the time seemed ripe to rebuild The Globe on

A Mnemonic Globe Theatre, 1619. *By permission of the Folger Shakespeare Library.*

the original site. The area was being cleared of the warehouses hastily put up after the blitz of World War II, and there would be space close to a restored theatre for hotels and restaurants to take care of students and tourists who might be expected to visit, especially if a World Center for Shakespeare Studies were established, with the restored theatre as a laboratory. With faith in this dream, the American actor Sam Wannamaker, who had settled in England, and others who became interested, arranged for lectures in London in the summer of 1970 or 1971 and for a company of actors to perform in a tent theatre on the site of the old Globe. And when Hodges, who had helped promote the reconstruction project, found that compromises demanded by real estate men and others would not result in a Globe Theatre in Southwark that was authentic, he and others promoted, as a substitute, a Shakespeare company playing in an Elizabethan-type theatre reconstructed in an old Church of St. George in London. Production survived there for several years.

In the late 1970s the spark of the restoration idea took fire in Detroit, Michigan. Leonard Leone of Wayne State University was the leading spirit of a new restoration project. In 1979 he gathered in conference in Detroit the dozen or so scholars from Britain, Canada, and the United States who had done notable research on the Elizabethan theatre in the past several decades. At the meetings the scholars pooled their ideas of what an authentic Globe Theatre should be and came near enough to agreement so that building plans could be made. But then architects and builders had their say: "The fire laws will not permit building a wooden structure," "If you use a glass overall cover, there is the problem of noise in a rainstorm," etc., etc. The idea of compromise was accepted, however, and a money-raising campaign to continue over a long period was undertaken. But the project has lapsed for lack of money.

Renaissance Drama in England

A NEW VIEW OF HISTORY: THE HISTORICAL PLAYS

The Elizabethan stage façade, symbol of a throne, a castle, a realm, was also a symbol of historical order. Shakespeare and some of his contemporaries put on the platform in front of that façade one of the world's greatest visions of man in history.

Medieval writers collected stories of the fall of princes, showing how the wheel of fortune would raise them to the height of power, then cast them down to defeat and death. The wise man scorned the world and turned to heaven. Yet in these collections of historical examples can be traced a gradual emergence of a sense of man's responsibility for his own fate. In *The Mirror for Magistrates*, published in several versions in the 1560s, there emerges a tragic sense that man and his will and deeds have significance in this world. The *Mirror* had a great influence on the historical plays of Shakespeare and his contemporaries. Elizabethan tragedy developed in close relationship to the history plays, and many plays now classified as tragedies were published as histories.

Development of the great English historical plays came in the 1580s and 1590s, when the international situation was very tense and there was a sharp sense of England's peril. The defeat of the Spanish Armada in 1588 was only a great crisis in a long conflict with Spain. Spain controlled most of America and most of Europe, including Italy and Austria. The Low Countries were struggling for freedom from Spain. While Queen Mary of England was married to Philip II, Spain dominated England, and when Mary died, Philip hoped either by marriage to Elizabeth or by conquest to regain that domination. But the English were determined to remain independent and take their place in the world. Books of history showed them that they had a glorious past and a destiny in the world. The stage brought much of that history to life and was more effective than books in giving the people as a whole a sense of history.

The idea of the great individual and the idea of a united nation were closely related. As man stood at the center in the Neoplatonic structure of the cosmos, looking up to God, so also did he stand at the center of the political picture, looking up toward a benign king. The idea of a centralized nation meant a radical break from the feudal system, and civil war in nearly every country in Europe destroyed the power of the feudal barons. The Renaissance saw the emergence of the absolute ruler.

Spain and England were the first countries to achieve strong unity. When the Spanish princess Katherine of Aragon was married first to Arthur, Prince of Wales, and then to his brother Henry VIII, it seemed that the two nations could lead the world. But problems of religious diversity and competition in exploration and settlement of the New World kept them enemies.

Englishmen were thankful for the strong Tudor government which had brought together York and Lancaster and healed the wounds of the War of the Roses. Protestant leaders under Edward VI and Catholic leaders under Mary had gone to such extremes that the middle course of Elizabeth seemed a marvel of sense and security. The northern lords did rebel in 1569, near the beginning of Elizabeth's reign, and Essex led a rebellion in 1599 near the end of the reign. English soldiers were repeatedly sent to help the Protestant towns in the Low Countries against the Spanish armies. Sir Philip Sidney, the most popular hero of the time—poet, chivalrous knight, prince—lost his life in Holland in 1586. The massacre of Protestants in France on St. Bartholomew's Day in 1572 was a shocking event. Civil war in France was not ended until the last rebellion was put down in 1628 and the power of Richelieu brought the nobles to bay.

What was to happen to England after Elizabeth's death? No provision was made for the succession until Elizabeth was a very old woman, and it was clear that James Stuart of Scotland would be acceptable. The problem was repeatedly dramatized. Several times lawyers invited the queen to their Inns of Court where they put on plays showing ancient examples of the chaos of a divided kingdom. Though played to only a small group, they had great influence on the dramatists of the popular theatres.

The four greatest literary achievements of Elizabeth's reign were all studies of the education of a prince and expressed concern over public affairs. They were *The Mirror for Magistrates;* Philip Sidney's *Arcadia* (1590), the greatest prose tale of the age; Edmund Spenser's *Faerie Queene* (1590), the greatest poem; and, greatest of all, the series of histories and historical tragedies of William Shakespeare.

Shakespeare's age was convinced that while an extreme tyrant might justify rebellion, it was far better to endure a bad king than to rebel. Henry Bolingbroke, who became Henry IV, had rebelled against Richard II, and this wrong brought wars and dissension for nearly a hundred years. Henry's son, Henry V, brought a moment of peace, but after his death the boy king Henry VI was unable to hold the nobles in check. The English were defeated in France because of dissension at home. The chaos led to the bloody tyranny of Richard III before it was resolved by the first Tudor, Henry VII. Shakespeare's eight plays about these events form two closely knit tetralogies. *Henry VI* (three plays) and *Richard III* were written before the four plays about the earlier time.

In the first part of *Henry VI* (1589–90) the glorious achievements of Henry V are lost. The great soldier Talbot is defeated and killed in France because the headstrong English nobles quarrel. Joan of Arc is presented as a strumpet-witch

338

The flower portrait of Shakespeare. *From the RSC Collection, with the permission of the Governors of the Royal Shakespeare Theatre, Stratford-upon-Avon.*

who rules the French and magically defeats the English. In *2 Henry VI* (1590–91) the bitter contention between the houses of York and Lancaster begins. As in a morality play, the good advisor to the youthful king is disgraced and killed, leaving the field open to the ambitious Duke of York. Jack Cade leads a noisy rabble in rebellion to destroy not only the rich and the titled but books, schools, and records of the realm. The crowd deserts Cade, and a country squire captures him and sends his head to the king. The third play of *Henry VI* (1590–91) presents civil war in full sweep. Two vivid figures emerge and come together at the end: King Henry VI, whose saintly patience and compassion give pause to some of the fighters, and the demonic Richard Crookback, who becomes Richard III. *Richard III* (1592–93), the last play in the tetralogy, is based on Thomas More's history of Richard III. Shakespeare, like More, believed that chaos leads to violence and tyranny.

Shakespeare reached the height of his powers in writing the tetralogy about the beginning of the trouble: *Richard II* (1595), the two parts of *Henry IV* (1596–98), and *Henry V* (1599). They are studies not only of political turmoil but of great individuals caught in the mesh of political problems. Shakespeare led his age in his increasing interest in the psychology of human character as it interacted with the social order. In the next decade he took one more step in the penetration of the inner life of the individual, and his plays became tragedies.

The two-part structure of Richard II shows the difference between Richard as a bad ruler and Henry as a good one. At the beginning of the play Richard is faced with a difficult problem which he solves in the wrong way, provoking Henry to rebel and depose him. At the beginning of the second part (Act IV) Henry is faced with the same problem and solves it in the right way by reconciling his quarreling subjects and consolidating his rule. But Shakespeare did not develop the characters in a simple good and evil contrast. Richard was the rightful heir and the anointed king. Even if he had been involved in the murder of an uncle (a hidden crime) that lay beneath Henry's accusation of treason, it was not right for Henry to depose him. Shakespeare's Henry is a rather prosaic man of action; the playwright's sympathy went to the sensitive Richard, who was forced to abdicate and was finally murdered.

In the two plays on Henry IV, Shakespeare set up a more complex structure, with better integration of the parts than in *Richard II*. The two plays are a kind of morality play about the education of a prince. They carry on the morality play tradition of the Lusty Juventus or prodigal son, with scenes of revelry leading to repentance and new dedication. They surround the growing knight with a variety of characters and experiences, of war, chivalry, revelry, vice, and of justice and responsibility. The knight (Prince Hal) casts off play to become Henry V, a better monarch for having known the companionship of the common people. On the other hand, seen as part of the course of history following the deposition of Richard II, the two plays show the disorder that Henry IV might well have expected. The more distant nobles who had helped him in rebellion rebel against him in turn, and his son, Hal, becomes a truant in London taverns showing no interest in the military or civil duties of a king. The quick-tempered Hotspur, in pursuit of honor and fame, young leader of the new rebels, seems a better knight than Prince Hal. But Hal rallies to the call of war. The rebels are defeated, Hotspur is killed, and the prince is reconciled with his father.

Falstaff, Hal's companion in revelry, is one of Shakespeare's great creations. He is far more than the chief tempter in a morality play. He is a drunkard, glutton, braggart, coward, thief, and liar, but a man of wit and imagination with a great zest for living. He robs for the fun of telling his exploits. His cowardice is a very practical sense of self-preservation, and Shakespeare gives him a wonderful speech on the uselessness of "honor" to balance Hotspur's outdated desire to "pluck bright honor from the pale-faced moon." Falstaff's lying comes from an inventive mind. His prank of claiming the bodies of the enemies Hal has killed reduces even war to a game. Hal, the warm, friendly prince, can enjoy the prince of players and in his own way play the game.

In 2 *Henry IV*, Shakespeare gradually separates Falstaff from the prince, and at the coronation shows the young king, now taking mature responsibility, cast off the companion of his carefree youth. If Hal had a real affection for Falstaff, the rejection seems cruel. But it may be argued that Hal had a real affection for Falstaff while realizing that their association must end. In a number of his comedies Shakespeare shows his feeling for the passing of youth and carefree days. His histories show his regard for kingship. What is more natural than to show both feelings through a carefree prince who in time accepts the necessary attitudes of a good ruler?

The second part of *Henry IV* presents an interesting reconciliation with Justice, the highest of royal virtues. The Lord Chief Justice expects harsh treatment from the monarch because he had once had Prince Hal arrested. But the king makes no reprisal. In the tableaux vivants, Justice occupied a heavenly throne above the king himself, and in Elizabeth's reign the law held that position. It is notable that a few years after *Henry IV* was performed, the new monarch, James I, dismissed his Lord Chief Justice and thus began the undermining of his dynasty.

The last play of the tetralogy, *Henry V*, shows the triumph of Hal as king and the triumph of England. Shakespeare presents Henry V in a complex political order. He is head of an integrated state, the servant of England. He defies and conquers the enemy but with less bragging than the fiery Dauphin, his opponent. In contrast to Christopher Marlowe's Tamburlaine, he is humble before God and his men. A group of four British nationalities—an English, a Welsh, an Irish, and a Scotch soldier—symbolizes the coming together of the parts of the kingdom. Henry is shown again making contact with the common people, this time in concern over their welfare and his responsibility for their lives. For warfare brings a new companionship between the prince and the commons, celebrated as a ritual

341

in Henry's St. Crispin's Day speech, which declares:

> And gentlemen in England now a-bed
> Shall think themselves accurs'd that were not here
> And hold their manhoods cheap whiles any speaks
> That fought with us upon Saint Crispin's day.

Henry V solved the problem of order in the state by making war on another state. His father had advised him to "busy giddy minds with foreign quarrels." Patriotism and national unity may receive a great reinforcement from the play, but there is a touch of tragic irony in the picture of the prince who repudiated the petty intemperance and thievery of his boyhood companions and set out to steal a kingdom.

THE ROMANTIC PLAY

The historical plays are significant not only because of their vision of English history but because of their close relationship to a new genre of the English Renaissance, the romantic play. Reaching its own perfection in the 1590s, the new romantic play stands in sharp contrast to Greek drama, which presents one human situation in the most compact and spare form possible. The English playwrights added subplots, spectacle, and all manner of detail, until their plays might seem full to bursting—yet they are also unified, in a different and exciting way. The historical plays are romantic in their epic sweep, in the number and variety of colorful episodes, and in their spectacle. But the serious tone is unlike that of most romantic plays, and history does not always manage a happy ending, as the author of a romantic play usually does.

The immediate ancestors of Elizabethan drama were complex in structure. The medieval cycle plays were long epics with scenes that moved from the Garden of Eden to Jerusalem, from Herod's throne to the gates of hell. They included adventures as exciting as those of the knights errant. To such adventures the Elizabethans added tournaments, battles, sieges, conspiracies, triumphs, processions, all sorts of colorful spectacle. The French classicists of the seventeenth century saw no order in such drama. Yet the romantic play has its own kind of unity and a firm structure, and must be considered one of the great genres of the theatre.

In many romantic plays, form and imagery are related to the basic meaning of the play. In *Romeo and Juliet* (1595–96) for instance, the interaction of the two feuding houses gives an enclosing form as well as a constant motivation. A fight between the houses opens the play, and a reconciliation ends it. One series of episodes brings Romeo and Juliet together, another series tears them apart. The

lovers are separated as each endures a series of trials, and they finally come together in the tragic mishaps at the tomb. Juliet has a comic nurse and Romeo a
picturesque friar as advisor. Romeo's friend Mercutio not only reinforces the impetuosity of Romeo's youth but, by his boisterous contempt for love, sets in sharp
relief the depth and sincerity of Romeo's passion. All of the large cast define the
plight of the central couple by contrast. Juliet's parents give her no sympathy and
insist on her immediate marriage with Paris. Even the nurse lets her down. Left
alone to face her problem, she becomes one of the memorable figures of romantic
literature. She discovers the strength of a desperate ego. "If all else fail," she says,
"myself hath power to die."

But it is more than the tragic-romantic story of the two lovers, set off by many
contrasts, that holds the play together. The imagery and the musical pattern of
the verse give it unity and also embody the basic meaning. In *Shakespeare's Imagery*
(1935) Caroline Spurgeon first pointed out the sets of images that dominate Romeo
and Juliet. They all concern something that is too quick or brilliant, like sparks,
fire, lightning. Looking at the play as a musical pattern, we discover that it is a
series of slow moments, each followed by the sweep of relentless speed. The
lovers are forever meeting and parting; time is forever lingering, then rushing on
with overwhelming compulsion. The young blades are in a hurry to get to the
party, but they linger for Mercutio's vision of Queen Mab, then for Romeo's presage
of sorrow; then with pounding drum they all rush off. The brisk tempo is picked
up immediately on the Elizabethan stage by the servants of the Capulets in a
hurry to finish arrangements for the party. Romeo lingers a moment with Juliet,
and then the guests rush in. Mercutio lingers a moment on his way home to make
bawdy, satiric comments on love, and Romeo lingers a longer time for the balcony
scene. Friar Lawrence tries to persuade Romeo to curb his passion and proceed
carefully, and the nurse teases Juliet by a mischievous delay. The contrast in speed
permeates the imagery. In the scene of the lovers' last parting they think at one
moment of dawn: "Jocund day stands tiptoe on the misty mountain tops"; the next
moment they feel an intangible dread, as of the tomb where they will meet next.

This pattern of tempo, or surging forward and pulling back, or reaching upward
while being held down, suggests the basic meaning of the play. It is a romantic
tragedy that does not depend for its effects on the pattern of tragic fault and responsibility. Romeo and Juliet achieve their glorious assertion of individual rights
against the traditional world of feudal hatreds. They are the wellsprings of all romantic characters in their glorious, if short-lived, assertion of the human will.
And they define forever one type of tragedy. If the universe is full of old tradition
and hatreds, of blind chance and accident, of malignant stars, man can still, by
supreme assertion of his own values, snatch a moment of ecstasy in the face of
disaster. Assertion is all the more magnificent if it is made in full knowledge that
the moment will soon pass "like lightning that is gone ere one can say it lightens."

Not only do the characters Romeo and Juliet mark a new point in the emer-

343

gence of the individual, they also mark a new chapter in the literature of love. The ideal of romantic love created by the troubadours was outside of marriage. Shakespeare's play, written about 1594, was the first instance in drama of the reconciliation of courtly love with marriage. The love of a young man for the girl he marries becomes the central ideal of the rising bourgeois world.

Even when Shakespeare wrote *The Comedy of Errors* (1592–94), a comedy of Plautus adapted for his audience, he was not willing to keep it simple. He gave the farce an enclosing action that is in the greatest possible contrast with the spirit of Plautus, opening the play with a man about to be put to death but given one day in which to hunt his long-lost sons. The note of sorrow and anxiety modifies considerably the comic effect of the whole. At the end of the play the man finds not only his sons but the long-lost wife and mother, and this gives a wider context to the action than Plautus provided.

An enclosing action also serves Shakespeare for *A Midsummer Night's Dream* (1595–96), a romantic play. Theseus, Duke of Athens, announces his marriage at the beginning, and his wedding celebration ends the play. But the enclosing action is more thoroughly integrated with the rest of the action than in *The Comedy of Errors*. The Duke and his lady are brought in more than once, and at the end provide a commentary on the play within the play.

David Garrick and Anne Barry in *Romeo and Juliet*, London, 1750. *Courtesy of the Trustees of the British Museum.*

344

The central theme of the play, marriage, is enhanced by a number of variations. The happy marriage of the Duke is set in contrast to the quarrels of Oberon and Titania and the farcical misunderstandings and mismatings of the four young lovers. As played by the homespuns, the tragic love of Pyramus and Thisbe becomes "very tragical mirth." Harmonious love is parodied in a gross key by Titania's doting on Bottom, transformed into an ass. The Duke's sympathetic response to the rustics' play transforms their comic efforts to pure devotion. Puck, with the aid of night and his magic flower, transforms the young lovers into mismatches, then turns them back to their right relationships. But the transformations are not at all like the farcical mistakes of a Plautine comedy. They are effected by the imagination.

From another point of view, *A Midsummer Night's Dream* is an epitome of the Renaissance state. At the head is the noble, accomplished prince, returned from conquests to devote himself to the civil arts. Like him, Oberon is a creature of the highest refinement, ruler over the night, the night that will release not only youthful mischief but also the charm and ennobling power of the imagination. These two princes, mirrors of each other, blend noble citizens and humble artisans, the public life of courtly ceremony, the courtship and quarrels of youth and parents, the moonlight magic of fairy revels, and the fascination of the grotesque and miscalculated. They bring together the folklore of the pagan Celts and Saxons, the classic ideal of an aristocrat, Plautine laughter over distraught lovers, and the clumsy attempt to present a classic play in naïve medieval terms.

The Merchant of Venice (1596–97) is another fine example of the romantic play having unity in complexity, where many characters, plots, contrasts, and overtones are all brought together in a rich poetic harmony. The play is about getting and using money, trade and finance, ventures at sea for gain and ventures on land for love, bonds and forfeitures, caskets made of lead, silver, and gold that puzzle the choice. It was a play very timely for a London replacing Venice in sea ventures, trade, and finance. Antonio, the merchant, signs a bond to Shylock. There is a smoldering hatred between these representatives of trade and finance, and at the court trial they are locked in battle that has no decent solution until Portia comes in disguise from that other world to free them. Then the trick of the rings creates a new suspense which is resolved in the moonlight return to Belmont. The trial is like a medieval morality play where Mercy defeats strict Justice and love triumphs over usury.

ROMANTIC COMEDY

Of the romantic plays cited here, one is a romantic tragedy (*Romeo and Juliet*) and one a romantic play with very serious undertones (*The Merchant of Venice.*)

345

Frontispiece to the Rowe edition of *The Tempest*, 1709. *By courtesy of the Board of Trustees of the Victoria and Albert Museum.*

A Midsummer Night's Dream is, of course, a romantic comedy. In this genre Shakespeare and several of his contemporaries excelled. Romantic comedy is quite distinct from Plautine farce, the satiric comedy of Aristophanes, and high comedy, which was the great achievement of the middle and late seventeenth century. It differs from the folk comedy of the medieval villagers or the incidental comedy of the mystery cycles, though it incorporated some elements from both. Its ancestors were age-old popular festivals, with their spirit of release and joyful celebration, and the courtly romances of medieval chivalry. The very structure of romantic comedy shows a mixed derivation: it regularly combines scenes of highborn aristocrats with scenes of amiable lowly characters.

Robert Greene's *Honourable History of Friar Bacon and Friar Bungay* (published in 1594) set the romantic pattern. Young Lacy is on a jaunt in the spring countryside when he falls in love with the Fair Maid of Fressingfield, and he is finally permitted to marry her, though she is of humble birth. We are to suppose that the spring charm of the courtship will touch every day of the lovers' lives, for romance assumes that people of imagination and warmth can sustain the glow of the spring long after the flowers are dead.

The festival spirit permeates the romantic comedies of Shakespeare. *A Midsummer Night's Dream* is a play of a magic night of midsummer, the only night when all the fairies are out and mortals are likely to be transformed beyond recognition. The audience can stand with Puck to look down in amusement and delight at the foolishness of men and the perversity of the universe: "Lord, what fools these mortals be!" *Twelfth Night* (1601–02) must release two women from too great care over love, and eliminate the threat of the love-tormented Malvolio. At the end the wedding festivities proceed with music and gaiety. Feste the fool has assured the audience that journeys end in lovers' meetings, and his last song is sad only because the carefree companionship, revels, and courtship are too quickly lost amid the cares of a practical world. *As You Like It* (1599) is the very essence of a holiday, a brief renewal of simple sanity. All the characters return to the court at the end, completely transformed. Though *The Tempest* (1611) differs from these comedies, with philosophical implications which they lack, Prospero's island is a bit of magic illusion, a free-association, hypnotic dream induced by the trauma of shipwreck. The experience is brief, but the characters have found their true selves and are ready to return to the responsibilities of everyday life. Romance insists that only in the escape of a festival holy day, only as one puts on the special garment of the celebrant, the motley of the fool, the mask of illusion, only as one puts to sleep the conscious mind and escapes to the seacoast of Bohemia, can one find the true self. It is not only in religion, in Christ's forty days in the wilderness or Mohammed's hegira, that withdrawal is renewal, and that holiday is holy day.

347

THE RENAISSANCE HERO: TAMBURLAINE

In 1587 the actor Edward Alleyn, leading player of the Lord Admiral's Men, stepped out on the open stage platform, proud and free. In one gesture he broke the medieval chains that bound men to humility. He was Tamburlaine, the peasant shepherd who conquered the world. He invited not only his rival, General Theridamas, but the whole English audience into a proud new world of achievement:

> Forsake thy king and do but join with me,
> And we will triumph over all the world.
> I hold the Fates bound fast in iron chains,
> And with my hand turn Fortune's wheel about,
> And sooner shall the sun fall from his sphere
> Than Tamburlaine be slain or overcome.

Christopher Marlowe, the shoemaker's son from Canterbury, created the character. Marlowe might well have been fascinated by this peasant who achieved fame not by birth but by will and aspiration. Neoplatonic man, at the center of the universe, was drawn by his view of heavenly beauty to realize himself, not in the other world but by the highest assertion possible on this earth, in the Renaissance symbol of royal man. Tamburlaine gives a magnificent description of that aspiration:

> Nature, that framed us of four elements
> Warring within our breasts for regiment,
> Doth teach us all to have aspiring minds.
> . . . .
> Wills us to wear ourselves and never rest,
> Until we reach the ripest fruit of all,
> That perfect bliss and sole felicity,
> The sweet fruition of an earthly crown.

Like a medieval knight, Tamburlaine is inspired by a lady, a symbol of aspiration toward the highest. His longing for beauty is the counterpart of his longing for heroic conquest. When Zenocrate is captured he leads her away in silence, and as she comes to understand his gentle though relentless strength, she joins him on his throne.

As the pageant of Tamburlaine's triumphs in honor and love sweeps across the stage platform, there is little conflict or suspense but considerable contrast, with spectacular climaxes and magnificent verse. The generals of Persia desert their king to go with Tamburlaine, responding like small boys to his promises of triumphs and kingships: "Is it not passing brave to be a king / And ride in triumph through Persepolis?" The battle is a walk-away, and the silly king of Persia is left

348

Portrait of Christopher Marlowe, 1585.

alone on the battlefield. Tamburlaine gently takes his crown from him, then gives it back, and the king flees in terror when he realizes whom he is facing.

Bajazet, Emperor of the Turks, is a more formidable opponent, but the battle is built up not by running and sword-clashes but by a set of beautifully balanced speeches of defiance, the emperor and his three kings on one side of the stage being answered from the other side by Tamburlaine and his three kings. When the men on both sides leave, their ladies, in balanced splendor, brag how each is going to make a servant of her opposite number, until news comes that Tamburlaine has won the battle.

On his way to conquer the third enemy, the Soldan of Egypt, Tamburlaine carries with him in a cage the Turkish Emperor and his Empress and mounts his throne stepping on the crouching Emperor. The conquest of Egypt is presented in a pageant of colors. On one day Tamburlaine's men and his tents are dressed in white to promise mercy if the city surrenders, on the next day in red, and finally in black to signal complete destruction to those who have continued to defy the conqueror. Tamburlaine has evolved as a Renaissance hero under the teaching of beauty, honor, and aspiration. At the end of the first play he places a crown on Zenocrate, his inspiration, now his queen.

Scene from the national theatre (London) production of Christopher Marlowe's *Tamberlaine the Great*, 1970, directed by Peter Hall. First production of *Tamberlaine* since Elizabethan times.

350

Tamburlaine Part II (1588) shows a quite different aspect of the hero and of Marlowe. In the first part of the play Tamburlaine had reached an ideal maturity and balance. But extreme individualism, as the nineteenth-century romantics rediscovered, is a greater help in carrying a person from youth to manhood than in carrying him on to maturity and old age. The problem of the future catches Tamburlaine. Fame is not enough for him; he wants his sons to continue his triumphs. One of them, however, has no inclination for warlike deeds. So Tamburlaine must face the diversity of human wills in the defection of his son, the loss of beauty in the death of his wife, and extinction in his own death.

The final magnificence of Tamburlaine is that he refuses to accept these limitations. Like a willful boy, he screams to the heavens. In his fury he would destroy the universe. He burns the town where his wife died and vows he will wrap her body in gold and keep it always with him. With Zenocrate gone, he turns more violently against weakness, kills the son who would prefer a life of peace, and becomes "the scourge of God and terror of the world." He whips the two oriental kings who pull his chariot crying, "Holla, ye pampered jades of Asia." He looks at a map and, outraged that something is beyond his grasp, cries, "And shall I die, and this unconquered?"

In this two-part play Marlowe established one of the major patterns of tragedy. The defeat is inevitable because the hero challenges the limits of existence. There is tragedy in the lack of balance: too much of qualities that in themselves and in a balanced context were the highest values. But the final impression is not of defeat but of magnificent assertion.

In *Dr. Faustus* (c. 1589–92) the two aspects of the Renaissance hero's story—the bursting of old bonds and then defeat as the hero discovers that not all limits can be transcended—are encompassed in one situation, and an even more terrifying play than *Tamburlaine* results. We have what is probably only a fragment of the play Marlowe wrote, and some scenes are vastly inferior to the concept as a whole, but the play must still be considered as in the first rank of all plays ever written.

Faustus, too, is a great Renaissance individual. Like Tamburlaine, he comes from a humble family and rises beyond all medieval heights. But instead of seeking achievement in earthly conquest, he looks to a mental realm that "stretcheth as far as doth the mind of man." On the surface the play resembles a medieval morality play, replete with devils, clowns, good and evil angels, and a pageant of the Seven Deadly Sins; and at the end, devils carry off the sinner. But Marlowe has internalized these allegorical figures and created a central character very different from the Mankind of the morality play. Even Mephistopheles is little more than a projection of Faustus' wish. The morality located the source of evil outside of man in wicked influences sent by the devil. Faustus, with the springs of measureless good and evil within himself, is a modern man. Mephistopheles is a medieval foil for the Renaissance Faustus. He is terrified of heaven and hell, while Faustus is proud of being a man with a man's superior fortitude.

Where Tamburlaine comes gradually to learn his unwelcome limitations, Faustus

351

is tied to them from the beginning. But by making his contract with the devil he is able to forget them for a definite time. By pretending that heaven and hell are fables, Faustus releases his ego and becomes more powerful than popes and emperors. Yet it is knowledge he most craves, and some of that knowledge is very exciting. He travels over the world and learns the secrets of foreign potentates—a reflection of the Renaissance interest in India, Africa, America, the East. And he can recreate the ancient world, one exciting enough to banish despair:

> Was this the face that launched a thousand ships
> And burnt the topless towers of Ilium?
> Sweet Helen, make me immortal with a kiss.

But Faustus repeatedly wants answers to metaphysical questions—what is behind the visible creation—questions Mephistopheles cannot answer since he, like Faustus, is cut off from God. In the middle of the play Faustus busies himself with

Frontispiece from Marlowe's *Faust*. Faust has been identified as the actor Edward Alleyn.

clowns' tricks and fetching a duchess some grapes out of season. These scenes seem trivial in comparison with Faustus' early hopes. They suggest that Marlowe foresaw the barrenness that must follow when humanistic study neglects metaphysical and religious questions. At the end there is the devil to pay, and the final scene, in which Faustus cries out to Christ and offers to burn his books, has been called the most intense scene in all dramatic poetry. Faustus' anguish is a measure of the magnificence of man's spirit: it can storm the very gates of heaven in its restless search for knowledge infinite.

Marlowe left two other plays, *The Jew of Malta* (c. 1590) and *Edward II* (c. 1591–92), vivid expressions of two minor aspects of the great liberated individual. *The Jew of Malta* develops further the impulse of the hurt individual to strike back. Barabas the Jew, like the stricken Tamburlaine, responds with evil. But the setting now is social rather than cosmic. Where Tamburlaine wanted to "march against the powers of heaven and set / Black streamers to signify the slaughter of the Gods," Barabas seeks to outsteal and outpoison the hypocritical Christians around him. Edward Alleyn had a part almost as large as that of Tamburlaine, if more subtle, sly, and bitter.

In *Edward II*, Marlowe made the weakness that Tamburlaine despised the central quality of the English king. Like a weak ruler in a morality play, Edward chooses corrupt advisors and falls a victim to Mortimer, an ambitious, Machiavellian villain, who in turn must be destroyed. In Edward, Marlowe showed the suffering of a sensitive soul, a kind of character Shakespeare was to develop so well in *Richard II* and *Hamlet* (c. 1600). Marlowe moved even further than in *The Jew of Malta* in putting his hero in a social context. If he had lived longer, he might have matured beyond the love for ruthless, titanic heroes.

In Marlowe we get glimpses of a personality that is in many ways characteristic of his time. He had broken away from family and village and religious ties. Perhaps an interest in homosexuality set him further apart from the world around him. He apparently worked as a spy. He was patronized by the nobility and consorted with writers and actors but remained an enigmatic individual. In his plays he expressed some of the bitterness and ultimate failure of the lone individual. But he is best remembered as the creator of towering, self-asserting Renaissance characters.

Ambitious men fascinated George Chapman as much as they did Marlowe. The heroes of *The Revenge of Bussy D'Ambois* (1610) and *Charles Duke of Byron* (1608) are nonconformists who conspire against the social order. Their lack of balance and control soon leads to defeat. At the end the playwright condemns them as monsters. But in the passing moment these heroes are glorified by aspiring thoughts that continue the high tone of Marlowe. Bussy wants to "Do a justice that exceeds the law." He is sure of fame, "Doing those deeds that fit eternity." Chapman, the Renaissance man, is fascinated by the aspiration, the intensity of a hero "Whose strength, while virtue was her mate / Might have subdued the earth."

353

Shakespeare, too, created his versions of the magnificent Renaissance hero. His fullest portrait of heroic evil in a Machiavellian tyrant is Richard III. His finest man of triumph is Henry V. Henry confidently meets the defiance of enemies, storms their cities, wins his lady from his enemies and holds the ardent devotion of his followers.

Both the glorious conqueror and the superhuman villain live in *Othello*. The Moorish general is not himself an aristocrat, but he bears a princely mind and wins his lady from his enemies as easily as Tamburlaine. With the help of the villain, he finds his limitations in his home. Yet his jealousy is part of the intensity of his love. He loved "not wisely, but too well."

Shakespeare's most splendid conqueror is Mark Antony of *Antony and Cleopatra* (1606–07). This couple neglected their duties and threw away an empire. But they had known royal magnificence. They are Tamburlaine grown to maturity, just as they are Romeo and Juliet grown to maturity. The play was written after the four great tragedies that express disillusionment and despair. After the Renaissance belief in unity and order had begun to fade, Shakespeare could return to the sure confidence of the high Renaissance, with greater depth and maturity.

Shakespeare achieves the heroic assertion in this play in two ways. One is the large sweep of events across the Elizabethan stage. Shakespeare dared to open the play with a full expression of Roman disgust at "The triple pillar of the world / Transform'd into a strumpet's fool." Then he builds up gradually the sense of regal splendor, until Cleopatra raises Antony, for his dying farewell, into a high moment, symbol of eternal fame, and she herself dies with such dignity that the new Caesar, ruler and representative of the new social order, has to pay tribute to the great individual: "Bravest at the last, / She levell'd at our purpose, and being royal / Took her own way."

But Shakespeare reinforced the visual splendor on the stage of the Globe Theatre with some of his richest imagery. Antony is a man beyond measure, to be compared to sky and ocean and continents. Cleopatra is of infinite variety. She is sure Antony will not stay with Octavia, a woman of so little royal bearing: "The man hath seen some majesty and should know." Antony throws away kingdoms because with Cleopatra he knows the meaning of royal *space*: "Let Rome in Tiber melt, and the wide arch / Of the ranged empire fall! Here is my space." Cleopatra remembers Antony in terms of cosmic grandeur: "His face was as the heavens, and therein stuck / A sun and moon, which kept their course, and lighted / The little O, the earth . . . ." At the end Cleopatra rises to her true royal dignity. When she dies she will be properly robed and crowned: "Give me my robe, put on my crown, I have / Immortal longings in me." And Charmian recognizes a great Renaissance individual:

Now boast thee death, in thy possession lies
A loss unparalleled. Downy windows, close
And golden Phoebus, never be beheld
Of eyes again so royal.

354

But the Renaissance ideal of heroic man was expressed on the Elizabethan stage not only in kings but in merchants and even apprentices. The *Four Prentices of London* won distant ladies and riches and conquered Jerusalem. Simon Eyre, the madcap hero of Thomas Dekker's *Shoemaker's Holiday* (1599) is a glorious match for Tamburlaine, Faustus, and Antony. He has the conquering confidence of the age, and he is as much a symbol of an ordered realm as any king. All his apprentices and journeymen love him. He begins as an ordinary master of a shop, but the foresight of his men, the friendliness of noblemen, and the business enterprise of a new age give him the chance to buy and sell in a big way, and he becomes a rich man, the sheriff of London, and finally the Lord Mayor.

Success delights Simon but in no way spoils him. He is constantly concerned about the welfare of his men. At the beginning he tries to get a military deferment for his Ralph, who has just taken a bride. There is dignity in his racy individuality: "I am a man of the best presence. I'll speak to them and they were popes: gentlemen, captains, colonels, commanders: brave men, brave leaders, may it please you to give me audience. I am Simon Eyre, the mad shoemaker of Tower-street." The play ends not only in the marriage of a nobleman to a member of a bourgeois family but in a feast that unites workman, master, and king. Simon Eyre says: "Soft the king this day comes to dine with me, to see my new building. His Majesty is welcome: he shall have good cheer, delicate cheer, princely cheer. This day my fellow prentices of London come to dine with me too: they shall have fine cheer, gentlemanlike cheer. I promised the mad Cappadocians when we all served at the conduit together that if ever I came to be mayor of London, I would feast them all, and I'll do it."

But these assertive heroes of the English stage, lower class or princely, would soon give way to a very different sort of character as Renaissance confidence was replaced by Mannerist doubt and confusion. But meanwhile, drama in Spain was experiencing its own Renaissance spirit at this time.

The Commercial Theatre of Spain

In the middle of the sixteenth century, Lope de Rueda was able to earn a living with a small traveling company playing in city halls or for noblemen's banquets, on an improvised platform at festivals, or merely on the streets. Such a troupe produced mainly short interludes. By the 1560s several companies were performing long plays in Madrid in the *corrales*, or open courtyards, which were a regular feature of Spanish buildings. Making a temporary arrangement with the residents or shopkeepers of a building, they would set up a stage with curtains and use windows or an upper gallery for a higher level. There was room for a large standing audience, and seats and windows were hired by the more affluent. But in the 1570s, at about the same time as in London, theatres were built. The first permanent theatre, called the Corral del Principe, was built in Madrid in 1579 and was followed in 1582 by the Corral de la Cruz. Seville and other Spanish cities followed almost immediately, and even the cities in the New World: Lima, Peru, in 1594 and Mexico City in 1597.

Like the earlier corrales, open-air theatres had a platform at one end, a gallery or *cazuela* ("stew-pan") for women at the other, and windows or galleries and a row of raised seats around the sides. Benches near the stage seated some important people, and in Seville a stool on the stage could be had for a high price. But a large number of groundlings stood in the open pit. An awning gave some protection, but there are many references to performances cancelled because of rain.

In Spain, as in Paris and London, the commercial theatre brought together a mixed populace—nobles, merchants, artisans, peasants. It was an open-air court before a platform stage backed by a system of curtains to reveal a structure symbolic of cities, castles, and heaven. For that stage Spanish authors created a great romantic drama, mingling kings and clowns, tragedy and comedy, violence, passion, and poetry. In Madrid and Seville, and sometimes in Valencia and other cities, the free man of the Renaissance, like his London counterpart who had recently arrived in the city from the farm or the artisans' shop of the small town, could see on the stage the image of his own new-found individuality—but an individuality dependent on the glorious stability of the king. Like England, Spain had as writer for its popular folk theatre one of the world's great geniuses. Lope de Vega, like Shakespeare from humble provincial stock, caught the excitement of an expanding world.

356

"All I need is four trestles, four boards, two actors and a passion," Lope de Vega claimed, and the Spanish stage was little more than that. Sometimes the audience saw only plain curtains around three sides of the stage. The actors entered from openings in the curtains, and by their words and actions they made the audience see gardens, streets, forests, royal palaces, village festivals, citizens' houses. Action and counter action, love scenes, battles, pursuits, and processions passed across the open platform with no need for scenery. But at any moment scenery could be brought on by the actors, with the help of stage attendants who might be part of the mob in the play. Shrines, towers, castles, tents, walls, clouds, fountains, and boats—the elaborate mansions of a medieval cycle—were brought on to indicate several places at the same time. Some of the mansions had complex machines: trees suddenly turned around or the trunk or the top opened for the magic appearance of a lady, angel, or vision.

At times a façade structure similar to that on the Rederyker stage was disclosed in back of the curtains, part by part. Formal doorways were shown at the sides when needed, or were turned into shopfronts or tents. Behind the center curtain was an inner stage or *nicho* for an enclosed room or cave, and above, behind the upper curtains, was an upper stage, which could serve as the upper window of a house or as the wall of a fortified city. Or sometimes a Last Judgment was played with the throne and heavenly host above the doors to heaven and hell below. For

A performance in the Corral de la Pacheca, c. 1660. Drawing by Juan Comba y Garcia, Madrid, 1888.

357

some plays, paintings, still tableaux, or dumb shows like the figueren of the Rederyker plays were shown on this upper stage. Directions for Lope's *Lo fingido verdadero* (*The Feigned Truth*) (c. 1608), a play about the baptism of a converted actor, read, "Let the doors above be opened to the accompaniment of music and on them let two images appear: one of Our Lady and the other of Christ in the Father's arms and on the steps of this throne some martyr." Later in the same play, in the upper gallery two angels bring water in a salver and ewer and baptize the actor, while a third angel holds a candle and a fourth looks on from a cloud.

Many Spaniards, inclined to a very strict morality, disapproved of the popular theatre, like the Puritans in England, yet they marveled at it. But though the theatre might shock the straitlaced, it kept its respectability by a connection with some charitable institution, usually a hospital, which had a share in the profits, sometimes receiving as much as two-thirds of the receipts. In some cities a pious confraternity contracted with players to come to their town and give two plays "divine fashion" (that is, religious plays) in the morning and two "human fashion" in the afternoon. Whereas English actors became servants of a nobleman in order to acquire a legal status, many Spanish authors and some actors had protection as members of religious orders.

THE DRAMA OF LOPE DE VEGA

Across this open platform stage passed a vigorous poetic drama. Besides presenting the poems, dances, and songs of entertainers, Lope and his contemporaries gave theatrical expression to the whole range of their own exciting age: the great loves and exploits of medieval knights, the acts of the saints, and the entire sweep of ancient as well as Spanish history.

Lope knew that the classicists thought comedy must be concerned with only the middle and lower classes, but he filled his comedies with kings, knights, generals, heroes, poets, and noble ladies. He was familiar with the standard farce plots of disguise, pretense, and mistaken identity, but when he used them he created a new kind of drama: the comedy of cloak and dagger, where intrigue and disguise produced scenes of great excitement, and the suspense was serious because the characters were admirable. Often the character in disguise was the king himself, and the outcome was the solution of an ethical problem in the relation of a ruler to his friends and subjects.

Lope himself was an expression of the expansive vitality of the age. Born of humble parents who had moved to the city from a small village, he managed to get a university education and to become the friend of a number of the greatest lords of the land. He sailed with the Spanish Armada that in 1588 undertook the defeat of England, and his ship was one of the few that escaped and returned to Spain. His young days were filled with the pursuit of women and pleasure and the fathering of a miscellaneous brood of children. In his later days he is said to have flailed his own back until the blood spattered the walls of his penitential cell. But always he wrote. His friends claimed that he wrote more than 1,800 stage plays, besides several hundred *autos sacramentales*, or religious plays. Almost a fourth of this number are extant.

Lope knew that the classic thinkers considered prose suitable for comedy, and dignified, smooth verse suitable for tragedy. But for use in both comedy and tragedy, his generation achieved a new form of dramatic verse that, like blank verse in England and the alexandrine in France, was more flexible than the long stanzas of medieval drama and yet was lifted above prose. As in London, the Spanish public was intoxicated with the excitement of spoken poetry, and actors were famous for good delivery. Orators were said to frequent the theatre to learn perfection of diction and gesture. The inflated verse of the nineteenth-century English translations has no resemblance to the vigor, suavity, and wit of Lope's verse.

In many of Lope's plays a self-confident, independent man appears. Like Marlowe, Lope put on his stage the great scourge of God, Tamberlan of Persia. In another play he dramatized that great Renaissance man Columbus.

Lope's proud Renaissance women are the equals of the Renaissance prince—indeed, in wit and clever intrigue, his superiors. The Spanish stage began in Lope's day to use women for the roles of heroines. At first they played along with boys impersonating women, and there were occasional attempts to prevent women from appearing on the public stage. But the actresses won the day. Their beauty was one of the great attractions, but some were praised even more for beautiful speaking.

The presentation of the Renaissance individual in the larger context of a new absolute monarchy appears most vividly in Lope's *Los desposorious de Hornachuelos* (*The Betrothals of Hornachuelos*), a lively comedy about the conflict between the individual and authority. Lope Melindes, the "Wolf" of Estremadura, is a rough local lord who defies the king. He is in love with a high-spirited woman who defies him. In turn her peasants defy her orders to marry. When the king arrives he wins over the Wolf by persuasion and the power of his personality. But love can recognize no external authority, and the king must allow both the noble lady and the peasants to choose loves to suit themselves.

The authority of the royal government was a dynamic new reality in Lope's time. As in France and England, the greatest political achievement between the fifteenth and the seventeenth century was the breaking of the power of the feudal lords and the transfer of the people's loyalty to the central government. Spain had driven out the Moors and united the scattered kingdoms under Ferdinand and Isabella in the 1490s. Yet, as in France and England, it took more than a century to establish fully the royal authority. Fear of chaos and local tyranny was still alive in

Lope's time, and a number of his plays, together presenting a great epic of Spanish history almost as impressive as Shakespeare's vision of English history, served as rituals to exorcise that fear and unite the kingdom under a strong central rule.

Three of Lope's most vivid plays dramatize the shift of loyalty from local lord to king. They show noble heroes and heroines of peasant stock and peasants uniting against the misrule of the feudal lord. For that reason Lope was hailed by

Lope de Vega in 1625.

360

early Soviet critics as a great proletarian writer, and the play *Fuenteovejuna—The Sheepwell*, the name of a village—(1614), had a number of productions in Russia. But the Russians failed to notice the wider context of the play. Where the local lord is tyrannical, it is His Glorious Catholic Majesty, the king, who brings peace, security, and justice.

In Lope's *Peribañez* (1610?) the local *comendador* (governor) happens on the wedding of a peasant couple, and, entranced by the bride, sends the husband away as head of a company of soldiers so that he may serenade her. The bridegroom returns in disguise and kills the intruding governor, then flings himself at the feet of the king, asking that at least his widow may have the reward offered for his capture. The king lives up to his title of *justiciero* and makes the peasant the captain of a new company. A similar local lord in *El mejor alcalde el Rey* (1622?) interrupts a wedding and has the bride carried off. The groom appeals to the king. When the royal letter commanding redress is ignored, the king arrives, orders the offending lord to marry the girl, then has him beheaded and gives half his lands to the poor but noble groom. It is the local lord who is irresponsible and predatory; the king brings wisdom and strong justice.

Even more explicit is the shift of loyalty in *Fuenteovejuna* (1623?). A powerful noble makes the mistake of opposing Ferdinand and Isabella as well as outraging his own peasants by pursuing their women. One lusty peasant turns his crossbow against him to protect his girl. The king defeats the rebellion, but the lord escapes and steals the girl away from her wedding. The aroused villagers attack the castle and kill the noble and several of his lords. When the king puts them to torture to learn who is guilty, they all cry "Fuente Ovejuna did it"—that is, the entire village did it. There is nothing the king can do but forgive them. One soldier cries, "Spain turns already to the Catholic King, a name by which our rulers have come to be known, and the nation renders obedience to their laws." The peasants beat down their lord's scutcheon with stones and boast outright that they will set the royal arms above the portal in the village square where their lord's has been. When a local master threatens the people, he hears the reply that their loyalty is to the king. The Master then promises to subdue his rage and do obeisances to the crown.

Tirso de Molina in *Antona García* (1622) wrote a feminist version of the transfer of loyalty to the king. The king is Queen Isabella, fighting for the throne of Castile. The heroine is a common woman, Antona, who stirs up the peasants to fight the tyrannical wife of the local lord and give their support to the queen.

In Lope's *La estrella de Sevilla—The Star of Seville*—(c. 1623) the anarchy to be overcome is located not in an irresponsible local leader but in the king himself. This king tries to seduce Stella and corrupt her brother, but everyone so magnanimously refuses to take advantage of the guilt that the king is shamed into a higher respect for his own honor and duty. The play illustrates a combination of the spirit of the Renaissance and new attitudes that will be discussed in the following chapters.

361

VII

The Age of Displacement:
Mannerist Art

Macbeth in an eighteenth-century English barn theatre, 1788. *Courtesy of the Trustees of the British Museum.*

363

Introduction

THE CRACK IN THE HUMANIST FAÇADE

By 1600 a new mood dominated thinkers, poets, artists. An age of belief in man as the center gave way to a new generation watching Hamlet, the displaced prince, Lear, the old king thrust out of doors, Macbeth, the man of action losing his grip on reality—all disillusioned, baffled by complexity in the universe.

The discovery of sea routes to America and around Africa at first tended to enlarge the mind of man, but soon made him feel that there were too many worlds, too many ways of life, to be combined into unity. Gold and trade brought enormous opportunities for the individual, but they also brought insecurity and doubt.

The Reformation started with high hopes and ideals but soon created baffling problems of a divided Europe. The many people who hoped for radical economic reforms from Luther were disappointed. Not only did the Lutherans, the Anglicans, and the counter-reforming Jesuits each fail to win all Europe, but new schisms appeared and religions multiplied. In 1600 the religious conflicts seemed insoluble. France had had decades of civil war; Germany held tensions which soon led to the Thirty Years' War that left her devastated for many years; England had its plot to blow up Parliament, and the conflicts between Parliament and court broke out later in civil war.

The new capitalism of the sixteenth century, by breaking the restrictions of guilds and city councils, set the individual free to develop unlimited riches; but it cut him off from the security of town and guild, and often plunged him in failure. The Renaissance princes of church and state had offered the artist the exciting task of celebrating the highest ideal in the murals, poems, public ceremonies, and plays they created. But both the Counter-Reformation and the new Protestant authorities brought all art under suspicion, censorship, and repression. The individualism of the Renaissance could not turn every person into a great, proud, self-confident prince or trusted advisor. It left many people lonely and insecure. A new spirit developed in art to express the confusion and anguish of the individual displaced from old certainties.

The Italian states had barely achieved the prosperity of the Renaissance when they were overwhelmed by the two nations to the west, France and Spain, which, as soon as they attained unity and power, overran Italy. The Italians were disillusioned when Charles V, Emperor of Germany and King of Spain, invaded Italy to drive out the French. He fostered wide trade and capitalist expansion—at his own price. He had paid the pope one hundred thousand ducats for supporting his election as emperor, but in 1527 he let loose his armies, who sacked Rome, besieged the pope in his castle, plundered churches, raped nuns, killed priests, quartered horses in St. Peter's and soldiers in the Vatican. Next Charles put an end to the last vestiges of the Florentine republic by making the Medici hereditary princes. The Inquisition was introduced in 1542 to apply its bloody torture to anyone suspected of being an individualist in religious thought.

Michelangelo, who had brought Florentine control and clarity to a climax in the ceiling of the Sistine Chapel, came back many years later to paint there the tortured, twisted bodies of the Last Judgment. But shortly after the masterpiece was finished, the fear of humanist classicism, following the Council of Trent, made painters hurriedly cover with loin cloths the nudity of the all-too-human figures. Soon the firm linear perspective of Florentine painting had given way to the nebulous aerial perspective of the Venetian school. The clear central-vanishing-point perspective with its single viewpoint, gave way to the diagonals and off-the-picture vanishing lines of Tintoretto, to the shifting planes, the multiple viewpoints, the exciting but baffling chiaroscuro of Mannerist art. The three-dimensional stage wings of the sixteenth century gave way to the flat wings of the seventeenth century, which magically shifted with the multiple painted scenes or disappeared behind the descending cloud machines of the Baroque theatre. Classical unity was gone. The certainty of the microcosm-macrocosm relationship dissolved into a sense of a fragmented universe that shifted its point of view, like revolving mirrors, every moment.

Machiavelli had already expressed a new "realistic" attitude. Montaigne developed a more charming, humane detachment. All influences were leading to one of the greatest changes in modern thought. As Alfred North Whitehead and Bertrand Russell point out, the great creative idea of the seventeenth century was to split the world in two. Whitehead calls this the "bifurcation of nature," the dichotomy of reality. Inner experience was separated from the outer world, the subjective from the objective, private reality from public truth, man from nature. Galileo, Descartes, and Newton chose to concern themselves not at all with qualities but with quantities—mass, weight, number, motion—the measurable aspects of nature. They dismissed as subjective, perhaps unreal, the reactions of the other senses—color, taste, smell, sound—and all the affective qualities such as sweet, disagreeable, desirable, lovely. Since 1600 the world has been split into the scientific world of nature and the subjective world of religion, art, and values.

The first reaction of the generation of disillusionment was a protesting bitterness that dwelt on revenge, destruction, decay, suicide, death. It did not accept displacement. It released a titanic energy, as though it could span the new abyss that had opened up, or by some paradox, could bring two into one. Rupert Brooke wrote in a book on John Webster a description of the mood.

The nature of man became suddenly complex, and grew bitter at its own complexity. . . . The most gigantic crimes and vices were noised, and lashed immediately by satire, with the too-furious passion of the flagellant. For Satire flourishes, with Tragedy, at such times. The draperies of refinement and her smug hierarchy were torn away from the world and Truth held sway there with his terrific court of morbidity, skepticism, despair, and life. The veils of romanticism were stripped away: Tragedy and Farce stood out, for men to shudder and to roar.

Most important of all disturbances was the radically different explanation of the solar system. The position of man at the center had been closely tied to the concept of the world as the center of the universe, but now that concept was questioned. Copernicus published his "hypothesis" in Latin in 1543, in the decade when the Council of Trent was putting an end to the last vestiges of medieval drama and bringing the exuberance of Renaissance art under tight control. He made little impression at the time, and it was decades before the church thought it necessary to put his book on the Index. But gradually the idea spread that perhaps the earth was not the center of all but only one of many planets circulating around the sun. In 1600, about the time Shakespeare was beginning to write *Hamlet*, Giordano Bruno was burned at the stake for supposing that there were countless stars, complete worlds, suns, universes, each with its own life, its own time, but no one center of the universe. The new complexity was baffling. John Donne, writing in the mood of the early seventeenth century, gives one of the most vivid expressions to the feeling that nothing was left but a twisted universe for the moral order as well as the stars:

And new Philosophy calls all in doubt,
The Element of fire is quite put out;
The Sun is lost, and th' earth, and no mans wit
Can well direct him where to look for it—

In England both the Renaissance and the new period of displacement were more intense and concentrated than in France or Italy. The main blossoming of the Renaissance, much later than in Italy, took place in the 1590s. Then suddenly, at the turn of the century, the mood changed and in one decade English writers gave full vent to attitudes that El Greco, Tintoretto, and Bernini developed over a much longer time.

Shakespeare suddenly experienced the change in the midst of his career. *Twelfth Night*, written about 1601, is the last of a series of romantic comedies, while *Hamlet* and *Troilus and Cressida* (1601–02) begin a series of tragedies and bitter comedies with only *Julius Caesar* (1599) for transition—and *Caesar*, for all its ironic picture of the disintegration of idealism, belongs with the heroic Renaissance plays of the 1590s. All London showed the change of mood. The queen was growing old and sick and there were threats of disorder both within and without the realm. There was already disillusioned satire of the new-rich, and in 1597 Ben Jonson made a tremendous hit with *Every Man in His Humour*, played by Shakespeare's company. In 1601 the Earl of Essex, the principal star of the kingdom for ten years, overreached himself, led a revolt, and was beheaded.

England now woke to some grim realities. The queen died, and James the Scotsman, almost a foreign monarch, was brought in. His court had little dignity or discipline. He was extravagant and given to drink, fancy lace, and girls. The Jesuits were intriguing against the government, and the Gunpowder Plot was discovered just in time to prevent the conspirators from blowing up Parliament. The mood of London in this first decade of the seventeenth century was one of anxiety, suspicion, and cynicism.

Nowhere is the new mood caught more brilliantly than in Shakespeare's *Troilus and Cressida*, the epitome of broken faith, a broken society, a broken universe. The play may never have been seen in the public theatre, and one guess is that it was written for the cynical young lawyers and law students of one of the Inns of Court. The Middle Ages had created a glamorous vision of Troy. Did not both the French and English claim their nations were founded from Troy? Chaucer and Lydgate had portrayed Troilus as a great knight. But Shakespeare paints a very different picture. Here is a comparison of the claims of Menelaus versus Paris for Helen:

He, like a puling cuckold, would drink up
The lees and dregs of a flat, tamed piece;
You, like a lecher, out of whorish loins
Are pleased to breed out your inheritors.

Troilus discovers that the love he had thought so solid was only fragments, and that the greasy relics of faith were already pledged to someone else. The whole play is a bundle of shifting points of view, of results that belie hopes, actions that contradict words. Ulysses makes a long speech, insisting that all difficulties have come because the Greeks have quarreled among themselves, have violated "degree," the hierarchical order by which the planets, as well as states and brotherhood, are held together, the order that protects society from the anarchy of envy and disdain. But immediately, in complete disregard of degree and order, Ulysses himself is involved in a scheme to trick Ajax and Achilles.

Throughout the play somebody is watching somebody else. Both the lechery plot and the war intrigues have a gallery of spies. Ajax is watched as he rises to the bait, and Cressida's flirting with Diomed is watched not only by Troilus but by Ulysses and Thersites. Two of the most vivid characters are observers, and what a pair! Pandarus, whose name has given a word to all western languages, is the master of ceremonies of the corrupt show of love. Thersites, the coarse, bitter observer, presides over the corrupt show of war.

The most characteristic new dramatic figure of the age of disintegration was the disinterested observer though he has lost his illusions too recently to be completely detached; he is still bitter over his loss of security, not yet accustomed to being a displaced person. Two important ways of thinking were to emerge from this state of detachment. One was the attitude of modern science. The other was comedy. But at first there were anguished expressions of the new mood. Most of the observing characters in the drama of the period have just been banished or disillusioned and have not had time to find it humorous.

In *Measure for Measure* (1604) Shakespeare dramatizes one of the strongest disillusionments the age of breakdown had to face—that the judge may be as guilty as the judged. The duke who exiles himself, to return incognito, is the main observer. He is paired with the depraved railer Lucio. The action is a series of judgments, of judges being tested, of petitioners refused. At the end the Duke reestablishes justice with mercy. Since the play is a comedy, order and harmony win out.

The Tragedy of Displacement:

Hamlet, Lear, Macbeth

The greatest dramatization of the theme of man displaced from old certainties is in Shakespeare's three tragedies of 1600–1606: *Hamlet, King Lear,* and *Macbeth.*

HAMLET

Hamlet is the first hero in literature to face the baffling complexity of many aspects of reality. He stands at a moment in history when ritual does not suffice. Of course the play also has ritual aplenty. It opens with an impressive changing of the guard and a court address by the new king, and ends with an elaborate court hearing and duel and the arrival of another king and a military funeral. But the rituals are all dubious and perverted; they do not bring certainty. There are abundant tokens from heaven; but Hamlet is never sure whether they are good or evil, or at what price he should obey them, or which of the many Christian, chivalric, family, civic, or individual duties he should follow. Here is modern man, having to look at all sides, to examine, probe, weigh, replan, experiment, hold a dozen mirrors up to nature. Yet, complex and disjunctive as the play is, it has unity. It shows a fascinating multiplicity, but by its structure creates artistic order and affirms a belief in order.

Throughout, Hamlet is a displaced man. There are three kings—the dead king, demanding revenge; the present usurper, his uncle, on his father's throne and in his mother's bed; and Hamlet himself. His is faced with three fathers—the armed ghost of his idealized father; his mother's husband, constantly speaking as his father; and his prospective father-in-law, Polonius. But all his important ties are broken. His father is dead and speaks only from an unhallowed warlike shell, demanding the most terrifying vengeance. His mother is identified with her new husband—"Father and mother is man and wife; man and wife is one flesh"—and that flesh is loathsome to him. His father in prospect is plotting against him. He is cut off from his love not only by the horrible example of his mother's love but by Ophelia's repulse, inspired by her father.

In the old Hamlet saga Amlothi bided his time as a fool, lying on the ground in disorder and dirt, talking in riddles and abusive language, showing special harshness to his mother and his foster sister. In fact, the word Amlothi meant fool. Throughout the play Hamlet acts as jester and fool. But lo, there is another fool already in his place: Polonius, with no more understanding than a simpleton. Hamlet repeatedly calls him fool—"Thou wretched, rash, intruding fool." So Hamlet, the displaced king and fool, is faced with a usurper king and usurper fool.

There are many actions in the play but they are mirror-images of one another. Fortinbras, like Hamlet, must try to recoup the losses of a dead father, and finds himself opposed by an uncle. Laertes, returning home to find his father murdered and buried, his last rites scanted, demands vengeance. One function of these subplots is for sharp contrast with the indecision and delay of Hamlet. Fortinbras is persuaded by his uncle to abandon the plan for revenge as unjust, but when he finds his honor involved in a war with the Polacks, this "delicate and tender prince," daring death and danger for an eggshell, moves into action; while Hamlet, afraid, "thinking too precisely on the event," hesitates. Laertes, again unlike Hamlet, has no hesitation about moving to his revenge. Those readers and playgoers who think the tragedy of the play is that Hamlet thought and feared too much, consider these two men of action a reproach to him. Hamlet certainly envies them their ability to go straight to their purposes and clear their honor. Those readers and play goers more respectful of thought can see these two mirror plots in a different light. The Quaker scholar Harold Goddard has suggested that the last thing Hamlet ought to do is follow the demands of his warlike father, and that it is his Christian decency that makes him try to avoid violence. From that point of view Fortinbras and Laertes are examples of un-Christian violence which mislead Hamlet. The sight of Fortinbras' expedition ready to send twenty-thousand men to their graves for a fantasy and trick of fame stirs Hamlet to his most violent: "From this time forth, my thoughts be bloody, or be nothing worth." Laertes dares damnation and casts "Conscience and grace to the profoundest pit." Accepting the king as a father image, he turns his anger toward Hamlet, will "cut his throat i' th' church"—this shortly before Hamlet, too, has cast off conscience and is ready to face any desperate eventuality—"the readiness is all." Fortinbras and Laertes show Hamlet how simple action is if one can disregard the future. The three avenging sons are mirrors of one another, but in the complexity it is not certain which is right or whether any of them is.

The actions in the middle of the play are likewise mirrors of one another. Hamlet plans the play-within-the-play as a mousetrap to catch the conscience of the king. Polonius, who advocates a policy of craft and trickery, who will "by indirection, find direction out," who sends a messenger to spy on his own son, sets first Ophelia and then the queen as his mousetraps to catch the motives of Hamlet. The king sets Rosencrantz and Guildenstern as spies.

The two most vivid mirror-images are furnished by the players, who, in fact, serve many purposes. Hamlet feels a great affinity for these displaced wanderers, old hands at dealing with illusion and reality. They bring out his best side, the creative. They reproach him by their power of imagination, their intensity, but they inspire his happiest plan, the one least fraught with violence: he will set a trap, he will use the powers of dramatic art, not to destroy the king but to make him cry out his own malefactions.

The play within the play, old-fashioned in its formal, rhetorical style, is a clear-cut mirror image of the king's crime and the queen's defection. The king, deeply shaken, might have let his conscience be caught if Hamlet had not added his wild threats to the actors' words. Now the fight between Hamlet and the king is brought out in the open. The play scene is fascinating in itself, making a great advance in the plot, and letting the audience as well as the characters see the main action from another angle. How like the serpentine sculpture of the Mannerist period, which twists and revolves, showing many sides but no complete definitive view!

Few notice that the speech of the Player King, about Pyrrhus' slaughter of old Priam and Hecuba's lament that sets off Hamlet's famous "What a rogue and peasant slave am I," is far more than a warm-up for the play within the play. It is indeed an epitome of the pattern of the main play. It describes the bloody Pyrrhus (Hamlet) looking for Priam (Claudius), the first blows, too wide (Hamlet's tentative efforts at revenge), the moment of suspended terror with sword uplifted (Hamlet's situation a moment later with the king at prayer), followed by the thunder and violence of destruction and the grief that would have "turned white the very eyes of heaven." This is the speech Hamlet remembered and wanted to hear again, for it is a mirror of his own bloody thoughts.

Irony is the very heart of a disjunctive organization. Juxtapose two actions that are concerned with the same kind of problem but have different moral attitudes and they make an ironic comment on each other. The art of most periods has a simple moral tone, but it is the essence of Mannerist painting that it sets different characters, stories, and draperies, on shifting planes of depth, splashing over them a scintillating light from contradictory directions. Don Quixote is no more mad than the world around him. The poetry of John Donne ties together the dignified and the homely, reveals paradoxes by trying to capture the divine in the ugly or bawdy or familiar. El Greco achieved unity out of flame-like bodies, draperies, and clouds, all flowing in luminescent highlights without any evidence of solid bone or structure underneath. The problem of the age was to express the insecurity, the chaos which resulted when the medieval and Renaissance unities could no longer hold.

372

Hamlet's advice to the players, seen in this light, takes on new meaning. Notice its position in the play. Just after Hamlet makes the most uncontrolled attack on Ophelia and shouts half-veiled threats to Polonius and the king, he advises the players to "use all gently," to "o'erstep not the modesty of nature." He considers it villainous of Polonius to interrupt with his quips some necessary question of the play; but in the same scene he himself interrupts the play with his jests and taunts, giving the king's conscience no chance to consider the necessary question. Shortly, in his mother's room, he forgets all temperance and modesty of nature, stabs Polonius in a "rash and bloody deed," and then lectures his mother about letting blood rule over judgment.

Watching for ironic juxtaposition, one can ask why Shakespeare interrupts Hamlet on his way to listen to advice from his father by a scene in which Laertes and Ophelia listen to their own father. Did Shakespeare intend that Polonius' advice to Laertes should be remembered as Hamlet is listening to his father and making vows of vengeance by heaven, earth, and "shall I couple hell"? Mannerist art is all the more fascinating because it can be looked at in so many ways. Goddard finds it ironical that the ghost, with hellish advice, is so impressive and that Polonius, who gives good advice, is the usurper-fool. Ophelia, displaced from love and marriage, merges images of her father's funeral (which was suppressed) with images of the wedding she had not had and sings gaily of a deserted love. She makes jests of funerals and love, things which Hamlet had disrupted in trying to act seriously. She puts into serious action the madness which Hamlet had played in jest.

Yet throughout this play, in the midst of the displacements and ironic contradictions rise the outlines of the old belief in order, the philosophical basis of humanist belief. Christianity is a very positive element in the play. Immediately after the guards have seen this strange disturber of the night, moving away from day "like a guilty thing upon a fearful summons," they turn toward the dawn to think of the season near our Saviour's birth when no such spirit may walk abroad. Neoplatonic idealism is eloquently celebrated, even at those moments of greatest awareness of the lapses from such idealism. When Ophelia believes Hamlet completely out of his mind, she speaks of that "sovereign reason" which man shares with God, a power that could rule all the lower faculties and baser matter. When Hamlet is confessing to Rosencrantz and Guildenstern his despair, he lingers over the Neoplatonic vision of man as the center of the universe, the proud link between the divine and the animal, "The paragon of animals!"

The lonely Hamlet, like the desolate Tamburlaine of Marlowe's second play, could wander on the free forestage, displaced from throne and questioning the meaning of heaven. But the audience saw in back of the actor Burbage a splendid architectural structure which gave a real and a symbolic unity to the play. Hamlet could attack the throne and contend over his displacement from it, but there in the middle of most of the scenes was an actual throne. When Shakespeare spoke of the dangers to a state of the murder of a king, there on the stage was a large, three-storied symbolic backing for a throne. When he spoke of something rotten in the state of Denmark, there behind the actors, unchanging during the whole play, probably marked by a shield with the arms and name of Denmark, stood the symbol of the realm. Above the throne were the angels' gallery and the heavenly throne, witnesses to the divine order that endorsed the realm. When Hamlet spoke of "this goodly frame the earth," there behind him, over him, under him, were the medieval symbols of earth, heaven, and hell. When Fortinbras arrived to reestablish order, he stood in the center of an enormous throne, before a castle symbol of the realm, beneath the symbols of divine providence. Such a setting, beautiful, colorful, and impressive, standing unchanged behind and above the actors, reinforced all the elements of the play which imply that the divine, the political, the moral order are intact, no matter how complex and uncertain outward appearances may be.

KING LEAR

In *King Lear*, Shakespeare dramatized even greater complexity, yet study reveals that it has an even more solid structural pattern than *Hamlet*. The character scheme, the themes, and the imagery unite the diverse material. Shakespeare gave a full picture of displacement, disruption, anarchy, and chance. Yet through his artistic order we can see the conviction that the universe is relation, order, significance.

In *King Lear*, a whole generation goes awry, a kingdom is torn in war and hatred, the sky is rent asunder, and the mind is tortured into madness. Not only the king but the whole age suffers a convulsion. All the bases of social order are shattered and the citadels of reason toppled down. When the king is thrust out of doors, the heavens themselves erupt in tempests.

Now the front platform becomes a forlorn heath, buffeted by winds, lashed by rain and lightning. On it huddle a king and a fool and a beggar. In fantastic madness and anguish they hold a mock trial, not so much to try the villains who have thrust them out as to question the nature of the universe that can produce such cruelty. Certainly *King Lear* is the most tremendous artistic product of the age of Mannerist anguish.

The play begins with an amazing spectacle. The old king mounts his throne and gathers his children, counselors, dukes and earls, and suitor-kings around him. He is a strong ruler over a united Britain. But he divides the kingdom. He is so trustful that he turns over the whole realm to the young generation of calculating monsters. Cordelia cannot save him without becoming like those who will destroy him. Kent speaks out and the king banishes him. It is the same in the subplot. The one son of Gloucester who is faithful is driven out by the traitor son. Disguised and unrecognized, Edgar watches helpless as the old king staggers in exhaustion into the storm. He then becomes the seeing guide to his blinded father, though he cannot restore him to his rightful place. Nobody can stop the wicked forces until Goneril, Regan, and Edmund have destroyed themselves. The holocaust also destroys Lear and Cordelia. On the negative side, there is the great relief as the quiet dawn shows the enemy dead. But that is only part of the vision. There is a purification and redemption of Lear, who develops into an understanding, loving person as he faces the whirlwind. And Shakespeare organizes his vision of chaos in such a way that not only the love and religious concern of the main characters but the very structure of the play is a magnificent assertion of order and meaning in the universe.

Shakespeare develops the vision of order rhythmically and systematically by examples of disorder. One after another, the effects of disorder reverberate from a few centers until a kingdom and then the cosmic elements are shaken out of their peaceful ways. In other plays Shakespeare uses the second plot mostly for contrast. Here he doubles his trusting Lear with a trusting Gloucester; his wicked daughters with a ruthless son Edmund; his patient, plain-spoken Cordelia with a kind, long-suffering son, Edgar. Such schematic doubling gives the characters a more than natural intensity. The wicked daughters and Edmund become fiends of hell. No one has ever created characters more individual than Shakespeare's; but when he was swept by the tensions of the Mannerist age, he saw beneath the individual the abstract forces that can possess an individual and turn him into a fiend.

To the opposition of ruthlessness and patience is added that of flattery and plain speaking. The extravagance of the flattery of Goneril and Regan makes Cordelia react in the opposite direction. This contrast is developed further in the servants. Goneril's servant Oswald is "a serviceable villain, as duteous to the vices of his mistress as badness would desire," who so outrages Kent, in disguise as Lear's servant, that he attacks him on sight, precipitating the major conflicts between Lear and his wicked daughters. What the servants begin the masters must finish. The first act ends with Lear thrust out of Goneril's house. The second act is more complex, but again the servants begin the conflict and the act ends with Lear thrust out by both daughters. The third act contains the wild phantasmagoria of the storm, presented in three scenes that gradually grow more and more quiet until Lear is cast out even from the hovel, and out of his mind. But woven in counterpoint to the diminishing storm scenes is the sharp crescendo of the indoor scenes leading up to the blinding and thrusting out of Gloucester. The contrast between the two dukes gives a structural pattern to the two large parts of the play. Cornwall, man of war, dominates the end of the first part when he blinds Gloucester and he himself is stabbed. Albany, man of peace, takes the lead in the second half and reestablishes peace and order at the end. The doubling of examples gives a sense of universality and a firm sense of structure.

The structure is based on a concept of world order that the Renaissance inherited from the Middle Ages. But it is more than a scene for Lear's own emotions. When Lear is thrust out of doors, the entire world is wrenched with agony, the winds and lightning unleashed. The extent of the chaos is proof that all parts of the universe are tied together. Man is related to the state, to the physical universe, and when he goes astray, all other parts are torn from their course.

The third act, with the alternation of the scenes of Lear on the heath with scenes of the trap closing on Gloucester, is one of the world's most magnificent visions of universal turmoil—Aeschylus' Furies combined with Dante's Inferno. Lear is stripped of the remnants of his old illusions, and dancing around him are images of each of the terrors of his mind.

First is the great terror of insanity. In regular pulses of fear in the first two acts, Lear has been struggling to keep from madness. On the heath, his wild words and actions are combined with the ragings of the storm, and he matches quips with the professional fool. These are soon enlarged by the wilder ravings of Edgar, covering his identity as Poor Tom. As Lear focuses on a madness outside himself, he passes beyond the struggles of half sanity into a quieter delusion. Where the first scene on the heath has the drum and trumpet crashing of "Spit, fire! spout, rain!" and "Strike flat the thick rotundity o' the world," the second scene has the softer, stranger music, like woodwinds, of "Still through the hawthorn blows the cold wind." And finally Lear is completely insane, looking beneath the surface of all sanity, in the fantastic mock trial of the footstools as his daughters.

When nature is in order man occupies the great position at the center of the hierarchy, as the link between the beasts below him and the angels and God above him; but with order broken man sinks to the lowest level. In the first two acts, Goneril and Regan show themselves as serpents, kites, vultures, sharp-toothed. The imagery expresses horror at their cruelty. In the third act the theme of base animals becomes a repeated image of the degradation of all nature. Edgar is obsessed with animals. He chants of eating the swimming frog, the toad, the tadpole, the wall-newt, the old rat, and the ditch-dog. He brags of combining all the vices of the lower beasts—"hog in sloth, fox in stealth, wolf in greediness, dog in madness, lion in prey."

In the main plot Goneril and Regan destroy each other over lust for Edmund. The theme of lust is echoed in the imagery throughout the play, especially in Lear's mad scenes. There it is tied with one of the main themes of the Mannerist age—the ruler or judge guilty of the crimes he condemns. As for womankind, it is no longer the central link that unites the earth with the gods.

> But to the girdle do the gods inherit,
> Beneath is all the fiends';
> There's hell, there's darkness, there's the sulphurous pit.

The king and the fool, the one the center of social order, the other a satellite circulating at the outside, are the poetic symbols of man's plight and redemption.

For Lear, as he becomes the fool, discovers the paradoxical insight of the fool; as he is stripped of authority, he gains a new judgment. He discovers universal pity and prays for all houseless poverty, all human beings in need. He conducts a mock trial of all nature and sees evil for what it is. When he becomes the fool, the fool drops out of the play, and in the fourth act Lear must play the fool for Gloucester, reminding him in jests that he is blind, just as the fool had constantly reminded Lear of his folly. When the blind know they are blind, when kings know they are fools, that is the beginning of wisdom. When Lear suffers enough to need love, not the show of it, he finds it in full. The fool who never had a home, the banished Kent, Edgar in disguise, and the about-to-be-homeless Gloucester offer him service. When Gloucester is wandering, blind, his mistreated son takes him under his care and cures him of despair. All these, like fools, offer affection, sympathy, love. Cordelia cures Lear, partly by her care, but also because she restores order to the universe. Her love brings man back to his center, looking upward toward reason and love.

The Mannerist age was haunted by images of man's fall, by the fear that the whole universe was falling. Shakespeare could write the most profound expression of that age because he held on to the conviction that man was the key to an ordered universe.

King Lear is a play of chaos and destruction, but also of redemption. The fool, Kent, Cordelia, and Edgar learn patience. Gloucester is first a credulous, foolish man, so full of despair he believes "As flies to wanton boys are we to the gods; they kill us for their sport"—but later, after an attempt at suicide, a patient sufferer. The imperious old dotard Lear does not merely become meek and resigned but goes through a magnificent redemption, gaining deeper wisdom as he loses control of his mind.

King Lear has been the most popular of Shakespeare's tragedies in the later twentieth century. *Hamlet* kept the lead throughout the romantic nineteenth century and the first part of the twentieth century. But with the Communist and Fascist revolutions, with the emergence of new forces in all five continents, with world wars and cold wars throughout the globe, this dramatic image of an age in crisis and change has become the more compelling attraction. *Lear* had very few twentieth-century productions in English before 1940; but since the Second World War, London has seen a series of major productions, and practically every college drama department in America has produced it. The play is a reminder of the monstrous happenings of our own age, yet it gives the strongest reassurance that nightmares come to an end.

MACBETH

In *Macbeth* the scope is reduced to a single action, a few characters, and almost to one castle. The bonds that are broken are initially the same as those broken in *Lear*—loyalty, gratitude, love. A kingdom is reduced to a state of anarchy by the crimes of one prince. In *Lear* the effects of the breach are explored extensively. In *Macbeth* the breach is explored intensively, within the mind. Macbeth is not displaced in the same sense that Hamlet and Lear are. He grasps the kingdom near the beginning of the play and holds it almost to the last minute. But he is displaced in his own mind; he loses his grip on reality. Then the world around him is topsy-turvy—fair is foul and foul is fair. Nothing is what it seems; all is bewildering, contradictory, illusory.

More than the compact action, it is this enveloping atmosphere of nightmare that gives the play its power and unity. We can accept a Macbeth who does not understand his own motives, who watches himself in terror, yet is carried on to crime after crime, as though driven by some appalling duty. We can accept such actions because the play creates a sense of demonic forces let loose in the night. The three witches may be human beings who have sold their souls for hellish power, or they may be the powers of evil themselves. In Shakespeare's source, Holinshed's *Chronicle*, they are the "weird sisters, that is the goddesses of destiny, or else some nymphs or fairies." Or they are the projection, in forms of popular folklore, of the evil already working in Macbeth's mind. Lady Macbeth invokes the spirits, the murdering ministers, to

> Unsex me here,
> And fill me, from the crown to the toe, top full
> Of direst cruelty.

And through the rest of the play she acts as one possessed by a demon, until her somnambulism comes true literally, and, her conscious mind broken, she walks in her sleep and mutters in the simplest words the most appalling fragments of her crimes and terrors.

All is night. "Come thick night and pall thee in the dunnest smoke of hell." Night, where evil forces are released but where nothing is sure—"nothing is but what is not . . . Hurlyburly . . . won and lost . . . tempest tost . . . fair is foul and foul is fair . . . unsex me . . . unfix my hair." The characters do not understand themselves, but are constantly puzzled, amazed, amidst rumors, uncertainties, and fears. The fierce animals are mentioned—wolf, ram, bat, crow, and snake. There is the horrible suggestion of Duncan's horses that run wild, make war on mankind, and eat one another.

But contending with the forces of dark and evil are the forces of grace and innocence. The dark of night is broken not only by the lurid light of the witches' cauldron, the sickly smear of the murdered king's "silver skin, lac'd with his golden blood," and the glint of the dagger, but also by glimpses of angelic grace. Lady Macduff and her boy have a brave innocence unknown in *Hamlet* and *King Lear*, an innocence reinforced throughout the play by many images of babes, growing nature, sleep, cure, grace of heaven, of "heaven's cherubims, hors'd upon the

The heath scene from Nicolas Rowe's edition of *Macbeth*, 1709.

sightless couriers of the air." The Duncan Macbeth murders was, in Holinshed's *Chronicle* (1587), a weak king whose leniency provoked disorder and rebellion. With Shakespeare he becomes a gentle, able, even saintly king, full of trust, love, and honor.

The mirror images, not visualized in whole actions like the Players in *Hamlet* or the second plot in *Lear*, are verbal and mental, and they too dramatize the duplicity that torments Macbeth, the contrast between appearance and reality, the promise and the act, the hope and the fulfillment. Most curious is the compulsion of Malcolm, the young prince, to heap accusations on his own head. He rehearses all the sins of Macbeth and the woes of Scotland as a trick to test Macduff; but it also satisfies some need for the perverse, the reversed mirror. Very fitting is the drunken porter who jokes as he opens the door to let daylight and reality in after the nightmare of the murder. But he jokes of lechery and drink that stirs up desire but takes away the performance. Every token in the play stirs Macbeth's desire but cheats him of the fulfillment.

The mirror images of Macbeth's mind are in that *Doppelgänger* of the imagination, the desire always out of reach—the dagger that hovers in the air but cannot be grasped, the ghost of the man he murdered, the angels that plead trumpet-tongued against the deep damnation of his taking off, pity like a naked babe striding the blast, hands that will the multitudinous seas incarnadine.

So Macbeth's displacement is from himself. He particularly strives to cut himself off from consequences. "If it were done when 'tis done . . . we'd jump the life to come." He invokes night to cut all the bonds that hold any man to life:

> And with thy bloody and invisible hand
> Cancel, and tear to pieces, that great bond
> Which keeps me pale—

and which, of course, tears to pieces all bonds of sympathy he has with mankind. Most agonizing of all, he is alienated from sleep. He thought he could cut himself off from thinking, from imagining, but there is no rest. His first terror, when he realizes what he has done, is that he has murdered not Duncan but his own peace.

> Methought I heard a voice cry, "Sleep no more!
> Macbeth does murder sleep,"—the innocent sleep
>
> . . . .
>
> "Glamis hath murder'd sleep, and therefore Cawdor
> Shall sleep no more; Macbeth shall sleep no more."

So he suffers in all three titles, his three persons. Likewise in his public person he is cut off.

> And that which should accompany old age
> As honor, love, obedience, troops of friends,
> I must not look to have; but in their stead
> Curses . . .

380

He is cut off finally from time, meaning, significance. When he realizes that his wife is dead he mutters in anguish, "Tomorrow and tomorrow and tomorrow . . . signifying nothing."

Macbeth's curse is that he has a vivid imagination. His actions rise to haunt him—Banquo from his grave, the consequences he hoped to avoid. Fears take shape as the line of Banquo's descendants stretches out to the crack of doom, as Birnam Wood moves on Dunsinane.

Lady Macbeth's displacement is simpler. She is without imagination and can foresee nothing. When she does see the consequences she cannot face them. She thought she was not afraid to look on death. But faced with the actual sleeping man she could not kill him. She says, "Had he not resembled my father as he slept, I had done't." She had not reckoned on the actual sight of a man bleeding to death: "Who would have thought the old man to have had so much blood in him?" Right after Macbeth has done the murder she is sure "a little water clears us of this deed," but when she has faced the inner consequences, "All the perfumes of Arabia will not sweeten this little hand. . . . What's done cannot be undone." She is closer to real understanding after her mind has broken.

The structure of *Macbeth* is much simpler than that of *Lear*. The main pattern has

Sarah Siddons as Lady Macbeth and John Phillip Kemble as Macbeth in the dagger scene, 1803. *Courtesy E. T. Archive.*

381

two parts. The first starts from the witches and works out their three promises; the second again from the witches and works out, ironically, the three deceptive assurances. At the beginning is a double opening. There is no structural necessity for two witch scenes, separated by the bleeding sergeant scene, but it is effective to begin with a brief scene of the witches before bringing Macbeth into contact with them in the more spectacular second scene.

Again, as with *Hamlet* and *Lear*, the façade of the Elizabethan stage gave the play a unity that is scattered in most modern productions. In the first half of the play there was no reason for an Elizabethan audience to suppose more than one place, on the way to and at the castle of Macbeth. Immediately Lady Macbeth establishes the stage façade as Macbeth's castle. Duncan and his retinue come on the forestage on their way. Then they see the castle, and Lady Macbeth meets them and takes them in. Servants enter, preparing a feast, and we know we are glimpsing activities in the castle. By the conventions long established in pageantry, the symbolic structure which resembled the entire castle serves for all actions, inside and outside, connected with the ruler. Even the scene of Banquo's murder is near the gate of the palace—"hence to the palace gate." When a banquet is prepared, a variation of a throne scene, it is set before the symbol of the whole castle.

In the second half of the play, the scene shifts to the castle of Macduff. Immediately Lady Macduff enters and we know this is Macduff's castle. In the next scene Malcolm and Macduff speak of being in England, away from his castle. Probably the background was still supposed Macduff's castle, though he is speaking of it far away. If special banners or shields had been hung on it to decorate it as Macduff's castle, there would be no reason for removing them. With the sleepwalking scene, the action moves back to Macbeth's castle. The rest of the play alternates between Macbeth in front of his castle and the enemy forces coming nearer and nearer, undoubtedly on the forestage. At one point Macbeth has special battle banners hung on the façade with the command, "Hang up our banners on the outward walls." At the end Malcolm takes charge; the head of Macbeth is mounted high on the show-castle, and all hail Malcolm as the new king.

So at the end, the stage symbol of order prevails. The nightmare is over. The displaced mind of Macbeth has destroyed itself. In 1606 the British kingdom had just survived the crisis of losing a monarch who had no immediate heirs. Yet the heritage had passed without violence to the royal cousin, the King of Scotland, and two kingdoms were united. In the chronicles, Macbeth was the last of a long line of elected kings, every one of them murdered. Banquo's son established an order that had continued from father to son without disruption to King James of Scotland and England. Shakespeare's company, officially servants of the king's household, proud of the security of a strong monarchy, could celebrate the ancestor of James as a symbol of a return to peace and harmony in the realm.

The Comedy of Displacement: Ben Jonson

With a slight shift in outlook, it was possible to take a comic view of disintegration and chaos. What made Hamlet bitter and angry made Ben Jonson's characters bitter and gay. They attack the monstrous deformity of the age, expose it to public view, and hail it into court to gain a sharp judgment. By showing clearly the warped characters of his time, Jonson could satisfy the "Furor Poeticus" he describes in the induction to *Every Man Out of His Humour* (1599):

I will scourge those apes:
And to these courteous eyes oppose a mirror,
As large as is the stage whereon we act,
Where they shall see the time's deformity
Anatomized in every nerve and sinew,
With constant courage and contempt of fear.

Jonson satirizes the get-rich schemers of an expanding commercial age, the obsessions and moral subterfuges of individuals who have left the security of village and guild and set out to climb by their own devices, and the foolish fads of those who seek security in following the fashions of the moment. Like Shakespeare, he rediscovers order by exploring disorder, which he locates in man's psychological makeup. The Greek and Renaissance ideal of the well-balanced man has been lost and in its stead is the man dominated by one obsession. Borrowing the medieval theory that the temperament is determined by the four fluids or "humours"—choler, black bile, phlegm, and blood—Jonson defines his approach to the obsessed character by the metaphor of a "humour":

As when some one peculiar quality
Doth so possess a man, that it doth draw
All his affects, his spirits, and his powers
In their confluxions, all to run one way,
This may be truly said to be a humour.

Setting out to expose folly, Jonson created a kind of comedy that gives pleasure in contemplating distorted or monstrous characters. He accepted displacement as the norm and gave the audience a well-controlled aesthetic distance. His mirror brings all into focus, and from his anger at moral confusion he creates artistic order. In his lighter plays the order is controlled by sophisticated young men who set the fools on, sure that they will expose one another and that their follies will consume them. The tone is set by the zest of those who watch.

Ben Johnson. *Courtesy National Portrait Gallery, London.*

A more bitter tone is set in *The Alchemist* (1610), where the manipulators (the alchemists) cheat and rob fools rather than merely bait and watch them. But what brings the play into perspective is the fact that every one of the dupes deserves the robbing he gets. The druggist who wants to learn the superstitious lore about setting his door and walls in the right direction is an absurd fool, easy to gull. But when Tribulation Wholesome, agent of a pious religious sect, seeks money and power from the philosopher's stone to extend control over the world, Jonson shows that the narrow hatreds and ambitions of pious people are more dangerous than the wiles of the two fake alchemists. So vividly are the characters presented and so well is the comic tone sustained that the play is one of the most skillfully wrought of all comedies.

Jonson's greatest triumph is *Volpone* (1606). Here the playwright deals with criminal monstrosities. Hoping to please Volpone and be named his heir, one man disinherits his son and another offers to put his wife in bed with the supposed invalid. There is a superhuman dimension to the monstrosity, and at the end Jonson brings all before the court of Venice and deals out harsh justice. There is horror at human depravity, but the characters contrive their own downfall with zest and perform their dance of death in a brilliant key. Jonson did not quite achieve high comedy, which requires a more complete detachment. His separation from a monstrous world was still too bitter. But he began a new way of looking at human character that Molière and the English Restoration dramatists later in the century raised to a high artistic achievement.

For all its earthiness, Jonson's comedy holds much Renaissance splendor. Jonson was too much a classicist to use princes and noble characters in comedy, and he was not in the mood for charming young noblemen like Shakespeare's Bassanio, Orlando, and Claudio. His characters are mostly middle- and lower-class people of the town and not of the court. Yet there is grandeur about them. Mosca in *Volpone* is half medieval Vice and half Roman parasite, but he is an aristocrat in his taste and style. Though he has the nimble resource of a commedia dell' arte zany, he has some of the towering intensity of an archangel. Unlike Mephistopheles, who relentlessly pursues a victim doomed for hell, he collects damned souls for the profit and amusement of his master and himself. In the French film of *Volpone* Louis Jouvet made Mosca a sinister, over-dignified corrupter of souls, a character hardly suitable for comedy. On the stage Mosca delights a modern audience by nimble footwork, wit, and intense cynicism.

Although Volpone himself is a Venetian opportunist without position or rank except as money brings all money-lovers to his door, he is heir to the voluptuous luxury of the Renaissance. He has the most finely wrought gold table service, he possesses the rich heritage of classic and medieval literature, and he fills his house with songs and masques. He opens the play with an apostrophe in praise of his god, in the tradition of Elizabethan poetry; but the god is money: "Thou art Virtue, Fame, / Honour, and all things else. Who can get thee, / He shall be noble, valiant, honest, wise." When Volpone makes love he has at his command the richness of ancient and medieval love poetry. His wealth has the glamour of the storied East: "See, here, a rope of pearls, and each more orient / Than that the brave Egyptian queen caroused— / Dissolve and drink 'em." But Volpone is not a Renaissance prince making courtly love to a beautiful heroine; he is an unscrupulous debauché who wishes to rape the greedy Corvino's ninny of a wife. The glamour of ancient poetry is used to express the perverted lust of a jaded old man.

The grotesque was to become one of the dominant elements in Baroque art. In his court masques Jonson made use of it in the antimasque, where the vulgarity and awkwardness of ugly or rustic dancers enhanced the glamour of the aristocratic maskers when they finally appeared. In their paintings, Jordaens and Rubens liked to put a goat or a satyr next to a charming nude for contrast. But in Jonson's satiric plays, the grotesque is at the heart of the comedy. A generation that inherited the philosophy of Plato and of Christianity and the love poetry of Ovid, Petrarch, Dante, and Sidney, and might have been drawn upward to divine love, had gone mad over gold and the corrupt life it could buy.

Jonson's comedy is, with the limitations that have been noted, a comedy of detachment. In several plays the sophisticated young men are collectors of characters. Their game is to set their fools against one another and watch them destroyed or cured. With no personal concern for the fools, the observers are driven by a demonic fascination. Troilus cannot laugh as he watches Cressida rush to the arms of the other man, though Pandarus can make cynical remarks about love and Thersites snarling remarks about war. Shakespeare feels the anguish of detachment, whereas the younger Jonson finds that a certain zest for life becomes possible when detachment is achieved.

The new comedy burst on London in 1598 with *Every Man in His Humour*. Jonson was a classical scholar, and almost every character is a development from a character of Roman comedy. But this is no longer low comedy but the forecast of high comedy. The strict father and wild son, the clever servant with a dozen disguises, the jealous guardian, the braggart soldier, the gulls to be deceived—all the stereotypes are here but with a difference. For Young Knowell, the first of a long line of young men of fashion, winning his girl is merely one of the diversions of the town. Who's in, who's out, who's arrived, who's in disgrace, who's to be laughed at next—the whole world of society is here. Renaissance values of education are transposed into the values of fashion. The naïve cousin has just arrived from the country, eager to learn—not Latin and Greek but the language of hunting and hawking. From Roman comedy comes the braggart soldier *Boabdill*, who has his conventional accounts of exploits in battle and his expected moment of cowardice. But he too has adopted the preoccupations of the town.

In this new comedy the real enemies are not the slave owner who keeps the girl out of the boy's reach or the tyrannical father of the ancient pattern. Now the nuisance is the fanatical, stupid, or inflexible person. In low comedy the obstacle is external, something to be attacked and forced out of the way. In high comedy

386

the obstacle is psychological, a matter of character, something to be studied, manipulated, and if possible persuaded and transformed. In Shakespeare's *Twelfth Night*, Malvolio is a serious threat to the festivities. The gulling of Malvolio is both a ritual exorcism and a low-comedy trick. But the romantic atmosphere softens the harshness, the countess comes to Malvolio's rescue, and the play ends with a sense that the festival is over and the pranks of youth will soon be only a nostalgic memory. Jonson's comedy is very different. His fanatical characters must be brought to justice. The obsessive father is told he must trust his son. The jealous husbands and wives are shown how foolish they have been. But the judge is no impartial ruler; he is the merry old madcap Justice Clement, who has his own crotchets. It is a world where none of the old virtues remain. But the clever young men land on their feet. Individualism runs wild, but the individual obsession can be a source of endless amusement.

In *Epicene* (1609) the young men about town seek pleasure in fashion, sure that wit is more important than morals. Leave repentance to old age. Into the view of the two carefree young men sweeps Sir Amorous La Folle, granduncle of all the fops of the Restoration drama that was still to come, inviting them to a dinner where all the men and women of fashion will be seen. Though he wears a sword he only talks about fighting to make a social impression. Faced with a challenge, Sir Amorous is as ridiculous a coward as Shakespeare's Sir Andrew Aguecheek when he is forced to fight Viola disguised as a boy. But Jonson's dashing young men are less interested in a cowardly combat than in seeing how the pretentious fools will compete in bragging about their social accomplishments. Glad to avoid touching steel, the opponents are jostled into lying admissions that they had had favors of the bride.

In *Bartholomew Fair* (1614) Jonson shows the hypocrisies and ironies of the whole world in the microcosm of Bartholomew Fair, the popular London amusement park, with its roast-pig and gingerbread shops, ballad singers, and puppet shows. Though the play is brilliant, the scene is overcrowded and the reader gets lost in the proliferation of detail. In each generation some theatre enthusiast attempts to cut a good play from the mass of material, and there have been a few attempts at modern performance. But the play remains a heap of disparate scraps, a monument to the enormous vitality of a robust cynic.

The fantasia of enormities includes every imaginable form of cheating, stealing, gulling, pretense, and illusion. The religious hypocrite, Zeal-of-the-Land Busy, condemns the fair but finds pious reasons why he and his flock must go there. Justice Overdo disguises as a fool to expose the enormities, and adds to them. His preaching against pickpockets enables the pickpockets to work better. He is beaten twice and put in the stocks. Ursula, the fat pig woman, rails at those who make fun of her and gets burned in the scalding pan in which she tries to burn others. A suitor has to disguise himself as a madman because the woman he loves is in love with madness, while her real madman, tortured by the injustice of

Justice Overdo, wanders around begging for a warrant—for anything, good or bad, a warrant. In the puppet play, Hero and Leander, Damon and Pythias, famous lovers and friends, end up fighting. When Overdo denounces the puppet show the puppet Dionysius proves that the charge of immorality is without foundation since puppets have no sex. The puppets denounce Overdo's mistakes— "and remember, you are but Adam, flesh and blood! You have your frailty."

In the inferno of monstrosities in this play a few positive elements emerge. One is the humility of healthy disillusionment—awareness of the dangers of fanatical idealism. Another is the zest in the game. Absorption in the doing is basic, but it is self-defeating unless it leads to self-knowledge. Justice Overdo humbly seeks out the man he has made mad to indulge him in a blank warrant, and at some moments he sees that he deserves his beatings and looks forward to telling his friends and having them laugh at him. Here is the astringent remedy of laughing at oneself. The comedy of detachment is also the comedy of enlightenment.

Spain in the Age of Displacement

A shift from Renaissance confidence to displacement occurred also in Spain, though with considerable difference. *The Star of Seville* marked a change in Lope de Vega's work. In form it is comparable to the popular Renaissance drama of England. Public scenes of the king on his throne alternate with scenes of intrigue, in and out of the house, with disguises, pursuits, fights, escapes, duels, love scenes and travesties of love scenes. At one moment the upper curtains of the stage are pulled back and the king sees in the daylight, hanged on the balcony, the slave woman he had bribed the night before. The scene of the prisoner awaiting execution is enlivened by melancholy songs and a scene of the clown pretending to be in hell.

The extreme complexity and restlessness of *The Star of Seville* are Mannerist rather than Renaissance. Yet the play does not have the perplexing moral uncertainty expected in Mannerist art. The values associated elsewhere with the Baroque age were already fixed in Spanish drama: God, king, and honor. At the end of *The Star of Seville* a triumphant monarch is revealed in all his glory.

The corral stage rarely presented a unified picture of a prince standing before symbols of cosmos and realm. There was never the overwhelming assertion of a Renaissance individual like Faustus, and in the shift to Mannerist complexity the Spanish stage did not present the extreme of agony to be found on the English stage. In other European countries Mannerist complexity was succeeded by a Baroque resolution through the dream of royal glory. In Spain the resolution came through illusion, magic, and dream.

On the Spanish stage the back curtain was a floating veil of illusion. Whereas Shakespeare had in back of Romeo, Henry V, and Hamlet solid images of royal and divine order—a castle gate, a throne and canopy, clouds and zodiac above, all in gleaming gold and marble splendor—Lope had a curtain that covered most or all of the background. Whatever castle gateway, throne, or heavenly choir he needed was revealed a piece at a time in fragmented glimpses. Even the trees or towers brought on the forestage were as likely to open up for a magic vision as to serve as earthly forest or town.

The dream element increased in Spanish drama in the seventeenth century. Cervantes' prose narrative *Don Quixote* marks a dividing line. It was the first narrative to make a game of the uncertainty about which reality is real, which value is

389

Tirso de Molina.

valid; and the increase of objectivity in such a game was of prime importance for the development of both science and comedy. The Spanish dramatists were almost as much concerned as Cervantes with the baffling uncertainty of appearance. If there was no great questioning as in *Lear*, no anguished intensity as in El Greco's paintings, there was in the followers of Lope de Vega, as in many of the followers of Shakespeare, much playing with the fragments of appearance, much conjuring with madness, dream states, and illusion.

Lope himself had written plays about madness or pretended madness. Many of his disguises brought up the Mannerist question of which is the mask and which is the face. Many of his characters were infatuated by women they knew were unfaithful. Many were torn by the contradiction of love and jealousy. But seventeenth-century Spanish drama accepted contradiction as a basic condition of the universe and created a resolution of chaos through fantasy.

Many Spanish plays of the early seventeenth century have a strict, moral ending. Yet during most of the play the characters are at odds with a world where appearances are deceiving. The hero can go a long course before he meets anything real enough to stop him. This is true also of Ruiz de Alarcón's *La verdad sospechosa* (*Truth Suspected*—1628). The hero, who tells so many lies that no one believes him, finds himself married to a woman he had not intended to ask for. Unable to tell the truth, he is unable to know the truth. The play is too serious to be a good comedy. Corneille in *Le Menteur* (*The Liar*—1644), using the same plot, achieved a level of bright comedy.

TIRSO DE MOLINA AND THE MANNERIST TENSION

In between Lope de Vega and his most distinguished successor, Calderón, Tirso de Molina gave the *comedia* some new directions and explored several themes that became important in the Mannerist period. His great overreachers, like Marlowe's Faustus, are torn between doubt and faith, ready to defy heaven. Tirso's most famous sinner is Don Juan. In *El burlador de Sevilla* (*The Trickster of Seville*—1639) he introduced to European literature the first image of the irresponsible seducer who is carried off to hell by the stone statue of a father he had killed. In a world of fiery men proud of their honor and cold women proud of their virginity, Tirso's Don Juan is provoked to prove, by treachery, lies, or flattery, that all women are assailable. He thinks there is always plenty of time to be saved by a last-minute declaration of faith. He ends in hell.

A more fearful sinner is Tirso's hero in *El condenado por desconfiado* (*The Man Damned for Lack of Faith*—before 1625). Paulo, the hero, is at first a very pious hermit, sure that his austerity and good deeds will win salvation. When he is told, in a prediction actually from the devil, that he will have the same fate as a certain

391

bragging bandit, he defies the justice of God and becomes a bandit too. At the end he is taken off to hell, an outraged figure, while the bandit confesses and is absolved and saved.

The fearful uncertainty about salvation brought to the surface tensions almost forgotten in the more controlled art of the Renaissance.

THE CLASSICISM OF CALDERÓN

Changes in the 1620s moved toward more controlled tensions and toward a new classicism that foreshadowed the classicism of France in the time of Corneille, Racine, and Molière.

In the quarrels over the freedom in form and range of material for the popular stage, Lope and his defenders seemed to have won the day. But in the 1620s some playwrights abused their freedom, and new attacks on the stage criticized both the lack of morals and the lack of a classic form. In 1625 a reformation council demanded that the monk Tirso be forbidden to write any more plays and be sent to a monastery far from the city. Although the edict was not strictly carried out, it showed a growing opposition to the popular commercial stage. But Calderón de la Barca, while keeping much of the varied form of the popular theatre, was able to give the *comedia* a smooth consistency that mollifed the men of classic taste, and he wrote plays that had such excellent religious content that he pleased the authorities. He has been called the greatest theological playwright of the Catholic world.

Calderón was a first-rate poet. While the nineteenth-century reader preferred Lope de Vega and his spontaneous poetry based on the language of the street, a twentieth-century reader often prefers Calderón. He used the elaborate *culto* style which has chains of metaphors and elaborate balanced comparisons. The contrived prose of John Lyly's *Euphues* (1579) was similar. But Shakespeare showed that ingenious conceits could be witty in comedy and powerful in serious moments. And John Donne showed the power of extending a startling image. When people of the time repeated the remark of Cervantes that Lope de Vega was a *monstruo*, a prodigy of nature, they added that Calderón was the prodigy of art.

Calderón's *La devoción de la Cruz* (Devotion to the Cross—1633?) is a good example of the unresolved tensions of the Mannerist age. The hero knows he is set apart from the rest of mankind by a birthmark, a cross on his chest. Winning in a duel with a close friend, the jealous brother of his love, he finds a similar cross and carries the young man to a priest to be shriven before he dies. About to abduct the woman he loves, he finds a mark of the cross on her breast. At the end he is miraculously brought back to life long enough to be shriven, and then he and his

Pedro Calderón.

love are drawn upward on a platform with a large cross. But the play is not as simple as this summary suggests. It is a picture of man's confusion and misery. Because the cross repeatedly keeps the lovers from each other, they are desperate, and both go to the mountains to lead bands of desperadoes, eager to commit every crime. Not only does the cross prevent their desires, they are cursed by the unreasonable jealousy of the father, who did not trust his wife. There is tragedy for the old man when he learns that the young man and his love are both his children and hence brother and sister. In his last flight the hero falls down a mountainside—a symbol of his fall from grace.

CALDERÓN AND HONOR

El alcalde de Zalamea (The Mayor of Zalamea—1640s?) seems at first like another study of the triumph of the king's justice over that of an arrogant local lord. And it seems as if Calderón tried to outdo Lope de Vega with characters from every walk of life—common soldiers, camp followers, petty officers, peasants, a down-at-heels knight, a general, and finally the king himself. At the center is the rich old peasant Crespo, proud of the respect of his neighbors and contemptuous of bought titles. Yet the play differs from the Lope pattern considerably. The king arrives only after Crespo has defied the general.

And the point of honor is more complex than in the plays of Lope de Vega. Everyone has his pride in his function. The camp followers are proud of the games and songs that entertain the soldiers. When Crespo learns that the officer had abducted and raped his daughter, he prepares for direct vengeance. But at that moment he is made mayor of the town, and in his new role acts by a more just concept of honor; he gives the officer a chance to restore the girl's honor by marrying her. When the arrogant officer refuses, he has the town execute him. The king upholds the action. There has been a shift from private vengeance to public justice.

The concept of honor in Calderón has been much discussed. In the seventeenth century, as the feudal system was disintegrating and Spain no longer enjoyed the early prosperity of gold from the New World, the drama reflected a tense insecurity. Jealousy and suspicion could run wild at a time when certainty seemed impossible and trust and belief a desperate gamble. Recent students find that even in the plays that directly set honor against love, Calderón saw the shortcomings of the old code. In many plays his imagery associates love with warmth, light, and life, while honor is associated with cold, darkness, and death. A tragic effect is created when a man protests at the cruelty of a duty he cannot escape. The plot of *A secreto agravio, secreta venganza* (*Secret Vengeance for Secret Insult*—1635) has the excitement of the planning of the perfect crime—killing the suspected wife in a fire and the other man in the collapse of a boat. But the play is more than a romance of crime; it is a study of four unhappy people. The wife had been in love with a man reported dead in battle but now returned and unable to leave her alone though she is married. The fourth figure is a friend wandering like an outcast who had regained his honor by vengeance but now finds that no one remembers his honorable deed but only the disgrace. The ending is an example of one of the popular resolutions of the Baroque age: the sense of freedom when torment and conflict are over. The husband is free to serve his king in battle, and he adds, "and there may end my life—if indeed misfortune ever ends." The audience knew that the royal expedition referred to had ended in disaster.

CALDERÓN'S PHILOSOPHICAL MASTERPIECE

Two of Calderón's best plays deal with philosophical issues. The plot of *El Mágico prodigioso* (*The Master Magician*—1637) turns on discovering the relation between Aristotle's First Cause and the Christian God. It is a *Faust*-like play. Cyprian, a great magician and pagan philosopher, falling in love with a Christian girl, Justina, makes a pact with the devil to get her. But the devil cannot corrupt her and has to deliver a veiled phantom. When Cyprian tries to embrace her he finds only a skeleton. Freed from his delusions about the world, he forces the devil to admit that the First Cause is the Christian God. Then he and Justina are martyred together.

Calderón's most famous play *La vida es sueño* (*Life's a Dream*—1635) is a great philosophical drama. Although complex, dealing with a dozen or more philosophical issues, it brings each issue to clarity or new definition. The main theme derives from the sudden changes of fortune of Prince Sigismundo, brought up as a chained brute in a mountain tower, then waking in a royal bed and hailed as Prince of Poland, and then a third day finding himself back in chains in the tower. He concludes that his royal day was a dream, or he is dreaming now, or perhaps both are true and all life is a dream. When a rebellious army comes to rescue him and make him king, he does not want to risk disappointment again. The vision of Rosaura gives him a glimpse of heavenly beauty and a new insight that will enable him to live in the world and control his violence.

Rosaura appears in three different forms. In the first act, disguised as a man, she tumbles down a mountain side, her clownish servant with her, and comes upon the tower where the prince is confined. The prince is moved at the sight of a person more gentle than his brutal keepers. In the second act, at court, where she is a waiting maid for the Princess Estella, his released fury is calmed by her beauty. In the third act, while he is in battle against his father, he sees her as a woman with the armor and weapons of battle and desires her for himself. But when she invokes his help in regaining her honor, he sees his own role as prudent, unselfish ruler.

Just as important as the dream theme is the theme of fate. The old king Basilio was warned by eclipses and conjunctions of the stars that his son would be a monster and bring murder and chaos to his country, and humiliation to this father. To prevent this fate, the king had the son chained and imprisoned, to grow up more animal than man. When Rosaura has penetrated the secret, the king tests the son by having him drugged and brought to the palace to wake up as a prince. Of course the prince Sigismundo behaves as predicted, killing a servant immediately and causing chaos. But Calderón gives the prince full justification. Sigismundo's first speech as a prisoner is a brilliant lament for the lack of freedom. When the courtiers see his brutality he angrily retorts that they have made him a brute by chaining him. In trying to avoid tyranny, the king has become a tyrant. The death of Clarín, the *gracioso*, makes clear the futility of trying to avoid fate. Running away from battle, he hides only to be killed by a stray bullet.

Life's a Dream shows the process by which brutishness in man, often provoked by inhumane treatment, is transformed by experience, guidance, and philosophy. It endorses a decision to work for the best values, no matter how confusing and insubstantial the world may seem.

AUTOS SACRAMENTALES

The last phase of Calderón's career was devoted almost entirely to the *autos sacramentales*, a form in which he reached the highest expression of his classic learning as well as his moral and religious convictions. On the occasion of the opening of the court theatre, El Coliseo, in 1634, in the grounds of the Buen Retiro palace, he wrote a spectacular mythological play; and when Lope de Vega died in 1635 he was made court dramatist. He wrote a variety of plays in the 1630s—comedias, some tragic, for the corrales, spectacular shows for the Coliseo, and *autos* for the Corpus Christi festivals—but the 1640s saw a radical change in his life. He took part in the suppression of a rebellion in Catalonia and returned to Madrid ill. Because of mourning for the death of the queen and then the prince, the corrales were closed for several years and never regained their vitality. After the death of two brothers and his mistress he became a priest in 1651. Henceforth he confined his dramatic activity to writing two autos sacramentales for the city of Madrid each year. He dominated the form, and after he died in 1681 the city fathers did not expect new plays but made do with revivals of old ones. In the eighteenth century the autos disappeared; to the followers of the Enlightenment it seemed a foolish relic of medieval superstition.

The auto was a form peculiar to Spain. In a sense it was a continuation of the medieval procession of pageant wagons at Corpus Christi, with a play put on in the public square after the procession. As in the Middle Ages, there were many folklore images in the procession: dancers and giants, for instance, and a grotesque female dragon, the Taresca. As in the medieval procession, the main scenic devices for the play were built on wagons and carried in the procession and brought up to join a stationary platform before a structure that could seat part of the audience, leaving the rest standing or sitting as best they could. As in the Middle Ages, the play was financed by the city corporation and presented without charge to the public, once for the city officials and then at one or more other places in the city.

An auto sacramentales reconstructed by Richard Southern. A scene for Lope de Vega's *La Adultera Perdonada*. By courtesy of the Board of Trustees of the Victoria and Albert Museum.

397

The play was not a long mystery cycle but a short morality play. Nor was it a traditional play performed each year by amateur actors. It was a new play written by a professional playwright and performed by professional actors, both hired from the companies of the *corrales*. It was written by some of the best dramatic poets in European history. As R. G. Barnes writes,

The auto sacramental has long been neglected because its mode is allegorical not realistic, its theme transcendental, and its purpose not merely aesthetic but ritual. In its portrayal of human nature it tends toward the archetypal and the abstract rather than toward the individualized and mundane. For these reasons the auto sacramental ought to recommend itself to us now.

The generation that was waiting for Godot, that was haunted by the extremes of Marat and de Sade, or was longing for psychedelic, transcendental planes of being could understand the auto as the rationalist could not.

Calderón was of course not the only dramatist who wrote impressive autos sacramentales. Lope de Vega's *Auto Sacramental de la circumcision y sangría de Cristo nuestro bien* (*Auto Sacramental of the Circumcision and Bleeding of Our Beloved Christ*) at first glance looks like a medieval adoration that is shifted from the Nativity to the Circumcision, having a much more subtle and complex counterpoint of philosophical, poetic, and dramatic ideas. Even Joseph and Mary see in the human baby the later shedding of blood. The doddering old Simeon who performs the circumcision sees his own fulfillment and death in the act. The shepherds dance as for their village May King. The comic Roman soldier is outraged at the cutting and bleeding, and puzzled that the others find such significance in the new-born child. Around the suffering baby and blood the poetic imagery weaves a web of many strands and meanings.

Far more startling is the story of *De la Serrana de Plasencia* (*The Bandit Queen*), written by the priest José de Valdivielso. The plot situation is like many comedias. A wife estranged from her husband goes to the mountains and becomes a bandit queen, capturing all goodlooking youths on the road. Her aide is named Snares, and the young men she takes are Youth, Beauty, and Honor. Her spouse is not a jealous Spanish nobleman, but rather Christ, and the errant wife is the Soul, ever defiant and drawn by Delight. When she finally tries to embrace Delight, she finds a skeleton, and Disillusion and Snares have a name-calling contest. When the spouse comes like a handsome shepherd boy, the queen humbles herself, confesses, and awaits forgiveness. When the Brotherhood of the Order of Corpus Christi come to execute her, the spouse cannot stop Justice, but he stands in front of her and receives in his own body the five wounds from the five crossbows.

For this play the two scenic pageant wagons drawn through the streets and pulled up to join the open platform before the audience were spectacular. A cave high on a mountain was the mansion for the entrance of the bandit queen, and there she takes her youthful victims. For the spouse the other wagon was built as

398

the city of Plasencia. At the end one cart opened to show a tableau of the bandit queen tied to the stake and her husband with the wounds, and the other cart opened for a hell-mouth and within it Snares is pierced by crossbow bolts.

For Calderón's *La cena del Rey Baltazar* (*King Belshazzar's Feast*—1670s) the pageant wagons used elaborate machines. On one pageant wagon Idolatry held the bridle of a bronze equestrian statue, bringing it down from the sublime palace above. On the other wagon Vanity brought up from the caverns under the earth a temple for the worship of the statue. But the statue cried out a warning, and the machines brought the statue and tower back into place and both visions closed.

The auto, as the occasion required, always ended with the triumph of religion and a demonstration of the power of the sacrament. In that respect it is a perfect example of tension resolved in orthodox doctrine and impressive spectacle. Yet on the way to its solution it faces doubt and defiance. The land of the Spanish Inquisition and of the bullfight understood the desperation of a triumphant faith in a dangerous world. In the Golden Age, the auto sacramental measured the pain and anguish that had to be paid for the Baroque triumph.

COURT THEATRE AND POPULAR THEATRE

As in Paris, London, and Venice, the 1630s in Spain saw some blending of the traditions of court and town. In 1626 the Italian architect-designer Lotti, a specialist in gardens, fountains, and scenic effects, was brought to Spain. At first his productions used mansions and chariots of the medieval and Renaissance traditions. In 1635, when the new palace, the Buen Retiro, was finished, he staged a spectacular water play of Calderón called *El mayor encanto amor* (*Love, the Greatest Enchantment*—1635). The King and court followed in gondolas the action on the lake. Allegorical fountains with singers representing seas and rivers led Odysseus to Circe's island, where a mountain exploded to reveal Circe's palace and where men, transformed into trees, plants, and animals, were dancing. When the goddess Galatea rescued Odysseus, Circe turned her palace into a snowy wilderness where a volcano rose. This spectacular piece was performed by a professional company, and after the special gala opening it was performed a number of times for the paying public.

Many masques and spectacular entertainments were acted by the aristocrats themselves, but when in 1640 Lotti built a splendid new theatre, the Coliseo, in the palace grounds, it served both for court entertainments and for professional performances for the general public. The auditorium of the Coliseo was not much different from the open-air corrales, with a patio, box seats or *aposentos* at the sides, and a royal box that rose above the *cazuela*. But the stage seems to have had a proscenium and front curtain, apparently for the first time in Spain. For the traditional *comedias* the companies seem to have used the curtains, formal doorways, upper gallery, and moveable mansions, but for the court plays, Lotti and his followers, also mostly Italian, installed the painted wings and back shutters of the Italian perspective. Thus the Italian system was gradually established in the commercial theatre, though the corrales and the old staging lingered on through most of the century. Spain did not see the sudden change that came in England with the closing of the public theatres in 1642 and the reopening in 1660 with painted perspective settings framed by proscenium and front curtain; nor did it see the rapid change that came in Paris in the 1630s as perspective replaced the old simultaneous scenery in less than a decade. The connection between the theatre and the Spanish court did not die out even in the difficult days of the eighteenth century when Spanish theatre was only an echo of the Golden Age and a provincial follower of France.

The Professional Clowns:
Commedia dell' Arte

With the art of the poet, Shakespeare raised the popular buffoon and the court jester to a figure of universal appeal. He caught in his clown figures, personalized yet impersonal, an image for all future ages—the timeless face of a playful acceptance of the illusion and deceptive appearance of life. But his clowns left no progeny in the theatre.

The Italian clowns of the *commedia dell' arte*, however, while creating their own kind of theatre, established a theatrical tradition that was one of the most vital in Europe for a hundred and fifty years. This had great influence in the eighteenth and nineteenth centuries, and left some traces in the circus, Punch and Judy shows, as well as many music hall, radio, and television comedy acts. It was the great contribution of Italy to the western theatre.

DEVELOPMENT OF THE COMMEDIA

The commedia was a theatre of the actor. Dispensing with the playwright, the leader of the company sketched a scenario that was tacked up in back of the scenes to give the relationships of the characters and tell who entered in what order and what the main action of each scene would be. The rest was left for the actors to create as they went along. The commedia was spontaneous and completely devoted to the performance and the audience reaction. No layer of written text came between the thought and the act. A commedia actor's performance came from the depths of the personality that Stanislavsky and his followers have striven to rediscover and combine with fixed words of an author.

Improvisation permitted the actor to take advantage of every changing mood or accidental happening in the audience, to bring in local or contemporary references, and to make a comic point of every slip or accident on the stage. The characters were the same from one day to the next, and even if the general story was different, the same comic situations came up over and over again. The audience waited to see how the actor would pull off the trick this time. But improvisation

Comedians and charlatans in the Piazza San Marco, Venice. *Courtesy Museo Correr, Venice.*

did not mean a stumbling for words or a tongue-tied dependence on gesture. The commedia was one of the most eloquent of all theatres, each performance full of quick sallies and long poetic discourses. Behind the performers lay a tradition and the specialized skill of each player, who perfected one character during most of his professional life. Further, each actor had to have at the tip of his tongue hundreds of phrases, speeches, discourses, arguments, riddles, proverbs, and poems on which he could play variations as part of the full development of his role. He memorized opening speeches and closing tags, often ending a scene with a rhymed couplet. Skilled in mime, acrobatics, dance, and music, the actors were just as quick with speech.

Nor were performances shapeless and undisciplined. The name commedia dell' arte means comedy of the artists—the most highly skilled actors in Europe. They had the discipline of the type character, crystallized in the mask—such an entity that it could be handed on from one company to another, from one generation to the next. If the mask, the type character, limited the actor in some ways, it also gave him support and direction. He could take what others had created and add his own subtleties.

References to the commedia in the middle of the sixteenth century show that it was already important in Italy. By the 1570s companies had visited Bavaria, Paris, London, and Madrid, playing at royal courts and on the streets. Since the actors were able to make a living and delight the audience, even though speaking in their native Italian, they must have had a wonderful command of expressive movements and have been able, by inflection, intonation, and rhythm of speech, to make the audience understand what they were saying. By the end of the sixteenth century they had so captured the European imagination as *the* image of real life that French political satirists could allude to their characters and jests with confidence that everyone would know what was meant. When Shakespeare wrote his version of the popular concept of the ages of man for Jaques in *As You Like It*, he naturally thought of the image of an old man as the commedia character Pantalone.

> The sixth age shifts
> Into the lean and slipper'd pantaloon,
> With spectacles on nose and pouch on side,
> With youthful hose, well sav'd, a world too wide
> For his shrunk shank; and his big manly voice,
> Turning again toward childish treble, pipes
> And whistles in his sound.

The origin of the commedia is an intriguing mystery. The masks worn by commedia characters suggest a connection with the mimes of ancient Greece and Rome. It is unlikely that a masked theatre would suddenly appear without roots or precedent in a sophisticated era. In the Middle Ages masks had been used only for devils and animals or for persons blasted by light from heaven. Moreover, particular characters and actions in the commedia were remarkably like those of ancient mimes and clowns, especially the two old men and the pair of stupid servants of the Atellan farces. Yet no one knows how Roman comedy could have survived as an influence during a thousand years of scanty activity. Borrowing from Plautus and Terence was common in the sixteenth century, but the commedia was a theatre of such lively performance that it could hardly have been invented out of the literary tradition.

The early commedia stages were the square platforms of the mountebank, with a simple cloth hung at the back, sometimes with houses sketched in charcoal to indicate a street. When the actors were invited to play for princes, they were given a standard perspective street scene of two rows of solid houses, with plenty of doors and windows for escapes, serenades, and eavesdropping, and with separate street corners for running around, hiding, meeting, sneaking, or surprising.

From the Gothic age the commedia inherited reminders of devils and beast epics. Harlequin's black mask had the sooty face of the medieval devil Hellekin and the hairy skin of some companion of Reynard the Fox. Pulcinella's cock's crest, hunchback, barrel chest, and beak nose show his derivation from a primitive cock mask. The monstrous deformity, the warts, blotches, swollen noses, and long ears of many of the masks were reflections of an age obsessed by man's corruption. Yet all was placed in a world of make-believe, with much of the festival gaiety of a Venetian carnival. A few touches remained of the Danse Macabre, the hysterical flagellations of St. Vitus' dance epidemics in the fifteenth century.

But the Renaissance had softened the ugliness and grotesque comic elements of the Gothic. The young lovers introduced a romantic element, an idealism, an aristocratic note of the age of rich merchants and splendid humanist princes. Satire was changed by the Renaissance. Instead of the scornful anger at sin and corruption of the Gothic satires, it now had classic example and historical prestige. The Renaissance man, less bound by the church and the feudal order, was free to enjoy a comedy of intrigues about money and sex. He had a sense of the importance of man's activities in this world and so could get pleasure from difficulties and misunderstandings in human relations. When the Renaissance gave way to the Mannerist age, what could be better to express displacement than the commedia, a theatre of masks and disguises?

Yet the commedia not only suggested displacement but offered a solution, not through a dreamy acceptance of illusion as in *The Tempest* and *Life Is a Dream* but through acceptance of complexity and bafflement for the sheer fun of it. Partly the satisfaction is achieved from sheer virtuosity. The Baroque age that followed the Mannerist age worshipped the skilled performer, the virtuoso tenor or male castrato-soprano, the king who could dominate an assembly or a parade or a *ballet de cour*, a priest who could conduct a spectacular ceremony. And a most amazing virtuoso was the commedia actor who could leap through windows, box an ear with a foot, adapt the words of his song to a local situation, burst into the most absurd yet eloquent speeches. Laughter was a more successful, if more difficult, resolution of Baroque tensions than spectacular opera or operatic church and court.

404

Extreme Puritans could not enjoy it, yet many seventeenth-century religious people who had a strong sense of man's depravity were delighted. Here was a theatre that did not reject man while flaunting his weaknesses and absurdities. High comedy achieved the paradoxical power of making the most precise exposure of man's sins and follies while showing how he could be liked, accepted, and enjoyed. And the commedia, with its tremendous vitality and zest, moved a long way toward high comedy.

THE COMMEDIA TYPE CHARACTERS

The commedia masks set the types, gave distinction to the performance, and created a tradition greater than the art of any one performer. For the audience the mask was an enlargement, an intensification, a simplification. For the actor it was even more important. Any dancer or actor in a mask, like the performers in primitive rituals, discovers that his body movements respond to the intensity, scale,

Four scenes from *Balli D. Sfessania. Courtesy National Gallery of Art, Washington, D.C., the Rosenwald Collection.*

405

and special quality of the mask. He moves in the realm of fantasy and dream, of a comic caricature that is both human and superhuman, the realm of primitive dancers and magicians. He makes visible some of the basic patterns of the subconscious.

The better companies usually had a dozen major actors besides supers. Central are the old man, Pantalone, his valet, the young man, and the girl. But duplication is the essence of the comedy; there are two young lovers and two charming girls, two to four old men, a captain between young and old, two to four *zanni* (buffoons), and at least one soubrette, or rustic maid. The Gelosi company ("jealous of pleasing" company), under the leadership of Flaminio Scala, had regularly a dozen actors. Pantalone and Gratiano the Doctor were Scala's two old men, and his Capitano was Spavento. His young lovers always used the names Oratio and Flavio, and the girls, Isabella and Flaminia. There was a pair of zanni—Arlecchino, the quicker, and Pedrolino, the more rustic, who was sometimes a valet, sometimes an innkeeper. Franceschina, the robust, lower-class woman, was sometimes a maid, sometimes the wife of Pedrolino. The eighteenth-century company that Goldoni describes in his memoirs had pairs of lovers, the three old men— Pantalone, the Dottore, and the Capitano—and a pair of zanni, Arlecchino and Brighella. Pulcinella, important in many companies, might be either a valet or an old man, and sometimes he was the center of the company. He survives as the Punch of the puppet shows.

Most companies presented a cross section of society and a geographical cross section of Italy. The lovers used the aristocratic Tuscan speech of Florence. Pantalone, the rich magnifico, was always from Venice, the trading city, and spoke the dialect of that busy port. The Dottore, occasionally from Padua, was most frequently from the University of Bologna, a town famous for sausage as well as for the pretentious jargon of its learned men—two forms of a product named after the town: baloney. While trained in law or medicine, he always spouted more than he understood. The Capitano spoke Italian with a Spanish accent, but, like some of the zanni, the character originated in Naples. Arlecchino sometimes and Brighella regularly used the dialect and had some of the legendary qualities of Bergamo, famous as a town of fools.

The glamorous young lovers, without masks, were figures for audience identification. Handsome, well dressed, and perfumed, the actor carried in his hand the tiny edition of Petrarch's sonnets to Laura. He is a well educated aristocrat, but often he has lost his parents and fortune or falls on evil days. The old man is usually the father of the young man or of his love and is his main obstacle, sometimes even his rival for the girl or the husband of the young wife with whom he is carrying on an intrigue. But sometimes the lady herself makes the difficulties. She has learned from the Court of Love to be cold and to make her lover sigh and languish, or she is led to think that he is paying attention to someone else. She is proud and demands full respect. She is more than a good preliminary sketch of

406

the proud, independent heroine who appears in the English Restoration period in the plays of Etherege and Congreve.

The actor playing the innamorato must learn songs and serenades, sonnets and poems, and tirades of angry, rejected, jealous, or thwarted love, or of one who is planning suicide for love. He was expected to read the best books, study the devices of rhetoric, and have at the tip of his tongue metaphors, similes, paradoxes, proverbs, antitheses, quotations, *bon mots*, retorts, and sallies. The character he played was always in an ecstasy of hope or an agony of despair or in both states at the same time. Several actors and actresses were so eloquent that their poems and discourses were published and adored by scholars, princes, and public. Isabella Andreini was the most famous performer of her age, the toast of princes, famous for her virtue, learning, and charm, mourned by many admirers when she died in 1604.

Glamorous and romantic as the young couples were, they rarely had a scene untouched by laughter. While Fortunio is serenading his Lucinda, Pantalone can be seen hiding around the corner, mocking him, waiting to rush out and beat him. Or it is not Lucinda at all but Arlecchino in Lucinda's cape, grinning at the audience, grimacing at every phrase. Or Celia, receiving the addresses of Flavio, is actually directing her responses at her real love, who had slipped up behind Flavio. Or if no other double dealing is going on the zanni leaps through a window and interrupts the lovers.

Though the other characters are abstractions, they throb with the desires, subterfuges, and terrors of human beings. Pantalone tries to exercise the authority of "Il Magnifico" of Venice, but he is the butt of the intrigues of the young people and zanni. He wears a tight-fitting red vest and drawers that droop to his ankles, which survive as the pantaloons or pants of today. He has Turkish slippers, a brimless cap, and a dark brown mask with hooked nose and straggling gray beard. In the sixteenth century he wore a phallic appendage, sometimes draped with a napkin.

The Dottore, or Doctor Gratiano of Bologna, is the most frequent second old man. The earliest Dottore wore a normal academic robe, a black dress with a white collar and a sixteenth-century brimmed doctor's cap still used in some continental universities. But later the collar was elaborately ruffled and the hat was two or three feet wide. He cannot open his mouth without a quotation or a Latin phrase, though all is garbled. He is given to pedantic analyses and elaborate repetitions and summaries, and invents long lists of authorities and of towns and countries with fantastic names.

The Capitano is the braggart soldier of ancient comedy brought up to date as a Spanish captain when the Spanish ruled Sicily and Naples and frequently overran the whole peninsula. He enters roaring like a lion, bragging of the thousands he has killed, but he sneaks away when his bluff is called. He brags of his ancestors famous for massacre and of himself as a baby being "washed in molten lead, clad in

A series of pantalones from contemporary drawings. *Illustration by Martha Sutherland.*

A series of Il Dottore characters from contemporary drawings. *Illustration by Martha Sutherland.*

red-hot iron, and fed with hemlock juice and deadly nightshade." He had many names, all suggesting some terror of the earth: Spezzaferro, Crocodillo, Rinoceronte, Spavento of Hell's Valley. He wears a long sword and a high neck ruff, and has black mustaches curled at the ends.

Most vivid of all are the zanni. Some companies had one, some four zanni, but most frequently a pair. The most famous zanni was Arlecchino, or Harlequin. If his mask suggests ancient and medieval dark-faced devils and hairy animals, his costume of bright-colored patches is the symbol of the cheerful outcast. In the sixteenth century the patches were real rags, but gradually they were stylized into the conventionalized diamonds of bright colors. His sword, at first a phallus, became a wooden dagger, then a wide, straight sword. When the sword was made of two thin strips of wood it gaved a terrifying whack when used for beating, and it became known as a slapstick. In the eighteenth century, Harlequin was made more charming. He was often a silent mime in the new musical spectacles of Paris and London, and he became a regular figure in the English Christmas pantomimes.

Next in importance was Pulcinella, a vivid zanni from Naples. He is a stupid fool who is yet shrewd and even witty. His hump back and hooked nose are the most characteristic traits. His misshapen body and his feather or cock's comb hat, as well as his arrogant bluff, bring down from ancient times the character of the strutting cock.

A company of clowns, each a vivid performer, required skillful coordination. At some moments each character was given the stage for his turn or solo specialty, but much of the performance consisted of duets, trios, quartets, or long sequences involving the entire company. When everything clicked and the timing was right, the group gave a whirlwind sequence and climax that kept the audience roaring.

Each actor had his *lazzi*, his characteristic gag, trick, or turn. Some zanni involved two or more actors. The zanni distracting Pantalone while the lovers escape, stumbles, spills something on Pantalone's cloak and has to clean it, pretends that someone is chasing him, catches flies or spits cherry pits, sends other people on a wild goose chase, tries a dozen ways of committing suicide, then sets out to tickle himself to death, giggling, screaming, and rolling all over the stage. Scaramouche, sent on an errand, cannot bear to leave what he is eating and keeps running back for another bite. Two people, each thinking the other has been lost in a shipwreck, see each other as ghosts, then with starts and retreats approach, feel each other to be sure, and end in embraces, laughing and crying at the same time. The names of many standard lazzi give only a hint of what the action may have been: "kissing the hand," "take this and leave that," "he knows it already," "lovers on their knees." Some lazzi involve a number of people. The scenarios specify in what order the zanni come on, which may add an extra trick, and which must provide the climax or start another sequence.

A series of Harlequins from contemporary drawings. *Illustration by Martha Sutherland.*

The wildest kind of physical action was the rule. Some actors specialized in falls on the mouth, the back, the head. Bones were sometimes broken, but many commedia actors, among the most agile acrobats of history, kept the pace for years. An actor thrilled his audience by starting to run in fright, swinging out onto the gallery of the auditorium, and running around the house on the rail. For other effects trick doors, trap doors, collapsible furniture, and magic props added surprise on surprise. Mime sequences were developed. Rich, a famous London Harlequin of the eighteenth century, would demonstrate to his young Harlequin in a pantomime dance how the first man was hatched from an egg, chipping the shell, acquiring motion, feeling the ground, making a quick trip around the shell, and so on until he is a grown man.

The basic plot of a commedia might be a tragi-comedy or a romantic tale of charming shepherds and enchanted isles, but it was only a framework for the char-acteristic devices of the type characters. The scenario of *La Creduta Morta*, or *the Girl Who Feigned Death*, starts with the Juliet situation of a girl who takes a drug and is put in her tomb. But fantastic "Italian night" farce scenes follow. She is seen in the street and thought a ghost. Arlecchino brings her shroud back, puts it on and frightens others.

The commedia, far more than Plautus or modern farce, made the fullest use of technical patterns of farce—quick changes of speed and rhythm, patterned move-ments, with two or more moving in unison, sequence, imitation, duplication, one move followed by another, a formal proposition by a counter-proposition, a short question by a short answer, sequences of two, three, four, or five repetitions, with characters coming out of a door or window having the same reaction, stumbling, falling, or knocking over the same person.

THE INFLUENCE OF THE COMMEDIA

In the seventeenth century Molière was able to borrow freely from the com-media and transform it. But a hundred years later Goldoni found that the masked comedy had become so stale and inflexible that he tried to drive it out of the theatre. Instead of a mechanical coarse energy that was often bawdy, Goldoni wanted charm, grace, and warmth, and characters more like everyday people. His company preferred to continue the tired old routines, but occasionally he per-suaded them to present one of his new comedies with fresh characters. If it failed to make money he would return to writing new variations of the old plots, leaving places for the clowns to fill in with the same tricks they had used for centuries.

"Robust" is the word for the puppet versions of the commedia, and the principal way in which Pulcinella has come down to our day is as the violent wooden clown

Punch. In a version of the Punch and Judy show, Goethe first saw the possibilities of the Faust story, for Punch had become a symbol of man's defiance of the devil or of any obstruction. If the masks and fantastic costumes of the commedia actors set a comic key, an aesthetic distance removed from reality, the wooden image set that distance at the ultimate limit that could still give a suggestion of humanity. Pain and human responsibility are completely disregarded by this block-headed monster. When the cat is too noisy, Punch lures him near and beats several of his lives out. When Punch's baby cries he beats him, kills him, and throws him out the window. When his wife Judy protests she gets beaten and thrown out the window in turn, and so do all her relatives. He goes round the world in search of women and adventure. Back in England, he is taken by the police and is about to be hanged, but instead of his own head he manages to get the hangman's head in the noose and he goes free. When the devil comes to claim him with pitchfork and slapstick, Punch is more than a match for him—the eternal clown, symbol of man's inexhaustible ingenuity and will.

In the eighteenth century, Harlequin led the commedia characters into the new musical spectacles in which two great traditions were combined: the spectacular Baroque opera of magicians, supernatural transformations, and cloud machines, and the light, irreverently comic commedia. When Rich made a tremendous success with Harlequin Sorcerer in 1717, the "Harlequinade" and the Christmas pantomime were born. As an actor in the regular theatre he had been a failure because of his ugly face and poor voice, but as a masked dancer and pantomimist he was a wonderful Harlequin. In a slick black mask he created a more charming, dream-like Harlequin who for comic effects assumed the powers of the magicians of

The puppet name "Punch" is derived from "Punchinella." *Illustration by Martha Sutherland.*

412

opera. He and Columbine wandered over the world, sampling the exotic customs of the Arabian nights, the courts of Kubla Khan, and the corridors of the Emperor of the Moon. If demons or outraged officials pursued them, Harlequin had only to wave his magic stick, and his enemies were turned to statues, flower pots, wheelbarrows, or baskets. Prisons dropped down from the skies to pen up the pursuers; caverns and volcanoes and castles opened up to surround them with exotic dancing girls. Harlequin flew through the air on cloud machines or Arabian carpets. With acrobatic agility he leapt through windows or walls. He followed Dick Whittington and his cat around the world, Jack up the beanstalk, and Cinderella to the ball. In different disguises he fled through scene after scene and at the end he was rescued by some supernatural king in a spectacular scenic transformation. He lost the robust fun of his commedia existence and was softened into a dream figure haunting the fairy story spectacles that delighted children of all ages, especially for the Christmas festivities in England. In France, Thomassin gave Harlequin a sad countenance that moved his audience to tears.

Saddest of all characters descended from the commedia was Pierrot, a nineteenth-century creation who moved completely into moonlight fantasy. The earlier Pierrot, a relative of the zanni Pedrolino, was a country bumpkin. Molière uses him as a rustic lout in his *Don Juan*. But in the nineteenth century, with white

Italian masked actors and French farceurs. Molière is on the extreme left. *With the kind authorization of the Comédie-Française, Paris.*

413

An eighteenth-century commedia theatre in the Arena in Verona. © *The Art Institute of Chicago. All Rights Reserved.*

face, white jacket with pompom buttons, and loose white pantaloons, Pierrot became a charming symbol of forlorn hope. He sang serenades to the moon, adored a distant beauty who was stolen by the man of action, Harlequin, and had to content himself with the devotion of the mundane Columbine. The actor Deburau made him a popular image of man's brave endurance for the populace of Paris in the 1830s—a character romantically revived by Jean Louis Barrault in the film *Children of Paradise* (1945). Such a clown is preserved in the opera *Pagliacci* (1892). But Pierrot was most at home in the romantic world of the ballet. Pretty, charming, sad, and completely out of this world, he floated through ballets decade after decade.

Even the modern circus clowns have kept little of the costume of the commedia. A painted face and a loose white jacket with wide sleeves and pompom buttons is an occasional relic of the tradition. But such clowns as Emmett Kelly made a fresh start from the nineteenth-century stage tramp. His painted face and fantastic costume moved him as far from reality as the masks of Harlequin and Pulcinella, and he used many of the old gags and gadgets. Charlie Chaplin and many successors have invented special characters, and clowns in pairs or groups have appeared on stage and screen, but there has never been, in ancient or modern times, another scheme of clowns with the appeal of the commedia dell' arte.

The Baroque Resolution:
The Dream of Royal Glory

The church, the king, the theatre—these provided the Baroque age with a magnificent answer to the doubts that had tortured the generation of Shakespeare, Ben Jonson, John Donne, Cervantes, Calderón, and the Mannerist painters. The Catholic Church met doubt and division with splendid buildings decorated with gold sunbursts and clouds of angels, great services of installation or devotion, spectacular processions of bishops, the singing of hundreds of angels welcoming a saint to heaven, or the representation of the triumph of the Archangel Michael over the hordes of Satan. Audiences sat gaping at the splendor of the Jesuit pageants representing the triumphs of the saints, which were written and presented by experts. The new absolute monarch silenced disaffection or any impulse toward individualism by his magnificent coronation, his new castles, fountains, and grand stairways, and his elaborate tourneys, operas, and shows. The theatre of the Baroque age, a theatre of royal masques and ballets and of spectacular operas, gave the same answer to the troubled soul. The pain of Hamlet and Lear, the snarl of Volpone gave place to the splendor of the theatre of heavenly and royal glory.

The new theatre gloried in the sense of shifting reality. It kept no solid Elizabethan façade, no solid Serlian street scene. All was dissolving appearance. A palace suddenly melted before the eyes and became an enchanted garden, then at the gesture of a magician, a horrid cave; the cave gave place to a ship on a tossing sea, or it opened up to disgorge monsters. But at the end a great cloud descended to dissolve all earthly shows, and the gods appeared amidst choiring angels, with Jupiter singing praises of the earthly king. When the show was over, the only solid thing remaining was the proscenium frame of gilded canvas and plaster, a symbol of illusion, the separation of the spectator from the show.

Characters were constantly in disguise. The masque and the *ballet de cour* were dramatized masked balls. Opera abounded in plots of heroines disguised as pages and of heroes disguised as women, fantastic servants, music masters, or tradesmen or transformed by magicians into dancing monkeys, rocks, trees, or demons. Nothing was what it seemed: dissolution and transformation were sources of endless fascination. At the end the gods or a more powerful magician in the play or the wise king in the audience banished discord, making way for a triumphant chorus of praise and resolution.

416

THE ITALIAN *INTERMEZZI*

The new stage of magic transformation was created in Florence. That city had seen a structure of the cosmos visualized in neo-Platonic philosophy, in the serenity of the linear perspective of Renaissance painting, and in the new perspective stage, which Florence shared with nearby Ferrara and Mantua. Before the end of the sixteenth century, however, these enlightened cities saw the perspective wings and back shutters of the theatre fade away in the magic effects of the *intermezzi*. For although audiences were impressed by the plays of Plautus and Terence and their modern imitations and by charming pastorals, such plays alone were dull, and no revival was considered proper for a court occasion without elaborate intermezzi between the acts. Eventually the intermezzi smothered the plays and created a new kind of theatre that at first was extravagant but was eventually developed, through the new ideals of the Baroque age, into the spectacular opera.

Unlike the plays themselves, the intermezzi could be linked with the occasion. Some sixteenth-century intermezzi had a vague relationship to the plays they adorned. Thus for the Ferrara revival of Terence's *Eunuchus* in 1499, the performance was enlivened by intermezzi of dancing youths pursuing Fortune, young ladies choosing young men rather than older suitors, and young people singing

Cloud machine for the descent of divine characters in Turin. *Illustration by Martha Sutherland.*

417

love serenades and dancing morris dances. A comedy set in an ancient city was properly enlivened by intermezzi of gods, goddesses, nymphs, and heroes of ancient mythology. English tragedies of the 1560s and 1570s were enlivened by musical dumb shows of episodes illustrating the moral. But for Florentine wedding celebrations of the Medici court the scene and story of the play itself were almost forgotten in the machines and transformations as gods and goddesses were conjured up to bring praise, gifts, and blessings to the bride and groom. A Temple of Fame might be let down from above so that Fame, standing on a tower at the center, might present the famous ancestors of the couple and predict greater heroes to come. Even the caves of Vulcan and the dungeons of hell were forced into a relationship with the occasion, so that Vulcan and his furies might make a suit of armor that Mars would present to the duke in the audience. A paradise, with choiring angels and dancing cherubs, might be let down in the sky so that Jupiter could drive Discord and his cohorts into the abyss and sing a blessing on the noble pair.

The Italians anticipated the French and English in such shows, for they already possessed the Renaissance perspective stage. Onto that stage they now brought the spectacular effects so popular with the general public in street processions and religious pageants. Between the parallel cloth-covered sections of sky, machines

Rustic scene from *Il Giupizio di Paride*, Florence, 1608. *Courtesy Roma, Istituto Nazionale per la Grafica.*

418

Palace of Fame from *Il Giupizio di Paride*, Florence, 1608. *Courtesy Roma, Istituto Nazionale per la Grafica.*

The forge of Vulcan from *Il Giupizio di Paride*, Florence, 1608. *Courtesy Roma, Istituto Nazionale per la Grafica.*

could be let down and drawn up. The Glory that was popular in religious plays for bringing Gabriel or the Virgin from heaven could now take a dozen different forms. It might swing down on a counterweighted lever or be let down by ropes guided in wooden grooves. For the wings and borders of the perspective stage hid the backstage machinery. Juno's car, set in clouds and drawn by stuffed swans, could enter on one side of the sky, move and disappear on the other side, with the support of beams, grooves, and ropes hidden from the audience. Groups of clouds could be let down to cover parts of the sky or to fill the entire stage with a pageant of clouds, thrones, chariots, temples, and sunbursts. Little doors or front curtains in the clouds could be opened to reveal a brightly lighted throne or sun; clouds might be clustered in a small mass, then advance on a sliding beam, or spread apart on hidden jibs like the ribs of a fan or an umbrella. Sometimes separate clouds with seats for angels or deities were interconnected by hidden pins and props and wires so that they could change into two or three different formations.

At the back of the scene, Serlio in the 1530s had made miniature processions cut out of boards pass behind a small archway. But the Florentine intermezzi at the end of the century transformed the entire back of the stage into an elaborate machine. Rows of waves, either cut-out boards or painted revolving cylinders, pro-

From Venetian opera, *Adone in Cipro*, by Legranzi, 1675, a seascape with nymphs seated on dolphins and seahorses and tritons in water. Venus is above in a cart drawn by swans. *Phot. Bibl. Nat. Paris.*

420

Teatro de Medicio, 1617.

duced a tossing sea. Between the waves nymphs moved in sea cars, tritons astride dolphins, or Neptune in a car drawn by sea horses. Small boats or cars were built like miniature toys with sails and oars worked from below by means of little rods and strings, but entire monsters and chariots rode on wheels on a floor several feet below the rows of waves. Trap doors in the main stage could let rocks and mountains suddenly rise from the ground. From the sides large chariots could enter with dancing attendants, with the effect of a street pageant. Devices for changing the wings were clumsy and were superseded in the seventeenth century by a flat wing system.

From medieval drama came the use of hordes of demons as a contrast to the attendants of the favorable deities. The Florentine intermezzi presented them as demons helping Vulcan in his fiery cave, as vices and evil passion, or as storms and devils attendant on Discord. But elaborate as the effects became, the intermezzi remained separate, disconnected fragments, interlude diversions between the acts of the play. They expressed the sense of dissolution, the break-up of Renaissance unity that is visible in Italian painting before it appears in English drama; but they were also linked to a growing sense of the glory of the sovereign that reached fuller expression in the seventeenth century. It remained for the French and English masques, in their limited way, then for the Italian opera in its magnificent way, to give a full development to the Baroque theatre of Royal Glory.

THE MASQUE AND THE *BALLET DE COUR*

The theatre of dissolving reality and royal glory, patronized by the aristocracy and expressing their point of view, took two forms. The court masque was danced by the aristocrats themselves for their private enjoyment. The opera was performed by professionals for a wider public audience and was sometimes largely dependent on the box office.

The earlier form, known in England as the masque and in France as the *ballet de cour*, which was developed gradually in the middle of the seventeenth century, gave way to the more dramatic form of the opera. The court masque had all the elements of opera—story, song, dance, spectacular changes of scenery. But it was never a full drama because it was always associated with a court occasion, and the principal parts were acted by the nobles or royalty themselves as an introduction to their dance. It remained a ceremony rather than a work of art. It was a belated example of the dramatization of social ritual that was the great achievement of the Middle Ages. Hence the masque, in some ways a medieval form, partly amateur, partly professional, acquired new life and reached its significant development in Paris and London as an expression of the dawning age of the absolute monarch.

The court masque or ballet was a glorified masquerade ball, principally associated with festivities at the royal court. The spectacular development came in the dramatization of the arrival of the masked guests. Typically they were the whole group of lords to be honored; sometimes the arrival or disclosure of the honored ladies was also part of the drama. The regular pattern in Paris was for the king's ballets to present only the men, the ladies sitting as audience until the maskers asked them to participate in the general dance. At the queen's ballets, only the ladies were involved in the drama until they invited the lords to dance.

Renaissance maskers dramatized their arrival in the ballroom in the same way they dramatized their arrival on the tourney field, appearing in a fantastic chariot or a mountain or castle on wheels and introduced by an orator, singer, or a group of professional dancers. Late sixteenth-century ballets used a *décor dispersé*, with separate mansions and devices scattered around the ballroom. But at the beginning of the seventeenth century all the separate devices were placed on one platform at the end of the hall in imitation of the Italian perspective stage. Sometimes the Italian backdrop and wings were used, sometimes a French system of one cutout backing behind another, and sometimes the setting made use of such triumphal arches, pavilions, castles, mountains, and magic turntables as were used in the religious cycles and the tableaux vivants. Chariots were still used to bring on some of the dancers. Restricted to a shallow stage by the ballroom locale, the masque remained partly medieval in staging until in the 1630s it gradually adopted the deeper stage and flat wings that had been developed in the opera.

Allegory played a large part in masques and ballets. The story must provide for a disclosure of the maskers beautifully dressed and associated with a noble enterprise. One of the simplest forms was used in the ballet that Catherine de Medici presented for the visit of the Polish ambassadors to Paris in 1573. Six ladies of the court representing the six provinces of France entered the ballroom on a rock of silver in niches of clouds. They danced several elaborate figured dances and presented symbolic plaques to the royal family, the ambassadors, and various officials. The more complete form of a dramatic masque appears in the famous *Ballet Comique de la Reine* (1581), of which there is a beautiful souvenir booklet with several engravings. It used the motif that was later a favorite of the Baroque theatre—enchantment. The queen and her ladies were captives in the palace of Circe, and their rescue provided the main action that eventually brought them to view for the social dances. But the setting was still the old arrangement, with separate mansions spread around the hall. The king and the queen mother (Catherine de Medici), as the chief members of the audience, were seated on a dais, with the leafy bower of Pan and a grotto of illuminated trees at their right, and at their left a gilded cave with clouds outside and a splendid light inside where a chorus sang. At the end of the hall a platform with the garden and palace of Circe left passageways at each side for the entries and chariots. The musicians were placed behind Circe's palace. Sirens and Tritons sang to introduce the principal chariot, decorated with

Circe, Ballet Comique de La Raine. *Salle de Petit de Bourbon, 1581.* Phot. Bibl. Nat. Paris.

424

Ballet *La Polonais*, Salle des Tulleries, 1573. *Phot. Bibl. Nat. Paris.*

fountains, which carried sea gods and the queen and her ladies as Naiads. The ladies presented a figured dance, which was interrupted when Circe drove them into the castle. Four Virtues came to the rescue of the prisoners. Minerva arrived on another chariot, Pan danced out of his bower with his satyrs, and Jupiter descended from the ceiling, struck Circe with his thunderbolt, and delivered her into the hands of the king. The released Naiads danced figured dances, presented gold medals to the king and lords, and led them into the general social dancing. This story did not permit the return of the ladies to the prison as a conclusion, but the English masques regularly had some character summon the maskers back into the setting to vanish and conclude the evening's festivities.

In the ballet of 1581 only one thing was lacking—a stage form to unite the scenes into one picture. Inigo Jones used a platform stage for a masque in London in 1607. In 1610 the Duke of Vendosme presented the *Ballet d'Alcine* at the Louvre on one stage at the end of the hall. The front curtain fell to disclose a forest where monkeys performed a grotesque dance. A magician came out of the setting and advanced with his attendants to the king's seat in the audience to explain that he had transformed the knights of the court into grotesque objects. A series of separate entries of dancers followed. A group of towers and giants entered and opened up to release Naiads. Then in turn came on flower pots, viols, and windmills, from which emerged nymphs and dwarfs. When the dancers were chased back by the magician, the forest suddenly disappeared to disclose an enchanted palace, in front of which stood the knights, like statues. They came to life, assaulted the castle, and tore it down, then danced figured dances before they invited the ladies of the court into the general dance.

Early French ballets, presented on a shallow stage, used a mixture of medieval and Renaissance devices to secure the magic transformations. A turntable like that used in fifteenth-century tableaux vivants was a central device of the English masques. Sometimes angel wings at the sides were drawn offstage and a shutter at the back slid off to reveal another shutter behind it. But the small stage in the early seventeenth century was limited in its resources, and the ballet and masque did not attempt more than two or three changes of scene. Only with the perfection of the new system of sets of flat wings and flat shutters did the Baroque theatre of transformation come into its own. That was in Venice in the 1640s.

The masque in England was perfected by Ben Jonson, for several decades the chief writer of masques for the English court. With Inigo Jones as designer he gave the form more significant meaning. He wanted the entire masque to be a unified work of art, and he thought it should celebrate the idea of order, ceremony, reverence, and devotion to the body politic. One of his great achievements was to dramatize the dance entries or *intermedii*. This secondary part of the masque he developed into the "antimasque," which, while providing startling appearances for contrast with the main show, was also related in some way, often by allegory, to the main theme. Jonson said that he got from the queen the suggestion of adding a contrasting dance or show to a masque, to have the effect of a foil or false masque, but the idea was already an implied possibility in the contrasting scenes of the intermezzi. Since the masque celebrated the arrival of devotees for the rites of honor and worship, the simplest form for the antimasque was the exorcism of evil spirits or ugly intruders who had come to interrupt the rites or steal the offerings and blessings. This provided not only a contrast but dramatic action leading to the disclosure and triumph of the good. For the *Masque of Queens* (1609), Jonson planned his great presentation to show the queen and her ladies in a House of Fame, a variation of the throne of honor popular in the tableaux vivants. To build up to that disclosure he first showed a scene of hell, with witches representing ignorance and malice. When the scene gave way to the splendid palace of Fame, the ladies descended from a great globe and bound the witches to their chariots, symbolizing the triumph of virtue over ignorance and malice.

A long series of antimasques in William Davenant's *Coelum Britannicum* (1634) danced out a vision of the different ages of British history, suggesting first the natural deformities of the time of Atlas, then the retrograde movement of the sun down the zodiac, then the country pleasures released by Plutus, god of Wealth, and the gypsy life following Poverty. Battles were danced under the influence of Fortune, and the Five Senses danced under the eyes of Pleasure. After this extensive presentation of allegorical forces, human history was reached in the anti-

Baroque costume designs from English masques. *Illustration by Martha Sutherland.*

masque of Picts, the earliest inhabitants of Britain, who were replaced by a mountain that rose bearing the three thrones of England, Scotland, and Ireland. The mountain opened to permit the maskers to appear from a cave.

Jonson's *Hymenaei* (1606) is an example of a well integrated masque in which setting, drama, and dances carry out one central idea. It made the occasion of a marriage between two noble families a symbol of union, order, and rule throughout the life of man and of the realm. From a microcosm or globe representing man issued the antimasque, the unruly humours (phlegmatic, choleric, melancholic, and sanguine) and the four affections (desire, fear, joy, and grief), who danced in discord to disturb the wedding fête. But on top of the microcosm sat Reason, who brought them all under control. Still higher appeared Juno, who represented the harmonizing power of love. Finally Jupiter appeared at the very top in the clouds. The king and queen of heaven were reminders of the king and queen of the realm and of the union of the two kingdoms of England and Scotland under James.

The masque as developed by Jonson and other poets was an early expression of the Baroque dream of royal order. But the forces of dissension were powerful. Order was destroyed in England by the civil wars of the 1640s and 50s and was almost destroyed in the same decades in France during the minority of Louis XIV. When new strong governments appeared in England and France in the 1660s, a new opera and heroic drama expressed a new age.

In view of the civil wars that lay ahead, there is an ironic sadness in the last great English masque in 1640. The *Salmacida Spolia* (1640) of Davenant and Inigo Jones must have been one of the loveliest. With utmost confidence it proclaimed the magic power of the splendid presence of the king in dispelling the spirits of Discord. In an opening scene of storm and darkness, Fury sent evil spirits to bring discord to England, and the antimasque danced the Discord that must have been feared and dreaded in the country at that time. But Discord was dispelled by Concord sitting in a silver chariot in a peaceful landscape. The Good Genius of Great Britain invoked the people to honest pleasures. The many entries of happy dancers were a Cavalier answer to the Puritan objection to dance. In a scene of craggy rocks and mountainous paths Charles I, serene guardian of order, sat at the top in a throne of honor. The queen and her ladies, dressed as Amazons, descended in a cloud, and the nobles danced out their hopeful vision of peace and order. When the maskers had moved onto the ballroom floor, the scene on the stage changed to a view of London, with citizens passing over the bridges and the gods in the heavens giving their blessing.

The masques gave full expression to the sense of confusion in the early seventeenth century. The choruses and group songs included strong dissonances, and the solo parts might sing of the anguish felt because Fury had brought Disorder into the world and might call for a good knight to come to the rescue. But fear and chaos were always dispelled by a vision of heavenly rule as the skies opened and Jove spoke from the heavenly throne, giving full endorsement to his representative, the king on the earthly throne.

428

The Triumph of the Baroque in Opera

Opera achieved the most splendid resolution of the restlessness of the Mannerist age. It was both Mannerist in presenting dynamic forces and Baroque in bringing those forces into a triumphant image of power in the final scene.

The full Baroque theatre could not be realized in the disconnected spectacles of the intermezzi or the elaborate displays of the court masques. Both were bound by the limitations of a ceremonial occasion, a palace ballroom as setting, and amateur actors. The Church could show the glories of Christian salvation and the court the glories of the royal presence, but the full vision was realized symbolically in the music and grand spectacle of the opera. The heroes of romance and ancient history, dressed in elaborate "antique" costume of embroidered skirts, long capes, and high plumes, walked on a stage amidst long rows of theatre wings and asserted, with the rich melodies of Baroque music, the eternal sorrows of man and his heroic longing for love and fulfillment of his dream of glory.

The new theatre provided two scenic delights that never ceased to please the audience. One was a dynamic world of wings and back shutters that changed not two or three times, as in the court masques, but six, eight, or as many as fifteen times, and not during an intermission with the curtain closed but in two or three seconds before the eyes. The other delight was a dynamic interplay of heaven and earth. From the Baroque heaven, which was not fixed in one place, messengers descended in chariots, and cloud machines were released that covered the wings and shutters and opened up to display choruses of angels or translucent temples, thrones, and palaces of light.

The Baroque theatre took over the solid Italian perspective stage but transformed it almost beyond recognition. Painted flat wings at the sides replaced the solid angle wings of Serlio. These flat wings could slide offstage in grooves, and they were used in sets of four or five so that when one wing moved off another was disclosed just behind it. At the back of the scene the *prospettiva*, or backdrop, was equally changeable: a similar set of grooves held a set of half-shutters that divided at the center and slid off to the sides. Engineers soon devised a set of ropes attached to each wing and shutter and led by pulleys to one capstan under the stage, where two or three men, by a turn of the capstan, could slowly move all the setting in one smooth, coordinated change.

For operatic spectacles, the sloping floor of the perspective stage opened up in

429

Drawing for Dragons, seventeenth century. *Courtesy The National Swedish Art Museum.*

pits, especially at the distant back of the scene, to permit red clouds to rise for dawn, followed by the sun chariot of Apollo or Phaeton, to permit Neptune to rise from the sea or a set of revolving waves to appear, between which monsters, dolphins, whales, and ships might pass from one side to the other, fight, turn, or sink. The clouds at the top of the stage were no longer three-dimensional but were painted on flat strips of cloth to frame a spectacular skyway, a set of open passages for the busy traffic of heaven. Messengers plummeted down between them. Cloud chariots drawn by peacocks passed from one side to the other. Temples of gods and goddesses floated down to fill the entire stage picture. The Renaissance stage of solid architecture had given way to the Baroque stage of paint and canvas, lightweight changing forms, and dynamic transformation.

THE DEVELOPMENT OF ITALIAN OPERA

Baroque opera itself, like the scenery, was a spectacular transformation of a be-lated creation of the Renaissance. In the sixteenth century music was dominated by polyphonic forms, used either by the large choruses of the church or by small groups of madrigal singers. Monody lived on in popular song, but composers could not develop from that an expression of the surging emotions of drama. In the 1580s and 1590s an attempt was made to revive the dramatic music of the an-cients. The leaders were a group of music-loving scholars who gathered at the Duke's *camera*, an informal classical academy in Florence. Vincenzo Galilei, whose son was to become the famous scientist, published in 1581 *Dialogue on ancient and modern music*. He and his friends believed that the ancient Greek actor singing alone with an instrument of four strings must have been more expressive than a chorus singing the elaborate music of Palestrina. Galilei tried setting to music a passage from Jeremiah and a lament from the *Divine Comedy*. He and the other scholars were much interested in the production of *Oedipus Rex* that opened the Teatro Olimpico in 1585. Galilei had set the choruses to music and had included a few passages for solo voice. For the Duke's marriage in 1589 the musicians of Florence performed a combat of Apollo with the serpent Pytho, a subject that had had fa-mous music in ancient Athens. In the 1590s the poets Rinuccini and Corsi, with the musicians Peri and Caccini, began more extensive work in the new dramatic style. To express the passion of drama they developed a form more elevated than ordinary speech yet more flexible than pure song and called it *stilo recitativo*. Their first opera, *Dafne*, was produced with great trepidation in 1597. The audience ex-perienced a great revelation: a new form of art. The recitative style gained inter-national fame when in 1600 in Florence Rinuccini and Peri produced *Euridice* for the marriage of Marie de' Medici to Henry IV of France.

Model of the winged chariot system for eighteenth-century theatre. *Courtesy Accademia de Belle Arts di Palermo.*

432

In recitative style subtle changes of thought and emotion could be followed as they had never been in the repetitive melodies of the Renaissance. The glorious hero could dominate the stage in solo and express his grief, fury, or dedication as he had never been able to do as one element in a chorus or madrigal.

But the early Florentine recitative, the creation of poets and scholars, had not felt the hand of a musical genius. It was Monteverdi of Mantua, already successful in writing in the polyphonic forms, whose *Orfeo* (1607) realized for the first time in western Europe the possibilities of a drama in music.

Monteverdi gave the stilo recitativo vitality. For the active dialogue he kept the accompaniment by chords in imitation of the Greek, but for lyric moments he wrote *arioso* passages, or arias, with full musical development, and he used the rich color of an orchestra to accompany them. This form of composition set the musical pattern that has prevailed in opera—alternation of recitative and arias. The recitative was dialogue in free rhythm with only chords plucked on a theorbo or played on a harpsichord to punctuate the phrases, and the arias were set pieces that gave musical development to the emotions at crucial points in the story. In one sense this scheme separates the drama from the music. But devotees of opera find that good recitativo sets the dialogue so far above everyday speech that it easily blends into the more elaborate arias.

Arrangement for moving sky and village profile at the rear of an intermezzi scene, seventeenth century.

433

When a corps of dancers was added, opera became a complex and expensive form indeed. Monteverdi found already at hand a tradition of painters' "antique" costumes suitable for gods and for heroes as well, since pastoral characters and plots were frequent in the opera. Above all, opera took over the machines that had been developed over centuries in religious drama and civic pageantry and perfected them to serve the Mannerist vision of life as a kaleidoscope of scenes and characters constantly changing.

Opera was a court toy in Florence and Mantua, but in Rome from the 1620s and in Venice from the 1630s it became the rage of an entire city. In Rome the Borghese family produced operas for a wider public, and in 1632 the Barberini built a theatre near the Quattro Fontane that seated four thousand. Beginning in 1637 in Venice, opera became so popular that before the century was over some eighteen theatres were built in that city.

The aristocrats built most of the theatres and sponsored the productions for their own pleasure and as a public gesture, but the public gave support at the box office. Crowds pushed their way in by the light of their own candles to fight for the best seats. Carnival time, from December 26 to Lent, was the important season for opera, but soon two other seasons were added. The audience hailed the prima donna and cheered when they recognized their favorite bass in a new disguise. The greatest enthusiasm was for the *castrati*, who could sing the soprano roles with a power that no woman could achieve. Fathers sacrificed the manhood of promising choir boys in the hope of fame and fortune for the family.

In few ages has there been such love for showy effects and virtuosity as in the seventeenth century. The extravagances of opera were no more artificial than those in painting and architecture—a high dome in a church painted with clouds and columns and heavenly hosts, for instance, or an altar with twisted columns framing an oil painting of a saint wildly gazing up to heaven.

The opera audience got its money's worth in music, plot, and spectacle. The heroes of romance and history in magnificent embroidered "Roman" costumes sang the sorrows of love in soft song and the defiance of battle in high declamation. They sang against a violin, a trumpet, or a whole orchestra. Their *recits* of terror in witches' caverns were answered by echo choruses and ghost arias. Their professions of faith at a pagan altar were reinforced by a chorus of priests and worshipers. The composers wanted scenes of love, battle, solemn oaths, and sacrifices. The chorus leader wanted great battle scenes with marches, conclaves of gods or heroes, and showy coronations. The machine operator wanted to show his mechanical devices: flying demons, chariots in air, land, and sea, and skies lit up with hundreds of lamps or darkened to allow a sky full of peephole stars to spell out the name and motto of the king. The dance director wanted a dozen "entries" of satyrs, fauns, naiads, peasants, Africans, Americans, cobblers, peddlers, monsters and demons, or enchanted rocks and flower pots. Monteverdi objected to the monsters and supernatural beings, wishing to hold the opera to hu-

434

manistic themes. He said, "Ariane moves us: she is a woman, and the Orpheus, because he is a man, but how can I write music for a wind?"

Venetian opera offered an especially wide range of excitement and contrast. Rapes, kidnappings, murders, duels, battles, fires, and pillage abounded; clowns, buffoons, servants, or peasants provided frequent comic contrast and sometimes entered into the serious scenes. Penelope, waiting for Ulysses, was surrounded by pairs of shepherd lovers who sang love songs and popular songs, and a court jester added a cynical note for contrast. Grandiloquent declamations were followed by soft duets, burlesque dialogues, popular airs, or comic songs. Disguise and transformation were constantly in use, and the world of the supernatural enclosed everything, initiating and resolving the action. Jealous gods or wicked magicians were the source of terror and confusion. Jupiter himself, with the whole conclave of heaven, ended the confusion in a colorful finale of glory.

The opera transformed the humanistic pastoral almost beyond recognition. What had been a poetic image of man in an ideal simple setting became a spectacular image of a marvelous universe. Not only willful magicians but all the gods of Olympus might interfere in shepherds' lives.

Opera offered extreme examples of a general theatrical craze for spectacle. The popular town theatres of Madrid, London, and Paris offered some scenic variety. Even when there was no change of setting, the old simultaneous decor at the Hôtel de Bourgogne could present spectacular effects. For one play we read, "In the middle of the stage a hell, covered . . . above the hell, the heaven of Apollo, and above Apollo the heaven of Jupiter, at the side of hell, the mountain of Sisyphus . . . all to close and open." But opera could present the whole phantasmagoria far better, and the simple shepherds and nymphs of Arcadia were absorbed into the court of Ulysses or the train of Hercules or of Theseus, to rescue Andromeda.

THE TRIUMPH OF SPECTACULAR OPERA

Andromeda started the rage for popular opera in Venice in 1637, and in 1641 Torelli began his fantastic career as designer with the *Marriage of Thetis and Peleus*. Scenes exploded into one another, with mountains followed in turn by groves, the glittering throne of Jupiter, the smoky caverns of Hades (where jealous Juno stirs up Discord), the mountain slopes of Peleon and the groves of Ida (where knights, Tritons, Bacchantes, and fauns dance), and the assembly of the gods (where Love finally overcomes Discord). Scenic changes were made with such amazing brilliance that Torelli became known as "the wizard."

Torelli produced in Venice for four years, then Paris called. The followers of

Richelieu decided that the court of Louis XIV, already the richest in the world, should be the most splendid in show. Torelli came to Paris in 1644 and for a decade produced one great spectacle after another. His most famous, *Orfeo* (1647), was no simple story of a sad husband bringing his wife back from Hades. It was truly a Baroque spectacle: a rival prayed to Venus to stop the marriage and caused Euridice to die; Jupiter stirred up Prosperpine's jealousy of Pluto's attention to Euridice; the rival killed himself and his father Bacchus brought his Bacchantes to tear Orfeo apart in revenge; an apotheosis presented choruses in praise of love and conjugal fidelity; and Jupiter sang the praise of the queen mother in the audience. At the court of the Sun King gods must arrive in a chariot of the sun surrounded by flames and lit up by gold and brilliants. Torelli's settings for *Orfeo* were so wonderful that no one was willing to destroy them. Asked to provide another spectacle that could use the same splendid sets, Corneille wrote *Andromede* (1650).

But these productions, most in the Petit-Bourbon, a wing of the old palace, were still not splendid enough for the insatiable court. To build a new theatre for the marriage festivities of the young king, Louis XIV, Mazarin brought Vigarani of Modena to Paris in 1659, and in 1662 the new theatre in the Tuileries, called

Combat à la Barrière, Les Noces de Polée et de Thetis. Phot. Bibl. Nat. Paris.

Lully's ballet *Le Triumph de L'Amour* in the newly built Theatre des Tulleries, 1662. *Phot. Bibl. Nat. Paris.*

the Salle de Machines, was opened with *Ercole Amanti*. The distance from the front of the stage to the last perspective shutter was 167 feet, and the cloud machines could raise and lower a chorus of two hundred at one time.

The opera was indeed the Theatre of Machines. One expert found fifteen or sixteen types, among them celestial, military, rustic, maritime, civil, and academic machines, and machines of poetic history.

One of the most magnificent operatic productions of the century was the *Pomo d'Oro*, produced for the imperial court in Vienna in 1668 with scenery by Burnacini. A souvenir libretto was published for the imperial guests with engravings of the principal scenes. The prologue began with an address in praise of the emperor in a Theatre of the Glory of Austria. The first act opens in the Palace of Pluto where the Goddess of Discord is preparing the golden apple that will bring on the Trojan War. The scene changes to the convocation of the gods in the Palace of Jupiter. Next is disclosed a woodland on Mt. Ida, where Prince Paris is tending his sheep. For the Judgment scene the setting changes to the courtyard of the Palace of Paris, where the three goddesses descend from heaven in a great "gallery," a curved arcade of gold columns set with bright jewels, that comes to rest on top of a triumphal arch. Venus makes the scene change to a garden of pleasure with fountains, statues, nymphs, and cupids, then reveals the image of Helen, and the act ends with a ballet expressing the idea of beauty.

In the second act Paris is at a port, ready to embark, the theatre wings of rocks

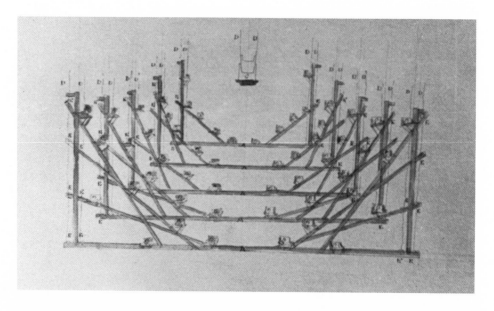

Configuration of cloud borders carrying heavenly personages without the cloud profiles and Venus's cart in the center. *Courtesy G. Lombardi Collection, Archiveo di Stato, Parma, Italy.*

in the foreground framing the distant view of the sea, where prows of ships rise and fall between the revolving cylinders of waves in the back pit. In front of this scene falls a great curtain painted as a hell-mouth, cut out to give a view of the boat of Charon on the waves, and behind that a painted scene of the City of Dis in flames. In an armed camp with tents as wings, a chorus of soldiers parades, and Athena appears on a chariot in the sky. The act ends with a chorus of Amazons.

The third act brings the wild forces of the universe into play, with Aeolus in his cave stirring up the dancing winds and zephyrs. Paris is glimpsed in a vessel on the sea, but of more interest are the dance of the sea nymphs, the chariots drawn by sea beasts, the chorus of sailors, and the entry of Venus reclining on a shell with her chorus of Nereids about her, and Neptune with his chorus of Tritons. Mars appears in his arsenal, and at the end of the act, in an amphitheatre of battle, Cecrops is captured by the soldiers of Mars.

The fourth act presents visions of Athena appearing in a cloud to her worshiping priests as Venus and Juno watch from fiery chariots in the air, and a series of triumphal chariots moves across on the stage: fire drawn by salamanders, the double triumph of Venus and Mars drawn by lions, and finally the great figure of Victory.

In the last act, Paris' Villa of Delight is invaded by Juno in a dark cloud and Jupiter on an eagle. There is a distant view of the palace of Mars with a tower in the center. Jupiter from his eagle strikes the tower, which, by means of a contrivance of hinges, falls in ruins. The eagle descends and gets the apple. Juno and Pallas demand it, but Venus emerges on her car from the fortress of the sky, and Jupiter, as the wise ruler, delivers the judgment and brings peace and order to the universe.

Opera had come a long way from the humanistic drama of man. The fantasy of wish fulfillment is fully released by beautifully clothed gods and goddesses sailing through the air, singing, receiving the homage of choruses and dancers. Conflict and confusion are dramatized in shifting color and spectacle, but man need have no anxiety since he has no real responsibility. The absolute monarch, the triumphant church, and the demands of duty justify suppression of private will and rebellious feelings. In the world of real terror in *Macbeth*, the witches' promise "Though his bark shall not be lost / Yet it shall be tempest-tost" is ominous. But in Baroque opera the tempest leads to a triumphant resolution.

FRENCH OPERA

In the 1670s the French developed their own composer, librettist, and designer. For a decade Lully had been composer for the court spectacles and comedie-ballets produced by Molière, but he broke with Molière and in 1672 persuaded the royal franchise to control all music-drama in Paris and to direct the Academie Royale de Musique that had been created in 1671. Lully took Quinault as his poet. Quinault had written many tragedies and tragi-comedies for the Paris stage, and he was familiar with the drama of concentrated will and conflict as developed by Corneille and with the more complex dramas of popular taste. In 1674, two years after Molière's death, Lully and Quinault secured the Palais Royal, the theatre which Richelieu had built next to his palace, and in 1680 Jean Berain, a great designer, joined forces with them. A number of Berain's designs, especially of costumes, have survived to show what charm and imaginative fancy were possible within the balanced, stately outlines of the operatic conventions.

The French opera of Quinault and Lully came more than thirty years after *The Cid* had opened a new era of "classical" drama on the Paris stage. Inevitably the new opera showed some influence of the critics' battle with the dramatists over unity of place, time, action, and tone. The complexity of Italian opera was greatly

Baroque setting in the manner of *Pomo D'Oro* apotheosis scene for *Serrio Tullio*, Munich, 1685.

Costume plates for court theatricals of Louis XIV. *Phot. Bibl. Nat. Paris.*

441

reduced; subplots were almost eliminated, buffoonery was subordinated or occasionally omitted, and the plot was made more unified. But the differences between the Italian and the French seem minor. Spectacle was of the essence, and in spite of the critical ideal of unity of place many changes of setting were used. The different "entries" of dancers in fantastic costume continued. The opera played in a public theatre (though in a royal palace building), but it kept the royal orientation, and the enclosing action must include ceremonial praise of the king and allegorical reference to his recent activities. *Thésée* (1675) began with a prologue in the gardens before the palace of Versailles. The vision of the universe as an arena of magical forces whose transformations are beyond human control had not changed: the incantation and magic sequence of scenes continued. In 1686 Quinault and Lully in *Armide* used Ariosto's story of Roland the Crusader, who fell under the spell of the eastern sorceress Armide. The character Hate, surrounded by demons, is the main motivating force. The scenes flow from palace to city square to woods to the banks of a river. Then a desert is covered by a rising cloud of mist, caves open, and terrible monsters come out. Next appears a verdant glade with trees full of fruit, which in turn changes to the enchanted palace of Armide. Demons tear down the palace and Armide flies away in a chariot.

Opera was called lyric tragedy, but no drama that gave such a large role to magic and the supernatural and such a small role to the decisions and responsibility of man could be really tragic. The French did try some tragic scenes. *Atya* (1676) has a situation similar to that of Euripides' *Bacchae*. Atya kills Sangaride while under the spell of Cybele, then discovers his crime and in horror commits suicide. But Quinault and Lully followed the death with a pastoral fête and an apotheosis.

VIII

Neoclassic Drama:
A New Form for a New Age

English Restoration theatre, London, c. 1700. *Illustration by Martha Sutherland.*

Introduction

The most important development of Baroque drama was in France. From the triumph of Corneille's *The Cid* in 1637 to the death of Molière in 1673 and the retirement of Racine in 1677, neoclassic drama, based on a reinterpretation of Greek and Roman dramatic principles, offered an alternative to opera and to the popular theatre of Alexandre Hardy at the Hôtel de Bourgogne. In the opinion of critics and most philosophers, it was far superior to either; and it brought three playwrights—Corneille, Racine, and Molière—to a peak of achievement that placed them among the greatest dramatists of world history.

The French classic drama won the acclaim of the learned world. Along with the palace of Versailles, it became the symbol of French superiority in European culture. French artistic domination of Europe was not seriously challenged until the end of the eighteenth and the beginning of the nineteenth century. To this day neoclassic drama, with a complex plot based on conflict of wills, created by Corneille and Racine, remains for the playwright one of the great models of dramatic action.

We have noticed that at the beginning of the seventeenth century Paris had at the Hôtel de Bourgogne a noisy, vulgar theatre crowd which Alexandre Hardy catered to while wishing for a more refined audience. Refinement did come, though it was some time before aristocrats were drawn to the popular theatre or a playwright was invited to the salons of courtly society.

The refinement was the result of deliberate and concerted effort on the part of a serious-minded segment of society to improve manners and morals. Three dates mark the beginning and early achievement of the movement. In 1607 was published the first volume of H. D'Urfey's *L'Astrée*, a prose romance that became the bible for those seeking a life of better manners. It was a new kind of pastoral, with shepherd-princes as heroes who spent more time in discussing how to behave properly and how to please a lady than how to win a battle. They espoused a tender love, with cajolery and banter but without sensuality.

As provincial nobles spent more time at the royal court and as administrators and clerks increased in number, larger and larger palaces were needed. In Fontainebleau, built by Francis I, in the various wings of the Louvre added by Henry IV and Louis XIII, and in Louis XIV's Versailles, the epitome of lavishness and elegance, many men and their wives and daughters must learn to live in amity. Observers noticed that, unlike Spain and Italy, where women were never seen, France had a society in which women appeared with their husbands. But even more important than occasions at court were the gatherings in the salons of Paris, where choice spirits met regularly to discuss etiquette, relationships within a refined society, and diction and literature. The second date in the development of a refined society and a refined theatre is 1613, when Mme. de Rambouillet began to hold regular receptions at the Hôtel de Rambouillet. Here for four decades gathered not just aristocrats but cultivated spirits from several walks of life: learned churchmen, grammarians, critics, poets—all intent on establishing new standards of social behavior and new artistic norms.

The third important date is 1626, when Jean Mairet presented at the Hôtel de Bourgogne a pastoral play called *Sylvie*, which became the rage of a decade. It played for weeks until the actors begged the audience to let them present some of their other plays lest they forget them. *Sylvie* went through fourteen editions, and many people could recite long passages. There are stories that even two decades after the first performance of the play, when it was no longer given regularly, provincial brides wanted it performed at their weddings.

In most aspects *Sylvie* is a conventional tragicomic pastoral, with a prince disguised as a shepherd in love with a beautiful shepherdess. Sylvie escapes the plot of her jealous shepherd-suitor, but she is put under an enchantment that can only be broken by the prince Florestan. However, there are several departures from the conventional pastoral. Gone are the bestial satyr, the coarse, bawdy poltroon, and the magician and his demons. Of the supernatural there remains only a short scene in a grotto, with lightning and thunder, when the prince breaks the magic mirror and delivers the shepherdess from enchantment. There are sensible discussions by the shepherd parents on the problems of children in love and by the royal parents and advisors on the conflict between personal choice and political duties. Besides the tender dialogue of lovers, there are witty scenes of badinage and clever retort that raise courtship to a playful level, and the shepherdess makes a game of her determination to keep some independence of mind. She is not as independent and witty as Shakespeare's Beatrice of thirty years before, and it was more than four decades before Molière and then Congreve would define fully the social role of a woman of spirit; but in a tentative way the independent woman made her appearance on the French stage.

Mairet's chief accomplishment was to bring an elite group, especially women, to the popular theatre. At last Paris had an audience that combined the taste of the court with the taste of the town. Ten years after the opening of *Sylvie*, that audience, dominated by the insistent critics who wanted plays to accord strictly with the neoclassic rules, was ready for the triumph of Corneille's *The Cid*.

446

Heroic Drama of the Will: Corneille

The great achievements of Pierre Corneille were to reassert the central position of man in the universe, recovering the humanism of the Renaissance, and to recreate a drama of human aspiration in an age of operatic spectacle. As Jupiter descended in clouds of glory in the theatre, the role of the spectator was passive: he had only to be impressed. But Corneille swept aside spectacle and magic and rejuvenated the drama of human conflict that had languished without order or power in the hands of the popular playwrights. In a time and city of exacting artistic standards, he had the genius to create a new kind of drama and raise the stage to a position of highest respect. Critics and thoughtful theatregoers were ready for rededication to the ideal, and in 1637 Corneille, a young man from Rouen who had written several ordinary comedies, created in *The Cid* a young hero who embodied that dedication.

Corneille wrote at a turning point in philosophical thought. Starting with the isolated individual, the philosopher Fénelon led the way to deliverance from solitude through God. In its less earnest way, opera did the same: there is no place for loneliness beneath a sky full of gods and goddesses and choruses of angels. But the philosopher Descartes, who developed his analysis of the passions at the same time that Corneille developed his concept of man, did not evade the problem of the solitary ego. Both Descartes and Corneille provided man with a new relationship to his passions. If man's consciousness is independent of the outside world, it is also separate from the passions and man can watch and control them. Renewing the ancient stoicism that had had many followers in the Renaissance, Descartes gave this philosophy a positive purpose. Admitting the body as well as the soul, he sought not avoidance of the passions but direction of them. Corneille found the positive side of man's emotional experience in the triumphant heroism of the will. His characters are torn by passion, but they reach a new clarity, not by suppression but by a full release of passion in a chosen direction.

The result of this view is a new concept of tragedy. Corneille rejected the tragedy of weakness and faults, designed to evoke pity. His purpose was to stir the spectator to admiration, to induce contemplation, understanding, and "compassion" that was active and dedicated to a high ideal. Corneille's Oedipus protests that we are not slaves of the imperious stars; he reasserts the rational human

447

Pierre Corneille, 1644. *Phot. Bibl. Nat. Paris.*

being. Similarly, to Descartes "admiration" was the highest of the passions, the "rational" passion. In the active will of the ego Descartes and Corneille found a new concept of freedom and necessity.

Descartes, however, denied all external certitude and rested his philosophy on individual consciousness. But Corneille's characters discover a world outside themselves that calls forth their highest idealistic endeavor. They discover that they live in a dynamic society led by a glorious king. Devotion to their country often demands sacrifice of other interests, but it is a great realization. They often find that their duties to the state are linked with old traditions: the dedication of a knight to the ideals of chivalry, of a lover to the code that will make him worthy of his love, of a Renaissance courtier to the principles of the trusted advisor and administrator of a king. In this will to fulfill the ideals of a knight and prince, Corneille's hero brought into the modern world the humanist tradition. Corneille gave a vivid image of a universe of ideals at just the moment when Europe was ready for it.

The year 1637 was a critical moment in the European theatre. The drama that had flourished so vigorously at the turn of the century was languishing. This was the year when Venetian opera began, bidding fair to inundate the spoken drama of humanism. Ben Jonson and Lope de Vega had died in 1633. The London theatres, which were playing to a small circle of court followers, would be closed by Parliament in 1642, not to be reopened until 1660. In Paris, Hardy had died in 1631 or 1632, and the drama of adventure which he had popularized no longer pleased the Paris audience. More sensitive people looked not to the drama but to the prose romances of Madame de Scudery and other writers of fiction for an expression of their ideals. Corneille's rediscovery of tragedy and his redefinition of man in terms of conflict, struggle, and choice answered a deeply felt need.

In an age of absolute monarchy, when local lords and squires must give up their independence and submit to the discipline of a central royal court, Corneille made the drama the chief expression of the conflict between personal desire and the necessity to conform to a social pattern.

The Cid is in some ways a hero of medieval romance. He is in love, and he conquers the invading Moors almost singlehandedly. But the real involvement of Don Rodrigue is not battles or even duels to avenge his father, but his relationship with Chimène, the woman he loves. She is outraged when he kills her father, but she loves him, and, what is just as important for the audience, she has great admiration and respect for him. Her conflict is not a struggle against fate or enemies or evil but for a new integration in her own soul. Corneille has internalized the drama. When the world conqueror comes home from battle, he finds that his greatest battle is before him; his final achievement is to conquer himself.

449

PSYCHOLOGICAL TRIUMPH IN CORNEILLE

Corneille created a great psychological drama. It is hard in the twentieth century to realize the fresh impact of that drama in its day. The debates between the claims of love and duty, of love and honor, of love and country, the concern over "my glory," "my honor," "my renown" may seem mechanical. Many readers and theatregoers find little to which they can respond in a seventeenth-century play in which a hero kills his sweetheart's father for his honor's sake or a hero is glad that his enemy is his beloved brother-in-law because there is more virtue and renown in sacrificing what one loves for one's country than in killing an unknown enemy. But once they penetrate the shell of the heroic characters of Corneille, they can respond to a drama that seeks a solution for psychological conflict in dedication to a higher cause.

The psychological drama of Corneille does not offer suppression or denial. It differs radically from the Puritan view, which denied value to love or other impulses that might interfere with duty. Corneille's heroes never take for granted the values they have to consider when some new situation comes on them. Don Rodrigue in *The Cid*, happily engaged to Chimène, is suddenly asked by his aged father to avenge the family honor by fighting Chimène's father. He is swept into the chivalric code of an older generation, a code he had not chosen. His father thinks love is worth nothing in comparison with the family honor. No cold-blooded, single-minded man like his father, Rodrigue knows it is just as infamous to betray his love as to abandon his father. With passionate thoroughness he brings both sides to light and debates with himself. When he concludes that the family honor is his concern, he takes on the higher duty, knowing that it means the loss of Chimène.

Neither this nor any other play of Corneille is a sad, romantic play of self-sacrifice like the Japanese Kabuki dramas, where killing one's love or oneself is a noble exit from an impossible situation. Corneille's heroes work their way through a higher synthesis. And in *The Cid* Chimène also experiences psychological conflict and finds her own solution. Where Rodrigue's conflict expressed the determination of seventeenth-century man to direct the passions to a higher cause, Chimène's conflict expressed his resentment at being overwhelmed by authority. Submission to the absolute monarchy meant giving up a great deal of private liberty, and although there were glorious advantages, many a man doubtless felt resentment. At the time *The Cid* was produced the queen of France was watching her husband at war with her father, the king of Spain, and it is said that her secretary suggested the subject of the play to Corneille. Chimène has mixed emotions. Her father has been killed, and a champion must fight Rodrigue to release her hatred. But she also loves Rodrigue, and when he comes back from battle covered with

450

new glory she admires him still more. Just before the duel she confides to him that she wants him to win her, showing that she had made the choice herself. At the end the king suggests that she wait a year before marrying Rodrigue. A triumphant monarch can afford to be gentle and to encourage his subjects to take time to turn resentment to reason. The drama recognizes that one can adjust oneself to a conqueror if the conqueror is admirable and lovable. But a residue of resentment must be expressed in some symbolic act.

For contrast, Corneille alternates the scenes of Rodrigue and Chimène with the plaints of the Infanta to her confidante. The Infanta is hopelessly in love with Rodrigue but must not marry outside the royal family. By suppression of desire, she can perform the higher duty. But there is no suppression for Rodrigue. In each episode he reaches a new understanding of himself. In the end, when he is sure of Chimène's love, all is clarified, and hatred and revenge have been expiated on both sides. By his high ideals Rodrigue has won the love and admiration of both his lady and his king. His glory is complete.

Resentment of a difficult choice made for one's country is stronger in *Horace* (1640), where again the conflict is within the family. When Rome is at war with its close neighbor Alba, Horace and his two brothers must fight the three Curiace brothers in a test combat, though Horace is married to their sister, and one of the brothers Curiace is engaged to Horace's sister. In varying degrees the men revel in the glorious privilege of putting their countries above private ties. But the case is more difficult for the women. When her brother has killed her fiancé and his brothers, Camille cannot restrain her hatred, and she denounces Horace and Rome. Horace pursues her offstage and stabs her. Undoubtedly the audience had gloried in her expression of resentment, but such resentment must never prevail. In the last act Corneille brings in a wise king of Rome to be the judge at a trial. All sides are considered, and while Horace's life is spared because he has served Rome well and because his motivation for the killing came from love of country, it is made clear that he had been too cruel. The drama of Corneille deals with tremendous emotions, but it brings them to the understanding of the conscious mind and subjects them to reason. Out of confusion and conflict comes a new synthesis.

In *Cinna* (1641), Corneille traces in detail the steps by which mutinous hatred is overcome by the generosity of the monarch. The Emperor Augustus, a new absolute monarch, seems a tyrant to Cinna, the grandson of Pompey, and is especially hated by Emilie, who wants to destroy him to avenge an old injustice to her father. Cinna and Maxime are both in love with Emilie and both are plotting the death of the emperor. But when Augustus openly asks their advice in deciding whether to rule as a monarch or to restore the republic, and entrusts them with new responsibilities, Cinna is won over. When Emilie is still implacable, he declares that he will fulfill his oath to her and kill the emperor but that he will then kill himself since she is a greater tyrant than Augustus. Jealous of Cinna, Maxime plans to take Emilie away, but his confidant betrays them to the emperor. All confess and expect death, but Augustus forgives them. They are now ready to give up resentments inherited from their fathers, for they have discovered that the emperor is not a tyrant and that there is a greater glory and honor in serving him than in clinging to old hatreds. Corneille could assure his generation that authority can be loving and generous, completely devoted to the welfare of the subjects. He gave full expression to the resentment that was inevitable in the establishment of authority, but he offered a symbolic exorcism of the resentment and a new dedication of the personality to the public good.

Polyeucte (1642) gives an even fuller picture of the generosity that results from high ideals. When Polyeucte, the Armenian leader, is converted to Christianity and about to be put to death for his heresy, he generously urges his wife to turn to his rival, and both his rival and his wife plead for his life. The three vie with one another in magnanimity. Again the large gestures and pompous speeches may seem too inflated. Like St. Peter's in Rome and the Baroque churches of Italy and the Spanish countries, they take a little getting used to. But behind the large scale of Corneille's heroic characters is the yearning of a great age for a new integration of the personality.

The four great plays of Corneille are variations of one theme: the reconstruction of a torn personality by appeal to long-enduring values. In *The Cid* it is the chivalric duty of a knight to fight for his father and his king. In *Horace* (1640) love of country must be put above love of family, even at the risk of destroying some of the family. In *Cinna* the political ideals of a generous ruler win the loyalty of those who were outraged by the process of his coming to rule. In *Polyeucte* religion activates a full realization of the higher humanity, even in the face of martyrdom. Two of the plays bring one important character to death, but not the other two, and in all there is a glorious fulfillment. Corneille at first called *The Cid* a tragicomedy, but he later spoke of it as a tragedy. In no sense are these plays of defeat. Yet in their dignity and the moral reassessment of the characters they are tragedies.

A bourgeois of Rouen, Corneille wrote of kings, emperors, and magnificent heroes for a Paris audience that was oriented toward the court, and he put his heroes in the elaborate court version of "Roman" costumes. But his plays are not as aristocratic as they seem at first. In the sixteenth and seventeenth centuries the bourgeois merchant thought of himself as aspiring to nobility. But nobility of rank was but a symbol of nobility of character. The characters of Corneille have the moral integrity that has always appealed to citizens of moderate means and that has meant the stability of Western civilization. The integrity may become complacency, the enemy of individualism or change. But Corneille did not support complacency. His characters win their moral certainty only after the most painful reappraisal of old conventions, and in the final synthesis they see clearly why they were wrong. They never resort to hypocrisy, and eventually they bring their private conflicts before public authorities. In the long run they trust their king, their law, their country, their fellow man and integrate their private aspirations with the ideals of the society in which they live. They are successful men and Corneille's plays have happy endings. Since the bourgeoisie emerged into self-conscious importance in the Gothic cities of the fourteenth and fifteenth centuries, they have been successful and have believed in success. They have thought it possible to combine religious idealism with active participation in the work of the world. They have believed in action and in happy endings. After their reassessments, Corneille's heroes have energy and will for new accomplishment.

But Corneille's plays are great tragedies, whereas much literature directed to the middle class is shallow. Either the characters are too good and solve their problems in a conventional way, as in sentimental comedy, or the dangers and conflict are external, as in melodrama. Corneille's characters face the tragic conflict between man's impulses and his ideals. They undergo the pain of growth from adolescence to maturity and emerge from neurotic evasion to adult responsibility.

CORNEILLE'S COMPACT DRAMATIC FORM

Corneille created a new form for drama, of which Ibsen's dramas and other well-made plays are direct descendants. Renaissance critics had talked about unity and a classic form and had complained of the episodic religious folk plays and of the complex popular dramas of London, Paris, and Madrid.

The neoclassic critics called for plays that observed the unities of action, place, and time, providing a simple, uncluttered line of action involving the personal relationships of a very few characters, a single location, and a limited period of time, ideally no more than twenty-four hours. Subplots and public ceremonies and spectacle of all kinds were to be eliminated. Such dramas were completely unlike the plays of the great dramatists of the Renaissance in England and Spain, the melodramas in public theatres such as the Hôtel de Bourgogne, and of course the scripts of operas. A few classicists had tried to write imitations of the ancients. It remained for a genius to sift the same material the popular stage was using and give it form.

The nature of that form appears when we compare *The Cid* with its source, *Las Mocedades del Cid*, a play of considerable dramatic power that had been compacted from the legends about the famous Spanish leader who defeated the Moors. It shows the injured father testing his three sons in turn by twisting their hands before he tells the most fiery one, the Cid, that he must fight to avenge the family honor. The Cid stops on his way to battle to share food with a leper and has a vision of Saint Lazarus. The scenes of battle are enacted, and for further excitement bloody handkerchiefs and the head of an enemy are brought on stage.

Corneille not only reduced the cast and eliminated some episodes but shifted

the emphasis from outer story to inner conflict. Yet compact as it is, *The Cid* is not
the ultimate in compression, and the stricter critics of Corneille's time, demanding classical unity, were not fully satisfied with it. Corneille himself recognized
that, although the scenes of the Infanta presented a variant of the theme of the
conflict of love and duty, they were not completely integrated with the main action. In the scenes of the king receiving the Cid after the battle there were a few
attendants and some spectacle—superfluous elements by strict classical standards.
Later plays of Corneille and the plays of Racine included no such ceremonial
scenes. The French neo-classic drama was not to be concerned with the public
activities of the king but only with his private relationships. There was no processional entrance of the court; the king never sat on a throne to receive ambassadors or announce public decisions. The scene was never a throne room but a
private anteroom.

In the process of simplification and concentration, all the court attendants were
abstracted into the rather impersonal "confidant." The confidant was not always
merely a listener. Nero's tutor in Racine's *Britannicus* opposes his crime, and in
Cinna the confidant exposes the conspiracy. Sometimes two confidants get together and may even become spies. But if a confidant betrays the major character
he is paired with, he must die, by his own hand if no one else is ready to kill him.

The confidant served a very useful purpose. He did not prevent soliloquy, for
he could be forgotten when he was not needed. But he was an aid to ease and
suppleness in a style tending to the too formal and grandiose. He was a kind of
alter ego, to listen and question. He could punctuate the major character's remarks
by interjections and now soften the emotions, now stir them to a higher pitch.
Newton and Descartes and the other scientists and philosophers of the seventeenth century sought laws that were public, universal, and clear to all. Corneille
sought psychological conclusions that were public, lasting, and equally valid for
all thinking men. The confidant was the symbol of the listening world that must
ultimately be satisfied with the hero's choice of values. Finally, he was a technical aid on a stage that had little furniture and no steps or platforms, for he had
knees, shoulders, arms, and hands that the more important character could grasp.
He was, and in modern plays of the classic form still is, a very convenient three-
dimensional object to give the actor resistance and definition of space.

THE SIMPLE STAGE OF HEROIC HUMANISM

The new concentrated drama required a unified stage that was simple and dignified. The critics were just as impatient with the half-medieval setting of five mansions strung together on one stage as they were with the half-medieval drama of
many episodes, violent action, and tonal contrasts.

Fortunately we have the notes and sketches of Mahelot, the stage manager of the Hôtel de Bourgogne, for this decade when the transition was made from the old simultaneous setting to one organized and unified by Italian perspective. A crowded stage would have made it difficult for the audience to remember what mansion the actor had come out of or where he was supposed to be, and thus the introduction of perspective lines brings all the mansions into unity. The Italian theatre had already provided two examples of new possibilities: the solid, three-dimensional street scene of Serlio and the flat, painted scenes of the opera. The French evolved a simple setting that shows the influence of the two Italian stages and their own simultaneous stage.

In *The Cid* Corneille still used the simultaneous setting. From some of the comments of critics of Corneille's time it is hard to tell whether they are objecting to the form of the play or to the form of the stage. In his later plays Corneille settled on a simple unified stage with classic columns.

The new type of unified setting evolved by Mahelot at the Hôtel de Bourgogne and by Corneille and his friends at the Marais Theatre eliminated separate mansions. The stage became one place, and although the setting was important for style and dignity it was no longer important for identification of place. In bringing the theatre back to a drama of humanism, Corneille went to the opposite extreme from the gaudy scenes of opera and eliminated all spectacular effect. The plays he wrote before *The Cid* had been planned for particular settings, but after *The Cid* the heroic characters were almost completely abstracted from any setting. This does

Setting by Mahelot for *La Cornelie* by Alexandre Hardy, 1634. *Phot. Bibl. Nat. Paris.*

455

not mean, however, that Corneille can be produced on a modern space stage with black curtains and shifting shafts of light. Although his characters never use the setting, it is very much there. Its classic columns lift the action into the world of the Golden Age of the ancients. The columns may be merely painted on one or two wings at each side and on a flat cloth backdrop, but the simple, dignified design unifies the play with an image of a complete world of public order. Here are no frivolous Rococo ornamentations; these men and women are battling for their souls. Here are no charming branches of trees that were to soften the architecture of the eighteenth-century stage; these heroes must work out their salvation on an austere human plane. Here are no glamorous clouds to bring help from heaven, no dark magician's cave to ease man of the responsibility for facing his own suffering. Man is not completely alone, but he must come to terms with the long tradition of humanistic values that started with the Greeks. On the stage are the two images of that reconciliation: the one or two actors dressed in idealized "antique" costumes, and surrounding them the never-changing columns and cornices of an idealized classic architecture.

Corneille's genius was acknowledged even by Jean Racine, the dramatist who was thirty-three years younger and who became his bitter rival. Corneille continued to write plays after the fifteen-year period of his important tragedies, but they were less successful than the great tragedies of Racine, whose career reached its height in the 1660s and 1670s as Corneille's powers declined. Speaking at the Academie François, Racine gave perceptive and generous praise to his great precursor:

In what state was the French stage when Corneille began to work? It was art without order, regularity, taste, morals, characters or any perception of true dramatic beauty. Most of its subjects were extravagant enough to be destitute of all probability: its language depended for effect upon miserable quibbling. Every rule of art, of self respect and decency was constantly neglected. Corneille after endeavoring for some time to strike into a higher path was impelled by an exceptional genius to bring *reason* upon the scene—reason accompanied by all the majesty and embellishment of which our language is susceptible, and combined the semblance of truth with the marvelous. . . . How noble his subjects, how energetic his pictures of passion, how grave his sentiments, how dignified and varied his characters . . . he could yet descend at will to the most simple naïveté of comedy, where he was likewise inimitable.

Jean Racine: Baroque and Anti-Baroque

Jean Racine and Pierre Corneille are often lumped together as writers of tragedies in the neoclassic form. Yet there are great differences. Corneille created the classic form and Racine perfected it, and where Corneille used complicated plots and simple psychology, Racine simplified the plots and complicated the psychology. While Corneille typified Baroque impulses, Racine shows a mixture of the Baroque and the anti-Baroque. He illuminates the characteristics of the Baroque partly by contrast. The plays of Corneille seem full of energy and tumult, even though violent action is offstage, ready to break out of the compact form forced on the material by the author. Racine, on the contrary, seems in perfect control. More important, he does not create characters like Corneille's who choose and triumph, but rather characters who cannot support their choices with the will and fail miserably and suffer greatly.

Early orphaned, Racine grew up with his grandparents in Port Royal, a center and refuge for the Jansenists, a puritanical religious group within the Roman Catholic Church who turned away from the commerce of the cities, the splendor of the royal court, and the pomp of the Church. Following ideas of St. Augustine, the Jansenists believed that man's will was so corrupt that only by the extraordinary grace of God might a few people be saved from damnation. Many people moved to Port Royal to live a monastic life, others to lead a quiet family life. Many others, while remaining in the active world, kept contact with this center of anti-Baroque feeling. Although the Jansenists stayed within the Roman Church, they incurred the suspicion and hostility of bishop and king, and of course the opposition of the Jesuits, who took a very active part in the world in order to direct and control it. Where the Jesuits emphasized Latin literature, Jansenist teachers gave Racine a thorough grounding in Greek, including the tragedies. But the stage, of course, was too sinful to be thought of. Though the nobles and even the bishops might enjoy the theatre, and the king have the players perform in the palace, the Church did not permit actors or other vagabonds to take communion. How then account for the action of young Racine in defying the Jansenists, moving to Paris, making a reputation at court, working with theatre people, living with glamorous actresses, and devoting a decade and a half to writing for the stage? This spanning of the two extremes creates an ambiguity and offers an interesting problem in psychobiography.

457

Frontispiece to the collected works of Jean Racine, Amsterdam, 1743.

Racine arrived in Paris early in the 1660s, when royal majesty was at its most spectacular. Palace life was ceremonial, elegant, passed in splendid surroundings. Women were gorgeously clad, and men's costumes were elaborate, with wigs, petticoat breeches, lace, ribbons and bows. Racine's charm and his poems praising the king won him access to the court and attention and favor from young Louis XIV. Molière, who was nineteen years older, produced Racine's first heroic play, *La Thébaïde* (1664), at the Palais Royal, but Molière's company was better in the more realistic style of comedy than in the grand style of tragedy, and Racine gave his next play, *Alexandre le Grand* (1665), to the rival company at the Hôtel de Bourgogne. Further, he lured Mlle. du Parc from Molière's company to play his leads and become his mistress. The Jansenist as a person was indeed transformed.

Comparison with John Milton throws light on Racine and the Baroque age. In relation to the Baroque/anti-Baroque division (in England, Cavalier/Puritan), both Racine and Milton changed sides, or bridged the chasm, as each moved from one extreme a long way toward the other. Milton was more than thirty years older than Racine, but *Paradise Lost* was published and *Andromaque* was produced in the same year, 1667. While Racine left the puritanical austerity of Port Royal to join the pleasures of the court and town, Milton moved in the opposite direction, from the world of the Cavaliers to that of the Puritans. He grew up in a house of aristocratic leisure, devoted to music and poetry, enjoying the theatre, writing delicate, sensuous poetry. Though it was for a modest occasion, he wrote a masque to glorify an aristocrat. He spent months in Italy in 1637–38, the year of the great rage for opera, and he dreamed of writing an opera himself. When the Civil War broke out in England, Milton found himself involved in the battle of ideas, writing pamphlets and essays against tyranny on any side. While he defended those who beheaded Charles I, he wrote one of the great defenses of freedom of the press. When the Puritan Commonwealth was set up, Milton became Cromwell's Secretary of State. After the collapse of the Puritan cause and the restoration of Charles II in 1660, he found himself isolated by politics and blindness and turned to his great epic, *Paradise Lost*.

Both Milton and Racine took forms of verse that were nearly a hundred years old and patterns of epic and tragedy more than two thousand years old and polished them to the highest degree of perfection. Since both men were first-rate poets, they left a very impressive legacy. Tragedies about man's corruption and damnation may never be favorites with modern playgoers and readers, yet, as Eugene O'Neill and Tennessee Williams show, dramatic studies in the self-destructive psychology of those who feel godforsaken can have more meaning for the twentieth century than the cosmic completeness of *Paradise Lost* in Milton's vast arena of conflict. Racine is one of the world's masters of vivid studies of the contentions of godforsaken characters.

Racine's first great success, *Andromaque* (1667), was recognized immediately as a first-rate play, but also as a very disturbing one. It is not about the cost of choos-

459

ing the nobler of two loyalties. The emotions of the four tortured characters in this play are not noble. Andromaque, the widow of Hector, so dignified in her grief in Euripides' *The Trojan Women*, is here faced with a choice of letting the Greeks kill her small son Astyanax or marrying King Pyrrhus, her captor, and thereby violating the memory of Hector. But instead of choosing, she tries a trick, agreeing to marry Pyrrhus and expecting to kill herself after the ceremony. Pyrrhus only half believes her offer, however, and Hermione, daughter of Helen and Menelaus, reacts violently. She has been waiting almost a year, engaged to King Pyrrhus but seething with anger and hurt pride as he keeps postponing the wedding, hoping to win Andromaque. The circle of hopeless loves is completed by Orestes, who is in love with Hermoine.

When Hermione learns that Pyrrhus repudiates her, her rage knows no bounds. She persuades Orestes that he must show his love for her by killing Pyrrhus, but when he reports to her that his men have committed the murder, she turns on him her full fury: he should have done what she really wanted, not what she said; he should have saved her from herself. Orestes goes mad. The play ends with news that Andromaque has been welcomed as queen, with no more worry over losing

Setting for *Andromaque*, Hôtel de Bourgogne, 1667. *Illustration by Martha Sutherland.*

her son or violating her loyalty to Hector. The tragedy is not the cost of the higher choice but the cost of a degrading passion.

With four major acting roles, the play has held the stage for more than three centuries. Here are no tongue-tied, stumbling persons but articulate kings, queens, and princes. They analyze their feelings to the tiniest nuance. They think they are motivated by noble passions, but Racine shows that their passions are riddled with petty jealousies, resentment, cruelty, shame, humiliation, and hurt pride. Love is mixed with hate and never persuades the loved one. Destructive passion that cannot be controlled is the fate of human nature in its depraved condition since the fall of Adam. Love is not a joy or a blessing but a shameful madness that tortures and destroys.

Yet these violent emotions are expressed in the most carefully controlled verse. No writer has achieved more clarity of expression. The speeches, episodes, acts, the details of character, the turns of plot, all are given form in the most meticulously calculated proportions. The four characters form a circle as each is pulled two ways, and any move by one will break the unendurable static tension.

The struggle of youth to gain freedom from dominating parents, the central theme of classical comedy from Plautus and Terence to Molière, is given a tragic treatment in Racine's *Britannicus* (1669), where the young emperor Nero is determined to establish his independence from his mother, Agrippina. Racine presents Nero as a monster but gives him a great deal of provocation. His mother will never let him forget that he owes his position as emperor to her. She consorts with his enemies and is so pleased with the budding love of Nero's attractive half-brother Britannicus and the shy girl Junie that Nero fears that she might manipulate him out of his position and make Britannicus emperor. Nero has had Junie abducted and tries to win her himself, but she cannot be won by force. Nero's frustration turns to violent resentment. Pretending to invite Britannicus to a love-feast of reconciliation, he has him poisoned. Junie escapes by becoming a Vestal Virgin, and Agrippina, knowing that she will be the next to be killed, has the melodramatic satisfaction of telling Nero the future she sees for him: one bloody crime leading to another, a course that can only end in self-destruction and the reputation for being a model for all bloody tyrants.

Berenice (1670) is the one play of Racine's that follows Corneille's favorite pattern: the choice of a higher duty at the expense of love and happiness. When his father, the emperor Vespasian, dies, Titus hurries back to Rome from the Near East bringing with him Berenice, Queen of Palestine, whom he expects to marry. But when he realizes that Roman laws and the Roman people will never accept as empress a woman who is both a foreigner and a queen (so strong are the memories of wicked kings and queens who had to be driven out before Rome could become a republic), he gives up his love and sends Berenice home. It is a simple story that could be dealt with in one episode, but Racine adds psychological complication by making Titus so tender-hearted that he cannot face Berenice himself, and

461

Berenice so ardent that she will not believe it when someone else tells her she must leave. Racine completes his complex of relationships by adding a third person to be buffeted by the other two. This is Antiochus, King of Comagene, who has been in love with Berenice for some time, though he has never told either her or Titus of his love. When, on behalf of Titus, he tells Berenice that she must leave, she believes that he is lying for his own advantage and turns on him a violence of anger she would not have shown Titus himself. Racine's tragic characters will never accept compromise or second best. She finally faces the inevitable, and the three separate forever and go their own ways. There is no death in the play, and in his Preface, Racine cites the example of the Greeks, who felt that death was not absolutely necessary in a tragedy. Racine wrote, "It is enough that the action be grand, the actors be heroic, and the passions stirred, and all work together to create that majestic sadness that constitutes the pleasure of the tragedy."

Racine's *Iphigenie* (1674) was the most popular of his plays in the eighteenth and nineteenth centuries. It is based on Euripides' posthumous play, *Iphigenia in Aulis*, but there are some striking differences. Racine despised Euripides' ending: the goddess coming down in a cloud machine to spirit away the girl about to be sacrificed to ensure favorable winds for the expedition to Troy, and when the cloud is lifted a hind lies on the altar, as a substitute for the human sacrifice. Racine's last-minute rescue is achieved by an added character called Erephile, a mysterious, ill-starred girl who does not know who she is, but only that she will find out at the peril of her life. She was brought as a captive by Achilles, with whom she is hopelessly in love. The procession to the altar that seemed intended for the wedding of Iphigenie to Achilles turns out to be a procession for the sacrifice of Iphigenie. Then the priest reveals that Erephile is the daughter of Helen and Theseus and that her real name is Iphigenie. Erephile stabs herself at the altar, thus sacrificing as "Iphigenie," leaving the other (the real?) Iphigenie to marry Achilles and live happily ever after. Is this ending an evasion of tragic responsibility? Is Erephile the central tragic character who will not accept a world of compromise? Or, looking at the play from our distance, shall we say that the self-destruction of one neurotic loner was a small price to pay for the rescue of the family life of Agamemnon and Clytemnestra (or was that such a happy family life?), and an ironic, cheering send-off of the boys setting out for a glorious plunder of Troy? How ironic was Racine?

There is no question of irony about *Phèdre* (1677), the last play Racine wrote for the professional theatre and his greatest. The tragic values are completely integrated with the action, and the complex, destructive emotions are given the fullest expression. Phèdre sees with the utmost clarity what she is doing and how vile she is, yet she cannot help herself.

Phèdre is closely based on *Hippolytus* by Euripides, with a few important differences. Euripides' Hippolytus is devoted to Diana, goddess of chastity and the hunt. Like an athlete who will not break training for sex, he neglects the altar of

Venus. To make sure that his masculinity is unquestionable, Racine gives him a sweetheart, Aricie. This relationship adds an interesting complexity to Phèdre's emotions. It is shameful to be rejected by her stepson when she confesses her uncontrollable love for him, but when she finds that he has a secret sweetheart, she is enraged: it seems that he can love anybody but her. Chagrin, jealousy, hurt pride, all the petty emotions, are added to the basic passions: love, shame, and fear.

Like Hamlet in English-speaking countries, Phèdre has been the top acting role in French theatre. A complex, varied, and subtle role, its range is never exhausted. It was first created by La Champanesle, Racine's mistress. According to report, Racine, who was an excellent reader, taught her the declamation verse by verse. She was especially good in the scenes when Phèdre is sick and world-weary. The great eighteenth-century actress Clairon wrote an analysis of the part as she prepared it. In the scenes of remorse she worked for simple diction, noble and sweet, the voice filled with tears, but in the scenes of love, for a kind of drunken delirium, as though a sleepwalker were trying to wake from the fire that consumes her. The two great French actresses of the nineteenth century made Phèdre one of their most successful roles. In 1843 Rachel changed the course of theatre history by reestablishing classic acting after more than a decade of romantic furor. In 1873 Sarah Bernhardt, a small, red-headed, fiery actress made an unforgettable impression in the part and continued to play it for years. Percy Fitzgerald, writing in 1881, described the impact of Bernhardt's Phèdre in London. He tells how the English were amazed and delighted that a small creature with a boyish head could have such passion.

She approached the Hippolytus of Mornet-Sully with an irresistible seductiveness, to win him and wind him in her spell. Then with a recoil of horror, abrupt and magnificent, appeared to loathe herself and wish the very earth to open, [was] again drawn to him pleading, until the final burst of almost fiendish despair, when with the frantic madness of a wild animal she clutched and tore at his sword to end her life. Literally spent and inanimate, she was borne off by her attendants . . . the listeners were aghast and swept away.

In the last act, Bernhardt's Phèdre, already near death, declaimed her confession on a single note in a dry voice, biting each syllable in a steady pounding rhythm, to terrific effect.

RACINE'S RELIGIOUS PLAYS

After *Phèdre* Racine left the theatre as suddenly as he had come into it. He had provocation: a claque who hated him saw to it that *Phèdre* was a failure. But there was more than that: he experienced a kind of religious crisis. He made peace with Port Royal and the Jansenists and married a pious girl who never read one of his plays. But he stayed in Paris working for the king as historiographer. He even worked on the libretto of an opera, that extreme Baroque form that seemed to the Jansenists worse than the sinful theatre. The king also had a religious conversion, abandoning his frivolous mistress and taking on the pious Madame de Maintenon. It was she who persuaded Racine to write two religious plays for the girls' school she sponsored at St. Cyr, near Versailles. He chose the stories of Esther and Athalie from the Old Testament, and, copying the Greeks, wrote choruses that could be sung by the schoolgirls.

Athalie (1691), the second and last religious play, though it shows the providential interference of God, gives almost as desolate a picture of the human condition as the tragedies. As in a fairy story, a guardian priest brings the true prince out of hiding to rally the people and destroy the wicked queen. But Racine created so complex a queen, haunted by dreams and touched by pity and longing for the unknown prince, that it has been one of the great roles for star actresses. The palace revolution is not a great success, since neither the priest nor the prince will be much better in ruling than the queen, but the prince, as a descendant of David, will be an ancestor of Christ, hence outside of this wicked world. Some day in the distant future will come the Messiah.

Racine creates complex, passionate characters. He shows the mixed hate-love that develops between father and son (*Phèdre*) and the jealous resentment between brothers (*La Thébaïde*). He gives an appealing picture of the asymmetry of love. Love is rarely requited, and when it is it has no chance in competition with other relationships.

It is possible to see the unhappy characters as reflections of the ambiguity of Racine's relation to Jansenism on the one hand and to the court on the other. One critic sees Racine's entire work as a progressive revelation of the wilfulness, vanity, cruelty, and futility of court life. Another thinks that in *Andromaque* and *Britannicus* consciousness of the court is at the center of the play, whereas in the later plays the court becomes less and less central while the tragic character moves more toward the center. With *Phèdre*, the critic thinks, this process has been completed. Then the long silence that followed, with Racine once more allied to the pious Jansenists, is natural: with *Phèdre* he had achieved both his personal liberation and the most perfect expression of his tragic vision. Yet in his last plays, activated by religion, the principal character is still a passionate, complex being, of shifting moods and uncertain will.

464

The Comedy of Enlightenment

One great achievement of the seventeenth century was the creation of a comedy of enlightenment, which is commonly called high comedy or comedy of manners. Terence gave a glimpse of the possibilities of this sophisticated drama to a few aristocrats in ancient Rome, and his influence on the Baroque age was great. Some of Shakespeare's plays gave promise of a new comedy of wit. Ben Jonson expressed the zest of disillusionment that was necessary for the new comedy, but satire dominated his plays. For comedy both detached and committed, both critical and accepting, the world had to wait for Molière and the English Restoration drama of the 1660s.

High comedy, or the comedy of enlightenment, seems at first glance a comedy of rejection, mainly concerned with ridiculing the limitations, obsessions, and petty commitments that impede the free individual. Yet it is in fact a comedy of affirmation.

Donatus, Bishop of Carthage in the fourth century, in a Latin comment on Terence that became a standard text in humanist teaching, defined comedy as "a story of various habits and customs of public and private affairs, from which one may learn what is of use in life and what must be avoided." "From which one may learn" is the key phrase for the comedy of enlightenment. The central concern of the characters in the plays (and presumably of the audience as well) was learning to get along with oneself and with other people. Comedy became an institution for human education. Voltaire was right when he said that Molière "founded among the French the school for civil life." It is no accident that several high comedies bear the name of school: *School for Husbands, School for Wives, School for Scandal*, etc.

The source of the comedy of enlightenment is in the humanistic education of the Renaissance. To be sophisticated is to know oneself and other people, to know the way of the world. Tight moralists, whether medieval, Puritan, or Victorian, know what is wicked and base their philosophy on avoiding contact with danger and keeping from their children the knowledge of evil. But the humanist believed that the best way to meet danger was to know something about it and that the best way to learn was vicariously—through literature and the theatre. Hence Roman comedy held a central place in humanist education. Terence had been central in monastic education throughout the Middle Ages because his conversational style was considered the finest model for Latin, but many churchmen deplored his worldly subject matter. To the humanists, however, the subject matter was useful. *The Governor*, by the English humanist and schoolmaster Thomas Eliot, defends comedy against the Puritans in these terms:

> First, comedies, which they suppose to be a doctrinal of ribaldry, they be undoubtedly a picture, or as it were a mirror of man's life, wherein evil is not taught but discovered, to the intent that men beholding the promptness of youth unto vice, the snares of harlots and bawds laid for young minds, the deceit of servants, the changes of fortune contrary to men's expectations, they being thereof warned may prepare themselves to resist or prevent occasion.

Learning, education, the formation of an ideal personality, became the central interest of sixteenth-century literature. Edmund Spencer's *Faerie Queene* (1590), like John Lyly's *Euphues* (1579) and Philip Sidney's sonnets, is a study in the development of an ideal gentleman. Alongside these serious works, a few English comedies showed a process of learning. Katherine is educated in a rough way in *The Taming of the Shrew*, and in *Love's Labour's Lost* four women educate four men. Comedy is one part of Prince Hal's education in *Henry IV* and *Henry V*. But in the sixteenth century education was regarded as primarily the experience of a prince or knight in the midst of great struggles and affairs of state. When in the seventeenth century self-development and the art of living became ends in themselves, modern comedy of learning flourished.

The basic assumptions of the high comedy of enlightenment are two interrelated developments in human thought: a new skepticism and the idea of plurality and complexity.

A new skepticism was implied in the shift from a religious orientation in the Middle Ages to a secular orientation in the Renaissance. Humanistic education, with the use of non-Christian classical literature and the concern with practical government and public activities, encouraged detachment from old ways of thinking. Self-knowledge and the ability to enjoy love as a game—both essential to high comedy—were possible after a century and a half of skeptical speculation. The high comedy of the seventeenth century is comparable to the serene skepticism of Montaigne. In the midst of civil and religious wars at the end of the sixteenth century, he refused to lose his composure. He would not join those people who cried out that the world was near dissolution and the Day of Judgment was at hand, but considered that many worse things had been seen in other ages and that at that very time people were merry in a thousand other parts of the earth. He cheerfully accepted complexity.

In the fifteenth century Boiardo and Ariosto had shown how to deal with complexity in a non-tragic way. They could not treat the loves and tournaments and battles of the court of Charlemagne with the absorption of a romancer of the

Middle Ages but used the material with playful grace, smiling as they wrote. The result was burlesque. A little later, Rabelais in France produced an even more topsy-turvy mixture of classic, romantic, and realistic material, burlesquing pedantry and scholarship. Burlesque came more slowly in the mass art of the theatre. The first full-length English dramatic burlesque, *The Knight of the Burning Pestle*, came in 1607.

The 1660s saw the dawn of toleration after a century and a half of religious turmoil. France had been torn by war in the 1560s and had seen the horrible massacre of Protestants on St. Bartholomew's Day in 1572. Henry of Navarre was able to establish a balance of opposed factions under a strong central government. But the rest of Europe was plunged into the Thirty Years' War that ended in exhaustion in 1648. In England in the 1640s civil war destroyed the monarchy. Presbyterians hoped to control the government and force everyone into their Church. But Anabaptists, Levelers, and other Protestant sects banded together to prevent uniformity. Laws of toleration were placed on the books in the 1650s. By 1660 too many people had grown weary of Puritan rigidity, and the monarchy was restored. Under a sophisticated and tolerant king, the English might solve complexity by the peaceful and sometimes comic adjustment of human relations—the subject matter of the comedy of enlightenment.

Shakespeare's half-high comedy of the late sixteenth century took a long step toward liberation of the mind and of the individual; Molière in his plays of the 1660s presented that liberation, especially in women, much more fully; and English Restoration comedy in the last four decades of the seventeenth century reached a peak of liberation to become high comedy.

SHAKESPEARE'S HALF-HIGH COMEDY

In bringing romantic comedy to its highest perfection, Shakespeare almost invented high comedy. The central figures of the genre, as Etherege and Congreve perfected it late in the seventeenth century, were a proud man and a proud woman, working out a relationship that would combine love with independence, faith with skepticism. The proud, witty couple achieve their difficult balance in a society filled with foolish prudes and fops, naïve bumpkins fresh from the country trying to acquire the manners and social graces of the town, and oversophisticated couples trying to rescue a little pride and independence from their easy loves. The one superior couple, for all that wit threatens at times to part them, finally respect each other's pride and wit.

In *Much Ado About Nothing* (1598–99) and *Love's Labour's Lost* (1594–95) Shakespeare developed situations based on combats of wit between men and women,

467

but his characters abandon their wit as they come to grips with the problem of love and marriage. Shakespeare recognized that a game of antagonism is one form of courtship, and his Beatrice and Benedict court each other in their sparring, but it is not pride and wit that bring about marriage.

Shakespeare defines and demonstrates wit in the verbal combat between Romeo and Mercutio in Act II, Scene 4, of *Romeo and Juliet*. Each quickly takes up the other's play on a word or an idea, aware that they are fencing and that each wins points when he parries the other's thrust. One criterion of their wit is speed. When Romeo extends a jest of Mercutio's into several new variations, Mercutio in mock breathlessness cries, "Come between us, good Benvolio; my wits faint." Another criterion is the power to wound. Mercutio complains, "Thy wit is a very bitter sweeting: it is a most sharp sauce." But the sharp sauce serves its purpose by lifting Romeo out of his solitary heaviness. The duel is a game, and after the duel is over the players are still friends.

The definition of wit is more precise in *Much Ado About Nothing*. The qualities of speed and sharpness are invoked in a short exchange of wit between Benedict and the waiting maid Margaret. Throughout the play, wit is associated with disdain, scorn, cutting, and stabbing. But in this play and others of Shakespeare, wit is particularly associated with pride. The attitude suggests the medieval concept that pride is chief of the Seven Deadly Sins and causes all the rest. Describing Beatrice, who is eavesdropping, Hero attributes her disdain and cruel wit to pride and self-love. When Beatrice gets this clue to self-knowledge and then hears Hero and Ursula say that Benedict is in love with her, she resolves to reform. This resolve is not a reversion to the medieval court of love requiring the lover to become the abject vassal of the beloved, but neither is it the full high comedy of the Restoration requiring that lovers keep their independence and that each take pride in the independence of the other.

Nor is Shakespeare's solution to the lovers' dilemma the solution of high comedy. Congreve and Sheridan have their characters work out a new relationship themselves, but Shakespeare resorts to the Plautine ruse of deception and the romantic threat of danger. Each of the lovers is brought to overhear an arranged conversation that indicates the other is madly in love, and when each admits his own love he drops the antagonism. Benedict and Beatrice are not brought together until the main plot has involved them in danger, and Benedict then becomes the medieval knight ready to fight for honor.

Love's Labour's Lost consists almost entirely of combats of wit between the four lords who had planned to spend three years in studious retreat and the four ladies who intrude upon them. The plan emphasizes the impulse to resist love, and in this play the whole purpose of wit is to attack and bring the opponent low, humiliate him, and drive him away. Even crueler than in *Much Ado About Nothing*, the witty remarks are often metaphors associated with shooting, and at one point the ladies start on an actual shooting party. Boyet describes their tactics in terms of warfare, and when he reports to the ladies that the men are coming to attack them disguised as Muscovites, he cries, "Arm, Wenches, arm! Muster your wits: stand in your own defense." The princess considers that exchanging tokens and wearing masks to confuse the men is a justified counter-attack. When they have put the disguised gentlemen quite out of countenance, Boyet concedes, "The tongues of mocking wenches are as keen as is the razor's edge invisible." And Berowne, completely broken down, admits defeat. The ladies describe their gifts from the lords with contempt and resolve to torture them to the limit. When the princess enters a mild protest, Rosaline replies, "They are worse fools to purchase mocking so. That same Berowne I'll torture ere I go!"

That sharp wit, amusing as it may be, is a fault as stated at the beginning of *Love's Labour's Lost*, and witty insult is much too cruel to last to the end of the play. When the princess receives word that her father is dead, the game of combat is dropped. For to Shakespeare a game of wit is only a beguiling interlude that must come to an end when the serious business of life intrudes. At the end the ladies agree to keep the men waiting for a year to prove them, and Berowne especially must be exorcised of his "mocks . . . flouts . . . wormword." Rosaline will not have him as he is, but has a plan to test and reform him. He must spend a year jesting to the sick in a hospital. If he can make them laugh, good, "but if they will not, throw away that spirit / And I shall find you empty of that fault / Right joyful of your reformation." This is a comedy in which a half-high dance of wits is resolved with the same romantic warmth that suffused the ending of Shakespeare's farce *The Comedy of Errors*. To the Shakespeare of the 1590s wit was an amusing disorder of growing up that kept friends or lovers apart. His characters would mature and come together only by renouncing it.

To triumph over others is comedy at a low level; to recognize the right of others to triumph is one level higher; but high comedy exists only when a character achieves full self-awareness and then learns to laugh at himself. Shakespeare's characters achieved the second level, but fell short of the final stage.

Shakespeare portrayed well the character who comes to a moment of clarity, when the deception and delusion drop away and in irony and bemusement he is aware of his situation. In the tragedies, the high point comes as the hero recognizes his fate. Comedy involves so many plots of deception and delusion that only occasionally does a character stop and observe himself. In *Love's Labour's Lost*, Berowne is from the first skeptical of the proposal to spend three years in seclusion, out of sight of women. All through the action he stands aside and comments on the others. He falls from his oath as do the other men, but he knew that he would and had watched himself with a sense of irony.

Even Bottom in *A Midsummer Night's Dream*, after his strange encounter with Titania, the queen of fairies, shows some self-awareness. He savors his comic experience and wants a ballad written and entitled "Bottom's Dream." One of Shakespeare's most charming moments approaching high-comedy awareness comes in

Twelfth Night when Viola, disguised as a boy, first realizes that Olivia has fallen in love with her. Her low-comedy amusement that her disguise has deceived the countess, who thinks her a youth, is immediately transformed into a more serious amusement as she realizes that she herself is hopelessly in love with the Duke. For a moment she becomes a high-comedy character—clearheaded observer and participator at the same time.

Shakespeare's great achievement in self-awareness is Falstaff. Who can name another character in all literature as free from self-deception as Falstaff? Seeming a coward, he yet is courageous enough to live with zest and disregard all fear of the future. Seeing through the pretenses of honor in his age, he yet does what he has to about the war. He hopes that Hal will protect him from the sheriff and bravely goes to sleep behind the curtain. If Hal protects him, good; if not, he is ready to ride the cart to prison. In either case he knows banishment and death are merely postponed. The most heart-rending scene is the play-acting game, with Falstaff and Hal alternating roles as stern royal judge and plaintiff, and Falstaff facing the possibility of Hal's rejection of him in the future. But Hal, play-acting, speaks the relentless words of fate: "I do. I will."

Hal and Falstaff are separated not by lack of understanding but by the rigidity of the feudal system. Hal had no flexibility but knew only extremes. He either broke away completely from his position as heir to the throne, wandering the byways and taverns to enjoy uncalculating companionship, to live each adventure for its own sake, totally free from concern for the future, or he accepted a place in the feudal system and foreswore the generous companionship of his youth.

For all the group scenes of companionship, of playing pranks, or robbing for the adventure of it, of play-acting,— *Henry IV* does not provide a model for high comedy. With Falstaff, for a few passing moments of youth, life becomes for Hal an end in itself, the life of the imagination, with its whimsical inventions and enterprises, its jests and group pranks. From the point of view of respectable society Falstaff is an evil parasite who refuses to work or take responsibility for his own deeds. His companions, all outlaws, create a group life for its own sake, not as a means to food or trade or government. The tavern group is not a model of sophisticated society: it is a special subculture as isolated and encapsulated as the wanderers in the forest of *A Midsummer Night's Dream* or on Prospero's island. It is a model of man's relation to fate, not to society; hence the play has had no more influence on high comedy than its near contemporary *Don Quixote*.

Since both Shakespeare and Molière start with the basic structure of Plautus and Terence—a blocking character that must be removed or circumvented if the young man is to get his love—it is instructive to notice how far each varies from the formula. Most notable is the greater prominence given women by both dramatists. Not only does the young girl in love figure more prominently than in Plautus but there is a great variety of other women: mothers, helpers, aunts, and housekeepers. Sometimes a woman takes the place of Plautus' intriguing slave or para-

470

site who must do the lying and tricking for the couple in love. But most interesting is the girl who must manage her own intrigue. Here Shakespeare seems in advance of Molière as he has a number of enterprising, independent young ladies, usually in the disguise of a boy, who go after the man. Rosalind and Orlando take on a new dimension if Orlando is played as fairly certain that this youth is a girl and surely the same princess he met at court. But he is completely in her power and cannot stop her game until she is ready. Olivia in *Twelfth Night* is not a blocking character, and she has no stern father keeping her locked in. Except for her own psychological obsession with mourning and seclusion, she is a free, adult woman. She must be transformed, but, as with Benedict and Beatrice, Shakespeare falls back on a Plautine low-comedy trick of deception to effect the change.

Molière's characters are so preoccupied with deception in order to escape from childhood and the home that they have no time for more complex adult relations of high comedy. But Molière goes further than Shakespeare in that direction.

Molière: His Comedy and His Life

"Who is the greatest man in my reign?" asked Louis XIV of the critic Boileau. When Boileau answered, "Molière, Sire," the King and many others were surprised. The King liked Molière and his theatre. But also active in the same fifteen years were generals of the army, architects, musicians, poets, religious thinkers, not to mention the great Colbert, a financial wizard who reorganized the fiscal system of the kingdom and laid the basis of great prosperity. But these people, important in their time, are now unknown while Molière still lives, a great man who wrote—and acted in—great plays.

One might think of Molière as an objective writer who made use of the conventions of comedy already developed and brought them to a final perfection. Or one might picture him as a sharp observer who delighted his age by adding to the old comic formulas satiric portrayals of the affectations and obsessions of the Paris of his time. One might picture him as crowning a happy moment of equilibrium between two emotional periods: after Corneille's generation developed a social attitude of tragic heroism and before Racine's generation watched the disintegration of that social ideal. Looking at Molière's gallery of funny characters, his many scenes of lovers escaping from difficulties, his gentle fooling of the bourgeois gentleman and his imaginary invalid, one might classify him as a happy comedian. No one of these classifications suits perfectly, yet each is partly right.

If the bloody wars of religion had subsided by the 1660s, the private quarrels at court were almost as bitter, and, in spite of enlightenment, Paris was hardly the home of a mature society. Molière made many people furious by implying that they should behave more sensibly, and particularly that they should laugh at themselves.

Molière acquired his wisdom through the experiences of a life of unusual variety and stress. His delightful comedy, which is both relaxation and reaffirmation, is a triumph over as much personal difficulty and anguish as was ever expressed in tragic drama or lyric poetry. If his plays show the world how to rise above difficulties, it is because he learned how to rise above his own. This man, who teaches how to adapt one's life to the attitudes of society, had a most unhappy time as a clown of his society. The man who gave the world a vision of free, adult relations between men and women built that vision out of the painful trials of his own rela-

472

tions with women. The man who shows how to make an artistic game of life learned by making a game of dying in six years of a losing struggle with tuberculosis.

The sensible people in Molière's plays constantly advise the foolish characters to be reasonable and to avoid extremes, to adapt themselves to public opinion, to do nothing to provoke anger. Nineteenth-century readers of Molière accepted this attitude as a full expression of his doctrine. But if we glance at Molière's life and take a deeper look at the plays, the meaning is not so simple. It is easy for those sensible creatures in the plays to preach prudence because they do not have problems of their own. In his own life Molière never followed the respectable way of bourgeois security and caution. He was educated at the Jesuit College Clermont, was a good Latin scholar, and he might have led an agreeable life in the company of intellectuals. Also, a business career was open to him. His father was upholsterer for the royal palaces, and Molière as a youth was marked for his successor. But he gave up that prospect to join the disreputable profession of acting. Actors might win the fleeting favor of kings and public, but they were still outlaws of state and church, classified with vagabonds, thieves, and prostitutes. When Molière was dying he was refused the last rites of the church and the promise of Christian burial. When the king intervened, the family was permitted to take the body by candlelight, with a minimum of ceremony, to the section of the graveyard kept for the unbaptized. Later it was whispered that churchmen secretly had the body removed from the proximity of the respectable and saved.

For two seasons the young Molière and his actor friends tried to establish themselves at a theatre in Paris, but failed. They took to the road, and for fourteen years made their living and perfected their art by competing on street corners with jugglers, peddlers, and the clowns of the commedia dell' arte. Sometimes they won the applause of cities and princes and rose in the world. For a time they won the favor and friendship of the Prince of Conti, who had been a student at Clermont with Molière. But he became ill and pious and abandoned his vagabond friends. In 1648 other princes finally arranged for the company to play before the king. Molière tried presenting a tragedy, but the actors were not players of the grand style and they were a failure. Molière stepped forward, apologized for his presumption in playing tragedy in Paris, and offered to show the king one of the little farces that had been successful in the provinces. The farce was a great success, and the king asked the company to act in Paris and to share the royal hall that was rented part of each week to the Italian clowns of the commedia dell' arte.

Molière could have played it safe with light entertainment for the crowd and the court. But he saw too clearly the ridiculous pretenses of the people around him. The women who had set out to refine French manners and language were a powerful group, but Molière put their fad on the stage in *Les Précieuses ridicules* (1659). The play was a tremendous success, but it made enemies.

In the middle of his career Molière wrote *Tartuffe* (1664). It was an imprudent play and he realized it. It delighted the royal family and many nobles, but it brought down on his head the wrath of the clergy. A number of religious groups were competing for influence, and Molière had managed to infuriate them all. The Jesuits were exhorting people in the active world of court and city, and the Jansenists, a more ascetic group, were insisting that people should lead a pu-

Molière as Sganarelle. *Phot. Bibl. Nat. Paris.*

474

ritanical life. The Society of the Holy Sacrament trained and promoted advisors to be placed in families as guides in piety. Eventually all three societies were to be suppressed or controlled by king and pope for their corruption in seeking power. But in the 1660s few people dared say, as Molière showed in *Tartuffe*, that a pious manner was no guarantee that a person was equipped to run the lives of others. Molière pointed out that his play made clear the difference between real piety and unscrupulous hypocrisy. He even tried a version with his hypocrite dressed not as a churchman but as an ordinary citizen and got the tacit approval of the king. But the archbishop forbade anyone to act in the play, see it, or listen to it, on pain of excommunication. The Commissioner of Police said that he respected the play but that it was not the business of actors to meddle in moral affairs. The king gave in to the Church and told Molière that he must not play *Tartuffe* publicly. After five years, when tempers had cooled and the archbishop had established peace among religious parties, the king permitted *Tartuffe* to be played.

The dévots were right in insisting that the play was subversive, for it implies, as most of Molière's work does, skepticism about authority. The play means more than the doctrine of prudence preached by Cléante. Modern critics have pointed out that Orgon is the kind of father who wants to lord it over his family and that Tartuffe gives him a religious excuse. When Tartuffe's perfidy is exposed, the sanction for Orgon's authority is gone and he has to face his family with no more right to dominate than any adult has to dominate another. Molière denounces not only hypocrisy but the cherished human right to tell other people what to do. He insists that true dévots attend to their own business and do not undertake to run other people's.

If Molière had believed completely in the doctrine that his softer characters preach, he would not have stirred up a hornet's nest as he did with *Tartuffe*. The play delighted many bright minds and must have been a joy to the *libertins*, high-spirited men about the court who prided themselves on their disdain for rules and restrictions. Molière was friendly with many of them, but perhaps one of them crowed too loudly over the attack on excessive piety. In his next play, *Don Juan* (1665), Molière showed the plight of the complete skeptic. In the last act Molière took a slash at both the *libertins* and the hypocrites. After Don Juan sends his father away deceived, he rises to a climax of denunciation of the weak and wicked age, determined to confound his enemies by setting them at each other's throats and letting them destroy each other under the cloak of religion and virtue. The speech is only one moment in a play of complex form and balance, but it turns loose so much private anger that it is a reminder of the bitter comedies of Ben Jonson.

While Molière was writing comedies, Corneille was writing of man's heroic sacrifice of private interests in dedication to a larger cause, and Racine was fascinated by man's compulsion to follow his dark passions into the whirlpool of destruction. Molière's vision is perhaps more profound than theirs. His characters are just as much involved as the tragic writers' in the anguish of being themselves in complex human relationships. The sum total of his comedy shows the way to adjustment and the release of tension in laughter. He achieves comedy and the ability to laugh, but out of personal knowledge of anger and frustration at the outrageous wickedness of the world. Molière knew well the impulse to attack all authority and live the life of a skeptic and *libertin*, but he saw how empty and destructive such a life would be.

Even more than his professional career, Molière's love life shows the triumph of comic understanding over emotional distress. In his late thirties Molière found himself in love with Armande, the teen-age girl growing up in his own household, daughter of Madelaine Bejart, the woman who had been his mistress and chief actress for nearly two decades. Armande passed as Madelaine's sister. Molière's enemies did not hesitate to say that she was his own daughter, while his friends insisted that she was Madelaine's daughter by another man. She was ambitious and loved the thought of being the wife of the successful actor-author and head of the theatrical troupe. The charming young girl received a great deal of attention from other men, and it appears that the marriage was beset with difficulties. But she bore Molière several children and played the gay young girl in his plays for the rest of his life and for years afterward. When he was first in love with her he wrote *The School for Husbands* (1661). Taking the plot of Terence's *Adelphi*, with its contrasting pairs of parents and children—a strict father and a rebellious son, a more understanding father and a loyal son—he substituted for the sons two girls being brought up by two brothers instructed by the girls' father to marry them themselves or secure them other husbands as they came of age. Molière wrote for himself the part of the strict guardian who is outwitted by the girl while the lenient guardian finds that his ward is glad to marry him in spite of his age. Molière was exorcising from himself the impulse to be harsh with his girl and trying to feel that love and understanding could bridge the twenty-year difference in their ages.

But after the marriage the problem did not look so simple, and the next play, *The School for Wives* (1662), has a much more difficult situation as its comic base. Molière wrote himself the part of an old guardian who is conscious of every step of the courtship of his ward, whom he loves, and her young man but can do nothing but grimly bear it. Molière had watched his own delightful Armande escape from her mother-sister and from the rest of the company to be with him. Did he now have to recognize that it was perfectly natural for her to prefer the company of young men to that of a husband of his age? Right after the marriage the company spent weeks at Versailles taking part in the festivities of the court. Molière could understand the impulse to lock up a flirtatious young girl and to wish she knew nothing about the world of fashion. But his intelligence told him that that would do no good. So he wrote the play about the possessive guardian, Arnolphe, who was so obsessed with fear that he kept the ward he intended to marry under lock and key and tried to keep her innocent and ignorant. Molière lets Arnolphe have it from both sides. The young man does not know that Arnolphe is the guardian and tells him about the courtship; and the ward, Agnes, tells him of her love for the young man. Plautus' old men could beat the slaves who tried to deceive them, but Molière's Arnolphe is tied to his "deceivers" by love and family and friendship. When he fails he falls to his knees, begging Agnes to stay with him, under any conditions she wishes to make. He is pitiful, but Molière, the comic actor, made him ludicrous, with a comic rolling of the eyes and a frantic voice.

Molière as Arnolphe in *L'Ecole des Femmes*, 1670. *Phot. Bibl. Nat. Paris.*

A man's relation to a difficult woman appeared again in *The Misanthrope* (1666). This play came after suppression of *Tartuffe*, and Molière had reason to hate the whole world. But he knew that to show such an attitude in a stage character would be foolish. He wrote himself the part of a foolish misanthrope to express his feelings but at the same time put them in perspective. Alceste is the most complex and subtle character in all Molière's plays. The part has been played with excellent balance, as a charming, accomplished man of the world, friendly and needing the love that people offer him, but so possessed by the frustration of trying to make people do what he decides they should do that he exhausts himself and gives up trying to maintain human relationships. He is tortured by guilt until he collects evidence that proves to him that the world is all wicked and deserves every criticism he makes of it.

Alceste is furious because so many people agree with their friends just to be pleasant, yet he goes to the other ridiculous extreme, refusing to keep an opinion if he finds that other people have it. Sure that no one ever loved as he does, he claims unlimited rights over Célimène. He insists that the more one loves the more frankly one points out the faults of his beloved. He is not ready for the fine discrimination of the lover who sees the faults and still loves the lady. To the last he hopes to "correct" Célimène. He daydreams of a Célimène who is alone and mistreated so that he can come to her rescue. But the real Célimène is a quite self-sufficient person, and she has no intention of giving up the world to join Alceste in the lonely world of his ego.

Célimène was the first large part Molière wrote for his young wife. She had made an excellent impression in the musical spectacles he had helped produce at Versailles and in several short plays. Here she could develop into a full portrait the woman of wit, vivacity, and cruelty. As Alceste, Molière could not understand Célimène, but as the author he understood all too well her right at twenty to go her own lively way.

In this play we have a glimpse of Molière in 1666, settling down to the long pull, making the most of a difficult world. He had been married for several years and knew that Armande could never change. But she was an excellent actress, and he could put his feelings, and perhaps some of hers, into a form of art. He had just had the first unmistakable symptoms of tuberculosis, and he knew the doctors had no cure for that. But he got seven more years of very active life before death came in 1673.

In the course of those years he went still further in the dramatization of his life by making a comic game of his ill health and the threat of death. After 1666 there were many months when he was unable to play at all. Because he was afraid when he acted that he would have to cough in the middle of a speech, he made a cough a part of his characterizations. In *The Miser* (1668) the matchmaker flatters him by telling him he coughs with such grace that it becomes him. In the summer of 1672 Molière was confined to his bed for weeks, and his company was desperate for lack of work. He gathered his strength and wrote a play in which he could act mostly sitting or lying down. In *The Imaginary Invalid* (1673) Argon is a gourmand savoring all the details of illness: the medicines, enemas, bloodlettings. But everyone knows he is not really ill. Like the fathers in *Tartuffe* and *The Miser*, he is ready to sacrifice his daughter in order to get a son-in-law to indulge his obsession. When Argon's brother proposes to take him to see some of Molière's satires on doctors, he bursts out in a rage: "He's an impudent one, to make a play of such honest men. If I were a doctor, I'd have my revenge. When he got sick I'd let him die without any help at all—not the least little bleeding, not the least little enema, and I'd say to him, 'Die, die, that'll teach you to make fun of the medical academy." To every symptom Argon mentions, the mock doctor comments triumphantly, "the lungs." Making a game of his own impending death, Molière has Argon counterfeit death in order to test his second wife and his daughter. Thinking him dead, the wife describes the disgusting thing he has been, with all his medicines and coughing and spitting, and she rejoices that he is dead.

The Imaginary Invalid had an excellent ballet at the end of each act, and Molière hoped to play it at Versailles, but he had had a quarrel with the composer Lully, who with his new Academy of Music was lording it over everyone. He had Molière restricted to six singers and an orchestra of twelve, and when Molière asked someone else to write music for his play, the king sided with the outraged Lully and did not ask to have the new play at court. Molière opened *Le Malade imaginaire* on February 10, 1673, and it was a tremendous success. But during the fourth performance he had a hemorrhage and choked on his last word in the initiation ceremony. He bravely continued the play to the end, and was taken home coughing blood and died soon after.

Molière's humor in *The Imaginary Invalid* was born of a strong skepticism combined with a strong faith in nature. His own physician was a skeptic who so disagreed with the Academy of Medicine that for some years his membership was suspended. Molière had repeated in play after play the joke that was probably true, that more people died of their doctors' treatments than of diseases. The invalid's brother expressed Molière's belief, and doubtless that of his own physician, that doctors know very little and that they had better prescribe complete rest and give nature a chance to cure. Molière anticipated modern ideas about psychosomatic illness in his belief that many of the ills of the body have their origin in the mind. He never denied that illness and evil existed, but he believed in the power of the human spirit to triumph over them. In the little comedy-ballet *The Doctor Love* (1665), the young daughter is sick because her father won't let her marry the man she loves, but when the man comes dressed as a doctor and proposes marriage as a cure, she is bright and well.

Looking at Molière as an actor—and by all accounts he was one of the greatest actors of all time—we see how he changed the tone and silhouette of the character he played to fit the changing spirit and shape of his own life. In the commedia dell' arte a man would play the same character all his life, and in one sense Molière played the part of one clown all his life, even using the name Sganarelle in five plays. But he made interesting changes. When he first arrived back in Paris from fourteen years on the road, he played the exuberant Mascarille, who loved disguises and fun and fooling. But as he settled down he turned himself into Sganarelle, an older man, hard and aggressive, obsessed by one idea and sure that he is right. As Sganarelle he wore a moustache, and he used a nervous, acid laugh that usually ended in a defeated grimace. As the guardian in *The School for Wives* (1662) and Orgon in *Tartuffe*, he used similar makeup and characterization. But for *The Misanthrope* he left off the moustache and made Alceste much more charming. After the suppression of *Tartuffe* and the only moderate success of *The Misanthrope*, he repeatedly returned to his variations on the Plautine clown. He gave himself some very rough treatment in his roles, not only in *The Forced Marriage* (1664), when he was still fairly vigorous, but in *George Dandin* (1668), *Monsieur de Pourceaugnac* (1669), and *Scapin* (1671), a masterpiece of whirlwind action that gives a vision of life as a series of mishaps, disappointments, and beatings. But after 1668 a new silhouette appears, a thinner, older, weaker man, with a cough. Not strong enough to be a terrifying tyrant, Molière made his Miser only a ridiculous, pitiable old man. As the Imaginary Invalid, Molière the actor showed real terror of illness. His genius as playwright and actor enabled him to make his miser and invalid pitiful and human and at the same time ridiculous.

Molière's plays demonstrate that the dramatist believed in equality and in absolute freedom of the individual. In basic relationships—father and child, husband and wife, master and servant—he showed that force produced a tyranny that destroyed human relations. The master could beat the servant, but unless he won his trust, the servant could always deceive him. In several plays the distrust of a husband is a provocation to the wife to betray him. In *The Miser* (1668) the daughter speaks up to the father: she will die before she will obey his orders. Only loving

Frontispiece from Molière's published plays.

480

trust between equals can create contentment. Most of Molière's plays show the tension of a father, guardian, or husband trying to enforce his authority and the victim having to trick and deceive him to break or divert his power. At the end the young people have gained their freedom and are ready to explore more mature relations as free people.

Molière fell short of creating full high comedy, though he came nearer that end than did Shakespeare. His characters are so preoccupied with Plautine deception in order to escape from childhood and home that they have not much time for the more complete adult relationships that occupy the characters in full high comedy. In *Tartuffe, The Miser,* and *The Bourgeois Gentleman* (1670), the daughter has a quarrel with her lover, angry that he is not giving her more help. In pride the two clash, but the quarrel is brief, and it is not pride and wit that bring them together.

For all his contribution to high comedy, Molière remains a master of farce. It is not the harsh farce of Plautus: in only a few plays are there beatings and wild pursuits. But there are disguises, deceptions, misunderstandings, and crises aplenty, and these proceed at times with great speed. Only *The Misanthrope* is free from farcical action.

Pattern is far more important in Molière than in modern farce. Verbal sparring in balanced phrases, movement of two characters in unison or in opposition, or dancelike interweaving of several characters give comic intensity to a situation and add a pleasure that lifts the material close to high-comedy level. We expect a living being to make fine adjustments, but a character obsessed by one idea or blinded by a narrow passion will be caught in a mechanical pattern of assertion and response; and Molière abounds in such situations.

In Molière, farce is given psychological complexities entirely different from the rough and tumble of Plautus. There are levels of irony that are rarely suggested in Roman Farce. In Plautus the young lover or his slave sets out to outwit a stupid father, who is completely duped. But Molière almost eliminates the servant, gives

PSICHÉE

LES FEMMES SCAVANTES

L'IMPOSTEUR

LE TARTVFFE

the girl in love an active part, and often makes the father conscious of what is going on but unable to do anything about it. Again and again the dupe is self-deceived because of his obsession with money or nobility or doctors. And always more pleasure than pain is created, for the characters and for the audience, more fun than anger. Even the monstrous fathers with their extreme obsessions have likable traits and moments.

Molière filled his plays with music, using a small orchestra and a corps of trained singers and dancers. Most of the plays are, in fact, *comedie-ballets*. His practice was to concentrate the music and dance at the end of each act, sometimes as an entire act, but sometimes he integrated it into the play. The doctor's initiation at the end of *The Imaginary Invalid* and the spectacular mamamouchi Turkish ceremony in *The Bourgeois Gentleman* are the unforgettable climaxes of the action of the plays. There are some songs at other places, and *The Bourgeois Gentleman* has almost as much music as an opera. Molière used his corps of singers and dancers and gave few songs to his main actors. Modern audiences are more used to the pattern set in *The Beggar's Opera* in 1728 and which continued in modern musical comedy, where the main characters sing songs, expressing their feelings and reactions to what is happening.

In English Restoration comedy there is much less farce than in Molière. The plays concentrate on the high-comedy elements of ironical situations, verbal sparring, and the display of pride and wit in the development of a love affair that is without romantic ardor and ends in a marriage of equals who expect to retain their independence.

But if Molière did not quite achieve the full possibilities of high comedy, he raised comedy to a height of excellence comparable to the achievement of Corneille and Racine in tragedy. He produced a large body of work of high literary quality and a view of humanity that stresses the rights of the individual, woman as well as man. Seeing clearly the shortcomings and wickedness of human beings, he does not deny them essential dignity. The extent of his influence on other dramatists is debatable, but it is certain that, as he drew upon Plautus, he was drawn upon by some English Restoration and eighteenth-century playwrights, among them John Dryden, Thomas Shadwell, William Wycherley, and Colley Cibber. Moreover, he has survived into the twentieth century, not only as a classic in the repertoire of the Comedie Française and in productions by other professional and amateur groups in Europe and America, but in adaptations on the British and American stage. A notable example is *Scapino*, based on *Les fourberies de Scapin* (1671), given in New York in the mid-1970s, with incredibly agile Jim Dale, a London actor with music-hall background, playing brilliantly the role created and played by Molière.

Restoration Comedy:
High Comedy in Full Flower

After Charles II came to the English throne following two decades of Puritan domination under Cromwell, another comedy of enlightenment was created. Similar in some ways to Molière's comedy, more cynical and libertine and not so well controlled by common sense, it developed in its narrow range a greater maturity. Though some people have found it shocking and immoral, it in fact made one of the two major attempts in literature to find a higher basis for courtship and marriage than the physical lure of sex.

To express their disapproval of the Puritans, the aristocrats went to opposite extremes. Where the Puritan had insisted on plain clothing, men of fashion now blossomed out in the most elaborate costumes Europe has ever known: wigs so enormous that the large plumed hat was often worn on the arm, petticoat breeches made of many yards of embroidery and lace and decorated with yards of ribbon at shoulders, hips, and knees, and lace gathered at neck, chest, wrists, and calves. A man might be so plain that he could not "by nature move a cookmaid," but with this enhancement he would undertake to "melt down a countess." With perfumed gloves, snuff box, mirror, muff, and long cane added to the costume, there was an ostentatious style that has never been equaled.

From 1642 to 1660 the theatres were closed, although there were some surreptitious performances and a few traveling troupes put on short versions of plays in the provinces. In the reaction against the dreariness of these decades without fun, Charles himself, the Merry Monarch, led the way. An astute politician, he kept the different factions balanced and calm; he had no wish to go into exile again. But off duty he went about the town as "Old Rowley," drinking in the taverns, gossiping in the coffee and chocolate houses, and enjoying the tumultuous audience gathered in the afternoons in the playhouses. He and his noblemen had returned from exile skeptical of dogmas and impatient of restraint. One great lord ended a drinking party by appearing naked high on the front of a tavern and addressing the crowd that gathered in the street.

Behind the spontaneous release of long-suppressed impulses was an urbane disillusionment and reaction against metaphysical speculation. Thomas Hobbes, whose *Leviathan* (1651) was a study of man from a naturalistic point of view, became the man of the hour. He was popular at court for his sharp wit, attractive personality, good nature, and facetiousness. Accepting enthusiastically his view that men are motivated by pleasure and displeasure, his friends and followers were determined to get as much pleasure as possible in a world with no absolute rules. He gave philosophical justification for sexual pleasure as the satisfaction of natural appetite, but at the same time he thought sexual pleasure less permanent and important than intellectual pleasure. If Restoration comedy seems full of people absorbed in temporary pleasure, it regularly shows a few who are searching for something more lasting.

The new scientists taught people not to look for values in the everyday world of facts and even to question the senses. Some of the same men who saw themselves mirrored in Restoration comedy were founders and supporters of the Royal Society, England's great scientific academy. Freedom from old dogmas enabled some men to devote themselves to science, and others, or often the same men, to give their lives to the enjoyment of passing pleasures. It is all the more amazing that a Restoration comedy regularly ended with an effort to reconcile the world as it is with a world of higher values.

In the economic sphere, wealthy businessmen held the view that the world of trade was separate from the world of religion and subjective values and that it should operate by natural self-interest. Though the main characters in Restoration comedy are contemptuous of tradesmen, their lives are dominated by trade and the standards of the marketplace. Nearly all the plays open with the evasion of tradesmen's bills and end with a property settlement. In between, all relations are in the open market. Each person tries to make the best bargain he can and is skeptical of the claims of other people. In William Wycherley's *The Plain Dealer* (1676), Fondlewife says, "In the way of trade, we still suspect the smoothest dealers of the deepest design." In the human market, as in trade or a game of cards, the feelings are carefully hidden: no one makes more than tentative commitments until he finds out what offer the other can make. Much of the sexual imagery in the plays is in terms of trade: offers, bids, contracts, and payments. Of course the cultivated gallant can far outplay the businessman in the sexual market. Restoration comedy shows no mercy for the losers in a ruthless competitive world. Only at the end of a play do the few who still have a glimmer of outlawed love and faith resort to the old institution of marriage and take themselves out of the competitive market.

Restoration comedy begins when the young people are already free from families, in fact free from all institutions and standards, and it considers how their characters evolve as they improvise casual human relations and strive to create more lasting ones.

In the Restoration plays the young man is living by himself in his own rooms in town and making his own high-handed arrangements with tradesmen and servants. He has found a sophisticated companion, a man of his own age, to help explore the fashionable world. He has already paid suit to an experienced older

The Plain Dealer, 1676.

woman, sampled various lower-class girls in passing, and is currently having an affair with a woman of wit and fashion. Then he finds the one girl proud and witty enough to challenge him. The women, too, are adult and free from the restrictions of parents. Harriet Woodville in *The Man of Mode* (1676), Sir George Etherege's most famous heroine, has a country home that may be limiting, but we see her on a trip to the town and not in the least restricted by the presence of her mother.

The town gives these characters, fine or shallow, their maturity. The English dramatists take advantage of their theatrical tradition and show the gallant and the belle not only in their own receiving rooms but in the public places that make London life a liberal education: taverns, a fashionable shop at the Exchange, the Mall, and other places in the park.

Almost as much as the operas, the London scenes express playful deceptions and unmaskings. The mazes and cross walks of London parks are a reminder of the interweaving of purposes: the arbors and trees are nature, but nature patterned and methodized. The large forestage brought these free individuals almost as far into the audience as the Elizabethan stage. The proscenium doors—two sets, and apparently in one theatre three sets—not only permitted interruptions and surprises but gave a sense of many alternatives: no clever person could be forced in any direction he did not want to go. Far at the back of the acting stage the scenery changed before the eyes of the audience in seconds. Never was an actor enclosed by the setting.

The character of the proud gallant or the high-bred belle is defined not in isolation but as part of a cross section of a community that includes men and women who in various ways fail to live up to the best ideals. At the center of the picture is the lively couple, playing a dangerous game with their future at stake. At one side of the mercurial center pair are those who are rude, countrified, or naïve, not wise or sophisticated enough for the complex life of the town. On the other side are those who are too sophisticated, who have no character because they yield completely to fashions. By showing the wrong way, these lesser characters define the better way of the central couple. The reputation the comedies have gained for immorality and triviality is largely due to these minor characters, but when the whole scheme of characters is looked at in perspective, there is no doubt that the central couple see the triviality of those around them and work for salvation, not by leaving sinful society to become hermits but by shaping their own lives independently. For this solution nineteenth-century Romantics could never forgive them since their own ideal for countering the evil of the world was withdrawal to the desert or a mountain top.

The characteristic pattern does not appear at first glance in Wycherley's famous plays *The Plain Dealer* and *The Country Wife* (1674–75) because the sincere couples are undeveloped minor characters. Wycherley allows the country wife and the easy amorous ladies and cynical ranters to crowd his picture so that few people

486

notice Alithea and Harcourt, who quietly work out a match that is not shallow. As a brilliant development of the negative part of the canvas, *The Country Wife* is a delight, but the full picture could not be understood without the more balanced plays of Etherege and William Congreve.

Most picturesque of the foolish characters are the fops—overdressed, affected coxcombs. Their names flaunt their qualities: Sir Courtly Nice, Sir Fopling Flutter (Etherege's *The Man of Mode*), and Sir Novelty Fashion (Colley Cibber's *Love's Last Shift*, 1695), who in a sequel by Sir John Vanbrugh (*The Relapse*, 1696) was raised to the peerage as Lord Foppington. Vanbrugh shows him trying on a new periwig "so long and so full of hair it will serve for a hat and cloak in all weathers." But "passitively" he thinks it shows too much of his face. "I'll wear it today," he declares, "tho' it show such a monstrous pair of cheeks, stap my vitals, I shall be taken for a trumpeter."

In the twentieth-century production the fop is likely to appear effeminate, with ballet steps, gushing speech, and much handkerchief-waving, but he was played in the seventeenth century as an infantile exhibitionist. He has no tastes or ideas of his own. Even his lovemaking is not a vital drive but only another way of being in the mode. Etherege's Sir Fopling Flutter, when set on by the mischievous gallants, makes an approach to Mrs. Loveit, but when he is repulsed he easily turns his thoughts to a way of pleasing the whole society of women rather than "throw away that vigor on one, which I mean shall shortly make my court to the whole sex in a ballet." Making a fetish of clothes and ornaments and generalizing erotic interest through social events, the fop becomes a pre-Freudian study of sublimation and substitution.

Less picturesque than the fop are the frail women who offer themselves easily. Unable to play the game of courtship with skill, they are deserted or tricked into marriage with some pretender. They are hypocrites, and, like the fop, they are not concerned with character but with reputation. In *The Country Wife* Lady Fidget, Mistress Dainty Fidget, and Mistress Squeamish disdain the "filthy" men and will not hear Sir Jasper Fidget speak of the "naked" truth. Of Horner, the rake who has just told everyone that he is impotent, Mrs. Fidget says, "Truly, not long ago, you know, I thought his very name obscenity; and I would as soon have lain with him as named him." Such pretense is a mask for lasciviousness. Horner feels no compunction in taking such women, who are brought to his house by stupid men of "business."

Molière's deceivers are young girls duping their guardians to get to talk to their beaux; Wycherley's are married women eager to be untrue to their husbands. But the emphasis is on the provocative stupidity of the husband. Sir Jasper Fidget is delighted that Horner can keep his wife occupied while he is off to his business.

Olivia in *The Plain Dealer* is a classic example of hypocrisy. Malicious and corrupt herself, she rails about those who gossip and pretends to be furious at the bawdiness of the playhouse. When she and her friends comment on the scene of double entendre in *The Country Wife*, where the ladies come to Mr. Horner's rooms to be given a sample of his "china," she reveals her own dirty-mindedness. Dramatist and audience were aware of the obsessive public prudery of those who are insecure in their private morals.

More than any other character in Restoration drama, Mrs. Margery Pinchwife, the Country Wife, has amused the twentieth century, crystallizing as she does the reaction against Victorian prudery. It is not Margery but her "dear Bud" who is obsessed with all the details of wickedness, and it is his incessant suspicions that arouse her interest in other men. He teaches her to write to the men, and by disguising her as a boy enables Horner to kiss her under his very eyes, and finally he brings her in disguise and delivers her into Horner's arms.

Congreve's Miss Prue in *Love for Love* (1695) is a more pleasing picture than the Country Wife of a country innocent who rushes into concupiscence, and her small part is a variation on the main themes. Even Tattle, the shallow rake, does not want to take a woman without opposition.

The most appalling frail women are the amorous widows who have taken a "long lease of lewdness." Lady Wishfort in Congreve's *The Way of the World* (1700) is one of the great comic portraits in all drama. She is seen first at the dressing table, sputtering in boudoir Billingsgate because Mirabell, who had once courted her, now calls her "superannuated frippery." Her agitation cracks her face paint and her maid must repair her. Next she appears coyly rehearsing how she will receive Sir Rowland, how sit, loll, dangle a foot, and suddenly start and "rise to meet him in a pretty disorder." When he arrives, she bubbles into elaborate speech, hiding the grossness of her desire in an affectation of modesty.

Where Molière chose one kind of comic monstrosity for each play, the Restoration dramatist put all the major kinds into every play, often balancing a character against the opposite extreme. In an age that used balance and symmetry in all aspects of life this balance of different kinds of fools defined a middle way of life that has been a principle of humanism since the Greeks. Thus in *The Country Wife*, Pinchwife, who is too jealous, is set in contrast to Sparkish, who is so completely without jealousy that he does not hold his fiancée's interest. In *The Man of Mode*, Sir Fopling Flutter is matched with Mrs. Loveit, the stale spinster who enters into an easy affair with Dorimant. Around Valentine and Angelica at the center in Congreve's *Love for Love* circulate the fop Tattle and an easy woman, Mrs. Frail, in contrast to the amiable Ben, fresh from life at sea, and the naïve Miss Prue, fresh from the country. Tattle and Mrs. Frail suppose that they can trick a young man and young woman into marrying them, but they are tricked into marriage with each other and cheerfully set out to make the best of a bad job. But Miss Prue and Ben, the naïve pair, easily seduced by Tattle and Mrs. Frail and as quickly abandoned, have honesty enough to confess their dislike of each other and part. The couple at the center of a balanced scheme of characters in each play surpass the fools and coxcombs by outplaying them at all levels of the game of living.

Like the court of love, the game of love played by these Restoration couples

Mrs. Pitt as Lady Wishfort. *The Way of the World*, 1776.

makes a major protest against the current debased pattern of marriage. But the game of love differs in most respects from the court of love. Where the medieval knight was ready to subordinate himself to his love, the Restoration gallant has no intention of giving up his own personality but expects to become a member of a lively partnership. The medieval lover expected to be totally transformed by a love that would last forever. The Restoration gallant does not expect love to become a substitute for all other interests though it might add zest to them. He wants a proud, independent woman who has her own interests and will leave him his.

Many of the minor characters are cynically cheerful about the failure of marriage. Hippolita's maid in Wycherley's *The Gentleman Dancing Master* (1672) advises her lady to marry the fool her father has picked and then find other men, since this one is "handsome enough to lie with in the dark . . . and for the day-time, you may take the privilege of a wife." But no one could be enthusiastic about such a situation. As Ben, the honest sailor in *Love for Love* says, "A man that is married, d'ye see, is no more like another man, than a galley-slave is like one of us free sailors: he is chained to an oar all his life, and may-hap forced to tug a leaky vessel into the bargain." And it is that same danger that seems a nightmare to the Old Bachelor in Congreve's play by that name. After a narrow escape he will never go near a woman again. Etherege's Lady Cockwood has no right to expect her husband to show affection. "If you did but know, Madam," she is told, "what an odious thing it is to be thought to love a wife in good company." And in *The Way of the World*, Witwood apologizes for absentmindedly asking his friend about his lady's health: "I beg pardon that I should ask a man of pleasure, and the town, a question at once so foreign and domestic."

Restoration stage lovers are expected to be as practical as scientists and as calculating as tradesmen. Mature and sophisticated, they cannot abide the nauseous cant of puppy love. Congreve's heroines, adolescent or mature, will listen to no romantic passion. Belinda in *The Old Bachelor* (produced 1693) won't be pestered with "flowers and stuff" and says " . . . don't come always, like the devil, wrapt in flames—I'll not hear a sentence more that begins with an *I burn*." Etherege started his writing of comedy with *The Comical Revenge* (1664), in which there is a heroic plot, but he used two other plots that were a travesty of the poetic scenes. Dryden and others tried combinations of the heroic and the comic, but although the new high comedy had high-born characters and was written in polished prose, the emotions and language were unheroic.

The new love was also a revolt against a fad for praising Platonic love. The Précieuses in France had revived the medieval Court of Love, and D'Urfey's *Astrée* had long analyses of love as worship without possession. Queen Henrietta Maria and her ladies introduced the discussion of Platonic love in England in the 1630s, and a few Restoration plays tried to develop the idea. But the temper of the time was against it.

On the positive side the new love gave full recognition to the independence of each person. Perhaps the greatest achievement of high comedy is a vision of a zestful human relationship not merely in spite of differences but because of them. Where the English plays include many instances of deception and trickery and even romantic surrender, they point the way to mutual understanding in which thoughtful laughter is an affirmation of love.

In the famous proviso scene in *The Way of the World*, Millamant states the terms of her independence, a Magna Carta for women who hope to be respected persons and not mere subjected wives:

. . . liberty to pay and receive visits to and from whom I please: to write and receive letters without interrogatories or wry faces on your part: to wear what I please; and choose conversation with regard only to my own taste: to have no obligation upon me to converse with wits that I don't like, because they are your acquaintance: or to be intimate with fools, because they may be your relations. Come to dinner when I please, dine in my dressing-room when I'm out of humor, without giving a reason. To have my closet inviolate: to be sole empress of my tea-table, which you must never presume to approach without first asking leave. And lastly wherever I am you shall always knock at the door before you come in. These articles subscribed, if I continue to endure you a little longer, I may by degrees dwindle into a wife.

In the midst of skeptics and calculators a few characters in Restoration comedy believe that by grace and faith some may escape the general damnation of trivial living. Several plays use the imagery of faith and salvation. Near the beginning of *The Man of Mode*, Medley, the skeptical rake, teases young Bellaire, who is about to be married:

You have a good strong Faith, and that may contribute much towards your Salvation. I confess I am but of an untoward constitution, apt to have doubts and scruples, and in Love they are no less distracting than in Religion: were I so near marriage I should cry out by fits as I ride in my coach, Cuckold, Cuckold, with no less fury than the man Fanatick does Glory in Bethlehem.

Dorimant says to his mistress, "Constancy at my years! You might as well expect the fruit the autumn ripens in the spring. . . . Youth has a long journey to go, Madam: should I have set up my rest at the first inn I lodged at I should never have arrived at the happiness I now enjoy." But as he becomes interested in Harriet, his span of time is longer—he could keep Lent in expectation of a happy Easter. At the end he is still teasing the other women and Harriet does not demand much assurance of fidelity, but now he does have faith. *Love for Love* effects a conversion at the end that changes even some of the trivial characters. Valentine has been trying to win Angelica by deceptions aimed to mislead her. Each time she comes to his rescue she finds him surrounded by people with no faith in human constancy. But at the end even Scandal says, "I was an infidel to your sex, and you have converted me." In the midst of general cynicism the best Restoration comedies achieve salvation by faith for the few true wits.

The highest salvation for the central couple is achieved in *The Way of the World* (1700), the last of the true Restoration plays before the characters were sentimentalized in the eighteenth century. Mirabell has known Millamant for a long time. While her whimsicality can still surprise him, he has a deep acquaintance with her faults and her charms. Still girlish and thriving on attention, she is mature enough to have perfected the art of teasing. She is so sure of her social group that she can play with witty comparisons with Witwood and tease Mirabell with a mixture of cruelty and laughter. Beneath her security is the melancholy realization that friendship is fleeting, that love is touched with cruelty and pain, and that joy in love depends on the ability of the playful imagination to keep the spirits high. She knows that Mirabell is angry with her for spending time with fools and she teases him for his "violent and inflexible wise face," and leaves him thinking of her as a whirlwind. Millamant is Congreve's greatest triumph. Taking people as she finds them, she is never surprised into despair. Taking the world as she finds it, she knows where to find values.

THE HERITAGE OF HIGH COMEDY

High comedy presents a difficult attitude toward living that has never won the widest popularity. Most people of the eighteenth and nineteenth centuries rejected it, and not a major high comedy was written between the 1780s and the end of the nineteenth century, when the witty plays of Oscar Wilde and Arthur Schnitzler had a limited vogue. Only in the twentieth century have playwrights and audiences come back to a full interest in the form.

There was opposition even among theatre people of the Restoration period. Thomas Shadwell, whose own plays seem coarse enough, was shocked at the central couple of the plays, the "swearing, drinking, whoring, ruffian for a lover, and an impudent ill-bred tomrig for a mistress . . . their chief object is bawdry and profaneness." Jeremy Collier, a dissenting parson, published a sizable pamphlet, *A Short View of the Immorality and Profaneness of the English Stage* (1697–98), which prepared the way for the sentimental comedy of the eighteenth century. Collier found the language of the plays immodest and would not admit satire or realism as an excuse for presenting immoral behavior. He was especially outraged that plays made fun of the clergy, and he even objected to light treatment of pagan priests or devils. He had strong opinions about dramatic form and showed how English plays violated classic rules. To show a person of the upper class as foolish seemed to him wrong, and to let the principal character sow wild oats and then reward him with a good-looking heiress was beyond endurance. He could be comfortable only with neat poetic justice and with the simpler kinds of comedy in which exalted characters were taken seriously and funny characters were of low class. Partly as a result of Collier's diatribe, the eighteenth-century theatre reformed its rakes and made its heroes virtuous young men, respectful of parents and tradesmen, and so created a different kind of comedy.

A few nineteenth-century romantic critics could not leave Restoration comedy alone. The more urbane among them envied it for its gaiety and unashamed concern with social amenities. They formed a picture of Restoration drama as an artificial comedy removed from serious cares and responsibility. William Hazlitt grew ecstatic in the *Examiner* in 1817:

Happy age, when kings and nobles led purely ornamental lives. When the utmost stretch of a morning's study went no farther than the choice of a sword-knot, or the adjustment of a side curl: when the soul spoke out in all the pleasing elegance of dress: and beaux and belles, enamored of themselves in one another's follies fluttered like gilded butterflies in giddy mazes through the walks of St. James' Park.

Charles Lamb made an ardent defense of his liking for Restoration comedy by supposing that the plays were free from moral concern. For him the characters lived in a cloud-cuckoo land, a "Utopia of Gallantry." Later in the century critics still found the characters "shadowy creatures," "puppet semblances of humanity." "Touch them," said one critic, "and like ghosts of Elysium, they turn to empty air in our grasp." Even in the early twentieth century these characters were liked because they seemed superficial. As anti-Victorianism was added to Romantic revolt against society, new meanings were attached to the terms "artificial comedy" and "comedy of manners." If the plays had enormous appeal because of their frank treatment of sex, they still seemed "artificial" because their characters spoke politely to one another. In a period of naturalism and proletarian interest it was assumed that the "natural" impulses were hate and distrust and that an impulse to be agreeable was "artificial." In his theatre studies in the early 1930s, John Palmer wrote that artificial comedy is a holiday from the sublime and beautiful, from the coarse and real; that it is the sublimation of the trivial, that the comedy of manners is "life in terms of a muffin." Bonamy Dobrée suggests in *Restoration Comedy, 1660–1720* (1927) that the world of the comedies is a charming illusion: "We are permitted to play with life, which has become a charming harlequinade without being farce. It is all spontaneous and free, rapid and exhilarating; the least emotion, or appeal to common sense, and the joyous illusion is gone."

In the late twentieth century a different view of high comedy is possible. Restoration plays seem important as dramatizations of major intellectual trends of the seventeenth century and as early definitions of the relationship of the individual to society. The question of morality no longer carries weight. After twentieth-century experiments in liberation in both art and actuality, there is as much freedom as the cavalier rakes ever wanted. T. S. Eliot wrote: "The morality of our Restoration drama cannot be impugned. It assumes orthodox Christian morality, and laughs at human nature for not living up to it. It retains its respect for the divine by showing the failure of the human."

In its treatment of sex, Restoration drama brings into the open the varying attitudes in a compact society and emphasizes the situation of the persons who search for genuine relationships. The Victorians wanted no such frankness. Macaulay wrote of the Restoration dramatists: "None of them was aware that a certain decorum is essential even to voluptuousness, that drapery may be more alluring than exposure, and that the imagination may be far more powerfully moved by delicate hints which impel it to exert itself, than by gross descriptions which it takes passively."

Historically the Restoration gallant is the logical next step after the Renaissance courtier. Freed from the military duties of feudalism, the Renaissance courtier could cultivate the arts and graces and perfect his body and his mind. A useful magistrate and counselor for the prince, he was still a public figure. The Baroque gallant expected, at least for a season in town, to be free from duties to the king and to his own estates in order to devote his attention to the fine art of self-realization.

Two characteristics of high comedy repel romantic audiences. One is that it shows a positive affection for fools. But to be tolerant does not mean to be blind; to withhold condemnation does not mean to forego judgment. The skepticism of the Baroque age made thinking people very dubious that they could improve their neighbors by jailing them or correct private sins with harsh sermons. In Molière and Restoration drama skepticism became a deep respect for the right of each fool to work out his own folly so long as he allowed his children and neighbors to do the same.

The other characteristic of high comedy that outrages the romantic is the admission of complexity and variety in love. High comedy offers no guarantee of eternal fidelity but only points out the ways that have the greatest chance for long life. It looks at marriage not in terms of all or nothing but in the context of complex lives where sex is one of many considerations. In the middle of the twentieth century Eric Fromm defined love as spontaneous and positive, "based on equality and freedom." This kind of love has been demonstrated in high comedy since the 1660s.

494

IX

The Eighteenth-Century Theatre

Tony Lumpkin in *She Stoops to Conquer*, London, 1776. *Courtesy of the Trustees of the British Museum.*

495

Introduction

A number of descriptive terms have been used to suggest the essential quality of the eighteenth century. The art and culture called Baroque merged into the Rococo. In art and architecture, Rococo implies elaboration and ornamentation. The painting of Boucher and Fragonard has pleasing softness of design and color; the work of lesser artists was often merely artificial and fussy. As applied to culture in general, Rococo suggests a relaxation of Baroque standards and more softness of feeling and judgment. In discussions of English literature, the period is usually referred to as the Augustan Age, suggesting a height of Neoclassicism. The eighteenth century is also called the Age of Reason, in reference, especially, to Voltaire and the *philosophes*. Combining these various terms, one may arrive at a fairly accurate impression of the century; yet something must be added. Beginning even before the middle of the century, there were indications of dissatisfaction with prevailing social conditions and attitudes, and of change, and in the last quarter of the century came revolution, political and cultural.

TRANSITION TO SERIOUS COMEDY

The attitude toward life suggested in the high comedy of Etherege and Congreve was too skeptical and cold for the eighteenth century. Even before the end of the seventeenth century several new devices were developed that increased the emotional impact of a play and furnished the lovers with an idealistic challenge. A new kind of ending went far to change comedy to a more serious form, though Plautus and Shakespeare had already demonstrated the effectiveness of a serious ending after confusion and laughter.

Colley Cibber's *Love's Last Shift* (1695) made an immediate sensation, partly because of the fop Sir Novelty Fashion, a role Cibber wrote for himself, but partly because of the appeal of the ending. After years of wandering, the libertine Loveless is lured into the bedroom of the wife he had abandoned but does not recognize. When the next day she reveals who she is he admits that he had found a very passionate virtue that he was not able to appreciate as a young bridgegroom. In Sir John Vanbrugh's *The Relapse* (1696), a sequel to *Love's Last Shift* and a parody of it, Loveless finds a new adventure in infidelity and his wife considers a counter revenge, but she does not pursue it. Even in admitting the difficulties of virtue, playwrights and audiences of the 1690s showed a liking for a more serious turn in the ending of love comedies.

The ending of George Farquhar's *The Beaux' Stratagem* (1707) is made exciting with both moral conversion and a rescue from robbers in the night. Aimwell and Archer are disguised as a lord and his servant to catch a woman of fortune in the country. Just as Aimwell is succeeding, he is so impressed by the trusting innocence of the young lady that he confesses he has deceived her. His sincerity appeals to her, and she will take him poor. Then there is news that his brother has died, and now he really is the lord he pretended to be. The robbers add a touch of melodrama, a middle-class version of the rescue by the dashing knight. The robbers also are the means of getting the papers of the drunken dolt, Squire Sullen, who is willing to divorce his wife but had hoped to keep her fortune.

By the 1770s the serious note and conversion at the end are regular even for high comedy and farce. In Oliver Goldsmith's *She Stoops to Conquer* (1773), Kate Hardcastle keeps control and sustains a more playful attitude. Like Amanda in *Love's Last Shift*, she must win her husband on more than one level. She has won him as the brisk barmaid, but before she can confess that she is also the great lady he had not dared look at, she lets him think she is a poor relative and has him in tears of pity.

This softening of emotional attitudes in plays which might still be classified as high comedy prepared the way for the mode characteristic of the late eighteenth century in England: sentimental comedy.

Sheridan's *The School for Scandal*

Richard Sheridan's *The Rivals* (1774) and *The School for Scandal* (1777) are in the tradition of Etherege and Congreve, but are adapted to the changed taste of the eighteenth century. *The School for Scandal* is considered by many the finest example of the comedy of manners in English, and it has been one of the most effective of all plays on the stage. In the list of successful plays in the London *Who's Who in the Theatre* it stands second only to *Romeo and Juliet* and *As You Like It* and ties with *Othello* for third place. Next to the balcony scene of *Romeo and Juliet* the screen scene in the fourth act is the most famous single scene in English drama. Among twentieth-century critics it has been the fashion to consider the play vastly inferior in wit and characterization to Congreve, to deplore the concessions Sheridan made to the prudery and sentimentality of eighteenth-century taste, or to praise it only for its theatricality. Kronenberger says in his edition of Sheridan's plays, "It belongs wholly to the stage, with no overtones of real life."

Yet there is much more to the comedy than a good story and the first-rate farcical scene in which Joseph hides Sir Peter in a closet and Lady Teazle behind a screen. Even if the ingenue Maria is too nice to be interesting, she does not demand much attention, and every other character is alive every second of the play. The scandalmongers are as vivid in their "humours" as any character Ben Jonson created; the generous brother, Charles Surface, is treated consistently as a high-comedy character; and sentiment is satirized in the hypocritical brother, Joseph Surface, one of the best comic acting roles in English. In addition, the central pair, Sir Peter and Lady Teazle, solve some of the most difficult problems of human adjustment.

Though Sheridan began two different plays—one about the Teazles and one about Lady Sneerwell and her crew of gossips—the two stories combine well. Sir Peter is concerned with what the world of gossip thinks of his young wife, and he learns to laugh at himself and to adjust to his marriage at the same time that he learns to distinguish between the public appearance and the true nature of the two Surface brothers.

Sheridan was right to surround the stories of Sir Peter's marriage and the two brothers with a chorus of scandalmongers. To the Victorian audience the gossips seemed vicious, and they were delighted when Lady Teazle promises to resign from the college of scandal. But the treatment is not really harsh. Lady Sneerwell and Snake spread trouble-making lies from malice born of bitterness. But Mrs. Candour, Crabtree, and Sir Benjamin Backbite merely make wild guesses and repeat the inaccurate reports of others. What these harmless gossips laugh at are timeless subjects for gossip and laughter: husband and wife who quarrel, older women who paint and pretend to be young, the fat woman who diets on whey and tries to reduce by riding a pony. Only those who do not know human nature or themselves, in short, those without a sense of humour, need beware of this college of scandal. Sir Peter, the violent critic of all gossips, who makes dangerous misjudgments and was "never mistaken in his life," is finally brought to say, "Sir Oliver, we live in a damned wicked world, and the fewer we praise the better."

The play defines several attitudes toward the enjoyment of gossip. The main question is how far "wit" is to be based on ill-nature and malice. Lady Sneerwell insists "Psha! there's no possibility of being witty without a little ill nature. The malice of a good thing is the barb that makes it stick." When Sir Peter suggests, "Oh, Madam, true wit is more nearly allied to good nature than your ladyship is aware of," the others do not disagree: they are only aware of the difficulty of realizing that ideal. Lady Teazle suggests a witty acceptance of man's failure with, "True, Sir Peter: I believe they are so near akin that they can never be united." And Sir Benjamin adds, "or rather, madam, I suppose them man and wife because one seldom sees them together." Mrs. Candour pays lip-service to Maria's disapproval but does not pause in her own gossip. Lady Teazle sees interest in the activities of neighbors as the inalienable right to freedom of discussion that any good sportsman will respect. When Sir Peter objects, she cries out, "What, would you restrain the freedom of speech?" When he protests that the gossips have made her as bad as any of the society, she smilingly admits: "Why, I believe I do bear a part with a tolerable grace. But I vow I bear no malice against the people I abuse: when I say an ill-natured thing, 'tis out of pure good humour: and I take it for granted they deal exactly in the same manner with me. . . . But Sir Peter is such an enemy to scandal I believe he would have it put down by parliament."

Sir Peter's experience is comparable in many ways to that of Molière's Misanthrope. But Sheridan was more optimistic than Molière about the ability of man to learn and change. Sir Peter disapproves of the fashionable world and is as distressed as Alceste that his lively young wife loves the social game. But he learns to see his own mistakes and finally to laugh at himself.

The more complex English form of drama, with subplots, large cast, and many changes of scene, makes the plot of a man learning to adapt himself to the people around him more credible than the compact French classic form of the 1660s. Where Molière made the solution of his plot depend entirely on Alceste's demand that Célimène leave the world of fashion, Sir Peter is more involved with the lives of other people. If Molière gives a deeper psychological study, Sheridan gives a wider social picture. As guardian of Maria and de facto guardian of Charles and

Joseph, Sir Peter is tempted to force Maria to follow his estimate as to which brother she should marry, an estimate based on the wrong report. He cannot run off to the desert when he meets social disaster but is forced to face his own share of public opinion. He is more committed to his friends than is Alceste to his. He drives the gossips out of his house in a farcical scene, but when his two close friends begin to laugh at his embarrassment over the screen episode, he must accept their good-humored teasing and laugh at himself. And he is more devoted to his love than is Alceste: he enjoys Lady Teazle's high spirits and teasing manner even when they quarrel. Where Molière's stiff-necked Misanthrope demands that other people change, Sir Peter knows it is up to him to reform.

Later critics doubt that Lady Teazle's contrition has totally converted her into a pious prude, and the outraged remark of a writer in the *Gentleman's Magazine* at the time tells that the original Lady Teazle carried her twinkling smile to the end. High comedy is wary of too large a promise, but, as Charles says, "Why as to reforming, Sir Peter, I'll make no promises, and that I take to be a proof that I intend to set about it." Sir Peter shows his new sense of humor with "May you live as happily together as Lady Teazle and I—intend to do."

The Theatre of David Garrick

A revolution in acting came in England in 1741 when Charles Macklin defied the tradition of a red-wigged, comic Shylock and played him in a quiet, natural manner. In the same year an actor in his early twenties, little David Garrick, arrived in London with his schoolmaster, Samuel Johnson, to make his fortune. When the two regular theatres (Drury Lane and Covent Garden) turned him down, he played Richard III in the off-season theatre in Goodman's Fields and made such a sensation that Drury Lane immediately hired him. A director and leading actor for three decades, he made the Drury Lane company the best in Europe. His acting was a startling break with the methods that had prevailed since the Restoration, especially in tragedy, for he despised the sustained inflections and large movements that had made Baroque acting grandiose. One admirer said that "he threw new light on elocution and action; he banished ranting, bombast, and grimace; and restored nature, ease, simplicity, and genuine humour." He set himself against the regular rhythm of speech and the decorative costume usual for Shakespearean actors, for, he said, "I hate your roarers." The actor James Quin, who intoned tragedy like plainsong and played Coriolanus in a Roman tunic as wide as a ballet skirt, said, "If the young fellow is right, I and the rest of the players have been all wrong."

Garrick's vivid eyes and mobile face were a marvel to all who saw him. The young actor would entertain his fashionable friends by putting his head between two folding doors and changing his expression "successively from wild delight to temperate pleasure, from this to tranquillity, from tranquillity to surprise, from surprise to blank astonishment, from that to sorrow, from sorrow to the air of one overwhelmed, from that to fright, from fright to horror, and thence . . . up again to the point from which he started." Garrick's greatest acting strength, one critic thought, lay in "surprise, impatience, interruption," adding, "his sudden transitions, in particular, he has the happy art of making extremely swift. . . . He falls from fury into tears with a breath: and is pure and entire in both." For these effects he made great use of broken sentences and pauses. He was said to have taught his actors that "the great art is to give variety & which only can be attained by a strict regard to ye pauses—the running the different parts of a Monologue together, will necessarily give a Monotony & take away ye spirit and Sense of ye author."

502

Naturally he did not please everyone. Some ridiculed his "false pauses, stammerings, hesitations and repetitions" as claptrap contrived to gain applause. At first Macklin accused him of over-active strutting and playing with his handkerchief to the point of stealing scenes. He wrote of Garrick's restless style,

Garrick huddled all passions into strut and quickness,—bustle was his favorite . . . he was all bustle! bustle! bustle! The whole art of acting, according to the modern practice is comprized in—bustle! . . . all Garrick wanted in order to make him a great actor were consequence, dignity, eloquence, and majesty of figure.

But Macklin and Garrick soon became good friends and, with the beautiful actress Peg Woffington, shared a menage, and Garrick learned much from Macklin's criticism. In spite of a stature of less than five and a half feet, a restless temperament, and a voice that could not sustain the strongest tones and was sometimes hoarse, Garrick became one of the great actors of all time. Edmund Burke declared, "He raised the character of his profession to the rank of a liberal art." The dramatist

David Garrick as Lethe. *Published with the permission of the Birmingham Museum and Art Gallery.*

Richard Cumberland gave his impression of Garrick's charm and the importance of his achievement in his reminiscence of the performances of Garrick and James Quin in the same plays in 1746–47. Quin seemed to him insipid and dull "in an enormous full-bottomed periwig . . . with very little variation of cadence, and in a deep full tone accompanied by a sawing kind of action which had more of the senate than of the stage in it, he rolled out his heroics with an air of dignified indifference . . ." Of Garrick Cumberland wrote, "When I first beheld little Garrick, then young and light and active in every muscle and feature, come bounding on the stage—heavens, what a transition! It seemed as if a whole century had been stepped over in the transition of a single scene." That quick fire Garrick was always able to make convincing. John Hill wrote, "Mr. Garrick has more fire than any actor in the world probably ever possessed: but did anybody ever suppose that Mr. Garrick had too much? None ever thought of it."

Garrick increased the prestige and appreciation of Shakespeare. Critics found that his reading threw light on many passages, and for students and public alike he became the high priest of the increasing Bardolatry. He promoted a Shakespeare Jubilee for the second centennial at Stratford, which finally came off in 1769 a few years late, with some mishaps but much acclaim. No plays were performed at Stratford, but in his own theatre and with his regular devoted audience Garrick kept the major plays more than alive, constantly restudying them and trying to improve the performance and occasionally providing new scenery and costumes. But for the most part the actors used the same dress for *Hamlet*, *Macbeth*, and *Lear* that they used for the kings and nobles in plays of more recent times. The texts used, which were often major revisions to suit Restoration taste, are shocking to twentieth-century taste. Yet in nearly all instances Garrick changed the scripts of his predecessors, putting back much of the original Shakespeare that they had cut or rewritten.

The fresh interpretation of Hamlet was the subject of general comment. For the traditional entrance with pompous music, Garrick substituted a quiet entrance, and in the "To be or not to be" soliloquy he gave the subtlest modulation of voice and face at each change of thought. But his fire burst forth at the meeting with the ghost. Dr. Johnson was not sure that the effect was natural. When Boswell asked him, "Would not you, sir, start as Garrick does if you saw a ghost?" he replied, "If I did, I should frighten the ghost." From a German visitor, Lichtenberg, there is a detailed account of how Garrick produced such an electric effect.

As Romeo, this short, unglamorous actor triumphed in competition with a tall, handsome actor, Spranger Barry. During most of his career Garrick had this actor in his company and presented him and Mrs. Susannah Cibber as Romeo and Juliet with great success. But when they both went to the rival house, Covent Garden, where the manager immediately announced *Romeo and Juliet*, Garrick took up the challenge and played Romeo himself. For weeks the town was buzzing over this war of the theatres, and two excellent performances were analyzed and discussed in every point. Finally it was decided that Garrick drew the most applause but Barry the most tears. Most theatregoers agreed that Barry was best in the first part of the play but that Garrick was unsurpassable in Romeo's anguish and violence in Friar Lawrence's cell and in the final scene, where, in the eighteenth-century version, Romeo remains alive long enough for a farewell duet with Juliet. It is said that some enthusiasts went to see Barry in the first part, then rushed to Drury Lane to catch Garrick and Mrs. Bellamy in the last acts.

For little Davy to play Lear was an even greater challenge, but he made it his most impressive and touching part, exploiting his wide range and quick transitions to the fullest, moving from fury to tears in a breath. It was said that even the red-coat guards wept. Until he reclothed the play in his last year, he had little help from costume. With a grey wig and knee britches of his own time and the same short ermine-trimmed coat he used for all kings, he looked more like a petty comedian than a figure of tragedy. Yet he achieved grandeur by sheer intensity of acting. Throughout his career Garrick studied the part, made improvements in his acting, and tried different versions of the play. He started with Nahum Tate's version, a major rewriting of 1681 that left out the fool, softened many of the characters, and ended with Lear happily restored to the throne and Cordelia and Edgar married. Although Garrick never dared use the original ending or the fool, he gradually put back many of the lines that Tate had omitted or rewritten. Only a few urged the full Shakespearean version, and even the great arbiter of taste, Dr. Johnson, thought Shakespeare's ending, with the undeserved death of Cordelia, unendurable. The classic taste of the eighteenth century required that there be no comic distraction in a serious play and that an ending show the triumph of virtue.

When Macklin was critical of Garrick's first performance of *Lear*, Garrick held the play off the boards for six weeks to restudy it in the light of his suggestions. It is told that Garrick went to study a madman, who, having dropped his child out a window, was forever obsessed with acting over again the child's joy in playing and his own horror at discovering that he had killed his child. Garrick would enact the character in his parlor entertainments and found this study very helpful for his Lear.

Theatregoers were amazed that an actor could keep such violent intensities in perfect control and make them convincing. A detailed description of the scene in which Lear throws his crutch away, gets on his knees to curse Goneril, and bursts into tears appears in the report of a conversation between Garrick and Samuel Foote. Foote says: "You fall precipitately upon your knees, extend your arms—clench your Hand—set your Teeth—and with a savage Distraction in your Look—trembling in your Limbs—and your Eyes pointed to Heaven—begin—with a *broken, inward, eager* utterance; from thence rising every Line in Loudness and Rapidity of voice."

Although his prestige was based on Shakespearean roles, Garrick delighted his age equally in comedy. He played the adventurer-gallant Archer in George

505

Top: Garrick as Lear. *Courtesy of the Board of Trustees of the Victoria and Albert Museum. Bottom:* Garrick as Richard III. *Courtesy of the Board of Trustees of the Victoria and Albert Museum.*

Farquhar's *The Beaux Stratagem* with dash and elegance and even in the disguise of a servant, dressed in beautiful sky-blue livery. The small part of the tobacconist, Old Drugger, in Ben Jonson's *The Alchemist* became one of his most famous roles. Not the stock buffoon of Theophilus Cibber or the stupid lout of other actors, he gave to his Old Drugger such a flood of warm feeling, half hidden from the other characters, that he charmed the audience while they laughed heartily. According to one spectator, at the end, when Drugger found himself duped, he "stripped off his clothes, rubbed his hands, clenched his fists, and threw himself into all the attitudes of a modern Broughtonian bruiser."

An equal delight for the audience was the role of Sir John Brute in Sir John Vanbrugh's *The Provoked Wife* (1697). Instead of a morose, ill-natured, drunken boor, Garrick made him a wicked dog, with a touch of the attractive rake and a suggestion of a worn-out fop, with a small beribboned hat jauntily perched on the top of his wig and a fashionable oak stick in his hand. The drunken orgy at the tavern was a triumph of high spirits. The street scene that follows became wild farce as Sir John, threatened by the constable and the watch, put on the dress the tailor was taking to his wife and with a watchman's staff held off the watch in lively combat. His imitation of feminine ways was a hit. But most delightful of all was the scene in which Sir John returned home, his wig over part of his face, now breaking into coarse talk and now becoming "so wise and merry in his cups that the whole audience bursts into a tumult of applause." That the same actor could give such a coarse performance one night and rise the next to the majesty and dignity of Hamlet or Lear never ceased to impress his contemporaries.

Besides the careful coaching and directing of his actors, Garrick in his career as manager is noted for great improvements in staging. The Elizabethan practice of allowing a privileged few to sit on the stage had not been abandoned, and Garrick took a position long overdue in canceling the privilege. Stage lighting was still inadequate, and Garrick performed a service in introducing methods that had been introduced in Alsace by Philip James de Loutherbourg. In England the chandeliers that lighted the stage were part of the lighting of the house. In an eighteenth-century picture of *Romeo and Juliet*, Garrick stands on the forestage below the stage box looking up at Juliet and the chandelier far from the painted backdrop of garden, clouds, and moonlight. As long as the main lighting was from the front chandeliers and the footlights the actor had to stay well out on the apron. But with better lighting within the scene he could move back into the picture. Not only the actor but the setting benefited by the placing of vertical strips of lamps behind the side wings and behind the cut-out backdrop. Garrick created a sensation when he introduced the new lamp system after a trip to the continent in 1764–65. The effect of new lighting is apparent in an engraving of Juliet's tomb, with strong unseen lights behind a darker drop painted as a tomb in night.

Still more romantic effects were achieved by De Loutherbourg when Garrick hired him for the Drury Lane Company. He developed transparencies with caves and mountain glens only half revealed in the midst of wings and borders and cut-

507

out shapes. Strong lighting of the audience was retained, however, and these romantic stage effects were created from relative darkness, so that there was still no full contrast of dark and light.

Particularly as an actor, but also as manager, director, acting coach, and technical innovator, Garrick is a colossal figure in the development of the English theatre.

The Kembles

In England it was no new playwright, such as Schiller or Goethe, but two actors who expressed the taste of the last of the eighteenth century: John Philip Kemble and his sister, Mrs. Sarah Siddons, perhaps the greatest actress the world has ever known. Both brought to the stage the dignity and simple greatness that are called classic.

After several years of playing in the provinces, Mrs. Siddons was brought to London by Garrick in his last season in 1775, but she made no great impression and the new managers did not rehire her. She returned to the provinces and built a strong reputation, especially in Bath. By 1782 she was a matured artist, and London was ready for her. Appearing as Isabella in Thomas Southerne's *The Fatal Marriage* (1694), she made one of the greatest sensations in theatre history. Only the debuts of David Garrick and Edmund Kean compare with it. Here was a tall, dignified woman without the least touch of flirtation, yet warmly feminine. Here was the wronged heroine to stir eighteenth-century sensibility. Here were proud grief and majestic desolation. In an old play she showed the age both the agony of a world of wrong and the fortitude to face it. She proceeded to other brave, suffering women: Euphrasia in *Grecian Daughter*, Calista in *Fair Penitent*, and Belvedera in *Venice Preserved*. London was at her feet—pit and society, artists and royalty.

The last spurt of Rococo taste had spent its force in women's dress in the 1770s. Wigs were ornamented with windmills or sailing ships or built so high that satirists declared the dresser must mount a ladder to arrange them. Bodices were stiff and long, and panniers held the skirts out very wide. Mrs. Siddons wore neither wig nor powder and braided her hair very close to her head. She wore a soft waist and a simple skirt. The new styles brought out her easy dignity. Sir Joshua Reynolds was entranced and painted her portrait as the Tragic Muse, putting his name, the story says, to go down to posterity on the hem of her skirt.

She had a wide range. In gentle, domestic woe she had no rival, yet she could raise passions more furious than the winds. Always she was simple, commanding. She could listen with such intensity that the audience looked only at her; she could sweep into an archway as an outraged queen and, motionless, dominate the scene. She studied sculpture and did some herself. She was especially impressed by the Apollo Belvedere at the Louvre and by the intensity of feeling of Egyptian

509

statues with arms close down by the sides and hands clenched. Her Hermione, the statue that comes to life in Shakespeare's *The Winter's Tale*, seemed the perfection of both sculptural beauty and acting.

Sara Siddons.

510

Her most famous part was Lady Macbeth, to which her brother's Macbeth seemed only support. Her concept of Lady Macbeth was a woman captivating in feminine loveliness, who could fascinate an honorable hero like Macbeth. But she added to that captivating charm her turbulent and inhuman strength. She hurried Macbeth on in a mad career of ambition and cruelty that, without her influence, his nature would have shrunk from. Then came sickness, remorse, and despair, the "flagging of her spirit, the melancholy and dismal blank beginning to steal upon her," as one witness described Siddons' Lady Macbeth. No one who saw it could forget her sleep-walking scene. Dressed in a white drapery, like a statue, or as in a shroud, she appeared quite suddenly, listening eagerly, speaking in a melancholy tone and a strange whisper, ending her soliloquy with a convulsive shudder that suggested madness.

John Philip Kemble, her brother, did not have the beautiful voice or the ease of Mrs. Siddons. But he had the same dignity and strength and an even more towering grandeur. He worked very hard, developing a diction so precise it often went to the extreme of pedantry. He joined the Drury Lane Company the year after Mrs. Siddons did, making a considerable success in *Hamlet*. But he excelled in the Roman parts. Even before David in France, he rejected the elaborate costumes for a simpler tunic and drapes studied from Roman statues. His Cato in Addison's play of that name was magnificent. He excelled in parts requiring the development of a single dominating passion. Coriolanus was probably his greatest role. He gave it impetuosity, haughty dignity, and unbending sternness. Coriolanus was at once a rebel against society and a proud aristocrat who had to submit to the demands of the people. Here were dignity and bravery and self-respect amidst the painful insistence of a new democracy.

Always the Kembles gave fresh, intelligent readings, carefully planning every move and inflection. John Philip sometimes maintained such an even power that he seemed monotonous, but when he suddenly made one moment stand out, the effect was tremendous. The Kembles well represented their age. But it is easy to understand that after thirty years of them London might welcome the short, impetuous, fiery Edmund Kean.

Late Eighteenth Century: Revolution

The last quarter of the eighteenth century saw one of the most dramatic reversals of history that Europe has even known. The ideal of the Baroque-Rococo synthesis, the product of more than three hundred years of development, was in a quarter of a century attacked, repudiated, and banished. The harmony among town, court, country gentleman, scientist, parson, and poet turned to discord. The cultivated young man at the beginning of the eighteenth century found an agreed-on ideal of aristocratic behavior, agreed-on models in education and all the arts, and above all a concept of society as the highest expression of human ideals and the scene of man's most satisfying work and play. But the sensitive man at the beginning of the nineteenth century found himself isolated, cut off from society, seeking out the most remote wilderness or Alpine peak, plotting bloody vengeance on his fellow man, and sure only of the surging passion within his breast, the deep longing for love and the ideal. The eighteenth-century man hoped that his cultivated society would go on forever, but it did not last the century out.

The French Revolution was a violent and bloody climax to a movement that was to shake the old regime to its foundations and transform government, social classes, economic institutions, religion, philosophy, science, education, customs and costumes, taste for both nature and art, and the ideals of what a man should be and what his goals should be.

What began with criticism ended with assault. Voltaire began by praising his own enlightened era and what it was achieving in throwing off the superstition of the Middle Ages. The generation that followed him carried his worship of reason to the point of idolatry and tried to rebuild the world in its name. But they saw their ideals threatened at every turn by entrenched tyranny. Their most popular novels and plays were filled with tyrants in castles and the storming of forts and prisons, and this was true not only in France, where a king was killed and old fortresses were actually stormed, but in England, Germany, Italy—among gentle souls who would never have joined rebels on the barricades. The revolt of the mind proved just as violent. From the 1760s and 1770s the dramatists Goldoni and Beaumarchais were making fun of aristocrats in terms which seem mild today but which aroused fiery enthusiasm at the time.

512

Rousseau saw clearly that the old order was corrupt and doomed. He saw what the social ideal did to particular men, what the neglect of childhood did to particular children, and he insisted that society and education must be remade. He believed that the only basis for society was freedom of the individual. He looked to the achievement of a "general will," but he recognized that that must come out of adjustment in the give and take of conflict and not out of the suppression of most of the people. He was aware of the weight of opposition to anything new— hence his great emphasis on the fiery genius, on originality and creativity. A curious, contradictory man, he confessed to as much meanness in himself as he saw around him. But from his wide experience, his own sense of guilt, arose a strong cry for a new beginning. Against the seventeenth-century insistence on the depravity of man he declared that man is by nature good and if he seems depraved it is because of the corruption of society. Back to nature! Against the eighteenth-century acceptance of a world where everything that is is right, he saw all of man's deeper needs thwarted by traditions, institutions, and conventions. Back to nature! The Baroque grand opera, the playful decoration in Rococo art he found sterile and artificial. Back to nature!

Political revolution erupted in 1789. In the spring Louis XVI at long last called an assembly of the three estates—nobility, clergy, and the "Third Estate," or merchants and mere people—to help solve the financial crisis of the nation. The third estate felt loyal to the king, but in contention with the clergy and nobility stood firm. Then on July 12 news reached Paris that the king had dismissed his liberal minister, Necker, and was bringing royal troops into the city. The assembly protested in vain and the city began mobilizing its own guards and militia to protect the assembly. On July 14 a mob of new city militia and angry citizens took the arms stored in a soldier's home and started looking for more. When someone suggested the Bastille, the crowd, without leaders and without a plan, laid siege to the prison.

Actually the event was no great triumph: the Commander of the Bastille lost his nerve and let down the drawbridge, the arms found were negligible, and there were only seven prisoners to be set free. But citizens had stormed and taken the most hated symbol of power and tyranny. For four centuries its ugly towers had loomed over the workingmen's section of Paris. For two centuries it had been the chief prison for state prisoners. The king gave noblemen blank warrants, "lettres de cachet," by which they might have anyone arrested. No prisoner knew how long he would be held. There were rumors of terrible tortures. Some of the highest persons of the realm had been held prisoner. Once a man in an iron mask had been carried in and never came out; nobody knew who he was. The Paris mob avenged not only the years of legal injustice but every insult, privation, or misery they had ever experienced, whether from aristocrats or from the course of life itself. They paraded the streets carrying chains, keys, and other symbols of tyranny. They dragged the Commander in front of the city hall and cut off his head with a pocket knife.

513

When the king was told of the storming of the Bastille, he exclaimed "But this is revolt." "No, Sire," was the reply, "it is Revolution." Paris remained armed. The king left his soldiers in the provinces, recalled his minister, and went to the city hall, where the mayor put on his hat the new tricolor cockade, a combination of the red and blue of Paris with the Bourbon white. All over France the people, stirred by excitement and rumors of bandits, attacked local forts and chateaux and forced noblemen to destroy feudal deeds giving them rights to personal service. Presently the nobility and the clergy in the assembly in Paris, in an orgy of renunciation, gave up their age-old privileges, rights, taxes, titles, and symbols.

The effect of the Revolution on other countries was tremendous. Many people were greatly alarmed. Edmund Burke, who had defended the American Revolution, wrote, "The age of chivalry is gone. That of sophisters, economists, and calculators has succeeded; and the glory of Europe is extinguished forever." But the idealistic young were ecstatic over the promise of a new age. Wordsworth expressed that hope in a famous passage in *The Prelude*:

Bliss was it in that dawn to be alive,
But to be young was very heaven!

. . . .

Not favored spots alone, but the whole Earth
The beauty wore of promise

THE THEATRE OF REVOLT

The theatre of the last quarter of the eighteenth century shows the same patterns, emotions, and symbols as the French Revolution. The playwrights might be aristocrats and the audience might despise the violence of the French Revolution, but in the theatre they responded to impulses of revolt. In imagination they deserted society to go with the noble outlaw, free from old restraints, avenging injustice and wrong. They identified with the innocent heroine of the Gothic plays, shut up, pursued, and tortured in a gloomy medieval castle by a tyrant himself half-mad with guilt. With some nameless "stranger" they broke from all their false friends and started life over again, mysteriously and anonymously doing good, never asking any return from a wicked world. Or in brighter moments, seeking the simplicity and nobility of a new beginning, they loved the honest strength of Mrs. Siddons' acting and the stalwart grandeur of her brother, John Philip Kemble, the noblest Roman of them all. They watched Brutus, the leader of revolt against the Tarquins, sacrifice his own son to protect new-won freedom. In the theatre, as in the assemblies of Paris, Philadelphia, and Washington, Greco-

514

Roman heroes, architecture, and costumes seemed right for the heroic beginning of a new age.

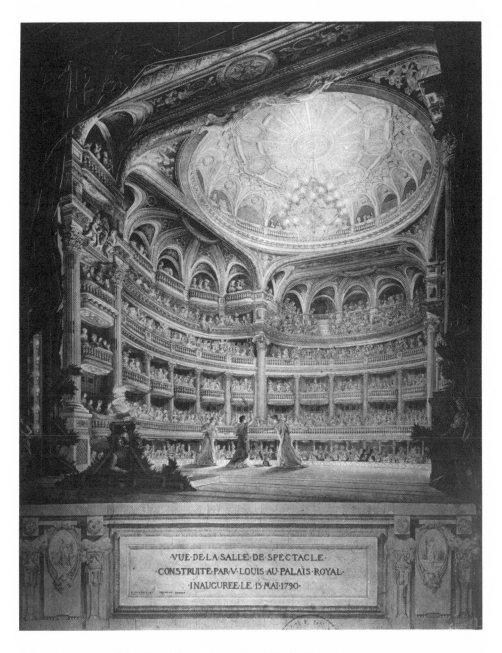

Salle de Spectacles, Palais Royal, Paris, 1790. *Phot. Bibl. Nat. Paris.*

Goethe and Schiller, in a country that was just waking to its cultural development, created the first plays of revolt. Goethe led off by publishing *Goetz von Berlichingen* in 1773, sixteen years before the outbreak in Paris. He chose for his hero one of the last of the independent medieval knights. Though loyal to the distant emperor, Goetz of the Iron Hand will not bow to the neighboring court. His manliness and self-reliance are set in contrast to the intrigue and luxury of the court. Betrayed by friends and enemies alike, Goetz defends himself with a few loyal followers but is crushed. Goetz is surrounded by a mob of rioters who insist on his being their leader. He accepts on condition that they cease lawless robbery and burning of towns. But they get out of hand, and his one loyal page is killed. Goetz dies brokenhearted—it is a wicked world.

This pioneering play was never very popular on the stage, but it had a great influence on other writers. Sir Walter Scott was fascinated by it, made a translation, and followed it in working out his own way of presenting history.

Goethe created a more successful picture of noble revolt in *Egmont* (1788). This hero of the Netherlands revolts against Spain, despising danger or prudence, goes about encouraging self-reliance and resistance and tells the Spanish governor what he thinks of him. He is so frank and noble himself that he is surprised to be put in prison and condemned to death. At first he despairs, but Goethe shows his two great sanctions: the recognition of self-reliant nobility and the promise of the future. His enemy's son comes to his prison to express admiration. The back wall of the prison opens to show a vision of Freedom in classic garb assuring him that his death will bring the freedom of the provinces. He marches to his death with drums and music.

The most successful play of revolt was Schiller's *The Robbers* (1781). Few plays in the history of the theatre have had such influence. Before the end of the century it was well known in Paris, London, and New York, and it remained in most repertories for almost half a century. It shaped patterns of melodrama which lasted into the twentieth century on both stage and screen.

Karl Moor, Schiller's hero, embodied more aspects of the age than any other literary character. Alienated from his father and his home, bitter because of injustice done him, he turns against society, organizes a band of robbers who swear vengeance on all authority, and sets about rescuing the victims of injustice and righting the wrongs of the world. He is contemptuous of all restraint and law. "They curb honest nature with absurd conventionality," he declares, ". . . never yet has law formed a great man; 'tis liberty that breeds giants and heroes." He broods not only on vengeance but on the titanic possibility that lies before a man who has thrown off shackles and chains. "Set me at the head of an army of fellows like myself, and out of Germany shall spring a republic compared to which Rome and Sparta shall be but as nunneries." He defies the priest sent by the city to demand his surrender. "Tell your masters that my trade is retribution—vengeance my occupation!" He justifies his robbing and burning by the wickedness of the

516

victims. He points to the rings on his fingers and lists the corrupt, venal officials and churchmen they were taken from. At last Karl Moor is plunged into anguished remorse, and as a final gesture he stabs his faithful sweetheart and gives himself up to authority.

The repudiation of the established order could scarcely be stronger than in Schiller's *Love and Intrigue* (1784), a play almost as popular as *The Robbers*. The basic situation starts like a Baroque comedy of intrigue; the son loves a bourgeois sweetheart, while the father wants him to marry a woman with a title. Lady Milford, the mistress of the prince, sees the young man as her chance of salvation. But the honest young couple are such a reproach to her that she sells her jewels, denounces the court, and returns to England, poor but honest. The father intrigues, like a father in sophisticated comedy, to convince his son that the girl has a lover. He forces the girl to write incriminating letters to save her father's life. But the young man is now a new kind of hero. Already tormented by his father's cruelty and taking his love and his ideals very seriously, he kills the girl and himself.

Perhaps the richest and fullest expression of revolt was Schiller's *William Tell*. It was written in 1804, ten years after the excesses of the Reign of Terror had turned many people against the French Revolution. But hatred of tyranny is as strong as ever. The Swiss citizens, proud and independent, are outraged not only at the unjust acts of the Austrian Governor but at the building in their midst of a fortress to ensure his power and imprison rebels. William Tell, refusing to bow to the cap of the Governor, submits to the famous trial by shooting an apple from the head of his young son, but denounces the Governor, escapes from prison, and kills the Governor in a mountain pass. By 1804 Schiller is ready to make a distinction between patriotic defense of freedom and the revolt of anyone brooding over a personal slight. Tell repudiates the man who had wantonly murdered the Emperor.

The sentimental variation of the rebel appeared in August Friedrich Ferdinand von Kotzebue's *Misanthropy and Repentance* (1781), which had an enormous vogue for half a century. Translated as *The Stranger*, it was one of the most popular plays in England and America. It was imitated by Richard Cumberland in *The Wheel of Fortune* (1698), which furnished one of John Kemble's best parts. Kotzebue's "stranger" has disappeared from society because a close friend stole the affections of his young wife. He lives anonymously in a small village helping the needy but refusing to see visitors or accept thanks. He longs to go away and bring up his children uncontaminated by society. His wife, now repentant, has taken service under a new name in the nearby castle and is likewise anonymously relieving the needy. The two are brought together and, in a scene of sorrow and anguish, say farewell forever. But when the children are brought on, in a scene without a spoken word, the two rush into each other's arms, creating one of the most emotional curtain tableaux in the history of the theatre. For the benefit of Victorian taste, some performances omitted the original ending of *The Stranger* and let the two go their separate ways, forever blighted by sin.

The mysterious stranger, usually anonymous because of some great wrong done him, was a commonplace in the Gothic drama and hence in the melodrama that came later. He is humble and undemanding, turning his aggression on himself. Quietly he rescues other victims of injustice and builds up the case against the real villain. At last he is reinstated and his nobility recognized. While the rebel takes the audience completely away from society in order to attack it with vengeance, the stranger enables them to cut off their normal connections with society temporarily, then when they have righted the wrongs of other victims, to reassume their positions. Needless to say, the stranger was more popular than the rebel.

The French Revolution began with a symbolic gesture—the storming of a Gothic castle (the Bastille)—such action as had already appeared in a number of plays. The Revolution developed with a cult of Greece and Rome that was equally symbolic and dramatic. The new kind of Neoclassicism in painting, architecture, and drama had already made its appearance in the 1780s, but the style became the liberating symbol of simplicity and republican dignity for the revolution. French patriots acted out the Gothic nightmare and the Greek dream that haunted a generation and in modified form still persisted for much of the following century.

At first glance it seems contradictory that a Gothic castle and a Greco-Roman architectural style should appear together in the decade of the Revolution. It has puzzled art historians that the political revolt adopted the neoclassic painting, architecture, and stage designs of David, while the generation of Victor Hugo and Delacroix in the 1820s looked on the "classic" from Racine through David as the dead hand of the old regime. We must make a distinction between the new generation appearing in France in the 1820s—the generation usually called the Romantic—and the earlier generation of the Revolution. Both were trying to destroy the vestiges of the Baroque-Rococo culture and bring a new age into being. The earlier generation had rather simple objectives: to destroy by violence all visible evidence of an old regime and start the new by political fiat with a rationalistic constitution and a simple style of architecture, dress, and behavior suggested by the Greek and Roman republics. After the Revolution the new generation repudiated the simple rationalistic objectives, as well as the Greco-Roman style, and began to seek deeper religious, philosophical, and psychological bases for their new world. In England, where there was a quick revulsion against the French Revolution and a reactionary government that made political action seem hopeless, the two phases overlap. It is much easier to trace the relation between style and history in France, where the first impulse burst into sudden and overwhelming violence and where the Napoleonic wars delayed the second impulse for a generation.

THE GOTHIC CASTLE

Even more than the outlaw rebel, the Gothic castle focused the fear and anger at entrenched society. The most thrilling plays at the end of the eighteenth century scared the audience with the destruction of a tyrant in a frightful castle and often, with thunder and lightning, the whole castle.

Horace Walpole, who had already added Gothic architectural details to his estate, Strawberry Hill, created the first Gothic novel, *The Castle of Otranto* (1764), and started a long fad. He made his ruined castle and monastery embodiments of terror, superstition, and torture. He exposed an innocent girl to the night terrors of secret passageways, subterranean chambers, ghostly figures in armor, a statue that bleeds, a helmet large enough to crash into a vault and crush a human being, monks, nuns, hermits, and a tyrannical old monster who is guilty of a secret ancient crime.

The greatest popularity of the Gothic castle came in the decades of Revolution. In 1781 *The Castle of Otranto* was dramatized. In the same year Schiller in *The Robbers* showed an innocent girl pursued through medieval castle corridors by the wicked Francis Moor. In the same year, Henry Fuseli, a strange Swiss-English artist, painted "The Nightmare," showing a lovely maiden hanging half out of bed, almost in the claws of a frightful demon.

In 1789, the year of the beginning of the French Revolution, Ann Radcliffe began her prolific output of Gothic novels, which were almost immediately dramatized. Her most famous was *The Mysteries of Udolpho* (1794). By the 1790s, from English and German sources, Gothic tales and plays had become popular in all Western Europe and in America. They roused terror at the uncanny and supernatural in the ruins of a cursed castle, horror at the tyrant consumed by his secret guilt, and passion by the sufferings of the persecuted maiden. Any history or local color in the plays is merely an afterthought. Whether the setting was medieval or modern, in Italy or in Germany, a fully equipped Gothic castle needed dungeon, tower, secret corridors, spiral staircase, vaulted rooms, closets hidden in the walls, trap doors, grated doors, tapestried room, portrait gallery, or armored hall where statues or paintings come to life, a set of subterranean passages, vaults, catacombs, crypts, and chapels, where the hero and heroine can meet at last, make love, hate, fight, surprise, assassinate, or marry each other. Nearby were forest, ruined convent, and cavern, equally gruesome settings for action. The time was often dark night, and sometimes there was little light on the stage except a flickering candle, a dim lamp, or a swinging lantern. Sound was important: the clank of chains and the midnight bell were standard, and sometimes choruses of religious or heavenly singers rang out.

The main characters were the tyrant, often a usurper, the unknown imprisoned in the dungeon, the persecuted maiden fleeing the tyrant, now penetrating into the mysteries of the castle, and the young hero, who is mostly outside bringing help to storm the castle. Sometimes the tyrant enlarged his power with a secret tribunal, a special terror in a decade that had memories of Jesuit societies recently abolished and of Jacobin Clubs so active in the French Revolution, a decade seething with rumors of secret "illuminati" societies plotting to destroy the world by revolution. There were attacks on the Freemasons in both Europe and America. The rumors were fantastic, but the fear of violence was real.

The ruined Gothic convent was almost as frequent in the plays as the castle. Corrupt monks and priests appear, and when the heroine seeks sanctuary she may be tormented by those who want to force her to become a nun.

The high point of the Gothic fad was reached by M. G. Lewis, whose novel *The Monk* (1797) became so popular that he has been known ever since as Monk Lewis. In 1798 Lewis wrote *The Castle Spectre*, the best of the Gothic plays and the most successful play of the age. It had an enormous run of 47 nights and was revived for years. Seven printed editions appeared in the first year.

In *The Castle Spectre*, the hero penetrates the castle with the help of a jolly friar and a motley fool. He hides in the armor of the good former lord of the castle. Long ago the tyrant had ordered his brother and his sweetheart killed when the brother won her love, and he will not be thwarted this time. When he hears that the hero has escaped to bring help he cries "No, rather than resign her, my own hand shall give this castle a prey to flames; then plunging with Angela into the blazing gulf, I'll leave these ruins to tell posterity how desperate was my love, and how dreadful my revenge!"

The story takes a new turn when the repentant villain's assistant (a figure established in *The Robbers* and standard in later melodrama) discloses that the lord, Angela's father, is still alive in a secret dungeon beneath the castle. This gives the villain a new power. Unless Angela gives in to him he can kill her father. But first she has a vision of her mother's ghost, the Castle Spectre. The back wall opens up to disclose a brightly lighted oratory, where the mother sings a lullaby and a chorus sings "Jubilate."

The last act begins with a series of movie-like scenes, showing hero, heroine, and tyrant separately approaching the dungeon. The tyrant is ready to kill the father unless the daughter gives in, but the spectre of the mother intervenes. While he stands terrified, Angela stabs him. And then the hero arrives. Regularly in a Gothic play the hero takes no part in the final conflict. Audiences may have identified with him, recognizing the existence of danger and necessity for violence but trusting that someone else will take the responsibility. In melodrama and the movie Western the hero is equally innocent, and the villain has to be taken care of by a less attractive victim or by an accident.

Less Gothic and more revolutionary was Beethoven's *Fidelio* (1803). Into the agony of a dungeon scene comes the trumpet call of deliverance. A scene of bright sunshine follows in which the released prisoners sing of freedom.

While the Gothic castle had its main popularity with the first generation of revolt, from 1789 to 1815, it was too good a setting to throw away. The more complex Romantic hero Bertram in Alexandre Dumas' *La Tour de Nesle* (1832) was surrounded by most of the standard furnishings of the castle. In spite of a new sympathy for the Middle Ages, the castle continued to serve as a setting for horror and villainy.

GRECO-ROMAN SIMPLICITY

If the Gothic castle was the symbol of the dark aspects of the age of revolt, a brighter side was represented by the cult of simplicity, expressed principally by a new kind of imitation of the Greeks and Romans. The Gothic and the Neoclassic existed side by side, complementary expressions of the same impulses: hatred for the aristocratic relics of the past and longing for a new republican beginning.

Rousseau had been calling for a return to nature and simplicity in life and the arts, and in 1753 he brought out his village opera, *Le Devin du Village*. In 1762 Isaac Bickerstaffe had a great success in London with the ballad opera *Love in a Village*, in which the young man disguises as a gardener and the young lady as a maid, before they can be brought together. In 1773 Kate Hardcastle found that she had to stoop to pretending to be a barmaid to conquer the man who was afraid of aristocratic ladies. Soon afterward Marie Antoinette and her ladies, in charming costumes, played at being dairy maids in buildings just out of sight of the great palace at Versailles.

In the 1770s Benjamin Franklin made a great impression in Paris in plain clothes, without wig or sword. He appeared from the New World as a symbol of simplicity and virtuous revolution, almost a saint. He was elected master of the most important Masonic Lodge in Paris and through the Freemasons won the devotion of many of France's leaders, not only to the cause of the American colonies but to the ideal of a universal benevolence which would overcome tyranny and superstition.

Fresh interest in antiquity, substituting for the Baroque interpretation of the ancients a realistic imitation of simple architecture and simple costume, grew from a new study of the ancients. Pompeii and Herculaneum were explored, and much information was obtained about Roman culture. A variation of the Baroque style, the Louis XVI style, was much more severe as it assimilated fresh details from ancient Rome. Of great influence was the Stuart and Revell *Antiquities of Athens*, the first volume of which appeared in London in 1762.

The prophet who led the western world back to a worship of fifth-century Athens was Johann Winckelmann. This son of a Prussian cobbler, impatient with the elegant Baroque of Dresden and the Rococo of his age, created a new vision from Greek coins, engraved gems, plaster casts, and books. He brought out in 1755 a small pamphlet, *Thoughts on the Imitation of Greek Works in Painting and Sculpture,* which stated the ideal of classic art that has prevailed to this day: the noble simplicity of Greek sculpture. His vision of a simple Greek art swept like a cool breeze over those stifled by the hothouse Rococo.

After spending years in the Vatican Library, Winckelmann brought out in 1764 his *History of Art among the Ancients,* a philosophical interpretation of ancient art. He explained the superiority of the Greeks to other ancients by their climate, free political institutions, joyous nature, delight in physical beauty and in games and festivals, and noble character. Such a study of the relation between the arts and local geography, institutions, and race cut sharp against the eighteenth-century idea of a universal art and a fixed standard of taste. It anticipated the historical interpretation that was to be so important in the nineteenth century. The immediate impact of Winckelmann was to identify Greek art with a noble, joyous republican life.

Perhaps because his sources of study were colorless—statues long since washed white, plaster casts, drawings and engravings—Winckelmann's vision of Greece was white. To this day, in spite of the knowledge that Greek statues and even buildings were painted in rich colors, most people think of fifth-century Greece as white.

Goethe, ever responsive to the forces of his day, after dramatizing the medieval in *Goetz* and *Egmont* in the 1770s, turned in the 1780s to a Greek theme. He was under the spell of the Strassburg Cathedral in the 1770s and he later made a trip to Italy to admire the relics of the ancient world. But Gothic and Greek did not alternate in Goethe's life as inconsistent modes. They were variants of the same impulse: to create a new beauty out of the ruins of an old culture.

Goethe's *Iphigenia in Tauris* (c. 1789–90) deals with a guilt-stained Orestes rescuing a persecuted heroine—just the material for a Gothic play. But what a difference without the Gothic castle! How gently melancholy Iphigenia is in the Greek sunlight; how noble victim and tyrant become in Greek architecture! The kind king who is pursuing the heroine generously lets her go with his blessing.

When the French Revolution broke out it found its Neoclassic symbol in a painting by David, *The Lictors Bringing Back to Brutus the Bodies of His Sons.* The government was in the act of suppressing the picture. It became a *cause célèbre,* and when openly exhibited was immediately popular. Brutus, who sacrificed his own traitor sons to defend liberty, became the symbol of the defenders of republican freedom.

Jacques Louis David, a follower of Winckelmann, had studied several years in Rome, painting ancient buildings and statues. He had won some favor from the French aristocrats and was even elected to the conservative Academy. But he became the artistic leader of the Revolution, suppressing the Academy as a stronghold of privilege and opening the Salon to all artists to exhibit. He undertook to paint the great events of the Revolution. He designed Roman costumes and settings for the theatre and even planned a new costume for the whole nation. Most important of all, he designed in the Neoclassic style the great public fêtes, where, far more than in the theatres, were dramatized the events the French people were living through.

The first great fête was on the anniversary of the storming of the Bastille. A classic altar of the "nation" was erected, where Talleyrand celebrated Mass and Lafayette administered an oath of loyalty to king and nation. The fête the following year was the apotheosis of Voltaire as Father of the Revolution. Since the clergy had denied him burial in holy ground, David gave the occasion à strong pagan Roman quality to express his anticlerical feeling. When the Jacobins gave a pageant culminating in a ceremony in honor of a statue of Liberty, their opponents, to balance it, had an enormous procession as a "Triumph of the Law." The symbols, architecture, and costumes were all based on antiquity.

The two greatest fêtes came during the Terror. When a new constitution was presented in 1793, it was celebrated by a festival of Unity and Indivisibility. At the site of the Bastille, representatives from all parts of the nation drank the waters from a Fountain of Regeneration. In the great procession, groups representing the commingling of all classes and trades bore symbols of the trades. The ashes of heroes were borne with garlands and music, while carts carried plunder taken from aristocrats. At the Place de la Revolution, before a great Statue of Liberty, a pyre, with flags and symbols of tyranny, was burned. Finally at the Champs de Mars, beyond a Gateway of Equality and Liberty, each man placed on the great altar of the Nation some token of his trade or the fruit of his labor. The last great display, the Festival of the Supreme Being, was the most pagan of all. Just before the fall of Robespierre, it came at the crest of the anti-clerical movement, when many hoped to drive out all vestiges of medieval religion as well as aristocracy. The new cult had impressive ceremonies. Robespierre preached a sermon and with a torch set fire to a cardboard statue of Atheism, which burned away to reveal a slightly smudged image of Wisdom. The procession carried patriotic and humanitarian emblems to the Champs de Mars, where David's picture of the *Oath of the Horatii* was re-enacted and new patriotic hymns were sung.

The allegorical figures in all these fêtes David clothed in the simplified costumes based on ancient statues rather than on the "antique" costumes that Baroque actors and artists used. By 1789, the actor Talma, copying some of the simpler Roman costumes he had seen Kemble use, had carried David's costumes to the stage in the part of Proculus. The other actors were alarmed at his naked arms and knees, and made fun of him. But in 1792 David designed in a similar style settings and costumes for Chenier's *Caius Gracchus*, which dramatized the fight of the Roman sans-culottes against the aristocrats.

The hall where the convention met in 1793 was decorated in the new style, with statues of four Greeks and four Romans. Most prominent was Brutus, near the orator's tribune. In several cities religious honors were paid the bust of Brutus. Charlotte Corday, who assassinated Marat, saw herself as reenacting the heroic patriotism of the ancients, especially the Mother of the Gracchi. She wrote from prison that she anticipated "happiness with Brutus in the Elysian Fields."

Personal names and names of streets and towns that suggested aristocratic or religious origin were changed to classic names. The Revolutionists abolished the Christian calendar and in 1792 started to number the years from 1. They renamed the months with poetic names taken from nature, with Vintage, Fogs, and Frost for autumn; Snowy, Rainy, and Windy for winter; Germinal, Florial and Prairial for spring; and Messidor, Thermidor, and Fructidor for summer. The inconsistent system of weights and measures was replaced by the metric system based on a scientifically calculated portion of the size of the earth. The metric system, adopted around the world, has been one unquestioned gain from the Revolution.

Daily clothing was already simplified in the 1780s, but with the Revolution it was copied from workmen. Wigs were discarded. The long pantaloon (named after the *commedia* clown) and the short *carmagnole* were admired more than the knee-length *culottes* or the long coat. The stiff bodice worn by women was replaced by a higher, softer waistline, with a fichu or scarf over the shoulders. The patriotic colors, often in stripes, were popular.

In America there was no such extreme as the worship of Reason in a Greek temple erected in Notre Dame, but the Greek revival became the official style of the young republic. Washington, Franklin, and Jefferson were Deists and Freemasons, looking to freedom, tolerance, and equality in both politics and religion. The Methodists and other revivalists, though opposed to the "natural religion" of the Deists, repudiated the harsh intolerance of the Puritans and opened the doors of salvation to all.

A new age needed a monumental style, and there was the style of the Greek and Roman republics for inspiration. When a triumphal arch was built in Philadelphia for the celebration of peace in 1783, Washington was represented on it as Cincinnatus resigning his sword for a plow. The veteran officers of the Revolution called themselves the Cincinnati. Greenough did a statue of Washington in classic garb, nude to the waist. Jefferson, Hamilton, and Madison argued over the faults and failures of Sparta, Rome, and Carthage, and for the next half-century orators made frequent reference to the ancient world.

Jefferson, especially, hated the frivolity of the English Baroque and its American imitations. More than anyone else he inspired the architecture of the American republic and designed a number of buildings himself. In New York, Philadelphia, Richmond, and above all Washington, the new public buildings were based on a fresh adaptation of the classic. The classic took new life during the Greek struggle for independence in the 1820s, and from southern mansion to New England or Ohio farmhouse, a style of quiet dignity was established. The style long outlasted the anticlerical feeling of revolutionary days and was adapted to churches as well as to courthouses.

524

Talma in Roman toga. *Alinari/Art Resource, N.Y. Biblioteca a Raccolta Teatrale del Burcardo della SIAE—Roma.*

525

X

The Age of Romanticism

Setting for Pixerecourt melodrama *Le Château de Locu Levan. Phot. Bibl. Nat. Paris.*

Introduction

GOETHE'S *FAUST*, A ROMANTIC MASTERPIECE

Goethe's *Faust*, Part I (1808), the finest drama to come out of the Romantic age, is an epitome of the period. The new indirect methods which poets and dramatists were striving for are more nearly achieved in it than in any other play. The character Faust has seemed the symbol of the Romantic, perhaps the symbol of western civilization. He is melancholy and restless and fluctuates from suicidal despair to the deepest yearning, to ecstasy, and finally to bitter remorse. He throws off the old to make a new beginning. He yearns for the transforming experience of love. Yet he cannot rest with love but must explore the meaning of history and man's destiny.

Working on the play most of his life, Goethe gathered the major interests of his day. The new concepts of nature, science, folklore, ballads, history, psychology, politics, and religion are reflected in it. It is at once a new dramatic form and an anthology of poems and methods imitated from Hindu drama, the Hebrew scriptures, Greek drama, the mystery and morality plays, medieval ballads, Hans Sachs, the commedia dell' arte, the opera, and Shakespeare. It is clear and bold enough to hold the stage to this day, but contains subtle symbolism which scholars have not yet completely explored. The play is fragmentary and incomplete, the love interest has soured a little for modern taste, and the English translations are dull; still it can be a very rewarding study, both as a work of art and as a document of its age.

The two prologues project the play at once far beyond the scope of the ordinary eighteenth-century drama. In the Prologue in the Theatre, an idea borrowed from the Hindu play *Shakuntala*, the manager brings on the singer, actor, and dramatic poet, promises a complex method using tears and laughter, sense and nonsense, and many-colored pictures and suggesting both truth and the delight in illusion. The Prologue in Heaven owes something to the morality plays but more to the Book of Job. It goes far beyond human society to the reverberations of the spheres. There God and the Devil are concerned with the destiny of man and the nature of evil. Thus the duality which men of the Romantic period found in their own lives—the conflict between the longing for infinite love and good and the perversion of good into evil—was projected into the heavens.

Faust has been seen by some as a symbol of the Middle Ages giving way to the wider exploration of the Renaissance or of the humanistic spirit of the Renaissance

wrestling with the materialistic spirit of modern science. It is perhaps most important to see the play as an epitome of late eighteenth-century man throwing off old
traditions of learning and seeking a new vision of himself in the universe in terms
of nature, experience, and history.

Faust is melancholy and rebellious, given to contemplation in moonlight and
ready for some heroic act of violence. His worldly achievement seems worthless,
and all his science has not persuaded nature to open up her secrets. Like all mankind, he has gone astray; he has missed what was all-important. He has no power
over the world around him and thus finds existence a burden and wishes for death.
But when he is about to take poison, the sound of an Easter service rouses memories of childhood and calls him back to life.

When Marlowe's Dr. Faustus makes his compact with Mephistopheles he asks
for twenty-four years, but Faust refuses to fix a limit to his desires. He is so sure
that nothing can finally satisfy him that he is willing to risk all. He says in his
compact, "Show me one experience so perfect that I will say to the moment—
'Stay yet! You are so beautiful!'"

The relationship with Gretchen (Marguerite) as the climax of Faust's experience
is typical of the Romantic movement. A Romantic hero, denied adjustment to society, yearns for something worthy of his ideals, something noble, young, pure,
and innocent. The pure maiden is a great fulfillment. But as he has built up his
ideal far beyond the earthly, there is profanation in winning her. In his remorse he
often joins her in death. Romantic loves are usually fatal, and since the destructive
forces as well as the creative are considered part of the nature of the universe, the
hero does nothing to prevent death.

As an incident in the life of Faust, the Gretchen episode is out of proportion.
Goethe writes much of it from her point of view and makes almost a separate play
of it, only just remembering to bring Faust back at the end of her story. Since no
Romantic hero could make an adjustment to another real human being, the heroine is not a real character and has no mind of her own. A reader of *Faust* may be
repelled by this trembling innocence, but on the stage Gretchen can be made acceptable if not quite credible. Goethe has given her scenes a power and com-
pactness greater than most of the scenes involving Faust. The death scene, which
borrows much from Shakespeare, compares in lyric intensity with any scene of
Shakespeare's.

Not only does the play have poetry and philosophical observations that make
it unquestionably the most important work of German literature, but the stage
method, while borrowing from Elizabethan drama and old ballads, made innovations in techniques that are again important in the twentieth century. Goethe uses
not only the lyric power of verse but the indirect method of Romantic poetry. He
juxtaposes many contrasting scenes on various levels of the supernatural and the
fantastic. He uses poetic images that reflect the basic themes, rather than stating
them directly. He introduces songs, ballads, and choruses to reinforce theme as

well as create atmosphere. Gretchen has two songs that echo important themes of the play, one just before she finds the golden jewels which win her for Faust and love and destruction, and a little later, after Faust has a scene of remorse, her simple song, "My peace is gone. My heart is sore."

The Walpurgis Night Witches' Sabbath is the first major attempt since Greek drama to present a lyric equivalent on stage for some offstage catastrophe, and it is more complex and ambitious than anything the Greeks attempted. Goethe gives a dramatic equivalent of Gretchen's madness, anguish, and terror in a fantasy of a procession of witches. He has just shown Gretchen fainting in the cathedral, overcome by her guilt, her time near. Then the wild scene comes as if the lid had been taken off the universe. When it is over Faust knows she has been imprisoned for murdering her child and he hastens to her.

Up the sides of the Brachen, the traditional mountain gathering place of witches, a great procession whirls, to the same heavy, pushing rhythm as Longfellow's *Hiawatha* (1855). There are whirlwinds, owls, will-o'-the-wisps, seducers, witches and half-witches, brewing witches' messes, dancing, chattering, drinking, and making love. There are caricatures of pompous generals, ministers, and authors, and several contemporaries of Goethe's who were known as doubters of any mystery in the universe. There are Adam's first wife, Lilith, and other wraiths of Eden. In the midst, Faust sees a phantom of Gretchen, her lovely neck decorated by a scarlet thread no thicker than a blade of a knife. Then comes a dream, in the guise of an intermezzo, of the golden wedding of Oberon and Titania. Goethe inserts a group of epigrammatic stanzas which, though not closely relevant, reinforce the haunting scene. This Witches' Sabbath is not entirely successful as drama, but it was a great theatrical achievement in a new direction.

Much more effective is the expression of Gretchen's half-disordered mind in the last scene, a dungeon. Like Ophelia, she is a pitiful girl tormented beyond sanity. Her anguish is expressed in lyric verse that mixes the shocking, the tender, and the fantastic. She is swept by visions of her baby drowning and of her mother sitting dumbly on a stone. She gives directions to bury her mother, her brother, her baby, and herself. She now remembers that this was to be her wedding day and instead sees herself dragged to judgment. In the lyric she sings, Goethe has adapted the images of a macabre fairy story to give overtones to the scene.

Goethe published the combined Faust and Gretchen scenes as a complete play in 1808, realizing that though the ascent of Gretchen to heaven made a good stopping-place, he had not made a complete statement for Faust. In the last years of his life, he finished a second part, which is more complex, allusive, and cryptic.

Among many other things, the second part of *Faust* is an allegory of Western history, showing the breaking up of the Augustan Age before the impact of science, new thought, the industrial revolution, and the expansion of trade. The Revolution, Napoleon, and the Restoration of the monarchy in France seem represented in the wars and the two emperors of the play.

In the last act of the second part, Faust, now blind, is busy on a reclamation project, a rationalistic scheme for making a new home for men. Like a tyrant, he destroys a church and the happy peasant family who are in the way. When he has a vision of men dwelling on the reclaimed marshland, he experiences the highest bliss, and crying the magic words, "Linger on, thou art so fair," he dies. Mephistopheles claims him, but a host of angels, so charming that Mephistopheles is entranced, spirits Faust away. In a scene in heaven full of imagery and symbolism drawn from Swedenborg, Gretchen begs mercy for Faust, and the play ends with praise for the eternal longing that ever draws man on.

Goethe died in 1832 without being able to explain just what he meant by the reclamation project. Victorians, turning from the individualism of the Romantic period to a social ideal, said that of course he meant that selfish desires could never bring satisfaction, that only in working for society could Faust find a true ideal. That is still the standard interpretation. But some students in the twentieth century wonder whether Goethe perhaps thought that a theoretical scheme for improving mankind, in complete disregard of traditions and human feelings, was just as illusory as the other projects of Faust's long history. Goethe is known to have disapproved of the socialistic schemes of the St. Simonists discussed at the time of the 1830 Revolution in France. A plausible explanation of the last scene is that Faust found friends in heaven not because of a final right action but because of his lifelong striving.

The Wider Revolution

The French Revolution set out to release men from tyranny, to abolish titles and hereditary rulers. But in less than five years the Committee of Safety, during the Terror, became far more tyrannical and bloody than royalty had been, and in another ten years Napoleon was emperor. The Committee set out to defend liberty and destroy the military power of government and invented the greatest Moloch of the modern age, the conscript army. It armed the French to defend their republic, but they invaded the republics of Switzerland and Venice. French armies were expected to liberate their neighbors and establish harmonious republicanism, but they proved the greatest stimulant to nationalism that Germany, Italy, Spain, or England had known. The Revolution set out to establish a rationalistic order over the world, and it released the forces of unreason and disorder. The ideal of rationalistic universal order died with the Revolution.

Clearly there was no hope for an immediate establishment of a glorious new age. The idea of a perfect rational plan was replaced by a vision of individual struggle and the improvement of mankind through the gradual nourishing of institutions. That called for reexamination of basic philosophical, historical, and cultural ideas.

After the Terror of 1792−94, when faction and counter-faction sent each other to the guillotine, even the friends of the Revolution were sick at heart. Wordsworth and Coleridge, youths in their twenties, were in despair. Wordsworth had gone to France where he found friends among the revolutionists and a girl he loved. Full of revolutionary zeal, Coleridge made plans for a pantisocracy on the banks of the Susquehanna. These sensitive poets did not give up their hatred of tyranny or return to the aristocratic social and poetic ideals of the Rococo period. Wordsworth rediscovered the friendly hills of his childhood and became the great poet of nature and the simple life. He based his longest poem, *The Excursion* (1814), on a character in despair after the Revolution who found a new orientation and mental health. Coleridge studied the new transcendental philosophy of Germany and used neglected elements of the supernatural, the exotic, and the medieval in poetry of surpassing imagination and lyricism.

The melancholy and pessimism of the disillusionment remained features of the whole Romantic movement. If no political action was possible, the idealistic individual must turn his emotions of hope, longing, and desire into art and dreaming.

There began the separation of art from life that has been a major dislocation in civilization. As though to add to the frustration, Malthus brought out his *Essay on Population* in 1798, the same year in which Monk Lewis's *The Castle Spectre* and the *Lyrical Ballads* of Wordsworth and Coleridge were published. Malthus believed that population tended to increase faster than the food supply until checked by war or starvation. It was futile to try to improve the lot of the masses as any improvement would only increase the population and plunge all into misery. Especially in England, the new factory towns crowded workers together in appalling conditions. But labor unions had been outlawed in 1799. In 1811 and 1812, rioting workers in Yorkshire destroyed the machines that replaced individual home weaving. Workers who met in 1819 to protest were shot down in what became known as the "Peterloo Massacre."

The eighteenth-century optimistic belief in benevolence was radically modified. In its stead appeared a dualistic view of the universe: good in sharp conflict with evil. In the days of disillusionment, poets and dramatists were much occupied with devils, cruelty, and crime.

In reaction to the Revolution, the eighteenth-century cult of reason was re placed by a cult of the instincts and the imagination. Men turned from eighteenth-century philosophy, with its emphasis on the abstract and the universal. The Romantic poets led the philosophers in dealing with the subjective qualities—colors, warmth, and infinite variety of concrete experience. Along with reason and the abstract, the mechanistic view of the universe was repudiated. After the paganism of the revolutionary age came a strong revival of religion. Eighteenth-century deism, with its god of nature, was too cold for either poet or ordinary citizen. The Romanticist was sure the universe was spirit and mystery. Philosophy, following Immanuel Johann Kant and Johann Fichte, had to find room both for an idealism that could transcend the evidence of the senses and for the will of the individual.

Yet the Romantic age continued in new ways the main task of the French Revolution. It was basically just as determined as the revolutionary age to replace feudal aristocracy with a wider democracy. Many artists such as Scott, Byron, and even Victor Hugo looked to the aristocracy as a defense against a vulgar public. Yet as a whole the age was devoted to democracy. Lord Byron fought hard in Parliament for liberal measures, and in Greece he gave his life for "the people." The heroes of romantic plays are often high-born and aloof, but they are as much opposed to the traditional aristocrat as any Frenchman who stormed the Bastille.

The Romantic age is the wider revolution, the nonpolitical revolution. Jean Paul wrote in 1799, "A spiritual revolution, greater than the political revolution, and just as violent, beats in the heart of the world." That spiritual revolution must complete the liberation of mankind, by slow, individual action; it must explore wider and deeper bases for the new civilization by developing visions of man in nature, in history, and in culture; and third, it must develop new sanctions for individuals to live by while they were waiting for the new society: it had to develop a mythology of maladjustment.

534

INDIVIDUALISM, LIBERALISM, AND THE ENDLESS STRUGGLE

The idea of achieving freedom by a gradual struggle of individuals is the basis for the liberal movement of the nineteenth century. The word "liberal" implies the liberation of minds from old forms and prejudices. Pressure might be necessary, through public opinion, demonstrations, even boycott and strikes. But liberals worked mainly for gradual change through education, concession, and law. In some things they worked to widen the franchise so that restrictions of the vote by property, race, or sex would be removed. At other times they sought to improve the wages and environment of labor so that workers might be liberated from degrading conditions. Always they sought to protect the rights of the individual. While sometimes for a limited objective liberals took on various union, cooperative, and even socialist goals to use against entrenched power, they visualized each individual free from all limiting ties, whether political or mental. Liberals in the Romantic age had a strong sense of the inviolability of the individual soul. Accepting his loneliness, man built a sustaining sense of self-reliance.

In the 1830s, when Ralph Waldo Emerson was making self-reliance the keystone of his philosophy for pioneer America, Bulwer-Lytton drew in the play *Richelieu* (1839) one of the strongest stage characters of the period: an idealist in a treacherous world who cannot be beaten because he puts his final trust in one absolute, dependable thing: himself. "Old, childless, friendless, broken—all forsaken—all—all—but—." His companion asks "What?" and Richelieu replies, "The indomitable heart of Armand Richelieu." The play was as popular across America as it was in London.

The search for a multiform ideal based on a wide knowledge of many cultures had begun in the eighteenth century, but it had been obscured in the fervor of political revolution. In the beginning of the nineteenth century new explorations in history, folklore, religion, philosophy, psychology, science, and nature had brought in so many new points of view that no simple synthesis was possible. Yet the Romantic age achieved a revolution in culture that was not merely a repudiation of the eighteenth-century reliance on the Neoclassic culture but was based on positive concepts of man in relation to religion and philosophy, nature, history, and multiplicity of cultures.

MAN IN RELATION TO RELIGION AND PHILOSOPHY

A new vision of religion and philosophy must allow for the duality of good and evil, of man's dream of the glorious and his debasement before the actual. That duality is vivid in Goethe's *Faust*. Where Locke had treated the person as a passive receiver of sense impressions from the outside, Kant showed that the person himself has *a priori* forms of knowledge. Thus he gave a philosophical basis for the growing concept of man as a creative being. To counter the objection that *a priori* knowledge might vary in different egos, Kant supposed a "transcendental ego" which is the same in all individuals.

In *The Critique of Practical Reason* (1781), he gave the creative will of the individual greater freedom, thus setting religion free from the world of science—a doctrine very congenial to the new age. Men of thought and purpose did not like the industrial cities which applied science was giving them. They did not like to see merchants and manufacturers getting rich from the labor of overworked men in crowded quarters. They did not like the abstract physical sciences which neglected not only private aspiration but aesthetic experience. Hence poets were as active as evangelists in seeking deeper religious ways of feeling.

The industrial world could never satisfy the need to devote one's self to a creative mission beyond the selfish motives of the marketplace. Many Protestants turned to the Catholic church. Poets and artists made a religion of their art, expecting it to furnish the vision that could unite the soul with the sky. Not only the poets but the prophets—St. Simon, Renan, Taine, Carlyle, and above all Wagner—felt the need for a new-old mythology to take man back to a time of pure will and pure passion, when great heroes dominated life. Romantic drama and opera were much concerned with mythology, with ancient and primeval heroes, with titanic men of indomitable will.

Throughout the nineteenth century, religion was an important background of nearly all the plays. The playwright often asked the scene designer to provide a ruined abbey, a tomb, or merely a quiet glade in the forest where the forlorn heroine might pray. In Protestant countries the kind of religion was usually left vague, though designers from London to modern Hollywood have had high-church leanings because of the greater chance for color, music, and spectacle.

Music and spectacle in the theatre was one of the great achievements of the Romantic age. Naturalistic critics have jeered at music and spectacle as superfluous ornaments that might entertain the crowd but could only cheapen a true dramatic effect. But most spectacular effects in nineteenth-century drama were a direct expression of some important aspect of the play. In the Victorian drama, isolation was usually from the social group and the spectacle presented a group at a dance or important party so that the alienation of the disgraced or misunderstood hero or heroine was made vivid. At the beginning of the century, before the Victorian emphasis on society developed, man's fear of alienation and hope of support were directed toward the heavens. Hence religious chants, processions, tableaux, and spectacles were popular.

Monk Lewis's *The Castle Spectre*, the theatrical sensation of 1798 in London, has an effective religious scene as reinforcement to the faltering spirits of the tormented heroine. Religious spectacle was used just as powerfully to dramatize alienation in the last act of Charles Robert Maturin's *Bertram, or The Castle of St. Aldobrand* (1816). The scene is the chapel of St. Anselm, a religious shrine on the coast of a tempestuous sea, where the forlorn heroine Imogine is rejected by the church after her sweetheart, the rebel Bertram, has murdered her father. Monks and knights march in procession with banners, chanting a hymn in honor of the peace and security of the temple. They are interrupted by a scream. Imogine rushes in but sinks under the Prior's gaze. She clings to his robe, begging for pity, but he casts her off, saying, "I do pronounce unto thy soul—despair." The procession marches off chanting, leaving her alone with terrifying visions of her murdered lord. No amount of solo acting with classic monologues could make desolation so sharp. The nineteenth century was learning to use the full means of the theatre.

Religious spectacle served admirably to give not only an emotional tone to an action but a sense of wider significance. Schiller made the killing of the tyrant in *William Tell* (1804) more magnificent by bringing in symbols of local freedom and justice as well as of divine justice. The tyrant is caught in the midst of denying justice to a woman and her children who stop his path through the mountains. A bridal party with music brings on stage the theme of the local people, and after the tyrant dies six Brothers of Mercy form a circle around him and sing of God the Judge on High.

MAN IN RELATION TO NATURE

Partly from the scientific study of biology, partly from the intuitive discovery of nature by the poet, the new age found in nature a basis for man's health and spiritual life which seemed far superior to the discredited Baroque vision of man in society.

In the physical sciences, some uniform, consistent, timeless laws had been found, and some people expected to apply them to all aspects of culture. In the nineteenth century, however, as biological sciences came into greater prominence, men, institutions, the arts, and all of culture were studied in terms of genesis and growth. Thus nature furnished man with a new way of viewing himself, as

537

a living, growing organism, shaped by inheritance and environment, seeking to fulfill the inner purposes of nature. He began to see his institutions as developing gradually in history according to the character of the particular climate, geography, race, and nation.

On the poetic side, nature furnished not only a fresh delight but the chief solace to the lonely Romantic who had given up the old ideal of society. He could call on the trees, the mountains, the torrents to bear witness to "what man has made of man." Nature could echo his most violent moods and yet bring him peace and health. The rediscovery of the kinship between man and nature was one of the greatest spiritual gains of the period and of profound importance for modern scientific and philosophical thought. Here the poets led the philosophers. In all probability, the stage had an even greater impact on the wider public than poetry. The closeness of man and nature was one of the most persistent themes in the theatre throughout the century.

The love of nature has never been completely lost, but we have seen in Restoration drama the fashionable attitude of the time toward the country. Only boors could be expected from rural lanes, or, as James Russell Lowell was to put it later, only wildcats come out of the wilderness. The eighteenth century admitted gentle landscapes. But the Romanticist needed to lose himself in nature, finding at first a reflection of his own intensities, then through the sense of kinship with all nature, a spiritual significance in the universe.

Rousseau turned to external nature out of the sense of the stagnation of society. "I must have torrents," he wrote, "fir trees, black woods, mountains to climb or descend, and rugged rocks with precipices on either side to alarm me." He made good use of background in his novels, putting strong emotions among mountains and storms and restful moments in placid surroundings. A poem by Dalton in 1768 had the effect of making the English poets Thomas Gray and Edward Young visit the Lake Country, and in a few years such a tour was the height of fashion. Some theologians had considered mountains the unreclaimed home of the devil. As late as the 1760s Winckelmann, the discoverer of the nobility of Greek sculpture, drew down the shades of his carriage as he passed through the ugly Alps.

Byron made perhaps the most vivid poetic use of wild nature. He looked on the turbulent waters of the Po and felt himself "wild as thy wave and headlong as thy speed." Repeatedly Childe Harold finds wild nature to reverberate his emotions. The finest expression is in the semi-dramatic *Manfred* (1817), one of the best poems of Romantic torment.

In the north, poets and playwrights discovered the spiritual health of nature. Goethe wrote, "Nature, we are surrounded and enclosed by her . . . She is everything. . . . I trust myself to her. She may do with me as she likes."

Wordsworth turned from the Neoclassic reason of William Godwin, from the abstractions of mathematics and science, from despair over the moral and political turmoil of his day, to discover the healing power of a simple life near the lakes and mountains where he had spent his childhood. While Wordsworth tended to emphasize the wise passiveness of identity with nature and the simple delight in a flower that "enjoys the air it breathes," he could experience large philosophical thoughts while contemplating a violet, an aged neighbor, a highland reaper, or childhood itself. Even Byron, who at first made fun of him, learned by Shelley's help to understand Wordsworth's insight.

In Romantic theatre the scene designer had dark and gloomy forests so heavy that the sunlight scarcely penetrated. He had rocks and crags to match the torment of lonely heroes. Sometimes he painted the whole scene on a large drop fairly far downstage. Sometimes he used the full depth of the stage, painting the wings as rock crags or heavy trees. The Baroque designer often used his row of wings to lead the eye back to an open view of the sea, with special lighting, sea waves, and trick ships and monsters worked from the back pit. The Romantic scene designer was more inclined to close the back with a cave or mountain. A favorite effect was a bridge from one side of the stage to the other, affording a high place for distant entries and overlooking the scene in the foreground. Underneath the bridge was room for a cave or waterfall. In many a melodrama the bridge crashed with the villain's last fight.

Victor Louis Theatre at Bordeaux, 1890. *Phot. Bibl. Nat. Paris.*

539

MAN IN RELATION TO HISTORY
AND TO MULTIPLE CULTURES

But nature was not enough; man did not rebel against eighteenth-century society in order to be a hermit. While thousands did move to the American frontier
to build a new world, few people lost hope of a new *society*. In the plays, the robber outlaws took to the woods only to come back to get revenge on society. The
"stranger" who appeared in so many plays, though the victim of a great injustice,
lingered near society to lend aid to other victims and was at the end very happy to
be restored to his family and friends.

While man could adjust to some loneliness and accept the idea of the gradual
emergence of a better world, he must have some comprehensive vision of himself
in relation to the social culture around him, and he gained strength by seeing himself as the heir to a long tradition of history. He took a fierce pride in his tribe,
race, and nation. He cherished those things which made his folk different from
the rest, and by projection developed a great fascination with the folklore and
local color of other areas.

The biologists set the pattern for the study of the growth of institutions and
nations through different phases from infancy to maturity. The Romantic poet,
playwright, and scene designer studied how each folk, tribe, and nation exhibited
different characteristics because of inheritance, climate, and physical and social
environment. By the beginning of the nineteenth century both biologists and
poets were seeing life in the new dimensions of genetic development in time and
organic relation to environment.

Up to a certain point the concepts of history and of multiple cultures over-
lapped and reinforced each other. Newly discovered medieval ballads were valued
both because they were old and for the special dialect and qualities of the local
folk. Eighteenth-century culture, with its roots in Greece and Rome, had been
developed to the highest point in France, and Paris had become dominant, although England had partly held her own. The publication of old ballads was
hailed because the ballads proved that people who never heard of Greece and
Rome or of the court of Louis XIV could produce fine poetry. When the Ossian
poems, reputedly translated by James Macpherson from Gaelic originals, were
published in 1760–63, they were a literary sensation. Here supposedly was a
Gaelic epic to match Homer, giving western Europe and northern races a respectable antiquity. Though some people accused Macpherson of perpetrating a hoax
(and he never showed a Gaelic manuscript), he may have had, it is now conceded,
some old manuscripts to work on. In any case, he contributed more to the interest

in medieval history and to the idea that different countries and different ages might have their own characteristics than any scholarly translation of fragments of old Celtic poems could possibly have done.

The multiplicity of folk cultures was developed as a basis for aesthetics by the young German Wachenroder, who published a book in 1797 with the characteristic title *The Outpouring from the Heart of an Art-Loving Cloister-Brother*, which praised Gothic architecture as Germanic and was one of the first books to proclaim the kinship of the German spirit with music. Like many of the best Romanticists, he saw art as the most important spiritual achievement of man.

A more influential exponent of the concept of multiple cultures was Madame de Staël. In 1800 she published *Literature in Relation to Social Institutions* and in 1810, *On Germany*, though it was suppressed by Napoleon's censors and brought out in 1813 in London. These two books became the basic sources for the Romantic movement in France. The author emphasized the close relations between literature and the climate, nature, language, government, and especially the history of each country. She admired German literature and popularized in France the newer developments in German. But she would not have France blindly imitate northern models, either ancient or modern. She thought that each country should study and respect the particular qualities and diversities of all nations, but should develop according to its own character. If the Germans have greater depth than the French, she wrote, the French have better taste.

Nationalism and patriotism were greatly stimulated by the French Revolution and Napoleon's conquests. In 1807, a year after the German defeat at Jena, Johann Gottlieb Fichte's *Addresses to the German Nation* stirred patriotism to a pitch of religious ecstasy. From then on, freedom did not mean to the Germans freedom of the individual from the state, it meant freedom of the Germans to develop their country and culture according to their own folk character without the domination of any foreign culture, in particular the French.

The most important pioneers in the recognition of multiple folk cultures were Goethe and Johann Gottfried Herder. Goethe grew up in the 1750s and 1760s in a Germany dominated by French culture. He went to school for three years in the very French city of Leipzig in a university dominated by Gottshed, the main German advocate of French culture. After an interruption caused by a lung hemorrhage, he transferred to the University of Strassburg, an institution entirely French in atmosphere. He fell in love with the cathedral of Strassburg, an unfinished Gothic structure that had been built by Germans who could create without the help of Greece and Rome, and he met Herder, in Strassburg for eye treatment but eager for conversation in his darkened room. Herder was only five years older than Goethe, but he had traveled widely and had gathered the most progressive ideas of the day. He stirred Goethe with the idea that France represented an effete civilization and that a new age must be started by peoples of the north. From a prodigious memory Herder recited from English, Finnish, and German ballads and from the Icelandic eddas. He started Goethe reading Shakespeare and Homer and the Book of Genesis as folk art—all products of primitive peoples.

Herder's essay on Shakespeare was one of several new studies presenting the English dramatist as an example of vigor, contrast, spirituality, and freedom. With the translations of Schlegel and Tieck and Schlegel's lectures early in the nineteenth century, Shakespeare was to be fully established as the greatest German dramatist. Since then Shakespeare has probably been performed more in German than in English.

Herder laid the foundations for the literary study of the Bible as the unsophisticated poetry of a richly imaginative people, showing the special qualities of a particular nation as it was shaped by its geography and history.

But while theorists discussed new concepts of history and folk culture, the theatre did its part by interesting audiences in London, Paris, and New York in local color: a Swiss village, a Sicilian fishing port, a Gypsy camp, a midland cottage, or the weavers, peddlers, thieves, dancers, soldiers of a particular city. Symbolic of reassurance from the local is the play *Guy Mannering,* or *The Gypsy's Prophecy,* based on Scott's novel. It is a poor play, but in the middle of the nineteenth century Charlotte Cushman had a tremendous success in her electric performance of Meg Merrilies, the Gypsy Queen. The hero is a wanderer who does not even know who he is. But when he comes upon the Gypsy Queen, she sings the traditional family lullaby and restores his identity, then saves him from threatening smugglers and returns him to his rightful place in society. It seemed quite fitting to nineteenth-century audiences that Scott's symbol of local folk culture should cure the ills of the homeless romantic hero.

THE NEW MEDIEVALISM

The discovery of the medieval was one of the most important developments of Romanticism and remained one of the major interests of the nineteenth century. Here was the largest single section of history and culture that the eighteenth century had ignored—a whole world of ballads and romances, art and architecture, that seemed fresh to people weary of Baroque-Rococo standards. But even more important, the discovery gave western and northern Europe a history of their own. If so many attractive things lay outside Augustan culture, what became of its claim to universal validity? The new theorists who wanted art and literature to be less regular and more complex, less urbane and more spiritual, found in the ballads, romances, and other medieval creations a wealth of examples to cite against eighteenth-century taste.

The Renaissance placed the classic and the new Italian culture far above the medieval. While Tasso, Shakespeare, Spenser, and Ben Jonson found that medieval traditions were still very much alive at the end of the sixteenth century, the Baroque and Rococo tastes of the seventeenth and eighteenth centuries had no place for them. Dryden rewrote Chaucer, Shakespeare was greatly modified, and interiors of Gothic churches were almost hidden by the Baroque altars, paintings, columns, and clouds. The word "Gothic" was a synonym for barbarous.

But in 1744 Richard Dodsley published by subscription twelve volumes of *A Select Collection of Old Plays* that contained brief sketches of the early drama in each country in western Europe and a large selection of English plays from the fifteenth, sixteenth, and seventeenth centuries. In 1778 Thomas Hawkins brought out his *Origin of the English Drama: Illustrated in Its Various Species*, with examples of miracles, moralities, comedies, and tragedies from the fifteenth and sixteenth centuries. The *Niebelungenlied* was discovered in 1755 in a castle in the Tyrol and soon published with songs from the Minnesingers. *Aucassin and Nicolette* was published in 1756 and dramatized in 1779. Beginning in 1776 a *Bibliothèque des Romans* was published by the Comte de Tresson, and French poets began in imitation to write romances about medieval knights and their loves.

Of most lasting value was Bishop Percy's *Reliques of Early English Poetry*, published in 1765. Northern ballads gained a very wide audience and were almost as well known on the continent as Ossian. In 1773 Gottfried August Burger published *Lenore*, the first of a long line of literary ballads based on the traditions of the folk ballads. In the same year Goethe published the first important dramatization of medieval material in *Goetz von Berlighingen*. Richard Hurd's *Letters on Chivalry and Romance* (1762) showed admiration for the manners, virtues, and general magnificence of the age of chivalry. Thomas Warton published the first volume of his *History of English Poetry from the Twelfth Century to the Close of the Sixteenth Century* in 1774. He was one of many who could not be happy within the confines of Augustan taste and found in medieval poetry and Gothic architecture traditions more worthy.

Walpole's *Castle of Otranto* of 1764 is of course an important part of the story of interest in the medieval. Many people were drawn to a greater interest in Gothic architecture and armor and medievalism in general by the Gothic novel. But the revolutionary decades used this genre principally as a symbol of the hated old regime. During the Revolution a favorable view of the Middle Ages was obscured.

It was in reaction to the French Revolution that the great vogue for the medieval came in. After deism, rationalism, and the paganism of the revolution, there was a return to traditional Christianity. Chateaubriand led the new movement at the beginning of the nineteenth century. In *Génie due Christianisme* (1802) and *Les Martyrs* (1809) he explored the Middle Ages to show that Christianity had furnished a strong basis for nobility, culture, and art. He had great influence on Victor Hugo and other poets. Sir Walter Scott, who translated Goethe's *Goetz von Berlichingen* in 1799 and was a constant student of Shakespeare and collector of ballads, began the English vogue for the medieval in poetry in the first decade of the century and the vogue in the novel in the next decade. His novels and most of his poems were dramatized and had a long theatrical life.

Perhaps the high point in "medievalism" is Thomas Carlyle's *Past and Present* (1843). Carlyle uses thirteenth-century culture as a whip to castigate the materialism, self-seeking, and dissatisfaction of his own day.

The medieval furnished Tennyson and Wagner and many other mid-nineteenth-century authors with their most important material. Stage and opera built up such a fascinating world of knights, battles, crusades, sacrifice, love potions, and love-deaths that the rising realists felt they might never be able to persuade audiences to face contemporary problems. But the medieval plays served as definitely as plays about contemporary life in expressing the changing patterns of personal adjustment in the Romantic age.

HISTORY BEFORE THE EYES

The stage perhaps contributed more than any other factor in public life to the clarification and acceptance of the idea of history. A large audience saw on the stage the details of the past in a complete picture. The needs of the designer were a great stimulation to the antiquary to hunt out the details that distinguished one age from another.

It was more than a half century before enough was known and assimilated to view man in an extended range of history. In the 1780s Kemble had substituted fairly accurate Roman details for the highly conventionalized and fanciful Rococo Roman. But he had used details of imperial Rome. By the 1820s it was possible to distinguish the early Rome of the Republic from the Rome of the Empire. By the 1850s wide audiences were able to make finer distinctions in history than even the best informed men of the 1820s.

In the nineteenth century, theatre people of each generation, even of each decade, bragged that their productions were the first to use really accurate historical settings and costumes, only to be despised in the next decade for carelessness and lack of interest in history. Many "first" times were necessary, many advances, many refinements in the vision of history, before the richly detailed Shakespeare productions of Charles Kean and Samuel Phelps in the middle of the century were possible.

Gordon Craig and many others in the twentieth century deny that it was worth the trouble to develop such a concept of history. They put style above history. Yet, considerable use is still made of the historical approach, and many movies and television programs strive for documentary accuracy. With the camera and modern organized research many refinements have been made in the dramatization of history.

544

The first style that attempted to reproduce a past age consistently with fresh observation and research was the Neoclassic style popularized by the French painter David and put on the stage in the 1780s by Kemble in England and Talma in France. In the 1790s the antiquarian interest in the Gothic reached the stage. The leading influence was William Capon, who became Kemble's scene designer at Drury Lane in 1794. He had studied many of the ancient buildings of England with the zeal of an antiquary and had drawn many plans and sketches attempting to represent how they must have looked in their prime. As scene designer he painted a number of Gothic stock settings that were to appear in repertory for years. For oratorios he painted a Gothic cathedral. For *Richard III* he painted backdrops of the ancient English palace of Westminster and of the Tower of London and a chapel of pointed arches. For the repertory of old English plays he painted wings showing ancient English streets. For George Colman's *The Iron Chest*, produced in 1796, he designed a baronial hall and a library copied from some of the best fifteenth-century buildings extant. More truly historical was the gorgeous church interior Capon provided for Joanna Bailie's *De Montefort*, produced in 1799.

As the years passed, designers brought into settings and costumes more and more details of the past. The critics praised Kemble's *King Lear* in 1809 for its appropriate costumes "Generally of the Saxon character." But the next year a correspondent in *The Examiner* complained of Kemble's *Much Ado About Nothing*, that al-

Design by William Capon for a medieval scene of Bosworth Field, *Richard III.*

though the scene is laid in Messina over two hundred years ago and the characters are Sicilians, Benedict was shown in the uniform of a British infantry officer of the day and Leonato as an English gentleman of the year 1730.

The first great landmark in costuming an entire play accurately for a particular year of history was Shakespeare's *King John* of Charles Kemble in 1823. James Robinson Planche designed and supervised the costumes without pay, making use of newly published books on medieval antiquities and doing considerable fresh research.

So powerful did the interest in history become that it tended to drive out any other consideration in design. If the year and rank were right, an actor would wear the same costume for comedy as for tragedy. The history-minded producers ran roughshod over all earlier stage conventions.

In architecture the interest in the study and revival of old styles was so great that the entire nineteenth century produced no style of its own, and indeed rarely showed much vigor in the Greek Revival and Gothic buildings. What in the twentieth century is considered the creative spark was blocked out almost completely by the historical. For all its cult of originality and creative genius, the Romantic age did not set its architects or its stage designers on the task of original creation. It set them on one of the major intellectual adventures of the modern world: the creation of a vision of man in history.

Romanticism in France

Political revolution came to France with the fall of the Bastille in 1789, but literary revolution was delayed by the conflict and then by Napoleon's grandiose programs and wars of conquest. It was not until the 1820s that poets and prophets for the new Romantic age appeared in France. After Napoleon's defeat at Waterloo in 1815, the restoration of the Bourbons marked a reactionary return to pre-revolutionary ways. But the time was ripe for a resurgence of religion and other elements of Romanticism, which Chateaubriand made widely popular. His *Génie du Christianisme* (1802) praised the medieval religious emotion that was expressed in the Gothic cathedrals. His novel *René* (1802) had a romantic hero, and *Les Natches* (1826) gave a romantic view of the Indians and primeval forests of America. The young generation of Frenchmen, weary of wars and political strife, found their poets in Lamartine and Alfred de Vigny. In the handsome and already famous young social lion, Victor Hugo, they found a leader.

In art, the followers of David were still spreading pale colors in imitation of Greco-Roman motifs. But the young rebels found more vivid subjects and colors in the paintings of Gericault and Delacroix. The romantic Gericault took the shocking incident of the raft of the ship *Medusa* as a subject. One hundred and forty-nine shipwrecked people had drifted for twelve days on a raft, dying, eating human flesh, and turning mad. Only fifteen had survived. Gericault took a studio near a hospital and made studies of corpses, dying people, and the insane. When he exhibited his painting in 1819 it was too strange for most Parisians, but the young painter Delacroix was excited by it. Delacroix was a restless, tormented man in a restless, maladjusted age. The subjects of his paintings ranged from the bright local color of Morocco and Algiers, to massacres and martyrs, to lions, tigers, and the angry sea. He painted scenes from the Bible, from Goethe, Byron, Shakespeare, and the legends of the Middle Ages. He brought to his paintings live colors and emotional intensity. He had much to teach the Impressionists later in the century.

The literary Romanticists gained their first glory in the 1820s in poetry, but it was soon overshadowed by drama. Madame de Staël pointed to the drama of Schiller and Shakespeare as inspiration. Victor Hugo was convinced that drama must be the characteristic expression of the modern age.

547

Schiller's *Mary Stuart* was produced in Paris in 1820 in an adaptation a little nearer the classic French form than the original. Still, the play brought movement, crowds, and picturesque background onto the stage. But Shakespeare was the most exciting discovery. Since Voltaire, the French had known something of his plays, but had seen them only as rewritten in the classical form. In 1823 the novelist Stendhal published an essay, "Racine and Shakespeare," calling for a new approach to Shakespeare, not imitating him but adapting him to the new developments. Racine, he considered, was incapable of showing the change of passion, whereas Shakespeare had created Othello, first loving Desdemona extravagantly, then killing her, and Macbeth, an honest man at first, an assassin at the end.

In 1827–28 an English company began playing in Paris, and at various times William Charles Macready, Edmund Kean, and Charles Kemble joined them to play leads. Alexandre Dumas felt that he had discovered the secret of a new art. Hugo found his predilection for the drama confirmed. He wrote, "The drama subsists on reality—it flows from one source, Shakespeare."

Hector Berlioz, the musician, was excited about Shakespeare. He afterwards testified, "Shakespeare, coming upon me unawares, struck me down as with a thunderbolt." It was not only the drama but the leading lady that conquered. Miss Smithson's Irish accent in Shakespeare had been a joke in London, but Parisians lost their hearts to "La Belle Smidson." In a typical romantic gesture, Berlioz fled to Italy and tormented himself with dreams of her. He read Alfred de Musset's version of Thomas De Quincey's *Confessions of an English Opium Eater,* and from its atmosphere developed the program for his *Symphony Fantastique.* After writing his dream in music, he came back to Paris and married Miss Smithson.

In 1827 Hugo published *Cromwell,* a play he had started for the actor Talma. After Talma died he had finished it as a play to be read, a piece too long and complex for the stage. But the preface became the Bible of the Romanticists. It ranks with Wordsworth's Preface to *Lyrical Ballads* of 1798 as one of the great critical documents of the age.

The preface to *Cromwell* is mainly an essay on the grotesque. Hugo takes as the basis for an aesthetic the duality in man and the universe, which he relates to the Christian dichotomy of good and evil. The ancient world had developed an ideal of pure beauty. The Christian Middle Ages reveled in the grotesque. The modern age must strive for a balance. Shakespeare above all, with Dante and Milton as companions, had surpassed in using the grotesque to enhance the sublime. Hugo called for breaking down all restraints on art: the unities, poetic diction, the monotonous dignity of classic French drama. He wanted the poet to be free to mix comedy with tragedy, to show action on the stage, to use crowds and many picturesque scenes, to choose any words, whether colloquial or archaic, that would suit his characters and lyric effects that would express the interests of his day. The essay was received by his admirers as the law of Moses from Mt. Sinai.

By the end of the decade of the 1820s, the young Romanticists were ready to assault the last citadel of the classic drama, the Comedie Française. The minor theatres of the boulevards had already succumbed to the new taste for romantic melodrama, but without poetry. The opera had just hired a scene designer, Cicerci, from the boulevard theatres, who was creating new stage effects. In 1825 Baron Taylor had been brought from one of the vulgar theatres to manage the Comedie Française, and he made a number of changes in settings. But the principal actors and the audience of the chief theatre of France expected to go on with the classic routine of Racine and his imitators.

The main assault began when in 1829 the Comedie Française produced Alfred de Vigny's translation, *The Moor of Venice*, the first undiluted Shakespeare on the French stage, and Dumas' *Henry III and His Court*, an historical play with much of Shakespeare's sweep. The climax to this theatre revolution was to have been a poetic play by Hugo, *Marion Delorme*, about an innocent young man at the time of Richelieu who falls in love with the famous courtesan and when he learns what she is refuses to save his own life. But the government refused to allow the play to be presented. There was already strong opposition to Charles X, and it was no time for a play which showed the corruption of a royal court. So the battle of the Romanticists against the entrenched Classicists was postponed until the following spring, when Hugo could finish another play, *Hernani* (1830). The delay only increased anticipation. Both Romanticists and their opponents were ready. Nowhere in theatre history has the issue been so clearly drawn between tradition and change.

THE BATTLE OF *HERNANI*

The battle of *Hernani* in 1830 was as important to the young Romanticists as the storming of the Bastille had been to the Revolutionists of 1789. Like the Bastille, the Comedie Française was a symbol of power, and it was controlled by the old regime. *Hernani* was expected by Hugo and his friends to end the rule of Corneille, Racine, and Voltaire, to drive out the old tyrannies and open the way for freedom, ideals, youth, and progress.

Hugo read scenes of the play as he finished them to a group of friends and followers in his home. The devotees were wildly enthusiastic. The artistic world of Paris seethed with gossip and excitement. Newspapers and reviews began the battle long before the opening. There were threats against Hugo, and placards with the words *Vive Victor Hugo* appeared on the streets. Lines and passages of the forthcoming play were quoted and the classicists parodied them. A burlesque of the play appeared before the play itself was given. The classic actors quarreled with the author and fought against their parts. There was talk of conspiracies to ruin the play. The regular paid claque of the theatre could not be depended on and had to be dispensed with. There was grave danger that Hugo would be defeated.

A plea for defense of the author and his play was circulated. Poets, painters, musicians, bohemians, all who loved poetry or art or battle tramped into Hugo's house for tickets and instructions. They were handed red cards with the word "Hierro," the battle cry of a proud old Spanish house celebrated in a poem of Hugo's which they all knew by heart. Shouting "Hierro! Death to the wigs," they tramped to the theatre. Flaunting long hair, big mustaches, Spanish cloaks and bright silk caps, these young men thought themselves champions of the ideal, defenders of free art, knights of the future.

During the afternoon before opening night, they filled the top gallery of the dark theatre. They sang, they recited, they argued, they drank, they ate. When at last the lamps were lighted and the lords and ladies began to arrive, the hall reeked of sausage and garlic.

The quarrel in the house began with almost the first line of the play. The word dérobé for "hidden," considered by the classicists improper for poetry, was the excuse. From then on enemies of the revolutionary Hugo hissed or denounced, while friends applauded or yelled "Bravo!" Only in the last act was the audience silent, swept away by the poetry and the double suicide of the lovers. The opposition continued for forty-five nights. But *Hernani* triumphed, and the new kind of play would thereafter be accepted.

The first night opening of *Hernani. Courtesy Maison de Victor Hugo Museum, Ville de Paris.*

Hernani did indeed represent a radical change in drama, and especially in the concept of the hero. Hernani is the 1830 version of the outlaw rebel of Schiller's *The Robbers* (1781) and its many imitators. Like Schiller's Karl Moor, Hernani is the wild, handsome leader of an outlaw band. He has sworn vengeance on the king, Charles V, who had executed his father. He had grown up in poverty, deprived of his noble ancestral rights. He comes to the castle to rescue his beloved Donna Sol from the old man who plans to marry her. So much is like the typical Gothic tales and dramas of fifty years before. Like Karl Moor, Hernani denounces himself for bringing death to all who join him. He is torn by violent forces within, wanting only to love but fated to live by hate. But Romantic rebellion had grown more complicated since Schiller wrote. Now taking vengeance on the old was not so simple: the rebel found he had many obligations to the old.

Hugo and many of his followers had turned violently against the Bourbon monarchy and a few months after the play was produced joined in the 1830 revolution which drove the Bourbons out. During most of the rule of Napoleon III Hugo lived in exile. But his play is a cry for peace, a call for reconciliation between revolution and tradition. Hernani goes through a series of refusals to follow the path of violence or vengeance. When he discovers that the king is his rival, we expect the fight to be intensified. But in the first act the king spares him; in the second act he spares the king (with less reason than Hamlet had for sparing Claudius); in Act III Don Gomez spares Hernani out of a traditional sense of hospitality; and in Act IV the king, after communing with the tomb of Charlemagne over his approaching coronation as emperor, forgives everybody, gives up Donna Sol, and restores Hernani to his ancestral position. Yet Hernani cannot take his happiness without being false to the demands of the past. He has stolen his love from the older generation and has sworn an oath on his unavenged father's head. So he kills himself, and his love dies with him. The very settings embody the changed attitudes toward the lone individual and the past. The medieval castle of Act I is a place for lovers' meeting, for defiance of the old, but also for a noble gesture saving the rebel's life. The ancestral picture gallery of Act III reinforces pride in tradition and the nobility that derives from tradition. The tomb of Act IV speaks of generosity and forgiveness, of a larger view of history. By 1830 the individual act of defiance is hedged in by the longing for a reconciliation with tradition and by the need for a self-sacrificing gesture.

A DECADE OF ROMANTIC DRAMA

Romanticism remained the dominant mode in France through the thirties and in music and poetry throughout the century. But the vogue for Romantic plays lasted only a little over a decade. It was not drama but the lyric, the novel, and music that proved best for expressing the private, idealistic yearnings of Romanticism.

The dancing sensation of the 1830s in France was Fanny Ellsler, who made her reputation in concert versions of native character dances: Gypsy, Spanish, or Polish. Now the arts were harvesting the creative impulses of many peoples and building up in the public mind that sense of the special characteristics of each nation that Herder and Madame de Staël had extolled. By the 1840s dancing Paris was caught up in the rage for the polka, a "folk" dance imported from Poland that had wildness and fury and yet a strict pattern. The romantic interest in new and wider sources for European culture had spread down to the most thoughtless citizen of Paris.

After the "July Revolution of 1830" and the banishment of the Bourbons, the merchants brought in Louis Philippe, "the citizen King," and though few of the wider hopes of the revolutionists were realized, there was more freedom for new ideas under the new regime. Hugo and Dumas found the Comedie Française now open to their romantic plays, but both turned more and more to the boulevard theatres where melodrama reigned. Several very good actors who could speak verse well emerged in the minor theatres. Frederic Lemaitre, who grew up in the

Hernani, Act II. Phot. Bibl. Nat. Paris.

552

Mlle. Mars as Donna Sol in *Hernani. Courtesy Maison de Victor Hugo Museum, Ville de Paris.*

melodramas and pantomimes, created some of the more vigorous roles of Hugo and Dumas.

A typical play of the 1830s was Hugo's *Le Roi s'amuse* (The King Takes His Pleasure), set at the corrupt court of Francis I. In a cynical world a misshapen jester named Triboulet cherishes one good thing, his innocent daughter Blanche, but he unwittingly helps the king seduce her. In revenge he hires a ruffian to kidnap the king, and stabs the sack he thinks contains the seducer. But he hears the king singing "Woman is fickle," and discovers that he has killed his daughter.

In England and America the play had a long theatrical life in the rewritten version of Tom Taylor called *The Fool's Revenge*. The jester, now called Bertuccio, was considered Edwin Booth's greatest part. The critic Clement Scott never forgot the last scene in which Booth began in vengeful glee but showed the father's frantic grief and broke at last into cries of anguish. Hugo's play is still seen as *Rigoletto* (1851) in Verdi's operatic setting.

Dumas' *La Tour de Nesle* (1832) was probably the most popular romantic play in France. It caught the strong feeling against Louis Philippe and presented one of the most monstrous portraits of the *femme fatale* that haunted the age. To the love that kills and the trappings of castles and dungeons was added the theme of incest. The Queen of France, a drunkard and a nymphomaniac, each night lures a man to her tower and the next day has him killed. But one young victim gets word of the situation to a certain Captain Buridan, just arrived in Paris to look for his long-lost twin boys. The captain discovers that the queen was his first partner in crime and the mother of his sons. He learns that one of his sons has already been a victim of his mother's lust and that the other is about to fall into a trap she has set. He arrives too late to save the boy's life but kills the queen and is himself shot.

But in a little over a decade the main interest in romantic drama had run its course. When Hugo's *Les Burgraves* was produced in 1843, it was a failure. In this decade came a return to the classic tragedy of Corneille, Racine, and Voltaire and for a good reason. A new actress, Rachel, gave the classics a vitality they had not had since the seventeenth century.

Perhaps the greatest actress France has ever had, she was no friend of the Romantics. She acted in some of their plays when she first appeared in the 1830s but made her greatest success as Racine's Phèdre. Yet she had qualities which transformed the classic parts. To the simplicity and dignity and innocence expected in classic parts, she added a demoniacal fierceness. She excelled in scenes of defiance and denunciation. George Henry Lewes compared her terrible beauty and undulating grace to that of a panther ready to spring. She brought into classic acting one very important innovation taken from the acting in melodramas and romantic plays. She listened to the other characters and related more to the people in the scene and less to the audience. This short, queenly woman was notorious for tyranny over the other actors, for grasping financial ways, and for a series of famous lovers, but she was popular with the lowest and highest society of Paris and London.

554

Taste was turning from the extremes of romantic drama. The emphasis on domestic security and community tranquillity—the various developments that came to be called "Victorian"—established a compromise between the individual and society. Hence there was a revulsion against "monsters," so frequent in romantic plays.

Hugo and Dumas had already discovered that the novel was a better medium than the drama for their romantic interests. In *Les Miserables*, written in the 1860s, Hugo expressed many of the finest values of Romanticism and the liberal movement: sympathy for the oppressed, the loneliness of sensitive people, the deep need to give oneself for love or for ideals.

French Romanticism was not dead of course. It was yet to produce such superb dramatic pieces as *Cyrano de Bergerac* (1895) and the movie *Children of Paradise* (1945). *Ruy Blas* (1838) held the stage most of the century, and the twentieth century has rediscovered the little romantic comedies of Alfred de Musset, written in disdain of the spectacular effects of the Romantic stage. In the legitimate theatre

Rachel from *La Juive* in London, June 1841.

Hugo and Dumas were done for by 1843, but their kind of theatre was being taken over by the "grand opera" of the composers Auber, Meyerbeer, and Donizetti.

GRAND OPERA:
THE ROMANTIC MUSICAL SPECTACLE OF PARIS

"Grand Opera," a musical expression of the Romantic movement, arose in Paris in the same years as Romantic drama. Although Wagner was contemptuous of it, calling it "effect without cause," and later musicians do not rate the music very high, it seemed to express better than the theatre could the taste for the strange, demonic, and picturesque. Music gave romantic themes a greater aesthetic distance, and the vocal display and spectacle furnished more casual entertainment than the poetic drama.

La Muette de Portici, with a libretto by Eugene Scribe and music by Auber, was first produced in 1828, but its great success came in the exciting days of the revolution in 1830. In this opera the mob was the hero. In newly painted settings of the streets of Naples milled the many picturesque characters of a romantic locality.

After 1830 bourgeois taste determined the course of the opera as well as of the government. An astute banker initiated a new regime under a manager who had a gift for publicity and brought the rich merchants to the opera. To provide new operas the manager brought together three masters of their trades: Scribe for the book, Meyerbeer for the music, and Cicerci for the staging.

The first big opera of the new regime was *Robert the Devil*, produced in 1831. In music, French declamation was combined with Italian *bel canto*, but much more important than the solos were choral crowd scenes, large orchestral effects, and melodramatic spectacle. There were processions, marches, and dances. Scribe had learned from the melodrama to set two characters in conflict, then as the scene developed to have the chorus take over the plot in elaborate ensembles. A pure girl contends with the devil over the soul of Robert, an earthly son of the devil, in the midst of picturesque medieval scenes. Statues in the ruined cloisters of a monastery come to life, and sinful nuns dance and sing around the silent tombs. There are tournaments, troubadours, and ballads, and finally a big cathedral scene in which the church music triumphs over the devil.

Gas was used for the first time in opera for lighting the production, and English stage traps were introduced. The designer persuaded the librettist and the composer to plan for genuine medieval effects in settings and costumes.

A high point in spectacular effect and scenic splendor was achieved in *La Juive* in 1835. This story of vengeance of an old Jew and his daughter Rachel on her

556

Christian lover who had betrayed her was played against the processions of emperor and cardinals at the Council of Constance. In the ceremonies appeared warriors in real armor of iron, silver, and gold, ladies in flowing robes, heralds with banners, knights on fully caparisoned chargers, Capucine Friars, and crowds of peasants. At the end a public burning in oil was shown.

XI

Tradition and Change in
Nineteenth- and Twentieth-Century Theatre

Edmund Kean as Richard III. *Courtesy the Museum of the City of New York.*

559

Edmund Kean

In England the conflict between tradition and change came earlier than in France since theatre conditions were different. Drury Lane and Covent Garden theatres had held government patents since the Restoration, bestowing exclusive rights to produce spoken drama. But they were not so strongly entrenched as the Comédie Française and had not been arbiters of taste for all Europe. A number of lesser theatres in London, roughly comparable to the boulevard theatres in Paris, gave ballets, "horse ballets," short operas, and other varieties of entertainment. Tradition was now represented by the Kembles, who reached the peak of their careers about the turn of the century. In 1802 melodrama invaded Drury Lane with the production of Kotzebue's *Coelina, or A Tale of Mystery.*

More sensational than the introduction of a new genre was the debut of a new actor, Edmund Kean, at Drury Lane on January 26, 1814. Like David Garrick in 1741, he appeared in the role of Shylock without the traditional red wig. To audience and critics alike, these Shylocks seemed "natural," showing real human emotions, getting startling effects by rapid transition from one emotion to another, through pregnant pauses and strong attack. David Garrick's widow said in fact that Kean was the only actor she had seen who approached her husband's kind of genius. Kean was a phenomenon. After that one night at Drury Lane his career was assured—and he knew it. The story goes that he told his wife, "You will ride in your carriage and Charlie will go to Eton." He was one of England's supremely gifted actors. Discriminating writers like Leigh Hunt, William Hazlitt, George Henry Lewes, Coleridge, and Byron pronounced him great.

A month after his appearance at Drury Lane as Shylock he had an equally enthusiastic reception as Richard III. In the spring he played Hamlet and Othello and Iago on alternate nights. When he added the role of the evil hypocrite in *Riches* and Bertram in Mautrin's *Bertram, or The Castle of St. Aldobrand,* he had a repertory that, with few additions, would last him until his death in 1833.

From 1804 to 1813 Kean had served an apprenticeship in provincial theatres, as most young actors had before aspiring to Drury Lane or Covent Gardens. He married an actress of little talent, and they had two sons. When luck favored them and they went to London, Kean could not join the Drury Lane company at once because he had previously signed a contract with one of the lesser theatres. The

561

family lived in extreme poverty, and the older son died. The triumph of January, 1814, changed their domestic life; but Kean was the same man, reckless, a heavy drinker, and susceptible to the charms of women who found him irresistible. In 1825 there was a public scandal when an alderman and member of the Drury Lane Committee sued him for an alleged affair with his wife and was awarded a large sum of money.

Kean played to crowded houses at Drury Lane or Covent Garden in the winter season and in summer toured the provinces. In 1821 and 1826 he toured the United States from New York to Charleston, and in 1826 Canada was included, where in Quebec he was admitted into a Huron Indian tribe. He was childishly proud of his Indian name and costume and enjoyed showing off to his English friends in his Indian role.

In the late 1820s Kean experienced the humiliation of forgetting his lines in two roles that were new to him, but he never lapsed in plays he had played earlier. His last stage appearance was at Drury Lane on March 23, 1833, nineteen years and three months after his first appearance on that stage. He played Othello, his son Charles was Iago, and Ellen Tree played Desdemona. Edmund was ill when the performance began, but he persevered until the third act, when he collapsed in Charles' arms. The next day he was driven to his home in Richmond, where he died several days later. He was forty-six years old.

Romanticism Lingers

The nineteenth century brought important political, economic, social, and scientific changes: expansion of the British Empire, the Westward Movement in the United States before and after the Civil War, amazing growth of industry, the rise of a wealthy middle class of businessmen and industrialists with limited culture and aesthetic taste and with respect for a stable society that had been lost in the period of revolution, and Darwin's troubling theory of evolution. But in theatre the main interests of the period of Romanticism carried over until the end of the nineteenth century and into the first two decades of the twentieth century. By then, realism, and, even more, "naturalism," introduced to literature by Émile Zola in the late nineteenth century, had modified Romantic ideals, and new goals for theatre were offered by Adolphe Appia, Gordon Craig, and other innovators. Shakespeare was still of prime importance in the second half of the nineteenth century and was produced with more and more elaborate settings. Nature, local color, religion, and history unfolding before the eyes still influenced the stage director and designer. Most of all, melodrama kept a dominant position, and some interesting offshoots developed.

Cyrano de Bergerac (1898) by Edmond Rostand is a classic of Romanticism. The opening scene is in the famous old Parisian theatre, the Hôtel de Boulogne, in the seventeenth century. The beautiful heroine, Roxanne, is loved by Christian, a handsome cadet, and by Cyrano, a gallant gentleman, an expert swordsman, a poet, and wit. But Cyrano cannot believe that any lady can love him because of his enormous nose. Finding that Roxanne loves Christian, Cyrano supplies him with the tender, eloquent words that can win her. Christian goes off to the wars, is killed, and Roxanne devotes her life to mourning. In a final autumnal scene many years later, Roxanne learns that it was Cyrano who wooed her and whom she really loves. The play has all the essentials of Romance: excitement, danger, brave action, love, sacrifice, and sorrow.

Cyrano has had a good many productions, amateur and professional, in the twentieth century. In 1987 Steve Martin, an American comedian, used the plot in a film set in modern times and acted the part of a hero with an enormous nose, certain that many members of any audience would recognize the source of his material.

Replacing Edmund Kean in Shakespearean roles were William Charles Macready (who had been a serious rival of Kean and lived forty years after Kean's death), Edwin Booth, Edwin Forrest, and others. Charles Kean, though no genius, became a competent actor, and in the 1850s he and his wife, Ellen Tree, had a successful company in London, specializing in Shakespeare and famous for lavish productions. In a production of *Richard II* the lonely, unhappy, defeated Richard was shown in striking contrast to the overwhelming spectacle of the triumphant Henry Bolingbroke. Henry Irving became the leading director of Shakespeare in the 1870s, and through the first two decades of the twentieth century there were usually one or more companies playing Shakespeare in London or New York or touring throughout England and from coast to coast in the United States. Shakespeare at Stratford-upon-Avon became increasingly important after the opening of the new theatre in 1932; Stratford, Ontario, added its festival, and Shakespeare festivals proliferated from Connecticut to Oregon. In the last decades of the twentieth century the National Theatre Company and the Royal Shakespeare Company in London were the guardians of the Shakespeare tradition. To productions in the accepted manner were added many that were unorthodox and experimental. This kind of Shakespeare reached a peak in the Peter Brook *Midsummer Night's Dream* (1970), in which one setting was like a gymnasium, with Puck on a hanging bar.

The local color valued by the Romanticist was acceptable to realists and remained a pleasing element in many twentieth-century plays. Though spectacle and history before the eyes became less important for the stage when the movies took them over, they were not easily banished. *Ben Hur* (1880), with a chariot race on a rolling platform, was still touring the United States in the first decade of the twentieth century.

Meanwhile, *The Birth of a Nation* (1915), *Intolerance* (1917), and other colossal films show how much bigger if not better was the display of history and religion on the screen. The fiction of Victor and Alexandre Dumas, Romantic rebels of the 1840s in France, was perfect material for the movies, and *Gone with the Wind* (1939) was a late example of cinematic treatment of history, offering an extensive view of romanticized plantation life and Civil War devastation. The documentary as a means of presenting crises of the past and problems of the present became a rival and substitute for "historic" films as well as for stage spectacle.

A creative use of history—not for display but for reinterpretation of character, reassessment of historic forces, and presentation of philosophical ideas—came with George Bernard Shaw's *Back to Methuselah* (1921) and *Saint Joan* (1923) and Thornton Wilder's *Our Town* (1938) and *The Skin of Our Teeth* (1942). An ironic view of a segment of history appeared in Tom Stoppard's *Travesties* (1975).

But of all the Romantic inheritance, nothing was more pervasive or persistent than melodrama.

Nineteenth-Century Melodrama

Nineteenth-century melodrama was a deliberate attempt to create a new audience by combining several popular forms of writing and acting with mime, dialogue, and spectacle, all tied together by a simple accompaniment—just the opposite of Wagnerian opera. Wagnerians emphasized long, slow sequences of sound, saving climaxes for the end. Rarely would Wagnerian style put an accent on each phrase or word. The melodramatic style, however, does just that; each short phrase or single word is given its place in the melody. Single commands may have loud chords just before or after the word, or if the actor and musician are careful not to blur the words, they may coincide.

The first play to be called a melodrama was Kotzebue's *Coelina*, or *A Tale of Mystery*, performed in Paris in 1789, adapted and produced in London in 1802 in a version by Thomas Holcroft. Kotzebue was among the first to use such terms as Hero and Villain for the psychology of conflict. The audience had no chance to forget that mime was the principal medium of performance; the central character, spoken of as the Mute Victim, can never tell on his torturers: they have cut out his tongue. Here, there was no rush of blood or cry of pain as in popular modern melodrama.

All through the nineteenth century many actresses based their careers on melodrama, although Shakespearean roles carried more prestige. *East Lynne* and many other melodramas had hundreds of performances. As a "horse ballet," *Mazeppa*, or *The Wild Horse of Tartary* (1840), served Adah Isaacs Menken well. After *Uncle Tom's Cabin* was dramatized in Drury Lane in 1853 it became an inexhaustible resource on both sides of the Atlantic. Much more important than exposure of the evils of slavery were the tears, the faintings, the death of Little Eva, the prayers, the suffering, the sorrow, and the thrill of Eliza crossing the ice. Audiences could accept as reality the plot of this and other melodramas, the black and white of completely evil and completely good characters. And of course the Gothic plays, superb examples of melodramas of action and horror, though without theme music, were still seen, and the Stranger, in various guises, lingered on. People of taste who might scorn the popular melodramas could accept Arthur Wing Pinero's offerings of melodramatic material in elegant settings with aristocratic characters, and without music. A notable change in the patterns of melodrama was a shift from the innocent, misunderstood heroine to a sinful woman who reformed but must die, like the Lady of the Camellias, who had a long life on the stage and a much longer one in opera.

Nineteenth-century melodrama was reenacted, using means of the modern theatre, in the remarkable production by the Royal Shakespeare Company of *Nicholas Nickleby* in London and New York in 1980–81. Stephen Sondheim's *Sweeney Todd* (1979) was an effective musical version of the story of the Demon Barber of Fleet Street, not too greatly altered by modern staging from the several earlier dramatic versions. Nineteenth-century melodrama had planted a fertile seed, though the early playwrights, directors, and actors of the genre would have been astonished at some of the later growths.

The Traditions of Melodrama
and Charlie Chaplin's "Little Man"

In the development of various forms of stage platform, proscenium frames, king's throne, and so forth, a number of different structures and iconographical images have served as symbols of the meaning of the play. We have noted that the medieval king, with raised and decorated frames, served as a permanent symbol of the feudal lord. Then in the moving decoration of rising and setting sun, the Baroque and Rococo machines symbolized both the triumph and versatility of an age of mechanical repetition. In the same way, the realistic characters of Eugene O'Neill and the ambiguous "Fog people" of John Steinbeck float in and out of a dissolving, vague world of the twentieth century. Many images are also drawn into the billboard architecture of the modern streets and highways. But one image that seems determined to take the center of attention as the central type of twentieth-century man is the "little man"—an image evoked by Steinbeck in *Of Mice and Men* (1937) and by Miller in *Death of a Salesman* (1949), but perhaps most memorably by Charlie Chaplin, as the tramp and the harrassed working man.

Hollywood in its formative years evoked a world that seemed frozen in the time of myths, when people were created in three forms: men, women, and a characterless form with no position in the universe. Douglas Fairbanks took on the masculine identity of the rugged adventurer teeming with physical prowess—the idealized hero. Mary Pickford became the feminine figure with a dulcet voice—the figure of love and romance, "America's sweetheart." Chaplin was the faceless neuter of comedy, having no personality or sexual identity—a Mr. Zero, and thus, paradoxically, taking on an all-inclusiveness and universality that genuine comedy demands.

As a popular performer, Chaplin employed all the mechanical tricks and surprises of the music-hall clowns with whom he had worked since his childhood in England and who inherited the nineteenth-century traditions of popular melodrama. Indeed, the emphatic musical underscoring characteristic of conventional melodrama works well for broad comedy of the twentieth century. Through the music, dance, and mime of his films, Chaplin was able to heighten the uniqueness and significance of each dramatic or comic moment. The piano solo, violin solo, and dance solo, as well as piano and violin duets and dance duets were especially effective, Chaplin thought, in helping to articulate, almost "speak" the emotions

567

or ideas he wished to evoke in his otherwise silent characters and situations. Chaplin, himself an accomplished musician, composed nearly all the music that was to accompany his films and hired his own orchestra.

One of Chaplin's most ambitious creations in the tradition of melodrama occurs in *The Great Dictator* (1940) with a take-off on duet-dance, depicting the visit of Mussolini to Hitler—dramatized as the Italian dictator visiting Hynkel in Germany (Backteria). Jack Oakie, a hick Vaudeville performer, played Benzino Napaloni visiting Hynkel, the Dictator of Backteria. The two soon were dancing in competition, and the duet dance became a high point in the career of both Oakie and Chaplin—two stern dictators gracefully tossing a globe-balloon over the head or under the ankles.

Some members of the audience did not consider this scene proper for ballet, but others pointed out that this was not ballet—nor yet theatre acting. It was mime, or pantomime, and Chaplin in all the discussions of silent movies of the twenties and thirties insisted that if speech were given to a film character, his relation with the audience would be destroyed. Chaplin hoped that the scene of the global dance, universal in its language, could be part of an epic, leading to a major comment on mankind.

Yet although Chaplin's entertainment grew out of the tradition of melodrama, they are not plays. As film mimes (a new form of theatrical art performed in a commercial studio for the screen rather than on a stage for a localized audience), they are not reproducible in print, and since they are so much a product of Chaplin's unique artistic style and characterization, they cannot be reproduced by actors on the stage. Indeed, although Chaplin did a great deal of acting and directing, he himself was not primarily an actor but used the techniques, forms, and sensuous appeals of the musician, the dancer, the acrobat, and the mime to evoke *an abstract image* of man's humanity—of man's efforts to understand himself. He was essentially a performer, and as a screen performer he pushes this abstract image out of the theatre proper and into a more accessible medium.

As the "little man," Chaplin often portrays the unsuspecting workman starting on a job and stopping for the lunch hour. His most unforgettable image follows a man getting caught up in the belts and gears of a big machine; the result is an experience of genuine terror. When he frees himself from the contraption the boss fastens him into a feeding machine that pushes a pile of food into his mouth. Finally running out into the street, he turns a corner and is swept along at the head of a meaningless political demonstration. In another role, he struggles with the difficulties of a pawnbroker—finally setting about repairing a watch with the tools of a clock repairman, and at last sweeping all the parts into an envelope and smugly returning them to the owner. Both *Modern Times* (1936) and *City Lights* (1931) use images of the man against the machine, whether the army, the circus, or the modern factory. His shoes too large, his hat and coat too small, and his trousers too wide, he is constantly getting trapped into groups with no individu-

568

ality—dancers, cops, pilgrims, waiters—involved in the petty needs of the universe around them. He is at once absorbed in the crowd and almost spontaneously becomes one with it, taking on a disturbing anonymity; he becomes Mr. Zero.

Yet behind such haunting blankness often lies a monster, similar to that underneath Lennie Small in Steinbeck's *Of Mice and Men.* Unlike the Mute Victim in Kotzebue's melodrama who accepts his fate of entrapment by the Guardians, Chaplin's silent "little man" is an individualist who himself, after confronting many obstacles, finally resists these impersonal commercial forces through pure personal skill, and sometimes even violence. Through perfect synchronization, he likes to show off his commercial skills of speed-handling money, for example, or as a tramp, finding himself in the splendid stairwell of a department store and accidentally stepping into a pair of rollerskates, rolling toward the edge of the stairwell, but always adeptly averting disaster. This flirting with physical danger brings the audience to screams of laughter—and how much more so when combined with a melodramatic, sentimentalized character (the lone waif, the blind flower girl, the helpless workman pursued by the oversize machine).

Chaplin transcends conventional melodrama not only in his character's comic resourcefulness in counteracting the forces which assault him, but in the artistic development of his own unique character which reveals many subtle nuances and variations not found in the more simplistic themes of melodrama. Chaplin, then, is a kind of modern hero, the perfect figure of identification, especially for the early twentieth-century industrial worker who lived in the age of the New Deal. He is a seemingly inadequate working man who must face often meaningless forces and tasks, but who eventually triumphs through the perseverance of an individualist, the resourcefulness of a survivalist, and the often awesome coordination of an artist. He is the source of so much laughter and pleasure that we see in him the ironic triumph of a wise man of the ages.

So unconscious was Chaplin of his popularity before he took his famous train ride to New York in 1914 (an almost symbolic movement from California eastward) after several years' personal uninterrupted work in his own studios, that he was completely surprised by the crowds who came to meet him. People at every station crowded into the train when they discovered he was on board. The mayor at Santa Fe telegraphed Oklahoma City to prepare it for his arrival; Chaplin continued to Amarillo, across the plains to Chicago where police wired warning ahead to New York so that Chaplin and his company could get off the train at 125th Street Station and not try to go to Grand Central Station. Though still a young man, he had become a commercial celebrity and probably the most widely known public figure in the world. Moreover, he was to become the first performer to receive a salary of more than a million dollars a year.

Indisputably, then, Chaplin was an important figure of the twentieth century—a century of amazing inventions and changes: aircraft for war and travel, exploration of space, radio, T.V., nuclear power. From 1920 onward, there was also a revolution in social customs and attitudes toward religion and morals, and in the theatrical world, too, there was a great burst of innovation: a loosening of the structure in the writing of plays, as well as much greater variety and freedom in their production. Thrust stages and theatre in the round became familiar; warehouses and the streets provided theatre space. But even extreme changes had a basis in tradition. The early chapters of this book tell that Schechner, Grotowski, and other twentieth-century directors and producers found inspiration in their interpretations of primitive ritual and practices of the ancient theatres of India, China, and Japan. Greek tragedy, variously interpreted, has remained a staple of theatre to the present. The blend of tradition and change can be found also in the survival, though not dominance, of neoclassic theory that resulted in "the well-made play." Medieval and Renaissance abundance and variety still affect the theatre, as do nineteenth-century melodrama and the ideals of Romanticism. Theatre absorbs but does not discard. Through the age-old kinetic balance of tradition and change, theatre must inevitably continue to respond to current social conditions and to exercise its historical and time-honored influence on audiences everywhere.

Selected Bibliography
& Indexes

Eight Greek masks, tragic and comic. *Illustration by Martha Sutherland.*

Selected Bibliography

I
PRIMITIVE THEATRE

Benedict, Ruth. *Patterns of Culture*. New York, 1959.

Breasted, James H. *The Development of Religion and Thought in Ancient Egypt*. New York, 1912.

Brown, Ivor. *The First Player: The Origin of Drama*. New York, 1928.

Budge, E. A. W. *Osiris and the Egyptian Resurrection*. 2 vols. New York, 1911.

Caillois, Roger. *Man, Play, and Games*. London, 1918 and 1962.

Campbell, Joseph. *The Masks of God: Primitive Mythology*. New York, 1959.

————. *The Masks of God: Occidental Mythology*. New York, 1964.

————. *The Mythic Image*. Princeton, 1974.

Eliade, Mircea. *Rites and Symbols of Initiation: The Mysteries of Birth and Rebirth*. New York, 1958.

Fairman. H. W. *The Triumph of Horus*. London, 1974.

Frankfort, Henri. *Ancient Egyptian Religion*. New York, 1948.

————. *Kingship and the Gods*. Chicago, 1948.

Frazer, Sir James. *The Golden Bough: A Study in Magic and Religion*. 12 vols. London, 1911–1915.

Freud, Sigmund. *Totem und Tabu*. Vienna, 1913.

Gaster, Theodor. *Thespis: Ritual, Myth and Drama in the Ancient Near East*. New York, 1950.

Harrison, Jane Ellen. *Ancient Art and Ritual*. New York, 1931.

Havemeyer, Loomis. *The Drama of Savage Peoples*. New Haven, 1916.

Huizinga, Johann. *Homo Ludens: A Study of the Play Elements in Culture*. Boston, 1955.

Hunningher, Benjamin. *The Origin of the Theatre*. The Hague, 1955. New York, 1961.

Jones, Robert Edmond. *Dramatic Imagination*. New York, 1941.

Kirby, E. T. *Ur-Drama: The Origins of Theatre*. New York, 1975.

Levi-Strauss, Claude. *The Savage Mind*. Chicago, 1966.

Macgowan, Kenneth, and Herman Rosse. *Masks and Demons*. New York, 1923.

Malinowski, Bronislaw. *Myth in Primitive Psychology*. New York, 1926.

Mertz, Barbara. *Temples, Tombs and Hieroglyphs: The Story of Egyptology*. New York, 1964.

Montet, Pierre. *Eternal Egypt*. New York, 1969.

Murray, Gilbert. "Excursus on the Ritual Forms Preserved in Greek Tragedy." In *Themis*, ed. Jane Ellen Harrison. New York, 1912.

Nicholson, Irene. *Mexican and Central American Mythology.* New York, 1967.

Osterley, W. O. E. *The Sacred Dance.* Cambridge, 1923.

Renault, Mary. *The King Must Die.* New York, 1959.

Ridgeway, William. *The Drama and Dramatic Dances of Non-European Races.* Cambridge, 1915.

Schechner, Richard. *Essays on Performance Theory 1970–76.* New York, 1977.

Schechner, Richard, and Mady Schuman, eds. *Ritual, Play, and Performance.* New York, 1976.

Turner, Victor. *From Ritual to Theatre.* New York, 1982.

II

THE ORIENTAL ART OF THE THEATRE

Adachi, Barbara. *The Voices and Hands of Bunraku.* Tokyo, New York, and San Francisco, 1978.

Ahuja, R. L. *The Theory of Drama in Ancient India.* Ambala, 1964.

Alley, Rewi. *Peking Opera.* Peking, 1957.

Ambrose, K. *Classical Dances and Costumes of India.* London, 1950.

Anand, Mulk Raj. *The Indian Theatre.* New York, 1951.

Ando, Tsuruo. *Bunraku: The Puppet Theatre.* London, 1970.

Araki, J. T. *The Ballad-Drama of Medieval Japan.* Berkeley and Los Angeles, 1964.

Arlington, L. C. *The Chinese Drama from the Earliest Times until Today.* Shanghai, 1930.

Arnott, Peter. *The Theatres of Japan.* New York, 1969.

Awasthi, Suresh. *Drama: The Gift of Gods. Culture, Performance and Communication in India.* Tokyo, 1983.

Baumer, Rachel V., and James R. Brandon. *Sanskrit Drama in Performance.* Honolulu, 1981.

Bharata. *Natyasastra.* Trans. M. Ghose. Bengal, 1950.

Bowers, Faubion. *Theatre in the East: A Survey of Asian Dance and Drama.* London, 1951.

———. *Japanese Theatre.* New York, 1952.

———. *The Dance in India.* New York, 1953.

Brandon, James R. *Theatre in Southeast Asia.* Cambridge, Mass., 1967.

Brandon, James R., William R. Malm, and Donald H. Shively. *Studies in Kabuki: Its Acting, Music, and Historical Context.* Honolulu, 1978.

Buss, Kate. *Studies in the Chinese Drama.* New York, 1930.

Chen, Jack. *The Chinese Theatre.* London, 1949.

Chu-Chia-Chien. *Chinese Theatre.* Trans. James A. Graham. London, 1922.

Crump, James I. *Chinese Theatre in the Days of Kublai Khan.* Tucson, 1980.

Dolby, William. *A History of Chinese Drama.* London, 1976.

Dunn, C. J. *The Early Japanese Puppet Drama*. London, 1966.

Dunn, C. J., and Bunzō Torigoe, eds. and trans. *The Actor's Analects*. Tokyo, 1969.

Edwards, Osman. *Japanese Plays and Playfellows*. London, 1901.

Ernst, Earle. *The Kabuki Theatre*. New York, 1956.

Fenollose, E. F., and Ezra Pound. *Noh, or Accomplishment*. New York, 1917; revised as *The Classic Noh Theatre of Japan*. New York, 1959.

Gargi, Balwant. *Theatre in India*. New York, 1962.

————. *Folk Theater of India*. Seattle and London, 1966.

Gerstle, C. Andrew. *Circles of Fantasy: Convention in the Plays of Chikamatsu*. Cambridge, Mass., 1986.

Guhathkurta, P. G. *Bengali Drama*. London, 1930.

Gunji, Masakatsu. *Kabuki*. Trans. John Bester. Tokyo and Palo Alto, 1969.

————. *Buyo: The Classical Dance*. New York and Tokyo, 1970.

Gupta, Chandra B. *The Indian Theatre*. Benares, 1954.

Haar, F. *Japanese Theatre in Highlights: A Pictorial Commentary*. Tokyo, 1952.

Haas, George C. O. *Dasarupa: A Treatise on Hindu Dramaturgy*. New York, 1912.

Halford, A., and G. Halford. *The Kabuki-Handbook*. Tokyo, 1964.

Halson, Elizabeth. *Peking Opera*. Oxford, 1966.

Hamamura, Yonezo, et al. *Kabuki*. Trans. Fumi Takano. Tokyo, 1956.

Hare, Thomas Blenman. *Zeami's Style: The Noh Plays of Zeami Motokiyo*. Stanford, 1986.

Hironaga, Shuzaburo. *Bunraku, Japan's Unique Puppet Theatre*. Tokyo, 1964.

Horrwitz, E. P. *The Indian Theatre*. London, 1912.

Howard, Roger. *Contemporary Chinese Theatre*. Hong Kong, 1979.

Hsu, Tao-Ching. *The Chinese Conception of the Theatre*. Seattle, 1985.

Hung, Josephine Huang, trans. and adaptor. *Children of the Pear Garden: Five Plays from the Chinese Opera*. Taipei, 1961.

Inmoos, F. T. *Japanese Theatre*. London, 1977.

Inoura, Yoshinobu, and Toshio Kawatake. *The Traditional Theatre of Japan*. New York, 1981.

Iyer, K. Berriedale. *Kathakali: The Sacred Dance-Drama of Malabar*. London, 1955.

Johnston, R. F. *The Chinese Drama*. Shanghai, 1921.

Jones, Clifford R., and Betty True Jones. *Kathakali*. New York, 1970.

Kale, Pramod. *The Theatric Universe (A Study of the Natyasastra)*. Bombay, 1974.

Kawatake, Shigetoshi. *An Illustrated History of Japanese Theatre Arts*. Tokyo, 1956.

————. *Kabuki: Japanese Drama*. Tokyo, 1958.

Keene, Donald. *Bunraku: The Art of the Japanese Puppet Theatre*. Tokyo, 1965.

————. *Nō. The Classical Theatre of Japan*. Tokyo and Palo Alto, 1966.

————, trans. *Major Plays of Chikamatsu*. New York, 1961.

Keith, A. B. *The Sanskrit Drama: Its Origin, Development, Theory and Practice*. Oxford, 1924.

Kenny, Don. *A Guide to Kyogen*. Tokyo, 1968.

Kincaid, Zoe. *Kabuki: The Popular Stage of Japan*. New York, 1925.

Komparu, Kunio. *The Noh Theatre: Principles and Perspectives*. New York, 1983.

Kusano, Eisaburo. *Stories Behind Noh and Kabuki Plays*. Tokyo, 1962.

Lee, Sherman E. *Tea Taste in Japanese Art.* New York, 1983.

Leiter, Samuel L. *The Art of Kabuki: Plays in Performance.* Berkeley, 1979.

————. *Kabuki Encyclopedia: An English-Language Adaptation of Kabuki Jiten.* Westport, Conn., 1979.

Lombard, Frank Alanson. *An Outline History of the Japanese Drama.* London, 1928.

Mackerras, Colin. *The Rise of the Peking Opera 1770–1870.* Oxford, 1972.

————. *The Chinese Theatre in Modern Times.* Amherst, 1975.

————, ed. *Chinese Theater: From Its Origins to the Present Day.* Honolulu, 1983.

Malm, William P. *Nagauta: The Heart of Kabuki Music.* Tokyo and Rutland, Vt., 1963.

Maruoka, Daiji, and Tatsuo Yoshikoshi. *Noh.* Osaka, 1969.

Mathur, Jagdesh. *Drama in Rural India.* New York, 1964.

Miyake, Shutaro. *Kabuki Drama.* 6th ed. Tokyo, 1958.

Miyamori, A. *Masterpieces of Chikamatsu, the Japanese Shakespeare.* New York, 1926.

Nogami, Toyoichiro. *Japanese Noh Plays, How to See Them.* Tokyo, 1935.

Obraztsov, Sergei. *The Chinese Puppet Theatre.* Trans. J. T. MacDermott. London, 1961.

O'Neill, P. G. *A Guide to Nō.* Tokyo, 1953.

————. *Early Nō Drama; Its Background, Character and Development, 1300–1450.* London, 1958.

Pe-chin, Chang. *Chinese Opera and Painted Face.* New York, 1979.

Pronko, Leonard C. *Theater East & West.* Berkeley, 1967.

————. *Guide to Japanese Drama.* Boston, 1973.

Rangacharya, Adya. *The Indian Theatre.* 2nd ed. New Delhi, 1980.

Richie, Donald. *Three Modern Kyogen.* Tokyo, 1972.

Sakaniski, S. *Kyogen.* Boston, 1938.

Schuyler, M. *A Bibliography of the Sanskrit Drama with an Introductory Sketch of the Dramatic Literature of India.* New York, 1906 and 1965.

Scott, A. C. *The Kabuki Theatre of Japan.* London, 1955.

————. *The Classical Theatre of China.* London, 1957.

————. *Chinese Costumes in Transition.* Singapore, 1958.

————. *An Introduction to the Chinese Theatre.* New York, 1959.

————. *The Puppet Theatre of Japan.* Tokyo and Rutland, Vt., 1963.

————. *Theatre in Asia.* New York, 1973.

Shaver, R. M. *Kabuki Costume.* Tokyo, 1966.

Shekhar, I. *Sanskrit Drama, Its Origins and Decline.* 2nd ed. New Delhi, 1977.

Shih, Chung-Wen. *The Golden Age of Chinese Drama: Yüan Tsa-cnü.* Princeton, 1976.

Tarlekar, G. H. *Studies in the Natyasastra, with Special Reference to the Sanskrit Drama in Performance.* Delhi, 1975.

Toita, Yasuji. *Kabuki, the Popular Theatre.* Trans. Don Kenny. New York, 1970.

Waley, Arthur. *The Nō Plays of Japan.* London, 1921.

Wells, Henry W. *The Classical Drama of India.* New York, 1963.

Wilson, H. H. *Select Specimens of the Theatre of the Hindus.* Calcutta, 1955.

Winsatt, G. *Chinese Shadow Shows.* Cambridge, Mass., 1936.

Yajnik, R. K. *The Indian Theatre.* New York, 1934.

Zeami. *Kadensha*. Trans. Chuichi Sakurai, et al. Kyoto, 1971.

————. *On the Art of the Nō Drama. The Major Treatises of Zeami*. Trans. J. Thomas Rimer and Yamazaki Masakazu. Princeton, 1984.

Zucker, Adolphe Edward. *The Chinese Theatre*. Boston, 1925.

Zung, Cecilia S. L. *Secrets of the Chinese Drama*. Shanghai, 1937; New York, 1964.

III

THE THEATRE OF ANCIENT GREECE

Allen, James Turney. *Greek Acting in the Fifth Century*. Berkeley, 1916.

————. *Stage Antiquities of the Greeks and Romans*. New York, 1927.

————. *The Greek Theatre of the Fifth Century before Christ*. New York, 1920 and 1966.

Anderson, M. J., ed. *Classical Drama and Its Influence*. New York, 1965.

Arnott, Peter D. *An Introduction to the Greek Theatre*. Bloomington, 1953.

————. *Greek Scenic Conventions in the Fifth Century* B.C. Oxford, 1962.

————. *The Ancient Greek and Roman Theatre*. New York, 1971.

Ashby, Clifford. "The Case for the Rectangular/Trapezoidal Orchestra." *Theatre Research International* 13 (Spring 1988): 1–20.

Bacon, Helen H. *Barbarians in Greek Tragedy*. New Haven, 1961.

Bain, David. *Actors and Audience: A Study of Asides and Related Conventions in Greek Drama*. Oxford, 1977.

Baldry, H. C. *The Greek Tragic Theatre*. New York, 1971.

Bieber, Margarete. *The History of the Greek and Roman Theatre*. 2nd ed. Princeton, 1971.

Bowra, C. M. *The Greek Experience*. London, 1957.

Brooke, Iris. *Costume in Greek Classical Drama*. New York, 1962.

Butler, James H. *The Theatre and Drama of Greece and Rome*. San Francisco, 1972.

Conacher, D. J. *Euripidean Drama: Myth, Theme and Structure*. Toronto, 1967.

Cornford, Francis M. *The Origin of Attic Comedy*. London, 1914.

Deardon, C. W. *The Stage of Aristophanes*. London, 1976.

Ehrenberg, Victor. *The People of Aristophanes*. New York, 1962.

Else, Gerald F. *The Origin and Early Form of Greek Tragedy*. Cambridge, Mass., 1965.

Flickinger, Roy C. *The Greek Theatre and Its Drama*. 4th ed. Chicago, 1936.

Graves, Robert. *The Greek Myths*. New York, 1959.

Haigh, A. E. *The Attic Theatre*. Oxford, 1907.

Hamilton, Edith. *The Greek Way*. New York, 1942.

Harriott, Rosemary M. *Aristophanes: Poet and Dramatist*. Baltimore, 1986.

Harsh, Philip W. *A Handbook of Classical Drama*. Stanford, 1944.

Hathorn, Richmond Y. *Crowell's Handbook of Classical Drama*. New York, 1967.

Herington, John. *Aeschylus*. New Haven, 1986.

Hunter, R. L. *The New Comedy of Greece and Rome.* New York, 1985.

Kitto, H. D. F. *Greek Tragedy, A Literary Study.* 2nd ed. London, 1950.

———. *Sophocles: Dramatist and Philosopher.* London, 1958.

———. *The Greeks.* Chicago, 1964.

Lawler, Lillian B. *The Dance of the Ancient Greek Theatre.* Iowa City, 1964.

Lesky, Albin. *A History of Greek Literature.* Trans. James Willis and Cornelis de Heer. New York, 1966.

Lever, Katherine. *The Art of Greek Comedy.* London, 1956.

Long, Timothy. *Barbarians in Greek Comedy.* Carbondale and Edwardsville, Ill., 1986.

Lord, Louis B. *Aristophanes: His Plays and Influence.* Boston, 1925.

McLeish, Kenneth. *The Theatre of Aristophanes.* New York, 1980.

Murray, Gilbert. *Euripides and His Age.* New York, 1913.

Nicoll, Allardyce. *Masks, Mimes, and Miracles.* New York, 1931.

Norwood, Gilbert. *Greek Tragedy.* London, 1920; New York, 1960.

———. *Greek Comedy.* London, 1931.

Pickard-Cambridge, A. W. *The Theatre of Dionysus in Athens.* Oxford, 1946.

———. *Dithyramb, Tragedy, and Comedy.* 2nd ed., revised by T. B. L. Webster. Oxford, 1962.

———. *The Dramatic Festivals of Athens.* 2nd ed., revised by John Gould and D. M. Lewis. Oxford, 1968.

Podlecki, Anthony J. *The Political Background of Aeschylean Tragedy.* Ann Arbor, 1966.

Reckford, Kenneth J. *Aristophanes' Old-and-New Comedy: Six Essays in Perspective.* Chapel Hill, 1987.

Rees, Kelley. *The Rule of Three Actors in the Classical Greek Drama.* Chicago, 1908.

Reinhardt, Karl. *Sophocles.* Trans. Hazel Harvey and David Harvey. New York, 1979.

Rosenmeyer, Thomas G. *The Art of Aeschylus.* Berkeley, 1982.

Scott, William C. *Musical Design in Aeschylean Theater.* Hanover, N.H., 1984.

Sifakis, G. M. *Studies in the History of Hellenic Drama.* London, 1967.

Simon, Erika. *The Ancient Theatre.* Trans. C. E. Vafopoulou-Richardson. London, 1982.

Spatz, Lois. *Aristophanes.* Boston, 1978.

Taplin, Oliver. *The Stagecraft of Aeschylus.* Oxford, 1977.

———. *Greek Tragedy in Action.* Berkeley, 1978.

Trendall, A. D. and T. B. L. Webster. *Illustrations of Greek Drama.* London, 1971.

Vickers, Brian. *Towards Greek Tragedy.* London, 1973.

Vince, Ronald W. *Ancient and Medieval Theatre: A Historiographical Handbook.* Westport, Conn., 1984.

Vitruvius. *Ten Books of Architecture.* Trans. Morris H. Morgan. New York, 1960.

Walton, Michael J. *Greek Theatre Practice.* Westport, Conn., 1980.

———. *Living Greek Theatre: A Handbook of Classical Performance and Modern Production.* Westport, Conn., 1987.

Webster, T. B. L. *The Tragedies of Euripides.* London, 1967.

———. *An Introduction to Sophocles.* 2nd ed. London, 1969.

————. *The Greek Chorus*. London, 1970.

————. *Greek Theatre Production*. 2nd ed. London, 1970.

Whitman, Cedric H. *Sophocles: A Study of Heroic Humanism*. Cambridge, Mass., 1966.

Winnington-Ingram, R. P. *Sophocles: An Interpretation*. Cambridge and London, 1980.

————. *Studies in Aeschylus*. Cambridge and London, 1983.

IV

THE THEATRE OF ANCIENT ROME

Allen, James Turney. See Chapter III.

Arnott, Peter D. See Chapter III.

Barrow, R. H. *The Romans*. Chicago, 1964.

Beare, William. *The Roman Stage: A Short History of Latin Drama in the Time of the Republic*. 3rd ed. London, 1963.

Bieber, Margarete. See Chapter III.

Butler, James H. See Chapter III.

Casson, Lionel, ed. *The Plays of Menander*. New York, 1971.

Dorey, T. A., and Donald R. Dudley, eds. *Roman Drama*. New York, 1965.

Duckworth, George E. *The Nature of Roman Comedy*. Princeton, 1952.

Fowler, W. Warde. *The Roman Festivals of the Period of the Republic*. London, 1916.

Friedlander, Ludwig. *Roman Life and Manners Under the Early Empire*. 3 vols. New York, 1910.

Hamilton, Edith. *The Roman Way*. New York, 1932.

Hanson, J. A. *Roman Theatre-Temples*. Princeton, 1959.

Humphrey, John H. *Roman Circuses: Arenas for Chariot Racing*. Berkeley, 1986.

Hunter, R. L. See Chapter III.

Lucas, Frank L. *Seneca and Elizabethan Tragedy*. Cambridge, 1922.

Nicoll, Allardyce. See Chapter III.

Norwood, Gilbert. *Plautus and Terence*. New York, 1932 and 1963.

Pallottini, Massimo. *The Etruscans*. Rev. ed. Bloomington, 1975.

Saunders, Catherine. *Costume in Roman Comedy*. New York, 1909.

Segal, Erich. *Roman Laughter: The Comedy of Plautus*. Cambridge, Mass., 1968.

Sifakis, G. M. *Parabasis and Animal Chorus*. London, 1971.

Vince, Ronald W. See Chapter III.

Vitruvius. See Chapter III.

V
MEDIEVAL DRAMA

Adams, Henry. *Mont Saint Michel and Chartres*. Boston, 1905.

Anderson, M. D. *Drama and Imagery in English Medieval Churches*. Cambridge, 1963.

Axton, Richard. *European Drama of the Early Middle Ages*. Pittsburgh, 1975.

Bevington, David. *From Mankind to Marlowe: Growth in Structure in the Popular Drama of Tudor England*. Cambridge, Mass., 1962.

Boas, F. S. *An Introduction to Tudor Drama*. Oxford, 1933.

Bolton, Brenda. *The Medieval Reformation*. London, 1983.

Brody, Alan. *The English Mummers and their Play*. London, 1970.

Bryan, George. *Ethelwold and Medieval Music-Drama at Winchester: The Easter Play, Its Author, and Its Milieu*. Berne, 1981.

Bucknell, Peter A. *Entertainment and Ritual 600–1600*. London, 1979.

Chambers, E. K. *The Medieval Stage*. 2 vols. Oxford, 1903.

Cohen, Gustav. *Le théâtre en France Au Moyen Age*. Paris, 1928.

———. *Histoire de la mise en scene dans le théâtre religieux français du moyen age*. Paris, 1951.

Collins, Fletcher. *The Production of Medieval Church Music-Drama*. Charlottesville, 1972.

Craig, Hardin. *English Religious Drama of the Middle Ages*. New York, 1960.

Craik, Thomas W. *The Tudor Interlude Stage, Costume and Acting*. Leicester, 1958.

———, et al. *The Revels History of Drama in English*. Vol. 2: *1500–1576*. New York, 1980.

Crawford, J. P. W. *Spanish Drama before Lope de Vega*. 2nd ed. Philadelphia, 1937.

Denny, Neville, ed. *Medieval Drama*. London, 1973.

Donovan, R. B. *Liturgical Drama in the Medieval Spain*. Toronto, 1958.

Edwards, Robert. *Montecassino Passion and the Poetics of Medieval Drama*. Berkeley, 1977.

Evans, Marshall Blakemore *The Passion Play of Lucerne*. New York, 1943.

Frank, Grace. *The Medieval French Drama*. Oxford, 1954.

———. *The Medieval Drama*. Oxford, 1960.

Gardiner, Harold C. *Mysteries' End: An Investigation of the Last Days of the Medieval Religious Stage*. Hamden, Conn., 1946.

Hardison, O. B., Jr. *Christian Rite & Christian Drama in the Middle Ages*. Baltimore, 1965.

Helterman, Jeffrey. *Symbolic Action in the Plays of the Wakefield Master*. Athens, Ga., 1981.

Hoyt, Robert S., ed. *Life and Thought in the Early Middle Ages*. Minneapolis, 1967.

Hunningher, Benjamin. See Chapter I.

Johnston, Alexandra F., and Margaret Rogerson, eds. *Records of Early English Drama*. York 1: *Introduction, The Records*. York 2: *Appendixes, Translations, End-notes, Glossaries, Indexes*. Toronto, 1979.

Kahrl, Stanley J. *Traditions of Medieval English Drama*. Pittsburgh, 1975.

Kolve, V. A. *The Play Called Corpus Christi*. Stanford, 1966.

Lumiansky, R. M., and David Mills. *Chester Mystery Cycle: Essays and Documents. With an Essay, "Music in the Cycle," by Richard Rastall*. Chapel Hill, 1983.

Mackenzie, W. Roy. *The English Moralities.* London, 1914.

McConachie, Bruce A. "The Staging of the Mystère d'Adam." *Theatre Survey* 20 (May 1979): 27–42.

Meredith, Peter, and John Trailby. *The Staging of Religious Drama in Europe in the Later Middle Ages.* Kalamazoo, 1983.

Morrissey, L. J. "English Pageant-Wagon." *18th Century Studies* 9 (Spring 1976): 353–74.

Nagler, A. M. *The Medieval Religious Stage: Shapes and Phantoms.* New Haven, 1976.

Nelson, Alan H. *The Medieval English Stage: Corpus Christi Pageants and Plays.* Chicago, 1974.

Nicoll, Allardyce. *Masks, Mimes and Miracles.* New York, 1932.

Pederson, Steven I. *The Tournament Tradition and Staging The Castle of Perseverance.* Ann Arbor, 1986.

Pollard, Alfred W. *English Miracle Plays, Moralities, and Interludes.* Oxford, 1927.

Potter, Robert A. *The English Morality Play.* London, 1975.

Prosser, Eleanor. *Drama and Religion in the English Mystery Plays.* Stanford, 1961.

Purnis, J. O., ed. *The York Cycle of Mystery Plays.* New York, 1950.

Rossiter, A. P. *English Drama from Early Times to the Elizabethans.* London, 1966.

Rudwin, M. J. *Historical and Bibliographical Survey of the German Religious Drama.* Pittsburgh, 1924.

Salter, Frederick M. *Medieval Drama in Chester.* Toronto, 1955.

Shergold, N. D. *A History of the Spanish Stage from Medieval Times until the End of the 17th Century.* Oxford, 1967.

Simonson, Lee. *The Stage Is Set.* 3rd ed. New York, 1960.

Southern, Richard. *The Staging of Plays Before Shakespeare.* London, 1973.

———. *The Medieval Theatre in the Round.* Rev. ed. New York, 1975.

Sticca, Sandro. *The Latin Passion Play: Its Origin and Development.* Albany, 1970.

———, ed. *The Medieval Drama.* New York, 1972.

Stratman, C. J. *Bibliography of Medieval Drama.* Berkeley, 1954.

Stuart, D. C. *Stage Decoration in France in the Middle Ages.* New York, 1910.

Sumberg, S. *The Nuremberg Schembart Carnival.* New York, 1941.

Taylor, Henry O. *The Medieval Mind.* 2 vols. Cambridge, Mass., 1962.

Taylor, Jerome, and Alan H. Nelson, eds. *Medieval English Drama: Essays Critical and Contextual.* Chicago, 1972.

Tydeman, William. *The Theatre in the Middle Ages.* Cambridge and London, 1978.

Vince, Ronald W. See Chapter III.

Wickham, Glynne. *Early English Stages: 1300 to 1660.* 3 vols. New York, 1959–81.

———. *The Medieval Theatre.* 2nd ed. Cambridge and London, 1987.

Williams, Arnold. *The Drama of Medieval England.* East Lansing, Mich., 1961.

Woolf, Rosemary. *The English Mystery Plays.* Berkeley, 1972.

Young, Karl. *The Drama of the Medieval Church.* 2 vols. Oxford, 1933.

VI

THE RENAISSANCE THEATRE

Adams, J. Q. *Shakespearean Playhouses*. Boston, 1917.

Adams, John C. *The Globe Playhouse: Its Design and Equipment*. 2nd ed. New York, 1961.

Allen, John J. *The Reconstruction of a Spanish Golden Age Playhouse: El Corral del Príncipe 1583–1744*. Gainesville, Fla., 1983.

Baldwin, T. W. *The Organization and Personnel of the Shakespearean Company*. Princeton, 1927.

Barroll, J. L., et al. *Revels History of Drama in English. Vol. 3: 1576–1613*. New York, 1975.

Barry, Herbert, ed. *The First Public Playhouse: The Theatre in Shoreditch, 1576–1598*. Montreal, 1979.

Beckerman, Bernard. *Shakespeare at the Globe, 1599–1609*. New York, 1962.

Bentley, Gerald E. *The Profession of Dramatist in Shakespeare's Time, 1590–1642*. Princeton, 1971.

———. *The Profession of Player in Shakespeare's Time, 1590–1642*. Princeton, 1984.

Bergeron, David. *English Civic Pageantry, 1558–1642*. London, 1971.

Bevington, David. See Chapter V.

Blumenthal, Arthur R. *Theater Art of the Medici*. Hanover, N.H., 1980.

Boas, Frederick S. *An Introduction to Stuart Drama*. London, 1946.

Bradbrook, M. C. *The Rise of the Common Player*. London, 1962.

Brenan, Gerald. *The Literature of the Spanish People*. 2nd ed. New York, 1953.

Bristol, Michael D. *Carnival and Theater: Plebeian Culture and the Structure of Authority in Renaissance England*. New York, 1985.

Burckhardt, Jakob C. *The Civilization of the Renaissance in Italy*. 3rd ed. New York, 1961.

Campbell, Lily Bess. *Scenes and Machines on the English Stage during the Renaissance*. Cambridge, 1923.

Chambers, E. K. *The Elizabethan Stage*. 4 vols. London, 1923.

Cook, Ann Jennalie. *The Privileged Playgoers of Shakespeare's London, 1576–1642*. Princeton, 1981.

Crawford, J. P. W. See Chapter V.

Deierkauf-Holsboer, Wilma. *Histoire de la Mise-en-scène dans le Théâtre Français de 1600 à 1657*. Paris, 1933.

———. *Le Théâtre de l'Hôtel de Bourgogne*. 2 vols. Paris, 1968–70.

Dessen, Alan C. *Elizabethan Stage Conventions and Modern Interpreters*. Cambridge, 1984.

Foakes, R. A. *Illustrations of the English Stage 1580–1642*. Stanford, 1985.

Galloway, David, ed. *Elizabethan Theatre*. Hamden, Conn., 1973.

Gildersleeve, Virginia. *Government Regulation of the Elizabethan Drama*. New York, 1908.

Greg, W. W. *Dramatic Documents from the Elizabethan Playhouses: Stage Plots, Actors' Parts, Prompt Books, Reproductions and Transcripts*. Oxford, 1931.

Gurr, Andrew. *The Shakespearean Stage, 1574–1642*. Cambridge, 1970.

Harbage, Alfred. *Shakespeare's Audience*. New York, 1958.

Hattaway, Michael. *Elizabethan Popular Theatre: Plays in Performance*. London, 1982.

Herrick, Marvin. *Tragicomedy: Its Origin and Development in Italy, France, and England.* Urbana, Ill., 1955.

———. *Italian Comedy in the Renaissance.* Urbana, Ill., 1960.

———. *Italian Tragedy in the Renaissance.* Urbana, Ill., 1965.

Hewitt, Barnard, ed. *The Renaissance Stage: Documents of Serlio, Sabbattini, and Furttenbach.* Coral Gables, Fla., 1958.

Hodges, C. Walter. *The Globe Restored.* 2nd ed. London, 1968.

———. *Shakespeare's Second Globe.* London, 1973.

Hotson, Leslie. *Shakespeare's Wooded O.* New York, 1960.

Hussey, Maurice. *The World of Shakespeare & His Contemporaries.* New York, 1972.

Jacquot, J., ed. *Les Fêtes de la Renaissance.* 2 vols. Paris, 1956–60.

———. *Le Lieu Théâtral à la Renaissance.* Paris, 1964.

Jeffrey, B. *French Renaissance Comedy, 1552–1630.* Oxford, 1969.

Joseph, Bertram. *Elizabethan Acting.* 2nd ed. London, 1962.

Kennard, Joseph S. *The Italian Theatre.* 2 vols. New York, 1932.

King, T. J. *Shakespearean Staging, 1599–1642.* Cambridge, Mass., 1971.

Larson, Donald R. *The Honor Plays of Lope de Vega.* Cambridge, Mass., 1977.

Lawrence, W. J. *The Elizabethan Playhouse and Other Studies.* 2 vols. Stratford-on-Avon, 1912–13.

Lees-Milne, James. *The Age of Inigo Jones.* London, 1953.

Mahelot, Laurent. *La Memoire de Mahelot, Laurent et d'autres Décorateurs de l'Hôtel de Bourgogne et de la Comédie Française au XVIIe siècle.* Ed. H. C. Lancaster. Paris, 1920.

Mullin, Donald C. *The Development of the Playhouse: A Survey of Architecture from the Renaissance to the Present.* Berkeley, 1970.

Nagler, Alois M. *Shakespeare's Stage.* New Haven, 1958.

———. *Theatre Festivals of the Medici, 1539–1637.* New Haven, 1968.

Nicoll, Allardyce. *Stuart Masques and the Renaissance Stage.* London, 1937.

———, ed. *Shakespeare Survey* 12 (1959).

Oosting, J. Thomas. *Andrea Palladio's Teatro Olimpico.* Ann Arbor, 1981.

Orgel, Stephen. *The Illusion of Power: Political Theatre in the English Renaissance.* Berkeley, 1975.

Orgel, Stephen, and Roy Strong. *The Theatre of the Stuart Court; Including the Complete Designs . . . Together with Their Texts and Historical Documentation.* 2 vols. Berkeley, 1973.

Orrell, John. *The Quest for Shakespeare's Globe.* New York, 1983.

———. *The Theatres of Inigo Jones and John Webb.* New York, 1985.

Parker, A. A. *The Approach to the Spanish Drama of the Golden Age.* London, 1957.

Rennert, Hugo A. *The Life of Lope De Vega.* Philadelphia, 1904.

———. *The Spanish Stage in the Time of Lope de Vega.* New York, 1909.

Reynolds, George F. *The Staging of Elizabethan Plays at the Red Bull Theatre, 1605–1625.* New York, 1940.

Rhodes, E. L. *Henslowe's Rose: The Stage and Staging.* Lexington, Ken., 1976.

Rutter, Carol C., ed. *Documents of the Rose Playhouse.* Dover, N.H., 1985.

Schoenbaum, S. *William Shakespeare: A Documentary Life.* Oxford, 1975.

Shapiro, Michael. *Children of the Revels: The Boy Companies of Shakespeare's Time and Their Plays.* New York, 1977.

———. "Annotated Bibliography on Original Staging in Elizabethan Plays." *Research Opportunities in Renaissance Drama* 24 (1981): 23–49.

Shergold, N. D. See Chapter V.

Shoemaker, William H. *The Multiple Stage in Spain during the Fifteenth and Sixteenth Centuries.* Princeton, 1935.

Smith, Irwin. *Shakespeare's Blackfriar's Playhouse: Its History and Its Design.* New York, 1964.

Smith, Warren D. *Shakespeare's Playhouse Practice: A Handbook.* Hanover, N.H., 1975.

Strong, Roy. *Splendor at Court.* Boston, 1973.

Styan, J. L. *Shakespeare's Stagecraft.* Cambridge, 1967.

Surtz, Ronald E. *The Birth of a Theater: Dramatic Convention from Juan del Encina to Lope de Vega.* Princeton, 1979.

Symonds, John A. *The Renaissance in Italy.* 7 vols. London, 1909–37.

Thomson, Peter. *Shakespeare's Theatre.* London and Boston, 1983.

Vasari, Giorgio. *Vasari's Lives of the Artists.* Paris, 1927.

Vince, Ronald W. *Renaissance Theatre: A Historiographical Handbook.* Westport, Conn., 1984.

Vitruvius. See Chapter III.

Weinberg, Bernard. *A History of Literary Criticism in the Italian Renaissance.* 2 vols. Chicago, 1961.

Welsford, Enid. *The Court Masque.* Cambridge, 1927.

Wiley, W. L. *The Early Public Theatre in France.* Cambridge, Mass. 1920.

Wilson, Edward M., and Duncan Moir. *A Literary History of Spain: The Golden Age, Drama, 1492–1700.* New York, 1971.

Wilson, Margaret. *Spanish Drama of the Golden Age.* New York, 1969.

Wright, Louis B. *Middle-Class Culture in Elizabethan England.* Chapel Hill, 1935.

Yates, Frances A. *Theatre of the World.* London, 1969.

VII
THE AGE OF DISPLACEMENT: MANNERIST ART

Arnott, Peter D. *An Introduction to the French Theatre.* London, 1977.

Baur-Heinhold, M. *Baroque Theatre.* Trans. Mary Whittall. London and New York, 1967.

Beijer, A. *Court Theatres of Drottningholm and Gripsholm.* Trans. G. L. Frolich. Malmo, 1944.

Bentley, Gerald E. *The Jacobean and Caroline Stage.* 5 vols. Oxford, 1941–56.

———. *The Seventeenth Century Stage: A Collection of Critical Essays.* Chicago, 1968.

Bjurstrom, P. *Giacomo Torelli and Baroque Stage Design.* Stockholm, 1961.

Bliss, Lee. *The World's Perspective: John Webster and the Jacobean Drama.* New Brunswick, N.J., 1983.

Ducharte, Pierre Louis. *The Italian Comedy.* Trans. Randolph T. Weaver. London, 1929.

Ellis-Fermor, U. *The Jacobean Drama: An Interpretation*. London, 1936.

Esrig, David. *Commedia Dell'Arte*. Nördlingen, Germany, 1985.

Gordon, Mel. *Lazzi: The Comic Routines of the Commedia dell'Arte*. New York, 1982.

Griswold, Wendy. *Renaissance Revivals: City Comedy and Revenge Tragedy in the London Theatre, 1576–1980*. Chicago, 1986.

Kennard, James Spencer. *The Italian Theatre*. 2 vols. New York, 1932.

———. *Masks and Marionettes*. New York, 1935.

Knights, L. C. *Drama and Society in the Age of Jonson*. London, 1937.

Lancaster, Henry C. *A History of French Dramatic Literature in the Seventeenth Century*. 9 vols. Baltimore, 1929–42.

Larson, Orville. *The Theatre Writings of Fabrizio Carini Motta*. Carbondale and Edwardsville, Ill., 1987.

Lawrence, W. J. *Pre-Restoration Stage Studies*. Cambridge, Mass., 1927.

Lawrenson, T. E. *The French Stage in the XVIIth Century: A Study in the Advent of the Italian Order*. Rev. ed. Manchester, 1984.

Lea, Kathleen M. *The Italian Popular Comedy: A Study in the Commedia dell'Arte*. 2 vols. Oxford, 1934.

Limon, Jerzy. *Gentlemen of a Company: English Players in Central Europe, 1590–1660*. London, 1985.

Logan, Terence P., and Denzell S. Smith, eds. *The Later Jacobean and Caroline Dramatists*. Lincoln, Neb., 1978.

Lough, John. *Seventeenth-Century French Drama: The Background*. Oxford, 1979.

Mcgowan, M. *L'Art du Ballet de Cour en France*. Paris, 1963.

Maraniss, James E. *On Calderón*. Columbia, Mo., 1978.

Mayor, A. H. *The Bibiena Family*. New York, 1945.

———. *Giovanni Battista Piranesi*. New York, 1952.

Mittman, Barbara G. *Spectators on the Paris Stage in the Seventeenth and Eighteenth Centuries*. Ann Arbor, 1984.

Nicoll, Allardyce. *The World of Harlequin*. London, 1976.

Niklaus, Thelma. *Harlequin*. New York, 1956.

Noyes, Robert Gale. *Ben Jonson on the English Stage, 1660–1766*. Cambridge, Mass., 1935.

Ogden, Dunbar, ed. and trans. *The Italian Baroque Stage: Documents by Giulio Trioli, Andrea Pozzo, Ferdinando Galli-Babiena, Baldassare Orsini*. Berkeley, 1978.

Oreglia, Giacomo. *The Commedia dell'Arte*. Trans. Lovett F. Edwards. New York, 1968.

Ornstein, R. *The Moral Vision of Jacobean Tragedy*. Madison, Wis., 1960.

Pandolfi, V. *La commedia dell'arte: Storia e testo*. 6 vols. Florence, 1957.

Parker, A. A. *The Allegorical Drama of Calderón*. Oxford, 1943.

Ribner, Irving. *Jacobean Tragedy: The Quest for Moral Order*. New York, 1962.

Rolland, R. *Histoire de l'opéra en Europe avant Lully et Scarlatti*. Paris, 1931.

Salerno, Henry F. *Scenarios of the Commedia dell'Arte*. New York, 1967.

Scholz, Janos. *Baroque and Romantic Stage Design*. New York, 1962.

Schwartz, Isidore A. *The Commedia dell'Arte and Its Influence on French Comedy in the Seventeenth Century*. Paris, 1933.

585

Silin, Charles. *Benserade and His Ballets de Cour.* New York, 1940 and 1977.

Sloman, A. E. *The Dramatic Craftsmanship of Calderón: His Use of Early Plays.* Oxford, 1969.

Smith, Winifred. *Italian Actors of the Renaissance.* New York, 1930.

———. *The Commedia dell'Arte.* Rev. ed. New York, 1965.

Worsthorne, S. T. *Venetian Opera in the 17th Century.* Oxford, 1954.

VIII
NEOCLASSIC DRAMA: A NEW FORM FOR A NEW AGE

Abraham, Claude. *Pierre Corneille.* New York, 1972.

Avery, Emmett L., and Arthur H. Scouten. *The London Stage, 1660–1700: A Critical Introduction.* Carbondale, Ill., 1968.

Boswell, Eleanore. *The Restoration Court Stage.* Cambridge, Mass., 1932.

Brenner, C. D. *The Théâtre Italien: Its Repertory, 1716–1793.* Berkeley, 1961.

Brereton, Geoffrey. *French Comic Drama from the Sixteenth to the Eighteenth Century.* London, 1977.

Bulgakov, Mikhail. *The Life of Monsieur de Molière.* Trans. Mirra Ginsburg. New York, 1986.

Cibber, Colley. *An Apology for the Life of Colley Cibber.* New York, 1914.

Clinton-Baddeley, V. C. *The Burlesque Tradition in the English Theatre after 1600.* London, 1952.

Cook, John A. *Neoclassic Drama in Spain: Theory and Practice.* Dallas, 1959.

Dobrée, Bonamy. *Restoration Tragedy.* Oxford, 1928.

Fernandez, Ramon. *Molière: The Man Seen Through the Plays.* Trans. Wilson Follett. New York, 1958.

Fujimura, T. H. *The Restoration Comedy of Wit.* Princeton, 1952.

Gooden, Angelica. *Action and Persuasion: Dramatic Performance in Eighteenth-Century France.* Oxford, 1986.

Gossip, C. J. *An Introduction to French Classical Tragedy.* Totowa, N.J., 1981.

Gossman, Lionel. *Men & Masks: A Study of Molière.* Baltimore, 1963.

Harbage, Alfred. *Thomas Killigrew, Cavalier Dramatist.* Philadelphia, 1930.

Harwood, John T. *Critics, Values, and Restoration Comedy.* Carbondale, Ill., 1982.

Holland, Norman. *The First Modern Comedies.* Cambridge, Mass., 1959.

———. *The Ornament of Action: Text and Performance in Restoration Comedy.* Cambridge, 1979.

Hotson, Leslie. *The Commonwealth and Restoration Stage.* Cambridge, Mass., 1928.

Howarth, W. D., *Molière: A Playwright and his Audience.* Cambridge, 1982.

Hubert, J. D. *Molière and the Comedy of Intellect.* Berkeley, 1962.

Hume, Robert D. *The Development of English Drama in the Late Seventeenth Century.* Oxford, 1976.

———. *The Rakish Stage.* Carbondale, Ill., 1983.

———, ed. *The London Theatre World, 1660 to 1800.* Carbondale, Ill., 1980.

Joseph, Bertram. *The Tragic Actor.* London, 1959.

Jourdain, Eleanor. *Dramatic Theory and Practice in France, 1690–1808.* London, 1921.

Jump, John D., ed. *The Diary of Samuel Pepys.* New York, 1964.

Koon, Helene. *Colley Cibber: A Biography.* Lexington, Ken., 1986.

Krutch, J. W. *Comedy and Conscience After the Restoration.* New York, 1924.

Lancaster, Henry C. *The Comédie Française, 1680–1701.* Baltimore, 1941.

Leacroft, Richard. *The Development of the English Playhouse.* Ithaca, N.Y., 1973.

Loftis, John, et al. *The Revels History of Drama in English: Vol. 5, 1660–1750.* New York, 1976.

Lough, John. *Paris Theatre Audiences in the Seventeenth and Eighteenth Centuries.* Oxford, 1957.

Lynch, J. J. *Box, Pit, and Gallery: Stage and Society in Johnson's London.* Berkeley, 1953.

McAfee, Helen F., ed. *Pepys on the Restoration Stage.* New York, 1964.

McBride, Robert. *The Sceptical Vision of Molière.* New York, 1977.

McCarthy, B. Eugene. *William Wycherley: A Biography.* Athens, Oh., 1979.

McCollum, John I., ed. *The Restoration Stage.* Boston, 1961.

Miles, Dudley. *The Influence of Molière on the Restoration Comedy.* New York, 1910.

Milhous, Judith. *Thomas Betterton and the Management of Lincoln's Inn Fields, 1695–1708.* Carbondale, Ill., 1979.

Milhous, Judith, and Robert D. Hume, eds. *Vice Chamberlain Coke's Theatrical Papers 1706–1715.* Carbondale, Ill., 1982.

––––––. *Producible Interpretation: Eight English Plays, 1675–1707.* Carbondale, Ill., 1985.

Moore, Will Grayburn. *Molière.* 2nd ed. New York, 1964.

Muir, Kenneth. *The Comedy of Manners.* London, 1970.

Nicoll, Allardyce. *A History of Early Eighteenth Century Drama, 1700–1750.* Cambridge, 1929.

––––––. *A History of Restoration Drama 1660–1700.* Cambridge, 1940.

––––––. *History of English Drama, 1660–1900.* 6 vols. Cambridge, 1952–59.

Odell, G. C. D. *Shakespeare From Betterton to Irving.* 2 vols. New York, 1920.

Palmer, John. *Molière. His Life and Works.* London, 1930.

Powell, Jocelyn. *Restoration Theatre Production.* London, 1981.

Rosenfeld, Sybil. *Strolling Players and Drama in the Provinces, 1660–1675.* Cambridge, 1939.

Southern, Richard. *Changeable Scenery: Its Origin and Development in the British Theatre.* London, 1952.

Spencer, Hazelton. *Shakespeare Improved: Restoration Versions.* Cambridge, Mass., 1927.

Styan, J. L. *Restoration Comedy in Performance.* Cambridge, 1986.

Summers, Montague. *The Restoration Theatre.* London, 1934.

––––––. *The Playhouse of Pepys.* New York, 1964.

Thaler, Alwin. *Shakespeare to Sheridan.* Cambridge, Mass., 1922.

Turnell, Martin. *The Classical Moment: Studies in Corneille, Molière and Racine.* New York, 1948.

Weber, Harold M. *The Restoration Rake-Hero.* Madison, Wis., 1986.

Weinberg, Bernard. *The Art of Jean Racine.* Chicago, 1963.

Williams, Aubrey L. *An Approach to Congreve.* New Haven, 1979.

Yarrow, P. J. *Racine.* Totowa, N.J., 1978.

Zimbardo, Rose A. *A Mirror to Nature: Transformations in Drama and Aesthetics 1660–1732.* Lexington, Ken., 1986.

IX

THE EIGHTEENTH-CENTURY THEATRE

Aikin, Judith P. *German Baroque Drama*. Boston, 1982.

Aikin-Sneath, Betsy. *Comedy in Germany in the First Half of the 18th Century*. Oxford, 1936.

Anderson, M. S. *Historians and Eighteenth-Century Europe*. Oxford, 1979.

Appleton, William W. *Charles Macklin, An Actor's Life*. Cambridge, Mass., 1960.

Baker, Herschel. *John Philip Kemble*. Cambridge, Mass., 1942.

Beijer, Agnes. See Chapter VII.

Borgerhoff, Elbert. *The Evolution of Liberal Theory and Practice in the French Theatre, 1680–1757*. Princeton, 1936.

Bruford, Walter H. *Theatre, Drama, and Audience in Goethe's Germany*. London, 1957.

Burnim, Kalman A. *David Garrick, Director*. Pittsburgh, 1961.

Carlson, Marvin. *The Theatre of the French Revolution*. Ithaca, N.Y., 1966.

———. *Goethe and the Weimer Theatre*. Ithaca, N.Y., 1978.

———. *Theories of the Theatre*. Ithaca, N.Y., 1984.

Downer, Alan S. "Nature to Advantage Dressed: Eighteenth Century Acting." *PMLA* (1943): 1002–37.

Fiske, Roger. *English Theatre Music in the Eighteenth Century*. London, 1973.

Gascoigne, Bamber. *World Theatre. An Illustrated History*. London, 1968.

Goldoni, Carlo. *Memoirs of Carlo Goldoni*. Trans. John Black. New York, 1926.

Gozzi, Carlo. *The Memoirs of Count Carlo Gozzi*. Trans. J. A. Symonds. 2 vols. London, 1890.

Heitner, R. R. *German Tragedy in the Age of Enlightenment, 1724–1768*. Berkeley, 1985.

Highfill, Philip H., Jr., Kalman Burnim, and Edward Langhans. *A Biographical Dictionary of Actors, Actresses, Musicians, Dancers, Managers, and Other Stage Personnel in London, 1660–1800*. Carbondale, Ill., 1973.

Hogan, Charles B., ed. *The London Stage, 1660–1800*. 3 vols. Carbondale, Ill., 1968.

Hughes, Alan. "Art and Eighteenth-Century Acting Style." *Theatre Notebook* 41 (1987): 24–31; 79–89; 128–39.

Hughes, Leo. *The Drama's Patrons: A Study of the 18th Century London Audience*. Austin, Tex., 1971.

Karlinsky, Simon. *Russian Drama from Its Beginnings to the Age of Pushkin*. Berkeley, 1985.

Kelly, Linda. *The Kemble Era*. London, 1980.

Kenny, Shirley Strum, ed. *British Theatre and the Other Arts, 1660–1800*. Washington, D.C., 1984.

Kistler, Mark O. *Drama of the Storm and Stress*. New York, 1969.

Klenze, Camillo von. *From Goethe to Hauptmann*. New York, 1926.

Lancaster, H. C. *Sunset: A History of the Parisian Drama in the Last Years of Louis XIV, 1701–15*. Baltimore, 1945.

———. *French Tragedy in the Times of Louis XV and Voltaire, 1715–74*. 2 vols. Baltimore, 1950.

————. *French Tragedy in the Reign of Louis XVI and the Early Years of the French Revolution, 1774–92.* Baltimore, 1953.

Leacroft, Richard. See Chapter VIII.

Leacroft, Richard, and Helen Leacroft. *Theatre and Playhouse: An Illustrated Survey of Theatre Building from Ancient Greece to the Present Day.* London and New York, 1984.

Loftis, John. *Sheridan and the Drama of Georgian England.* London, 1976.

————. See also Chapter VIII.

Mackintosh, Iain, and Geoffrey Ashton. *The Georgian Playhouse: Actors, Artists, Audiences and Architecture 1730–1830.* London, 1975.

Manvell, Roger. *Sarah Siddons.* New York, 1970.

Marker, Frederick J., and Lise-Lone Marker. *The Scandinavian Theatre: A Short History.* Oxford, 1976.

Meserve, Walter J. *An Emerging Entertainment: The Drama of the American People to 1828.* Bloomington, 1977.

Molinari, Cesare. *Theatre Through the Ages.* Trans. Colin Hamer. London, 1975.

Nicoll, Allardyce. *The Garrick Stage.* Manchester, 1980.

————. See also Chapter VIII.

Odell, G. C. D. See Chapter VIII.

Pascal, Roy. *The German Strum and Drang.* Manchester, 1953.

Peacock, Ronald. *Goethe's Major Plays: An Essay.* Manchester, 1953.

Pedicord, Harry W. *The Theatrical Public in the Time of Garrick.* New York, 1954.

Price, Cecil. *Theatre in the Age of Garrick.* Oxford, 1973.

Prudhoe, John. *The Theatre of Goethe and Schiller.* Oxford, 1973.

Rankin, Hugh F. *The Theatre in Colonial America.* Chapel Hill, 1965.

Reed, T. J. *The Classical Centre: Goethe and Weimar, 1775–1832.* London, 1980.

Richards, Kenneth R., and Peter Thomson, eds. *Essays on the Eighteenth Century English Stage.* London, 1972.

Roach, Joseph R. *The Player's Passion: Studies in the Science of Acting.* Newark, Del., 1985.

Robertson, J. G. *The Life and Work of Goethe, 1749–1832.* London, 1932.

————. *Lessing's Dramatic Theory.* Cambridge, 1939.

Rosenfeld, Sybil. *A Short History of Scene Design in Great Britain.* Oxford, 1973.

————. *Georgian Scene Painters and Scene Painting.* Cambridge, 1981.

Slonim, Marc. *Russian Theatre from the Empire to the Soviets.* Cleveland, 1961.

Southern, Richard. *The Georgian Playhouse.* London, 1948.

Stone, George Winchester, Jr., ed. *The Stage and the Page. London's "Whole Show" in the Eighteenth Century Theatre.* Berkeley, 1981.

Stone, George Winchester, Jr., and George M. Kahrl. *David Garrick: A Critical Biography.* Carbondale, Ill., 1979.

Varneke, B. V. *History of the Russian Theatre.* New York, 1951.

Watson, E. B. *Sheridan to Robertson.* Cambridge, Mass., 1926.

Williams, Simon. *German Actors of the Eighteenth and Nineteenth Centuries: Idealism, Romanticism, and Realism.* Westport, Conn., 1985.

Willoughby, Leonard A. *The Classical Age of German Literature, 1749–1832.* London, 1926.

Wilmeth, Don B. *George Frederick Cooke: Machiavel of the Stage.* Westport, Conn., 1980.

Woods, Leigh. *Garrick Claims the Stage: Acting as Social Emblem in Eighteenth-Century England.* Westport, Conn., 1984.

X
THE AGE OF ROMANTICISM

Abrams, M. H. *The Mirror and the Lamp: Romantic Theory and the Critical Tradition.* New York, 1953.

Brown, Frederick. *Theater & Revolution: The Culture of the French Stage.* New York, 1980.

Carlson, Marvin. *The French Stage in the Nineteenth Century.* Metuchen, N.J., 1972.

———. *The German Stage in the Nineteenth Century.* Metuchen, N.J., 1972.

———. *The Italian Stage from Goldoni to d'Annunzio.* London, 1981.

———. See also Chapter IX.

Collins, Herbert F. *Talma. A Biography of an Actor.* London, 1964.

Daniels, Barry. *Revolution in the Theatre: French Romantic Theories of Drama.* Westport, Conn., 1983.

Hewitt, Barnard. *History of the Theatre from 1800 to the Present.* New York, 1970.

Lacey, Alexander. *Pixérécourt and the French Romantic Drama.* Toronto, 1928.

Lee, Briant Hamor. "Origins of the Box Set in the Late 18th Century." *Theatre Survey* 18 (1977): 44–59.

Mayer, David. *Harlequin in his Element: The English Pantomime, 1806–1836.* Cambridge, Mass., 1969.

Meserve, Walter J. *Heralds of Promise: The Drama of the American People in the Age of Jackson, 1829–1849.* Westport, Conn., 1986.

Moody, Richard. *America Takes the Stage: Romanticism in American Drama and Theatre, 1750–1900.* Bloomington, 1955.

Peers, E. A. *A History of the Romantic Movement in Spain.* 2 vols. Cambridge, 1940.

Penzel, Frederick. *Theatre Lighting Before Electricity.* Middletown, Conn., 1978.

Quinn, Arthur H. *A History of the American Drama from the Beginning to the Civil War.* 2nd ed. New York, 1943.

Richardson, Joanna. *Rachel.* New York, 1957.

Root-Bernstein, Michèle. *Boulevard Theater and Revolution in Eighteenth-Century Paris.* Ann Arbor, 1984.

Stein, Jack M. *Richard Wagner and the Synthesis of the Arts.* Detroit, 1960.

Storey, Robert F. *Pierrot: A Critical History of a Mask.* Princeton, 1978.

Watson, Ernest B. See Chapter IX.

Witkowski, Georg. *The German Drama of the Nineteenth Century.* Trans L. E. Horning. New York, 1968.

XI
TRADITION AND CHANGE IN NINETEENTH- AND TWENTIETH-CENTURY THEATRE

Altick, Richard D. *The Shows of London.* Cambridge, Mass., 1978.

Antoine, André. *Memories of the Théâtre Libre.* Trans. Marvin Carlson. Coral Gables, Fla., 1964.

Appia, Adolphe. *The Work of Living Art.* Trans. H. D. Albright. Coral Gables, Fla., 1960.

———. *Music and the Art of the Theatre.* Trans. Robert W. Corrigan and Mary Douglas Dirks. Coral Gables, Fla., 1962.

Appleton, William W. *Madame Vestris and the London Stage.* New York, 1974.

Artaud, Antonin. *The Theatre and Its Double.* Trans. Mary Caroline Richards. New York, 1958.

Arvin, Neil C. *Eugène Scribe and the French Theatre, 1815–1860.* Cambridge, Mass., 1924.

Bablet, Denis. *Edward Gordon Craig.* New York, 1967.

Baker, Michael. *The Rise of the Victorian Actor.* Totowa, N.J., 1978.

Banham, Martin and Peter Thomson, gen. eds. *British and American Playwrights 1750–1920.* 16 vols. Cambridge, 1982–87.

Beacham, Richard C. *Adolphe Appia: Theatre Artist.* Cambridge, 1987.

Bentley, Eric, ed. *The Theory of the Modern Stage.* New York, 1976.

Bigsby, C. W. E. *A Critical Introduction to Twentieth-Century American Drama. Vol. I: 1900–1940.* New York, 1983.

Booth, Michael. *English Melodrama.* London, 1965.

———. *Victorian Spectacular Theatre: 1850–1910.* Boston, 1981.

———. *Prefaces to English Nineteenth Century Theatre.* Manchester, n.d.

Braun, Edward. *Meyerhold on Theatre.* New York, 1969.

Brockett, Oscar G., and Robert R. Findlay. *Century of Innovation: A History of European and American Theatre and Drama Since 1870.* Englewood Cliffs, 1973.

Brown, T. A. *History of the New York Stage, 1836–1918.* New York, 1923.

Brustein, Robert. *The Theatre of Revolt.* Boston, 1964.

Carlson, Marvin. See Chapter IX.

Carter, Huntly. *The New Spirit in the European Theatre, 1914–1924.* New York, 1925.

Carter, Lawson A. *Zola and the Theatre.* New Haven, 1963.

Cheney, Sheldon. *The New Movement in the Theatre.* New York, 1914.

Cole, Toby, and Helen K. Chinoy, eds. *Directors on Directing.* 2nd ed. Indianapolis, 1963.

Bibliography

Craig, Edward Gordon. *On the Art of the Theatre.* London, 1911.

Cross, Gilbert. *Next Week "East Lynne": Domestic Drama in Performance, 1820–1874.* Lewisburg, Penn., 1976.

Dahlstorm, C. E. W. L. *Strindberg's Dramatic Expressionism.* Ann Arbor, 1930.

DeHart, Steven. *The Meininger Theater, 1776–1926.* Ann Arbor, 1981.

Disher, M. Willson. *Blood and Thunder: Mid-Victorian Melodrama and Its Origins.* London, 1949.

————. *Melodrama: Plots That Thrilled.* New York, 1954.

Donohue, Joseph W., Jr. *Dramatic Character in the English Romantic Age.* Princeton, 1971.

————, ed. *The Theatrical Manager in England and America.* Princeton, 1971.

Downer, Alan S. "Players and the Painted Stage: Nineteenth Century Acting." *PMLA* 61 (1946): 522–76.

Dukore, Bernard. *Dramatic Theory and Criticism: Greeks to Growtowski.* New York, 1974.

Esslin, Martin. *Brecht: The Man and His Work.* New York, 1960.

————. *The Theatre of the Absurd.* New York, 1961.

Eynat-Confino, Irène. *Gordon Craig, Movement, and the Actor.* Carbondale, Ill., 1987.

Felheim, Marvin. *The Theatre of Augustin Daly.* Cambridge, Mass., 1956.

Findlater, Richard. *Six Great Actors: Garrick, Kemble, Kean, Macready, Irving, Forbes-Robertson.* London, 1957.

Foulkes, Richard, ed. *Shakespeare and the Victorian Stage.* Cambridge, 1986.

Fuchs, Georg. *Revolution in the Theatre.* Trans. C. C. Kuhn. Ithaca, N.Y., 1959.

Fuegi, John. *Bertolt Brecht: Chaos, According to Plan.* Cambridge, 1987.

Fuerst, W. L., and S. J. Hume. *Twentieth-Century Stage Decoration.* New York, 1928 and 1967.

Fulop-Miller, Rene, and Joseph Gregor. *The Russian Theatre. Its Character and History.* London, 1930.

Gassner, John. *Form and Idea in Modern Theatre.* New York, 1956.

Glasstone, Victor. *Victorian and Edwardian Theatres.* Cambridge, Mass., 1975.

Gorelik, Mordecai. *New Theatres for Old.* New York, 1940.

Grimsted, David. *Melodrama Unveiled: American Theatre and Culture, 1800–1850.* Chicago, 1968.

Grube, Max. *The Story of the Meiningen.* Trans. Ann Marie Koller. Coral Gables, Fla., 1963.

Henderson, Mary C. *Theater in America: 200 Years of Plays, Players, and Productions.* New York, 1986.

Hewitt, Barnard. *Theatre USA, 1668–1957.* New York, 1959.

Hill, Errol. *Shakespeare in Sable: A History of Black Shakespearean Actors.* Amherst, 1984.

Hillebrand, Harold Newcomb. *Edmund Kean.* New York, 1933.

Hoover, Marjorie L. *Meyerhold: The Art of Conscious Theatre.* Amherst, 1974.

Hughes, Alan. *Henry Irving, Shakespearean.* Cambridge, 1981.

Hunt, Hugh, et al. *The Revels History of Drama in English. Vol. 7: 1880 to the Present Day.* New York, 1979.

Innes, Christopher. *Erwin Piscator's Political Theatre.* New York, 1972.

————. *Edward Gordon Craig.* New York, 1983.

592

Irving, Laurence H. *Henry Irving: The Actor and His World*. New York, 1952.

Izenour, George. *Theatre Design*. New York, 1977.

Jasper, Gertrude. *Adventure in the Theatre: Lugné Poë and the Théâtre de l'Oeuvre to 1899*. New Brunswick, N.J., 1947.

Jones, R. E. *The Dramatic Imagination*. New York, 1941.

Knowles, D. *French Drama of the Inter-War Years, 1918–39*. New York, 1968.

Koller, Ann Marie. *The Theater Duke: Georg II of Saxe-Meiningen and the German Stage*. Stanford, 1984.

Larson, Orville. "New Evidence on the Box Set." *Theatre Survey* 21 (1980): 79–91.

McArthur, Benjamin. *Actors and American Culture, 1880–1920*. Philadelphia, 1984.

MacCarthy, Desmond. *The Court Theatre, 1904–07*. London, 1907.

Macgowan, Kenneth, and R. E. Jones. *Continental Stagecraft*. New York, 1922.

Mander, Raymond, and Joe Mitchenson. *The Lost Theatres of London*. Rev. ed. London, 1975.

―――. *The Theatres of London*. Rev. ed. London, 1975.

Marker, Lise-Lone. *David Belasco: Naturalism in the American Theatre*. Princeton, 1975.

Matlaw, Myron, ed. *American Popular Entertainment*. Westport, Conn., 1979.

Mayer, David, and Kenneth Richards, eds. *Western Popular Theatre*. London, 1977.

Mazur, Cary. *Shakespeare Refashioned: Elizabethan Plays on Edwardian Stages*. Ann Arbor, 1981.

Meisel, Martin. *Realizations: Narrative, Pictorial, and Theatrical Arts in Nineteenth-Century England*. Princeton, 1983.

Meyer, Michael. *Ibsen: A Biography*. New York, 1971.

―――. *Strindberg: A Biography*. New York, 1985.

Miller, Anna Irene. *The Independent Theatre in Europe, 1887 to the Present*. New York, 1931.

Moderwell, H. K. *The Theatre of To-day*. New York, 1925.

Moynet, J. P. *French Theatrical Production in the Nineteenth Century*. Trans. Allan S. Jackson and M. Glen Wilson. Binghamton, N.Y., 1976.

Murphy, Brenda. *American Realism and American Drama, 1880–1940*. New York, 1987.

Nagler, A. M. *A Source Book in Theatrical History*. New York, 1977.

Nemirovich-Danchenko, V. *My Life in the Russian Theatre*. London and Boston, 1936.

Odell, G. C. D. *Annals of the New York Stage*. 15 vols. New York, 1927–49.

Patterson, Michael. *The Revolution in German Theatre, 1900–1933*. Boston, 1981.

Planché, J. R. *The Recollections and Reflections of James Robinson Planché*. 2 vols. London, 1872.

Postlewait, Thomas. *Prophet of the New Drama: William Archer and the Ibsen Campaign*. Westport, Conn., 1986.

Quinn, A. H. *A History of the American Drama from the Civil War to the Present Day*. 2nd ed. New York, 1949.

Rahill, Frank. *The World of Melodrama*. University Park, Penn., 1967.

Rees, Terence. *Theatre Lighting in the Age of Gas*. London, 1978.

Reynolds, Ernest. *Early Victorian Drama, 1830–70*. London, 1936.

Richards, Kenneth, and Peter Thomson. *Essays in Nineteenth-century British Theatre*. London, 1971.

593

Robinson, David. *Chaplin: His Life and Art*. New York, 1985.

Roose-Evans, James. *Experimental Theatre: From Stanislavsky to Peter Brook*. Rev. ed. London, 1984.

Rowell, George. *The Victorian Theatre, 1792–1914*. 2nd ed. Cambridge, 1978.

———. *Theatre in the Age of Irving*. London, 1981.

Rudlin, John. *Jacques Copeau*. Cambridge, 1986.

Sachs, Edwin O., and E. A. E. Woodrow. *Modern Opera Houses and Theatres*. 3 vols. London, 1897–1898.

Sanderson, Michael. *From Irving to Olivier: A Social History of the Acting Profession, 1880–1983*. New York, 1985.

Saxon, Arthur H. *Enter Foot and Horse: A History of Hippodrama in England and France*. New Haven, 1968.

Saylor, Oliver M., ed. *Max Reinhardt and His Theatre*. New York, 1926.

Segel, Harold B. *Twentieth-Century Russian Drama*. New York, 1979.

Senelick, Laurence. *Gordon Craig's Moscow Hamlet: A Reconstruction*. Westport, Conn., 1982.

Shattuck, Charles H. *The Shakespeare Promptbooks, A Descriptive Catalogue*. Urbana, Ill., 1965.

———. *Shakespeare on the American Stage: From the Hallams to Edwin Booth*. Washington, D.C., 1976.

———. *Shakespeare on the American Stage: From Booth and Barrett to Sothern and Marlowe*. Washington, D.C., 1987.

Shattuck, Roger. *The Banquet Years: The Arts in France, 1885–1918*. New York, 1961.

Shaw, George Bernard. *Our Theatre in the Nineties*. 3 vols. London, 1932.

Sheaffer, Louis. *O'Neill: Son and Playwright*. Boston, 1968.

———. *O'Neill: Son and Artist*. Boston, 1973.

Slonim, Marc. *Russian Theatre from the Empire to the Soviets*. Cleveland, 1961.

Southern, Richard. *The Victorian Theatre: A Pictorial Survey*. London, 1970.

Speaight, Robert. *William Poel and the Elizabethan Revival*. London, 1954.

Stanislavski, Constantin. *My Life in Art*. London, 1924.

Stanton, Stephen, ed. *Camille and Other Plays*. New York, 1957.

Styan, J. L. *Chekhov in Performance*. Cambridge, 1978.

———. *Modern Drama in Theory and Practice*. 3 vols. New York, 1981.

———. *Max Reinhardt*. Cambridge, 1982.

Symons, James. *Meyerhold's Theatre of the Grotesque: The Post-Revolutionary Productions, 1920–1932*. Coral Gables, Fla., 1971.

Tairov, Alexander. *Notes of a Director*. Trans. William Kuhlke. Coral Gables, Fla., 1969.

Toll, Robert C. *On With the Show: The First Century of Show Business in America*. New York, 1976.

Trewin, J. C. *The Edwardian Theatre*. London, 1976.

Vardac, A. Nicholas. *Stage to Screen: Theatrical Method from Garrick to Griffith*. Cambridge, Mass., 1949.

Volbach, W. R. *Adolphe Appia, Prophet of the Modern Theatre: A Profile*. Middletown, Conn., 1968.

Waxman, S. M. *Antoine and the Théâtre Libre*. New York, 1964.
Willett, John. *The Theatre of Bertolt Brecht*. New York, 1959.
————. *The Theatre of Erwin Piscator*. New York, 1979.

Subject Index

Topics under subtitle headings are listed sequentially. Illustrations are identified by italic numerals.

597

Index of Plays

Index